Quo Vadis

QUO VADIS

HENRYK SIENKIEWICZ

In Modern Translation by

W.S. KUNICZAK

HIPPOCRENE BOOKS
New York

This modern translation was made possible by grants from the Polish National Alliance of the United States of North America and the Kosciuszko Foundation. I wish to express my sincere gratitude to Edward J. Moskal, president of the PNA and the Polish American Congress, to Joseph E. Gore, president of the Kosciuszko Foundation, and to their trustees, directors and members.

—W. S. Kuniczak

Hippocrene paperback edition printed with permission of
  Macmillan Publishing Company, 1997
Hippocrene paperback edition, tenth printing, 2010.

Macmillian Publishing Company edition, 1993.

Library of Congress Cataloging-in-Publication Data

Sienkiewicz, Henryk, 1846-1916.
        [Quo vadis, English]
        Quo vadis / Henryk Sienkiewicz; translated by W. S. Kuniczak.
              p. cm.
        ISBN-10: 0-7818-0763-8 (hc)
        ISBN-13: 978-0-7818-0550-6 (pb)
        ISBN-10: 0-7818-0550-3 (pb)
        1. Rome—History—Nero, 54-68—Fiction. 2. Church history—Primitive
    and early church, ca. 30-6000—Fiction, I. Kuniczak, W. S., 1930- . II. Title.
PG7158.S4Q43   1997
891.8'536--dc21

                                                              97-2694
                                                              CIP

Printed in the United States of America.

FOR EWA KUNICZAK,
an artist in her own right

ACKNOWLEDGMENTS

This modern translation was made possible by grants from The Polish National Alliance of the United States of North America and the Kosciuszko Foundation. I wish to express my sincere gratitude to Edward J. Moskal, president of the PNA and the Polish American Congress, to Joseph E. Gore, president of the Kosciuszko Foundation, and to their trustees, directors and members.

—W. S. Kuniczak

⟨ I ⟩

IT WAS CLOSE to noon before Petronius came awake, feeling as drained and listless and detached as always. He was a guest at one of Nero's banquets the evening before and the orgy dragged on late into the night, and his health hadn't been all that good anyway for some time. He told himself that waking in the morning was a kind of mental and physical paralysis where neither his mind nor his body was capable of action. But an hour or two spent at his private baths, followed by a thorough kneading of his flesh by skilled slave masseurs, gradually quickened the sluggish flow of blood in his veins, roused him, revitalized him and restored his strength so that he would leave the anointing room as if resurrected, with eyes full of wit and aglow with humor, restored to youth, full of life again, so incomparable in his poise, fastidiousness and brilliance that even Otho couldn't match his style; he would be truly what everyone said he was: the undisputed arbiter of all that was elegant and tasteful.

He seldom went to the public baths, unless it happened that some particularly well known or widely publicized master of rhetoric was performing there or if the young wrestlers in the *ephebeum* were especially interesting that day. Besides, he had his own baths that had been built for him within his compound by Celer, the famous partner of Severus, who enlarged the *insula*—or the adjoining servants' quarters of his city villa—and then equipped and decorated them with such exquisite taste that Nero himself saw them as superior to the imperial baths, although those were immeasurably larger and more opulent.

After that orgy at the emperor's palace, where he was bored close to tears by the mindless posturing of Vatinius, he took part in a debate with Nero, Lucan and Seneca as to whether women possessed a soul; and now, having risen late, he was indulging himself at his baths as usual. Two huge bath attendants had just stretched him out on a cypress slab covered with a snow-white sheet of Egyptian linen, and started to rub perfumed oils into his well-formed body. He, in the meantime, closed his eyes and waited until the scented warmth of the steam room and the heat of their hands penetrated his flesh and eased the weariness of his whole body.

But after a while he began to talk. He opened his eyes and started asking what the weather was like outside and if the jeweler Idomeneus had brought the selection of gems he ordered for that day. He was told that the weather could hardly be better, with a light breeze blowing from the Alban hills, but that no one had brought any jewels. Just as Petronius had let his eyelids fall shut again and had ordered that he be carried to the *tepidarium*, where he could be rinsed off in barely tepid water, the *nomenclator*, or the slave who was charged with calling out the names of his guests, peered from behind a screen. He informed Petronius that young Marcus Vinicius, who was home from the legions that fought in Asia Minor, had just come to visit.

"Have him taken to the *tepidarium*," Petronius ordered quickly, "and take me there as well."

The visit pleased him. Vinicius was a son of his older sister who had married the older Marc Vinicius, once a consul in the Tiberius era. The young man had served in the latest Parthian war under Corbulanus and had just returned to Rome now that the fighting on that eastern border dwindled for a while. Petronius had a certain weakness for his handsome and athletic nephew, due in large part to the tempered judgment and sort of an aesthetic selectivity that the young man showed in his pursuit of vices, which was a gift Petronius valued more than any other.

"Greetings to you, Petronius!" The young soldier marched into the rinsing room with a smart quick stride. "May all the gods bless you, but especially Asclepios and Cypris. Nothing bad can happen to your health if those two have their eyes on you."

"Welcome to Rome, rest and relaxation!" Petronius stretched his hand from the soft folds of the fine carbasus linen in which he was wrapped. "You've earned some sweet times now that the war is over. So what's the good word from Armenia these days? And did you happen to brush against Bithynia while you were in Asia?"

Petronius had once been the proconsul in Bithynia, a fair and energetic one, which showed a strange juxtaposition of virtue and vices in this effeminate and pleasure-loving man. He liked to hark back to those times that proved what he could do and what he could have been, if that's what he felt like being and doing.

"I was in Heraclea for a while," young Vinicius told him. "Corbulanus sent me there to train reinforcements."

"Ah, Heraclea! I once knew a girl from Colchis over there, and I'd give all our Roman divorcees for her any day, including Nero's Poppea herself. But that's ancient history. Tell me instead what's happening on the Parthian border? It's true that I'm bored to death by all those Vologensians and Tyredatians and Tigranians, and the rest of those barbaric hordes who still walk on all fours, as young Arulanus insists, and pretend to be human only when we're there. But there's a lot of talk about them in Rome nowadays, probably because they're the safest subject."

"That war's still going badly." Vinicius shook his head and shrugged with distaste. "It could turn into a real disaster if Corbulanus wasn't there."

"Corbulanus!" Petronius was amused. "By Bacchus, a true god of war. A great commander who's a veritable Mars on a battlefield: fiery, impulsive, righteous and dumb as an ox. I'm really fond of him, if for no other reason than that he frightens Nero."

"Corbulanus is no fool," young Vinicius said.

"Maybe you're right. Besides, it's all the same. Stupidity is no worse than wisdom, according to Pyrrho, and doesn't amount to much less in the end."

Vinicius started talking about the war and Petronius closed his eyes again. His face seemed gaunt with weariness and gray with fatigue.

"Are you all right?" Worried about this sudden loss of energy, the young man changed the subject. "Have you been ill? Aren't you feeling well?"

Petronius looked at him with lackluster eyes.

Well? He was far from well. True, he had not yet reached the stagnant, passionless condition of young Sisenius, who had sunk into such a torpid state that he had to ask "Am I sitting?" when he was carried to his baths, but good health was something else again. Vinicius wished him the benign protection of the two deities charged with medicine and healing, Asclepios and Cypris, but Petronius didn't place much faith in their ministrations. Who was this Asclepios anyway? Nobody even knew whether he was the son of Arsinoe or Coronis, and if there is doubt about a mother, who could tell the father? There were few patricians in Rome nowadays who could swear to their own paternity, so what about the progeny of Zeus?

Petronius started laughing.

"I sent three dozen live cocks to Asclepios' temple in Epidaurus a couple of years ago," he said, "along with a cupful of gold. But do you know why? I told myself that it couldn't hurt even if it didn't do me any good. People still make sacrifices to the gods, but I doubt if anyone who matters takes them seriously. Maybe the mob does. Maybe there's still faith in some divinity among the mule drivers who rent themselves to travelers at the Porta Capena, but that's about all. Besides Asclepios, our great god of healing, I also had some dealings with the lesser healers when I had trouble with my bladder last year. I knew they were fakes and cheaters, but so what? Fakery is in fashion. The world lives by deceit and life is an illusion anyway, so what harm is there in cheating and being cheated? The soul is also an illusion. The only thing that counts is to be intelligent enough to distinguish between the illusions of pleasure and pain. I burn cedar logs sprinkled with ambergris in my steam room because I'd rather smell perfumes than stenches around me. As for Cypris, in whose kind hands you've also placed my health, all I can say is that I keep getting shooting pains in my right leg, and she doesn't seem able to do much about them. Other than that, I suppose she's a decent goddess. Talking of sacrifices, though, and considering her other role as the patroness of midwives, I suppose you'll be taking some white doves to her altar soon enough."

"I hope so." Vinicius grinned. "The Parthians didn't manage to put an arrow into me, but Cupid did a nice job right outside the city!"

"Ah, by the white knees of the Graces! Really?" Petronius' brief moment of vitality had begun to ebb. "Tell me about it when we've a little time."

"That's why I've come here," Marcus said. "I need your advice."

Just then the manicurists entered and busied themselves with Petronius, and Marcus threw off his tunic and stepped into the water.

"Hmm. I don't need to ask if the girl shares your feelings," Petronius said, looking at the powerful young body that seemed as smooth and hard as if carved from marble. "If Lysippos ever caught sight of you, you'd be decorating the Palatine Gate as young Hercules."

The young man grinned with easy satisfaction, plunged into the bath and started splashing warm water across the inlaid floor whose mosaics portrayed Hera, the wife of Zeus and mother of the Gods, as she begged Sleep to overcome her husband. Petronius watched him with an artist's eye.

Vinicius had no sooner finished, stepped out of the bath and gave himself over to the manicurists when the house *lector* came into the room, the educated slave charged with reading poetry to his master. Petronius asked the young soldier if he wanted to hear anything.

"Gladly, if it's something you've written," Vinicius said. "Otherwise I'd much rather talk. Poets grab people on every street corner nowadays."

"Don't they just? You can't pass a single temple, bath, library or bookstore without some poet whirling his arms at you like a windmill. When Agrippa came here from the East, he thought they were all mad. But that's the way it is these days. The emperor writes poetry, so everybody wants to be a poet. The only danger is if you're the better poet, which is why I'm a bit worried about Lucan. I write only prose, which I don't thrust on anyone, including myself. What the *lector* was supposed to read today are the commentaries of that poor Fabricius Veientus."

"Why poor?"

"Because he was told to imitate Odysseus and go into exile until he's allowed to come home again. This Odyssey will be easier for him than it was for Homer's original wanderer because his wife is neither as beautiful nor as faithful as Penelope. It was a stupid order because it's a dull and boring book and nobody read it until the author was packed off to the provinces, but that's how things are done these days in the city. Nothing has any depth, and all that matters is what's on the surface. Now everyone howls '*Scandala! Scandala!*' and maybe Veientus did make up a few things. But I know the city, our leaders and our women, and I assure you it's nothing compared to how things really are. Still, everybody has his nose in those scrolls today, searching with terror for some allusion to himself and with delight for any slur on everyone he knows. A hundred scribes are copying the thing in Avirnus' bookshop, and the sales are terrific."

"Are you in it too?"

"I am. But the author missed the mark, because I'm both far worse and far less one-dimensional than he says. See, we've long lost our sense of good and evil here, and I'm starting to think there's really no difference between them, even though Seneca, Musonius and Trasca pretend that they see it. It's all one to me, and I say what I think. But at least I've kept enough perspective that I can tell ugliness from beauty, and that's something our ruling redbeard, our imperial poet, balladeer, charioteer and clown, doesn't grasp at all."

"I'm sorry for Fabricius, though," the young man said. "He's good company."

"He was too anxious to be the center of attention," Petronius shrugged. "Everyone suspected what the book was going to be about, but nobody knew for sure until he started babbling his stories all around the city. It was all supposed to be a big secret, as if anyone can keep a secret in Rome, and the gossip blew it up out of all proportion. By the way, did you hear the story about Rufinus?"

"No."

"Then let's go into the *frigidarium*. We'll cool off a little, and I'll tell you there."

A fountain splashed pink water in the middle of the cooling room, spreading the scent of violets. They settled in a pair of niches carved in the marble walls so that their body temperature might return to normal. There was a moment of protracted silence. Vinicius let his thoughts wander for a while as he stared at a bronze group in which a faun bent a reluctant nymph across his arm and greedily sought her lips.

"That one knows what's what," he said at last, nodding at the bronzes. "That's what counts in life."

"Could be," Petronius said. "But you're a warrior as well as a lover, aren't you? Impassioned about both your favorite occupations? Personally, I don't care for war. It's terrible on your nails. But what's the difference? Everyone has his own likes and dislikes anyway. Nero loves singing, particularly his own, and old Scaurus is mad about his Corinthian vase. He keeps it beside his bed and kisses it whenever he can't sleep. He's already kissed off all its edges. Tell me, though, you don't write verses, do you?"

"No. I never got a single hexameter together."

"And you don't sing or play the lute?"

"No." Vinicius shook his head.

"And you don't race chariots?"

"I did a bit of that in Antioch but I never won."

"Then I don't have to worry about you. What faction do you fancy at the hippodrome?"

"The Greens."

"Better and better!" Petronius smiled in relief. "You've some fine property, which could be a problem, but at least you're not as rich as Pallas or Seneca. The way to make a social hit among us nowadays, you see, is to write poetry, recite it in public, play the lute and race in the circus. But it's far better, by which I mean safer, not to write, play, sing, recite or race anywhere. The best assurance of security is to know how to fake admiration whenever Nero admires anything.

You're an extraordinarily handsome lad, so your only danger is that Poppea might want you for a lover. But she's too smart for that with all her experience. Her first two husbands let her have as many lovers as she wanted, but her cravings take a different form with Nero, our beloved copper-bearded poetaster, balladeer and king of the lute. Do you know that her discarded Otho is still mad about her? He climbs rocks in Spain and sighs like a bellows, but he's gone so far downhill when it comes to all his former fascinations, or even the proper rituals of caring for himself, that it takes him only three hours a day to get himself barbered. Who'd ever expect anything like that? Especially from Otho?"

"I know what he feels like," Marcus said. "But I'd do something more than sigh if I were in his boots."

"Such as what?"

"I'd create new legions loyal to myself. Those Iberian highlanders make excellent soldiers."

"Vinicius, Vinicius!" Petronius shook his head with amused compassion. "I'll risk the thought that you'd never be able to do it. And do you know why? Because one does such things but never talks about them, even as the remotest possibility. I'd laugh at Poppea, laugh at Copperbeard and form my legions out of the highland women, not the men. The worst thing I might do is write a few epigrams, but even that I'd keep to myself, unlike that miserable Rufinus I started telling you about."

"So what happened to Rufinus?"

"I'll tell you in the *unctuarium.*"

Their bodies cooled sufficiently for comfort, they passed into the anointing room, but here the young man found something else to think about. He was immediately surrounded by slave girls, handpicked for their beauty, who waited there for the bathers. Two of them, Nubians whose black bodies gleamed like polished ebony, began to work subtle Arabian fragrances into their skins; two others, Phrygians skilled in hairdressing, whose hands and arms seemed as swift and pliable as serpents, set about their heads with combs and hand mirrors made of polished steel; while two more, Greeks from Cos, and as breathtaking as a pair of goddesses, waited their turn to dress them and set the folds of their togas as fashion commanded.

"By Zeus the Thunderer!" Marcus Vinicius said. "What a selection you have here!"

"I prefer choice to numbers," Petronius said. "My whole Roman household is a mere four hundred. Only a jumped-up shopkeeper, a newly rich social climber, would need any more than that for his intimate personal attendants."

But Vinicius was busy sniffing the scented air that surrounded the perfumed young women. "Not even Copperbeard can own so much beautiful flesh. Or keep it for his guests."

Petronius gave a friendly and elaborately careless shrug. "You're my nephew. Besides, I'm not cheap like Bassus or as much of a stickler for propriety as Aulus Plautius. Cheapness and virtue are the enemies of pleasure."

But that last name knocked the girls from Cos right out of Marcus' head.

"How did you happen to think of Aulus Plautius?" he asked with lively interest. "Did you know that I hurt my arm a few miles outside the city walls and spent a couple of weeks in his home? He came by the moment it happened. I'd dislocated my shoulder, a stupid accident. I was in pain so he took me home. Merion, his slave physician, got me well again, and that's just what I wanted to talk to you about."

"Why? You didn't fall in love with Pomponia, did you? Aii, what a mistake that would be! She's not only virtuous but long in the tooth, and I can't think of a less interesting combination. Brr!"

"No, not Pomponia!" Vinicius grimaced.

"Then who?"

"I wish I knew! I don't even know what to call her, Ligia or Callina. She is a Lygian so they call her Ligia in the household, but she also has her barbarian name, Callina. It's a strange household. It's packed with every kind of servant and attendant, and busy as a beehive, but it's as quiet, peaceful and serene as the sacred groves. It took me several days to realize that a divinity is living there as well. One day at daybreak I caught her outside, bathing in the fountain, and I swear the rays of the sun passed right through her body. What is this, I thought, Aphrodite rising from the foam? I was sure she'd melt into the sunrise along with the dawn. I caught sight of her only twice since then and that's the last time I had any peace of mind. I want nothing else. I don't care what Rome can offer me. I don't want women, gold, Corinthian copperwork, amber or mother-of-pearl, wines, feasts or whatever! I just want Ligia! I'm telling you, Petronius, I dream about her like Morpheus dreamed of Psyche. I can't think of anything else, night or day."

"If she's a slave, then buy her."

"She isn't a slave."

"Then what is she? Some freed maid of Plautius?"

"How could she be freed if she was never a slave to begin with?"

"Then what in Hades is she?"

"I don't know. Some kind of a king's daughter or something like that."

"Hmm. Go on," Petronius showed his first sign of interest. "What kind of a king's daughter?"

"It's not a long story. Maybe you even know Vannius, the king of the Suevi, who lived so many years in exile here in Rome after his people chased him out. He got quite famous as a charioteer and for his luck with dice. Drusus, when he was emperor, put him back on his throne, and luck and his wits kept him there happily enough until he started skinning his own people as eagerly as he skinned and looted his barbarian neighbors. Then his two nephews, Vangio and Sido, sons of Vibilius, king of the Hermanduri who married Vannius' sister, decided to chase him back to his dice in Rome."

"I remember. That was in Claudius' time."

"That's right. So there was a war. Vannius got help from the Yazigi, and his loving nephews called in the wild Lygians who fix the horns of aurochs to their battle helmets. They came in such numbers, lured by loot and rumors of Vannius' riches, that Claudius himself started worrying about the peace of the frontier. He didn't want to get involved in some barbarian war, but he instructed Atelius Hister, who commanded the Danube legions at that time, to keep his eye on that war and make sure it didn't disturb our own peace. Hister convinced the Lygians to stay out of our territories and even got them to send hostages, including their king's wife and daughter. You probably know that those northern tribesmen go to war along with their entire families. Anyway, that daughter was Ligia."

"How do you know all this?"

"Plautius told me. The Lygians kept their word and stayed out of our borders, but you know how it is with the barbarians. They come like a hurricane and blow away like the wind. The Lygians were no different, along with their horns. They hammered Vannius' Suevi and Yazigi into pulp but their king got killed, so they went home to their forests with their loot and left the hostages behind. The mother died soon after, and Hister sent the daughter to Pomponius, the commander-in-chief for all of Germany, since he didn't know what else to do with her. Pomponius received a triumph when he came back to Rome from his campaign against the Catti, and she walked behind his chariot as one of the captives. Of course she was a hostage, not a captive, so she couldn't be treated like a slave, and Pomponius turned her over to his sister, Pomponia Graecina, the wife of Aulus Plautius, once his triumphant entry into Rome was over. And since everything in that household is as virtuous as the Vestals are supposed to be, starting with the master and the mistress and ending with the chickens, she is still a virgin. Unfortunately she's as chaste as Pomponia herself, and so beautiful that if you put Poppea beside her she'd look like an autumn fig next to a fresh apple."

"And so?"

"I tell you that from the moment I saw those streaks of sunlight running through her body I fell head over heels in love, and that's all I can think about."

"She's transparent, then?" Petronius was amused. "Like a lamprey eel or a baby sardine?"

"Don't joke about it, Petronius." The young soldier grew suddenly serious. "I might make light of my lusts, but that's just a pose. Don't let it confuse you. Sometimes the deepest wounds hide under the brightest robes. I spent one night in Delphi on my way from Asia, hoping for a prophetic dream, and Mopsus himself appeared in my sleep to prophesy that love will bring a great change in my life."

"Pliny says that dreams make more sense than all our gods together," Petronius observed, "and maybe he's right. My jesting doesn't interfere with thought, and I often think that there is only one eternal, omnipotent and creative deity, and that's Venus Genetrix, the mother of us all. She gave us our senses. Eros, her firstborn, brought the world out of chaos. I can't say if he did a good job of it, but it's enough to earn our admiration and allegiance. One can bow to his power even if it isn't necessary to do it on one's knees—"

"Ah, Petronius!" the young soldier broke in, anxious for advice. "It's easier to philosophize than to come up with a good practical idea."

"But what is it that you actually want?"

"I want Ligia! I want these arms of mine to clutch her to my chest, instead of clawing at this empty air. I want to suck her breath. If she were a slave, I'd give Aulus a hundred others for her, with white-washed feet to show that they'd never been auctioned off before. I want her in my house until my own thatch turns as white as the peaks of the Alps in winter!"

"Hmm." Petronius turned to the practicalities of the matter. "She's not a slave but she's a member of Plautius' household, almost a foster child, and he could pass her on to you without any trouble."

"That wouldn't happen if you know Pomponia! And besides, they're both as devoted to her as if she were their own natural child."

"Oh, I know Pomponia." Petronius was amused again. "A sheer weeping willow in perpetual mourning. She's been wearing black veils on her head ever since Julia was fed a poisoned apple in Augustus' time; you could rent her out as a wailer at the funerals. Even in life she looks as if she was wandering among the shades. Moreover she's an *univira*, married for life to one man, which makes her unique among all our reigning divorcees who go through four or five husbands like changing a scarf. She's as rare as the Phoenix that rises from his own ashes in the desert. By the way, did you hear that the Phoenix is said to have been born again somewhere in Upper Egypt? That doesn't happen to him more than once in five hundred years."

"Petronius, Petronius!" young Vinicius pleaded. "Can't we save the Phoenix for another time?"

"What's left to say, my boy? I know Aulus Plautius. He disapproves of my life-style, but he does have a certain weakness for me. Maybe he even respects me more than others because he knows I'm not an informer like Domitius Afer, Tigellinus and the rest of that gang that hangs around Nero. I don't pretend to be a Stoic, but I take a dim view of Nero's excesses, unlike Seneca or Burrus who merely ignore them. I'll do what I can for you with Aulus if that's what you want."

"I think you could do a lot. He does respect you. You can influence him. Besides, your mind rises to any challenge. If you could just check into this, see what can be done, and have a talk with Plautius. . . ."

Petronius showed a wry grimace, only half-amused. "Don't give too much credit to my influence." He smiled. "Or to my quick wits. But if that's all you need, I'll talk to Plautius as soon as they move back into the city."

"They've been back two days."

"In that case let's have breakfast. Then we'll have ourselves carried to Plautius' city villa."

"I've always thought the world of you," Vinicius said quickly, "but now I'll have a statue of you put up in my atrium and treat it like one of my household gods—one as beautiful as this one."

He pointed to the row of statues that lined one wall of the fragrant chamber, including one of Petronius himself in the role of Hermes, the winged messenger of the gods, with a caduceus in his upraised hand. "By the light of Helios!" he added in genuine admiration. "If Paris of Troy was anything like you, who'd ever blame Helen?"

His cry rang with as much sincerity as flattery. Petronius may have been the older, and his body lacked the muscled power of the athletic soldier, but he was even handsomer than the young Vinicius in his own special way. The women of Rome assessed his physical characteristics with the same approval they showed his wit, charm, manners and good taste, which won him the title of *arbiter elegantiarum* among his peers. This admiration shone also in the eyes of the girls from Cos who knelt before him now, adjusting the folds of his toga. The one named Eunice, who loved him in secret, stared up into his eyes as if in a daze.

He didn't seem to notice. Instead, he smiled at Vinicius and started quoting Seneca's famous dictum about the character of women: "Woman is an animal without shame . . . et cetera. " Then he threw his arm around Vinicius' shoulder and led him from the perfumed room into the *triclinium* where their breakfast waited.

Left behind in the anointing room, the two Greek girls, the Phrygians and the pair of Nubians started to clear away the jars of scents and unguents, and then the heads of the two huge bath-keepers poked through the folds of the curtain that screened the *frigidarium*.

"Psst!" one hissed softly.

One of the Greek girls, both the Phrygians and the pair of Nubians perked up at once and disappeared swiftly beyond the curtain. That quick, daily moment of the slaves' debauchery and frolic was about to start in the hot compartments of the bathing suite, with which the household overseer never interfered since he often took part in it himself. Petronius had some inkling of it as well, but as a worldly and understanding man, and one moreover who didn't like inflicting punishments, he closed his eyes to it and let it go on.

Alone now in the *unctuarium*, Eunice listened for a while to the laughing voices that dwindled in the direction of the steam room. Then she picked up the ivory and amber-studded stool on which Petronius had been sitting and put it down beside his carved image.

The anointing room was full of scents and sunlight, which reflected from the many-colored marble that lined the walls.

Eunice stepped up on the stool, and when her face was at the level of the statue's head, she flung back her bright golden hair and threw her arms around the marble neck. Then, pressing her rosy flesh to the pale carved body, she started kissing Petronius' stone lips.

‹2›

THEY CALLED IT BREAKFAST but they ate it long after any ordinary mortal had had his midday meal. Then Petronius suggested a short siesta; it was, he insisted, still too early to call on anyone. True, there were people who started their visiting at sunrise and actually thought this was an ancient Roman custom, but he thought it barbaric. In his view the civilized time for visits was late afternoon, after the sun had slid past the temple of the Capitoline Jove and slanted into the Forum from the western edge. Autumns were warm, he observed, and many people liked their postprandial nap after the noon meal; in the meantime it was pleasant to listen to the rustling of the atrium fountains, walk the required thousand paces to help the digestion, and then stretch out in the crimson light that seeped through the half-drawn purple vellum curtains on the divans in the *cubiculum*.

Vinicius agreed. They strolled for a while, chatting without much thought about whatever was new in the city and tossing in a few philosophic comments about life in general. Then Petronius lay down on a screened couch in the *cubiculum*, but he didn't sleep long. He came out in half an hour, ordered some verbena, sniffed it and rubbed it into his temples and along his hands.

"You won't believe how this refreshes me," he said with satisfaction. "Now I'm ready to go."

Their *lectica* or sedan was ready and waiting, so they stretched out inside it. Petronius ordered the African slave porters to carry them to the home of Aulus Plautius on the Vicus Patricius, where most of the great patrician families had their city houses. Petronius' compound lay on the southern slope of the Palatine hill, so their shortest way would have been just below the Forum. But because Petronius also wanted to stop at the shop of the jeweler Idomeneus, he chose a route along the Vicus Apollinis and then through the Forum in the direction of the Vicus Sceleratus, where all kinds of manufacturing outlets clustered at the corners.

The huge black porters hoisted the carrying chair and got on their way, preceded by runners known as *pedisequi*, while Petronius lay back on the cushions and lifted his verbena-scented hands to his face in silence; he seemed to be thinking.

"It strikes me that since your forest nymph is not a slave," he said after a while, "she could simply leave Plautius and move in with you. You could give her all the love and riches she might want, in much the same way as I treated my adored Chrysothemis, who by the way is just as bored with me these days as I am with her."

"You don't know Ligia!" Vinicius protested.

"And do you know her? You saw her, yes. But did you speak with her? Did you tell her how you felt about her?"

"I saw her only twice after that first glimpse at the fountain," Vinicius admitted. "I stayed in the guest house and dined alone as long as my arm was useless. I didn't see Ligia again until the eve of my departure when I joined the family for dinner, but I didn't get to say one word to her. Aulus did all the talking—first about his victories in Britain and then about the ruin of the small independent farmers throughout Italy, which is something that Licinius Stolo tried to prevent with his old reforms. That's all Aulus knows to talk about, and I'm afraid we're in for more of it unless you'd rather hear about how rotten and corrupt everything is today and about how we've lost all our Roman virtues. They keep pheasants in their chicken coops but they never eat them, believing that every eaten bird brings us that much closer to the fall of Rome."

"The next time I saw her she was sprinkling water on the irises that grow around their garden pool. She did it with the head of a reed she dipped in the cistern. Ah, by the shield of Hercules, look at my knees! They were as steady as a rock when swarms of howling Parthians charged our legionnaires, but they were rattling together by that pool like a pair of dice. I stood there gaping like a silly school-boy, as if I still had a child's amulet hung around my neck, begging her with my eyes to put me out of my misery. And I couldn't get a word out for the longest time."

"Happy man!" Petronius looked at him with something like envy. "Youth is the one worthwhile treasure in this world, no matter how miserable the rest of life might be." Then he asked: "So you didn't say anything to her?"

"Yes I did. Eventually. I finally got my wits a bit more together, told her that I was on my way home from Asia, that I dislocated my shoulder on the road and suffered great pain but that leaving that hospitable home was a lot more painful. I said that suffering there seemed more worthwhile to me than any pleasure I might find anywhere else and that even illness would be a better choice than health. She listened but seemed just as confused as I. She stared at the ground and scrawled some kind of symbol in the sand with the reed she used to sprinkle the flowers. Then she looked up at me, glanced back at that symbol, back at me again as if to ask me something, and then she fled like a water nymph startled by a stupid, witless faun."

"What are her eyes like?"

"As deep as the sea. And I drowned in them as if they were the sea! Believe me, the waters of the archipelago aren't as blue. Then Aulus' little son ran up and started asking something but I couldn't understand anything he said."

"O Athena!" Petronius cried out, amused, to the goddess of wisdom and experience. "Strip off that blindfold that Eros tied around this poor lad's eyes, or he'll crack his head on the columns the first time he enters the temple of Venus."

Then he turned to Vinicius. "What are you, anyway?" he asked with a smile of pity. "A fresh spring bud on the tree of life? A green vine sapling? Instead of carrying you to Plautius I should have you taken to the house of Gelocius where they teach adolescents about the birds and the bees."

"What do you want from me?" Vinicius demanded.

"And what did she scribble in the sand? Cupid's name? A heart with an arrow? Or was it something else that might suggest she heard a satyr whispering in her ear? How could you ignore a simple sign like that?"

"Who says I ignored it? I've been wearing a man's toga longer than you think. I know that girls scribble things in the sand, in Greece as well as in Rome, that they don't want to say out loud. I had a long, careful look at it before little Aulus came running up. But what do you think she drew?"

"I've no idea," Petronius said with a shrug, "if it's not one of the things I mentioned."

"A fish."

"What? She drew a fish?"

"That's what I said. A fish. I don't know what it means. Was she trying to say she's as cold-blooded as a fish? But since you're so quick to call me a spring bud, and you're so experienced, I'm sure you can tell me."

"My dear fellow!" Petronius started laughing. "Talk to Pliny about fish. He's an expert on them. If old Apicius was still alive, he'd tell you even more. He ate so much fish in his lifetime that the Bay of Naples wouldn't be big enough to hold them."

Their conversation ended then, because they were passing through crowded thoroughfares where they could hardly hear each other above the roar of city sounds and voices. From the Vicus Apollinis they turned into the Forum Romanum where idle mobs gathered before sunset on a clear day, to walk among the columns, gossip, hear the news, gape at the notables carried past in litters, and peer into jewelry shops, bookstores, money-changers' stalls, and innumerable stands, stores and barrows that sold silk and bronzes and every other luxury of the times, which lined all the buildings across the Forum from the Capitol.

Half of the Forum, the one that lay below the cliff face of the Capitol, was already buried in the shadows, but the columns of the temples placed higher up the slopes glowed like gold in the slanting sunlight, dazzling against the blue canopy of the sky. The lower columns threw their dark, elongated shadows on the marble pavement, so many looming everywhere that the eyes lost themselves among them as if in a forest.

Temples and buildings stood crowded together wherever they looked. Structures and columns clustered everywhere, huddled against each other as if for protection. Columns and porticoes thrust above each other, spilled to right and left, climbed the surrounding slopes, clung to the sheer rock and walls of the imperial palace or pressed against each other like a dense grove of marble tree trunks, some tall and thin, others squat and thick; some dazzling white and pink, others gilded by the sunlight; some flowering into marble vines and acanthus blooms under the architraves, others curled into Ionic horns or square-cut Doric corners. Triglyphs, or ornamental friezes, gleamed above this forest. Carved gods peered from the door panels and leaned out of the triangular areas of the pediments. Winged golden chariots seemed ready to leap into the sky off the peaks and summits and soar across the soft blue dome that hung so serenely above this crowd of temples.

A thick human river seemed to flow through this marketplace and along its borders. Crowds pushed among the arches of the temple of Julius Caesar, now an official god; other crowds sat on the steps of Castor and Pollux or swirled around the little temple of the Vestals, looking like a swarm of colored butterflies and beetles against the mass of marble that served as their background.

Fresh streams of people poured down the colossal stairway that led from the greatest of all the temples, the one dedicated to Jupiter Maximus Optimus, the ruler of all the gods. Impromptu orators harangued the passersby off the speakers' platform; peddlers hawked fruit, wine and watered fig juice; swindlers offered miraculous medicines and cures, soothsayers gazed into the future for a price, and tricksters and magicians located buried treasure and interpreted dreams. Here and there sounds of Egyptian sistras, sambucas and Greek flutes played counterpoint to this cacophony of cries and conversations. Elsewhere, the sick, the pious and those afflicted by anxiety and fear carried gifts and sacrifices to the temples, while flocks of pigeons, looking like animated dark and piebald stains on the marble slabs among the jostling people, gathered around the spilled grain, soared into the air with a hiss of wings, and settled down again after the mobs had passed.

Now and then the crowds parted, making way for gigantic porters who bore some curtained litter on their shoulders, with the harsh, set faces of senators and members of the Equestrian Order showing among the curtains or with the fashionable coiffures of great ladies resting in the cushions. The nobles' faces were uniformly weary and had features that seemed scarred by life and congealed into masks of waste and devastation, and the beautifully gowned, resplendent women glittered with jewels, decadence and corruption. The multilingual mobs cried out their names in Greek as often as Latin, frequently adding insults, praise or jeers, or some favorite nickname, and swirled aside before troops of soldiers marching heavily in step or the civil watch charged with the keeping of the public order.

Vinicius, who had been away from the city a long time, looked with some curiosity at this human beehive and at the Forum Romanum that ruled the known world but seemed swamped to the point of drowning by this tidal wave of subjects.

"The nest of the Quirites," Petronius offered, guessing the young man's thoughts. He used the name that the native Romans adopted for themselves when they had absorbed the Sabines into their community under Romulus, the founder of their city. "But without the Quirites."

"It seems so," Marcus said.

Indeed, the native element had practically disappeared in this seething mass composed of all the peoples of the Roman empire. He could see black Ethiopians, towering yellow-haired northerners from beyond the Alps, Britons, Gauls and Germans, slant-eyed inhabitants of Lericum, olive-skinned men from the banks of the Euphrates and the Indus with beards dyed the color of raw bricks, Syrians with luminous black eyes, people who seemed as dry and desiccated as old bones and came from the depths of the Arabian deserts, gaunt Jews with hunched shoulders and sunken chests, Egyptians with their never-ending smiles of aloof indifference, blue-black Numidians and gleaming Africans. There were the Greeks from mainland Hellas who ruled Rome along with the Romans and who dominated the city through their art, their sciences, their shrewd minds and their money-changing skills; and more Greeks from the Aegean Islands and their colonies throughout Asia Minor, and from coastal Italy and Egypt and Narbonic Gaul. Crowds of free Roman idlers of the lower orders moved leisurely and carelessly among the swarms of slaves with holes punched in their ears, along with free immigrants, settlers and specu-lators from other towns and countries of the empire, drawn to this vast sprawling city by its riches and its venality, and by the opportu-nity to make their own shrewd fortunes. The emperors gave these idle mobs bread and circuses, fed them and amused them, and even clothed and housed them just to keep them quiet, but they were a volatile and explosive element nonetheless.

Nor was there ever any shortage of priests and hucksters in the Forum. There were priests of Serapis with palm branches waving in their hands, and priests of Isis who gathered more offerings on her altars than the Capitoline Jove, and priests of Cybele who clutched golden rice stalks, and priests of all the nomadic divinities of the East. Oriental dancers with tall, brightly colored miters on their heads jos-tled with dealers in amulets, and snake charmers, and Chaldean wiz-ards; and finally there were the great noisy masses who did nothing at all but who came each week for free grain at the Tiber granaries, fought over lottery tickets and seats in the circus, slept in the rickety houses beyond the Tiber that crashed on their heads time and time again, and spent their days lounging in the shade of open porticoes, or in the foul soup kitchens of the Suburra, or on the Milvian bridge, or sprawled before the compounds of the rich where they were some-times thrown the scraps and scrapings of the slaves' kettles.

Petronius was well known to these crowds. Indeed, he was some-thing of a hero to them. Marcus Vinicius heard time and again as one or another of the idlers caught sight of him and cried *"Hic est!* It's Petronius!"

They liked him for his careless generosity. His strange popularity with the mob soared especially high when word seeped down to the populace that he protested the imperial verdict that sentenced to death the whole vast household of the prefect Pedanius Secundus, that is to say, every slave of both sexes, no matter their ages, because one of them killed that unspeakably cruel man in a moment of madness and despair. Petronius told everyone who would listen that he didn't care about the slaves one way or another. It was all the same to him. He spoke about the matter privately to Nero only in his role as the arbiter of taste, because the massacre offended his aesthetic sensibilities. It was, he thought, barbaric, fit for some savage Scythians, and quite beneath the Romans. But the mob that rioted in the streets, because of that slaughter, loved Petronius from then on, no matter what he said.

This, too, was a matter of indifference to him. He remembered that the street mob also loved Britannicus, whom Nero poisoned, and Agrippina, whom his praetorians murdered at his order, and Octavia, whom he starved in prison on Pantaleria—her wrists were slit in a steam bath by his command, and she was then strangled—and Rubelius Plautus, driven into exile, and Thrasea, whose death could come at any moment. The love of the mob could be seen as bad luck as much as anything, and Petronius was highly superstitious. He despised the rabble on two grounds: first as an aristocrat and then as a man of culture and refinement. In his view, men who smelled of roast lima beans, which the common people carried in their shirts for a handy snack, and who were always hoarse and sweaty from their games of "fish" which they bet on in the peristyles and on every street corner in the city, weren't even human. So now, ignoring the mob's applause and the kisses sent his way here and there, he told Marcus about the Pedanius affair, sneering at the fickleness of "the great unwashed" who applauded Nero the day after the massacre and their own rioting, as he drove to the temple of Jupiter Stator, the patron of stability and order.

But at the bookstore of Avirnus he ordered a halt, went inside and bought a decorative manuscript which he handed to Vinicius. "That's for you," he said.

"Thanks," said Vinicius as he glanced at the title. "*The Satyricon?* That's something new. Who wrote it?"

"I did, but keep it to yourself. I didn't want to make the same mistake as Rufinus, whose story I wanted to tell you, or Fabricius Veiento, so nobody knows it."

"You said you didn't write poetry"—Vinicius glanced quickly through the scroll—"but there's a lot of it here mixed in with the prose."

"Note Trimalchio's feast when you're reading it. As for verse, I've formed an aversion to it since Nero started writing in Homeric couplets. Ha! Whenever Vitelius wants to ease his stomach, he pushes an ivory stylus down his throat. Others induce vomiting with flamingo feathers dipped in olive oil or in boiled thyme. All I have to do is read Nero's epic, and the result is immediate. Then I can praise him on an empty belly if not exactly with a clear conscience."

Here he halted the litter at the workshop of Idomeneus, went in to take care of the gems he wanted, and finally ordered the bearers to take him straight to the Plautius villa.

"I'll tell you the Rufinus story on the way," he said, "to show you what an author's pride can do to a man."

But they turned into the Vicus Patricius before he could start it, and they were at the gate of Aulus Plautius only moments later. A muscular young doorkeeper swung open the doors to the *ostium*, the first of two antechambers before the main atrium where a caged mockingbird screeched "*Salve!*" above their heads.

"Did you notice that the doorman wasn't wearing chains?" Vinicius asked on their way to the atrium.

"This is an odd household," Petronius murmured softly. "You probably know that Pomponia was suspected of worshiping some kind of eastern idol—named Chrestos or something. I think that Crispinilla got that rumor going. She can't forgive Pomponia for one husband suiting her for a lifetime. Imagine! A one-man woman! It's easier to find a dish of Noricum mushrooms in Rome nowadays. They brought her up on charges at the domestic court but—"

"You're right," Vinicius nodded. "This is a strange household. I'll tell you later what I saw and heard when I was staying here."

Meanwhile they came to the atrium. The slave in charge of it, called the *atriensis*, sent the *nomenclator* to announce the guests, while other house slaves offered them chairs and footstools. Petronius, who imagined that only gloom could reign in this serious household, had never been there before; now he sat peering around in surprise, with perhaps a touch of disappointment, because the atrium had a rather pleasant and cheerful look about it. Bright sunlight streamed in from above through a large square opening and fractured into thousands of glittering prisms in the fountain and the rectangular pool below. The pool, called the *impluvium*, was actually a rain basin, used to catch the pure rainwater in autumn and spring, but here it served as a centerpiece for an indoor garden of anemones and lilies. Lilies seemed to be the favorite flowers in this home; they grew in profusion everywhere, in white and in crimson, along with clumps of irises, from sky blue to as dark as sapphires, their delicate petals gleaming with drops of water as if they'd been brushed in passing with a silvery pollen. Little bronze statuettes of children and water birds peered from among the fronds and out of the moss that hid the flowerpots, while in one corner of the pool a bronze doe bowed her greenish head toward the water as if about to drink. The floor of the atrium was laid in mosaic tile. The walls, either veneered in red marble or painted with trees, fish, birds and mythical animals, were especially appealing with their cheerful colors. The side doors that led to other rooms were tastefully decorated with carved tortoise shell and ivory, and rows of statues that represented Aulus' ancestors stood between them all along the walls. Wherever the visitors looked they could sense a calm and confident impression of plenty, by no means excessive but quite sufficient for the most demanding needs.

Petronius, who lived on a far more lavish and elegant scale, always seeking the exact balance between the exquisite and the ostentatious, could find nothing here to which he might object, and he turned to comment on that to Vinicius when the *velarius*, the slave whose job it was to draw and open curtains, drew aside the tapestry that hid the interior gallery or terrace where family records were normally kept in a Roman household. They saw Aulus Plautius hurrying toward them out of the corridors beyond.

He was a middle-aged man, fast approaching the sunset of his years but still hardy, with energy etched into his features and with a clenched, somewhat crumpled face that made him look like a watchful eagle. This time he showed a touch of alarmed surprise at the unexpected visit of Nero's friend, confidant and favorite boon companion.

Petronius was far too worldly to miss this telltale sign of consternation, and once the normal ritual of greeting was over, he launched into a soothing and urbane explanation, delivered in his most eloquent and diplomatic tone, that he came only to thank Aulus for the care that his sister's son had received in his house.

"It's just a matter of simple gratitude," he said, smiling at Aulus. "A normal and expected courtesy among men who have known each other as long as you and I."

"Delighted to see you," the old general assured him. "But it's I who am grateful to you, my dear fellow, although I'm sure you wouldn't guess why."

"Indeed." Petronius fixed his puzzled brown eyes on the ceiling and mentally scratched his head. He couldn't think of a single instance in which he might have rendered any kind of service to Aulus, or to anybody else for that matter. His planned intervention on behalf of Marcus was probably the first time he had ever done anything for someone other than himself. Oh, it might have happened sometime by accident, he supposed, but never as a conscious effort.

"You don't remember what you did for Vespasian?" Aulus asked. "I'm awfully fond of him and I value him, and you saved his life the time he fell asleep while listening to Nero's poetry. We were all quite sure he had run out of luck."

"On the contrary," Petronius said. "His luck was never better because he missed some really awful verse. But I admit it could have ended badly. Our Copperbeard was all set to send a centurion to him with a friendly suggestion to slit his wrists."

"But you, Petronius, turned it all into a harmless joke."

"True. Or rather partly true. I merely told our versifying emperor that he was now the equal of Orpheus who could sing wild beasts to sleep, which made his poetry divine. Nero can take a bit of criticism if it's wrapped in flattery, which is something our gracious empress, the much-loved Poppea, understands very well."

"Ah, what times we live in!" Aulus shook his head in sad disapproval. "I lost two front teeth in Britain where some Briton hit me with a stone, which is why I whistle a bit when I speak these days. And yet the happiest years of my life passed among those savages—"

"Because they were your glorious and victorious years," Vinicius tossed in.

But Petronius, worried that the general might regale them with some old war stories, quickly changed the subject. It appeared that some peasants found a dead two-headed wolf cub in the neighborhood of Praeneste, while a thunderbolt ripped off an angle in the temple of Luna during a freak storm at about that time, which was unheard of so late in the autumn. The man who told Petronius about it, a fellow by the name of Cotta, also added that the temple priests saw in this sign the fall of the city or at least the ruin of some great house that only some extraordinary sacrifices could avert.

Aulus agreed that such omens couldn't be ignored. "The Gods could be angry. It's hardly surprising. There's just too much wickedness these days, in which case special sacrifices are perfectly in order."

"Well, it can hardly be your house," Petronius observed lightly, "because it's quite small, even though a great man lives in it. Mine may be too big for such a worthless owner, but it also doesn't amount to much. But if we're talking about the destruction of some really great house, such as the imperial palace, for example, is it worth our while to avert its ruin?"

Plautius said nothing, and Petronius felt somewhat piqued by this obvious caution. For all his indifference to other people's welfare and his inability to tell good from evil, he had never played informer and it was safe to talk to him about anything. But he changed the subject again nonetheless and started praising the good taste of Aulus' house.

"It's an old home," Plautius said, "and I have changed nothing in it since I inherited it."

After the curtain between the atrium and the inner gallery had been drawn aside, the house was open from end to end. It was possible to see across the next peristyle and the salon beyond it, all the way to the garden that gleamed at the far end like a bright painting set in a somber frame. Children's laughter rang there happily and echoed through the house as far as the atrium.

"Ah, General," Petronius said, "give us a chance to hear that pure and honest laughter from close by. It's so hard to come by it nowadays."

"Gladly." Plautius rose and led the way. "That's my little Aulus and Ligia playing ball. But speaking of laughter, Petronius, I'd say that you've been listening to it all your life."

"I laugh," Petronius said with a shrug, "because life isn't worth a tear. But this laughter's different."

"Besides," Vinicius added, "Petronius does more laughing at night than in the daytime."

They walked the length of the house and came to the garden where Ligia and little Aulus were playing catch with balls that special slaves, called *spheristae*, picked up and handed to them. While Petronius threw a quick assessing glance at Ligia and little Aulus came running to greet Vinicius, the young soldier bowed in passing to the beautiful girl who stood with ball in hand; her hair was disordered, her face was flushed, and she was out of breath.

They made their way to a leafy arbor sheathed in grapes, wild woodbine and ivy. Pomponia Graecina sat on a three-sided table couch, the kind used for reclining during meals. Petronius knew her, even though he had never visited her at home, because he had seen her in the house of Antistia, the daughter of Rubelius Plautus, and in the homes of Seneca and Pollio. For all his mannered cynicism, he couldn't quite resist a certain admiration for her, struck as he always was by her quiet sadness, by the mild, pensive gravity of her face, and by the natural dignity of her pos-

ture, movements and bearing. Pomponia upset all his ideas about women
to such a degree that this thoroughly corrupt and self-indulgent man, for
whom her sex held no mysteries whatsoever, not only found himself
touched by a strange respect but actually lost some of his aplomb.
Now, thanking her for the care she had given Vinicius, he couldn't help
addressing her as *domina*, which never even occurred to him when he
talked to such great ladies of the Roman world as Calvia Crispinilla,
Scribonia, Valeria or Solina. Then, as soon as he was done with his
thanks and greetings, he started complaining that she came out so seldom
in society and that she was never to be seen at either the amphitheater or
the circus.

"We're both getting on in years," she said quietly, taking her husband's hand, "and we've become very fond of our peaceful home."

Petronius wanted to argue the point but Aulus Plautius interrupted
him.

"And we feel even less at home," he added, "among people who call
our Roman gods by Greek names."

"The gods have become mere figures of speech for quite a while
now." Petronius shrugged indifferently, with a quick admiring glance
at Pomponia, as if to say that no divinity could come to mind beside
her. "Besides, since Greeks teach us rhetoric, even I find it easier to
say Hera than Juno."

Then he started to contradict what she had said about aging.
"Some people do age quickly," he agreed politely, "but they live lives
totally different from yours. Moreover, there are faces that seem to
stay forever young."

To his own surprise, his mannered phrases sounded quite sincere.
Pomponia did look young even though she was past her youth. Her
skin was smooth and quite untouched by age, and her face and head
were delicate and small, so that despite her gravity and the somber
colors of her robes, she projected the impression of quite a young
woman.

Meanwhile little Aulus, who had become very fond of Vinicius
while he was staying in the house, ran up to ask him to join him and
Ligia at their game. She also came into the arbor, and now Petronius
could get a better look at her. With the sunlight filtering through the
fringed canopy of ivy and sparkling on her face, she seemed like some
woodland nymph, far more beautiful than at first glance. Since he had
said nothing to her earlier, he got up to greet her, bowed smoothly
before her, and rather than using the customary phrases, spoke to her

as Ulysses did when he met Nausicaa in the Odyssey. He quoted Homer:

> "Nymph, are you divine or mortal?
> If you are of this earth, then blessed is your father
> And your mother both,
> And blessed are your kin."

Even Pomponia was pleased by the exquisite gallantry of this worldly and cultivated man, while Ligia listened to him with her eyes cast down, blushing in confusion. But then a merry smile trembled gradually in the corners of her lips and modesty struggled briefly in her face with a desire to answer him in kind; this desire apparently won the fight. She looked up suddenly at Petronius and quoted Nausicaa's ironic reply, rather like a breathless schoolroom recitation.

> "Clearly, you're quite extraordinary yourself,
> And with a head to match."

Then she spun around and skimmed away much like a startled bird.

It was now Petronius' turn to gawk, thoroughly astonished to hear Homeric couplets coming from a girl who, as Vinicius warned him, was born a barbarian. Nor could Pomponia offer him an immediate answer, because she was looking at her husband, smiling at the flush of pride that spread suddenly in old Aulus' face.

Nor could the old man conceal his delight, first because he had become as attached to Ligia as if she were his own natural child, and then because he thought Greek the height of sophisticated usage, even though his old Roman pride and prejudice forced him to thunder publicly against it. He was secretly ashamed that he had never been able to learn it properly himself, so now he beamed with pleasure to have this refined and picky arbiter of good taste, who may have thought his household primitive by high society's standards, greeted in his home with Homer's words and language.

"We have a Greek tutor in the house"—he turned to Petronius—"who teaches my lad, and the girl listens in. She's a young sprite as yet but a very pleasant one, and my wife and I have both become very fond of her."

But Petronius' attention shifted to the garden. He was looking through the twisting ivy at the three young people who were playing there. Vinicius had thrown off his toga; dressed only in his indoor tunic, he was punching the ball high into the air, and the girl who stood across from him stretched her arms to catch it. She seemed too thin to him at first quick glance, but that impression vanished when he got a closer look at her in the arbor. That's what the first light of dawn would look like, he thought, if it were rendered in human form by a gifted sculptor—say Boëthus of Tanagra, a town in Boeotia and the birthplace of Hercules and Bacchus, who created such magic with silver and alabaster. As a true connoisseur of beauty he understood at once that there was something extraordinary about this girl, some inner quality that both defied and challenged his experience. Now he saw and assessed everything at once: her pink, translucent cheeks, her fresh young lips that seemed to be pouting for a kiss, the blue depths of a sea that glowed in her eyes, the clear alabaster whiteness of her forehead, the profusion of her tumbled dark hair, shot with amber lights of Corinthian copper where it curled and twisted, her delicate, smooth neck, the slope of her shoulders that brought to mind Diana and Aphrodite, and her entire body: slim, pliant, supple and projecting all the newness of May and fresh blooms.

The artist and the worshiper of beauty woke in him at once. There was only one title for a sculpture of her: Spring! Nothing else would do! And suddenly he thought of Chrysothemis, his kept lover of many years, and the envy with which all of Rome looked at him because he possessed her; he almost laughed out loud in self-derision and contempt. Compared to this untouched glowing freshness, that society beauty seemed like a half-wilted, comically faded rose, with her painted eyebrows and gold-dusted hair. Then he thought of Poppea whose fabulously famous face seemed suddenly like a lifeless mask. This Tanagran figure possessed the inner radiance of Psyche herself, and that deep-seated glow flowed through her fresh young body as a candle flame shines in polished alabaster.

Vinicius was right, he thought. And my Chrysothemis is as old as Troy!

"I understand now, *domina*"—he turned to Pomponia and gestured toward the garden—"that with so much life in the house you'd rather stay at home than sit through the circus or Palatine banquets."

"Yes." She nodded, looking at little Aulus and Ligia.

The old general launched at once into the girl's story, telling it as Vinicius had told it to Petronius and including whatever he had heard from Atelius Hister about the Lygian people who lived somewhere in the gloomy forests of the North.

The three outside, as pale against the dark cypresses and myrtles as three ivory statues, had finished their game a short while earlier. They walked slowly, talking to one another along the sanded paths, and now sat down on a stone bench beside the ornamental fish pond. Ligia had held little Aulus' hand, but he broke free and ran to tease the fish in the still clear water. Vinicius went on with what he was saying.

"Yes"—his voice was barely audible and trembled with feeling— "I'd no sooner stopped wearing a boy's tunic than they shipped me off to the Asian legions. I know nothing about Rome or life in the city. Life and love are both a mystery to me. I can recite a bit of Anacreon and Horace, but I can't imitate Petronius and speak poetry when the mind is numb with shock. I can't stumble on the proper words. I got my early schooling from Musonius, who taught that to be happy we have to want what the gods have in mind for us. In other words it's a matter of our own choice and will. But I think happiness springs from another source, a far deeper one that doesn't depend on will because it comes from love. The gods themselves search for it all the time so it must be the most precious of the lot. I do as they do, and since I've never felt love for anyone before, I keep looking for the woman who might give it to me."

Quiet for a moment, he listened to the soft plop of pebbles tossed into the water where little Aulus was stirring up the fish. Then he picked up again.

"Do you know Titus, Vespasian's son?" His voice sank even lower. "The story is that he fell in love so totally with Berenice, when he was barely out of boyhood, that he almost died of longing for her. I also could love like that, Ligia! I see no point in riches, fame or power. That's smoke! An illusion! A rich man can always find someone richer than himself. Somebody else's fame can always overshadow yours, and power falls before a greater power. But if the emperor and all the gods know themselves immortal only when they feel that one desired breast pressing against their own, and rise above those mundane satisfactions only when they kiss that one treasured mouth, then love makes us their equals."

She listened, startled and surprised but also fascinated, as if she were listening to a Greek flute or the music of a hand-held harp. It seemed to her at times that Vinicius was singing some wonderful strange song which seeped into her ears, making her blood flow faster, which frightened her, and making her feel confused and weak and at the same time filled with inexplicable joy. What he was saying seemed to find an echo in what she'd told herself many times before without quite realizing what it meant. She felt the first strong stirring of something new within her, something he was awakening. Her unformed dreams started to acquire shape, color and texture, becoming ever clearer step by step and much more beautiful at each transformation.

Meanwhile the sun rolled past the Tiber and began to sink into the Janiculum on its rounded hill. Red light suffused the air and framed the cypress trees. Ligia looked up, fixed her blue, half-dreaming eyes on Vinicius and saw a new image, something far more beautiful and appealing than imagination. With his head bowed toward her in that evening radiance and with a mute question trembling in his eyes, he seemed much more than any man she had seen or any deity glimpsed in the temple atriums.

His fingers closed lightly just above her wrist. "Can't you guess, Ligia, why I'm saying all these things to you?"

"No." Her whisper was so hushed that it barely reached Vinicius' ear.

But he didn't believe her. His grip tightened on her wrist, and he started to pull her toward him. His heart was pounding in his chest, spurred by the girl's beauty so close, within reach. He would have drawn her to him and let the hot words spill into her ears if old Aulus hadn't suddenly appeared on the path, framed by the myrtle hedge.

"The sun is going down," he warned. "Don't play any games with Libitina, you two."

"I don't feel any chill," Vinicius said, "and I don't have my toga."

"Well, the sun's half down, as you see," the old general growled and suddenly waxed poetic. "Ah, if this were only Sicily where, in the evening, the people gather in the marketplace and sing to send Phoebus on his way in his fiery chariot."

Spurred by the name, he started talking about Sicily where he had a country home and extensive farmlands. He quite forgot his own warning against Libitina, the goddess of corpses and patroness of funeral undertakers, whom he'd mentioned earlier.

"I've thought about moving there," he said.

"You have?" Vinicius was immediately alarmed.

"Certainly. Why not? I can't think of a better place for my final years. You don't need frost on the ground around you when your hair turns frosty white on its own."

The leaves had hardly started falling as yet, he went on, and the sky still wore its golden smile, but when the grapes turned yellow, the snow fell in the Alban Hills, and the gods sent the winds howling through Campagna, then who knew what he'd do?

"I might very well just pick up," he said, "and move myself and my entire household to that peaceful life in the country."

"Would you really want to leave Rome, Plautius?" the young soldier asked, bewildered by the possibility of losing sight of Ligia.

"I've wanted it for years. Life in the country is both calmer and safer."

And once again he began to extol his orchards, his herds, the house that crouched among the vines, the bees that swarmed in the wild cloves and the thyme that covered the hills. But Vinicius paid no attention to this country idyll. All he thought about was that Ligia might be taken away from him, and he kept shooting glances at Petronius as if he were his last desperate hope.

Meanwhile Petronius sat beside Pomponia and enjoyed the sunset, the garden and the sight of the figures clustered by the fish pond. The setting sun gilded their white tunics and togas against the dark backdrop of the myrtles. The evening sky turned into deeper violets and purples; the roof of the sky glowed lavender and lilac, as opaque as opal. The cypress trees stood black and stark against the sinking radiance, their silhouettes harsher than in daylight, and the quiet stillness of the evening settled on all of this, falling upon the trees, the people and the entire garden.

Petronius was particularly struck by the peacefulness he read in the faces of the Plautius household. The old general, Pomponia, Ligia and the boy seemed to contain and project some strange soothing light, a quiet inner joy that came directly from the sort of life they lived in this unusual home and something that he had never seen in faces elsewhere on any other night. He had spent his life in the pursuit of beauty and contentment, the perfection of the mind and spirit, and he never even brushed against them anywhere. They had eluded him time and time again so that he started counting them among his unattainable illusions. But now he thought, surprised, that they must be tangible and real after all, because he could sense them everywhere around him.

He couldn't hide that thought. "I can't help thinking how different your world is from the one ruled by Nero," he said to Pomponia.

She raised her delicate face toward the glowing sky. "God rules the world, not Nero."

They were both silent then. They listened to the footsteps coming near along the sandy path, but before Aulus Plautius, his son, Ligia and Vinicius came into the arbor, Petronius asked one last question:

"So you believe in the gods, Pomponia?"

"I believe in the one true God who is omnipotent and just," Pomponia said.

"SHE BELIEVES IN A GOD who is one, all-powerful and just," Petronius said as soon as he and Vinicius were back in their carrying chair. "If her god is all-powerful, he has control over life and death. If he is just, he doesn't send death unjustly. So why does Pomponia mourn Julia after all this time? By grieving for her she's accusing her own god. I'll have to repeat all this to our copper-bearded ape, because I don't think I've a thing to learn from Socrates when it comes to reasoning. I agree that every woman has three or four souls, but none of them is capable of reason. Let Pomponia ponder along with Seneca and Cornutus on the nature of creation. Let them call up the ghosts of Xenophanes, Parmenides, Zeno and Plato, because they must be as bored in the underworld as caged mockingbirds. I wanted to talk with Plautius and Pomponia about something else! Ah, by the sacred belly of the Egyptian Isis, how could I? If I'd told them straight out what we had come about, we'd never hear the end of it! Their virtue would rise up in arms, and they'd make more noise than a copper gong. I simply didn't dare! Can you believe it, Marcus? I just didn't dare. Beauty, yes. it's all very beautiful over there, but peacocks are also beautiful until they start screeching. The possibility of all that shouting simply scared me stiff. But I do have to compliment you on your choice. She's the true image of Aurora, *'the rosy-fingered dawn,'* to borrow from Homer. I thought of spring the moment I saw her, and not our own Italian springs when the olives turn gray the moment the first flowers bloom, but that young, fresh, bright green spring I saw one time in Helvetia. I'm not surprised that she got to you as she did. I'll swear it by that pale moon that's looking down on us. But watch yourself, Marcus. Loving her is like falling in love with Diana, and you know what happened to Acteon when he tried to carry off his moon goddess by force. Aulus and Pomponia will tear you apart like the wild dogs that devoured Acteon."

Slumped on the cushions, Vinicius said nothing for a while. Then he hissed out in sharp, broken phrases made breathless by passion.

"I wanted her before," he snarled. "Now I want her more. I thought I'd burn up when I grasped her hand. I've got to have her. I wish I was Zeus! I'd cover her like a cloud, the way Zeus threw himself on Io, or I'd fall on her like a shower of gold, the way he possessed Danae. I want to kiss that mouth until it hurts. I want to hear her shouting in my arms. I want to kill Aulus and Pomponia and seize her and carry her to my house. I won't sleep tonight, that's certain. I'll have some slave flogged and listen to his screams—"

"Calm down," Petronius snapped. "Your tastes are as crude as a common carpenter's."

"I don't care. I've got to have her one way or another. I came to you for advice, but if you can't give it, I'll find my own way. If Aulus thinks of her as his daughter, why should I see her as a slave? So let it be marriage if it can't be anything else. Let her rub wolf tallow on my doors, let her hang a red thread from the lintels, and sit by my hearth as my wife."

"Calm down, you madman," Petronius warned again. "You're a Roman noble. Your ancestors were consuls. We don't drag barbarians on a rope's end behind our war chariots just so that we end up marrying their daughters. Beware of extremes. Try all the simple, honest, ordinary means and win us both a little time to think of something useful. I also thought of Chrysothemis at one time as some sort of goddess, but I didn't marry her, did I? Nor did Nero marry his Acte, though she's supposed to be the daughter of King Attalus. So calm down, I tell you. Remember that if she decides to leave Aulus' household and move into yours, there's nothing they can do about it. She's not their property. The law's on your side. And you're not the only one who fell in love, my lad. I could see Eros working on her, too, and I know what I'm talking about, you can bank on that. Be patient. There's a key to every door. I've done enough thinking for today so I won't strain myself anymore tonight, but I promise you I'll give it a lot of thought tomorrow. I wouldn't be Petronius if I failed to find something that would work."

They were quiet again for a time. When Vinicius broke the silence a little later, his tone was much calmer.

"Thank you," he said. "And good luck."

"Easy does it, lad. Patience is the key."

"Where are you going tonight, by the way?"

"To Chrysothemis."

"You're lucky to be able to have the woman you love."

"I?" Petronius laughed. "The only thing about Chrysothemis that still amuses me is that she cheats on me with my own freedman, the lute-player Theocles, and thinks I haven't noticed. I did love her once, but now her lies and her stupidity are the only entertainment she provides. Come with me. If she starts flirting with you and scribbling love notes on the table with a finger dipped in wine, you know I won't get jealous."

They ordered themselves carried to Chrysothemis' house. They had barely stepped into the atrium when Petronius tapped Vinicius on the shoulder.

"Hold on a moment," he said with a grin. "I think I've found a way."

"May all the gods reward you—"

"Yes! That's it! It's a foolproof method." Petronius smiled, pleased with his own brilliance. "Hmm . . . listen. Do you know something, Marcus?"

"I'm all ears, my dear oracle."

"In just a few days your divine Ligia will be keeping house for you—or eating the seeds of Demeter, as the saying goes."

"If that's so," Vinicius shouted, "you're greater than Caesar!"

⟪4⟫

PETRONIUS KEPT HIS WORD. Next day, after his visit to Chrysothemis, he slept until evening and then at nightfall had himself carried to the Palatine where he had a confidential talk with Nero. The result was that on the following morning, three days after Vinicius had first confided in him, a centurion came to the Plautius house with a squad of praetorian guards.

The times were full of uncertainty and fear. Such emissaries were usually messengers of death, so terror swept through the entire household when the centurion hammered on the door and the overseer of the atrium sent word that the vestibule was full of soldiers. The family ran to Aulus, sure that the danger threatened him more than anyone. Pomponia threw her arms around his neck, pressed herself with all her strength against him, and her pale lips whispered something swiftly into his ear; Ligia, white as linen, covered his hand with kisses; little Aulus clung to his toga; and slaves, both men and women, poured out of all the corridors: from the upper rooms where the women lived, from the servants' quarters, from the bathhouse and from the basement cubicles below. Shouts of *"heu, heu, me misere"* filled the house. The women wept loudly. Some of the slave girls clawed their faces and covered their heads as if for a funeral.

The old general stayed calm. Years of war had taught him to stare death in the face. Only his tight-knit aquiline features clenched into a stony mask that concealed all feeling. He snapped an order for silence and sent the slaves back about their business, then turned to Pomponia.

"Let me go," he murmured, pushing her slightly aside. "If my time has come, we'll have time to say good-bye to each other."

"I pray that I may share your fate, Aulus," she said, "whatever it is."

Then she went down on her knees and began to pray as fervently as only fear for someone very dear allows a human being.

Aulus, meanwhile, passed into the atrium where he came face-to-face with the centurion. This, he saw at once, was Caius Hasta who had served under him in the Britannic wars.

"Greetings, General," the centurion said as he showed his commission written on wax tablets. "I bring you greetings and an order from the emperor. And here are the tablets confirming that I come in his name."

"I'm grateful for the emperor's greetings," Aulus said formally, "and I'm at his command. Be welcome here, Hasta. Now, what's it all about?"

"The emperor has been told that you have a hostage in your house," Hasta began. "She's a daughter of a Lygian king whom her people turned over to Rome when the divine Claudius was our ruling Caesar, as their guarantee of our imperial borders. The divine Nero is grateful to you, General, for all the years of care you gave her in your home. But wanting to free you of that burden, and bearing in mind that she's a state hostage who should be under imperial protection, he orders you to hand her over to me immediately."

Aulus was too much of a soldier to protest an order, and too much a man to permit himself one word of bitterness or complaint, but his eyes narrowed with a sudden spasm of anger and pain. There was a time when the British legions quailed before such signs of his displeasure, and fear flickered briefly even now on Hasta's face as well. But this time Aulus was quite helpless in the face of an imperial order. He stared a moment longer at the tablets, then fixed his eyes calmly on the old centurion.

"Wait here, Hasta," he said. "The hostage will be with you shortly."

He made his way to the other end of the house where Pomponia, Ligia and little Aulus waited fearfully in the salon known as the *oecus*.

"No one is in danger of either death or exile," he said, coming in. "But the emperor's message is tragic nonetheless. It's about you, Ligia."

"About Ligia?" Pomponia cried, astonished.

"Yes." The old general looked sadly at the girl. "Ligia, we raised you in our home as if you were our own and we couldn't love you more if you were our daughter. But you know you're not. You're a hostage given to Rome by your people and it's the emperor's job to look after you. Well, now the emperor is taking you away."

The old general spoke quietly and calmly, but there was an odd foreboding in his voice, something strange and threatening that he couldn't allow himself to say out loud, and Ligia listened to him as if she couldn't understand one word. Her eyes, fixed on his face in fear and confusion, blinked rapidly. Pomponia became as pale as death. The terrified faces of the slave girls appeared again in the doors leading from the corridors outside.

"The emperor's will must be done," Aulus said.

"Aulus!" Pomponia cried and threw her arms around the girl as if to protect her. "Death would be better for her!"

Anger and pain blazed again in the old general's face. "If I were alone in this world," he snapped, "I wouldn't give her up alive. But I can't doom you and our child, Pomponia. Perhaps our son will live to see better times. I'll go to the emperor today and beg him to countermand his order. I don't know if he will or not. . . . In the meantime, Ligia, good-bye. I want you to know that Pomponia and I bless the day you first joined our family."

He fought against an onrush of feeling, struggling for that Roman and soldierly control over his emotions, but when he placed his hand on Ligia's head and she looked up at him with brimming, tear-filled eyes, and when she seized his hand and covered it with kisses, his voice quavered with the grief of a bereaved father.

"Good-bye, joy of our lives," he said, then turned abruptly and went to the atrium before his feelings got the better of him.

Pomponia led Ligia to her bedroom. She tried to calm the girl, soothe her and quiet her fears. She tried to give her hope in words that sounded strange in that Roman house where right next door were the alcoves of the household gods; the new, hidden laws by which both these women lived in a pagan world made little sense beside the ritual hearth where Aulus, true to the traditions of his ancestors, made daily sacrifices to the family's protecting divinities and spirits. The time of trial has come, she whispered to Ligia. The emperor's house was a lair of crime, depravity and evil. There was another time, now hallowed in history, when Virginius thrust his sword into his daughter's breast to free her from Appius. And years before, Lucretia had taken her own life to wipe out her shame.

"But we know, Ligia, you and I, why we can't put an end to our own lives. We have no right to do that. Only God has that right. His law is greater and holier than the two of us—greater than Rome itself. It lets us resist evil and degradation to the point of martyrdom and death but not by our own hands."

Whoever leaves the house of depravity and corruption, she went on urgently, and does so untouched and undefiled, earns the greatest merit. The world of the flesh is such a house of evil. Mercifully, it's no more lasting or important than the blink of an eye, and after it comes resurrection in the light—where mercy rules, not Nero, and where there is joy instead of suffering, and happiness instead of tears.

Then she began to speak about herself. Yes, she was at peace, she followed the Master, but another kind of suffering cut into her soul. Her Aulus was still blind to the truth, unable to see the light of his salvation. Nor was she able to raise her son in the true religion, having to hide her own faith from them. She couldn't bear the thought that this terrible deception might outlast her life, that she might die before their conversion, bringing a far more painful and longer separation than this temporary parting that distressed her and Ligia so much at the moment. She couldn't see how she would find happiness even in paradise without her husband and her son; if they died as pagans they'd be denied the eternity of heaven.

"I've prayed so hard for God's mercy," she confided, "begging for that moment of joy and enlightenment." She spoke of nights filled with prayer and tears. "I've offered my pain as a sacrifice to God."

She waited and continued to believe, she said. And she'd go on believing even now when this new blow struck her, and when a brutal order robbed her of what her husband called the joy of their lives.

"I trust in God," she said, "and I'll keep on believing that there's a power greater than Nero's and that mercy is stronger than his cruelty."

She pressed the girl's small head tightly against her breast. Ligia sunk to her knees and hid her eyes in the folds of Pomponia's robe. She stayed like that for a long silent moment. But there was a measure of acceptance in her face when she rose again.

"I'm sorry, Mother, that you must suffer so," she said quietly. "And I'm sorry for the pain that Father and little Aulus must be feeling now. But I know that we can't refuse the emperor's order. Any resistance would destroy you all. I promise when I'm in Caesar's house I'll remember everything you said and told me and taught me."

The two women threw their arms around each other again and then went out to the salon where Ligia said good-bye to little Aulus, to the venerable old Greek who had been their tutor, and to all the slaves. One of them, a tall, powerful Lygian named Ursus who had gone with Ligia and her mother and their other servants to the Roman camp in the time of Claudius, now threw himself down on his knees before her and bowed to Pomponia.

"Allow me, *domina*," he said, "to go with my princess and look after her in the house of Caesar."

"You don't belong to us," Pomponia said. "You are Ligia's servant. But will they let you in? And how will you be able to protect her?"

"I don't know, *domina*," the huge Lygian said. "All I know is that iron crumbles in my fists, and that can be useful."

Aulus Plautius came back at that moment and agreed immediately with Ursus. They had no right to hold him anyway, he said. "If we're handing over a state hostage, we must hand over her entire suite." Then he whispered swiftly to his wife: "Give her as many slaves as she needs. The centurion can't refuse to take them."

This comforted Ligia, although not much, and it pleased Pomponia that she could surround the girl with hand-picked attendants whom she carefully selected from those who shared their faith. Besides Ursus, who had been a Christian for several years, she chose her old wardrobe mistress, two Cypriot hairdressers and two German bath maids whose loyalty she trusted. There was a certain sense of destiny in the thought that seeds of the new faith would now be scattered in the emperor's palace.

She also wrote a few words to Acte, Nero's freed confidante and once his favorite concubine and slave, whom the murderous tyrant was said to love if he was able to love anyone at all. She commended Ligia to Acte's care and keeping. She had never seen Acte at any of the secret gatherings where people went to hear the gospels of the faith or the teachings of visiting disciples and apostles, but she had heard from them that Acte never refused them any kind of service and that she was an avid reader of the letters sent by Paul of Tarsus. Besides, she knew that the young freedwoman lived in constant sadness, that she was nothing like the rest of Nero's depraved household, and that she was, in general, the good spirit of the imperial palace.

Hasta offered to hand the letter to Acte personally. Nor did he object to the slaves who trooped around Ligia; he had expected a far larger suite for the daughter of a Lygian king so this picked handful wasn't any problem. He did urge everyone to hurry, however, in case he was accused of insufficient zeal in carrying out his orders. So came the moment of parting. Ligia's and Pomponia's eyes filled again with tears. Aulus Plautius placed his hand once more on the girl's dark hair and a moment later the soldiers surrounded Ligia and her servants. Led through the house by the screams of little Aulus, who shook his small fists at the centurion in defense of his adopted sister, the praetorians carried her away.

The old general immediately ordered a litter for himself and led Pomponia to the picture gallery that lay next to the salon.

"Listen, Pomponia," he told her when they were alone. "I'm going to see the emperor. I don't suppose it'll do much good. I'll also go to see Seneca, even though his word means nothing to Nero nowadays. Today it's Sophonius, Tigellinus, Petronius and Vatinius who have the influence. As for the emperor, I doubt he even heard of the Lygian nation, and if he suddenly thought of Ligia as a hostage he must have been prompted. It isn't hard to guess who put the idea in his head."

She looked up suddenly. "Petronius?"

"Who else?" Silent for another bitter, angry moment, the old general snarled with helpless fury. "That's what happens when you let one of those treacherous, faithless men, without decency or conscience, into your house. I curse the day I brought Vinicius here! He is the one who thrust Petronius on us. I pity Ligia, because it's a bedmate they want, the two of them, not any kind of hostage."

Rage, helpless fury and grief for his adopted child made his speech even more difficult than before. A long time passed while he fought his anger, and only his tightly clenched fists showed how hard that inner struggle was.

"I worship the gods faithfully to this day," he hissed out at last, "but now I don't believe there is any divinity above us except one. A mad evil monster named Nero."

"Aulus!" Pomponia cried softly. "Nero is just a handful of rotten dust in comparison with God."

But now he was striding back and forth across the mosaic tiles that overlay the gallery floor. His life was filled with great deeds but bore remarkably few misfortunes, so he was puzzled by them and didn't know how to deal with them. The old warrior had grown more attached to Ligia than he realized, and he couldn't make his peace with this sudden loss. Moreover, he was bitterly humiliated; the corrupt power he had despised for so many years now crushed him to the ground, and he was helpless to do anything about it.

But at long last he stifled the rage that had gotten in the way of reason. "I don't think Petronius stole her from us for Nero," he suggested coldly. "He wouldn't want to antagonize Poppea. He took her for either Vinicius or himself. . . . I'll know about that later on today."

Soon afterward his litter carried him in the direction of the Palatine. Pomponia, left alone, went in search of angry little Aulus who wouldn't stop crying for his sister and shouting threats against the emperor.

《 5 》

AULUS WAS RIGHT in thinking that he wouldn't be admitted to Nero at the palace. He was informed that the emperor was busy with Terpnos, singing while the Greek tragedian played the lute. Besides, Nero never saw anyone for whom he didn't send. In other words Aulus was made to understand that any future attempts to see Nero would be equally useless.

But in the house of Seneca he found a different welcome. The old philospher and Stoic was ill and in fever but he received the general with all due respect.

"I can do only one thing for you, General"—he had given a wry shrug when he heard the story—"and that's never to let Caesar see that I feel your pain and that I'd like to help you. If he even suspected such a thing, he'd never let you have her back again. He'd do anything to spite me."

Nor did he think much help could come from Tigellinus, Vatinius or Vitelius. A bribe might work with them, or they'd do something to undermine Petronius whose influence they envied, but their most likely course was to tell Nero just how dear Ligia was to the Plautius family, in which case he'd have all the more reason not to let her go.

And here the Stoic thinker gave way to biting irony that he also turned on himself.

"You have been silent, Plautius, through all these years, and Caesar doesn't like people who are silent! How could you fail to go into fits of wonder at his beauty, his virtue, his voice, his recitations, his poetry and his chariot driving? Why didn't you laud the killing of Britannicus or make a speech praising him for murdering his mother or congratulate him on the occasion of Octavia's strangling? You're short on foresight, Aulus. That's something those of us who have the happiness of living near the court cultivate with a great deal of zeal and attention."

He took the small cup that dangled at his waist, dipped it in the water of the *impluvium* and freshened his parched lips.

"Nero has a grateful heart," he went on, aiming the irony at himself as well as at the times. "He loves you because you served Rome and made his name famous at the far ends of the world. He loves me because I was his tutor. That's why, you see, I know my water isn't poisoned and drink without fear. I'm not that sure about my wine, but if you feel thirsty, you can be quite at ease about the water. It comes by aqueduct from the Alban Hills, and to poison it you'd have to poison all the fountains in Rome. As you see, then, it's possible to feel secure in this world and to expect a ripe old age. It's true I'm ill, but that's rather a sickness in the soul. The body's well enough."

That, as Aulus knew, was true. Seneca lacked the moral fortitude of a Cornutus, say, or of Trachea, so that his life was a series of retreats before depravity, duplicity and murder. He knew it, and he also knew this much about himself: that a man who professed the philosopy of Zeno should have taken firmer paths and gone a better way. His suffering was genuine but it was due more to his growing contempt for himself, which hurt him more than any fear of death.

But the old general brusquely interrupted his bitter, self-derisive musing.

"Noble Annaeus"—he addressed Seneca by his given name—"I know how Caesar paid you for the care you gave him in boyhood, but it's Petronius who caused the theft of our child. Show me how to cope with him, tell me what can exert any pressure on him, and then use all your wonderful eloquence on him on our behalf. Perhaps our old friendship can help to inspire you."

"Petronius and I live in different worlds," Seneca said, sighing sadly. "I don't know how to deal with him. No one in Rome has any influence on him, which might be to the good. With all his decadence he may be worth a lot more than all those common cutthroats with whom Nero surrounds himself these days. But trying to prove to him that what he did was evil is a waste of time; Petronius is long past distinguishing between right and wrong. If I see him, I'll say that what he did was worthy of a freedman, not a cultivated noble, artist and patrician. If that doesn't serve him for a conscience, nothing will."

"Well, thanks for that much anyway," the old general said.

He had himself carried to the house of Marcus Vinicius whom he found fencing in the courtyard with a trainer of gladiators from the circus. This sight enraged him. The thought of this young man calmly going about his daily exercises while the plot against Ligia ran its course drove him to fury. The fencing master left them, but the curtains were barely still behind him when Aulus turned on Vinicius with a raging storm of abuse and insults.

Vinicius' reaction was another shock, however. Blood drained from his face. He became so deathly and unnaturally pale that Aulus couldn't believe for a moment he had anything to do with Ligia's abduction. Sweat beaded on his forehead and congealed like wax. The blood that drained out of his face now flooded back again like a wave of lava. His eyes shone with madness. His mouth spat out incoherent questions. Rage and envy shook him like a windstorm. He thought that Ligia was lost to him forever once she stepped across the threshold of the imperial palace, and when Aulus named Petronius as the instigator, suspicion flashed like lightning across the young soldier's mind. He thought at once that Petronius had played him for a fool and that he wanted either to curry fresh favor with the emperor by his gift of Ligia or to keep her for himself. His own lust refused to accept the idea that anyone who ever caught a glimpse of Ligia wouldn't want to have her.

Impulsiveness, which ran like a heedless, mindless cataract through his family, threatened to carry him away like a raging mustang and choked off his breathing.

"General," he grated out at last in quick, broken phrases. "Go home and wait for me. I'd settle this score with Petronius if he were my father. Go home and wait. Neither Petronius nor the emperor is going to have her."

Then he swung his clenched fists toward the death masks of his ancestors that lined the atrium shelves. "By these masks," he snarled, "I'll kill her and myself before that'll happen!"

With this he leaped up, threw a last "wait for me" at Aulus, hurled himself out of the atrium and into the streets, knocking people aside right and left as he ran toward Petronius' house.

Aulus went home with some hope. He thought that if Petronius got the emperor to seize Ligia for Vinicius, the young man would bring her home again. If the worst had already happened, then at least she'd be avenged and her shame would be erased by death. He was sure Vinicius would do everything he swore. He had seen his fury and knew how quick his family always acted, striking first and thinking only later if at all. He couldn't love Ligia more if he were her father, but he'd have killed her with his own hand before giving her to Nero. Only fear for his son, the last heir to his family's honorable traditions

and distinguished name, forced him to hand the girl over to Caius
Hasta. The old general had been a soldier all his life and had hardly
heard about the Stoics, but he was much like them; to his way of
thinking and to his sense of dignity, death was the better choice over
humilation.

Home again, he did his best to calm and soothe Pomponia and to
pass on to her a little of his hope. They settled down as best they
could to wait for whatever news would come from Vinicius.
Whenever they heard the soft footsteps of the slaves tiptoeing in the
atrium, they thought it was the young soldier returning their child,
and they were ready to heap blessings on them both. But time passed
and there was no news. Evening came before they heard a knocking
on their door.

A slave brought a letter.

The old general took pride in his self-control, but his hand was
shaking when he took up the tablet and read it carefully and swiftly,
as if the future of his entire family were at stake.

But suddenly his features sagged and darkened as if the shadow of
a cloud had passed over them.

"Read it," he said, passing it to Pomponia.

"Marcus Vinicius sends greetings to Aulus Plautius," Pomponia
read out. "What has been done was done by Caesar's will. Bow to it
as I and Petronius bow to it."

Then they sat in silence.

« 6 »

PETRONIUS WAS AT HOME when Vinicius arrived. The doorkeeper
didn't dare try to stop him as he hurled into the atrium like a thunderbolt. Told that the master of the house was in the library he
dashed there without breaking stride. Petronius was seated at his
writing desk, but Vinicius tore the reed out of his hand, snapped it in
two and hurled it to the floor, then clutched the man by the shoulders and brought his face within inches of his own.

"What have you done with her?" he snarled. "Where is she?"

Then a strange thing happened. The indolent, effeminate Petronius
grasped the young athlete's hand with one of his own, took hold of
the other, and clasped them in one fist as if in a vise.

"I'm useless only in the morning," he reminded Vinicius carelessly.
"I come back to my former self at nightfall. Try to break free if you
can. You must get your athletic training from a sewing circle. As for
your manners, they're straight from a stable."

He seemed neither angry nor surprised; only some pale stray
gleam of power, hidden strength and courage glowed briefly in his
chilly almond eyes. After a while he shrugged and let go of the young
soldier's arms, and Vinicius stood angry, humiliated and ashamed.

"You've a steel grip," he muttered, massaging his wrists. "But I
swear by all the gods of Hell that I'll shove a knife into your throat if
you've cheated me."

"Let's chat a little," Petronius said calmly. "Steel cuts deeper than
iron, so I don't have to be afraid of you, even though both my arms
would hardly make one of yours. But I'm sad to see how vulgar
you've become, and I'd be wondering about your lack of gratitude if
ingratitude could still surprise me among human beings."

"Where's Ligia?"

"In a whorehouse. That is to say, in the emperor's palace."

"Petronius!" Vinicius shouted.

"Calm down. Take a seat. I asked our Caesar for two things. First,

I wanted Ligia fished out of Aulus' virtuous little household, and then I wanted her handed over to you. Well, where's that knife? Do you have one hidden somewhere in your toga? But I'd advise waiting a few days before you try murder. You'll go to prison, and Ligia will be bored alone in your house."

Neither of them said anything after that. A short silence followed while Vinicius gaped at Petronius with astonished eyes.

"Forgive me," he muttered at last. "I love her. Love scrambled my wits."

"Then admire mine. I told our Caesar that my nephew fell in love with some skinny little wench and that his house feels like a steam bath with all that hot sighing. You and I, Caesar, I told him, who know what real beauty is about, wouldn't give a thousand sesterces for that bag of bones. But the boy was always as stupid as a ceremonial tripod, and now he's lost whatever brains he had."

"Petronius!" The young man was immediately offended.

"Relax! If you can't grasp that I said this to protect your Ligia, then I'll believe what I just said about you. I have Copperbeard convinced that such a refined aesthete as he couldn't possibly find any beauty in that girl. And he won't, since he can't tell the beautiful from the ugly unless I tell him which is which. So if he doesn't know she's beautiful, he won't want her. Simple, eh? You always have to protect yourself against that red ape and toss a net around him. Of course Poppea will know what's what at a single glance and do her best to have the girl sent away from the palace as fast as she can, but that's another story. I, in the meantime, couldn't have sounded more indifferent than if I were selling pullets at the market. 'Take the girl,' I told our Copperbeard as if I didn't care one way or another, 'and give her to Vinicius. She's a hostage so you've the law on your side, and you'll get to hurt Aulus Plautius at the same quick stroke.' He agreed, of course—first because he had no reason not to, and then because I gave him an excuse to inflict pain on some decent people. They'll make you the official guardian of the hostage and drop this Lygian treasure in your lap. You, on the other hand, as both an ally of the gallant Lygians and Caesar's faithful servant, will see to it that this treasure not only stays intact, in the sense that it doesn't dwindle, but that it swells and multiplies itself like a treasure should. Nero will keep her in the palace for a day or two to make the right impression and then have her dropped off quietly at your house. Anything wrong with that, you lucky lover?"

"Is that true?" Vinicius no longer took anything for granted. "Is she really safe in the Palatine?"

"Well, if she were to settle there for a while, Poppea would have a little word with her favorite poisoner, Locusta, but a few days won't do her any harm. There are ten thousand people in Nero's household, and chances are he won't even see her. He left it all in my hands to such an extent that I've just had a visit from the centurion who took her to the palace. I ordered her turned over to Acte, who's a kindly creature, and that's what he did. Pomponia must have had the same idea because she wrote to her, asking her protection. Oh, and there's a banquet at Nero's tomorrow night. I've reserved a place for you next to Ligia."

"Ah, Caius!" the young man exclaimed to his extraordinary uncle, using his given name, an affectionate form allowed in the family and among close friends. "Forgive my quick temper. I thought you had her carried off for either Nero or yourself."

"I can forgive impulsiveness," Petronius observed. "It's a youthful failing. But it's a lot harder for me to tolerate crude gestures, vulgar howls and a tone suited for dice throwing in an alley. Tigellinus does all of Nero's pimping; I play a different role. But I'll tell you this much: If I wanted to keep Ligia for myself, I'd simply tell you that I'm taking her and will keep her until she starts to bore me. And you wouldn't be able to do a thing about it."

He fixed his luminous almond-shaped brown eyes on Vinicius with such a cold and challenging contempt that the young man lost whatever composure he still had.

"I'm sorry," he said at last. "I was wrong. You're a good, thoughtful man, and I'm grateful to you with my heart and soul. But tell me one thing more: Why didn't you have Ligia taken to my house straightaway instead of this detour to the palace?"

"Because Nero's always worried about legalities. He's the chief magistrate of Rome and loves the idea that he's the fount of justice. People will talk about this, so he'll keep the hostage as long as they're talking. Once they're done, he'll send her quietly here, and that'll be that."

"Why should he care what anybody says?" Vinicius still wasn't entirely convinced. "He has the power to do anything he wants."

"And he uses it anytime he wants. But he's a coward. He knows that no one's going to object to anything he does, but he tries to justify each and every crime with some legal folderol. Have you regained enough control over your emotions for some philosophizing? I've often wondered why criminality always tries to cover itself with virtue even when it's as powerful and beyond anybody's reach as our emperors. Why bother? I happen to think that murdering your brother, your mother and your wife is a fit pastime for an Asiatic kinglet and quite beneath contempt for a Roman Caesar. But if something like that ever happened to me, I wouldn't write exculpatory letters to the senate. Nero, however, writes them all the time. Nero needs excuses because he's a coward. But come to think of it, Tiberius used to do the same, although he wasn't a coward. So why do they do it? Why do we have to show our respect to virtue even when we're vicious? Do you know what I think? I think we do it because crime is ugly and virtue is beautiful."

"Perhaps." Vinicius nodded.

"But take it a step further. If virtue is beautiful then a real connoisseur of beauty is a virtuous man. In other words I'm a virtuous man. Hmm, I'll have to spill a little wine today to the ghosts of Protagoras, Prodicus and Georgias; it seems there's some use for sophistry after all. But let's go on a little further with this train of thought. I took Ligia away from Aulus to give her to you. That's all well and good. Lisippus would carve a stunning group out of the two of you. You're both beautiful. That means that what I did was also beautiful, and being beautiful it cannot be evil. So here you have it, Marcus! You're face-to-face with living goodness embodied in Petronius! If Aristides were still alive, he would have to come here for a short course in virtue. I wouldn't charge him more than a hundred minas."

But Vinicius was more concerned with facts than academic musing or lectures on virtue.

"So I'll see Ligia tomorrow night," he said, "at the palace. And then I'll keep her with me in my house the rest of my life."

"Yes. You'll have your Ligia, and I'll be saddled with Aulus. He'll cry for vengeance to all the demons of Hell. Ah, if only he'd take a lesson in decent elocution, it wouldn't be so bad. But he'll rant and rave just like my old doorkeeper whom I finally had to send away to a country workhouse."

"Aulus came to see me," Vinicius said. "I promised to send him news about Ligia."

"Write him that the will of Caesar is the will of the gods and that you'll name your first son Aulus after him. We ought to give the old man something to console him. I think I'll have Copperbeard ask him to tomorrow's banquet. Let him see you and Ligia reclining together on the dining couches."

"No, don't do that." Vinicius was suddenly uneasy. "I'm rather sorry for him and his wife. Especially Pomponia."

Then he sat down at Petronius' desk and wrote the letter that robbed the old general of his final hope.

THE LOFTIEST HEADS of Rome used to bow low before Acte, the former lover of a youthful Nero, but she had kept out of the public eye even then, and if she ever used her influence on her enamored and impressionable young master, it was only to secure mercy for some victimized offender. She was too gentle, kind and self-effacing to win important enemies for herself, and even Nero's first wife, the jealous Octavia, found it difficult to hate her. Even those who envied her onetime access to the emperor didn't feel threatened by her. People knew that she still loved Nero, but this was a joyless sort of love, the kind that lives on memory rather than on hope. The image of her lover that she would carry with her the rest of her life was of a younger and a better Nero, one still capable of caring and not the monstrous and grotesque caricature he'd become. Everyone knew that she lived entirely in those memories but with no hope that they might ever become real again; and since it really was impossible for the older, cruel and corrupted Nero to go back to her, which made her totally defenseless, no one saw any need to bother about her and left her alone. Even Poppea thought of her as nothing more than a quiet and inoffensive servant, potentially so harmless that she didn't demand her exile from the palace.

But because the emperor had loved her at one time and had left her in a friendly and agreeable way without any kind of ill-feeling or rancor, she could count on some consideration even now. Freeing her from slavery, Nero assigned her a few rooms in the palace, with her own bedchamber, and a handful of house slaves to look after her. And since Pallas and Narcissus, both freedmen of Claudius, set the precedent by dining with the emperor, and taking high places at his table as his trusted ministers of state, she too was sometimes asked to come to Nero's banquets. Besides, since Nero had long given up caring who sat at his table, no one else did either. His nightly guests included the widest and most improbable assortment of people. There were senators, but mostly of the kind who could clown and posture and didn't mind making fools of themselves in public. There were patricians from the noblest families, both the young and the old, who craved depravity, luxury and sheer self-indulgence. There were great ladies bearing hallowed names, who liked to dress themselves in a harlot's wig and look for easy satisfactions in dark streets and alleys. There were high officials, and priests who jeered at their own gods when they drank enough, and a crude, grasping mob composed of singers, mimes, dancers, acrobats and poets who thought only about how much money could come showering on them for praising Nero's verses, and hungry philosophers whose greedy little eyes were always fixed on the serving dishes, and the best-known chariot drivers from the circus, sleight-of-hand magicians, self-styled wizards and miracle workers, backstreet story tellers, dressed-up jokesters and popular buffoons—and among them all were those various poseurs, posturers, fakers and nonentities who had been turned into the celebrities of the moment by either fashion or stupidity and who often hid a slave's punctured ears under their long hair.

Those who counted went straight to the tables. Those who didn't and who were there largely to provide amusement waited until the servants let them wolf down the leftovers and drain the emptied flagons. Tigellinus, Vatinius and Vitelius rounded up such guests because Nero felt most at home among them, and they often supplied the clothing suitable for the emperor's table. But it wouldn't matter if they didn't. The opulence of the court turned everything into its own mirrors, gilding everyone, and everything lost its shabby contours and trivial dimensions in that golden brilliance. Everyone fought to get there: the great and the small, the scions of old, distinguished families and the rabble swept out of the gutter, artists of towering talent along with literary pygmies; and all of them clamored to get invited, to be there, to devour those unimaginable treasures with their dazzled eyes and to stand near the living source of all wealth and riches. True, it was a risky and unpredictable source. It could bring utter ruin or kill without a thought. But it could also transform a slave into a magnate at a whim, change mediocrity into fame and public adulation, and send fortunes soaring with a single smile.

That night was to be Ligia's first at this kind of banquet and she didn't know what she ought to do. Fear, anxiety and a strange sort of listlessness in her struggled against a powerful wish to refuse to go. The listlessness, unsurprising after what had happened, made a decision especially difficult. She feared the emperor; she was afraid of people; the boom of voices that echoed through the palace, coming from everywhere at all times, frightened her as well; and she was terrified of Nero's famous banquets, well known for their perversions and depravities, that she had heard about from Aulus Plautius, Pomponia and their friends. Children learned about the world early in those days—few of its darker mysteries escaped their young ears— so even though she was still a young girl, barely out of childhood, she had a good notion of right and wrong. What she faced here, she knew, was her destruction. She would be lost. Nothing that mattered to her could survive within her, and she would never be herself again. Pomponia had tried to warn her when they said good-bye, and now she whispered a promise to defend herself. Her young spirit was still fresh, untouched by corruption; she had a faith that Pomponia had taught her, and she believed with all her soul in that lofty teaching. And now she swore to overcome her dangers. She made that promise to herself, to her adopted mother, and to that teaching God whom she not only followed but loved for his sweet compassion, the bitterness of his death and the glory of his resurrection.

Nothing she did now would reflect on Aulus and Pomponia, she was sure. They would not be called to account for her. She was free to refuse going to the banquet, and the consequences would fall on her alone. But why not go? Why not accept the challenge, take the test and show the same courage and endurance that all the other followers of her Teacher showed, proving their faith by risking death and torture? Wasn't this what God's teaching was about? Didn't his son show the way, dying on the cross? Didn't Pomponia say that the most fervent worshipers of the faith prayed for such an end?

Fear and anxiety were arguing on one side, her faith on the other, and then fantasy and imagination stepped into the picture. She saw herself as a holy martyr, with pierced hands and feet, white as the snow and glowing with unearthly beauty, carried by equally pale angels into sky blue space. She had enjoyed such musing in the Plautius home; it was a harmless, childish fantasy, innocent of reality and never very serious, even though Pomponia chided her now and then for her mild preoccupation with herself. But now, when thwarting Caesar's will could bring some savage sentence, when the sweet martyrdom of the imagination could become real torture, she felt the tug of yet another current. Curiosity moved in beside anxiety and fear. How would they punish her? And what sort of torments would they think up for her?

Back and forth she went, still half a child at best, swinging first to this side, then the other. But Acte was astonished when she heard about her hesitations. Was she sick? she asked. Did she have a fever? What was this about refusing to obey the emperor? Did she want his anger crushing her right at the beginning?

"You really have to be a child who doesn't know what she's saying to even think like that. Your own story proves that you're not really a hostage but a girl forgotten by her people. No law defends you. And even if one did, Caesar is powerful enough to tear it into shreds in a fit of anger."

It pleased the emperor to take her, Acte said, and now she was his to do with as he wished. His will was hers from this moment on, and that's how it should be, because there was no more compelling power in the world.

"Yes," she went on, "I read Paul of Tarsus. I know that there's a God and a resurrected son of God above the earth, but on this earth there is only Caesar. Remember this, Ligia. I also know that your faith forbids you to be what I once was and that, like the Stoics, your people must choose death before submission to shame and dishonor. But how can you be sure that death will be the worst that can happen to you? What makes you think you can choose death instead of shame? The law forbids the killing of a virgin, but haven't you heard about Sejanus' daughter? She was a young girl, a child and still a virgin, when Tiberius condemned her whole family to death. To satisfy the law, Tiberius ordered the jailkeepers to rape her so that she could be legally put to death. Ligia, I beg you, don't irritate the Caesar! When the time comes to make a choice, when you can't accept the life that's offered to you, you'll do what your faith says you ought to do. But don't destroy yourself of your own free will! Don't provoke this cruel, earthly god for some trivial reason."

Acte spoke with compassion. She was very moved. She was nearsighted and brought her lovely face close to Ligia's as though checking whether her words had any effect.

"Ah, you're so good, Acte," Ligia said, and she threw her arms around the Greek woman's neck with innocent impulsiveness.

"My joy is over," Acte said, hugging her. "My luck has run out. But I don't hurt people."

Then she freed herself from Ligia's arms and started pacing her room swiftly.

"No!" she said desperately, speaking to herself. "And he hurt no one either. Or he didn't used to. He wanted to be good. He tried to be. I know that better than anyone. The rest . . . well, that came later . . . when he stopped loving anything. Others made him what he is today. Yes, it was the others. And Poppea!"

Tears showed among her eyelashes. Ligia followed her across the room with her dark blue eyes, then said: "You pity him? You miss him?"

"Yes, I miss him." Acte's hands were clenched with loss, and hopelessness drifted across her face.

"You still love him, then?" Ligia's voice showed an embarrassed shyness.

"Yes, I love him." Then she added with a desperate pity: "No one else loves him. No one."

Silence hung between them while Acte put away her memories and regained her usual quiet and unassuming sadness.

"But let's talk about you," she said. "Don't even think about opposing Caesar. That would be pure madness. And calm yourself. Don't worry. It won't be so bad. I know what happens in this place, and I don't think the emperor intends you any harm. If Nero had you seized for himself he wouldn't bring you to the Palatine. Poppea rules the palace. Since she gave him a daughter, he's under her control more than ever. . . . No, he has nothing bad in mind for you, I'm sure of it. He did order you to be at the banquet, but he hasn't seen you, hasn't sent for you or even asked about you, so he's not interested in you. Perhaps he took you from Aulus and Pomponia just for spite. That's happened before. Petronius wrote asking me to take care of you, and so did Pomponia, so they must be working for you together. Perhaps she asked him to intercede for you. If that's so, and if Petronius is really on your side, you've nothing to fear. Who knows, maybe he can prompt Nero to send you back to the Plautius household. I don't know if Nero is all that fond of him, but he seldom goes against his views."

"Petronius called on us before they took me, Acte," Ligia said. "Mother was sure that Nero asked for me at his suggestion."

"That would be bad," Acte said.

She thought about that for a while, then shook her head.

"It could be that Petronius was simply careless, that's all. He could have dropped some passing hint to Nero at one of their suppers that he happened the see the Lygian hostage in the Plautius house. Nero is jealous of everything that pertains to his role as Caesar. After all, as our *imperator* he's only supposed to be the chief magistrate of Rome, carrying out the laws of the senate that rules the people. Hostages are state property and he's their custodian. He could have ordered you brought here because of that. Besides, he doesn't like Aulus and Pomponia and would want to hurt them. No, I think if Petronius wanted to take you from Aulus, he'd have found another way."

"Would you trust him, Acte?"

Ligia's quiet, childlike confidence in her saddened the older woman. She was moved to pity.

"I don't know if he's any better than those others that flock around Nero," she said carefully, "but he's certainly different. . . . And maybe there's someone else who'd speak for you and take your part as well. Did you meet anyone at the Plautius home who is close to Caesar?"

"I used to see Vespasian and Titus."

"Caesar doesn't like them."

"And Seneca," Ligia said.

"It's enough for Seneca to suggest a course, and Nero would go in the opposite direction."

The girl's fresh young face could never keep a secret. "And I saw Vinicius," she said, flushing brightly.

"I don't know him," said Acte.

"He's related to Petronius and just came back from Armenia."

"Do you think Nero likes him?"

"Everyone likes Vinicius," Ligia said, and her eyes opened wider and grew warm.

"And would he intercede for you?"

"Yes." Ligia was quite certain.

Acte smiled fondly. "You'll probably see him at the banquet, then. Yes, you'll go. First because you have to—only a child like you could've thought any different—and then because if you really want to go back to Aulus and Pomponia, you'll have a chance to ask Petronius and Vinicius to arrange your right of return. If they were here right now, they'd be the first to tell you that what I did—say no to Nero—was madness and disaster. He might not notice if you weren't there, but if he does notice and thinks you dared to go against his will, there'd be no help for you.

"Come, Ligia," she said at last. "It's time to get ready. Listen to all the hubbub in the house! The sun's going down, and the guests will soon start arriving."

"You're right, Acte," Ligia said. "I'll do as you say."

‹ 8 ›

LIGIA HAD NO IDEA how much her decision to go to the banquet was due to her need to see Vinicius and Petronius, and how much came from her curiosity, the simple inquisitive nature of children and women to see this kind of gathering just once, to watch the emperor from close by, to observe the court, to note as much as she could about the famous Poppea and other reigning beauties and to be dazzled, as all mankind seemed dazzled, by the rest of that vast and unbelievable display of wealth and raw power that all of Rome talked about all the time, and which she was hardly able to imagine.

Acte was right, she was sure. She had to be there. Impish curiosity took the side of necessity and reason and she made up her mind.

She followed Acte. There was never any shortage of slaves in the palace, and Acte had more than enough maids for her own service, but she decided to dress and anoint Ligia without any help. Why? She couldn't say. There was something about the Lygian girl that appealed to her protective instincts. Her beauty touched the heart. She was sorry for her. The trusting girl was so young, so clean, so free of guile, envy and corruption. Her childlike, natural artlessness made her seem defenseless, vulnerable in her inexperience.

She took the girl to her own anointing room, and suddenly her natural appreciation of the human body, the love of physical perfection that was so much a part of the Greek homeland she had left long ago, overshadowed her other feelings. Despite her mourning for her happy memories, despite the gray sadness of her life among all this glitter and despite all the writings of Paul of Tarsus that she had read, she gave way to the free, untrammeled Hellenistic spirit to which the beauty of the human form speaks much more clearly than anything else. She couldn't help crying out with simple admiration when Ligia dropped her robe. Naked, she was both bountiful and lissome. Her flesh seemed molded from mother-of-pearl and roses. Acte stepped back, as a sculptor might step back from a true masterwork, and stared with openmouthed appreciation at that image of spring.

"Ligia!" she gasped at last. "You beat Poppea a hundred times over!"

But the girl had been brought up in a different school. Strict modesty was the rule in Pomponia's household even when women were alone together. The flesh was never shown even though the short, sleeveless tunics worn about the house left arms and legs bare. She was almost dizzy with embarrassment. Lovely as a dream, as beautifully balanced and harmonious as a sculpture by Praxiteles, she stood with eyes fixed blindly on the floor, her knees pressed tightly together and her arms clutched across her breasts. Then her arms and hands flew suddenly to her hair. She pulled out the pins that held it coiled around her head, shook it free, and stood covered in it as if by a cloak.

"What beautiful hair," Acte murmured, coming close and touching the thick, dark coils that spilled almost to Ligia's knees. "So glossy. So full of natural lights. No, I won't put any gold dust on it. You've enough depth and richness, and there's enough gold and amber shining through the coils—although perhaps just a touch of gilding here and there to bring out the highlights. . . . Ah, but just a touch, ever so lightly, as if a sunbeam were caught and trapped in there. . . . You must come from a beautiful country if such lovely girls are born there."

"I don't remember anything about it," Ligia said. "Ursus told me that all we have at home are forests and more forests."

"Which are full of flowers." Acte smiled and dipped her hands in verbena to start moistening Ligia's hair.

Then, barely touching the girl's shy, warm flesh, she massaged Arabian perfumes into her skin all over her body, then slipped a soft, sleeveless tunic down over her shoulders. It was both an undergarment and a house dress, made of some delicate gold-colored material over which the formal snow-white *peplum* of a Roman lady would hang when she was fully dressed. But because Ligia's hair still had to be done, Acte wrapped her in a voluminous dressing robe known as a *synthesis.* She sat her in a chair and then handed her over to her slave attendants, whom she supervised and corrected from behind. Two other slave girls knelt to slip Lygia's feet into white court sandals, stitched and edged in purple, and laced them with golden ribbons to just above her alabaster ankles.

Done with the hair, the slaves brought the sleeveless, floor-length *peplum,* which they eased carefully over Ligia's shoulders. They worked on their knees to adjust its folds while Acte hung a string of pearls around her bare neck.

"Just a touch of gold here at the twists," Acte murmured, passing the dusting brush lightly over Ligia's hair. "Just the merest touch . . ."

She stepped back, admiring and content, and then ordered the same procedure for herself, all the while staring at the girl with eyes that reflected her own love of beauty.

She was soon ready. Since they had a lot of time left before the banquet, she took Ligia to the side portico that opened on the main doors and portals, creating a perfect observation point of the triumphal arch of the square-cut outer gate, the interior cloisters and the rectangular courtyard lined with colonnades of Numidian marble, just as the first carrying chairs appeared at the gates.

More and more guests began to pass under the lofty arch and its surmounting chariot, cast by Lisippus out of molten gold; its four charging horses seemed about to soar into the sun, carrying a gold Apollo and Diana. For Ligia, struck by the size and opulence of this careless splendor, piled on one another wherever she looked, the modest house of Aulus dwindled to nothing. She knew she would never have been able to imagine anything to match what she was seeing now. The sun had almost set, its last crimson beams sweeping over the Numidian marble and turning its slim yellow columns into gleaming pink-tinted gold. The marble images of the fifty daughters of Danaeus, the first king of Argos, stood between these golden pillars, among monuments to the gods and the busts of philosophers and heroes. The thick, flowing crowd of arriving guests seemed to reflect their glory, with each man and woman acquiring the sudden beauty of a living statue. The fading sunlight seemed to sink into the whiteness of their stoles and togas, catching each carefully hung and styled fold in each passing *peplum* and flowing gracefully, as if in submission, to the ground. A colossal Hercules, whose huge head was still glowing in the sun while his torso sank into the shadows of the colonnade, looked down at this moving human statuary of knights, notables and nobles, patricians, famous artists, senators—in widebordered togas and brightly colored tunics, with half-moons gleaming on their knee-high sandals—and Roman ladies, dressed in a variety of fashions. Some favored Roman dress, others swirled in the diaphanous colors of the Greeks or in the fantastic creations of the East, with hair piled and pinned into pyramids and towers or wreathed in flowers and brushed close to the head in the classic pat-

tern of the goddesses. Acte knew many of the men and women, and
she pointed them out to the avid Ligia, often including their brief but
horrifying histories and adding to her sense of shock, bewilderment
and amazement.

Ligia felt stunned. She couldn't come to terms with the contradictions of this unimaginable world that dazzled her with such astounding beauty. There was an overwhelming feeling of stability and order
in the red-rimmed sky; a deep tranquility rose from the rectilinear
rows of still and silent columns retreating into shadows and from the
people who resembled statues. Some strange, enchanted demigods,
newly stepped out of mythology and living lives of endless happiness
and contentment, should make their homes among the classic marbles, she was sure; instead, Acte's quiet voice went on listing, one
after another, the chilling secrets of the building and the men and
women. There, right before her, was the covered stairway whose floor
and columns were still splashed with the blood that had spurted from
Caligula under the knife of Cassius Chaerea; over there, under the
other portico, was the place where his wife was murdered and his
child was battered to death against a wall; beneath this wing of the
palace lay the dungeon where the younger Drusus gnawed on his
hands in hunger; in the other wing was the dining couch where the
elder Drusus died in the agonies of poison. Gemellus howled in terror here. Claudius and Germanicus died in convulsions there.

Every wall in this house echoed at one time or another with the
groans of victims, and the crowds hurrying to the banquet with their
flowers and jewels, their robes and togas, radiant in the dying light,
could be tomorrow's corpses, turned by a single whim into objects of
brutality and murder. And could she see terror and anxiety crouched
under those smiles? Did their godlike, marmoreal dignity mask the
fearful uncertainties that quivered inside them? And was it the fever
of crude open greed, avarice and envy that burned so brightly in these
carefree, half-Olympian creatures?

Ligia's startled thoughts darted about like birds. She couldn't keep
up with Acte's revelations. The more this earthly paradise pulled at
her and beguiled her, the more her chest constricted and tightened
with fear. With a force and urgency that shattered every gleam of
curiosity and pleasure, she suddenly longed for the kindness and gentleness of Pomponia, for the quiet home where love seemed to pulse
out of every wall just as crime and death seeped from the marbles
here, and for the peace of the Plautius house.

Meanwhile the Vicus Apollinis disgorged fresh waves of guests.

The road outside the gate rang with the loud good wishes of uninvited clients and retainers who had come with their patrons. The courtyard and the colonnades suddenly swarmed with imperial slaves, both male and female, cherubic page boys and grim praetorian soldiers. Now and then among the white and olive faces a black Numidian with huge gold rings dangling from his ears looked up from under a plumed helmet.

They carried lutes and citharas, oil lamps made of silver, gold and beaten copper, and armfuls of hothouse flowers in full bloom, although it was autumn. The hum of voices deepened and became indivisibly entwined in the silvery cascade of the splashing fountain, whose pink-tinted strands, still gleaming with sunset, fell from high above and shattered on the marble with a sound like weeping.

Acte stopped her stories, but Ligia kept on looking into the crowd, as if searching for some special person. And suddenly she flushed. She caught sight of Vinicius and Petronius moving among the columns. They had strolled into the open and now paced calmly toward the great dining hall—as detached, handsome and aloof in their snowy togas as a pair of gods. She thought a great weight had tumbled off her breast when she saw these two familiar faces, especially Vinicius'. She felt far less alone. The vast longing for Pomponia and the Plautius home that had overwhelmed her just a moment earlier now seemed less important. She had seen Vinicius. Soon she would talk with him. All other voices flew out of her head including Acte's stories and Pomponia's warnings. She struggled to remind herself of all the evil she had heard about Caesar's house, but that didn't help. Going to the banquet because she had to go was one thing, but now she wanted to be there. She was delighted that in a few more minutes she would be listening to that thrilling voice, the one that spoke to her about love and happiness that turned ordinary mortals into gods, and she was filled with joy.

And then suddenly she was afraid. That joy was dangerous. It seemed to her in all her confusion that she was betraying her new faith, the pure and clear teaching, Pomponia and herself. What happened to all that talk about resistance? To all those fantasies about martyrdom and angels? She had allowed herself to go because she was forced to. Going of her own free will and pleased to be going made her no better than the others who were crowding there. Guilt swept through her. She felt contemptible and lost. If she were alone, she'd be on her knees, beating her breast and whispering, "*Mea culpa, mea culpa,* I have sinned!" But now, as Acte took her by the hand and led her through a gallery of rooms to the banquet chamber, her heart was pounding so hard she could hardly breathe and could barely see or hear anything around her. Strange contradictory feelings swept through her and roared in her ears. Her eyes wouldn't focus; what she saw came to her as if in a dream. Thousands of lamps were flickering on the walls and tables. The shout that greeted Caesar thundered in her ears, and he himself seemed shrouded in a fog. The shouting deafened her, the glare made her blind. She was intoxicated by the perfumed air and thought she would faint. She barely even recognized Acte, who found Ligia's place at the table and then reclined beside her.

And then a low, familiar voice spoke to her from the other side:

"Greetings to you, most beautiful of the girls on earth and the stars in the sky! Greetings, divine Callina!"

Ligia looked up. Her sense of shock abated. Marcus Vinicius lay beside her on the dining couch.

⟨9⟩

VINICIUS HAD THROWN OFF his toga, as custom and comfort required during banquets, and wore only a scarlet short-sleeved tunic embroidered with silver palms. Two broad gold bands clasped on the biceps of his naked arms in the eastern fashion; they were a soldier's arms, heavily muscled and seemingly created for the sword and the shield, but also smooth, carefully plucked and hairless. With a wreath of roses on his head and a tanned olive-tinted face, his dark eyebrows forming a single line above the bridge of his nose and magnificent black eyes, he looked like the personification of youth at its strongest. Looking at him, Ligia thought him so beautiful that she could barely whisper even though the worst of her disorientation had passed and she was calm again.

"Greetings to you, Marcus."

"Happy are my eyes," he responded, "because they can see you. Happy are my ears because they hear your voice, dearer to me than the sound of citharas and flutes. Were it my place, divine girl, to choose between you and Venus as my dinner partner, I'd choose you."

His eyes were hungry as he stared at her. Fire seemed to leap out of her skin wherever they touched, scorching her. Their pressure slid from her face to her neck and then her naked shoulders; they brushed her hidden flesh, fondled her roundnesses, savored her, embraced her, devoured and consumed her; but they were also ecstatic, filled with love and happy.

"I knew I'd see you here," he said. "But everything inside me seemed to leap with joy when I actually saw you, as if it was the most unexpected surprise in the world."

She was quite steady then. Her jumbled thoughts and feelings had returned to normal. Nothing about this place made any sense to her. It was all foreign to her; everything was threatening. And because he was the only man there to whom she felt close, she turned to him for answers. How did he know she'd be in Caesar's house? And why was she there? Why did Caesar take her away from Pomponia? This place frightened her. She wanted to go home. Her only hope, she said, was that he would intercede for her with the emperor, along with Petronius. Otherwise she'd die of homesickness and anxiety.

Vinicius explained that he had heard about her abduction from Aulus himself.

"Why you're here, I don't know," he said. "Caesar never justifies his orders or accounts for anything he does. But you've nothing to be afraid of or worry about. I'm with you and I'll stay with you."

He'd rather lose his eyesight than her, he went on. "What would I need them for if I couldn't see you?" He'd trade his life for hers any day; he'd rather die than lose her. She was his soul, and he'd protect her just as fiercely as he'd fight for his own humanity.

"I'll build you an altar in my house," he said, "and I'll burn myrrh and aloes on it every day as if you were my personal divinity. In spring I'll sacrifice saffron and apple blossoms. I promise that you won't stay in Caesar's house if it frightens you."

He played a game, of course, skirting the truth and fabricating facts as he needed them. He was the Roman, the profligate, and still the seducer. But his commitment to her was quite real—she really did capture his imagination—and his strong young voice rang with passion and sincerity. Moreover he felt a shamed sort of pity for her; she deserved much better than to be used the way everyone used one another, without a thought beyond the pleasure of the moment. She stirred his compassion. Her anxious questions made him want to be generous and caring, and when she started thanking him and then assuring him that Pomponia, too would love him for his kindness, he was convinced he'd never be able to refuse anything she asked him. She projected such a natural innocence, she was so free of guile, that he was strangely moved to look after her and even protect her even from people like himself. Her beauty made him drunk. He wanted her body but at the same time, in a way that had never troubled him before, he felt that she was very precious to him and that he really could worship her like a goddess. He also felt an overwhelming need to talk about her beauty and how he adored her, but the noise of the banquet was getting in the way. He drew closer to her and started whispering kind and gentle phrases, expressing the best of his feelings as he understood them.

He sounded to her ears as soothing as music and as intoxicating as wine. And he had an intoxicating effect on her. She saw him among all those strangers as someone close to her, someone she could trust and who could become ever dearer and more important to her, and who was wholly on her side. He had calmed her fears. He promised that he would whisk her away from Caesar's house and that he would never leave her. He spoke of his devotion. Before, when they had spoken to each other briefly in the Plautius home, he talked in general terms about love and the happiness it brought; now he told her directly that she was that love for him, that he adored her, and that no one else could make him as happy as she.

No other man had ever spoken to Ligia like that. She had never heard such words from any man before. Gradually, as she listened, she felt something awakening within her, a strange new feeling began to rise as if from a dream. She rose with it into a new awareness where some great joy lay mysteriously entwined with an equally powerful uneasiness. Her cheeks burned. Her heart pounded. Her lips lay parted as if in amazement. She was afraid to listen to such things, but at the same time she knew she wouldn't miss one word for anything. Most of the time she looked down and away from Vinicius, then raised her clear, open eyes and fixed them on him—questioning, wanting to believe, uncertain and luminous with feeling—as if urging him to tell her even more. The roar of voices all around her dazed and bewildered her; the thick scent of flowers and Arabian incense made her senses spin.

When Romans ate, they did so lying side by side on the *triclinium* couches; at home Ligia's place was between Pomponia and little Aulus. But here it was Vinicius who reclined beside her: a beautiful young man as finely sculpted as a marble Hercules, totally in love and burning with passion. Her body felt the heat that pulsed from him as if from a brazier, and she found herself adrift in a pool of shyness, a bewildering new joy and anticipation. She sensed herself stepping into a reality she had never imagined, where she was fearful, helpless and excited all at the same time and gripped in an oddly thrilling lassitude; and then she gave way, abandoning resistance and slipping away from everything around her as peacefully and gently as if she were dreaming.

But her nearness had its effect on him as well.

His face was pale with intensity. His fine, sharp nostrils flared like a Parthian stallion's and began to quiver. His heartbeat quickened in excitement, his breath came faster and his words boiled out of him in sharp, broken phrases. He, too, had never been so close to her. He could no longer think. He was convinced that his blood was burning and tried to extinguish the fire with more wine. But he knew it wasn't the wine he flung down his throat that made him drunk. What fired his senses was the miracle of her beauty, the lovely face, naked arms and shoulders, young breasts lifting and falling under her golden tunic, and the full but delicate contours of her body—lying so near to his along its whole length and barely hidden in the soft folds of her *peplum*.

"I love you, Callina," he hissed into her ear. He reached out and caught her arm just above the wrist as he had that time in Aulus Plautius' garden, and pulled her toward him. "You're godlike . . . divine . . ."

"Let me go, Marcus," Ligia begged.

But he no longer could. His eyes were dimmed and clouded as if by a mist. "Love me!" his cracked voice rattled in her ears. "My goddess . . . my divinity!"

"Caesar's watching you," Acte spoke suddenly across Ligia's body, and anger swept at once across Vinicius. Damn Caesar but damn the woman too! How dare she interrupt him? The magic of enchantment was gone, shattered beyond repair in a moment. Damn that Acte! Even a friend's voice would jar the young man at this moment; moreover, he thought at once, she had done it on purpose.

He raised his head and glared at her across Ligia's shoulder. "It's long past the time when you lay with Caesar at the banquets, Acte. And aren't you going blind? Maybe you can't see him as well as you used to."

"I can still see him," she said with her usual sadness. "He's also shortsighted, like me, and he's looking at you through his emerald."

Everything Nero did called for the utmost watchfulness even among those closest to him, and Vinicius was immediately sobered and on guard. He started watching Nero in return, but carefully, with swift sidelong glances.

Ligia also looked at the emperor for the first time. At the beginning of the banquet she saw him only as a misty shape caught blindly through her panic and confusion. Later, entranced with Vinicius and charmed by his words, she didn't look at him at all; and now she turned toward him with wide open eyes, both curious and fearful.

Acte was right. The emperor, hunched over the table, squinted at them with one eye shut and the other hidden behind a flat, round emerald the size of a walnut but polished to the slimness of a coin. This was his monocle. He never looked at anything or anyone without it. It was in part a charm against black magic, in part belief in the healing powers of gem stones, in part a real magnifying crystal like the spyglasses recently invented by Egyptian sailors, and also one of Nero's artistic affectations. Now he was clutching it in two fingers, holding it up to his hidden eye and staring straight at them.

For just one moment his glance locked with Ligia's, and her whole being filled with sudden fear. As a child she had spent some time in the Sicilian countryside, in the simple rural setting of Aulus Plautius' estate, and an Egyptian slave woman told her about dragons that made their lairs in caves in the mountains. Now she was certain that the cold green eye of just such a dragon was glaring down at her. She clutched Vinicius' hand like a panicked child and a swarm of feelings, questions and impressions whirled into her head. So that was Nero, the awesome, terrifying man who could do anything he wanted. Whose power was so total and beyond all question. Who had absolute control over everything and all life and death. This was the first time that she really saw him, and she had imagined him as something quite different. She had expected almost ghastly features, terrifying with the evil frozen into a stony mask, but all she saw was a short, broad face, still terrifying but as incongruous as that of a child when seen from a distance, and a heavy head that slumped on a thick soft neck. She might have laughed nervously if he didn't frighten her so much.

Nero caused such conflicting feelings in everyone who saw him. He wore his hair on his forehead in four rows of curled fringes, twisted into lovelocks one above the other in the style introduced to Rome by the exiled Otho. He was clean-shaven at the moment, having burned his beard recently on the altar of Jove. All of Rome paid homage to him for this sacrifice, although there were whispers that he had gotten rid of his beard because it was a bright copper red like all the facial hair in his family, and for some reason he thought red hair was vulgar. There was, indeed, something Olympian about the lofty bulge of his forehead just above the eyebrows; those dark, drawn eyebrows projected full awareness of his power, shorn of all restraint and quite without limit. But this forehead worthy of a demigod ended just below, dissolving into the empty muzzle of an ape, a mindless buffoon and a drunken clown. His eyes seemed scrunched in suet. His image was corrupt, a whim-driven man overtaken by his own excesses; he was still young but was drowning in the rolls of his accumulated fat, was prone to quick illness, and was corroded by debauchery and slimy with spittle.

She thought him dangerous, an enemy to be feared, but most of all she saw him as repulsive.

Meanwhile he put down his emerald and stopped looking at her. She saw his bulging blue eyes blinking in the glare of too many lights. They were as glazed and void as brightly polished pebbles and empty of either thought or feeling like the eyes of a corpse.

REPELLED, LIGIA GLANCED AWAY while Nero turned to Petronius, who reclined beside him at the center of the wide, low, three-armed table bordered by the couches. "Is that the hostage that Vinicius loves?" he asked.

"That's the one," Petronius said with a shrug.

"What's the name of her people?"

"Lygians," Petronius said.

"Vinicius finds her beautiful?"

"Dress a rotten olive stump in a woman's *peplum* and Vinicius will think it beautiful." Petronius grimaced with contempt. "But you know the difference. No one understands the elements of beauty better than you, divine connoisseur. Ah, I can see the true assessment in your expert eye. You've no need to state it! She's too thin, she's like a dried-up twig, too skinny for a godlike authority like you, too unappetizing. A pretty face, perhaps, but perched on a frail stalk like a roadside poppy. While you, great aesthete that you are, know how to value the trunk of a woman. And you're right, of course, the richer the better! I've learned a lot from you about aesthetics even though I don't have your unerring eye; but I'm ready to gamble on it with Tullius Senecio if he would stake his mistress. It's hard to judge figures at a banquet where everyone is prone, but I'll bet you've already assessed hers correctly. 'Too narrow in the hips,' you told yourself."

"Too narrow in the hips." Nero grunted and let his eyelids slump across his eyes.

Petronius allowed himself a flicker of a smile that caught the eye of Tullius Senecio, who was busy arguing with Vestinius. Arguing was perhaps the wrong word for it; he was jeering at Vestinius' well-known faith in dreams, but he thought Nero and Petronius were disputing something and saw a quick chance to side with the emperor. "You're wrong!" he shouted at Petronius. "I agree with Caesar!"

"Please yourself," Petronius said with a smile. "I tried to prove that you have at least one pinch of brains in your skull, and Caesar holds that you're a brainless jackass."

"*Habet!*" Nero grinned and thrust his thumb down, the gesture with which a gladiator, fallen in the arena, was dispatched by a knife thrust to the throat.

"But I believe in dreams!" Vestinius shouted, still thinking that this is what the argument was about. "What's more, Seneca also told me once that he believes in them!"

"Last night I dreamed that I became a Vestal." Calvia Crispinilla leaned across the table so that her *peplum* gaped open to the navel. She was divorced too many times for anyone to remember. Her depravities rivaled the dead Messalina, and she was famous throughout Rome for her public orgies.

Nero clapped his pudgy hands, delighted with the joke, and everyone else broke immediately into loud applause. But Crispinilla wasn't bothered in the least.

"Well, why not?" she asked archly. "They're old and ugly, every one of them. Only Rubria still looks like a human being, so there'd be two of us even though she gets freckles in summer."

"Your life, purest Calvia, is an example to all Roman women," Petronius said smoothly. "Permit me to observe, however, that you could become one of the vestal virgins only in your dreams."

"And what if Caesar wanted me to be one?"

"Then I'd believe in dreams, no matter how fantastic."

"They come true, there's no doubt about it," Vestinius insisted. "I can see how people can stop believing in the gods. But how can someone not believe in dreams?"

"How about prophecies?" Nero asked. "A fortune-teller told me once that I'd rule over the entire East even though Rome no longer existed."

"Dreams and prophecies are all linked together," Vestinius went on. "There was a certain proconsul who was a great skeptic. He sent a slave to the temple of Mopsus with a question inside a sealed letter to see if the god could answer without actually hearing it said out loud. The slave slept in the temple to have a prophetic dream, then went home and said he'd seen a youth, bright as the sun, who spoke only one word. The word was 'black.' The proconsul went white as a sheet when he heard this. His guests couldn't imagine what was in the letter, but they didn't believe in dreams any more than he did."

Here Vestinius left the story hanging in midair and reached for a flagon.

"So what was in the letter?" asked Senecio.

"One question: Shall I sacrifice a white ox or a black one?"

But here Vitelius broke in, bellowing with laughter, as thick and mindless as the man himself. He was already half-drunk when he staggered into the banquet hall and had been drinking like a fish all night.

"What's that tub of tallow cackling about now?" Nero wished to know.

"Laughter is what makes the difference between man and beast," Petronius said. "It's his only proof that he's not a hog."

Vitelius cut his laughter. He smacked his greasy lips—smeared and splattered with cooking fat and sauces—and gawked at everyone around him as if he had never seen any of them before. Then he peered at his swollen hand, puffy as a cushion, and tried to flex his thick sausage fingers.

"I've lost my knight's ring," he muttered, wagging a naked finger.

"It's a miracle you had one in the first place," Petronius said with a shrug.

"No, it's not. It was an inheritance." Vitelius hiccoughed. "I got it from my father."

"Who was a sandalmaker," Nero tossed in.

But Vitelius howled with more unexpected laughter and started groping for his ring in Crispinilla's *peplum*. Vatinius shrieked, imitating the cry of a frightened woman, and Crispinilla's friend, Nigidia—a young widow with cold, knowing eyes in the sweet face of a little child—grinned in cynical amusement.

"He's looking for something he never lost," she said, "since he never had it."

"And which he won't know what to do with when he finds it," finished Seneca's nephew, the poet Lucanus.

The banquet was getting noisier and wilder by the minute, roaring to its climax. Throngs of slaves served one course after another, and drew corked flagons with every kind of wine from a huge ivy-wreathed vase constantly replenished with fresh mountain snow. Everyone was drinking, pouring the wine down their throats until it seeped and dribbled from their mouths. Meanwhile rose petals rained from nets in the ceiling onto the tables and the banqueters.

"Caesar"—Petronius turned to Nero—"why don't you bring some beauty to this table while there's still someone sober enough to hear it? Will you sing?"

"Sing! Sing! Yes, sing!" a drunken chorus bellowed in support but

Nero demurred. He wanted to be coaxed. Ah, it wasn't just a question of temerity, he explained, although he was always diffident and modest about his own talent. The gods knew how much a public performance took out of him. True, he did not refuse—"One must do something for art, after all"—and since Apollo gifted him with a fair voice, it would be wrong to hide it. "Yes, yes, I understand it's my duty to the state"—he made a helpless gesture—"but I'm too hoarse tonight. I even slept yesterday with lead weights on my chest, but it didn't help." He was even thinking of a trip to Antium to breathe some fresh sea air.

"Have mercy, divinity!" Lucanus appealed to him on behalf of mankind itself. "Everyone knows that you've just composed a new hymn to Venus that makes the old one, written by Lucretius, sound like the howling of a yearling wolf. Give us a feast for all our senses, not just the gut and the gullet. Teach us art and beauty. A ruler as good and kind as you shouldn't deprive his people. Don't be cruel, Caesar!"

"Be kind to us," cried everyone who sat within hearing. "Don't be cruel!"

Nero resigned himself. Sighing, he spread his hands in a helpless gesture. Gratitude, or what was meant to portray gratitude, glowed at once in every face around him. All eyes turned on him, wide in expectation. But first he sent word to Poppea that he was going to sing. She wasn't feeling well tonight, he explained, which is why she hadn't come to the banquet, but since no medicine did her more good than his singing, he didn't want to deprive her of this chance.

Poppea entered shortly afterward, as beautiful as a dream, glowing like a goddess, sweet-faced and golden-haired and as radiant in her freshness as a virgin child, although she had gone through two husbands before Nero. She ruled him as completely as if he were her slave, but she knew better than to test his ego as a singer, charioteer or poet. Now she swept in, dressed in the amethyst-colored robes reserved for the Caesars and wearing a necklace of gigantic pearls. Shouts welcomed her. She was greeted as the divine Augusta.

Ligia stared at her—awestruck, entranced but also repelled—because this was a woman whom Christians saw as the personification of viciousness and evil, and she had never seen such beauty anywhere before. Poppea Sabina was, she knew, one of the few truly vile women alive; she had heard about her from Pomponia, her guests and her servants. She knew it was this maddeningly beautiful, calculating woman who had driven Nero to murder his wife and mother, whose statues were pulled down and smashed at night throughout the city, and whose name, scrawled in hatred on walls everywhere, appeared every morning despite savage punishment for the perpetrators. She knew Poppea, as she was known throughout the Roman world, as evil incarnate. She couldn't tear her eyes away from this ruthless, murderous, unforgiving, cruel and angelic beauty, as ethereal as some celestial spirit, and she cried out before she could stop herself: "Ah, Marcus, how can this be?"

But he wasn't listening. The wine inflamed him and made him impatient. He was annoyed that so many things were distracting her and drawing her attention from him and what he was saying.

"Yes," he snapped. "She's beautiful. But you're a hundred times more beautiful. You'd fall in love with your own reflection, like Narcissus did, if you saw yourself as you truly are. She bathes in asses' milk, but Venus must've bathed you in her own. You've no idea, *occele mi*, my darling, how lovely you are! Don't look at her. Look at me, my darling. Touch this wine cup with your lips, right here, and I'll press mine to the same spot."

He pushed toward her, and she started to shrink back to Acte. But Nero rose just then. There were shouts for silence. The singer Diodorus handed him a three-sided, five-string lute, the kind known as *delta*. Terpnos, another singer who was to accompany him, approached with a twelve-string harp known as a *nablium*. Nero raised his eyes. Only the soft whisper of the falling roses broke the silence. Then he began to sing, or rather speak in rhythmic, modulated phrases, his ode to Venus, to the music of the harp and lute.

Neither his voice nor his poetry was especially bad, and poor Ligia was immediately in another quandary. Could she have misjudged him at first sight? Was she being fair? The hymn lauded Venus, the pagan goddess of carnality, but she thought it beautiful enough. And what about Caesar? With the gold leaves of his laurel wreath framing his tall forehead and with his upraised eyes, he seemed far more splendid than at the start of the banquet, not as terrifying and far less repulsive.

Applause burst like thunder. Ecstatic voices shouted, "Oh, heavenly voice!" all over the chamber. Women sat entranced, as if transported into unimaginable bliss, long after the song was over; others wiped their eyes or raised their arms in gratitude to the gods; and the whole gathering hummed and boiled like a roiled beehive. Poppea bowed her golden head to Nero and pressed her lips to his hand for a long, silent moment. The young Pythagoras, the same beautiful Greek singer and elocution teacher whom an older, half-mad Nero would later order to marry the four winds, now knelt in mute admiration at his feet.

But Nero's eyes were fixed solely on Petronius whose praise he wanted more than any other.

"When it comes to music," Petronius observed, "Orpheus must be as green with envy as Lucanus here. As to the rhymes, I've no words for them."

Lucanus shot him a glance of gratitude. "Damn the fates anyway," he muttered in pretended anger. "Why am I a contemporary of such a great poet? I'd hoped for a spot on Parnassus or some note in human memory; instead I'll be just a candle beside the sun."

But Petronius, who had an astounding memory, started to recite whole passages from the hymn, examining single lines and sections, and analyzing the best of the phrases. Lucanus threw in his own admiration as if the sheer beauty of what he had heard overwhelmed his envy. Nero's dull, empty face took on a glow of blissful vanity.

"What about this line?" he offered eagerly. "What about this phrase? Isn't it beautiful? Don't you think it the best of the lot?"

They praised him. His vanity was so all-consuming, the adulation that came his way each day so universal, and his godlike image of himself so monumental, that he took their replies as his due.

Dazed by his own perfection and moved to superior kindness, he had some words of encouragement for Lucanus. "Don't give up," he urged him. "Don't lose courage. You are what you were born, and there's nothing you can do about it. But just because mankind worships Jupiter doesn't mean it can't praise lesser gods."

Poppea really didn't feel well enough to be there, and Nero rose to take her to her chambers. He ordered the guests to stay where they were; he would be back. The banquet was not over.

‹ I I ›

NERO RETURNED soon afterward to steep himself in the clouds of Arabian incense that made him feel godlike and to watch the show that he and either Petronius or Tigellinus put on for the banquets.

The guests declaimed more poetry or listened to dialogues in which ornamentation took the place of wit. Paris, the famous mime, followed with the adventures of Io, daughter of Inachus, king of Argos, who was seduced by Jupiter in the form of a cloud and then changed into a cow by the jealous Juno; she went on to become a cow-headed goddess worshiped by the Egyptians under the name of Isis. Those banqueters who never saw a skilled mime before, and especially Ligia, thought they were watching miracles and magic. Paris' hands and body created an entire populated stage, filling it with graphic images and seductive action that seemed impossible to express in dance form. His palms stroked the air, creating a cloud of lust and subterfuge, full of life and fire, quivering and lascivious, gripping the fainting, semiconscious form of a girl shaken by spasms of pleasure. This was a living painting rather than a dance, a clear representation of illicit loving, shameless and bewitching and baring all the secrets of a lover's couch. Priests of Cybele, the earth goddess of lust and reproduction, came in with flutes, cymbals, citharas and hand drums, a glittering swarm of Syrian dancing girls running in behind them, and staged their ritual Cretan dance that celebrated fecundity and procreation, full of wild screams, flailing arms and legs, and even wilder music. Ligia felt shrunk, diminished, shaken and excited; she thought she was on fire and about to turn into a heap of ashes. She couldn't understand why a thunderbolt didn't strike and destroy this house or why the ceiling didn't crash down on the heads of the banqueters.

All that fell tumbling down, however, were the roses that rained from the golden nets fastened to the ceiling, while the half-drunk Vinicius mumbled in her ear.

"I saw you at the fountain in Aulus' garden. That's when I fell in love with you. You didn't see me, didn't know I was watching you. It was early, first light, and you thought you were alone. I still see you like that even though your body's hidden in that *peplum*. . . . Take it off, like Crispinilla did. You've seen the dance. There's nothing like loving, nothing in the world! Gods and men are always after it. Come here, lean on me. Put your head here on my chest and close your eyes."

She felt an oppressive pounding in her arms and temples as if she were falling. An abyss had opened under her, and she was hurtling down, and this Vinicius who seemed so close and trusted only moments earlier, did nothing to help her. Indeed, he was pulling her into the pit behind him; she felt cruelly disappointed.

Fear returned. Fear of this place, the banqueters, him and herself as well, gripped her as before. Some inner voice that sounded like Pomponia's urged her to save herself, but something else told her that it was too late. It was too late! Someone who felt this surging heat was already lost; nothing could help her or anyone who saw everything that happened at that banquet, whose heart hammered as wildly as hers when she heard Vinicius, and who trembled with such anticipation when he pressed against her.

She became dizzy and disoriented. She thought she would faint and then something terrible would happen. She knew she couldn't run away because anyone who left the banquet without permission risked the emperor's anger. No one could even rise or leave the table as long as he was there. . . . But even if that weren't so, she knew she had no strength to do it.

Meanwhile the end of the banquet was nowhere in sight. The slaves kept serving new courses and dishes, and filled all the cups the moment they were drained, and now two naked wrestlers appeared at the open end of the three-armed table. Massive oiled bodies gleamed when they closed and formed one quivering shape, straining against each other; the bones and tendons grated in their steel embrace, and a thick, dangerous growl seeped out of their clenched teeth. Their feet thudded on the saffron-strewn floor under them as they struggled for a better hold; or they stood still and silent, locked into each other, so that the spectators could believe they were seeing statues.

Roman eyes fixed with pleasure on the straining flesh of necks, massive legs, muscled arms and shoulders, but the bout didn't last long. Croton, the champion of the empire and supervisor of the gladiators' school, left no room for doubt that he was the strongest man in Rome. His opponent's breath quickened rapidly, and then he began to groan. His face turned purple, and blood gushed out of his mouth, and finally he hung limp across Croton's arm.

Applause thundered again while Croton threw his victim facedown on the floor, stepped on his back, crossed his huge arms on his chest and rolled his eyes around in a triumphant glare.

Too drunk to see much of anything around them, the banqueters paid scant attention to the jugglers, tumblers, clowns and animal impersonators who followed the wrestlers. The banquet slid gradually into a drunken orgy. The Syrian dancing girls now rolled with the guests on the dining couches. The music turned into a wild cacophony of citharas, lutes, Armenian tambourines and cymbals, Egyptian rattles, brass horns and copper trumpets. The guests who wanted to talk but couldn't make themselves heard in all that chaos howled for the musicians to get out of there. The air was hot and stifling, thick with the scent of flowers and aromatic oils that beautiful little boys sprinkled on the diners' feet throughout the banquet, and heavy with human exhalations and the smell of saffron. Lights flickered with a pale glow, wreaths hung cockeyed on heads and foreheads, and faces grayed and glinted under beads of sweat.

Vitelius rolled under the table. Nigidia, naked to the waist, rested her childlike head drunkenly on Lucanus' chest; he, just as drunk as she, amused himself by blowing the gold dust off her hair and laughing as it swirled. Vestinius, oblivious of anyone around him and driven only by drunken stubbornness, went on repeating Mopsus' answer to the doubter's letter. Tullius, who despised all the gods, jeered at them in a slow, drawn-out monotone that stumbled on hiccoughs.

"'Cause," he choked out. "You understand . . . if the globe of Xenophanes is round, and if it represents all the celestial bodies people worship, then you could roll such a god like a barrel, kicking it before you."

Offended by this blasphemous impiety, old Domitius Afer shook with indignation and spilled Falernian wine all over his tunic. A greedy, grasping thief and a paid informer, he believed in every god and goddess in the Pantheon, and the more the better. People say, he ranted, that Rome wouldn't last forever. Some say it's already falling. And why not? And who was to blame? Youth was to blame, that's who. They asked too many questions. The young had no respect for faith, and without faith there could be no virtue. All the strict old customs had gone by the board, and no one even thought that Epicureans might not be able to stop the barbarians. Ah, those

Epicureans and their *"carpe diem!"* Seize the moment, indeed, and feed all the senses! Live one day at a time and make each pleasure count! Well, that was just too bad. Too bad. As for him, he was sorry he lived to see such times where dissipation was the only sane refuge from reality and where debauchery was the surest antidote for the grief that racked a man of conscience.

With this the old thief clutched one of the Syrians and pressed his toothless mouth to her neck and shoulders. The bald old consul Memius Regulus sniggered at this sight, wobbled his head with its cockeyed wreath, and babbled in derision.

"Who says Rome's falling? Nonsense! I should know. I'm a consul, aren't I? *Videant consules.* Keep an eye on your generals, and you'll soon see what's what. Thirty legions guard our *Pax Romana!*"

He clenched a fist, pressed it to his temple and howled: "Thirty legions! Thirty legions from Britain to the Parthian border!" Then he paused and scratched his head in doubt.

"Or is it thirty-two?"

This finished him. Thinking was too much effort, and counting was worse. He rolled under the table where he began to throw up flamingo tongues, roast and frozen mushrooms, locusts dipped in honey, meats of all kinds, every sort of fish, and everything else he had drunk and eaten.

But Domitius Afer wasn't reassured by the number of the legions that guarded the borders. No, no, he wailed, Rome was bound to fall. It had lost its faith in gods and the strict old customs. Rome was doomed! Ah, what a pity, when life was so good, the emperor so kind and the wine so tasty! Ah, what an awful shame!

Then he buried his face between the shoulders of the dancing girl and burst into tears.

"Who cares about that promised afterlife," he mourned. "Achilles was right: It's better to be an errand boy on earth than a king in Hades. Lack of religion is what destroys our youth. Still, it's an open question if any gods actually exist."

Meanwhile Lucanus had blown all the gold dust off the hair of Nigidia, who snored on his shoulder. Most of her clothes had slipped off altogether, and now he decorated her with ivy that he pulled off one of the vases. "A sleeping nymph, what? Well, what do you think?" he mumbled to everyone around him, immensely pleased with his own creation.

He wrapped ivy around himself as well. "I'm not a man at all," he said with deep conviction. "I'm a faun."

Petronius had stayed sober, but Nero was drunk. Anxious that his "celestial voice" should hold up through his recitation, he drank comparatively little at the start, but then he drained one goblet after another and became quite tipsy. He burst into another singing declamation, this time in Greek, but he forgot his own verses and ended up singing an ode by Anacreon. Pythagoras, Diodorus and Terpnos tried to follow him, but they became lost in the discordant music and had to give it up. Nero, in turn, focused his eyes on Pythagoras, entranced by his beauty, and started kissing his hands in maudlin homage.

"Where did I see such beautiful hands?" he mumbled, clutching his wet forehead and trying to remember. Then a spasm of fear twitched across his face. "Aha! It was my mother!" Agrippina, as everybody knew, was also his first lover; she introduced him to debauchery through the joys of incest.

Gloom settled on him like a boulder. "They say," he mumbled, "that she walks on the sea at night in the moonlight between Baiae and Bauli. She walks and walks, nothing more than that, as if looking for something she lost. And when she comes to a boat, she just stares at it, that's all, and walks away again. But the fisherman she sees there dies at once."

"Not a bad theme for a tragic poem," Petronius remarked.

"I don't believe in gods," Vestinius whispered in a hushed, mysterious voice, stretching his long neck like a heron in the face of danger. "But ghosts . . . that's something else . . . that's another matter."

Nero ignored them both. "I went through all the rituals to appease the dead," he was muttering. "Five years ago. That whole three-day festival in May that's supposed to put the ghosts at rest, that entire *Lemuria*. So why is she walking on the sea? What's she looking for? I don't want to see her! I had to do it, you know. I had to condemn her. She sent me an assassin, or wanted to send one. If I hadn't struck first she'd have got to me and you wouldn't be able to hear my singing today."

"Thank you, almighty Caesar, in the name of the city and the world!" cried Domitius Afer.

"More wine! More music! Make them pound those cymbals!"

Lucanus, swathed in ivy, staggered to his feet and tried to shout through the sudden din that swept through the hall. "I'm not a human! I'm a forest faun! Ee-e-e-hoo!"

Then everyone was drunk and stumbling to oblivion. The emperor, men, women, everybody. The whole world was reeling. Vinicius was no soberer than the rest. The wine inflamed him, made him quarrel-some, and spurred all his cravings. His tanned olive features turned gray under his sweat, and his tongue tripped and stumbled among his bubbling words.

"Give me your mouth!" he ordered, angry and impatient. "Today, tomorrow, what's the difference? Come here. I've had enough of this! Caesar took you from Aulus so that I could have you, under-stand? He promised you to me in advance! You're mine! I'll send for you at sundown tomorrow, is that clear? You're mine and that's that. You have to be! Give me that mouth right now! I don't want to wait until tomorrow. Hurry up, give it here at once!"

He clutched at her, and Acte started to defend her. She herself struggled as best she could, but she had next to no strength left and felt she was sinking. She couldn't lift his thick, lifeless arm from around her body. He didn't hear the fear and anguish in her voice when she begged him to let her go, to be different, to be what he had been before and to show her some feeling and compassion. She recoiled from his hot wine-sodden breath as he pressed against her and pushed his face up against hers. He had turned into a drunken, vicious animal, a satyr driven by blind lust. Where was that former, good Vinicius who stirred such sweet longings in her soul? All she felt now was disgust and terror.

Her struggling was starting to fail her, however. He was too strong for her; she couldn't fight him off. It didn't help that she twisted in his grasp, trying to avert her face and avoid his kisses. He lifted him-self to his knees, seized her with both arms, pulled her head hard into his chest and started crushing her mouth with his own.

And then something happened. Some great force swept his mus-cled arms from around her neck as simply and as easily as if they were the weak arms of a puny child, and tossed him aside with as little effort as if he were a dry twig or a wilted leaf.

Vinicius lay dazed. He couldn't understand what had happened. He rubbed the fog from his eyes and saw the huge body of Lygian Ursus, whom he had seen in passing in the Plautius villa, towering silently above him. The Lygian was calm and quiet. He didn't seem particularly hostile. But there was something so telling and so terrible in his sky blue eyes that the young soldier felt his blood run cold and the marrow freeze in his bones. He watched the giant stoop and lift up his princess and carry her out of the banquet hall with a firm, quiet stride.

Acte went out behind him.

Vinicius sat frozen for a moment, as if turned to stone. Then he leaped to his feet and ran toward the doors.

"Ligia! Ligia!" he howled.

But passion, wine, rage and stupefaction pulled the floor out from under him, and he staggered into a naked dancer, tripping over her. "What happened?" he mumbled, clutching her shoulders.

"Drink!" she said, passing him a cup. Her glazed, drunken eyes were full of professional seduction.

Vinicius drained the cup and toppled facedown on the floor.

Most of the banqueters were dead drunk and prone under the table. Others staggered about the room, tripping on one another. Yet others slept on the dining couches, either snoring loudly or throwing up what they had drunk and eaten. The roses went on falling on the drunken consuls, drunken senators, drunken members of the Equestrian Order, drunken poets and philosophers, drunken dancing girls and patrician ladies, and on all that omnipotent world without a soul, still wreathed in laurels of conquest and civilization and sprawling over half the earth, but already dying.

Outside, dawn had arrived.

‹ 12 ›

NO ONE STOPPED URSUS. No one even questioned him. The banquet
guests who weren't lying dead drunk under the table had staggered
out of their places anyway, so the slave servants, seeing a giant carrying a senseless diner, thought Ursus was just another slave bearing his
drunken mistress to her sleeping quarters. Moreover, Acte walked
beside them, which removed any possible suspicion.

They left the banquet room, slipped into an adjoining chamber and
followed the colonnaded gallery that led to Acte's quarters. Lygia was
so spent that she hung limp in Ursus' arms as if she were dead. But at
the cooling touch of the clean dawn air, she opened her eyes.
Daylight became brighter. After a while, still walking among the
columns, they turned into a side portico that opened on the palace
gardens rather than on the courtyard, and caught sight of the tops of
the pines and cypresses reddening in the first crimson rays of sunrise.
This part of the palace edifice was empty, and the last bleats of music
and the yelling of the banqueters dwindled rapidly behind them. Ligia
felt as if she had been torn bodily out of Hell and carried into the
clean, clear light of God's good earth. Ah, so there was something
other for her than that banquet foulness. There was the sky, the lights
and colors of the sunrise; there was a cooling silence. She burst into
sudden tears—in part relief, in part gratitude, in part the residue of
disgust and remembered terror—and buried her face in the giant's
shoulder.

"Take me home, Ursus," she sobbed. "Take me home to Aulus!"

"That's where we'll go, then," Ursus said.

In a little while they found themselves in the small atrium of
Acte's apartment. Ursus sat the girl on a marble bench not far from
the fountain. Acte encouraged her, urging her to go to bed and rest,
and assuring her that she wasn't in any special danger since the
drunken diners were sure to sleep all day. But Ligia neither could nor

would calm down. She pressed her hands to her temples and went on pleading like a lost child to be taken home.

"Home!" she cried over and over. "I want to go home. Take me there, Ursus."

Ursus was ready. His reasoning was simple: The praetorians at the gate made no difference to him. The guard was there to keep out intruders, not to stop anyone from going out, and if they tried to stop him, he'd go right through them anyway. Once through the arch there would be no problem. The street outside was full of hired litters. People would soon start pouring out of the palace in throngs, and they'd go right with them and then head for home. Besides, what difference did it make? His dead king's daughter told him what she wanted, and that was all Ursus had to know. That's why he was there.

"Yes, we'll go, Ursus," Ligia kept repeating. "We'll get out of here."

Acte had to do the thinking for them both. So they'd get out! Certainly. Why not? Nobody would stop them. But anyone escaping from the house of Caesar commits a crime against the state and insults the emperor. They'd go out, but in the evening a centurion would march a troop of soldiers to the Plautius villa, hand a death sentence to Aulus and Pomponia, and take Ligia back to the palace. What hope would she have then? If Aulus and Pomponia took her under their roof, their death was a foregone conclusion.

Ligia let her arms fall weakly to her sides and hang there limp and useless. What could she do? She didn't have a choice. It was either death for Aulus, his boy and Pomponia, or her own submission. There was nothing else. She hoped, going to the banquet, that Vinicius and Petronius would convince the emperor to set her free and send her to Pomponia, but now she knew it was they who had her abducted in the first place. And for what? She felt that she had toppled into an abyss where only God and a miracle could save her.

"Acte," she wailed in despair. "Did you hear Vinicius when he said that Caesar gave me to him and that he'd send slaves for me this evening?"

"I heard him," said Acte. She spread her hands as if to say there was nothing she could do about it.

Nor could she. Ligia's despair found no echoes in her own experience. She herself was once Nero's concubine and lover. For all her gentleness and kindness and sympathy and pity, she couldn't feel what the Lygian girl was feeling; to her way of thinking, there was nothing abhorrent in that kind of union. She had been a slave; the rules of slavery were familiar to her. Besides, she was still in love with Nero; if he gave any sign of coming back to her, she would stretch out her arms to him as if he were happiness itself. Since it was clear to her that Ligia had to be the lover of the young and beautiful Vinicius if Aulus Plautius and his family were to go on living, she couldn't understand why she hesitated.

"You won't be any safer here than in Vinicius' house," she said after a while, not realizing what she was really saying.

On the surface it was true enough, but there were conditions. It was as if she had told Ligia to bow to her fate, accept the role in which others had cast her and become the plaything of Vinicius. But Ligia could still feel his hot animal breath scorching her neck and shoulders, and tasted the bitterness of his drunken kisses, and her whole face flamed with shame and loathing.

"Never!" she burst out. "I won't stay either here or there! That'll never happen!"

Acte watched her quietly for some moments, surprised by the violence of the outburst.

"Do you hate Vinicius so much, then?" she asked.

But Ligia couldn't answer. Sobs racked her body, and she gave way to another paroxysm of tears. Acte hugged her and murmured soothing phrases while Ursus, his huge fists clenched, towered over them like a brooding cloud. His doglike devotion to his princess made him sick with grief to see her in tears. Murder was stirring in that primitive, half-barbaric mind; cold rage demanded simple Lygian vengeance. He began to think about going back to the banquet hall and throttling Vinicius and Caesar, even if he had to kill them. The way he saw it, it wasn't all that much to be concerned about, and the only reason he hesitated, not quite daring to suggest it now, was that he wasn't sure if such a simple answer went along with the teachings of the meek and the mild.

Acte, meanwhile, managed to calm Ligia and asked her again: "Do you hate him that much?"

"No." Ligia shook her head. "I am a Christian. I'm not allowed to hate."

"I know," Acte nodded. "I also know from the letters of your Paul of Tarsus that you can't stoop to shame, or fear dying more than you fear sinning. But does this teaching allow you to bring death to others?"

"No," Ligia murmured.

"Well, then, how can you draw Caesar's vengeance on Aulus and Pomponia?"

Ligia said nothing. The abyss opened before her as before.

"I ask because I'm sorry for you," said the young freedwoman. "And I'm sorry for good Pomponia and Aulus and their child. I've lived a long time in this place, and I know what it means to anger Caesar. No, there is no way for you to escape from here if it means death to others. The only thing left for you to do is beg Vinicius to send you home again."

But Ligia had slid to her knees to beg someone else. Ursus knelt beside her after a short while, and both began to pray.

Acte had never seen such praying—not in Caesar's house, not in the pagan glow of a Roman sunrise. She couldn't tear her eyes away from Ligia. Seen in profile, with her arms raised and her head thrown back, the girl seemed to focus her entire being on something that Acte couldn't see, as if waiting for rescue or a sign. The dawn glowed in her eyes, streaked her dark hair and gilded her white *peplum,* so that she seemed to radiate a light of her own. Some otherworldly trust and dedication flowed from that pale, strained face, those reaching arms and soft, parted lips, so that she seemed transported and exalted. Now Acte understood why Ligia couldn't turn herself into a kept mistress. A veil that concealed a whole world of being, quite different from anything she knew or imagined on her own, parted suddenly for Acte. Such a profound faith amazed her in this home of depravity and murder. A moment earlier she was sure that Ligia was lost, that there was no way out for her in her terrible dilemma, but now she started to believe that something extraordinary was about to happen; help would come after all, she thought, and it would be so utterly overwhelming that even Caesar would give way before it. Winged armies would descend to protect the girl, or perhaps the sun would lay a stairway of light at her feet and lift her to another plane. She had heard of many miracles witnessed by the Christians, and now she could believe them.

Then Ligia rose. Her calm, restful features were alight with certainty and hope. Ursus also got off his knees and squatted by the bench; his pale blue eyes fixed quietly on his lady, and he waited for her orders. But her own eyes became suddenly dark with grief and still with acceptance, and two great tears rolled slowly down her cheeks.

"May God look after Aulus and Pomponia," she said at last, resigned but determined. "I can't bring disaster on them, so I'll never see them again."

She turned to Ursus and told him that he was all she had left now, that there was no one else in the entire world on whom she could rely and that he would have to be her guardian and her father from now on. They couldn't go to the Plautius home for refuge because that would doom everybody there. But she could neither stay here in Caesar's house nor go to Vinicius. Ursus must take her out, smuggle her from the city, and hide her someplace where neither Vinicius nor all his slaves could find her. She would go anywhere with him, suffer any hardships; let them go cross the sea, go beyond the mountains; let them live with barbarians beyond the reach of Caesar, so far away that the people never even heard of Rome.

"Take me away and protect me, Ursus," she commanded quietly. "You're all I have left."

The Lygian nodded with the same quiet confidence as Ligia's. He pressed his head to her feet in a sign of fealty and obedience. But Acte was disturbed and disappointed. Was that all? Where was the miracle? Was this what that fervent and exalted praying was supposed to bring? When you broke out of Caesar's house and fled without permission, you were committing blasphemy and a crime against the state, and that called for ruthless retaliation. Even if Ligia vanished into the unknown, Nero would extract vengeance from Aulus and Pomponia. If there was to be escape, let her escape from Vinicius, not from Caesar. Nero didn't like helping anybody. He might not want to get involved in Vinicius' personal affairs. But even if he did join the pursuit and find her, there would be no crime against the state to face or blasphemy to pay for.

Acte didn't know it, but this was exactly what Ligia was thinking. No one in Aulus' household, not even Pomponia, would know where she was. No, she wouldn't try escaping from Vinicius' house. She'd do it on the road. He had babbled that he would send slaves for her at sundown, which had to be true because he was drunk; if he had been sober, he'd never have said it. Both he and Petronius must have seen Caesar before the banquet and got him to agree to give her up the following evening.

"It could be that they'll forget about it or become distracted in some way," she said, turning to Ursus with urgent but thoughtful instruction. "But if they don't send for me tonight, they'll do it tomorrow."

But Ursus would save her. He would lift her out of the carrying chair and bear her away as he had from the banquet hall, and they'd go wherever safety beckoned. No one could stop Ursus. Even that dreadful wrestler who had crushed a man last night wouldn't be able to win over him. But since Vinicius might send many slaves to guard her, Ursus would go to the Christian bishop, the beloved Linus, and ask his help and guidance. Linus would understand at once what had to be done and would take pity on her. He wouldn't let her stay in Vinicius' hands. He'd order the community to go to her rescue, and they would set her free. Then it would be up to Ursus to find a way out of the city for them and to hide her somewhere beyond Roman reach.

Color arose on her cheeks once more, and her eyes shone with laughter. There was hope again, the possibility of rescue, and she saw it as if it had already taken place. She jumped up suddenly, threw her arms around Acte's neck and pressed her soft light lips to the woman's cheek.

"But you won't tell on us, Acte?" she whispered. "I can believe that?"

"I swear to you by my mother's spirit." The Greek freedwoman's voice was shaken with feeling. She had never felt so profoundly shaken or as moved. "I won't betray either one of you. But pray to your God again. Ask him to help Ursus in his part of it. Vinicius will fight to the death to keep you."

But the trusting, sky blue eyes of the childlike giant reflected only a vast inner happiness. He had racked his brains, such as they were, for just such a plan, and he came up with nothing. But doing his assigned part was as simple as tripping on a tree trunk. Let it happen at high noon or midnight, it made no difference; he would get her out of everybody's hands. He would go to the bishop. The bishop was a wise and holy man who read in the sky what to do and what not to do. He would get the Christians together anyway, bishop or no bishop.

He grinned. Ha! Didn't he know enough of them among the slaves, gladiators, freedmen and a slew of others from the Suburra slums to beyond the bridges? He'd get a thousand of them, two thousand if necessary, and carve a way to freedom for his lady. He knew how to smuggle her out of the city, and he'd go with her too. Where? Ursus grinned again. To the edge of the world, if that's what it took; anywhere as long as it was far. And—who knew, who could tell—maybe even to those forests they both came from, where no one even knew that there was a Rome.

His eyes focused on distances known only to himself, as if to catch a glimpse of something long vanished in his past and immeasurably far from his reality.

"To the forests?" His voice dropped to a growling whisper. "Hey, there, that was some forest."

He shook himself free of visions. There were things to do. He had to get to the bishop right away. He would have at least a hundred men in ambush before sundown. Let her escort be praetorian guards, not just a mob of slaves, it would make no difference! Just let them stay away from under his fist, even if they were in armor.

"There can't be much to this iron everybody thinks is so strong," he muttered. "Even the head inside the iron cracks with a good knock."

But Ligia, never more childlike than in her sudden gravity, raised a small finger and pointed at the heavens. "Ursus!" she commanded. "Thou shalt not kill, remember?"

The huge Lygian started rubbing the back of his neck with his massive fist. "Well, I don't know . . . I don't know," he worried, thinking about something that hadn't glimmered in his skull until now. She was "his light," as his barbarian custom taught him to regard her; he had to tear her out of whatever captivity she was in, there was no question in his mind about that. She said herself it was now up to him, it was his turn. Well, he would try not to hurt anybody, he'd do the best he could, but accidents could happen. And what if one happened? He remembered how easily accidents happened and she had to be free at any cost. Say something happened without his actually wanting to hurt anybody, if it simply happened. He would do heavy penance and would say how sorry he was to the flawless Lamb up there on the cross and would beg the Lamb to have pity on him. And the Lamb would hear him. The Lamb would know, as he knew everything, that Ursus wouldn't hurt him for the world. It's just that his fists were so huge and heavy.

A vast contentment spread across his face, a feeling of immense relief combined with gratitude, but he hid his face in another deep bow before Ligia.

"Well, then," he said. "I'd better see his holiness, the bishop."

Acte hugged Ligia and started to weep. She understood once more that there was yet another world, a different world, in which more happiness could come from suffering and endurance than from all the opulence in the house of Caesar. She saw again what she had seen before; it was as if a dark door had come ajar before her and she caught a glimmer of the light. But she also knew and understood that she wasn't clean enough to go through that door.

« 13 »

LIGIA KNEW SHE WOULD MISS Pomponia Graecina, who had been a mother to her for so many years, and she felt sick with loss. She knew she would miss all of the Plautius household just as much. But her despair was gone.

It pleased her that she was giving up so much for what she believed, that she was doing something for the truth she followed and going off into the unknown, away from the comforts and security of home. Perhaps there was something of a curious child in this anticipation of a life somewhere far away, among wild animals and exotic peoples. But there was also a profound conviction that she was doing what her Master wanted and that from now on he would watch over her like a father over a trusting and obedient child. If that was so, what did she have to fear? If there was pain, she would meet it in his name. If there was unexpected death, he would take her to him, and sometime in the future when Pomponia died, they would be together. It had often troubled her when she was a little girl in the Plautius household that she, a Christian, could do nothing for the dear, crucified, sacrificial offering that Ursus spoke about so simply and with such total trust. Now she had a chance.

She had a sudden need to share this with someone, perhaps to ask for help in understanding this strange new excitement even though so much else made her so unhappy, but Acte couldn't seem to grasp what she tried to say. How could she? It simply made no sense, to her way of thinking, to give up all she had, abandon everything dependable and familiar, cut all ties with Rome, leave all the gardens, temples, porticoes and monuments behind her, turn her back on all the splendid beauty and reject a warm land under a shining sun along with everyone who loved her. And for what? To hide from the love of a young and handsome patrician? There was no room in Acte's head for that kind of thinking.

Yes, she did glimpse something beyond her reach in isolated moments; now and then this seemed like the right thing to do. Yes, she conceded there could be some vast mysterious happiness at the end, but she couldn't see the clear and tangible core of the matter or grasp the totality of Ligia's faith and feelings. Besides, as Acte was all too well aware, the girl still faced a stormy passage in her break for freedom. It could end badly for her. She could still be killed.

By nature Acte was quite timid. She worried about what the evening might bring. She feared what might happen. But she didn't want to infect Ligia with that fear and started urging her to get a little rest after her sleepless and exhausting night. The day's light was now shining bright and clear, with the sun high enough to peer into the atrium, and Ligia was quite eager to oblige.

She followed Acte to the spacious bedroom, fitted out with the richness and abundance left from her days as Nero's favorite lover, and they lay down together on the sleeping couch. Tired as she was, however, Acte couldn't sleep. She was used to sadness and a sense of her own misfortune but now she felt the stirrings of a fresh anxiety, a new one she couldn't understand. Up till now her life had seemed only empty and without a future; now she thought it also shameful. Her thoughts, she noted, were becoming ever more chaotic. Illumination flashed and disappeared, as if the door between her and enlightenment cracked open intermittently and then slammed again, and when she did catch a glimpse of that blinding glare, it dazzled and confused her. She sensed more than saw that this light contained some immeasurable joy, something so vast and deep that all else was simply insignificant beside it. Her love for Nero was so absolute that she thought him at least a demigod, but she knew that if he suddenly drove Poppea from the palace and came back to her, it would seem like nothing next to that unknown happiness. It came to her suddenly that this demigod, this Nero she adored, was no more significant in the scheme of things than any other slave, and this palace with its Numidian marbles no better than rubble.

This seesaw struggle between light and darkness made her feel as if her head would burst. She was worn out and tired. She wanted to drift off to sleep, but anxiety kept her awake. At last, thinking that Ligia must also be too nervous, worried and upset to sleep—what with all the uncertainties and dangers that loomed over her—she turned to her to talk about the evening's planned escape. But Ligia slept quietly. A few stray beams of sunlight shot into the darkened bedroom through gaps in the curtains and caught the flecks of gold that swirled in the air; they brushed against Ligia's face as well. Acte watched her delicate, finely molded features, the childlike face so peacefully composed and laid lightly across a naked arm, the closed eyes and the slightly parted lips. Her breath was soft and even, as in untroubled sleep.

"She can sleep," Acte sighed. "She is still a child."

And then it came to her again that this child would rather run than be Vinicius' lover, that she picked homelessness and hunger over a life of ease in a splendid home near the Carinnae, the most celebrated quarter of Rome where stood the villas of men such as Pompey, and that she found more joy in a wanderer's satchel and a threadbare robe than in the rich silks, jewels, banquets, citharas and lutes she was abandoning.

"Why?" she asked aloud.

She peered at the girl as if to read the answers in her sleeping face. She looked at the clear young forehead and the untroubled arch of a perfect eyebrow, at the dark fringe of lashes that shaded her cheek, at the parted mouth and at the quiet rise and fall of her breath. How different she is from me, Acte thought.

And suddenly Ligia seemed almost mythical, a miraculous creation, some vision glimpsed only by the gods or some god's own goddess. She was a hundred times more beautiful than all the flowers in Caesar's gardens and all the sculptures in his Palatine, yet the young Greek woman looked at her without a shred of envy. She looked at the sleeping girl with enormous pity. All the dangers that threatened this dear, dreaming child, who was herself as beautiful as a dream, made her feel protective and anxious, like a mother. She loved this child, she knew, and bent down to kiss her.

Ligia slept as quietly as if she were at home, looked after by Pomponia Graecina. She slept fairly long. It was past noon when she opened her blue eyes and started looking around the bedroom with great curiosity. She seemed surprised not to be in her own bed in the Plautius house.

"Is that you, Acte?" She caught sight of the young Greek woman in the darkened chamber.

"Yes, Ligia."

"Is it night already?"

"No, dear. But it's past noon."

"Has Ursus come back?"

"Ursus didn't say he was coming back. He told us he'd be waiting for you in ambush with his Christians."

"Ah, that's right," Ligia recalled. She seemed untroubled by everything she remembered.

They left the *cubiculum*, and went to the bathing rooms where Acte bathed Ligia. Then she led her to breakfast and took her to the palace gardens. It wasn't likely they would meet any danger there, because Caesar and all his banquet cronies wouldn't be up for hours. This was the first time Ligia was seeing these gardens, one of the wonders of the Roman world, full of cypresses, wild pine, oaks, olive trees and myrtles, and with a whole population of white marble statues scattered in their shade. She caught sight of quiet pools as still as silvered mirrors, breathed the scent of roses that grew in thick groves throughout the park and glinted in the sun under spraying fountains, passed the mouths of enchanted grottoes framed in vines or ivy. Silvery swans drifted on the mirrors. Tame desert antelope from Africa wandered among the trees, and bright-hued birds brought from all over the world clustered around the statues.

No one was walking there other than Acte and Ligia. There was nobody about except scattered groups of ditch-digging slaves who grunted a low rhythmic chant as they swung their spades; others watered the roses and the pale blue petals of fresh-blooming saffron; still others, given a breathing spell, squatted by the pools or stretched out in the shade under the oaks.

Ligia and Acte walked a long time among these natural treasures. The girl had plenty to occupy her mind, but there was so much of the child still in her that she became totally absorbed while curiosity and wonder overran all her other senses. It even occurred to her that if there ever was a kind and decent Caesar, he could be truly happy in such a park and palace.

Tired at last, they rested on a stone bench almost entirely hidden in a cypress thicket and began to talk about what troubled both of them the most. The evening and its dangers drew steadily toward them. Acte was far less optimistic about Ligia's chances than the girl herself. She was alarmed to think that this could all be madness, an act of desperate folly that couldn't possibly succeed. She pitied Ligia more than ever and thought it would be a hundred times safer for her to work through Vinicius.

"How well do you know Vinicius?" she asked after a while. "It might be possible to win him over. He could return you to Pomponia on his own."

But Ligia merely shook her lowered head. "No. He was different in the Plautius home. But now I'd rather go to the Lygians. I'm afraid of him."

"But in the Plautius home," Acte hinted, "you liked him?"

"Yes." Ligia's head dipped lower.

"The thing is that you're not a slave, as I used to be," Acte said after a long pause. "Vinicius could marry you. You're a state hostage, the daughter of a king. Aulus and Pomponia think the world of you, and I'm sure they'd adopt you as their legal daughter. Vinicius could marry you, Ligia."

Acte could barely hear the girl's soft, sad voice: "I'd rather escape to the Lygians."

But she persisted. "Listen, Ligia, I'm ready to go to Vinicius straightaway, wake him if he's sleeping, and tell him just what I said to you. Do you want me to do that? Yes, dear girl, I'll go to him and tell him you are a king's daughter and a member of the Plautius family as well, the beloved child of the famous Aulus. He can return you to them and take you back again as his wife."

The girl's voice was now so low that Acte had to bend toward her mouth to hear: "I'd rather have the Lygians." And two large tears hung among her lashes.

Their silence, deep and thoughtful as it was, lasted but a moment. They heard the rustle of approaching footsteps, looked up and saw Poppea Sabina passing their bench with a retinue of slaves. Two of the girls fanned her lightly, and shielded her from the sun with bunched ostrich plumes they held over her head on flexible gold rods. Walking just before her was an Ethiopian woman, black as ebony and with milk-swollen breasts distending her tunic; she carried an infant swathed in imperial purple fringed with gold. Acte and Ligia rose, thinking that Poppea would just pass them by, but she stopped before them.

"Acte," she said, "you didn't sew those bells to the doll well enough. The child tore one off. She would have swallowed it if Lilith hadn't stopped her."

"Forgive me, Augusta." Acte bowed her head and crossed her arms across her chest and shoulders.

But Poppea saw Ligia. "Whose slave is that?" she asked after a pause.

"She's not a slave, divine Augusta," Acte murmured. "She's the daughter of a Lygian king, given to Rome as a pledge of peace and raised in the house of Pomponia Graecina."

"And she came to pay you a little call?"

"No, Augusta. She has been staying in the palace since yesterday."

"Was she at last night's banquet?"

"Yes, she was, Augusta."

"By whose order?"

Acte wished desperately that she didn't have to say what she had to answer.

"Caesar's."

"Oh?" Poppea's golden eyebrows rose slightly for a moment. She studied Ligia with far greater care, assessing her face, body, posture, youth and freshness with an expert's eye. Her attention sharpened as she watched the girl who stood bowed quietly and respectfully before her, but who couldn't help shooting curious glances up at her with her clear blue eyes. A deep vertical furrow cut suddenly into Poppea's forehead. She was immensely jealous of her beauty. It was the source of everything she was and had at her disposal, her most precious weapon, and she lived in perpetual fear of being surpassed. Some luckier bidder for Caesar's attentions might appear someday, as she had appeared in the court of Nero's first empress, and ruin her as she had ruined Octavia.

Made instantly suspicious by any lovely face throughout the palace, she took swift note of everything about this girl, judged and assessed all her shapes and contours, and all the details in each of her features.

She judged, compared and was uneasy. "This is a nymph," she told herself. "This is a child of Venus." And suddenly she felt a hot lick of fear she had never even thought about before no matter what beauties she was tabulating: I'm older, she thought. Much older. Her own admiration for herself trembled like a pane of glass that shudders before a storm; all her trained instincts cried out in alarm; threatening suppositions raced across her mind. Did Nero see her? Perhaps not yet, she thought rapidly. Or maybe he couldn't see her well enough, peering through that emerald. But what would happen if he came across her like this, in daylight, in the gardens, so beautiful and glowing in the sun?

That's a king's daughter, Poppea noted coldly, adding up her dangers. True, a barbarian king, but still royalty. By the immortal gods, she's as beautiful as I but younger! Younger!

The furrow deepened and darkened in her forehead, and a cold, calculating light glinted in her eyes. Her voice, however, when she turned to Ligia was balanced and calm.

"Did you speak to Caesar?"

"No, Augusta."

"Why would you rather be living here than with your Pomponia?"

"It's not my choice, great lady," Ligia murmured, still in her own trance over Poppea's beauty. "Petronius got the emperor to have me abducted from Pomponia, but I'm in prison here, great lady!"

"And would you like to go back to Pomponia?"

A softer, kinder note now quivered in her voice, and Ligia seized upon it like floating straw. "Great Lady," she said, stretching her arms toward her, "Caesar promised me to Vinicius for a slave, but you can speak for me and have me sent back to Aulus and Pomponia."

"Ah." Poppea felt much easier, even though the danger still remained. "So it was Petronius who talked the emperor into taking you away from Aulus to give to Vinicius?"

Hope hammered like a desperate bird in Ligia's breast. She knelt and clutched the hem of Poppea's *peplum*. "Yes, great lady. Vinicius is to send for me tonight. But you'll take mercy on me, won't you? You won't let that happen?"

She waited, straining for confirmation of that last quick hope while Poppea watched her; the smile in Poppea's eyes was radiant with malice.

"I promise you that you'll be in Vinicius' bed before this day is over," she said.

She walked off, still like a vision but an evil one. Only the screams of the child, who wailed for some reason out of sight, broke the silence.

Ligia's eyes also filled with tears, but she shook them off, rose and took Acte's hand. "Let's go back in," she said. "Help can come only from one place, and that's where we'll find it."

They came back to the atrium and sat there until evening. They were both very pale by the time it darkened beyond the colonnades and the slaves brought in their lighted four-armed candelabra. Their conversation was disjointed. Each of them strained for the sound of approaching footsteps. Ligia kept saying over and over that she was sorry to be leaving Acte, that she loved and trusted her and was grateful to her, but that somewhere out there in the darkness Ursus was waiting for her and she had to go. Her breathing sharpened and became more anxious as the moment neared. Acte raced through the room, snatching up whatever jewels she could find and knotting them in a corner of Ligia's outer robe. She begged the girl by all the gods not to reject this gift and the chances it could buy for her. Then there were long silences, a protracted stillness where both of them sat immobilized by anxiety, watching the sun go down and listening to imaginary footsteps. But all they heard through that deepening twilight were stray whispers that seemed to come from just beyond the hangings, the distant wail of a child and barking dogs.

Suddenly the hangings parted in the doorway that led beyond the atrium, sliding aside so softly they barely rustled, and a tall, dark-skinned man with a pockmarked face materialized before them. Ligia knew him—he was Atacinus, a freedman of Vinicius. She had seen him at the Plautius home while Vinicius was convalescing there.

Acte cried out, really frightened now, but Atacinus only bowed respectfully. "Marcus Vinicius sends greetings to Ligia," he said formally. "He waits for her with a celebration feast in a house decked with greenery and garlands."

The girl's lips were quite bloodless then. "I'm ready," she said.

The last thing Acte would remember of this moment was the girl's arms thrown around her neck in gratitude and love.

‹14›

THE HOUSE OF VINICIUS was ablaze with light and as green with garlands as Atacinus had said when he came for Ligia. Ivy and myrtle looped across the walls, wreathed all the lintels and bunched above the doors. Grapevines coiled in spirals up the fluted columns. The opening above the atrium, screened off to keep out the night chill, was covered with a hand-knitted purple tent made of oiled wool; inside, the rectilinear hall around the *impluvium* was as bright as day. Eight- and twelve-armed candelabra and lamp stands shaped like birds, trees, animals and flagons filled the atrium with a bright, multi-colored glow, as did the rows of marble and alabaster statues that held lamps filled with aromatic oils, and the tall freestanding candlesticks, taller than a man and glazed in gold over Corinthian copper. None of this was as awe inspiring as the famous candelabrum stolen from the temple of Apollo—the beautiful, costly one made by noted sculptors that Nero was using for himself.

Scarlet, blue, yellow and violet lights glowed behind stained glass from Alexandria and through delicate, handwoven lampshades from beside the Indus. The scent of sandalwood, which Vinicius had learned to like while serving in the East, lay thickly everywhere; and the dark, flitting silhouettes of house slaves, both male and female, drifted across a similar multicolored brightness seen in the far interior of the house. The low table within the flat, squared arch of the *triclinium* couches was set for four since Petronius and Chrysothemis were to join Vinicius and Ligia.

Vinicius had done everything Petronius suggested: "Don't go for her yourself," the supreme arbiter advised. "Anxiety is vulgar. Send Atacinus after you get permission from Caesar." Moreover he was to receive the girl here in his own home with every sign of courtesy and respect.

"You made a pig of yourself last night," Petronius observed. "I watched you. A quarryman from the gravel pits in the Alban hills couldn't show worse taste. Don't throw yourself at her so hard. A good wine should be savored slowly. And keep in mind that while it's sweet to want, it's a lot sweeter to be wanted."

Chrysothemis had her own, rather different opinion about that, but Petronius started lecturing her on the differences between a veteran charioteer and a bare-lipped boy who was climbing into a four-horse chariot for the first time. "What applies to you, my virtuous vestal, need not apply to anybody else.

"Win her trust," he said, turning to Vinicius. "Make her laugh. Be generous and high-minded. I don't want to sit through a gloomy dinner. Swear by Hell itself that you'll take her back to Pomponia, and then it'll be up to you if she decides in the morning that she'd rather stay.

"That's what I do with my own devoted, timid little dormouse" — he nodded at Chrysothemis—"and I've had no complaint in five years, at least none I've felt obliged to voice."

Chrysothemis hit him archly with her ostrich fan. "Complaints? I should say not! When did I ever say no to you, you satyr?"

"Hmm. Now and then, I seem to recall—perhaps out of respect for my predecessor?"

"Don't tell me that you weren't on your knees before me, begging me to leave him and come to you. You even kissed my toes!"

"All the better to get the diamonds on them."

Chrysothemis threw a quick, involuntary glance at her feet and her sparkling toe-rings, and both she and Petronius burst into knowing laughter. But Vinicius paid no attention to their verbal sparring. His heart was beating far too fast under the brightly patterned robes of a Syrian shaman he put on for Ligia.

"They should've left the palace by now," he said, stirring uneasily.

"They should have," Petronius agreed. "I could tell you about the predictions of Appolonius of Tyana to help pass the time. Or that story about Rufinus that I never finished, though I can't think why."

But Vinicius couldn't have cared less about Appolonius of Tyana or the misfortunes of Rufinus. His thoughts were centered wholly around Ligia, and even though he felt it was far better to receive her here than go to the palace for her like a common bailiff collecting a debt, he regretted that he hadn't gone. He would have seen her sooner. He would have stretched beside her in the curtained darkness of the double litter.

Meanwhile the slaves brought in hot coals in three-legged copper bowls, decorated with carved ram's horns at the edges, and started sprinkling them with small chips of myrrh and sandalwood.

"Now they're turning into the Carinnae," Vinicius blurted out as if talking to himself.

"He'll either burst with impatience," Chrysothemis observed, "or he'll run out to meet them and miss them on the way."

"I won't burst," Vinicius said with a tight, cold smile, but his nostrils whitened in anticipation and he began to breathe heavily like a bellows.

"There's not an ounce of the philosopher in him," Petronius said, sighing sadly. "I'll never turn this hotheaded son of Mars into a human being."

But Vinicius didn't even hear him. "Now they're in the Carinnae," he said.

And he was right. The litter and its escort were entering the Carinnae quarter. The slaves, known as *lampadari*, led the way with lanterns, and the *pedisequi*, or footmen and runners, trotted beside and behind the chair. Atacinus walked right next to Ligia, watching over everything and keeping an eye on the street ahead.

They made their way slowly. There was no public lighting in the streets at night, and their hand lanterns didn't give much illumination. The streets near the palace were almost deserted; only rarely did some skulking figure pass by with a hooded lamp. But later on, and especially in these narrow sidestreets, they appeared in surprising numbers. Every nook and doorway seemed to disgorge three or four dark figures as the convoy passed; all of them, Atacinus noticed, were walking without any lights or torches and all wore black. Some kept close to the convoy, slipping in among the slaves and walking beside them or coming up behind out of the alleyways and tunnels. Others came head-on in thicker clusters, reeling about as if they were drunk.

"Make way for the noble tribune Marcus Vinicius!" the lampadari shouted into the unexpected throng but without success. Slow to begin with, and now squeezing through a jam of people, the pace of the convoy fell to a snail's crawl.

Ligia saw these dark clusters of men through the litter curtains and began to shudder with anticipation. Hope and fear alternated, coming to her like intermittent flashes of light in the darkness. "That's he," she whispered through trembling lips. "That's Ursus and the Christians." It'll happen any moment now, she thought. Help them, Christ! Protect them!

Atacinus also started getting worried. He didn't pay much attention to the unusual crowding, not at first, and not as long as the litter managed to inch forward. But there was something very odd about it, and it got worse the farther they went. Now the lampadari were shouting for room at almost every step, and the press of people was so heavy at the flanks that Atacinus ordered his slaves to beat them off with cudgels.

Suddenly a wild yell burst from the head of the column, all lights disappeared, cudgels struck, fists flew, and utter chaos erupted around the litter.

"They've jumped us!" Atacinus knew at once and froze with terror.

Everyone in Rome was aware that Caesar amused himself now and then by forming gangs of thugs out of his court cronies and leading them out at night in disguise to smash shops in the Suburra and elsewhere in the city, to attack passersby, and to loot whatever wasn't nailed down. He often staggered back to the Palatine with black eyes, bruises and knots on his head, but anyone who put up a fight was put to death at once, no matter what his rank. The nightwatch who guarded the peace of the city were usually struck deaf and blind at such time, and Atacinus didn't think they would come running now even though their building wasn't far away.

The scuffle around the litter was an all-out brawl. Men clutched and wrestled with each other. Fists smashed into faces, clubs knocked people senseless, and those who fell were trampled underfoot. Atacinus focused on the thought that he must save Ligia and himself and leave the rest to the demigods of fate. He pulled the girl out of the carrying chair, threw her across his shoulder, and started to run. Chaos and darkness helped him. He thought he had a good chance to slip away unnoticed; indeed, he had made some headway and had started to thank his gods and congratulate himself, when suddenly Ligia shouted "Ursus! Ursus!"

She was dressed in white and easy to see. Atacinus used his free hand to throw his own dark cloak over her, but some terrifying vise clamped itself on the back of his neck, and a huge, crushing weight landed on his skull.

He fell like a sacrificial ox stunned with a hammer on one of Jove's altars.

The slaves were either down on the ground or scattered, tripping and falling or running into walls, and the attackers disappeared in the darkness. The litter lay smashed. Ursus marched swiftly toward the Suburra, carrying Ligia in his arms. His companions followed, vanishing in the alleys behind him as they went.

The bruised, beaten slaves slowly gathered in front of Vinicius' house, but none of them knew what to do next. They didn't dare go back inside. They argued for a while in whispers, then made their way back to the dark, silent street where they had been attacked. There was nothing there now except a few corpses. The body of Atacinus lay there as well. He was alive when they found him, still twitching, but not for long. His body quivered in one last convulsion as they watched and then he was dead.

They carried the dead man back to their master's home but stayed huddled outside, whispering and uncertain, terrified of what would happen to them when they told their story.

"Let Gullo tell it," they whispered among themselves. "He's got blood all over his face and has been hurt as bad as any of us, and the master loves him. It's safer for him to break this kind of news than anybody else."

Gullo had been captured years ago in Germania and came to Rome as part of the triumphal march granted to the conqueror, the elder Vinicius. He had passed to Marcus with the rest of his mother's property and was used to carry him on his shoulders when he was a boy. "All right," he said. "I'll do all the talking. But the rest of you had better come as well. I don't want his anger to fall on me alone."

Meanwhile Vinicius had come to the end of his patience. Petronius and Chrysothemis laughed at him and poked fun at him, but he didn't listen. He paced the atrium angrily, his tolerance gone along with his composure.

"They should be here by now!" he snarled over and over. "They ought to be here!"

He wanted to go out himself to see what was keeping them, but the others stopped him.

"Impatience is so vulgar," Petronius started to remind him when footsteps clattered in the vestibule outside and a mob of slaves burst into the atrium.

"Aaaaa!" they howled like mourners at a funeral, stretching their arms high over their heads and huddled against the walls. "Aaaaa!"

"Where's Ligia?" Vinicius leaped toward them. His shout was a scream of fury and impatience.

"Aaaaa!"

"Gone, Master!" Gullo edged out, splashed with blood, and started babbling in a whining voice. "See the blood, Master! We fought! We did our best! Look at the blood, my lord! Look at the blood, Master!"

That was as far as he got before Vinicius seized a huge bronze candlestick and crushed his skull with one blow. Then he grasped his own head in both hands and dug his fingers deep into his hair. *"Me miserum!"* he grated out. *"Me miserum!* I can't stand this!"

His face was purple, thick with blood, his eyes turned up whitely, and spittle bubbled at the corners of his mouth. "Scourges!" he howled at last, his voice as thick and mindless as an animal's.

"Spare us, lord!" moaned the slaves. "Aaaaa! Aaaaa . . . have mercy on us, Master!"

"Come, Chrysothemis." Petronius rose with a look of wry distaste etched across his face. "If you want to look at bleeding meat, I'll have a butcher's stall knocked open outside."

He left. She followed. The groans of the whipped and the hiss of scourges echoed all night throughout that festive house, garlanded for a joyful celebration.

‹ 15 ›

THAT NIGHT VINICIUS didn't lie down at all. Some time after Petronius left, when the wails of whipped slaves failed to relieve his rage and humiliation, he gathered another retinue and led it out in a wild search for Ligia. He combed the Esquiline quarter, the Suburra, the Vicus Sceleratus and all its side streets, cul-de-sacs and alleys. He crossed the Fabricius bridge to the island and then searched part of the district that lay beyond the Tiber. But this was a chase without a quarry, and he knew it as well as anyone. He had no hopes of finding Ligia. He searched for her only to be doing something. This night had been more than just a shock to him; it was devastating. He couldn't pass the rest of it sitting on his hands.

The sun was rising by the time he called off the search. And by the time he returned home, bakers were already opening their stalls for business, and the mules and carts of the market gardeners clip-clopped and creaked through the city gates, bringing in produce. The corpse of Gullo still lay where he had left it, so he ordered his household slaves to dispose of it. He directed that all the slaves who had taken part in last night's disaster be sold at once to rural workhouses or shipped to the quarries, although death would have been the kinder punishment. Then he threw himself down on a padded stone bench in the atrium, but he didn't sleep.

His thoughts were jumbled, running into one another like incoherent lightnings. He searched the chaos in his mind for some way to find Ligia and get her back again. The thought that she was lost to him for good and he would never see her again drove him close to madness. This was the first time in the young tribune's life that something didn't happen the way he demanded. He was a patrician, an Augustan; he had been obeyed from childhood. He was a military tribune, commanding a cohort and with powers of life and death over a thousand men. His own nature, and whatever positive traits he developed, contained a strong, powerfully focused will, and this self-willed nature had never met resistance. He simply couldn't understand how anyone or anything would dare deny him what he wanted, and yet he recognized another iron will pitted against his own.

Vinicius was a product of his civilization, born to command like every highborn Roman, and he would rather watch the world end and the city tumble into ruins than see himself fail to achieve what he set out to do. Here he was ready to sip from a magic cup full of miracles and sweetness, and it had been torn from his grasp practically at the lip. Such things just couldn't happen! It was unheard of, so shocking that it cried for vengeance to all the gods, to the laws, and for every kind of human retribution.

But mostly, because he had never wanted anything as much, he would not accept the idea that Ligia was gone; it seemed to him he would not exist without her. He questioned how he would live through the next day and all the days thereafter. His rage came close to stifling him at such times, and now and then his anger turned on her. He wanted to beat her and drag her to his bedroom by the hair whenever that happened. And then there would come a longing just to hear her voice, look into her eyes, and merely sense the nearness of her face and body.

He felt enslaved by her, as if his proper place was on his knees before her. He shouted for her, bit his nails and clawed at his hair, but he couldn't force himself to think logically and calmly about how to get her back. One mad idea flashed after another, all of them quite useless. Then he fixed on the enraged conviction that it was Aulus who had torn her from his grasp. He would go at once to the Plautius house and either force them to give her up or find out where they had hidden her.

He leaped to his feet, ready to face Aulus and Pomponia. If they ignored his threats, he thought, if they refused to return Ligia to him, he would go to Nero and accuse the old general of failing to carry out an imperial order. That meant a death sentence. But first he would get the old man to tell him where she was. Nor would he forgo retaliation even if Aulus turned the girl over to him without any fuss. True, they had been kind to him in the Plautius house and had taken care of him when he needed help. But this one unforgivable challenge to his will erased any gratitude he felt; he was, he thought, free of any obligations. How dared they thwart him and humiliate him? How did they think they would get away with that? His ruthless pride demanded retribution. In fact he started savoring the picture of Pomponia's anguish when she heard the death sentence read out to her husband.

Aulus would die. Petronius would help to push Caesar in the right direction, but Nero might just do it anyway without any prompting. He seldom refused anything to his favorite fellow Augustans unless he happened to dislike them or if their wishes got in the way of his own whim and pleasures, which wasn't the case here.

But—and this thought seemed to freeze the blood in his veins—what if it was Caesar himself who had stolen Ligia from him?

It was no secret anywhere in Rome that Nero looked for refuge from boredom in occasional night banditry in the streets. Even Petronius sometimes participated in these cruel pastimes whose main object was to cause as much uproar as possible in the poor, crowded quarters of the city, catch some unlucky woman and toss her in the air on a soldier's cloak until she was unconscious. Nero called this game "pearl diving," because the woman was sometimes a real pearl of youth, charm and beauty. In that event the cloak-toss turned into an abduction, and the plucked pearl was hustled off to the Palatine or vanished in one of Caesar's innumerable villas, or he turned her over to one of his cronies.

This could have happened with Ligia. Vinicius recalled how insistently Nero had stared at her at the banquet, and he had no doubt she must have seemed the most beautiful woman Nero had ever seen. How else could it be? True, Caesar already had her at the Palatine and could have kept her there. But as Petronius so rightly observed, this Caesar didn't have the courage of his own convictions even in his crimes. He never acted in the open if he could find some surreptitious way. And in this case he might have been afraid of Poppea.

With this thought now planted in his mind, Vinicius started doubting if Aulus and Pomponia had the ruthless courage to abduct a girl given to him by Caesar; it would take a madman even to think of it. So who would have such courage? The blue-eyed Lygian giant who had marched into the banquet hall and carried Ligia out of there in his arms? Possibly. But where would he take her, and how would he hide her? No, this was beyond the means of a mere slave. That left only Caesar, and at this thought Vinicius lost sight of his surroundings. His eyes blurred. Sweat beaded his forehead. Those were the only hands in the Roman world from which he would never be able to tear her free; once Caesar had her, she was beyond his reach. "*Vae misere mihi!*" he groaned again, more justified in his despair than earlier. Imagination clawed at him with pictures of Ligia with Nero, an obese satyr ravaging a nymph, and it dawned on him as it never had before that some forms of thinking were simply past enduring.

With this thought came another. He had no idea how much he loved Ligia until he had lost her. He clutched at his every memory of her, saw her in all his remembered images and heard everything she said. He recalled how she had looked by the fountain in Aulus Plautius' garden and how she had responded to him early at the banquet. He reached for her nearness, the scent of her hair, the warmth of her body, the joy he drew from the kisses with which he crushed her lips. She seemed a hundred times more beautiful and desirable, but also as dear and unique as if he had handpicked her from among all the goddesses and mortals. He had never experienced this depth of feeling for anyone before.

Pain lanced through him in spasms when he thought that this personification of all his hopes and longings now belonged to Nero. He couldn't bear the idea or the images it brought. He wanted to smash his head against the atrium walls. Madness reached for him and seized him, and he would have given way if one raging, murderous impulse hadn't sustained him: If there was nothing left for him, at least he could have vengeance.

A moment earlier he had been sure he would never be able to live without Ligia; now he knew he would have no peace even after death unless he avenged her, and this realization brought him a little ease. "I'll be your Cassius Chaerea," he muttered to his images of Nero. "I'll do for you what he did for Caligula." He grasped a handful of soil from the flowers around the *impluvium,* and took a formal oath, swearing by Erebus, the god of darkness, son of Chaos and brother of Night, that he would punish Caesar. He vowed by Hecate, the three-headed goddess of spells and enchantments, and by his own household gods. Vengeance gave him focus. This would at least give him a mission and a sense of purpose, and that would let him live.

Still too distraught to think clearly, he had himself taken at once to the Palatine, with the vague notion that he ought to confirm his suspicions. If the praetorians stopped him or searched him for weapons, that might be a sign that Nero took Ligia, but he didn't take a weapon with him. Like most people driven by a single passion, all he could think about was settling his scores with Caesar, and he didn't want to strike any haphazard, premature blows.

The thought that he might see Ligia somewhere in the palace shook him like a fever. He had to talk to Acte before anybody. She would know what had happened and would tell him the truth. But— and another wild hope flared behind his eyes—what if Nero seized the girl last night without even knowing who she was? What if he hadn't recognize her in the dark? But then, finding out, wouldn't he have ordered her returned today? He dismissed the thought. No. If they were going to return her to him, they would have done it last night, right after the abduction. Acte, however, might be able to shed some light on everything and he had to see her straightaway.

Sure of at least that much, he ordered his bearers to quicken their pace. His thoughts, such as they were in the dark chaos of lost love and vengeance, narrowed to intermittent flashes on Ligia and revenge. He had heard that some Egyptian priests could inflict any disease they wanted, and he decided to find out how they did it. It was said in the East that Jews had some sort of curse that covered their enemies with boils. He had more than a dozen Jews among his slaves and made a note to have them scourged until they told their secret. But his most satisfying thought focused on his most familiar weapon: the Roman military short sword. It caused terrible wounds at close quarters and spilled streams of blood, like those that had fountained out of Caligula, Nero's predecessor, and stained the columns under the main portico forever. Racked and hate-driven as he was that morning, he would have murdered everyone in Rome, and if some bloodthirsty gods offered to exterminate all mankind except him and Ligia, he would have agreed to that too.

By the time his litter reached the palace portals, he had managed to bring himself under full control. The great arch and its praetorian guard reminded him that he would be stopped right here if Caesar had Ligia somewhere in the building. But the guard commander just nodded at him with a friendly smile.

"Greetings, tribune," he said as he came a few steps closer. "If you're here to see Caesar, you came at the wrong time, I'm sorry to say."

"Why's that?"

"Because his child, the divine Augusta, fell sick yesterday. It came on her just like that. Nobody knows why. Caesar and Poppea are with her, along with every healer in the city."

This was important news. It could shake the empire. Nero had gone practically mad with joy when Poppea gave birth to his little daughter and had put on a celebration normally reserved for the major gods. Even before the birth, the senate formally dedicated Poppea's womb to all the divinities of Rome and ordered votive offerings to be made in all the temples. The greatest games of all times were held in Antium, where the child was born, and a new temple was raised to the twin Fortunas, the two goddesses of prosperity and luck. The baby's health could affect all of the Roman world, but

Vinicius was so absorbed in his own affairs and so totally focused on himself, his lost love and his need for vengeance, that he paid practically no attention to what the centurion told him.

"I just want to see Acte, that's all," he said as he passed inside.

Acte, however, was also busy with the baby and he had to wait. She didn't appear until near noon, her face pale with exhaustion, but at the sight of him she lost whatever color she still had.

"Acte!" he shouted, catching her by both hands and pulling her deep into the atrium. "Where's Ligia?"

"That's what I wanted to ask you about," she said, staring at him with accusing eyes.

He had sworn to himself that he would question her reasonably and calmly, keeping his wild rage under strict control. But pain and anger twisted in his face, and he clutched his head with both hands.

"I don't have her," he grated out. "She was abducted on the way." He forced himself back under some control. "Acte," he said between clenched teeth, his face mere inches from the woman's, "if you like living . . . if you want to avert a tragedy you can't even imagine, tell me the truth. Did Caesar take her?"

"He didn't leave the palace all day yesterday."

"Swear by your mother's spirit! Swear by all the gods! Is she in the palace?"

"By my mother's spirit, Marcus, she's not in the palace, and it wasn't Caesar who carried her off. His little princess got sick yesterday, and he hasn't stepped a foot away from her cradle. Neither has Poppea."

That made sense, even to Vinicius. Nero did everything to excess, every whim and fancy could turn into a passion, and his love for his child went beyond all reason. Unbalanced to begin with, he was totally out of his mind about her, which is what gave Poppea such a hold on him and made her so powerful. Relieved, Vinicius could breathe again. The worst that he had imagined no longer threatened him.

"In that case Aulus has her." He clenched his fists and sat down beside Acte. "So now he can expect the worst."

"Aulus Plautius was here this morning," Acte said, shaking her head. "He couldn't talk to me because I was busy with the child, but he questioned others about Ligia. They couldn't tell him anything, so he left word that he'd come back to see me."

"He just wanted to divert suspicion," Vinicius snapped coldly. "If he doesn't know what happened to Ligia, he'd have come about her to my house."

"He did," Acte said. "I'll show you his message. He thought that since you and Petronius were behind Ligia's transfer to the palace, he'd find her in your house, and that's where he went first thing this morning. Your people told him what happened last night, and so he came here."

She stepped into her bedroom and brought a wax tablet on which Aulus had scrawled his hasty message. Vinicius read it quickly. All his suppositions vanished, along with every plan, threat, hope and idea. He didn't know what to say or think. But Acte seemed to read the dark, bitter thoughts that flitted through his mind.

"No Marcus," she said, shaking her head again. "What happened is what Ligia wanted."

"You knew she wanted to escape!" Vinicius shouted, his rage breaking free.

"I knew she didn't want to be your toy." Acte's grave, misty eyes fixed firmly on his own.

"And what were you all your life?" he yelled.

"I had no choice." She shrugged. "I was a slave before."

But Vinicius wasn't ready to reason. What did he care what Ligia had been before Caesar gave her to him like any other object? "She was a gift," he shouted. "That's all!" She belonged to him! He would dig her out of wherever she was hiding and do with her anything he wanted. She would be his toy, his plaything and his pillow if that's what he decided. He would have her whipped anytime he wanted. When he got tired of her, he would turn her over to the lowest of his slaves or have her grind corn on his African estate. "I'll never stop looking for her," he threatened. "And I'll crush her into the ground when I find her!"

He let his pain rip through him and sweep him so far away from reason that even Acte knew he would never do half of what he threatened. Anger and suffering were doing the talking here. She could find compassion for the suffering, but his bitter ranting exhausted her patience.

"Why did you come to see me?" she asked at last.

"I don't know."

And he didn't know. He came because he couldn't think of anywhere else to go. He thought she would tell him something he could use. Actually he had come to talk to Caesar, not to her, and he dropped by her quarters only because Caesar was unable to see him. Running away, Ligia challenged the will of the emperor, so now he would convince Caesar to order a pursuit and comb the city and all its territories for her, even if it took a house-to-house search throughout the empire by every legion.

"Petronius will back me." He nodded, still enraged but calmer. "We'll start the search today."

"Be careful you don't lose her altogether once Caesar's men find her," Acte warned.

Vinicius frowned. "What do you mean by that?"

"Listen to me, Marcus!" Acte became anxious. "Ligia and I went walking in the gardens yesterday. We met Poppea, the little highness and the black wet nurse Lilith. Later that afternoon the child became ill, and Lilith swears it's a spell, some kind of curse thrown by the foreign girl they had met. Nobody will think twice about it if the child gets well. But if she doesn't and if the worst takes place, Poppea will be the first to charge Ligia with witchcraft, and there'll be no help for her wherever they find her."

They sat in deep, thick silence that lengthened with worry.

"But what if she did throw some kind of spell?" Vinicius asked at last. "She threw one on me."

"Lilith tells everyone that the child started crying the moment it passed us—which is true, she did. She was probably already ill when they took her out to the gardens. Search for Ligia anywhere you want, Marcus, but do it on your own. Don't mention her to Caesar, at least until his daughter is well again, or you'll bring Poppea's anger down on her. You've hurt her enough. May all the gods protect her."

Vinicius nodded. His voice was low and gloomy. "You love her, don't you, Acte?"

"I learned to love her." Tears glistened in the woman's eyes.

"Because she didn't pay you back with hatred, as she did me," he said bitterly.

Acte hesitated. She watched him carefully for a moment, as if to judge how he meant this and how much he meant it. "You blind, headstrong man," she said at last. "Ligia loves you."

‹16›

TOUCHED BY HER REVELATION as if it were fire, Vinicius leaped up like a man possessed.

"That's a lie! She hates me!"

Words thick with doubt and anger poured out of him like a bitter torrent through a broken dam. How could Acte know that Ligia loved him?

Angry and wanting to hurt her, he sneered, "Don't tell me Ligia turned you into a confidante after just one day and spilled all her secrets!"

And what sort of love is it that runs from the lover, turns its back on a joyous welcome in a festive house, and picks homeless wandering, the shame of poverty, the grim uncertainties of day-to-day survival and maybe even death in some rotting gutter?

"Don't tell me things like that," he shouted, "or I'll go raving mad!"

Oh, he went on. He wouldn't give up the girl for anything, not for all the treasures piled in this palace. And yet she ran away! What kind of love panics before its own fulfillment and breeds only pain? How could anyone make sense out of that? Who could understand it? Only the thought that he might find her somewhere stopped him from killing himself with his own sword.

"Love is something you give, not take away!" he shouted. There were times in the Plautius house, he muttered, that he thought he was getting close to her and that his joy lay almost in his grasp. "But now I know she hates me, always hated me and always will."

But Acte—timid and self-effacing for so many years—suddenly had enough: "And how did you try to get her?" she burst out. "Did you ask Aulus and Pomponia for her, like any straightforward decent man? And what were you after?"

Acte didn't want to hear any more about his love. He took the girl from home by trickery, by devious conniving. He wanted a harlot in his house, not a wife and lover. And did he think that would be enough for a king's daughter who had been brought up in a decent home?

"You had her brought to this evil and inhuman place. You made her take part in a drunken orgy. You treated her like a common slut. And did it ever occur to you what kind of effect this would have on a girl like that, one who'd been brought up by people like Aulus and Pomponia?

"Oh, that's too much!" she cried out. Was he blind? Stupid? Didn't he have brains enough to guess that women like Ligia and Pomponia were worlds apart from the likes of Nigidia, Calvia Crispinilla, Poppea and all the others he met in Caesar's house? Couldn't he see at first glance that Ligia was a clean, good, self-respecting girl who would rather die than live the kind of life he promised and offered?

"How do you know what gods she worships?" she demanded. Maybe they, too, were different from the sensual Venus and dissolute Isis worshiped in Rome by thrill-seeking, pleasure-loving high society women.

"No." Acte shook her head. "Ligia didn't share her secrets with me. But she said she expected only you to help her. She thought—no, she believed!—that you'd take her side, beg Caesar to let her go, and have her sent back to Aulus and Pomponia. She trusted you. You were her only hope. Oh, I could tell she loved you. You can be sure of that."

And what did he do? How did he respond to the clean young love from one who trusted him so much and was so ready for him? He fed her fear, resentment and disgust. He shocked and repelled her. So let him comb the country for her now, with Caesar's soldiers hunting her like game, but he ought to know that if Poppea's child should die, she will be blamed for it and there will be no way to save her even when he found her.

Through his pain and anger Vinicius blinked tears. The news that Ligia loved him or had loved him shook him to the core. He saw her as she was in Aulus' garden, listening to him with a bright flush mounting on her face and eyes filled with light. Yes, it was possible. Acte could be right. Ligia could have really loved him then or started to love him. The joy he felt at this thought was a hundred times more powerful than all the ruthless pleasures of his anticipation. I could have had her and her love of her own free will, he thought. She could have hung the red threads of marriage on his doors, rubbed wolf tallow into the lintels to invoke the blessings of the city's founders,

Romulus and Remus, and sat as his wife on the ceremonial sheepskin by his hearth. He could have heard her speak that old, sacramental phrase, "Where you go, Caius, there go I, Caia," and they would be together the rest of their lives.

So why didn't I take that route? he thought. He had been ready to do it, had almost talked himself into it, and now she was gone. He might never find her. Or if he tracked her down somewhere, it might be only to expose her to Poppea's frightful retribution. And even if the child got well and Ligia was in no danger from Poppea, then she, Aulus and Pomponia would have no further use for him.

Anger clutched him again, but this time the sick, gnawing fury was aimed at Petronius. He was to blame for everything that had happened. He had forged the first link in the mad, vicious chain of misunderstandings and disasters. If it weren't for his machinations, Ligia wouldn't need to run or hide from anyone; she'd be engaged to him, they would be planning marriage, and there'd be no dangers hanging over her head.

But now, he thought, it's too late. What happened, happened. There was no way to call back the time, cancel the mistakes or mend what couldn't be repaired.

"Too late!" he said.

He was numb with pity and regret. He stared, bewildered, while the earth seemed to tremble and split at his feet and some bleak crevice yawned darkly before him. He didn't know what to do, how he should begin or even where to go. Acte echoed his "too late," and hearing this phrase from somebody else was like a death sentence. Only one thing was clear to him: He had to find Ligia. If he didn't, then something dreadful would happen inside him.

He didn't even realize it when he was wrapping himself in his toga, and then he turned to go. He didn't think to say good-bye to Acte; all his movements were mechanical and mindless. But suddenly the curtains parted in the atrium doorway, opening the way to the vestibule beyond, and Pomponia Graecina came into the room. She, too, must have heard about Ligia's disappearance and came to Acte for news, probably thinking it would be easier for her than for Aulus to win Acte's sympathy and compassion. Noticing Vinicius, she turned her small, pale face toward him and looked at him for a long, silent moment.

"May God forgive you, Marcus, for all the harm you've done to us and to Ligia," she said quietly.

Guilt and tragedy held him as still as death. He felt rooted to the marble tiles. His head hung low, and his eyes were fixed blindly on the floor. He couldn't think of any god who would or could forgive him. And how could Pomponia plead for his forgiveness rather than cry for vengeance?

He left, confused and understanding nothing, full of oppressive thoughts and a vast anxiety, bemused, dumbfounded and bewildered.

A thick, worried crowd was already milling in the courtyard and under the colonnaded galleries. Senators and patricians pushed in among the household slaves and other palace servants, asking for news about "the divine Augusta" and making sure they were seen and heard voicing their concern. Even such unimportant witnesses as Caesar's slaves were good enough for their demonstration. The news must have spread quickly through the city, because fresh figures came hurrying through the gate while huge crowds formed beyond the open arch. Since Vinicius was leaving while they crowded in, some of the new arrivals pestered him for news about "the infant goddess," but he pushed on, saying nothing, until he almost literally walked into Petronius.

Feeling the way he did about the man, he would have blown up at his sight on any other day. He would have hurled himself into mindless violence, oblivious of the consequences right here in Caesar's compound, which would have sent him at once to prison and execution. But he was so crushed by what he had heard in Acte's apartment, so drained and listless and so utterly exhausted and depressed, that even his normal hotheaded recklessness was too slow to boil over. He pushed past Petronius and tried to go on, but Petronius caught him and held him back.

"And how's our little goddess?" he asked carelessly.

The brute strength of Petronius' grasp woke all the pent-up furies that clawed at Vinicius. He let his rage spill over. "Let Hell devour her and everything in this place," he snarled through clenched teeth.

"Quiet, you wretched fool!" Petronius glanced quickly around to see who might have heard; the easiest way in Rome to gain Caesar's favor was to turn informer. Then he threw his arm around the young man's shoulders and hurried him out into the street.

"Come with me if you want to know something about Ligia," he urged. "No, I won't talk here. I'll tell you all about it in my litter."

Getting Vinicius out of the palace courtyard was all he wanted to achieve just then, because he had nothing new to tell him about Ligia. He was, however, a quick-thinking man, one who knew how to get things done, and he felt a fair amount of sympathy for Vinicius. The young man had disgusted him the night before. He had been revolted by his crude impatience, his lack of poise and his tasteless violence, but he felt somewhat responsible for everything that had happened and already tried to do something about it.

"I have two of my slaves watching each city gate," he said as soon as they had settled in his litter. "They have the girl's description. They're also watching for that giant who carried her out of Caesar's banquet. There's no doubt in my mind that he's the one who got her away last night. Listen to me! If Aulus wants to hide her in one of his country homes, we'll know which way to follow. And if my people don't catch sight of her at any gate, that'll mean she's still in the city, and we'll launch a citywide search today."

"Aulus and Pomponia don't know where she is," Vinicius said. "They have nothing to do with her disappearance."

"Are you sure?"

"I saw Pomponia. They're searching for her just as we are."

Petronius grew thoughtful. "She couldn't leave the city before sunrise because all gates are locked at night. Two of my people have been watching each portal since midnight. If they catch sight of Ligia and the giant, one of them is to follow them and the other is to come running to us with the news. We'll find her if she's in the city, don't worry about that, because that huge Lygian stands out in any crowd. Someone will have seen him. You're lucky it wasn't Caesar who carried her off, but I can guarantee he didn't. Nothing happens in the Palatine that I don't know about."

But now Vinicius let his feelings break out into the open, more with regret than anger. His voice cracked and faltered. He poured out everything he had heard from Acte. The new danger that hung over Ligia was so deadly that it made everything else trivial in comparison, and the two fugitives would have to be well hidden from Poppea after they were found.

Then he turned bitterly on Petronius. "If it weren't for your advice," he accused, "everything would have gone another way. Ligia would be safe at home with Aulus and Pomponia. I'd be able to see her every day, and I'd be happier than any Caesar who ever lived."

Grief swept over him as he let the words spill out of him, anger and bitterness gave way to sorrow, and tears of frustration glinted in his eyes.

Petronius was surprised. He never imagined that the young tribune could fall in love so totally or that he was capable of such depth of passion. The goddess of love must be the most powerful deity of the lot, he thought, watching those desperate tears.

"Great queen of Cyprus," he addressed himself silently to Aphrodite, the Greek form of Venus, who was born of sea foam off the coast of Paphos in the west of Cyprus, "you alone rule among gods and men."

« 17 »

NONE OF THE SLAVES posted at the gates had come back to Petronius' house by the time he and Vinicius got there, and the atrium supervisor, the *atriensis,* reported that he had sent food to these roving pickets, along with fresh orders to watch everyone who tried to leave the city.

"As you see," Petronius said, "your fugitives are undoubtedly still in town. We're certain to find them. But tell your own people to watch the gates as well, especially those who were sent last night for Ligia. They might be able to recognize her more quickly."

"I've had them shipped to the hard labor camps," said Vinicius. "But I'll rescind the order. Let them go to the gates, as you say."

He scrawled a few words on a wax tablet and gave it to Petronius, who had it sent at once to Vinicius' home. Then both passed into an inner portico where they sat down on a marble bench and began to talk. The golden-haired Eunice and another girl called Iras placed bronze footstools under their feet, then brought a small serving table and a pair of drinking dishes. They poured wine from beautiful long-necked flagons imported from Volaterrae and Caecina.

"Do you have someone among your slaves who knows that giant Lygian?" Petronius asked.

"Atacinus and Gullo both saw him a few times," Vinicius said. "But Atacinus was killed last night at the litter, while I killed Gullo myself."

"Pity," Petronius said. "I liked Gullo. He looked after me when I was a boy, just as he did you."

"Yes, it's too bad. I even thought I might free him someday." Vinicius shrugged. "But let's talk about Ligia. Rome is like a sea—"

"Which is exactly where one dives for pearls. I'm sure we won't track her down today or even tomorrow, but we'll find her eventually, there's no doubt about it. You're blaming me now for the idea of having her picked up for you by Caesar, but the idea wasn't bad in itself. It turned bad when everything turned out badly. You heard Aulus say that he's thinking of moving to Sicily. That would have put a fair distance between you and the girl anyway."

"I'd follow them," Vinicius said. "That's simple. And she would be safe. As things stand, if the baby dies, Poppea will not just convince herself that it's Ligia's fault, she'll convince Caesar."

"Yes, that's a worry," Petronius agreed. "Still, it's not ordained anywhere that this imperial dolly has to die. Maybe she'll get well. And even if the worst should happen, we'll find a way out."

Petronius grew thoughtful. "They say Poppea believes in ghosts," he said after a while. "She's said to be a follower of Jehovah and interested in the religion of the Jews, which is full of apparitions. Nero is also superstitious. If we spread the word that Ligia was carried off by some evil spirits, people will believe it, especially since it *is* something of a mystery. After all, if neither Caesar nor Aulus got her away from you, who did? That Lygian couldn't have done it alone. He had to have help. And where would a slave gather so many men in one day?"

"The slaves stick together throughout Rome," Vinicius said.

"Yes, and Rome will pay for it in blood someday. Oh, yes, they help one another, but not if it hurts one of their kind. And here it was clear in advance that your slaves would be held responsible and suffer the consequences. Slip a hint to your housemen about evil spirits, and they'll confirm it at once, because that'll shift the responsibility off their backs. Go on, try it on one of them. Ask if he didn't see devils swooping down and carrying Ligia off into thin air. I'll bet the godhead of Zeus himself that the fellow will start swearing on the spot that that's how it happened."

Vinicius was also superstitious, however. He was a soldier, ready to look for help from the supernatural, and he didn't take unknown forces lightly. Alarmed, he looked at Petronius with a sudden worry.

"If Ursus didn't have people to help him," he muttered, "and if he couldn't carry her off alone, then who did?"

But Petronius only started laughing. "There, you see? They'll all believe the story since you're almost ready to swallow it yourself. That's the way it is in this world where people jeer at gods but believe in spirits. Everyone will accept that version of events and stop looking for her. We in the meantime will hide her safely in some country villa of yours or mine."

"But who could have helped her?"

"Her coreligionists, I expect," Petronius said.

"Such as who? What god does she worship? You've no better idea than I about that, and who'd know more than I about Ligia?"

"Just about every woman in Rome worships a different god." Petronius shrugged, amused. "It's obvious that Pomponia raised the girl in her own faith, whatever it is. One thing I know about Pomponia is that no one ever saw her sacrificing anything in any of our temples. She was even accused at one time of being a Christian, but that's quite impossible. The civil court quashed that, as it should. The word about the Christians is that they not only worship the head of an ass but that they're the sworn enemies of mankind and indulge in all sorts of unspeakable practices in their rituals. Simple logic tells you that Pomponia cannot be a Christian since she is justly famous for her probity and virtue. Besides, no enemy of mankind could treat her slaves as she does."

"No one treats slaves anywhere the way they're treated in the Plautius home," Vinicius interrupted.

"Amazing, isn't it? But there you are. Pomponia mentioned something about some god who is supposed to be all-encompassing, all-powerful, merciful and unique. In other words the one and only god, the Logos, as the Greeks call it. I've no idea what she did with the rest of the pantheon, that's purely her business, but it's fair to suppose that this god of hers can't be all that powerful if he has only two worshipers, namely Ligia and Pomponia, along with Ursus. There must be more of them and they're the ones who came to help Ligia."

"That faith orders them to forgive their enemies," Vinicius remembered. "I met Pomponia Graecina as I was leaving Acte's, and she said, 'May God forgive you for the harm you did to us and Ligia.'"

"It seems as though their god is a good-hearted fellow. Ha! Let him forgive you, then. And signify his forgiveness by sending you the girl."

"I'd sacrifice a hundred bulls to him the very next morning. Ah"—Vinicius stirred, too restless to do nothing—"I don't want to eat, sleep or bathe here today. Lend me a dark cloak for disguise, and I'll go and wander the streets for a while."

He asked Petronius for a slave's *lacerna*, a kind of homespun hooded cloak that shrouded the whole body. It came originally from Gaul and was used mostly by poor travelers, the kind who did their wandering on foot, and no respectable Roman would wear one in public. To do so would place the wearer in the highest possible opprobrium.

"Maybe in this wretched guise I'll find her." His voice was dark and heavy with despair. "I'm diseased, I tell you!"

Petronius looked at him with a troubled fondness. It was quite true, the young man did look ill. There was a hot, feverish light in his eyes and dark rings around them. He had not shaved that morning, and a smear of stubble muddied his clean, sharply defined jawline. His hair was uncombed. Iras and Eunice also looked at him with pity and compassion, but he didn't even glance at them, as if they weren't there. That, of course, was normal. Neither he nor Petronius would be any more aware of the slave girls beside them than of the greyhounds that milled around behind them.

"Fever's gnawing at you," Petronius decided.

"Yes, it is."

"So listen. I don't know what some nostrum vendor would prescribe for your sensitive condition, but I'll tell you what I'd do in your place: I'd find something here to fill a pressing need—bridge the gap, so to speak—until I got back the one I really wanted. She'd supply what the other couldn't, not being here to do so. I caught sight of some beautiful bodies in your house. . . . No, don't shake your head, don't deny it. I know what you're thinking. I know what love is and that there's never a real substitute for what you truly want. But a beautiful young slave can at least amuse you."

"I don't want amusement."

But Petronius was no longer listening. He had a genuine weakness for Vinicius and set his mind to finding the best cure for the distressed young man and the best possible means toward it.

"Your slave girls might have lost their novelty. It happens. But take a look at these." He nodded at Iras and Eunice.

Petronius peered carefully at both girls, as if he had never really looked at them before either, and he put his hand on the hip of the golden-haired Eunice.

"This one, for example," Petronius went on. "She's Greek. A few days ago Fonteius the Younger offered me three angelic page boys from Clazomene in exchange for her, but I was not surprised. Scopas himself, great as he was among Hellenic artists, wouldn't have been able to sculpt a more perfect body. I can't understand why, or rather how, I have remained unmoved by her as long as I have. It surely didn't have anything to do with any feelings for Chrysothemis! So, anyway, I'm giving her to you. Keep her for yourself."

Golden-haired Eunice turned as pale as canvas. Her eyes were wide with terror as she stared at Vinicius, waiting for his answer. But he merely jumped to his feet and started rubbing his temples with both hands.

"No! No!" He broke out in a quick, stumbling voice like a sick, feverish man who doesn't want to talk about anything except his disease. "I've no use for her. No use for any of them. Thanks but no thanks. If you'd just get me that *lacerna*, I'll go look for Ligia. She might be in the slums across the Tiber if she's with that slave. Gods grant that I at least catch sight of that Ursus."

He left the room practically at a run. Petronius didn't try to stop him. What would be the use? The young man couldn't sit still for a moment. His rejection of Petronius' gift could be ascribed to a temporary lapse, a passing lack of interest in any woman other than his Ligia, but Petronius didn't want his lordly gesture to go to waste; after all, true munificence was a rare quality and he wasn't moved to such generosity too often.

"Bathe yourself, Eunice," he said to the slave girl. "Then oil your body, pay attention to how you dress yourself, and go to the house of Vinicius."

Her reaction took his breath away. She fell to her knees, stretched her arms toward him and pleaded not to be sent away. She wouldn't go to Vinicius' house, she cried out. She'd rather carry firewood and tend the stove in this house than be the center of any other household. She didn't want to go, she begged him. She just couldn't! Let him have her whipped every day if he'd just let her stay!

She quivered like a leaf as she begged and pleaded. Urgency struggled in her against the fear of the consequences of her disobedience, and—to his amazement—it was the urgency that won. He heard her, but his ears simply refused to listen. The idea that a slave would beg to be relieved of some responsibility lay beyond his grasp. A slave girl who said "I won't" or "I can't" in Rome or anywhere in the Roman world was a contradiction. Nobody ever heard of such a thing. It just couldn't happen!

But the amazement passed at last, and his eyebrows narrowed in displeasure. He was too refined for cruelty. His slaves were given a great deal of leeway, especially in their own pleasures with one another, as long as they rendered exemplary service at all times, and carried out the will of their master with the same unquestioning obedience they showed to the will of the gods. If they failed in these two respects, however, he had no objection to whatever punishment was normal or whatever the customs of the times demanded. Moreover, he loved his peace of mind. He treasured his tranquility, his philosophic objectivity and his aloof detachment. He couldn't stand any kind of opposition and hated to have his equanimity disturbed.

"Call Tiresias," he told the kneeling girl. "And come back here with him."

Eunice rose, still trembling and in tears, and left the room. She was back swiftly with Tiresias, the Cretan who acted as the atrium overseer and who disciplined all the other slaves.

"Take Eunice and lash her," Petronius ordered him. "Twenty-five strokes will do. Just make sure you don't break her skin."

Then he passed into his library, took his place at a pink marble table and began to work on his *Trimalchio's Feast.*

But Ligia's escape and the illness of Poppea's child lay too heavily on his mind, and he didn't work long. That illness, in particular, was a serious problem. It occurred to him that he might become the scapegoat if Nero got it into his head that Ligia had cast a spell on his precious daughter. It was he, after all, who induced Nero to bring her to the palace, and this could be deadly.

He was, he knew, not without resources of his own. First, he thought, he had to convince Caesar that such thinking simply made no sense, and he had to do it the first time he saw him. Second, he counted on a certain fondness for him that he sensed in Poppea, perhaps even a certain weakness and a definite interest; oh, she was careful to keep it out of sight, but not so careful that he'd fail to spot it. Perhaps the time had come to exploit that dangerous opportunity.

After a while, however, he shrugged and decided he wouldn't waste any more time on worry. He would go to his dining room and have a light meal, and then have himself carried to the palace, to the Field of Mars, and then to Chrysothemis. But on his way to the table he caught sight of the slender, golden-haired Eunice in a group of slaves standing in one of the service corridors. He had forgotten to order any more than a whipping for her, and now he looked around impatiently for Tiresias, but he couldn't see him anywhere among the other slaves.

He turned directly to the girl. "Have you been whipped?"

She threw herself at his feet just as she had before and pressed her lips mutely to the hem of his toga. "Oh, yes, my lord." Her voice trembled with a puzzling gratitude and joy. "Oh, yes, indeed, my master!"

She apparently thought the whipping took the place of going to Vinicius, and that now she would be able to stay in the household. Petronius understood this very well. He was surprised by her resistance to his stated wishes, but he could guess the reason. Human nature held few secrets for him; such stubbornness, he knew, could come only from overpowering love or truly reckless passion.

"Do you have a lover in this house?" he asked.

She looked up at him then. Tears filled her eyes. Her voice was so low that he could barely hear her.

"Yes, my lord, there's someone . . ."

She seemed so beautiful with those glistening blue eyes, that back-flung mass of golden hair, and all that hope and fear blending in her face that Petronius found himself strangely and unexpectedly moved. He was, after all, a philosopher of the senses and an aesthete who worshiped every form of beauty. A touch of kindness, perhaps even fondness, brushed against him briefly.

"Which of them is it?" he asked, nodding toward the slaves.

But she didn't answer. She merely pressed her forehead to his sandaled feet and stayed as still and breathless as any household object.

Nor did he read an answer in the faces of any of the slaves. There were some handsome, strapping lads in that group, but none of them signaled anything to his experienced eyes. Instead he noted strange, enigmatic smiles, as if they were amused by some peculiar secret. He looked down at Eunice for a moment longer, then went on.

After his meal he had himself carried to the palace and then to Chrysothemis where he stayed until late at night. But when he returned home he summoned Tiresias.

"Did you whip Eunice?" he asked.

"Yes, my lord. Just as you ordered. Without damaging the skin."

"Did I order anything else in regard to her?"

"No, my lord." The atrium overseer looked up in alarm.

"Good. Which slave is her lover?"

"None of them. She doesn't have one, master."

"What do you know about her?"

"Well, my lord"—Tiresias didn't know what this was about and his voice trembled slightly—"there isn't much to tell. She never leaves her cubicle at night. She shares that with old Acrisiona and Ifida, and she keeps to herself when she isn't working. She never stays behind in the steam room after your bath, master. The other women laugh at her and call her Diana—"

"That's all I need to know," Petronius interrupted. "This morning I gave her to my nephew, the tribune Vinicius, but he wouldn't take her. So let her stay here. That'll be all for now."

"May I say something else about Eunice, my lord?" the *atriensis* offered.

"I told you to tell me everything you know."

"The whole household is talking about the escape of that girl who was supposed to live in the house of the noble Vinicius. After you left her, master, Eunice came to me and said she knows a man who would be able to find her."

"Ah!" Interested, Petronius sat up. "And what man is that?"

"I don't know him, lord. I just thought I'd better report it."

"Very well. Have that man wait for the tribune Vinicius here in my house tomorrow. And have the tribune invited here first thing in the morning."

The overseer bowed deeply and left. To his continuing surprise Petronius found himself thinking about Eunice. At first thought it seemed obvious to him that the slave girl wanted Ligia found so that she wouldn't have to take her place in Vinicius' household. Then it occurred to him that this man whom Eunice was foisting upon him might be her lover, and he was oddly irritated and disturbed. There was a simple way to find out about the fellow; all he had to do was call for Eunice and demand an answer. But it was late. Petronius felt unusually drained after his long visit with Chrysothemis and badly wanted sleep. On the way to his bedchamber, however, for no reason he cared to think about, he focused on Chrysothemis as he had seen her earlier. He recalled the wrinkles in the corners of her eyes that he noticed for the first time. Her beauty, he thought with wry regret, was far less real than its reputation. The three beautiful little slave boys from Clazomene whom Fonteius had offered for Eunice seemed suddenly a very poor trade.

‹18›

PETRONIUS WAS STILL DRESSING the next morning when Vinicius arrived. The desperate tribune already knew from Tiresias that none of the gate watchers had sent any news, but instead of being pleased about it as proof that Ligia was still in the city, he became even more depressed. He had begun to think that Ursus took her beyond the walls right after he seized her, which meant before Petronius' slaves had begun to watch the city gates. In the short autumn days the gates were closed early, but that was only to keep out those who wanted to enter after sundown. Anyone leaving could do so, and sometimes there were many. There were also other ways to slip across the walls, and all of them were quite familiar to slaves who wanted to break out of the city.

Vinicius had also taken some steps of his own. He sent slaves out into the countryside to watch all the roads leading from the city and to post rewards with the subprefects in the provinces, but it was unlikely that local authorities would hold anyone just on his demand. Any official action of that kind needed an endorsement from the city prefect, and there wasn't time to apply for one. He also spent the night in a fruitless search, disguised as a slave in a black *lacerna,* poking in all the out-of-the-way corners of the city without finding the slightest trace of Ligia or even a hint of where to look next. He did come across a few of Aulus Plautius' men, who were apparently on an errand similar to his own, but this only confirmed that Aulus had no part in her abduction and didn't know any more than he of her whereabouts. He hurried to Petronius' house as soon as Tiresias told him there was a man who knew how to find her, and he asked about him just as soon as they exchanged greetings in the dressing room.

"We'll see him in a moment," Petronius said. "It's some friend of Eunice. She'll be along in a minute to set the folds of my toga and tell us more about him."

"Is this the same Eunice you wanted to give me yesterday?"

"The same you refused. Actually, I'm quite grateful to you, because she's the best pleat-setter in the city."

The pleat-setter entered while he was still talking, shook out the toga that waited folded across an ivory chair, and stood ready to throw it around Petronius' shoulders. Her face was serene and alight with a quiet happiness. Her eyes shone with joy. She really is beautiful, Petronius thought with pleasure. She wrapped him in his toga and stooped to adjust the hang of the folds, and he noted the muted pale rose color of her arms and the translucent glow of mother-of-pearl or alabaster in her breasts and shoulders.

"Eunice," he asked, "is the man here, the one you mentioned last night to Tiresias?"

"He is here, my lord."

"And what's his name?"

"Chilon Chilonides, my lord."

"What do you know about him?"

"He's a master of the healing arts, my lord. Also a sage and sooth-sayer who can read people's fate and foretell the future."

"Has he foretold your future?"

A bright crimson flushed Eunice, even her neck and ears. "Yes, my lord."

"And what did he see in your life?"

"He said I would experience both pain and happiness."

"Well." Petronius smiled. "Tiresias inflicted pain on you yesterday, so now all you have coming is the happiness."

"That has already come to pass, my lord," Eunice murmured.

"And how's that?"

Her whisper was so low that he hardly heard her. "I stayed with you, my lord."

"You've arranged these folds very well." Petronius looked down at his toga and laid a light hand on her golden hair. "I'm pleased with you, Eunice."

The touch of his hand seemed to bring a warm mist into her eyes and quickened her breathing. But Petronius and Vinicius were already on their way to the atrium where Chilon Chilonides bowed low when they appeared. Petronius grinned, remembering last night's annoying supposition that this man could be Eunice's lover.

That was quite out of the question. This man, he thought at once, couldn't be anybody's lover. He had never seen anyone who was so much a caricature of what he represented, repelling and ridiculous at the same time, and so grotesque in his ugliness as to be a joke. He wasn't old but seemed practically antique; he creaked and he rustled as he bowed and scraped. There was barely a touch of white showing in his thick, tousled hair and unkempt, tangled beard, but he seemed older than time itself. His belly was caved in and hollow, and his narrow shoulders hunched forward in a permanent crafty stoop, as if he were deformed, so that at first sight he looked like a hunchback. Over this unnatural protrusion wobbled a huge head with curiously piercing eyes set in a sly fox face, but his sharp, restless features also showed the puckered, gleeful mischief of a monkey. Scarlet boils erupted all over this unprepossessing clown mask and pocked the dry yellow skin wherever it showed, and his nose glowed in its own crimson affirmation of his love for the bottle. He wore a ragged goat's wool tunic and a dark cloak of the same material, full of rips and gashes as proof either of his utter poverty or its imitation. The first name that occurred to Petronius when he caught sight of his grotesque caller was that of Homer's Thercites whom Ulysses thrashed at the siege of Troy, so that's how he addressed him.

"Greetings, divine Thercites," he intoned. "How are those lumps that Ulysses pounded into your back? And how's he doing in the underworld?"

"Noble lord," Chilon Chilonides replied in kind. "Ulysses, the wisest among the dead, sends you his greetings as the wisest of the living, along with a request that you throw a new cloak over my poor injured back."

"By Hecate in all her three manifestations!" Petronius cried, amused. "That answer is worth a cloak."

But Vinicius had no patience with this pointless wordplay. "Do you understand what you're undertaking?" he asked, turning on the Greek.

"It's not hard to guess the subject or the object," Chilon shrugged, "when the two households of the noblest families in Rome talk about nothing else, and half of the city repeats it after them. Night before last, noble tribune, someone abducted a young girl whom your slaves were escorting to your house from Caesar's palace on the Palatine. Her name is Ligia, or more precisely, Callina, and she was raised in the home of Aulus Plautius. I will undertake to find her for you in the city, distinguished tribune, if she is still here, or to point out exactly where she went and where she is hiding, in the unlikely event that she has already gotten across the walls."

"Very well." Vinicius liked the sharp, decisive answer. "What means will you use?"

"The means are yours, my lord." Chilon shot him a sly, calculating smile and tapped his forehead with a yellow finger. "All I have is logic."

Petronius also smiled. He took a liking to his unexpected visitor. An odd fish, certainly, but as crafty as a viper. Something about his sharp, sly wit and penetrating eyes amused and intrigued him. This man really will be able to find that girl, he thought.

But Vinicius scowled in sudden warning. "If you're thinking of cheating me for profit, you moth-eaten beggar, I'll have you flogged to death," he snarled.

"I'm a philosopher, my lord," the man answered calmly. "A philosopher should shun material profit, especially the kind your munificence suggests."

"Ah, so you're a philosopher!" Petronius threw in, interested and curious. "Eunice said you were a healer and a fortune-teller. How do you know Eunice?"

"She has heard about me because I'm widely known. She wanted advice."

"On what?"

"Love, my lord. She wanted a cure for unrequited passion."

"And did you cure her?"

"Better than that, my lord. I gave her an amulet that guarantees she'll be loved in return. In Paphos on Cyprus there is a temple where they venerate the sash of Aphrodite, or the Girdle of Venus as it's known in Rome. I gave her two threads from that sash locked in an almond shell."

"And you drove a good bargain for it, I imagine."

"No price is too high for returned affections. As you see, my lord, I'm short two fingers on my hand, and I can't write without a scribe. I'm saving to buy myself a writer who can take down my thoughts and pass on my teaching to the world at large."

"To what school of philosophy do you belong, divine sage?" Petronius asked, ever more delighted.

"There are holes in my cloak, my lord, therefore I'm a Cynic. I'm Stoical in adversity, as you see by my quiet acceptance of my poverty. Also, since I don't own a litter and go everywhere on foot, I'm clearly a wandering witness to the truth, a Peripatetic, spreading my teaching as I go from one wineshop to another and bringing wisdom for a jug of wine. That's also a good bargain."

"To which your nose is yet another witness. And it's that wine jug that gives you your discourse?"

"Heraclites says that all that lives is fluid. You won't deny, my lord, that wine is a fluid and that rhetoric often flows?"

"He also says that fire is a god, whom I see flaming in full glory on your nose."

"Be that as it may, my lord, the divinely inspired Diogenes of Apollonia held that air was the true substance of all things. The warmer the air, the higher the order of beings it produces, so naturally hot air is the province of profundities and academic wisdom. It follows that since autumn chills the air, a true sage must warm his soul with a little wine. Nor will you deny, my lord, that even a cheap jug, such as that watery stuff they make in Capua, warms the coldest bones."

"Tell me, Chilon Chilonides"—Petronius was only partly mocking—"what country do you come from?"

"Messambria, my lord, in the old Mithradic kingdom, between Bithynia and Armenia, in the region of the Pontus Exinus, which some call the Black Sea."

"You are a great man, Chilon," Petronius decided.

"But an unrecognized one," the sage added sadly.

Vinicius, however, lost patience again. Rekindled hope burned hotly in his mind; he was a man of action and wanted Chilon to start searching straightaway. The entire conversation was just wasting time as far as he was concerned, and he became rather irritated with Petronius.

"When will you start the search?" he asked, turning to the Greek.

"I've already started. Even being here and answering your courteous questions is part of the search. Trust me, noble tribune. I'd be able to find a shoestring if you lost one, or point to the man who picked it up in the street."

"Have you been used for this kind of work before?" Petronius asked.

"Ah!" The Greek lifted his eyes as if appealing to the gods for simple confirmation. "Virtue and wisdom don't draw good wages in these times of ours. Even a philosopher must find a way to keep himself alive."

"And what is your way?"

"To see everything, my lord, and share what I know with those who wish to know it."

"And who pay for it?"

"What can I do, my lord? I have to buy myself a slave for a writer, and that takes money. Otherwise I'll take all my knowledge to my grave."

"Since you didn't save enough for a decent cloak," Petronius suggested, "perhaps your merits weren't worth rewarding."

"Modesty forbids their enumeration." The sly, sharp-eyed Greek looked anything but modest. "And just think, my lord, where are all those great benefactors of the past who'd shower a man with gold for his services as if they were gulping down a Puzzeoli oyster? Gone, sir, that's where they are. Little minds and little men replace them. It's not that my merits are so meager, sir, but that human gratitude has become tightfisted. Look at the record, sir. Who can track down and unearth a high-priced runaway slave better than I? When insults to our divine Poppea appear on the walls, who points out the criminals? Who sniffs out the couplets in the bookstores that aim a barb at Caesar? Who'll always report what senators and nobles talk about at home? Who delivers letters that are too important to entrust to slaves, and who listens for news outside barbershops? Who hears all the talk in the wineshops and on the bakery lines? Who is trusted by slaves and sees right through any household, from the atrium to the gardens, at a single glance? Who knows every street, alley, blind tiger and hideout in the city, and can sing *verbatim* chapter and verse of everything said in the public baths, in the amphitheater, at the markets, in the sword schools, in the slave dealers' sheds and even in the gladiators' compounds—"

"Enough, by all the gods!" Petronius cried out, laughing. "Enough, my dear sage! Or you'll swamp us with your merits, your virtues, your eloquence and your wisdom. Really, that's quite enough. We wanted to know whom we were dealing with, that's all, and now we know it."

Vinicius was also satisfied. Point a man like that toward his quarry, he thought, and he'll never stop. He'll run it down better than a bloodhound.

"Very well," he said. "What more do you need?"

"Weapons, my lord," the Greek said.

"What kind of weapons?" Vinicius was surprised, but the Greek spread out a dry palm before him and made counting motions in it with his other hand.

"Such are the times we live in," he said, sighing with regret and dipping his head humbly.

"So," Petronius said with a smile, "you'll play the role of the jackass that captures a fortress with a load of gold."

"I'm only a poor philosopher, my lords." Chilon dipped his head even lower, and his empty fingers fluttered in the air. "You're the men with the money."

Vinicius threw him a purse that the Greek caught in midair even though he did have two fingers missing on his right hand.

"I already know more than you expect, sir," he peered at Vinicius. "I didn't come here empty-handed. I know that Aulus Plautius didn't take the girl; I've already talked to his slaves about it. I know she's not at the Palatine where everyone is busy with little Augusta. And I've a good idea why you'd rather search for her alone, without help from Caesar's soldiers or the prefect's posse. I know that she was helped in her escape by a servant who came from the same country. He wouldn't have received any aid from the city slaves, because they all stick together and wouldn't work with him against your people. He could have gotten help only from the followers of his own religion."

"You hear this, Vinicius?" Petronius broke in. "Didn't I say the same thing, word for word?"

"I'm honored, sir." Chilon bowed to Petronius and turned again to Vinicius. "The girl, my lord," he rattled on, "is sure to worship the same god as the most devout of the Roman women, that true example of a virtuous matron, the lady Pomponia. I've heard she was suspected of making sacrifices to some foreign idol, but none of her slaves would tell me who he is or what his followers call themselves. If I knew that, I'd join them, become the most devout among them, gain their trust and learn all their secrets. I know that you, distinguished tribune, spent a few days in the house of the noble Aulus. Can you tell me anything about that religion?"

"I can't," Vinicius said.

"You asked me a lot of questions, noble lords, now let me ask a few. Did you happen to see anything unusual there, noble tribune? Like maybe strange statuettes and offerings, or odd amulets or badges worn by Pomponia or your divine Ligia? Did you happen to see any secret signs they might have scribbled between the two of them?"

"Signs?" Vinicius looked up. "Wait a minute! Yes, I once saw Ligia drawing a fish in the sand."

"A fish? Aha! Oho! Did she do it just that one time or a lot?"

"Just that once."

"Aha! And it was a fish, my lord? You're sure about that?"

"I am!" Intrigued and alert, Vinicius was becoming impatient and excited. "It was a fish. Are you getting an idea of what that's about?"

"Hah! Am I getting an idea!" Chilon cried. He displayed his crooked teeth in a yellow smile and bowed to leave. "May Fortune shower you both with every sign of favor, most distinguished lords."

"Tell my people to give you a new cloak!" Petronius called after him.

"Ulysses thanks you on behalf of Thercites," said the Greek. He bowed again and left.

"Well?" Petronius shot an amused glance at the younger man. "What do you think of our philosopher?"

"He'll find Ligia!" Vinicius cried out, happy and excited. "That's what I think of him! But I'll also say that if the scum of the world had their own country, he'd be the king."

"No question about that. I'll have to get to know this Stoic a bit better. But in the meantime I'll have the atrium aired out after him."

Meanwhile outside, Chilon Chilonides wrapped his new cloak around him and cackled at his remarkable good fortune. The purse rang with a sweet melodious sound, musical yet substantial, when he tossed it lightly up and down under the folds of the mantle. It had a comforting weight in his hand. It felt solid. He walked at a slow, measured pace, shooting quick backward glances now and then to see if anyone was looking out at him from Petronius' villa. He passed the shrine commemorating Livia, turned the corner of the Civus Virbius, and headed into the slums of the Suburra.

"I'll have to pay a little call at Sporus' tavern," he mused to himself, "and spill a few drops of wine in honor of Fortune. She's finally given me what I've been seeking for so long. Hmm! He's young, impulsive, as rich and generous as the mines of Cyprus, and he's ready to give half his wealth for that Lygian snippet. Yes. He's made to order, but he'll need special handling, I can tell. That glowering frown of his comes just too fast to be taken lightly. He'd leap before he thinks. Ah, young wolves rule the world these days, and more's the pity! I'd worry less about that Petronius. . . . But, dear gods, what can one expect from a civilization where pimping pays better than decency and goodness?"

His protest made, the Greek turned to deeper contemplation. Ha! So she scrawled a fish in the sand, did she? Choking on a piece of goat cheese would be easier than solving that riddle at the moment. But he would solve it soon enough. He would know what it meant. And since fish lived out of sight, breeding under water, searching among them was harder than on dry land. It followed, then, that Vinicius would pay extra for that fish dinner before he was done.

"One more purse like this one," he said, sighing with satisfaction, "and I'll get rid of this beggar's outfit and buy myself a slave. Ah, dear Chilon, but what if I advised buying a slave girl rather than a man? I know you, you rascal. I know you'd agree. You'd get your youth back with her if she was as beautiful as that Eunice, and she'd also be a good source of steady income. Ah, poor Eunice. I sold two threads from my old cloak to that silly twit, but it's not the beauties of her mind I admire the most. I'd take her if Petronius offered her for nothing. Yes, yes, my poor, dear Chilon, son of Chilon. You've lost your parents. You're a wandering orphan. Buy yourself a slave girl to sweeten life a little. Of course she'd have to live somewhere, so Vinicius must rent something for her, and you, too, would have a quiet corner for your head at night. She has to wear something and she has to eat, so Vinicius would pay for the food and clothing."

This brought him back to the reality around him, and he complained bitterly to the gods. "What a hard life this is! How much it takes out of a man these days to make an honest living. What happened to the times when one copper penny bought a double fistful of beans cooked with fatback or a length of blood sausage the size of a twelve-year-old's arm? Ah"—and he turned into a low, dark doorway—"here's the place where that thief Scopus peddles his cheap rotgut. A wineshop is the best place to find out anything."

He went in, ordered a jug of Negrito, as the better grades of dark red wine were known in the taverns, and watched distrust glint in the innkeeper's round, suspicious eyes. He eased a gold coin from his purse and let it clink softly on the tabletop.

"I spent the whole morning working with my friend Seneca," he announced, "and he gave me a little something for the road."

Sporus' eyes grew even rounder at the sight of gold and the wine appeared before Chilon as magically as ordered. But he didn't drink it. He dipped a finger in it and scrawled a fish on the table surface.

"What's that mean to you?" he asked.

"It's a fish," said Sporus.

"Yes, but what else could it be?"

"What's it supposed to be? A fish is a fish! What else is there for it to be?"

"You're a fool, Sporus." Chilon wagged his huge, scabrous head in ponderous contempt. "It's true you water your wine so much I could probably pull a fish out of it, but this is something else. It's a secret sign, a philosopher's symbol for the smile of Fortune. Maybe you'd also get rich if you could guess its riddle. Honor philosophy and respect philosophers, I tell you, or I'll take my business to another pothouse, which my friend Petronius has advised for some time."

⟨19⟩

No one saw Chilon anywhere in the next few days. Ever since Acte said that Ligia loved him, or that she had loved him, Vinicius wanted to win her back again a hundred times more fervently than before, and he launched a search of his own, unable to wait for Chilon's machinations. He neither could nor wanted to get help from Caesar, who seemed numb with terror anyway as he watched over his dying daughter.

Nothing helped the infant. Neither the temple sacrifices nor the votive offerings had any effect, nor was there much hope from the practitioners of the healing arts; and even sorcery, tried as a last resort, failed in the end. The infant died after a week's illness. Rome sank into mourning, along with the court. Caesar, who seemed to go mad with joy when the child was born, gave every sign of losing his mind with grief now that she was dead. He locked himself in his rooms for two days, refusing to eat. Senators, patricians and distinguished nobles crowded into the palace to offer their condolences and show their compassion, but he wouldn't see them. The senate met in a special session to deify the dead little princess, vote funds for a temple for this new divinity and set up the priesthood of her new religion. Fresh sacrifices were made all over the city in all the temples, foundries poured new monuments of the goddess out of precious metals, and her funeral was one immense outpouring of mass grief, public curiosity and sheer entertainment. The show of mourning put on by a weeping, sobbing Caesar entranced the avid mobs who howled along beside him, showing their own tears. Gifts showered into their outstretched hands as the funeral wagons rattled by. It was a spectacle many would remember, even though they would soon forget who died and was buried with such stunning splendor.

Petronius, however, was alarmed to hear it. All of Rome knew already that Poppea blamed witchcraft for the child's mysterious illness and death. It was a view hastily endorsed by the medical profession since it explained their own uselessness and failure; it was loudly echoed by the priests who proved themselves equally helpless before the unknown; it was fearfully confirmed by the soothsayers and spell-casters, who shook with fear for their own skins but whose arts were suddenly in demand and who were making tidy profits all over the city; and finally it was picked up and accepted by the populace.

Petronius was now glad that Ligia had escaped. But since he didn't wish any harm to Aulus and his family, and also because he was highly interested in Vinicius' future and his own position, he went to the Palatine as soon as the cypress planted on the roof as a sign of mourning was finally taken down. The occasion was a banquet for senators and the most distinguished members of society, and he wanted to see for himself just how far Caesar swallowed the tales of witchcraft, what this might imply for the times ahead, and how he could deflect any unpleasant consequences in advance.

Knowing Nero, he supposed this Caesar would put on a good show of belief in spells and black magic to take the edge off his own remorse, to have someone on whom to wreak his vengeance, and to sidestep the inevitable gossip that the gods were punishing his crimes at last. Petronius didn't think him capable of loving even his own child with any depth of feeling, no matter what a show he made of it in public; he had no doubt, however, that being as bad an actor as he was, Nero would inflate his grief out of all proportion, in the same way as he had exaggerated his joys as a father.

He saw at once that he had guessed correctly. Nero met the commiserating senators with a dull, glazed stare, as lifeless as if his face had hardened into stone, and with his eyes fixed emptily on the space before him, but it was clear he was playing largely for effect. There may have been some real sorrow under that unconvincing mask of grief-stricken mourning, but he seemed far too interested in the overall picture he presented, measuring his grief against the response he wanted from his audience, like an actor weeping tragic tears on the stage. He couldn't even keep a grip on that stony silence that the abyss of his grief demanded. Instead he moaned and mewled. He waved his arms and made weak fluttering gestures as if he were heaping ashes on his head. But he leaped to his feet when he saw Petronius, and his voice rang with a tragedian's sorrow.

"*Eheu!*" he wailed. "Oh, pity! Oh, the shame of it! You, too, are to blame for her death, Petronius! It's at your prompting that an evil spirit came into this house and sucked the life out of her with one greedy glance! Help me, gods! Pity me! I'd rather be dead and blind

to the light of Helios than live in a world without her! *Eheu! Eheu!*
Oh, pity me!"

His voice passed into a piercing screech, but Petronius moved at
once to avert disaster. Like a calm, practiced gambler with steel
nerves and nothing left to lose, he staked everything on a single
throw: He slipped the silk scarf that Nero always wore from around
his neck and pressed it softly against Caesar's mouth.

"Divinity!" he spoke urgently but gravely. "Burn down Rome and
wreck the world in your desolation, but don't hurt your voice!"

Dumbstruck, the guests stared mutely at one another, wondering
what other thunderbolts would fall before the night was over. Caesar
himself gaped in openmouthed amazement, his eyes wide and bulging
in their sockets. But Petronius gave no sign of worry, as if there was
nothing else anyone could do. He was unperturbed and seemingly in
absolute control. He knew what he was doing. He remembered that
Terpnos and Diodorus were under strict orders to gag the emperor
whenever he risked damage to his vocal chords by raising his voice.

"Caesar," he went on with the same gravity, admonishment and sadness, "we've suffered an immeasurable loss. Nothing can replace it.
Spare us at least that one unique treasure to console us in *our* desolation."

Nero's face quivered. Tears sprung from his eyes and trickled
down his cheeks. He reached out blindly, clutched Petronius by the
shoulders and pressed his head against his chest sobbing all the while.

"You're the only one to think of that!" he sniffed as he wept. "The
only one, Petronius! There's nobody like you!"

Tigellinus, moving as always at Caesar's elbow, turned yellow with
envy.

"Go to Antium," Petronius urged the beaming, grateful Nero.
"That's where she came into the world. That's where you were happiest. That's where you'll find solace for your grief. Let the sea breezes
fan your sacred throat. Let your lungs fill with health in that salty air.
We, your devoted followers, will go everywhere you go. And while
we ease your suffering with our love, you'll soothe our mourning
with your song."

"Yes!" Nero's voice was still an appeal for pity, although it was suddenly lively and intrigued. "I'll write a hymn to her, and I'll compose
the music!"

"And then," Petronius hinted, "you can relax your muse in the sun
at Baiae."

"And seek forgetfulness in Greece . . ."

"In the homeland of poetry and song."

The grim, gloomy atmosphere in the chamber began to thaw and dissipate, the way passing snow clouds uncover the sun, and the talk turned to lighter matters. Oh, there was still sadness and a sense of tragedy, nothing else was possible at the court this quickly, but Tiridates, the king of Armenia, had announced a state visit and innumerable receptions had to be planned in the Palatine for that, along with all the public readings, performances and concerts that Nero would give on his trip to Antium and Baiae. Tigellinus made one more try to reawaken the specters of witchcraft, but Petronius had the measure of him now.

"Do you believe that witchcraft can touch the gods?" he asked Tigellinus.

"Caesar himself was talking about it," Tigellinus muttered. He was perhaps the closest of Nero's cronies, already prefect of Rome and soon to be commander of the praetorians, but Petronius was still beyond his reach.

"That was grief speaking, not Caesar," Petronius reminded. "But what's your opinion?"

"The gods are too powerful to fear spells," Tigellinus said with a shrug. He knew where Petronius was leading him, but there was nothing he could do about it.

"So would you deny the divinity of Caesar and his family?" Petronius struck home.

"*Peractus est.* He's finished," Eprius Marcellus muttered right beside them. Mobs howled that phrase in the circus when a gladiator took a blow that killed him on his feet, without the necessary knife thrust in the back of the neck after he had fallen.

Tigellinus bit back his fury, but his face was gray, like coals under ashes. Petronius was his only rival in influence over Caesar, and so far Tigellinus had managed to hold the edge. His superiority over the cultivated arbiter of taste lay in the fact that he pandered to Nero's lowest instincts, pushing him deeper into decadence and debauchery, and Nero didn't really care how gross he was in his company. But whenever he locked horns with Petronius, Tigellinus got the worst of it, soundly gored by a mind as quick and searing as lightning.

Silent now, he stood and noted for his future reckoning all those senators who flocked around Petronius, assuming after what had just happened that he was now Caesar's reigning favorite.

Petronius then left the palace and called on Vinicius, whom he told what had happened.

"So I not only turned the danger away from Aulus and Pomponia and from the two of us," he reported, "but from Ligia as well. They won't bother with her, if for no other reason than that I convinced the copper-bearded ape to get out of Rome. He'll go to Antium and Naples and Baiae, and especially Naples where he's been itching to go on the stage. He doesn't dare try any theater in Rome, but he's not worried about the provinces. Then he'll be off to Greece where he's determined to give a concert in every major city. The Greeks are shrewd enough to load him down with so many prizes that he'll be able to make a triumphal entry into Rome when he returns after that long absence. All this will give us enough time to find Ligia and get her well hidden. Well? So what's new? Have you heard from our great philosopher?"

"Not one word!" Vinicius snapped. "Your great philosopher is a cheat, a mountebank and a liar! He never came back, never showed hide nor hair, and he never will!"

"Hmm. I think better of him. Not of his honesty, you understand, but of his shrewd wits and his understanding of how his bread is buttered. He has bled your money bags once already, and he'll come back for another go."

"Let him take care that I don't bleed him."

"Hmm. Don't do that. Show him a little patience, at least until you're sure he's just stringing you along. Don't pay him any more but promise him a big reward for sound information. Are you doing anything on your own?"

"I have sixty men in the streets under my two freedmen, Nymphinius and Demas. Any slave who finds her has been promised freedom. I've people out on every highway leading from the city, asking about Ligia and the Lygian everywhere a traveler might stop. And I comb the back streets on my own every night, hoping for blind luck."

"Let me know whatever you find out," Petronius reminded. "I have to go to Antium, I'm afraid."

"Very well."

"And if you wake up some morning thinking that no girl is worth all that pain and bother, come to Antium too. Join our fun and games. They won't run out of women over there."

Vinicius started pacing swiftly through the room, and Petronius followed him with his eyes for a while. "Tell me the truth," he said. "No, not like an enthusiast who talks himself into a great passion and fuels his own excitement, but as a rational man talking to a friend. Are you still totally committed to this Ligia of yours?"

Vinicius halted, turned and stared at Petronius as if he had never set eyes on him before, then swung around and resumed his pacing. It was quite clear he was struggling to control an outpouring of churned and contradictory feelings. Helplessness, pity, remorse, anger and an irrepressible longing combined to form two great tears in his eyes, and these spoke louder to Petronius than any words could.

He thought about this for a while, then nodded. "It's not Atlas who holds the world on his shoulders. Woman does that. And sometimes she plays catch with it."

"Yes," Vinicius said.

They started saying good-bye to each other when a slave entered with word that Chilon Chilonides was waiting in the vestibule, asking to be admitted to their lordships' presence.

"Send him in at once!" Vinicius ordered.

"Ha, didn't I say he'd come?" Petronius asked. "By Hercules, he couldn't have timed it better. Just keep calm, Marcus. Find yourself a chair and take control over this interview. Otherwise he'll control you."

Vinicius sat and waited with clenched fists until Chilon appeared in the atrium doorway.

"All hail to you, distinguished military tribune." He bobbed and saluted as he clip-clopped inside on his dusty sandals. "And to you, too, my lord. May your fortunes always match your fame, and may this fame spread across the world from the Pillars of Hercules to Parthia."

"And hail to you, too, fount of truth and wisdom," said Petronius, smiling softly.

"What do you have for us?" Vinicius asked with pretended calm.

"The first time I brought hope, my lord." Chilon creaked and rustled. "Now I bring assurance the girl will be found."

"Which means you haven't found her."

"That's so, my lord. But I know who carried her away and what god they worship. And that shows us where to search for her."

Vinicius wanted to leap from his chair, but Petronius leaned slightly forward and placed a soothing hand on the young man's shoulder. "Keep going!" he said, turning to the Greek.

"Are you quite sure, my lord, that the girl drew a fish for you in the sand?" Chilon asked. He seemed to want to protract the moment, as if tapping his way through unfamiliar country.

"Yes!" Vinicius burst out, his self-control forgotten.

"Then she's a Christian," the Greek said. "And the people who abducted her were also Christians."

There was a long silence.

"Listen and don't forget this, Chilon," Petronius said at last. "My nephew has a large cash reward earmarked for you when you produce the girl, but there's an equal number of lashes waiting for your back if you try to cheat him. In the first event, you'll buy yourself three writers if you want, but all the wisdom of the seven Magi along with your own won't help you in the second instance."

"The girl's a Christian, my lord!" cried the Greek.

"Think well, Chilon. You're not a stupid man. We know that Junia Sillana and Calvia Crispinilla accused Pomponia Graecina of dabbling in the Christian superstition, but we also know she was cleared by the domestic court. Would you really want to stir up those old charges? Are you trying to tell us that Pomponia, along with her Ligia, could be avowed enemies of the human race? Or that they're part and parcel of a gang that poisons public wells and fountains, worships an ass's head, murders babies and indulges in unspeakable debaucheries? Think, Chilon! Ask yourself if your theory won't bring an instant countertheory etched with a scourge onto your bloody back."

Chilon spread his hands. The fault, the gesture stated, couldn't be his own. "Master," he said, "give me the Greek translation for the phrase: Iesus Christos, Son of God and Savior."

"Very well. What of it?"

"Now take the first Greek letter in each word and make it into one."

"*Ichthos,*" Petronius said, surprised. "The fish!"

"And that's why the fish is the Christian recognition symbol," Chilon said, smiling with satisfaction.

This time the silence was as dumbfounded as it was protracted. Chilon's pronouncement made no sense, but it was so stunning in its implications that the two aristocratic Romans stared at each other like a pair of idiots.

"Marcus," Petronius said at last, "are you quite sure it was a fish she drew in the sand?"

"By all the gods of Hell!" Vinicius shouted. "I'll go mad with any more of this! It was a fish! If she had drawn a bird, I'd have said so!"

"Then she's a Christian," Chilon said again.

"That means Ligia and Pomponia poison public water?" Petronius shook his head in total disbelief. "That they murder kidnapped children and take part in disgusting rituals? What utter nonsense! I didn't spend as much time with Aulus and Pomponia as you did,

Marcus, but I know them and Ligia well enough to say that is utter stuff and garbage! If the fish is really a Christian symbol, which is hard to deny, and if those two women are truly followers of this Iesus Christos, then, by Persephone, we've a lot more to learn about the Christians than we think we do."

"Spoken like Socrates, my lord," said the Greek. "Who ever questioned any Christians about their beliefs? Who understands their teaching? When I came from Naples here to Rome—and oh, how I wish I'd stayed there!—I traveled with a man named Glaucus, a healer whom people called a Christian. But I discovered he was a good and decent fellow nonetheless."

"And he told you now about the fish?" Petronius wanted to know.

"Unfortunately no, my lord. Somebody stabbed this good old man in some roadside tavern, and his wife and children were sold to slavers. I lost two fingers in their defense, as you can plainly see. But since there is never a shortage of miracles among Christians, as I hear people say, I'm hoping to grow new ones."

"What? You mean you've also turned Christian?"

"Since yesterday, my lord! Just since yesterday! That fish did it to me. Amazing powers in that creature, wouldn't you say, my lord? In a few days I'll be the hottest zealot of the lot and get into their deepest secrets, and once I'm there I'll know where the girl is hiding. Then maybe my Christianity will pay off better than my philosophy. I also promised Mercury, the god of thieves and actors, that I'll offer him a matched pair of milk cows with gilded horns."

"So your new Christianity and your old philosophy allow you to believe in Mercury?" Petronius smiled, amused. "There's no conflict there?"

"I always believe what the moment calls for." Chilon made a deprecating gesture with a modest smile. "That's my philosophy in a nutshell, and it ought to suit Mercury down to his winged sandals. There's one bad snag at the moment, though, my good lords. Mercury is a very suspicious god. He doesn't trust even the most profound philosophers. He'd rather have those milk cows in advance, which is a heavy outlay for a man like me; I'm not Seneca with his private fortune. So if the noble Vinicius would care to advance me a little something on account of that reward he offers . . ."

"Not a tin penny, Chilon!" Petronius shook his finger. "Not a single copper! Vinicius' generosity will stun you when it comes, but it'll come only when we have the girl. Show us her hiding place, and you'll see the money. Mercury has to give you credit on those cows, although I can't say I'm surprised at his hesitation. He's not the patron of thieves and mountebanks for nothing."

But Chilon also wasn't what he was for nothing, as he began to prove straightaway.

"Distinguished lords," he said, "I may not have the girl just yet, but I'm headed in the right direction. My discovery is of enormous value since it points us to her hiding place. You've sent slaves and freedmen throughout Rome and into the country, but did one of them do you any good? Has one said anything worthwhile? No! I'm the only one! And I'll tell you more: There may be secret Christians among your slaves that you wouldn't know anything about because that superstition has spread like a plague in the lower orders. They might betray you sooner than be useful. It's even bad they see me coming here. Eunice, my lord Petronius, ought to be told to keep quiet about me, while you, my lord Vinicius, should pass the word that I'm here just to sell you an ointment that makes chariot horses run stronger and faster. I'll look for her alone and you have to trust me, or rather you can trust in the encouragement I'll get from an advance against my expenses. That'll be like a goad for me or a carrot dangled before a cart horse, tempting me with the promise of what'll be coming to me in the end."

Money, he continued, was of course a matter of supreme indifference to a real philosopher such as himself, although Seneca, Musonius and Cornutus didn't show as much contempt for it as they should.

"They didn't lose any fingers defending anybody, so they can write their own names into posterity anytime they please. Moreover, I need to pay for more than just a writer and the cows, and you know the prices nowadays in the cattle markets. And then there are all kinds of other costs connected with searching."

He launched into a detailed version of his efforts among all sorts of people, listing the bakers, butchers, olive oil peddlers and fishermen he talked to, and pointing to the raw blisters on his feet as proof of his miles of walking.

"I've been to every wineshop in every nook and alley," he assured Vinicius. "I've sat in the hideouts of the runaways. I've lost a hundred groats shooting dice while gathering information. I've been in every wash house, laundry loft and soup kitchen in the working quarter. I've talked to mule drivers and masons. I've talked to men who pull teeth and cure diseased bladders. I've pumped fig peddlers and questioned the mourners in the cemeteries. And why did I do that?"

One reason only, he assured: to draw the sign of the fish everywhere he went, watch the eyes around him, and catch any recognition signal he might see glinting there.

"For a long time there was nothing," he confided. "Then I caught sight of this old slave shedding tears while drawing water buckets from a fountain. I asked him why he wept. He told me he'd been saving all his life to buy his son out of slavery, but his master, a certain Pansa who also owns the son, kept the boy and the money when he saw it. 'So here I sit weeping,' the old man said, 'because though I keep telling myself it's God's will, I can't stop my tears.'"

That, Chilon said, was his inspiration. "I dipped a finger in his water bucket and drew him a fish. 'I trust in Christ as well,' he told me at once. So I asked whether he knew me by the sign I'd drawn, and he said, 'Yes, and may peace be with you.' After that everything fell into place."

The old slave, he said, opened up to him like his own gaping buckets and gushed with information. His master, Pansa, it appeared, was himself a freedman of the great Vibius Pansa, and he ferried cut building blocks on barges down the Tiber, which his slaves and hired hands unloaded and carried to construction sites all over the city, working at night so as not to block the thoroughfares in daytime.

"It's a killing job," Chilon said, echoing the complaint of the old man who had wept as he talked about his son and many other Christians who worked on those barges.

"I wept right along," Chilon said, sniffing and sniffling, "because I'm a soft-hearted man and quick to feel compassion, and since my feet were killing me with all that walking anyway. I also told him I'd just come from Naples and didn't know any of the brethren here, so I didn't know where to go for a prayer meeting. He was a bit surprised that the Naples brethren didn't give me any letters to the Roman branch, but I told him I had had them but lost them, or somebody stole them. Then he told me to come tonight to the riverside where he'll introduce me to some of the brethren, and they'll take me on to the prayer houses and the Christian elders. Which, my lord," he finished earnestly with a calculating glance shot toward Vinicius, "made me so happy that I paid on the spot the full amount he needed to free his son, and I dare to hope that you, my lord tribune, with all your high-minded munificence, might give that back to me with a little interest."

"Your story, Chilon, is as streaked with lies as oil spilled on water," Petronius interrupted. "You've brought important news, there's no denying that. I'll even say it's an important step to recovering Ligia. But stick to the truth and don't grease your facts with transparent fiction. Who told you that Christians recognize one another by the sign of the fish? Did he have a name?"

"He did and does, my lord," Chilon offered smoothly. "His name is Euricius. Poor fellow, he reminds me of Glaucus, my old traveling companion, whom I defended when murderers attacked him. Which, I expect, is why his story moved me to such a gesture—"

"Oh, I believe you met him." Petronius smiled grimly. "I believe you'll use him. I believe you'll turn a pretty penny on this new acquaintance. But what I don't believe is that you gave him money! You didn't toss him as much as a groat! Not a groat, you hear me?"

"But I gave him a hand with the water buckets," Chilon pointed out, "and spoke about his son with a lot of feeling. That shouldn't come for nothing. Nothing, I gladly concede, can escape scrutiny and judgment by such a perceptive mind as yours, my lord Petronius, but I gave this fellow more than mere money. I rendered him full payment in my mind and spirit, which would be enough for a true philosopher. And I gave what I gave because I thought it vital and essential for the search. Just think, my lord, how it'll help me win over the entire sect, what access it'll get me, and how they'll trust me now."

"That's true," Petronius nodded. "And that's what you should've done."

"That's just why I'm here now!" Chilon cried, grinning his yellow smile. "So I'll be able to do it!"

Petronius turned his amused, ironic eyes from him to Vinicius. "Pay him five thousand sesterces," he suggested, "but only in spirit."

But Vinicius decided on something different. "I'll send a boy with you," he said, "along with the gold that you'll pay to the old man in front of my slave. The news you've brought is valuable and important, so you'll get the same again for yourself. Come back for the boy and the money this evening."

"Now there's a true Caesar!" Chilon said. "You'll permit me, my lord, to dedicate my great work to you once I have it written. But I hope you'll also permit me to come tonight only for the money. Euricius told me all the barges are unloaded now, and a new fleet won't be hauled from Ostia for a few more days. Peace be among you, as the Christians say. I'll buy myself a slave girl, that is to say a slave. Ha! You catch fish with a rod, it seems, and Christians with a fish. *Pax vobiscum*, gentlemen! Peace be with you! *Pax! Pax! Pax!*"

And Chilon hobbled swiftly through the door.

⟨20⟩

A FEW WEEKS LATER there was an exchange of letters between the two Romans. Petronius wrote the first one.

"Your hand may be better suited to the sword and javelin than a quill or stylus," he wrote to Vinicius, "but I hope you'll answer without much delay by the same trusted slave who brings this from Antium. I left you well on track of your lovely fugitive and on an optimistic turn. I expect you've already slaked your fond fires in Ligia's loving arms, but if not, that you'll do it before the winter winds start howling through Campania. My dear Vinicius! May Aphrodite guide your hand in love and may your Lygian spring bloom under your touch. Always bear in mind that even the costliest marble is just a dead stone and becomes a masterpiece only in the hands of an inspired sculptor. Be such a sculptor in your love, *carissime.* Loving is not enough. One has to know how to love and how to teach loving. Even the mob is capable of delight and animals feel pleasure, but true human beings can turn it into an exalted art form, which is the difference between animals and man. To know this and still delight in love opens the mind to the gods' own vision of what it's really like, so that it thrills the soul as well as the body. When I think about the emptiness, the shallowness, the uncertainties, the folly, and the utter boredom of our lives at court, I sometimes wonder if you didn't make the better choice, going to a life in the military. Unlike this court, war and love are real. They seem to be the two fields left to us where life still has value.

"You were a good and lucky soldier. Be also such a lover. And if you're curious about our doings here at Caesar's court, I'll drop you a few comments now and then. We twiddle our divine thumbs in Antium, we pamper our heavenly vocal chords, but we detest Rome as much as ever and plan to winter in Baiae to give our Neapolitan performance. We expect a great success in Naples whose canny Greek inhabitants are sure to show us more appreciation than the snarling tribe that lives along the Tiber, descended as it is from the she-wolves that suckled Romulus and Remus. We'll have crowds flocking from Baiae, Pompeii, Puetoli, Cumae and Stabia, so we won't run short of clapping hands and triumphal wreaths, which will fan our enthusiasm for the tour of Greece.

"We also pay respects to the memory of our deceased Augusta; we still weep over her now and then; we compose such glorious hymns and sing them so beautifully that the mermaids have all dived to the bottom of the sea out of sheer envy. I'm sure the dolphins would be glad to listen if they could, but they have water in whatever they use for ears. Our suffering goes on unabated, and we display it in every form suggested by the sculptors on every possible occasion, but we take careful note if it becomes us, if it suits our costume, if we project the proper sense of tragedy and beauty, and if the audience appreciates the poetry of our mourning. Ah, my dear fellow! We'll be buried as clowns and comedians when the curtain falls.

"All of high society is here, the male and the female, including five hundred jackass mares whose milk provides Poppea with her daily baths, and our ten thousand servants. We do have our fun! Calvia Crispinilla is getting old; they say she begs Poppea to let her use the milk bath when she's finished with it. Lucanus slapped Nigidia in the face, because he thought she was having an affair with a gladiator. Sporus staked his wife in a dice game and lost her to Senecio. Torquatus Silenus tried to trade four matched chariot racers for my Eunice, but I didn't take them even though they're sure to win this year's crown at the hippodrome. Thanks, by the way, for letting me keep her! About Torquatus, incidentally, he's not long for this world and has no idea he's about to die. His demise is signed, sealed and ready for delivery. And do you know why he has to die? His crime is that he's a great-grandson of our first immortal, the great Augustus Caesar, and thus in line for a Caesar's chair. There's no hope for him, but such is our world.

"As you know we expected Tiridates of Armenia to join us here, but he didn't come; instead we got a snotty letter from Vologensis, whose Parthians have overrun Armenia, asking us to let him keep Armenia in trust for Tiridates. If we don't, he informed us, he'll keep it anyway. Sheer comedy! He'll have war instead, that's also been decided. Corbulanus will get a free hand in Parthia, just as the great Pompey got in his war on the Sicilian pirates, but Nero had some doubts about that at first. It seems he's afraid Corbulanus might win too many battles, get too famous and attract too much attention to himself. Our Aulus was a candidate for that command, but Poppea soon put an end to that. She can't stand Pomponia, whose virtue is like salt rubbed into her wounds.

"Vatinius has announced some extraordinary gladiator contests he plans to stage for us in Beneventum. It seems that even the spawn of a cobbler can rise to great heights among us, despite that saying about silk purses and pigs' ears. Look at them all, in fact! Vitelius is descended from a sandalmaker, and Vatinius is the son of one! I dare say he'd still be able to poke leather with an awl if he wanted to. The mime Aliturus gave us a wonderful version of Oedipus last evening. Since he's a Jew, I asked him if Jews and Christians were one and the same, but he said they weren't. The Jews, he told me, have their own religion, one that's been functioning for centuries, while the Christians are a new sect started in Judea not too long ago. Some fellow got himself crucified there in Tiberius' time, and now he's a god whose followers multiply like flies every day. It appears they don't want to hear about any other god, and especially ours. Strange people! I don't see what harm our gods could do them.

"Tigellinus is now challenging me out in the open; he no longer bothers to hide his hatred for me. He hasn't been able to score against me but enjoys one great advantage over me, or perhaps it's two: He's a bigger scoundrel, which puts him close to our Copperbeard, and he's far fonder of life than I and takes good care of it. Sooner or later the two of them will get their heads together, and then it'll be my turn for a dish of poison. I can't guess the hour or the day, but I know it's coming, so there's no point in caring. In the meantime one has to entertain oneself. Life wouldn't be so bad if it weren't for Copperbeard, whose company destroys a man's self-respect. I've tried to see my daily struggle for his favor as a chariot race or a wrestling match or some kind of exercise or game in which the winner can congratulate himself on his perspicacity and skill, but that's not enough. It only makes me think that I'm another Chilon on a higher level. Send him to me, by the way, when you've finished with him; I became quite fond of his lofty thinking.

"Give my regards to your beautiful Christian and ask her for me to be a little warmer for you than a fish. Write me about your health, report on your love, learn how to be a lover and how to teach loving, and be well."

Marcus Vinicius wrote back at once.

"Ligia is still gone!" he informed Petronius. "Only the hope that I may find her soon makes this letter possible, because writing is a pain when a man sees no point in living. I wanted to see if Chilon played it straight with me, so I followed him that night when he and my slave took money to Euricius. I watched them from behind a piling on the dockside, and Euricius turned out to be flesh and blood, not just imagination. There were several dozen men working by torchlight at the riverside, unloading rafts piled with cut stone and stacking them on the shore. I saw Chilon come up to one old slave, saw how he talked to him, and how the old man fell to his knees before him. The others crowded around them, shouting. I saw with my own eyes how my slave handed the bag of money to this Euricius, who seized it and started praying with both arms raised to heaven. Some other fellow, probably his son, fell to his knees beside him. Chilon talked to them a while longer and then started blessing them and the others, scrawling a sign like a cross in the air. They apparently worship the cross as well, because they all bent their knees before it. I had an urge to go down among them and offer three such bags to anyone who would take me to Ligia, but I didn't want to undermine what Chilon was doing, so I went back home.

"This happened about twelve days after your departure. Chilon has been here several times since then. He tells me he's acquired great standing among the Christians, and the only reason he hasn't found Ligia's hiding place is that there are swarms of these Christians in Rome today, so many that they don't know one another and few know everything that goes on among them. They're also cautious and talk very little. Chilon, however, is certain he can unearth their deepest secrets once he is among their elders, or presbyters as they call them. He's met a few already and tried to learn something, but he must be careful. If he moves too quickly, they might get suspicious, which would put a crimp in any further searching. I can hardly stand this waiting, but I see his point, so I arm myself with whatever patience I can find and wait.

"He also discovered that they pray together in out-of-the-way places, often beyond the walls, in abandoned houses and even in gravel pits and quarries. That's where they feast, sing and worship Christ. There are many such places all over the city, and Chilon believes that Ligia and Pomponia go to different ones on purpose, so that in case of arrest Pomponia could swear she doesn't know where the girl is hiding. It could be those presbyters gave them that advice. When Chilon sniffs out all those meetinghouses, I think I'll go with him, and I swear by the head of Jupiter himself that if the gods let me catch a glimpse of her, she'll never get away again.

"I keep thinking about those prayer places. Chilon is scared of getting caught and doesn't want me to go with him among the Christians, but I can't sit still. I'd know her at a glance, even if she was veiled or disguised. They meet at night, but I'd know her even in the darkness. I'd recognize her voice and the way she moved. I'll disguise myself and watch everyone who goes in or out. I expect Chilon here tomorrow and I'll go with him then, but I'll hide a short sword in my cloak. First we'll look into the places in the city, and then we'll go beyond the gates. Some of the slaves I sent out on the highways came back empty-handed, but I'm convinced she's right here in Rome—and maybe even near. I've gone through quite a number of places myself, pretending to be interested in renting, and I'm sure she'll be a hundred times happier in my house than in those wretched hovels of the poor. I know I wouldn't stint on anything for her.

"You say I made the better choice in life, but I don't know about that; it seems I picked a path of bitterness and worry. Hope looks for something fresh to feed it every day, otherwise life would get too grim to continue. You say that one should know how to love a woman. Well, I knew how to talk about love to Ligia, but now she's gone and I'm gnawed with loneliness and longing. I sit and wait for Chilon, and I can't abide any of my surroundings.

"Be well," Vinicius closed, but he was far from well himself. Petronius was an expert in reading between the lines, and he also worried.

‹21›

As IT HAPPENED, Chilon stayed away so long that Vinicius did not know what to think of him and the rest of it. It didn't help to remind himself that a successful search had to be made slowly. Neither his hot blood nor his reckless nature could react sensibly to the voice of reason. He hated feeling helpless. He couldn't stand seeing himself as unable to determine his own fate. The thought of waiting, doing nothing and sitting on his hands was so at odds with his way of thinking, heritage and experience, that he didn't know what to do about it. Darting through the alleys at night, hooded like a slave, was a waste of time. It may have helped him delude himself that he was doing something, but it did nothing to make him feel less futile and useless. Nor did his freedmen do better in searching than Chilon. They were all shrewd and experienced men, but they proved a hundred times less skillful than the Greek.

Meanwhile, besides his love for Ligia, he started feeling the passions of a driven gambler. He had to win no matter what it cost. This wasn't something new; Vinicius had always been like that. Even as a boy he went after everything with blind determination; he couldn't conceive of failure or imagine that anything was beyond his reach, nor did it occur to him to deny himself anything he wanted. Army discipline curbed his ruthless will, but it also deepened his conviction that any orders he gave must be carried out. His years in the East, among people who were used to servile obedience, simply confirmed him in the fact that his "I want" could ignore all limits.

What he was going through just then touched him to the quick and affected his self-esteem; he felt as if his whole inner being had been gored and was bleeding. There was something he simply couldn't understand in all these contradictions, in this resistance, and in the bare fact of Ligia's escape. It was a riddle that defied his comprehension no matter how he wrestled with thoughts and ideas.

He felt that Acte spoke the truth when she said Ligia cared for him. But if so, why did she choose misery, homeless wandering and life in hovels over his love, his caresses and happy days in his delightful house? He could find no answer. But he began to sense there was a profound though unidentifiable divergence between himself and Ligia, that their most basic rules had nothing in common, and that between his universe and that of Petronius, and the one inhabited by Ligia and Pomponia, was an unbridgeable chasm of contradictory perceptions. Whenever he thought of this, he was convinced he'd never be able to draw Ligia into his world even if he found her, and this undermined and toppled whatever comfort Petronius tried to offer.

All his notions whirled in doubt, anger and confusion; all his truisms crumbled. There were dark moments when he could not tell if he loved Ligia or if he hated her; all he knew for certain was that he had to find her and that he'd rather be buried alive than never touch or have her. She was so vivid in his memory, painted with such detail by his imagination, that he could almost see her standing before him just as he had last seen her. He remembered every word he had said to her, and each she said to him. He could feel her nearness. A craving for possession swept through him like fire when he imagined her straining against his chest and locked in his arms. He loved her and called for her, although sometimes that calling was a curse. And when he remembered that she had also loved him a short time before and could have given him anything he wanted of her own free will, he bowed under an overwhelming sorrow, and a tidal wave of regret washed over him.

But he had moments when his peremptory nature showed its darker side. Her escape was defiance, pure and simple, and he abhorred that. He grew pale with rage, and the torments and humiliations he imagined he would inflict after he found her heightened his excitement. He wanted her, yes, but he also wanted her as a broken slave. At the same time he knew he'd rather be her slave, in the full dreadful meaning of that word, than never get to see her. There were days he dreamed about the whip marks on her delicate white flesh, and then he wanted to heal them with kisses. Once or twice the thought of murder glinted in his mind. He thought he could be happy only if he killed her.

His health and even his good looks suffered from this strain of doubt, anger, anxiety and exhaustion. He turned into a cruel, unforgiving master. His household feared him. Slaves trembled when he called them. And when his savage and unfair punishments turned their lives into a living Hell, even his old-time freedmen started to hate him in secret.

He sensed this hatred and isolation, and avenged it even more. He was careful only when dealing with Chilon, fearing he might abandon the search if he was mistreated, and the shrewd Greek immediately perceived this opportunity and took advantage of it. He demanded more and started to impose his own will on Vinicius. Each time he had come before, he assured Vinicius that things would go quickly with very little trouble; now he came up with lists of obstacles and problems, still talking about eventual success but hinting that it would take a long time and a lot more money.

When he came again, after days of waiting, he looked so gloomy that Vinicius turned as white as bleached linen and leaped toward him.

"She's not with the Christians?" Vinicius barely had the strength to stammer out the words.

"Indeed she is, my lord," Chilon said, "but so is someone else. I found Glaucus among them."

"What are you talking about? Who's Glaucus?"

"Ah, you've forgotten, lord. He's the old man with whom I traveled from Naples to Rome, the one I tried to save from the cutthroats when I lost these two fingers, which makes it impossible for me to hold a pen. The bandits who carried off his wife and children knifed him and left him for dead in an inn near Minturnae, which is where I last saw him. I mourned him a long time, but I've discovered that he's still alive and belongs to the Roman Christians."

Vinicius choked back the anger that welled up inside him. He didn't know what Chilon was talking about; he couldn't care less about some old Christian. All he knew was that this Glaucus was some kind of fresh obstacle in the search for Ligia.

"So why isn't he helping you if you tried to save him?"

"Ah, distinguished tribune! Even the gods show ingratitude now and then, so what about us mortals? Yes, I agree, he ought to be grateful. But he's a feeble-minded old man whose wits are dimmed by tragedy and age, so instead of gratitude he offers accusations! He's charging *me* with selling him to the cutthroats and causing all his misery, as I hear from his fellow Christians."

"And I'm sure he's right, you sniveling cut-purse," Vinicius snapped, impatient. "I'm sure that's just what happened."

"Well, if you know that much, my lord," Chilon said with a shrug, unmoved, "then you know more than he does. He merely supposes. He doesn't know anything for certain. But that wouldn't stop him from turning me over to his Christians and getting his revenge. I'm sure he'd do it, and I'm sure they'd help him. Luckily he doesn't know my name and didn't see me in that house of worship where I spotted him. I was all set to throw my arms around him, so happy to see he was still alive! But I'm a cautious man. I look before I leap. I asked a few questions about him when the praying was over, and those who knew him told me he was a man whose traveling companion sold him to marauders on the road from Naples. I mean, how would they even know about such a thing if he hadn't told them?"

"How would I care? Get on with what matters! Tell me what happened in that house of prayer!"

"You couldn't care less, my lord," the Greek said, "but I care a lot. I care as much as my own hide is worth. I want my teaching to live long after me, and that's why I'd rather give up the reward you promised than risk my life in further searching. What's money? What's material wealth? What are the illusions of the temporal world? A true philosopher like me can live and search for the truth without them."

But Vinicius loomed over him with a malignant glint, his voice suffused with fury: "And what makes you think Glaucus will kill you any faster than I? How do you know, you miserable dog, that I won't have your carcass planted in my garden in the next ten seconds?"

Whatever Chilon was, he was not a hero. One lightning glance at the grim patrician convinced him that one more careless word would be the end of him. "I'll keep looking for her, lord!" he cried instantly.

Only Vinicius' labored breath and the soft, distant singing of the slaves who worked in the garden broke the silence while the young patrician struggled for control and the informer watched.

"Death brushed against me," the Greek said at last, sighing. "But I looked her in the eye as calmly as Socrates. No, no, my lord. I didn't say I'd stop looking for the girl. I merely said the search is now a great danger for me. You doubted at one time that there was a real Euricius, so you spied on me to see if I was a liar, and now you think I invented Glaucus! I wish I had! If he were just a figment of my imagination and I could still move among the Christians as safely as before, I'd gladly give you that old slave woman I bought three days ago to take care of my infirmities in old age. But Glaucus lives, my lord. And if he catches sight of me just once, you'll never set eyes on me again. And then who'll find the girl?"

Here he wept a little, mopped his eyes and sighed again. "But how am I to search for her as long as he's alive? I can run up against Glaucus at any moment, and it'll be good-bye—and not just to me but to any searching."

"Where's all this leading?" Vinicius demanded. "What are you really after, and what do you want to do?"

"Aristotle teaches that small sacrifices must be made to save greater goals. King Priam of Troy liked to say that old age was a crushing burden. If Glaucus has been crushed by age and his misfortunes for so many years, and if this burden is so unendurable and painful, shouldn't he look at death as a blessing? Seneca holds that death is a liberation—"

"Play your games with Petronius, not with me," Vinicius snapped.

"If virtue is a game, my lord, then let me play games forever. I want Glaucus out of the way, because as long as he's alive, both the search and I are in danger."

"So what's the problem? Hire a few thugs who'll club him to death. I'll pay for it."

"They'll cheat you, my lord. First they'll overcharge you, and then they'll blackmail you. There are more cutthroats for hire in Rome than sand in the arena, but you wouldn't believe how much they charge an honest man who needs to use their skills. No, distinguished tribune! The risks are too costly. And what would happen if the nightwatch caught them at their work? They'd sing out who hired them and give you a headache. I'll hire them for you. They won't know my name so they won't be able to get me involved. You're wrong not to trust me. Even putting aside my proven honesty, my lord, you ought to bear in mind what's at stake for me here. I'll be frank, my lord: I want to save my neck, that goes without saying, but I also want to get my hands on the reward you promised."

"How much do you need, then?"

"A thousand sesterces." It was a large sum at a time when a murderer could be hired for a hundred, but Chilon said he wanted honest murderers or cutthroats with a code of ethics, not the kind who would take a cash advance and vanish. "Good work needs good pay," he reminded, "because what's fair is fair. I'd also like a little something for all those tears I'll weep for poor old Glaucus. Let the gods testify how I loved him! If I get a thousand sesterces today, Glaucus' soul will be in Hades two days later. Then he'll realize at last what a friend I was to him, if souls can reason and remember. I'll have the men for the job today, and I'll set a penalty of a hundred sesterces for each day Glaucus is alive after tomorrow night. I also have another idea that can't fail."

"All right, you'll get your thousand. But I don't want to hear another word about Glaucus, understand?"

"Of course, my lord, of course. That's as good as settled."

Vinicius wanted news of Ligia. He wanted to know where Chilon had been all that time, what he had been doing, and what he saw and found out among the Christians. But Chilon couldn't say any more than he had said before. He had been in two more prayer houses. He kept a sharp eye on everyone, especially the women, but didn't see anyone who resembled Ligia. The Christians, however, accepted him now as one of their own; they saw him as a man who walked in Christ's footsteps ever since he had paid for the manumission of Euricius' son. He learned from them that one of their great preachers, a certain Paul of Tarsus, happened to be in Rome just now, jailed on some complaint from Jerusalem and the local Jews, and he decided to get to know him too. But what excited him the most was that the greatest Christian leader of them all was coming to Rome soon.

"This fellow, name of Peter, was actually one of Christ's disciples. They went about together, and Christ made him chief of all the Christians in the world. All of them want to see him and hear him preach. All of them, noble tribune, and that means your Ligia! There'll be some mass gatherings, you can be sure of that. I'll be there, of course, that goes without saying. But because crowds are a good cover, I'll be able to bring you there as well!"

Ligia, he said, was as good as found with that in the offing.

"It won't even be so dangerous," the Greek was pleased to say, "with Glaucus removed. I can't get over what a quiet and gentle lot they are, but they'd still give us a hard time if they caught onto us before we were ready."

Here Chilon wagged his huge head in puzzlement. An odd bunch, those Christians, that's for sure! He never saw one orgy among them—not one in all that time! In fact they seemed to be painfully honest, decent and law-abiding people. He didn't hear about them poisoning wells and fountains. He didn't see anybody worshiping any ass's head or eating the flesh of children.

"Oh, sure, there are bound to be a few we can hire to take care of Glaucus," he hurried to add. "They can't all be perfect. But I've heard nothing in their preaching that encourages any kind of crime. On the contrary, they're taught to forgive their enemies."

Vinicius thought again about the strange words he heard from

Pomponia in Acte's apartment. Forgiveness? How could anybody keep his self-respect without revenge for insults and humiliations? But what Chilon said seemed to confirm that the strange teachings followed by Ligia and Pomponia weren't some foul criminal conspiracy, and Vinicius listened to him with relief and joy.

In his confused thinking about Ligia, where so much hatred overlay a wealth of longing and where revenge pricked like a nervous reflex under the growing image of wholly new and unsuspected forms of love and loving, pride in her goodness was probably the strongest.

This pride, this joy he felt in what he barely understood led to another realization, and he began to fear and hate something far beyond her. The thought grew in him the moment it appeared, but it never got sharper or clearer than a stab of instinct. He started to feel it was exactly this sense of the new and the unknown, this mystery beyond his understanding, this inexplicable worship of an obscure, executed Jew in a distant province that brought about the vast void lying between him and Ligia.

‹22›

CHILON WAS REALLY ANXIOUS to get rid of Glaucus, who may have been along in years but was far from the decrepit old man created for Vinicius' consumption. There was a fair amount of truth in what Chilon had told him and what Vinicius supposed really happened. Chilon did know Glaucus at one time. They did travel together. He did betray him, sell him to the slavers, rob him of his family and everything he owned, and set the killers on him. He didn't, however, think much about him afterward; he left him to die in an open field outside Minturnae rather than an inn and didn't expect he'd lick himself back to health again.

When he saw Glaucus alive and well in Rome at a prayer meeting, the shock threw him into a panic. The idea of giving up the search flashed across his mind, but his fear of what Vinicius would do to him was far more immediate. He had to choose between a panicked fear and a real terror, wondering if he could outrun Glaucus' vengeance before he fell to the pursuit launched by an enraged patrician, especially with help from the far more feared and powerful Petronius.

This tipped the scale. Chilon stopped wondering which way to leap and made his decision. Weak enemies among little people are always better than the great and well connected. Too much a coward to risk the dangers inherent in anything involving bloodshed, he determined to have Glaucus murdered by somebody else.

What mattered now was finding the right men, and this was the foolproof idea he had mentioned to Vinicius. He thought he'd use Christians. They seemed a lot more dependable and honest than the gutter sweepings with whom he spent his time in the squalid wineshops, the nightmare creatures who made their lairs in the slums of the Suburra and across the Tiber and who would rob him, cheat him, take cash in advance and threaten to expose him to the prefect's people or start their murderous work with him if they smelled the money! Judging everything by his own character and experience, especially since he hardly bothered to scratch the surface of the Christian teaching, he assumed he would find willing tools for murder among them. Cynical as he was, Chilon was startled by the paradox that their scrupulous honesty made them his best choice. And there was even more; what if he could sell them on doing the job out of religious zeal rather than for money?

With this in mind he set out to talk with Euricius, who just about worshiped the ground under Chilon's feet and would do anything to help him. Not that the Greek would even hint what it was all about. He was far too careful to betray himself, especially since his goals were in such violent contradiction to the old man's goodness and his fear of God. But he wanted men who would do anything for him, and Euricius was a start. Afterward he would so arrange matters that those who did his work would also keep the secret, although that called for a few other murders.

He found the old man in one of the shabby little stalls clustered around the Circus Maximus, which the old man leased after buying his son's freedom and where the two of them now peddled olives, boiled elephant beans, unleavened wheat cakes and honey-sweetened water to the spectators going to the races.

"Praised be the Lord Christ!" Chilon greeted him, and then launched at once into the reason for his visit. A terrible danger threatened him along with all Christians. And just as he had saved young Quartus and won the love of his father Euricius, so now only he could save the rest of the Christian brethren. He needed two or three big, strong and fearless men to help him stave off this threatening disaster. True, he was a poor man himself, having given practically everything he owned to Euricius in his time of need, but he would pay these men for their services as long as they trusted him, remained loyal to him and did everything he wanted without question.

Euricius and Quartus listened to him as if he were an oracle.

"A saintly man like you, Chilon Chilonides, wouldn't do anything that went against Christ's teaching," the old man assured him. He could do no wrong as far as they were both concerned. "Just tell us what you want from us. We're ready to do anything you wish."

Chilon assured them that Christ's teaching always lay foremost in his mind, and he raised his eyes humbly to the ceiling as if he were praying. In reality he went through his options. Their offer was tempting; he would save himself a thousand sesterces if he agreed to use them. Euricius was an old man, however, drained by worry and sickness, and Quartus was barely sixteen. What Chilon wanted were tough, experienced volunteers with fists like twin boulders. His idea of trading zeal for money would probably save him most of his thousand anyway.

They pressed him to take them on for a while longer, but he finally refused.

"I know a baker, master, name of Demas," Quartus said at last, "who has some slaves and hired labor working in his flour mill. One of his hired hands is so strong he takes the place of four. I saw him myself, good master, hefting a millstone that four others couldn't budge."

Chilon thought he sounded like just what he wanted. "I'd like to meet him. If he's a godfearing man, willing to sacrifice himself for his fellow man—"

"He's a Christian, master," Quartus said at once. "Most of Demas' millhands are Christians. They work around the clock over there, and he's on the night shift. If we went right away, we'd catch them at their supper, and you could have your talk without any trouble. Demas lives close by the Emporium."

"Let's go, then." Chilon rubbed his hands.

They set out at once for the Emporium, the great covered market-place that lay at the foot of the Aventine, not too far from the Circus Maximus. There was even a shortcut along the river, past the Emilian Gate, that saved them the trouble of going around Rome's famous seven hills.

"Ah," Chilon sighed when he and Quartus entered the colonnade. "I'm getting old. My memory isn't what it used to be. Wasn't our Christ betrayed by one of his disciples? Imagine, I can't quite remember what he called himself."

"It was Judas, master." Quartus wondered briefly how anyone could forget that name. "The one who hanged himself."

"That's right!" Chilon nodded. "Judas! That's the one. Thanks, my boy."

The Emporium was shut down for the night when they reached it. They went around it, passed the public granaries, and turned left toward the homes that stretched along the Via Ostiensis up to Mons Testacius and the great bread market of Forum Pistorium. They stopped in front of a wooden building that rumbled with the thumps and clatter of revolving millstones. Quartus went inside, but Chilon thought it best to wait in the street. He wasn't fond of showing himself to large groups of people, and there was always the fear of running into Glaucus.

"I wonder what he's like, this Hercules with flour in his hair," he mused while peering at the moonlit sky and the full white moon shining on the river. "If he's smart and vicious he'll cost me some money. If he's stupid, virtuous and a Christian, I'll get him for nothing."

Quartus came back just then with another man and broke in on his musing, and the Greek sighed with satisfaction. The other man wore only a short one-armed tunic, the kind called *exomis,* which allowed for full freedom of movement and was the normal garb of Rome's labor force. It left the right arm and the right half of the chest quite bare, and Chilon had never seen such a huge arm or such a massive chest.

"Here he is, master," Quartus said, "the brother you wanted to see."

"May the peace of Christ be with you," Chilon told the giant, and he nodded at Quartus. "Tell this good brother, my boy, whether I can be trusted and then go back home. You mustn't leave your old father alone like that."

"This is a saintly man," Quartus told the giant. "He didn't know me from Adam, but he gave everything he had to buy my freedom. May our Lord and Savior reward him in heaven."

The huge workman bowed his massive back, seized Chilon's hand and kissed it.

"What's your name, brother?" asked the Greek.

"I was baptized Urbanus, father," said the man. "That's my Christian name."

"Do you have time, brother Urbanus, for a quiet little talk?"

"I expect so, father. Our shift doesn't start until midnight. They've barely got around to cooking our supper."

"Then there's time to spare," said the Greek. "Walk with me by the river, why don't you, and I'll tell you what I came to say."

They found a place to sit on the stone embankment. It was quiet there, with only the hum and clatter of the millstones in the bakers' quarter and the soft rustle of the river at their feet. The workman's face wore the same grim look of dulled, sullen anger and regret that was common to most barbarians who had to live in Rome, but Chilon also thought he looked simple-minded, good-natured and honest. That's my man, he thought, hiding a smile. He's both good and stupid. He'll kill Glaucus for nothing.

"Urbanus," he said at last, "do you love Christ?"

"With all my heart and soul, master," the huge workman said.

"And how about your brothers and sisters in the faith? And what about those who taught you Christ's truth?"

"I love them, too, father."

"Then peace be with you, son."

"And with you, too, father."

There was another silence. As before, only the distant rumbling of the flour mill and the soft whisper of the water intruded on the quietness. Chilon fixed his eyes on the full white moon overhead and started talking about the death of Christ. He spoke in a quiet but exalted voice as if to himself, as if merely reflecting on the suffering and the glory of the crucifixion. It seemed as if he was not speaking to Urbanus but confiding and sharing the mystery with the sleeping city. The giant wept. He was immensely moved. And when the Greek started groaning in turn, bemoaning the fact that there was no one to defend the Savior at the moment of his death—from the actual crucifixion and from the jeers and insults of the mob and the soldiers—the barbarian's massive fists opened and clenched with misery and a half-stifled rage. It was clear the tale of suffering and death moved him to tears. But the thought of the howling mob with its sneers and insults standing beneath the cross filled his simple mind with a savage craving for revenge.

"Urbanus," the Greek said, turning to him suddenly. "Do you know who Judas was?"

"I know!" the simple giant burst out immediately. "I know! He's the one who hanged himself!"

His voice, Chilon noted, quivered with regret that the traitor had already applied his own justice and was out of reach.

"But what if he hadn't hanged himself?" Chilon went on quietly. "What if a good Christian was to meet him somewhere? Wouldn't it be his duty to avenge the Savior's suffering and death?"

"If only I could meet him!"

"Peace be with you, faithful servant of the lamb!" Pity and sadness crept into Chilon's voice, and then it hardened into a note of warning. "But, yes, you're quite right! It's fine for us to forgive trespasses against us, but who has the right to forgive injury to our God? And just as one snake is hatched by another, just as evil breeds evil and treachery spawns more treason, there's now another traitor plotting death and betrayal among us. And just as the old Judas sold our Savior to the temple and the Roman soldiers, so this new Judas plans to throw Christ's lambs to the wolves right here in Rome! And unless someone cuts the head off this serpent before he strikes, he'll destroy all of us and put an end to the worship of the holy lamb who died for our sins."

The huge workman stared at Chilon in extreme alarm, as if not quite able to grasp what he heard, and the Greek ducked his head under his cloak.

"Woe to you who serve the one true God." His thick muffled voice seemed to boom and roll deep under the ground like subterranean thunder. "Woe to all you Christian men and women!"

The pounding of the millstones, the dull rhythmic chant of the miller's workmen and the whisper of the river again intruded on another silence.

"Father?" the huge laborer asked at last. "Who's this traitor?"

Chilon let his head droop as if in despair. Who was this traitor? Ah, who indeed! The son of Judas himself, that's who. The seed of the poison tree and the hatchling steeped in his father's venom! The spy who played the Christian and went to prayer meetings, all the better to make his case against the whole community with Caesar. And what was he after? He plotted to denounce the Christians for refusing to worship Caesar as a god, to accuse them of poisoning the public wells and fountains and of murdering children, and to charge them with conspiracy to devastate the city so utterly that there wouldn't be one stone left standing atop another. Any day now, Chilon wailed in horror, the Praetorians would get their marching orders, seize and jail these poor old men, good women and defenseless children, and drag them to execution as they had the slaves of Pedanius Secundus.

"That's who he is, this second Judas, and that's what he's doing!" the Greek told the giant. "But if the first Judas escaped proper justice, if no one rose to defend Christ in his final torments or avenged him later, who would rise up to deal with this second one? Who'd trample the snake before he whispered his poisons into Caesar's ear? Who'd crush him and destroy him? Who'd save all his Christian brethren from utter destruction and preserve the faith?"

Urbanus sat all this time in silence, hunched over on one of the pilings of the stone embankment. But now he rose quickly.

"I'll do it, father," he said quietly, looking down at Chilon.

The Greek also clambered quickly to his feet. Bright moonlight bathed and revealed every line and furrow in the dark, determined face of the huge volunteer, and Chilon studied it intently for a

moment. Then he reached out in a ceremonial gesture, as if bestow-
ing an apostolic blessing and passing on a command from heaven, and
placed his palm on the bowed giant's head.

"Go you among the Christians," he intoned as grave as a bishop.
"Go to the house of prayer and ask the brethren to point out Glaucus
the physician. And when they've done so, kill him in Christ's name!"

"Glaucus," the giant repeated as if to drive the name into his memory.

"You don't know him, do you?"

"No, I don't. There are thousands of Christians in Rome, and they
don't all know one another. But every brother and sister in the city
will gather tomorrow night in the Ostrianum. The great apostle, the
one who knew the master, has come to Rome, and he'll be preaching
there. Every living soul among us will want to hear him. If Glaucus is
what you tell me, then he's bound to be there, too, and the brethren
will point him out to me."

"In the Ostrianum?" Chilon pressed, immediately alert. "Down by
the gravel pits and the old ice cellars? But that's on the other side of
the city walls somewhere, isn't it? All the brothers and all the sisters,
you say? Tomorrow night? Outside the gates in the Ostrianum?"

"Yes, father. We bury our dead out there between Via Salaria and
Via Nomentana. But didn't you hear that the great apostle will be
preaching there?"

"N-n-no." Chilon knew how strange this would sound to the
gigantic Christian. "I'm sure he wrote me but I haven't been home
for a couple of days so I missed the letter. As for not knowing about
the old sandpits—I mean the burial ground—well, I've just come
from Corinth where I led our community of Christians. But be that
as it may, since Christ inspired you to do what you must, my son,
then go to that Ostrianum tomorrow night, find Glaucus and kill him
on his way back to town. Do that and all your sins will be forgiven.
And now peace be with you!"

Pleased with his night's work, Chilon turned to go, but the huge
man stopped him.

"Father—"

"What is it, my dear lamb of God?" Chilon was moved to sudden
generosity. "Speak. Tell me. I'm all ears."

A vast embarrassment settled like a cloud on the giant's troubled
and unhappy face. He had a bad problem. It just so happened that he
had killed a man a few weeks ago, maybe even two, and Christ taught
that killing was a sin. No, he didn't kill anyone in his own defense—

that, too, was forbidden! Nor did he do it for profit, Christ help him! The bishop himself gave him some brethren to help out but he insisted that there be no killing. Well, he hadn't wanted to kill anybody; God just made his fists too heavy, that's all, and that's how it happened, and he'd been doing hard penance ever since. Oh how sorry he was, how he begged the lamb to forgive him, how he wept! Others sang at their work but all he did was think about his sin and how he offended the lamb and how he had to make amends for it. And now he promised to kill the new traitor.

"Well, that's a good thing," he muttered. "Vengeance is the Lord's when it comes to paying off some hurt to yourself, but something like this, well, that's a different story. So I'll kill him right in front of everybody tomorrow if that's what it takes."

Only, he begged, couldn't the word come from the elders, like maybe the bishop or the great apostle? "I mean," he said, "there's nothing to a killing. . . . I mean, it's even a good thing when it comes to traitors. They're like wolves or bears . . ." But what if Glaucus wasn't even guilty? How would he be able to have this new killing on his conscience, commit a fresh sin, and offend the lamb one more time?

"There's no time for a trial," Chilon said, alarmed. This pang of conscience could wreck everything. "Listen, my son, the traitor is to go to Caesar straight from Ostrianum, or he'll hide with a certain patrician he's working for. Look, I'll give you a sign to show the bishop and the great apostle. You do the deed as you're supposed to and show them the sign, and they'll bless you for it."

He dug one of the small silver pennies out of his money bag, groped for a knife hidden in his robes, found it and scratched a cross on the face of the coin.

"Here's the bishop's verdict and Glaucus' death sentence," he said, tossing the coin to the troubled giant. "Show this to the bishop after you've taken care of Glaucus, and he'll forgive that other sin as well."

The workman hesitated. He caught the coin but something continued to bother him, as if the earlier killing was too fresh in his memory or the new sin frightened him even before it happened.

"Father," he stammered out in a begging voice, "did you hear this Glaucus selling out the brethren? I mean, with your own ears? Are you taking this sin on yourself?"

Something had to be done, Chilon knew, to save the situation. The dimwit giant had to be convinced.

"Listen," he said as inspiration struck him, "I come from Corinth, as I said, but I was born in Cos, and I've been teaching Christ's way to a certain slave girl who comes from my island. Her name is Eunice, and she's a pleat-setter for this rich patrician who's a friend of Caesar's. His name is Petronius. Well, it's in his house that I heard Glaucus swear he'd sell out the whole community. What's more, he promised another friend of Caesar's, a certain Vinicius, that he'd track down some Christian girl who ran away from him. . . ."

The change that flashed across the giant's face took Chilon's breath away. The worry vanished. The uncertainty was gone. A feral light glinted in his eyes. Primordial rage narrowed the broad features.

"What's wrong with you?" Chilon was suddenly afraid.

"It's nothing, father." The grim giant looked murderous and determined. "Glaucus . . . is as good as dead."

But now another supposition glimmered in Chilon's mind. He grasped the huge workman by the shoulders and turned his face into the moonlight where he could watch it closely. Urbanus, was it? But what was his name before he was baptized? Light gleamed on the wide barbarian features and the enormous shoulders. One more question would answer everything, but the Greek grew suddenly more cautious. He paused, wondering if he should let well enough alone. It was sometimes better to leave some things unsaid. Things said too fast or too soon might panic the quarry.

He sighed and took a deep breath. Caution was always the best choice. He placed his palm on the giant's bowed head as before.

"Urbanus?" he asked in his lofty, ceremonial tone. "That's your baptismal name, is that right?"

"That's right, father."

"Then go in peace, Urbanus," the Greek said. "Peace be with you."

‹ 23 ›

PETRONIUS WROTE from Baiae to Vinicius as soon as he got the reply to his earlier letter.

"Things are bad with you, *carissime!*" he warned. "Venus must have addled your wits, taken away your powers of reason, your memory and your ability to think about anything but love. Read your own letter to me, and you'll see how far down that road you've gone. You're numb to everything but Ligia. Your thoughts keep coming back to her and to her alone. You hover over her like a hawk over his picked prey. By Pollux! Hurry up and find her, or you'll burn into a cinder or turn into another Sphinx who fell in love with Isis, the pale Egyptian goddess of the moon, lost his interest in everything else and just waits for night so that he can stare at her with his stony eyes.

"Do what you like about your searching in disguise at night. Go to the Christian prayer meetings with your philosopher if that makes you feel as if you're doing something. All this helps to kill time, fuels hope and does you no harm. But do me one favor if you want my friendship: This Ursus, Ligia's slave, is said to be immensely strong, so hire Croton as your bodyguard and take him on your searches. If Ligia and Pomponia belong to the Christians, then the sect can't be as vicious as everyone believes, but they've already shown us once, in rescuing Ligia, that they don't fool around when it comes to helping some lamb from their flock. I know you won't be able to control yourself when you finally see her, and you'll try to carry her off at once. And how will you do that with nobody but Chilon? Croton, however, will manage ten like that Lygian Ursus. Don't let Chilon cheat you, but don't skimp on Croton; he's worth every penny. I can't think of better advice to send you.

"We've now stopped talking about our dead little divinity over here. Nor do we talk anymore about spells or witchcraft. Poppea still mentions her now and then but Caesar has other things on his mind these days. Moreover, if it's true that Poppea is pregnant again, she'll soon forget about that other child. We've been in Naples for a few weeks now, or rather the neighboring Baiae. If your mind was free to function with anything but Ligia you'd have heard about us, I am sure, since all of Rome must be talking about nothing else. We've made our imperial progress to Baiae, a place of poignant memories for our Copperbeard, and we had a bout of filial guilt about our murdered mother. But do you know how far our dear Copperbeard has now descended into depravity and madness? His mother's murder is now just a theme for his versification and pseudotragic clowning. He used to feel some real remorse now and then—as far as his cowardice allowed it. Now that he's again convinced the world is under his feet as it's always been and that no gods are going to extract any vengeance from him, he puts on his show of grief so that everyone might feel sorry for him. He leaps out of bed at night and insists that the Furies are after him; he wakes everybody. He strikes an actor's pose like an imitation Orestes who slew his mother, Clytemnestra, to avenge his father, Agamemnon, and it's a mediocre act at best. He declaims Greek verses at us and peers to see if we're all fainting from admiration. And, of course, we are! Instead of telling him straight out, 'Go to bed, you jackass,' we turn into posturing tragedians and defend the great artist from his Furies!

"By Castor! You must have heard he had his public performance in Naples at last. They filled the proscenium with every Greek ragpicker in town and the outlying cities, and they choked the arena with so much sweat and garlic that I thanked the gods I was backstage with Nero rather than in the stalls among the augustians. Can you believe he was scared witless? Really! He was in utter terror! He clutched my hand and kept placing it on his heart, and it really did pound like a frantic drum. He gasped. He could hardly breathe. He knew perfectly well that every row out front had its praetorians armed with whips and cudgels to stimulate the audience, but he turned as white as a corpse and sweated profusely when it was time to go out on the stage. As it turned out, the praetorians weren't necessary. No herd of Carthaginian apes ever howled louder than that mob. The stench of garlic just about overpowered the stage.

"Nero took bow after bow, clutched his heart, sent kisses to the mob and wept happy tears. Then he fell backstage among us, drunk with his success, howling that no one ever had such an artistic triumph. The mob kept yelling, stamping and pounding in applause, knowing very well that it was clapping out his goodwill for itself, along with gifts, a free meal, free lottery tickets and a chance to see their Caesar as a posturing buffoon. I can't say I blame them in this regard, because no one has ever seen such a show before. Meanwhile he kept repeating: 'There, you see? That's the Greeks for you!' I think his hatred for Rome and the Romans soared to a new level that day, even though special couriers went flying to the city with news of his triumph, and we expect a thanksgiving message from the senate any day.

"A strange thing happened here, though, right after this performance. The theater collapsed. Everyone was out and gone by then and I didn't see one corpse pulled out of the rubble, but many people including some Greeks see this as a sign of anger among the gods for such a profanation of imperial dignity. He, on the contrary, sees it as proof of the gods' approval of his artistry and their special blessings on those who hear him sing. That means a flood of thanksgiving sacrifices in all the local temples and more encouragement for his trip to Greece. He told me a few days ago, however, that he's afraid of what the people of Rome might say about all that since they may run short of bread and circuses if he's away too long.

"Now we are off to Beneventum to see the cobbler's monkeyshines staged for us by Vatinius, and then onto Greece. As for me, I notice that even a civilized man goes mad when madness is the rule and that there's even a certain amount of charm in going crazy along with everybody else. Greece is a journey to the music of a thousand lutes, a kind of triumphant Bacchanalian progress among nymphs and dryads dressed in myrtle, vines and honeysuckle garlands, chariots drawn by tigers, all those wreaths and flowers and voices shouting 'Evoe!' Music, poetry, all of Greece thundering in applause—that's all very well, but we've some bolder projects in our imperial skull. We're planning the creation of some fabulous Eastern empire, a land of palms and sunshine, of poetry and reality turned into a permanent ongoing dream, and life itself transformed into endless bliss. We want to forget Rome and fix the center of the universe somewhere between Greece, Asia and Egypt. We want to live like the gods, free of all human concerns with reality, and drift in golden galleys under purple sails among the Greek islands. We see ourselves as the single personification of Apollo, Osiris and Baal all at the same time, glowing pink with the dawn, made golden by the sun, turning silver with the risen moon and ruling, singing and dreaming forever.

"I may still have a few brains and a small quantity of judgment, but can you believe that I let these fantasies carry me away? They may be totally impossible, but they're at least sweeping and unusual. But if such a fabulous fairy-tale empire could ever exist, it would seem like no more than a dream to people living many centuries later. Life is meaningless in memory or imagination unless it manifests itself in art, and even Venus becomes an illusion unless she takes the form of a Ligia or a Eunice. However, Copperbeard will never make his dream come true, because there'd be no room in that Eastern paradise of poetry for treachery, vulgarity and murder and because under his poor disguise as a poet, he's a cheap comedian, a stupid chariot driver and a petty-minded tyrant.

"Meanwhile we pass the time in strangling people who get in our way. Poor Torquatus Silanus is now among the shades. He slit his arteries a few days ago. Lecanius and Licinius are scared to death they might be made consuls. Old Thrasea dares to be honest, so he won't avoid death before very long. Tigellinus still hasn't managed to get me an order to open my own veins; I'm still needed here as the arbiter of good taste and discrimination and as a man whose absence might spoil some of the Greek triumphs. I do think, however, now and then, that this too must happen sooner or later. When it does, my sole concern will be that Copperbeard doesn't get his hands on that exquisite vase of mine you admired. I'll give it to you if you're there when I die or smash it if you aren't. In the meantime we still have the cobbler's Beneventum ahead of us, along with Olympian Greece and whatever else the fates bring our way.

"Keep well and hire Croton or you'll lose Ligia for a second time. Send Chilon to me wherever I may be when you're finished with him. I might turn him into a second Vatinius, and then all the senators and consuls can quake before him as they do before that other knight of the cobbler's awl. It would be a sight worth waiting for. Let me know when you find Ligia; I'd like to offer two pairs of doves and swans for the two of you to Venus in her local temple. I saw your Ligia in one of my dreams, seated on your knees and seeking your kisses. Try to turn that dream into a prophecy.

"May there be no clouds in your sky," Petronius finished, "but if there are, let them have the color and perfume of a rose. Be well and good-bye."

‹24›

VINICIUS FINISHED READING just as Chilon slipped into the library, quiet as a shadow and not announced by servants, since the household had orders to let him come and go at will, at any time of day or night.

"May Venus, the divine mother of your ancestor Aeneas, be as kind to you," the Greek said on entering, "as Mercury, the divine son of Maia, was to me."

"What does that mean?" Vinicius leaped up from behind the table where he had been sitting.

The Greek looked up, eyes level with Vinicius'. "Eureka!" he said in imitation of that other Greek philosopher who sought the light of truth.

The young patrician was so swept by feeling that he couldn't say a word for quite a while. "You saw her?" he managed at last.

"I saw Ursus, my lord, and I spoke with him."

"And you know where they're hiding?"

"No, my lord. A lesser man might let himself be blinded by his own perspicacity into letting the Lygian guess he knew who he was, and so either get struck by a fist that would make him oblivious to all things thereafter or prod the giant's suspicions to the point that he changed the girl's hiding place that very night. That, my lord, I didn't do. It's enough for me that he works for a miller named Demas near the Emporium, the same name, by the way, as that of your freedman; and it's enough, my lord, because any trusted slave of yours can follow him home from work in the morning and pinpoint their hideout. I merely bring you proof that your divine Ligia is in Rome, since Ursus is also here, and that she's almost sure to be at the Ostrianum tonight."

"Ostrianum?" Vinicius broke in, looking ready to run there at once. "Where is that?"

"It's that area of old catacombs and cellars between Via Salaria and

Via Nomentana. The chief priest of theirs whom I mentioned to you is here now, much sooner than expected, and he'll be preaching and baptizing in that boneyard tonight. There are still no edicts to make them illegal, but they must be careful to hide their meetings because the people hate them. Ursus himself told me all of them will gather today in Ostrianum to see and hear that man. He was the first disciple of their Christ, and they call him the apostle, or the spreader of the faith. Since their women are admitted as freely as the men to all their practices, Pomponia will probably be the only one who won't be there tonight. Aulus Plautius worships the old gods, and she wouldn't be able to explain to him why she wanted to go out at night. Ligia, however, my lord, living under the care of Ursus and their elders, is sure to be there with every other woman."

Vinicius had lived through bitter weeks where only hope seemed to keep him alive. Now, watching that hope bloom into the start of life, he felt as spent as a traveler who comes to the end of the road with his last ounce of strength.

Nor did Chilon fail to read the signs or to read in them a chance for a profit.

"True," he observed, "the gates are watched by your men, my lord, and the Christians must know all about it. But they don't need a gate, they have the Tiber, and though it's a fair distance from the river to the other roads, it's worth the walk to see the great apostle. There are a thousand other ways to get across the walls, and I am sure they know every one of them.

"So, my lord," he went on, heading toward the point, "in Ostrianum you will find your Ligia. Or if she's not there, by some stroke of fate that I can't imagine, then you will have Ursus! He'll be there because that's where he's going to murder Glaucus for me. Yes, he's our hired killer! You get the point, distinguished tribune? No? Well, then, you'll either follow him home yourself and find out where they live or have him seized as a murderer and get the truth about her out of him one way or another.

"I've done my part." Chilon moved smoothly to his desired conclusion. "A lesser man would tell you he drank a vineyard's worth of the finest wine with Ursus before he got the secret out of him. Another would claim he lost a thousand sesterces playing twelve-card draw with him or matching dominoes, or rolling dice, or that he spent twice that much buying information. I know you'd double it for me, and rightly so, but let me be honest for once in my life . . . or, rather, as I've been through my whole existence. I trust that your munificence will exceed all my hopes as well as my expenses, as was suggested by that most munificent of patrons, the noble Petronius."

Vinicius was a soldier, used to coping with the unexpected of all kinds and quick to take action. Chilon's hopeful valedictory gave him time to recover from his surge of weakness.

"You won't be disappointed in my munificence," he snapped out, impatient, "but first you'll go with me to the Ostrianum."

"I, my lord? To the Ostrianum?" Going there was the last thing Chilon had in mind. "I promised to find Ligia for you, not abduct her. Just think, lord, what would happen to me if it dawned on that Lygian bear that he'd just torn Glaucus to shreds without a real reason. Wouldn't he point to me, wrongly as it happens, as the cause of his crime? The hardest thing for a philosopher, my lord, is to talk to idiots, so how would I answer the questions he asked me?"

Profit, however, had to be protected in any event. "But if you think I'm leading you astray, most distinguished tribune, then pay me in full when I point out Ligia's hiding place. For now, just show me enough of your generosity so that if some mishap should befall you, my lord—which may all the gods protect against!—I wouldn't stay entirely without a reward. Your great noble heart, my lord, would never allow that!"

"Here are some scrupula." Vinicius tossed him a satchel filled with the small gold sovereigns worth one-third of the gold denarius. "When I have Ligia in my house you'll get one like it full of denarii."

"O Jove," Chilon hailed him, "father of all the gods, who nourishes mankind!"

But Vinicius now wore a commanding frown. "You'll eat and rest here until dark. Don't even dream of stirring from this house. And when it's night, you'll go with me to the Ostrianum."

Fear and doubt showed briefly in the Greek's narrow foxlike face, but he soon calmed down.

"'Who can resist you, lord!'" he quoted words said to Alexander, the Macedonian conqueror of the East, by an Egyptian priestess whom he ordered seized. "Take this in the same spirit that our great Greek hero took in the temple of Ammon. Nobody can resist you, so it's best to surrender with good grace. As for me, your 'scruples'"—and here he jingled the purseful of sovereigns—"outweigh any of mine. Not to mention the joy of your company tonight."

But Vinicius had no patience with word games. He pressed Chilon for details: What else did Ursus say? And how did he say it? Two choices emerged from what he heard and both sent his expectations soaring. He would either know Ligia's hideout before this night was over, or he'd seize her on her way back from the prayer meeting and carry her off. A fierce joy gripped Vinicius at this thought. All the anger directed at Ligia vanished in an instant now that it seemed likely he'd have her back again. Grateful for the sudden sense of relief and fulfillment, he forgave her any bitterness or disappointment. He thought of her only as a precious being whom he needed with him, as if she were a lover who had been badly missed and was coming home after a long journey. He had an urge to order garlands strung throughout the house. He hated no one; not even Ursus merited a complaint. He was ready to forgive everyone for everything that had happened. Chilon, whom he despised no matter what services he rendered, now seemed to him both notable and funny. His eyes shone, his face glowed with life, and even the shadows of his house seemed cheerful and brighter. Youth and the joy of life awoke in him again. His gloomy suffering hadn't let him judge the full extent of his love for Ligia; he grasped it only now, expecting her return. He wanted her—oh, yes he wanted her—but the need was different; it was now something like the anticipation with which cold winter soil awaits the sun of springtime. Free at last of hurt and humiliation, he could see beyond the fierce imperatives of lust into a softer joy and a kinder feeling. He also felt immense energy and strength filling his whole body; nothing, he was convinced—neither all the Christians in the world nor Caesar himself—would be able to wrest Ligia away from him once he actually saw her.

His vast, brimming joy put some encouragement in Chilon, who now felt braver and better about his own prospects, and who started offering more advice. The game was not yet in the bag, he cautioned; they must exercise the greatest possible care or risk spoiling the whole painstaking plot. He begged Vinicius not to try seizing Ligia in the Ostrianum.

"We should go there in hooded cloaks, keep our faces hidden and just watch everything that happens out of some dark corner. Our safest way is to follow her home once we've spotted her, note the building she enters without coming out again and then surround it at dawn with a mass of slaves and take her in broad daylight."

The law, he pointed out, was on their side. She was still a hostage, officially under Caesar's jurisdiction, so the authorities wouldn't interfere. If for some reason Ligia wasn't at the Ostrianum, they'd follow Ursus with the same effect.

"We can't take a lot of men with us," Chilon warned. "They'd only alert the Christians. Then all they'd have to do is put out the lights, as they did the first time they abducted Ligia, vanish in the darkness and go to ground in some secret hideouts only they know about. But let's have weapons with us. And let's take one or two strong men we can depend on in case things go wrong."

Vinicius agreed with everything he said. Petronius' advice prompted him to send slaves for Croton, which finally set Chilon's last worries at rest. The Greek knew everybody in the public eye; he never missed the gladiatorial games in the arena and often admired the superhuman strength of the famous wrestler. Yes, he said, he'd go to the Ostrianum. Gladly! With Croton's help the promised sack of gold *denarii* seemed to be jingling a lot closer than before.

He sat down to his supper in good spirits, summoned soon afterward to the table in the servants' quarters, where he told the slaves all about the marvelous magic lotion he had just sold their master. It was enough to smear it on the hooves of the sorriest nag, he said, and it would leave every other racehorse in the dust. He, Chilon, learned how to mix the lotion from a certain Christian. The Christian elders knew more about miracles and magic than even Thessalonians, although Thessaly was famous for its witches. They held him in great veneration, he said, and trusted him implicitly, which would be clear to anyone who understood the sign of the fish.

He shot sharp questioning glances into all the faces hovering around him, hoping for some sign betraying a Christian whom he'd be able to denounce later to Vinicius. When this hope failed him, he shrugged and set about his meal, eating and drinking far more than he normally did, showering the cook with praise and promising to try buying him from Vinicius. Only the thought of going that night to the Ostrianum took some of the pleasure out of his satisfaction with himself, but that would all take place in the dark, in disguise, and he wouldn't be going there alone. One of his companions was the mightiest man alive, the killer idol of the populace, while the other was a high-born, powerful patrician, who was moreover an important military officer.

"They won't dare touch Vinicius even if they catch on to who and what he is," he reassured himself. "As for me, they'll be lucky to see the end of my nose."

That, he thought, was more like it, and he focused on his talk with the giant workman. This made him feel even better. He didn't have the slightest doubt the giant was Ursus. He knew about this man's enormous physical strength from Vinicius and from the slaves who had escorted Ligia from the Palatine. He had asked Euricius to find him a real strongman, hadn't he? So to whom would he send him if not Ursus? And then there was that flash of angry recognition when he mentioned Ligia and Vinicius; there was no question that the giant sat up at their names and that this was something which really concerned him.

Yes, he thought. No question about it. Everything else also fitted like a well-worn glove. The huge miller's helper talked about a penance because he had killed someone, while Ursus crushed the skull of Atacinus. Moreover he closely fit the description given by Vinicius. Only the change of name caused a doubt, but Chilon knew the Christians often took new names when they were baptized.

"If Ursus kills Glaucus," Chilon reassured himself, "that'll be just fine. But if he doesn't, it'll go to prove how hard it is for Christians to kill anyone, even to defend themselves, and that's good to know. Of course he ought to kill him. I would in his place. I painted him a picture of Glaucus as Judas' own son, maybe even more dangerous than the father and as the sworn enemy and betrayer of every living Christian. My reasoning and eloquence would have moved a cornice to fall off a roof and bounce on Glaucus' head, but I barely managed to convince that Lygian bear to lay a paw on him. He wasn't sure. He didn't want to. He mumbled about his remorse and his penance. Apparently bloodshed doesn't sit well with them. If they must turn the other cheek, as they say, and forgive any trespasses against them, and if they aren't allowed to seek revenge for others, just think, dear Chilon, what can threaten you? Glaucus can't go after what he thinks he has coming from you. And if Ursus doesn't murder Glaucus for as great a reason as mortal danger to all his fellow Christians, would he be likely to kill you for betraying a single one?"

Besides, he knew, once he pointed out the nesting ground of the little Lygian turtledove to the wild-maned Roman stallion he was serving, he'd be able to wash his hands of the whole thing and return to Naples.

"The Christians also talk about some handwashing. It must be a way to settle things among them. They're so strangely good, these Christians, but they have such a terrible reputation. Well, that's the justice of things in this world."

Chilon decided that he rather liked what little he had learned so far about Christian teaching. He was particularly impressed with their attitude about killing. It followed, as a simple philosophic line, that if there was no killing, there'd be no theft, cheating or perjury against others, which would make this teaching a hard one to follow. The Stoics taught how to die with dignity; the Christians seemed to teach how to live honest lives.

"If I'm ever rich," Chilon mused, "and live in a house like this one, with so many slaves, I might try a bit of this Christianity myself, for as long as I get something out of it. Why not? The rich can afford anything they want, even virtue. This is a rich man's religion, that's clear, but I can't quite understand why they have so many poor people among them. What can they ever get out of being good? Why let their goodness hamstring them like this? I'll have to give this a little thought sometime. Meanwhile hail to thee, Mercury or Hermes, winged messenger of the gods and patron of dexterity, for helping me smoke out this Lygian badger.

"But"—Chilon's satisfied murmur took on a mocking tone—"if you did that for those two white yearling heifers with gilded horns we once talked about, then I am amazed! Shame on you, god of thieves and tricksters. Such a smart god, and he couldn't foresee he wouldn't get a thing? I offer you my gratitude instead. And if you'd rather have two heads of cattle, then yours is the third, and you'd make a better drover than you do a god. Bear in mind also that I'm a philosopher, and it's best to get on a philosopher's good side. A good philosopher shouldn't have much trouble proving you don't exist, and then who'd make sacrifices to you?"

Ending this pleasant private chat with Hermes-Mercury, Chilon stretched out on a bench, bundled his cloak under his head and fell asleep the moment the slaves cleared the table. He slept until he was awakened at Croton's arrival and hurried to see him in the atrium. He found him closing his deal with Vinicius, and he looked with pleasure at the vast muscular figure that seemed to fill the entire atrium. Croton was the unbeaten fist fighter of Rome, a champion wrestler who taught sword fighting in the gladiators' school, and a great former gladiator himself. Now he was telling Vinicius about his next contest.

"By Hercules! It's a good thing you came to me today, sir," he said rather grandly. "Tomorrow I'll be going to Beneventum where the noble Vatinius called me to fight Syphax, the most powerful black ever spawned in Africa, before the court of Caesar. Hah! Can you hear his backbone crackling in my fists, my lord? I'll crush his skull with this one."

"By Pollux!" said Vinicius. "I'm sure you will."

"And you'll do well to do it," Chilon added quickly. "Yes! Crack his spine, crush his skull, and smash his chin as well! That goes with your image. I'm willing to bet you'll destroy his jaws with one blow! In the meantime I suggest you oil your muscles and get set to do your very best, because the man you might come up against is a real Cacus."

Cacus, as everyone in Rome knew, was a son of Vulcan, the blacksmith of the gods who manufactured thunder, and a proverbial giant of immense body strength who robbed and looted everyone around his cave in the Aventine until Hercules killed him for stealing his cattle. Croton didn't seem impressed, however.

"The man who guards the young lady that his distinguished lordship is concerned about is said to be exceptionally powerful," Chilon added to excite the wrestler.

"That's right," Vinicius tossed in. "I never saw him do this, but I'm told he can wrestle a bull and drag it anywhere he wants."

"Aii!" Chilon never thought Ursus could be that strong.

But Croton merely smiled with contempt. "This fist," he said, lifting a huge hand, "will seize and hold anyone you want, my lord. This other will keep seven such Lygians at bay while I bring the girl to your house. I'll do it even if all the Christians come howling after me like Calabrian wolves. And if I fail, sir, you can have me flogged right here in this *impluvium*."

"Don't do that, master!" Chilon cried, alarmed. "They'll stone us, and what good will his muscles do us then? Wouldn't it make more sense to take the girl quietly out of her own house, without risk to anyone including herself?"

Vinicius agreed. "That's how we'll do it, Croton!" he ordered.

"It's your money, sir." Croton shrugged. "You get what you order. Just bear in mind I'll be going to Beneventum tomorrow."

"I have five hundred slaves here in Rome alone," Vinicius said in answer. Then he waved them out, went to his library, and sat down to write a quick message to Petronius.

"Chilon has found Ligia. I'm going with him and Croton to Ostrianum, and I'll either have her seized there tonight or from her home tomorrow. May the gods pour all their good fortunes on you, my dear friend. Be well, *carissime*. My joy won't let me write any more for now."

The joy was one thing, but impatience also gnawed at him like a fever. He threw down his stylus and started pacing the room quickly. He kept repeating to himself that Ligia would be in his house tomorrow. He didn't know what would happen then or how either one of them would react; he knew, however, that if she felt and showed any love for him, he'd be hers to do with as she wished. He recalled Acte's words about Ligia's feelings and found himself shaken to his own emotional depths. It looked as if all he'd have to do was help her through some sort of modest virginal reluctance and whatever it was the Christians taught about such things. And if that was it, if Ligia was in his home at last and if she surrendered to either his urging or his superior strength, then surely she'd say, "Let it be if it has to be," and become his caring and willing lover from then on.

Chilon slipped into the room again and broke in on his musing.

"Something else occurred to me, my lord," he said. "What if the Christians have some special signs or passes to get into the catacombs today? That's how it is in their prayer houses, I know. In fact Euricius gave me such a pass right at the beginning. Let me check with him about all that and get whatever we'll need."

"Very well." Vinicius nodded, but something else occurred to him as well. "You're shrewd and cunning, my superb philosopher. I appreciate your foresight. Go where you please but leave your gold right here on this table just to make sure you come back to take me to the meeting. I wouldn't want you to think the job was done."

Chilon hated to part with the money, but he had no choice. He shrugged, allowed himself a wry, reluctant grin and went on his way. It wasn't far from the Carinnae to the Colosseum where Euricius had his stall, so he was back long before evening.

"Here are those recognition signs, my lord," he said, laying a few small objects on the table. "We wouldn't get in without them. I made sure to get the best directions, while I was about it. I told Euricius I needed these passes for some friends. As far as he knows I won't be there tonight. I told him it's too far for an old man like me. Moreover as far as he knows I'll be seeing the great apostle in private tomorrow, and he'll cite his best passages to me then."

"What do you mean you won't be there?" Vinicius wasn't paying all that much attention. His thoughts were soaring in clouds of their own. "Of course you will go!"

"Yes, of course, my lord. If I must, I must, but they won't know anything about it. I'll go well hooded, and I advise you and Croton to do the same. We wouldn't want to startle the birds, would we?"

Evening began soon after, and they started getting ready for the expedition. They put on thick, voluminous Gallic cloaks with deep hoods and carried small screened lanterns. Vinicius also armed himself and the others with curved Eastern daggers, while Chilon donned a wig he had picked up on his way back from Euricius' shop. They went out and hurried through the darkening streets, wanting to get to the Nomentan Gate while it was still open.

‹ 25 ›

THEY WENT THROUGH the Vicus Patricius and along the slopes of
Mount Viminalis, one of the seven hills of Rome, named for a willow
grove that grew there. They circled it all the way to the old Viminalis
Gate that led to the temple of Jupiter Viminius. Next to it spread a
sandy waste where Diocletian would later build his baths.

They passed the remnants of the wall built there by Servius Tullius
and walked through a gradually widening wasteland until they came
to the Nomentum road. They followed that until it turned left
toward Salaria. It may have been significant that the Via Nomentana
led to the old country of the Sabines, which the founders of Rome
had looted for its women. Here they found themselves in a hilly landscape, dotted with sandpits, gravel pits and quarries, and old burial
grounds.

The night was well settled by the time they got there, but the
moon had not yet climbed into the sky. They would have had a difficult time and gotten lost if—as Chilon had foreseen so wisely—the
Christians didn't help them. Shadowy figures slipping cautiously
toward the dunes, sandpits, and the old burial grounds beyond them
loomed in the darkness everywhere around them. Some carried
lanterns, shielding them under their cloaks when they could. Others,
who looked as if they knew the way, walked without a light. Even at a
distance Vinicius' sharp military eye caught the difference between
the firm movements of the young people, the stumbling stoop of the
old, and the quick fluid motion of the women.

He supposed that if such mass gatherings happened here often, the
few passersby and peasants who might catch sight of them that late
after sundown would take them for quarrymen heading for the pits
or for some burial society that held ritual observances at one or
another of the cemeteries.

As they went on, however, lamplight glowed and flickered more
openly around the young patrician and his two companions, and the

dark, shadowy figures began to grow in number and become increasingly more distinct. Some of them chanted hymns in low quiet voices that Vinicius thought were filled with strange sadness. He caught snatches of words and phrases such as "sleeper awake" and "arise from the dead," and the name of Christ was spoken with rising frequency by the men and women.

But Vinicius concentrated wholly on what he saw rather than on what he heard; his attention was scarcely diverted by words. He was focused on a single thought: Which of those nearing forms was Ligia? "Peace be with you," they said as they passed closer, or "Praise Christ," but his heart pounded all the harder, and anxiety settled on him like a cloud, because he thought he could hear Ligia's voice. A glimpse of a certain shape or silhouette in the darkness confused him; some well-remembered gesture or way of moving convinced him for an exhilarating moment. Only after a closer look revealed his mistake did he start to distrust his eyes.

The way seemed rather long to him. He knew the general area quite well, he had been there before, but he couldn't orient himself in it in the dark. There was a continuing run of narrow passages, sudden walls and ruins, and even buildings he didn't recall. Then at long last the moon began to edge out of the gathered clouds to brighten the landscape better than the lanterns. Something—a light—glowed up ahead like an open bonfire or the massed flames of torches.

"Is that Ostrianum?" Vinicius whispered to Chilon.

Chilon had not had a good time so far. The night, the distance to the city, and these shadowy forms that seemed like wraiths and spirits shook him quite a bit.

"I don't know, my lord," he quavered in complaint. "I've never been to Ostrianum. But they could've found themselves a place closer to the city to worship their Christ."

He apparently needed to talk just then, perhaps to put a little stiffness into his spine. "They're creeping together like bandits," he muttered, "but aren't they forbidden to kill anybody? Unless that Lygian lied to me, the ungrateful scoundrel."

Vinicius also wondered about that. Full as he was of thinking about Ligia, he was surprised by the secretiveness and caution with which her coreligionists gathered to hear their most important patriarch.

"Like most religions," he observed, "this one has supporters among our own kind. But the Christians are a Jewish sect, aren't they? So why do they gather here when the Trans-Tiber is full of Jewish temples where they could meet openly in daylight?"

"No, my lord." Chilon had the answer. "The Jews hate them more than anyone. It's some split in their religion or a heresy or some-thing, and they're very touchy about things like that. I've heard it almost came to war between Jews and Christians here in Rome in the times of our former Caesar. Emperor Claudius finally had enough of their riots and squabbles and drove out the lot of them, of whatever sect, but that was all a long time ago and they've all come back. The decree has been canceled anyway. . . . But these Christians hide less from the Jews than from our own people. As you know, my lord, they're hated by almost everybody because everybody believes they are criminals."

They walked in silence for a while, and Chilon became more uneasy the farther they went beyond the gates. He couldn't stop talk-ing.

"I borrowed a wig from a barber's stall," he said, as if this constant repetition made him feel better about his chances. "They shouldn't be able to tell who I am. I also stuck two elephant beans up my nose to make it seem wider. But they won't kill me even if they do recognize me. These aren't bad people. On the contrary they're a decent, hon-est lot. I've become quite fond of them and think highly of them."

"Don't be too fast with your accolades," Vinicius said. "Let's first see if they deserve your praises."

The ground dipped before them into a narrow defile, framed on two sides by broad trenches, with a tall stone aqueduct arcing above it at one point. The moon had cleared the cloud bank in the mean-time, and they saw a long walled enclosure overgrown with ivy that moonlight turned silver.

"The Ostrianum," Vinicius said, and his heart started beating faster than before.

Two grave diggers collected the passes and recognition signs at the open cemetery gate, and they passed between them. They found themselves in a wide, walled area, with solitary monuments and tombstones scattered here and there and with the entrance to the subterranean catacombs in the middle beside a rustling fountain. It was clear that the crypt itself was too small for so many people. Vinicius guessed that the rituals would take place in the open air. A dense crowd had been gathering for some time; lanterns glowed side by side wherever he glanced, but a great many people carried no lights at all. A few had bared their heads, but most remained hooded against the night chill or out of fear of being recognized. If that's how they stayed until the end, the young patrician worried, he'd find it impossible to identify Ligia in this dense, dark throng, considering how poorly lighted the place was.

But suddenly a few pine torches flamed beside the entrance to the catacombs and formed a small, smoky bonfire on the ground. The light became sharper. A strange hushed chant started quietly among the waiting thousands, and it gradually grew louder. Vinicius never heard this kind of music before. He picked up the same deep note of longing and regret he had heard on the road, hummed and sung in low voices by occasional passersby earlier in the night, but now, multiplied by a thousand voices, it swelled into a vast imploring sigh. Faith and a profound sense of hope and suffering rang in this pleading chorus, becoming clearer and stronger and more pronounced and pressing, until it seemed that the entire burial ground, along with the sandpits, hillocks and open land around it, was singing to the stars along with the people.

And there was something else in this strange, sad music, this cry in the night: It was as if a whole world, lost and confused in darkness, begging to be shown the way home, was sending up a humble plea for guidance and direction. Those trusting, upraised eyes seemed fixed on some being high in the sky. Those upthrust hands implored him to come down among them. In moments when the hymn dwindled, the hushed, suppressed longing turned into such a powerful and confident expectation, that Vinicius and his two companions shot anxious glances of their own into the stars, half-fearing something incredible would happen and that someone would step down from the clouds.

And there was yet another quality to the ritual that surprised Vinicius. He had been in every kind of temple in Asia Minor, Egypt and Rome itself and had been exposed to a variety of teachings and heard many anthems, but this was the first time he heard people calling out to God with overwhelming love, like children crying out to a good father or a loving mother, rather than as part of some required ritual. He would have to be blind, he knew, not to see that these people not only worshiped their god but actually loved him, and this was something new to him. No ritual or temple in any country ever showed him truly loving people; there simply wasn't any such thing in this era of the Roman empire. And those few people who still worshiped the gods in Rome and Greece did so either to enlist their help or to stay in their good graces, but no one would even think of offering them love.

His mind was almost totally occupied with Ligia and his attention was almost wholly focused on finding her in the hooded crowds, but he couldn't help noticing all these strange and astonishing things around him. Meanwhile a few more burning torches were tossed into the bonfire, and a sharp scarlet light spread through the burial ground, dimming the glow of lanterns. An elderly man, dressed in the same homespun hooded cloak as the rest but with the hood thrown back, came out of the crypt and stepped up on a boulder near the fire.

The crowd around Vinicius tensed and swayed. He heard quick voices whispering, *"Petrus! Petrus!"* Some people knelt, others reached out to him, as if to touch him across the distance. Their silence was so absolute that he heard the sputter of a single ember breaking off a torch, the far-off thump and rattle of cartwheels on the highway, and the sigh of the wind in the few pines that stood near the graveyard.

Chilon edged closer to his ear. "That the one they call the fisherman! Chrestos' first disciple."

The old man raised his arm, blessed the gathered Christians with a sign of the cross, and the whole vast throng sunk to its knees like a single creature. Chilon and Croton did the same to blend with the others, and so did Vinicius. The young man didn't quite know what to think of anything he felt. The old man seemed both extraordinary and simple, so unusual as to appear almost mythical, yet so ordinary as to be commonplace; and it suddenly occurred to Vinicius that this extraordinary power he sensed in the man came out of that simplicity. The old man stood with his head bared in the wind. He did not wear a cope, a miter or an oak-leaf wreath clasped about his temples, as did every other priest Vinicius had ever met; he didn't hold a reed or palm frond in his hands or have a gold tablet dangling from his neck; he did not wear white robes embroidered with stars or celestial symbols. There were more than two hundred major and minor gods worshiped throughout the empire, but he was like no Eastern, Egyptian, Greek or Roman priest Vinicius ever saw and showed none of their badges of distinction. He was struck again by the sense of mystery and difference he felt while listening to the Christian hymns. Nothing about this "fisherman" suggested a chief priest, skilled in the manipulation of ritual and dogma. He projected the patient, unassuming image of a simple, ordinary old man who has traveled far to tell about something real and important; a living witness to some truth he has seen and touched and in which he believes. It was clear even to an unbeliever that he perceived this truth as if it explained all of reality and that he loved it because he believed it. His face carried the power of unshakable conviction, the kind that came only from the truth.

By choice a skeptic, finding his explanations in nature and the world around him, Vinicius didn't want to feel himself enthralled or enchanted. But he caught himself biting his own lips with suppressed impatience, so anxious to hear this man that he seemed on fire with a fever. He couldn't wait to learn from the lips of this man himself— this first and last companion of the mysterious "Chrestos"—what that religion taught and why that teaching had become the faith of Ligia and Pomponia Graecina.

‹26›

WHEN PETER SPOKE, it was at first like a father admonishing his children and teaching them how to live. He told them to give up all excesses and the pursuit of material pleasures, to practice piety and virtue in every thought and deed, to turn their thoughts to God rather than the flesh, to be humble in their poverty, to love one another like sisters and brothers, to live simply and cleanly and always speak the truth. He enjoined them to show humility in the face of harm and persecution, to respect the laws of God and obey authority, to rid themselves of mistrust, treachery, hypocrisy and malice, and to offer an example of goodness to one another and to the pagans as well.

Some of this preaching irritated and upset Vinicius. Good, as far as he cared about it, was anything that would give him Ligia, while evil was everything that stood in the way. Moreover some of these shopworn homilies seemed pointed and offensive; in urging struggle against impurity and curbing the demands of the flesh, the old preacher struck directly at his love for Ligia. The young soldier was all the more alarmed by the likelihood that Ligia was out there in the night somewhere, listening to these injunctions, and that they would drive an even deeper wedge between them. If she took them to heart she would push him away even farther, he was sure; she would be confirmed and reinforced in her resistance to him, and fight all the harder. He had no doubt that if she still thought about him in any way at all, she would have to see him now as an enemy of her faith, a profligate and a scoundrel.

"What on earth is this?" he muttered to himself, angry and disdainful because he was uneasy. "What's new about this teaching? Where's the mystery? It's all common knowledge, old-hat rhetoric masquerading as some revolutionary new philosophy. The Cynics have long been preaching self-denial. The Peripatetics take pride in their poverty. Socrates himself recommended goodness as an old remedy for human frailty and folly. Any roadside Stoic praises moderation, even one as rich and spoiled as Seneca with his collection of five hundred tables; every true thinker recommends truth as a way of life, advises patience in adversity, and suggests endurance in misfortune."

All of this had the sound of an old wives' tale made dull by repetition. It nudged his senses with the smell of dry rot, like a pile of discarded corn turning to dust beside a road. "The world has had enough of that pap," he muttered in contempt. "People can't swallow any more of it, they don't want to touch it, which is why nobody even talks about it. So what are they after?"

Angry, he also found himself oddly disappointed. He had expected . . . oh, he didn't really know what he had expected. But it had to be at least a revelation, perhaps the plumbing of some unfathomable mysteries; if nothing else, he thought he would listen to some brilliant orator whose eloquence would give new meaning to the art of rhetoric. Instead he heard simple, unornamented phrases, bluntly if kindly spoken, and as plain and ordinary in style and context as a kitchen spoon. The only thing surprising about it all, he thought, was that this vast, hushed throng listened to the man in totally absorbed and attentive silence.

Meanwhile the man kept talking. He told his rapt listeners to be kind, gentle, modest in their needs and clean in their living. Why? Not merely to get through their temporal lives without a lot of trouble but "to live in Christ after death" and to bloom there forever in such joy, happiness and glory as no one on earth could ever imagine. Vinicius may have been annoyed and ill-disposed in advance toward this new teaching, but he was fair to note that there *was* a difference between this man's vision and that of the Cynics, the Stoics and all the other philosophers of the age. They proposed a clean, healthy use of the mind and body as a rational and sensible daily practice that would pay its own reward in the life of the practitioner; he, this strange old man with his simple phrases, promised immortality. And not just the gray arid vacuum inhabited in perpetuity by the wandering shades or lone souls doomed to an eternity of subterranean boredom but an eternity of glory that rivaled the magnificence of the gods. Moreover he spoke of this eternity as something absolutely certain, and in the light of such faith and such convictions, unblemished conduct acquired a value beyond price or limit. Life's tragedies, on the other hand, became insignificant; suffering for a while to achieve an eternity of joy was far different, Vinicius could suppose, than enduring pain as a law of nature.

But the old preacher went on to say in his ordinary, artless phrases that truth and goodness were to be loved for their own sake because they were God. Others might argue, but he merely stated as if it were obvious, that God was endless goodness and a timeless truth. It followed, then, with the authority of his absolute conviction, that he who loved these things loved God and thus became God's own beloved child.

This was especially difficult for Vinicius to grasp. He knew from what he had heard Pomponia tell Petronius that this Christian God was all-powerful and singular, drawing into himself all the powers of every other deity; now he was hearing that this Judean *avatar* was also the eternal good and the eternal truth. It flashed into his mind that Jupiter, Saturn, Apollo, Juno, Vesta and Venus Aphrodite didn't compare too well with such a demiurge. Beside such a godhead they seemed like a shrill clique of bickering adolescents who plotted and played malicious tricks on everybody else, alone and together. But the greatest amazement fell on the young man when he heard that God was also love, the beginning and the end of all understanding, caring and compassion, and that he who loved others worshiped him the best.

"Moreover"—the old man spoke now as a teacher as well as a father—"it's not enough to love just one's own kind; God died a man's death on the cross, he spilled his blood for all mankind, and even the pagans are turning toward him now, for example, the centurion Cornelius. . . . And it's not enough to love only those who love and treat you well. Christ forgave his executioners. He removed all blame from the Jews who turned him over to Roman justice to be crucified and from the Roman soldiers who nailed him to the cross."

The best love, he said, was the one that repaid suffering, unfairly imposed, along with forgiveness, "because evil must always be repaid with good."

Nor was that enough. Love, as these people knew it, was to be offered not merely to others of goodwill but also to those driven by the dark, malevolent forces of anger and hatred.

"Only love is more powerful than hatred," the teacher said simply. "Only love can clean the world of evil."

Chilon allowed himself a sigh of disappointment when he heard these words. All his work was wasted. Ursus or Urbanus or whoever he was wouldn't dare kill Glaucus after listening to such exhortations. No, not tonight or ever. On the other hand, Chilon took comfort in the thought that Glaucus wouldn't kill him, either, if he ever came across him and knew who he was.

But for Vinicius, who no longer thought there was anything new in this old man's message, these simple answers evoked a storm of questions: What kind of God was this? What sort of teaching could this be? And who were these people? His mind couldn't make sense of everything he heard; it was too much to cope with all at once, because these ideas, whether old or new, were a completely new way of looking at the world and totally rearranged everything known before. He sensed that if he were to follow the teaching, he would, for example, have to make a burnt offering of everything that had made him; he would have to destroy his thinking, crush all his perceptions, excise every habit, custom and tradition, erase his whole acquired character and the driving force of his current nature—burn it all to ashes, consign it to the winds, and fill the void with an entirely different soul and a life on a wholly different plane. A philosophy that taught love for Parthians, Syrians, Greeks, Egyptians, Gauls and Britons seemed like lunacy; love and forgiveness to an enemy and kindness in the place of vengeance were simply sheer madness; at the same time he sensed that within this madness lay something stronger than all philosophies. He knew instinctively that the full practice of such a religion could never be attained because it defied human abilities, and this made it godlike. His spirit rebelled against it, he pushed it away, but simultaneously he felt the tug of its beguiling sweetness as if the fresh scent of a field of flowers suddenly beckoned him; he breathed a strange intoxicating substance that seemed to come from the legends of the *Odyssey*, bringing forgetfulness from the country of the lotus eaters and ordering remembrance only of itself.

What he heard seemed totally divorced from reality as he understood it, and yet it made his reality so insignificant, it was hardly worth a passing thought. He felt drawn into a gentle but perplexing vortex, shrouded in a mist of contradictory confusions, and dimly aware of unknown colossi grappling beyond the stars. The burial ground acquired its own lunatic reality as he peered around it. It wasn't just a convocation of the mad, he thought, madly committed to their impossible commitments; it was much, much more. He saw it all at once as awesome and mysterious, a place filled with mysticism and secrets, as if it were the matrix of something unimaginable in mythology and unknown to man.

His mind fought back but failed. He had a moment of clarity akin to revelation, all the more brilliant for coming to him in intermittent flashes as blinding and remorseless as streams of lightning hurled by an angry Zeus. The young patrician grasped and absorbed everything he heard this night and looked at life, truth, love and this unfathomable new divinity through totally new eyes. All the events of the recent past seemed clear and ordained. There was a terrifying logic in everything that happened, but there was also an age-old twist to his new perceptions. Like all men whose lives have narrowed to a single focus, he understood everything in terms of his obsession; everything in him sprang from and returned to his love for Ligia. And one thought, the solitary survivor of his former thinking, emerged from this ordeal and remained burning in his head. He knew beyond doubt that if Ligia was on this ground tonight, if this was her true faith and if she heard and felt anything like what he had experienced, she would never be his lover in any way he knew.

It came to him with the jarring clarity of another vision that even if he got her back, as he now perceived it, it wouldn't be like recovering her at all. No matter what he took from her, he would receive nothing from her. Nothing like that had occurred to him before, not since the first day he saw her at the Plautius villa, and he couldn't make his peace with this realization. Why not? What did it mean? The shock stunned like a rock on impact and left him wobbling uncertainly among his ideas. He knew he would never comprehend the core of this unfathomable teaching, but he didn't care. He had less of a need to understand why things had to happen than a vague, gnawing sense of an irreparable loss that twisted in his belly like a poisoned dagger, and he had a sick premonition of some terrible disaster, some dreadful misfortune. Startled, alarmed and suddenly defensive, he turned a storm of anger on all the Christians and on the old teacher in particular. This bowed old Galilean fisherman, whom he had taken for a commonplace nonentity at the start, now projected the power of the supernatural, stirring him to such awe that it touched the boundaries of superstitious fear and loomed before him like some superhuman Fatum, the implacable demarcator of human destinies, who had dealt him a merciless and tragic hand to play.

A grave digger slipped a few more torches into the bonfire as he had been doing quietly all along, and the wind died down among the pines. The flame cut evenly and sharply, shooting straight up into the darkness like a frail sacrificial offering; it lifted toward the sky, slim and true, and sent its sparks soaring into the glittering profusion of the stars.

In the meantime the teacher touched upon Christ's death a little earlier, and then he started telling them what came afterward. The crowd was so still, plunged in such breathless silence that one could almost hear the pounding of their hearts. This was an eyewitness. He had seen what he was relating. And he related it like a man who carried every moment of it etched into his brain so that all he needed was to close his eyes and he would still see it exactly as it was. He told how he and John returned from Golgotha after the crucifixion and sat for two days and nights in their rented parlor, the same place they had eaten their last supper with the master. This time they neither ate nor slept except when exhaustion sent one or the other nodding off for a little while. They slumped against a wall, numb with the horror of it all, sick with pity, fear, doubts and defeat, each clutching his head in both hands and thinking that everything was over now that *he* was dead.

Oh, how hard and bitter life seemed to them then, he said. How hopeless and empty! Two days passed like that. The third dawn came and tinted the white limestone walls, and they still sat there, he and John, hopeless and grief-stricken, slipping into a brief, chaotic nightmare now and then because they had had no rest since the night before the crucifixion, and jerking awake to gnaw on their despair, when Mary of Magdala burst into the room. Her hair was wild. Her eyes were like saucers. She gasped for breath as she shouted: "They've taken the master!" They leaped up and ran like madmen to the tomb. John, being the youngest, got there first and found the stone rolled away, but didn't dare go in alone. It wasn't until all three of them stood huddled at the entrance that he went inside. He saw the shroud and the oiled linen wrappings abandoned on the limestone slab, but he found no body.

Fear clutched at them again because they thought the temple priests had stolen the body, and they slunk home in even deeper anguish than before. The rest of the disciples gathered there during the day, slipping in one by one, disguised and afraid, and wondering how to restore some sense to their devastated lives.

"Each of us wept and cried out to God alone," the frail old man quavered, racked with the memories that would stay with him forever, "and then we raised a great lament together so the Lord of Hosts could hear us all the better."

But nothing helped. The light had gone out of their lives, and their spirits crumbled. They thought the master would redeem their people, that he would restore glory to Israel and lead them all into the light of freedom, and here it was the third day since he had died and no miracles had happened. They couldn't understand why God had abandoned them, how he could have turned on his own true son. And they could neither face the day nor live with the crushing burden of their disappointment.

Two great tears spilled from the old man's eyes, caught the firelight and glinted in his beard. Those terrible hours were as real to him so many years after the event as they had been on that awful day. His old, naked skull quivered and began to shake. His voice sank into a strangled whisper. "This man is weeping for a great truth," Vinicius told himself. "What he is telling is what really happened."

Others around him also sobbed, moved by the old man's passion and anxious to hear him. All of them knew how Christ had died and that after his death came the resurrection, but this was the great apostle who was telling them what he had seen with his own eyes and felt in his heart at the time it happened. They wept along with him, twisting their hands and beating their chests in contrition, even though they knew this was a joyful story in the end. The old man barely kept his eyes open, as if to focus better on a distant moment, and the hushed throng settled down to listen.

"So as we wept and mourned," he went on, "Mary Magdalene burst in among us again, but this time she was wild with joy, shouting that she had seen the master back there by the tomb. He walked in light, she said, and it was so bright it dazzled her and she thought at first he was a groundskeeper or a tomb attendant with the sun behind him. But he spoke to her, she said, and called her by name, and she threw herself down before him, crying out: 'Great rabbi! Teacher!' Then, she said, he told her to find us all and gather us together, and then he disappeared.

"Well"—the frail old man spread his trembling hands, as if appealing for their understanding—"we didn't believe her. Some of us yelled at her, telling her to get herself together and stop her hysteria. A few of us thought she had gone off her head, driven mad by sorrow, especially since she said she saw angels in the tomb as well. We all ran there again, but the tomb was as empty as before. Later on in the evening, joined by Cleopas, a man who used to go with us to Emmaus, we all went home. Most of us agreed that what we saw was a resurrection. 'The Lord has risen!' we said to one another. 'He is truly risen!' Others still argued that it couldn't be, that it wasn't proven. We argued back and forth, hour after hour, hiding behind closed shutters so that nobody would hear us in the street outside, and suddenly there *he* was, standing among us even though the doors were barred behind him and the shutters closed.

"I saw him there," the old man said quietly, his eyes still focused on that inner vision. "I saw him as all the rest saw him, standing in great light, and this light filled us all and became our joy. We knew, you see, every one of us, that he had truly risen from the dead, and we said to one another what I'm telling you here: that the seas will dry up and the mountains crumble into dust, but his truth will go on forever.

"And after eight days," he went on, "Thomas Didymus put his fingers in the master's wounds because he still doubted. He was a rational man, a thinking man who didn't believe what he couldn't touch, and then he fell on his knees, crying out 'It is you, my Lord and my God!' To which the master said: 'You see, so you believe. Blessed are those who believe without seeing.' And I tell you now, if there is one who doubts it: We were there to hear him, and we saw him risen from the dead, because he came among us."

Something strange started happening to Vinicius. His hold on his surroundings seemed to slip so that he heard the words but couldn't put them together. Too many pieces of the puzzle clashed. He couldn't tell for a moment where he was or what was happening to him, nor could he engage his senses of reality, perception and judgment. It was impossible for him to believe what that old man told him; it just couldn't happen; yet he knew beyond doubt that this man couldn't be a liar. "I'd have to be blind, and deaf, to my own reasoning," he argued with himself, "to suppose this isn't an eyewitness."

Was he asleep? Dreaming? Was this an illusion? No. It couldn't be. He saw the silent crowd, the bonfire and the torches. He smelled the hot, acrid grease of tallow wicks and lanterns. There was the boulder, or perhaps a tombstone, with the old man on it—a stooped, worn figure with a bald, slightly palsied head twitching on his shoulders, almost tottering on the edge of his own grave—but he could not swear he was awake to see him.

But one thing was clear no matter how impossible it seemed: He watched tears trickling slowly down onto the man's white beard, judged the depth of feeling in that harrowed face, assessed the unassailable faith and conviction locked in that fragile body, heard the painstaking detail planted in the telling—details that no one could invent if he hadn't been there—and knew he couldn't doubt him.

"I saw it," the man repeated, and Vinicius knew that he spoke the truth. "I was there."

And he went on to tell it all up to the point when Christ was taken bodily into paradise. He had to rest now and then, because he spoke in detail and at length, but the picture he projected was as complete and timeless as if it were hammered into stone. His audience was spellbound, enthralled and ecstatic. They threw off their hoods to hear him all the better. They savored his words and hoarded them like treasures. Their fixed, inward stare carried them into another time; they were magically transported to Galilee, walking with the disciples among the olive groves and listening to the master. This hushed burial ground was suddenly the Sea of Tiberias, the borders of Judea, and Christ himself was standing on the distant shore, as radiant within the morning mists as he was when John first saw him from the fishing skiff. They were transported back in time. They were with John, the youngest and dearest of his followers, the time he hailed him as their messiah, God's messenger who would bring them peace and lead them to freedom, while honest, simple Peter leaped overboard to reach him all the faster and kiss the ground before him. Their set, ecstatic faces showed that each of them had stepped into another reality, lifted above their ordinary lives, oblivious of actual time and place, and burning with a boundless love and joy beyond expression. It was clear that some of them experienced visions during Peter's charismatic tale, and when he told how the clouds came down from the sky during Christ's ascension and how they formed a pillar at his feet and hid him from the eyes of the apostles, all eyes fixed themselves expectantly on the stars. Were they really waiting for this savior of theirs to reappear, return to them? To step down from the pastures of paradise to see how the old apostle shepherded the flock he had committed to him, and bless him and them?

Rome vanished for them then, Vinicius knew. There was no empire, no legions and no conquests. There was no mad, maniacal emperor anymore; nor were there any temples, gods, or pagans in their world. There was only Christ, who filled the earth, the seas, the sky and all existence.

Midnight came to the distant homesteads scattered along the Via Nomentana, and Chilon edged up to the young patrician.

"There, my lord," he whispered. "Over there behind the old man . . . I see Urbanus and some girl beside him."

The young soldier jerked awake, immediately alert, as if suddenly torn away from a deep dream. He looked where Chilon pointed and saw Ligia.

‹27›

EVERY DROP OF BLOOD in the young man's veins seemed to leap to life at the sight of Ligia.

He forgot the crowds. The apostle vanished from his consciousness. The shock of revelations among contradictions, and the clash of doubt, supposition and amazement at everything he saw and heard that night dwindled into nothing. He saw only her. At long last there she was. After all his efforts—the days of gnawing rages and impatience, the long anxious nights—he had found her again!

It never occurred to him before that joy could hurl itself on a man like a wild beast and crush the breath out of his chest. Nor would he recognize his own sudden image; he who believed that Dame Fortune was in some way obliged to grant all his wishes now found himself unable to believe his joy or trust his eyes.

That doubt was his salvation. His rashness might have hurled him into some hasty, unconsidered step, but he held back, not sure if what he saw was yet another illusion—a part of that skewed reality that transformed this graveyard—or if he was dreaming. But no. This wasn't a dream. She was there, with no more than twenty paces between them. She was in the light, fully bathed in the fire's glow, and he could feast his eyes on her all he wished. The hood had slipped off her head and disarranged her hair, her lips were parted, and her wide, upraised eyes were fixed on the apostle as if she was spellbound. In her dark woolen cloak she looked like any of the poor, ordinary people—perhaps a seamstress from the Suburra or a fruit peddler from the warrens across the Tiber—but her delicate, finely sculpted face betrayed her. She had never seemed this beautiful to him before.

Despite the chaos that raged in his head, Vinicius was struck by the purity and perfection of her patrician features in contrast with the coarse slave mantle she was wearing. Love swept through him like fire; colossal, overwhelming, it sent him spinning in some strange confusion of longing, adoration, animal lust and an immense respect. Just the sight of her filled him with delight, and he drank it in like a parched wanderer who finds and savors a cup of fresh water. Standing beside the gigantic Lygian, she seemed smaller, slighter, almost like a child; he also noticed that she was thinner now, almost ethereal in her new fragility, so that she seemed like a flower or a disembodied soul. But this only drove him all the harder to have this special being, so utterly different from all the women he had had in Rome and the East. He would have been glad to trade every one of them for her, and throw Rome itself into the bargain, along with the rest of the world.

He would have lost himself altogether in that sight, bemused beyond any thought of action, if Chilon hadn't tugged urgently at the edge of his cloak. The Greek was clearly terrified that the over-wrought patrician might do something dangerous. The Christians had started to pray and sing. Soon the *Maranatha* sounded, the great cry that affirmed their faith, and the apostle began the baptisms, sprinkling the candidates presented to him by the presbyters with water he drew out of the fountain. Vinicius was suddenly quite certain that this long, interminable night would never end. His patience was cracking. He wanted to follow Ligia out of there at once, seize her on the road or take her from her lodgings.

Some of the crowd started to trickle out of the burial ground just then, and Chilon edged closer. "Let's get outside the gate, my lord," he whispered. "We've kept our hoods on, and people are giving us strange looks."

That, Vinicius noted, was quite true. Most of the Christians had thrown back their hoods while the apostle spoke, all the better to catch every word, but the three intruders stayed hooded and hidden. Chilon's advice made sense in yet another way: Once they were past the gate, they would be able to watch everyone who left the cemetery, and the gigantic Ursus would be hard to miss.

"We'll follow them," Chilon murmured. "We'll see what tenement they enter. Then tomorrow, or rather later on this morning, you'll surround all the exits with your slaves, my lord, and take her."

"No!" Vinicius said.

"What will you want to do then, my lord?"

"We'll follow her into her lodgings and take her from there. Immediately! Are you ready, Croton?"

"I've been ready from the start," the sword fighter grunted. "You can have me free for a slave, my lord, if I don't break the back of the ox that guards her."

But Chilon started arguing, begging by all the gods that they keep to their original intentions. Wasn't Croton there just for their protection in case they were spotted? Taking the girl like this, practically singlehanded, was a risky business. They might be killed! Moreover, she might slip out of their hands somehow, hide elsewhere or break out of the city altogether. And what would they do then? Why not bet on a sure thing instead of staking the whole game on one roll of the dice that might prove quite deadly?

It took all his effort for Vinicius to control himself and not go after Ligia right there on the spot, seizing her in the middle of the throng in the cemetery, but Chilon struck some stray chord of reason in his mind. He almost agreed. But Croton was more concerned with how much he could make for this night's work.

"Tell that old goat to keep his mouth shut, master," he snarled, annoyed and contemptuous. "Or let me jam my fist through the top of his skull. One time in Buxentum, where Lucius Saturnius hired me for the games, seven drunk gladiators went for me in a tavern, and not one of them got out of there without broken ribs. I'm not saying to grab the girl right here, in this mob. They might stone us or trip us up some way. But once we're in her house, I can have her across my shoulder and on her way anywhere you say, sir."

This pleased Vinicius. He liked what he heard. "Then that's what'll happen, by Hercules!" he swore. "We might miss her somehow at the house tomorrow. But if we throw them all into a panic as soon as we get there, we can get her away tonight!"

"The Lygian looks awfully strong," Chilon groaned.

"Nobody's asking you to hold his hands," Croton snapped.

But they had to wait a long time beyond the gate. Dawn came and the country roosters were already crowing in the distance before they saw Ursus and Ligia coming out with several other people. Chilon thought he recognized the apostle, who walked with another, smaller old man, followed by two middle-aged women and a boy with a lantern. Some two hundred men and women crowded them, and the three intruders slipped into that throng.

"As you see, my lord," Chilon pointed out, "your girl is well protected. She's with that great apostle of theirs, way up there. See how they're going down on their knees before him."

People were indeed kneeling before the small group that included

Ligia, but Vinicius hardly saw them. He didn't let his eyes stray from the girl for even a moment. Her abduction filled his mind completely. He was a combat officer, quite at home with raids, ambushes and surprise attacks, and he composed his plan for the abduction with battlefield precision. His decision was a daring one, perhaps even risky, but audacity in war usually brought success. The bolder the stroke, he recalled, the better its chances.

The road back to the city was a long one, however. He had time to think about other matters, including the abyss between him and Ligia that this strange new faith had created. Now that it was too late, he understood everything that had happened and why. He was perceptive enough to see that he hadn't really known Ligia. He thought her beautiful beyond imagination, a ripe young woman who set fire to all his senses; now he could see she was an altogether different kind of being. This was a woman whose religion set her apart from others, and any hope that she would give way to physical desire, follow her senses into illicit pleasures or be impressed with riches was an idiot's dream. He grasped at last what neither he nor Petronius could comprehend before, that this new faith grafted some totally new idea onto the human soul, something that had never existed in mankind before, and that Ligia would not give up one fragment of her dedication even if she loved him. If delight had any meaning for her, it would be totally at odds with his vision of it; nor would Petronius, Caesar, the imperial court—or all of Roman society for that matter—understand it better. Any other woman he knew could become his lover; this Christian girl could be only a sacrificial victim.

Thinking about this, he felt a sharp, hot pain in the pit of his belly and a wordless anger, and he knew that both were useless. Carrying Ligia off didn't seem like much of a problem, he was almost sure to bring it off successfully; but he was just as sure that all his daring, skills, courage and resources were nothing beside her faith and that he would fail with her in the end. Something extraordinary passed across his mind and shocked this proud, Roman military tribune to the sole of his legionnaire boots; it was a thought that had never occurred to him before. He had lived all his years convinced that might ruled everything and that the steel swords and fists that won and held the empire could never be challenged. Now he saw something else at large in the world, and he couldn't affix an exact label to it.

What was it? He couldn't pierce the secret or find the words for it. All he could focus on in his staggered mind were images of that graveyard, of those gathered throngs, and of Ligia listening with all the concentration of her mind and soul to an old man who told about the torture, death and resurrection of some man-god who had redeemed the world and promised lives of unending joy in the lands of the dead across the river Styx.

Confusion threatened to split his head apart when he thought about it. He was almost grateful for Chilon's interruptions. The Greek groaned and whined about his fate and broke the grip of the patrician's worries. He had agreed to find Ligia, and he found her, didn't he? At quite considerable risk to himself, it ought to be remembered. So what more was expected of him now? He didn't sign on for any abductions, and who could expect it from a poor old cripple like himself, a man with two fingers missing and a mind given to learning, contemplation and good works? What would happen if someone as important as the distinguished tribune came to grief when carrying off the girl? True, the gods were supposed to protect the elite, but didn't it happen now and then that the gods were busy bowling on Olympus instead of keeping an eye on the affairs of men? Fortune is fickle because she wears a blindfold, the Greek pointed out, and doesn't see all that well in daylight, so what could she notice so long after sundown?

"Let something happen," Chilon moaned. "Let that Lygian bear hurl a millstone at the distinguished tribune. Let him hit the noble Vinicius with a vat of wine or a water cistern, and the reverberations would bury poor Chilon."

Wisdom, he said, must always bow before power and greatness— that was a law of nature. He had become as attached, he said, to the noble tribune as Aristotle was to Alexander. If only the great lord would trust him with that money bag he had watched him thrust into his belt before they set out, then if something were to happen, at least he would have the means to hire help or even bribe the Christians!

"Why," he groaned, "doesn't anybody listen to reason and experience?"

Distracted, Vinicius pulled the gold purse from inside his cloak and let it drop into Chilon's fingers.

"Take this and shut up," he said.

The weight of the gold tipped the scales in favor of the Greek's courage and lifted his spirits.

"Now I feel a lot better about all this," he said. "Hercules and Theseus also had their hard times and trials, and met them successfully, and who is Croton, my personal best friend, if not another Hercules? I won't refer to you, my lord, as a demigod, because you're totally divine, and you won't forget about your humble, loyal servant whose needs must be met now and then, because when he plunges into his books he forgets all else. A few shady acres and a little house would be a fitting gift from such a generous patron. Meanwhile I'll witness your heroic efforts, cheer you on from a distance, call on Jupiter to help you, and if things turn ugly I'll cause such an uproar that half of Rome will come running to help."

Tired from all the walking, he also thought to solve that problem for himself.

"What a hard, bumpy road this is," he observed. "Dark, too, with all the oil burned out of my lamp. If the great Croton, who is just as powerful as he is distinguished, were to pick me up and carry me at least to the city gates, he would have some practice for hoisting the girl later. He would also emulate Aeneas, hero of Virgil's epic and ancestor of all the patricians, which would win over all the decent gods and guarantee our success tonight."

"I'd rather lift the carcass of a mangy sheep that's been dead a month," Croton growled, "but I'll carry you to the gates if you give me that purse you just got from the distinguished tribune."

"May you stub your big toe!" the Greek shot back, annoyed. "Is this all you learned from that venerable old man who just preached that poverty and mercy were the greatest virtues? I see I won't be able to turn you into even a half-baked Christian. It would be easier for the sun to seep through the walls of the Mammertine prison than for the truth to pierce your hippopotamus skull."

"Don't worry," Croton said with a laugh. He was as deadly as any animal alive and had no human feelings whatsoever. "I won't turn into any kind of Christian, good or bad. I wouldn't want to risk my bread and butter."

"If you had any inkling of philosophy, you'd know that gold is merely an illusion."

"Great!" Croton laughed again. "You come at me with your philosophy and I'll ram my head into your gut, and we'll see who wins."

"An ox could say the same thing to Aristotle," Chilon said, shrugging.

Meanwhile it was getting gradually lighter. Dawn edged the walls with a pale glow. The roadside trees, structures and occasional tombs started to loom out of the graying shadows. The highway was no longer as empty as before; early as it was, the vegetable peddlers were already trudging along the road, heading for the city gates that would open by the time they got there, and leading mules weighed down with fresh produce. Carts creaked here and there, carrying loads of venison and beef. A low mist hugged the highway and the sandy roadside, heralding good weather. Seen from a distance, passersby acquired an intangible, ghostly quality, but Vinicius had eyes only for Ligia's slim back before him; she seemed brushed with silver as the daylight brightened.

"Lord," Chilon said behind him, "I'd be insulting you if I thought your generosity was about to end. I know it is endless. But now that you've given me a little on account, you can't suppose that I'm talking from self-interest only. Let me advise again that you find the building where your divine Ligia shelters nowadays, go home for your slaves and a carrying chair, and pay no more attention to the rumblings of that elephantine Croton. He's pushing for an immediate abduction only to squeeze more money out of you."

"What I have waiting for you here," Croton said, shaking his fist, "is a good crack between the shoulder blades. Which means you're a dead man."

"And what I have waiting for you is a cask of Cephalonian wine," Chilon offered. "Which means that I'll live."

Vinicius said nothing. They had now come to the city gates where the tribune had another shock. Two soldiers on guard at the portals went down on their knees as the apostle passed, and he placed his hand on their iron helmets and blessed them with the sign of the cross. The young patrician had never even thought that this Christianity might spread into the legions. He couldn't believe how quickly it was erupting everywhere, like a fire that leaps from house to house in a crowded city, seizing new converts every day with the speed of a real conflagration. He also thought of this proliferation in terms of Ligia; with Christians among the soldiers posted at the gates, he was now convinced she would find willing help anytime she wanted to slip out of the city. He offered fervent thanks to all his gods that she hadn't thought she needed to do that just yet.

Once they had crossed the empty, unpopulated spaces beyond the walls, the returning Christians started to break up into smaller groups and vanish among the houses. There were now fewer people to hide among, and the three intruders had to hold back a bit as they trailed Ligia. Chilon, who was getting more nervous with each step he took into the city, started to groan about bleeding feet and cramps in his legs; he fell back even farther, but Vinicius didn't care if he went or stayed. He didn't think he would need him anymore; the Greek would be useless in any kind of violence and might as well go home. But the philosopher didn't vanish in the side streets along with the Christians. He was apparently a genuine scholar, Vinicius thought coldly: at least as curious as he was pedantic. He even limped a bit faster now and then to catch up and renew his pleading for restraint and to speculate about the other stooped old man who walked with the apostle.

With a worried sigh he said, "He'd pass for Glaucus if he was a bit taller."

They had a long way to go, however, before they reached the tenements clustered across the Tiber. The sun was already over the horizon when the small group around Ligia broke apart. The apostle, an old woman and the lad with the lantern turned off along the Tiber, while the smaller old man, Ligia and the giant slipped into a narrow passageway. They walked another hundred paces and turned into a doorway between a bird shop and an olive stand.

That was the end of the road as far as Chilon was concerned. He stopped fifty paces behind the others, squeezed himself flat against a wall and hissed at them to come back to him for a moment.

"We need to talk," he whispered.

"We need to act," Vinicius snapped, impatient. "Go around the back and see if there's another way out of this building," he commanded.

The Greek may have spent an hour whining about his blisters, but now he ran out of the alley as fast as if Mercury's wings had sprouted from his ankles.

"No," he reported a few minutes later. "There's just the one door." Then he tried again: "I beg you, sir," he said with his palms pressed together, "by Jupiter, Apollo, Vesta, Cybele, Isis, Mithras, Baal and all the gods of the East and West! Give up this attempt. Listen to me. . . ."

But then he stopped. He could see there was nothing more to say. Nobody was listening. Vinicius had grown pale with feeling but his eyes were narrowed in a wolfish glint. One quick glance was enough to show that nothing would stop him now or turn him onto another course. He would never turn back. Croton, sniffing violence like an animal, looked more than ever like a killer bear caged in the arena. He started breathing heavily, filling his massive chest with air like a wrestler before a bout, and his thick, lowered skull swung from side to side. Other than that, he showed no sense of fear or alarm.

"I'll go in first!" he snarled.

"You'll follow me!" Vinicius commanded, and both of them vanished into the darkened hallway.

Chilon hopped around the corner of the nearest alley. He crouched there, shooting anxious glances from behind the wall, and waited for whatever would come next.

‹28›

VINICIUS WAS DEEP in the long, dark passage before he realized just how difficult his attempt could prove in a place like that. The tenement was a tall, narrow structure, one of those wooden warrens that had sprung up in Rome by the thousands to provide as much rental space as possible; they were built so hastily and cheaply that several of them collapsed every year, burying their tenants. These were real human beehives, full of closely crammed nooks and crannies where the vast population of the city's poor clustered in dank, dark spaces. In a dense, crowded city where many streets didn't have a name, these hovels had no numbers, and there was no way to tell who lived there at any given time. The landlords left the rent collecting to their slaves, who weren't obliged to report the lodgers to the city census and often didn't know who lived in the buildings. Looking for someone in such teeming ant heaps was immensely difficult, especially when there was no doorkeeper to question.

The long, dark hallway led Croton and Vinicius to a narrow courtyard walled on all four sides that served as a communal atrium, with a trickling fountain fixed over a stone basin. Wooden and stone stairways snaked up every wall, opening on inner galleries that led to living quarters. The ground floor was also dotted with apartment doorways, some crouched behind rickety pine-board doors and others merely screened from the yard by tattered curtains.

It was still early in the morning. No one was up and around as yet. Everyone in the building was still asleep, Vinicius supposed, except those who had just come back from Ostrianum.

Croton halted in the open space and peered about, sniffing the dusty air. "What do we do now, master?"

"We'll wait in the hallway." Vinicius stepped back into the shadows. "Maybe somebody we can ask will come by. In the meantime it's best if nobody sees us hanging about the yard."

It occurred to him that Chilon's urgings were practical after all.

Well, it was too late for second thoughts. If he had a few dozen slaves behind him now, he knew, he'd be able to block the gate and search all or most of the lodging rooms at the same time; as things were, he and Croton had to burst into Ligia's dwelling at the first try before she was warned. The building, he felt sure, was full of Christians who would let her know immediately that somebody was knocking on doors and asking about her. For the same reason it would be dangerous to question anyone who happened to come by. He was just wondering if he shouldn't go home after all, collect his slaves and bring them back to ransack the building, when he saw a man come out from one of the screened doorways along the far wall. He carried a large, filled colander to the water fountain.

"That's the Lygian!" Vinicius' whisper was hoarse with excitement.

"Am I to crush him now?"

"Wait!" Vinicius ordered.

They stood in the shadows of the hall. Ursus didn't see them. After the long, hungry night in Ostrianum, he was apparently getting breakfast ready and went on calmly rinsing the vegetables in the colander, then disappeared again behind the curtain from where he had emerged. Croton and Vinicius followed on his heels, sure they would burst at once into Ligia's quarters. But what they found behind the screen was another dark corridor that opened on a little garden with a few cypresses and myrtles and showed a small clay house snuggled against the blind back wall of the neighboring building.

This, both of them understood at once, made everything much easier. Any trouble in the bigger courtyard could have brought people pouring out of all the lodgings, but no one would see or hear anything in this little side court. Croton would make short work of any opposition and get rid of Ursus, and they would have Ligia out in the street before anyone noticed they were there. Once in the main street they were as good as home. No one would try to stop them in broad daylight. But if someone did get in their way, Vinicius would simply reveal who he was and send to the prefecture for help.

Ursus was almost at the door of the little cottage when he heard the rustle of footsteps coming up quickly behind him. He looked around, saw two swiftly moving men and placed his colander carefully on the balustrade before him.

"What are you looking for?" he asked.

"You!" Vinicius softly growled and then turned to hiss at Croton, "Kill him now!"

Croton sprang like a tiger at the Lygian before Ursus even knew he was in danger and wrapped his arms around him like an iron vise. But Vinicius didn't bother to wait for the outcome; sure enough of Croton's deadly reputation to doubt he wouldn't kill Ursus in another moment, he dodged quickly around them and shouldered the door. It burst open on a one-room cottage, a dark narrow place full of wavering shadows but with a small, bright fire burning in the hearth. The firelight fell fully onto Ligia's face and on the man beside her, the same short old man who had walked with her from the burying grounds. Vinicius' appearance was so sudden and violent among them that Ligia didn't have time to cry out before he caught her around the waist, lifted her overhead and headed for the door.

She didn't know who he was until his hood twisted to the side and she saw his face. He clasped her to his chest with one of his arms while he threw the old man aside with the other. The firelight caught his strong, familiar features, once so loved and now so fierce and terrifying, and she felt as if her blood were turning to ice. Her cry choked unuttered and died in her throat. She couldn't call for help. She did try to fight him. She clutched at the door frame as he bore her out, but her fingers slid off the weathered stone, and he rushed her out into the small garden.

Choked and dizzy, she felt that she would black out at any moment, and then a horrifying sight shocked her into full awareness. She caught sight of Ursus and the man he held clasped to his chest in his enormous arms. The man was folded practically in half, limp, his head dangling on a broken neck, and blood on his mouth. Ursus looked up, saw her and Vinicius, clubbed the bent bloody head with another blow, and hurled himself like a maddened animal toward them.

Here's my death, thought the young patrician, and then he ceased thinking. He may have heard Ligia's cry, coming to him on a strange dreamlike note as if through a fog: "Thou shall not kill." He felt as if a thunderbolt had burst open the hands with which he held her, and then the world was spinning all around him. He saw nothing more.

‹29›

CHILON FELT RATHER GOOD about everything as he waited around the alley corner, although he was too much of a coward ever to think himself absolutely safe. His curiosity was stronger than his fear, however. He also wanted to be close at hand when Vinicius carried the girl out; proximity at that time, he thought, could be very useful.

Ursus played no part in these calculations, because the Greek never doubted Croton would kill the Lygian on the spot; any other outcome defied comprehension. What he did count on, however, was that a crowd would form in the street, that the Christians might come running to help, and that he would appeal to them as the voice of reason and authority carrying out Caesar's will, which might impress Vinicius. If all else failed, he could run for help, bring the city watch to save the young patrician from the mob, and buy himself into his good graces again.

Truth to tell, he didn't like the way Vinicius handled this end of the affair. It showed a lack of foresight and was too impulsive. But he had great respect for Croton's massive biceps and thought the ploy could succeed, no matter how hasty. "If things become precarious for them over there," he mused as he waited, "the tribune will throw the girl over his shoulder and Croton will pave the way."

Time hung heavy on his hands, however, and he didn't like the long silence in the darkened hallway.

"If they don't find her hideout straightaway or cause a great hullabaloo about it, she'll flee." He worried for a moment, but even that had its positive side. In that event Vinicius would keep needing him, and he would be able to squeeze more sesterces out of him.

"Dear gods, keep aiding me," he prayed. "Whatever they do or don't do, I'm profiting. They're all working for me, and none of them knows it."

Something moved just then in the dark, silent hallway he was watching—he thought he briefly glimpsed some surreptitious object

—and he broke off his pleasant speculations to flatten himself against the wall again, peer around the corner and hold his breath.

Yes, he was right. A head, or perhaps half a head, showed in the doorway for a moment, checking the alley for any passersby. Then it disappeared. That was odd, he thought. It had to be either Croton or Vinicius. But if they had the girl, why wasn't she screaming? And why did they have to peer up and down the alley to see if the coast was clear? It can't be fear of being seen by anyone. They would be seen frequently going all the way to the Carinnae—the whole city would be up by the time they got there.

"So what is it, then?"

Suddenly every hair on his head lifted. He didn't have many left but was sure each of them rose in horror. A figure showed. Ursus filled the doorway, with the corpse of Croton slung across his shoulder; he started running down the empty street, heading for the river.

Now Chilon glued himself to the wall as if he were part of the plasterwork and whitewash. "I'm dead if he sees me" flashed through his mind.

But Ursus ran swiftly past his corner and disappeared behind the next building. Chilon knew there was nothing left to wait for. He set off at his own dead run down the side alley, his teeth rattling in his head in terror and his legs flying as if he were suddenly forty years younger.

"If he catches a glimpse of me on his way back here, he'll go after me and kill me," he gasped as he ran. "Help me, Jove! Help me, Apollo! Protect me, Hermes! Help, god of the Christians! I'll leave Rome. I'll go back to Messambria. Just keep me out of that demon's paws!"

The Lygian who had killed Croton couldn't be an ordinary human, he thought as he ran. Maybe he was some god disguised as a barbarian. Normally, as a matter of his day-to-day existence, Chilon laughed at gods, myths, faiths, rituals and religions, but at this moment he believed in every one of them. It also occurred to him that Ursus was an agent of a higher power, that Croton's real killer might have been the god of the Christians. He broke into a cold sweat at the thought of tangling with such might.

He ran past half a dozen alleys before he caught sight of a few laborers trudging toward him farther up the road. This calmed him down a little. He gasped, fought for breath, slumped on some threshold and started mopping the sweat off his forehead with the edge of his cloak.

"I'm getting old," he thought, wheezing. "I need peace and quiet."

The group of workmen turned into a side road up ahead, and he was left alone in the empty alley. The city was still sleeping. Mornings in Rome were busier in the richer quarters where household slaves had to be up at sunrise; in slum districts populated by free plebeians, who were fed by the state and didn't have to earn a livelihood, getting out of bed was a lengthy process, especially in winter. Chilon sat on the stone stoop for a while until he felt the sharp, morning chill. He climbed back to his feet, patted himself down to see if he still had the purses he had received from Vinicius, and headed for the river at his normal pace.

"I might see Croton's carcass floating somewhere in there," he thought as he went. "The gods preserve me! If that Lygian was a human being, he would be able to earn millions of sesterces fighting in the circus. Who'd be able to beat him if he could strangle Croton like a puppy? They'd pay him his weight in gold each time he stepped into the arena. Phew! Talk about a monster! He keeps a better eye on that girl of his than Cerberus keeps on the gates of Hell, and Cerberus has two heads to do it with. May he rot in Hell anyway! I don't want him near me. He's far too much of a bone-breaker for my taste."

But what was he to do? Where to start? A terrible thing had happened, and there was a lot more trouble on the way, he knew. If Ursus could mangle such a muscleman as Croton, the young patrician wouldn't last any better. Chilon was ready to swear before any deity that Vinicius was a ghost, flying above that cursed building at this very minute and begging for a funeral.

"By Castor! That's a patrician, a friend of Caesar, a relative of Petronius, a great noble known everywhere in Rome, and an army tribune on top of that. There'll be some bloodletting to go with that death, that's for sure. But what if I dropped a word in the praetorian barracks or paid a call on the city watch?"

He thought about that for a while but didn't like the prospects.

"Woe is me. I brought him to that house. His slaves and freedmen know I used to visit him. Some even know why. What if they accused me of causing his death? Even if it came out later at the trial that I didn't want him dead and didn't knowingly lead him into an ambush, they'll still say I did it. He's a patrician! They don't let one of those die without a scapegoat. And I'd look even guiltier if I kept silent about all this, slipped out of Rome quietly and hid myself somewhere in the provinces."

This time Chilon's choices lay between two evils. The lesser of the two was obviously the better. Rome was a vast city, but the Greek believed it might prove too tight for him in a day or two. Anyone else could go straight to the prefect of the city watch, report what had happened, and wait quietly for the investigation to reveal the facts, even though some suspicion might fall on him along the way. But Chilon couldn't do that. He would rather not make the personal acquaintance of the city watch or the city prefect; he had good reason to suppose that a close perusal of his past activities could bring some serious consequences and suggest lines of inquiry he would rather leave unexplored just now by the police.

On the other hand, if he ran for it, Petronius would believe him guilty of selling out Vinicius and of conspiracy to kill him. Petronius had colossal influence; he could have the civic guards of the entire state jumping at his orders, and he would comb the ends of the world for the perpetrators. It occurred to Chilon that his smartest step might be to go directly to Petronius, tell him the whole story and hope for the best. Calmness and tolerance were this man's most noted attributes; if nothing else, Chilon could count on getting the whole tale told without interruptions. Moreover Petronius would need fewer explanations since he was in on the whole affair from the start. He might find it easier to believe in Chilon's innocence than the city prefects.

But before he went running to Petronius, Chilon had to be sure of what had happened to Vinicius, and he had no ideas about that. Croton was dead. He had seen the Lygian carry the corpse to the river, and that was all he saw. Vinicius could be dead, but it was just as likely he was merely wounded and under lock and key until the Christians could decide what to do about him. And suddenly Chilon was convinced that this was what had happened. The Christians would hardly kill one of the Augustans, and a high-ranking army officer at that. Such a crime would bring massive retaliation, perhaps even punitive persecution of their entire sect. Yes! Chilon felt much better. It was far more likely they would just hold him captive for a while, long enough to hide Ligia somewhere else.

And that cast an entirely new light on the Greek's position.

"If that Lygian man-eater didn't rip him apart at first jump," he assured himself, "then he's still alive. If he's alive, he'll be my best witness. And if he testifies that I didn't lead him into any ambush, then not only are my troubles over but there's a whole new world of opportunity opening up before me! Thank you, great Hermes! You can start counting on those two cows again! I can send word to one of his freedmen where to find his master, and if he wants to go running to the prefect, that's strictly up to him. The main thing is I won't have to do it. Moreover I can sell Petronius on the idea of searching for Vinicius, after which it'll be back to Ligia. But the first thing I must know is whether he's alive."

He thought, but only for a moment, of questioning Ursus that night at the Demas bakery. He dismissed the notion as soon as it appeared; he didn't want anything more to do with Ursus. Since to his knowledge Glaucus was still living, some Christian elders must have warned the Lygian against murdering him, which meant he would now think of Chilon as a lying tempter. It might be better, he decided, to send Euricius for news into the building where the incident took place. In the meantime he needed a good meal, a bath and a place to rest. The long, sleepless night, the odyssey of his trek to Ostrianum and then the mad flight from across the Tiber had worn him out completely.

There was, however, one happy constant in his constellation of fears and ideas, one bright thought that kept him on an even keel no matter where his speculation pointed: He still had the money. Vinicius had given him one purse at home and threw him another on the way back from the cemetery, and he now had them both tucked inside his belt. This, along with all the shocks and terrors he had lived through that night, was reason for a celebration, and he promised himself a richer meal and a finer wine than he was used to having.

He did that part so well once the wineshops opened that he quite forgot about his bath. Sleep was all he wanted; the excitements of the night knocked him off his feet, and he weaved an unsteady path to his lodging in the Suburra and to the slave girl he had bought some days earlier with Vinicius' money. There, in a room as dark as a fox's burrow, he threw himself on a cot and fell asleep at once.

He snored all day. He stirred only in the evening, after sundown, when his slave girl told him there was someone at the door looking for him. Stir was the wrong word for it, however; he was instantly awake, sniffing danger, back in his cloak and hood and peering cautiously through a crack in the door, but what he saw made him weak with fear: The colossal Ursus loomed in the passageway outside.

Chilon's teeth rattled like Iberian castanets, his head and legs turned to ice, his heart lost a beat, and a swarm of fire ants surged up and down his spine. It took a few moments before he could speak, and even then his voice was like a tearful moan.

"I'm not in," he stammered to the girl. "Tell him I'm out. . . . I don't know . . . this good man."

"I already told him you're in and sleeping, master," the girl said. "But he said to wake you straightaway."

"I'll—" Chilon tried to threaten her, but all he managed was a frightened squeak. "O gods!"

Ursus seemed impatient. He stepped into the doorway and pushed his head inside. "Chilon Chilonides!" he rumbled like lava in a mountain.

"*Pax tecum! Pax tecum!*" Chilon rattled out. "Peace be with you, brother! *Pax! Pax*, best of the Christians! Yes, I'm Chilon, but this is some mistake. . . . We don't know each other!"

"Chilon Chilonides," Ursus said again. "Your master, Vinicius, wants me to take you to him."

‹30›

VINICIUS WOKE TO excruciating pain. He didn't know at first where he was or what was happening to him. His head was ringing, and his eyes seemed fogged. Consciousness crept back gradually; he tried to focus through a wavering mist and found himself peering up at three men who leaned over him. He recognized two of them—Ursus and the little elderly man he had bowled over while carrying Ligia out into the garden. The third man, whom he had never seen before, grasped his left hand and fingered the arm from the elbow to the shoulder and the collarbone, and it was this manipulation that brought such piercing agony he thought he was being tortured.

"Kill me," he grated out through clenched teeth, but they weren't listening. Ursus looked worried. His fierce barbarian face twisted with anxiety. He clutched an armful of clean white rags, torn into long, narrow strips to serve as bandages, while the old man spoke to the unknown torturer.

"Are you quite sure, Glaucus, he'll survive this head wound?"

"Quite sure, good Crispus," the physician said. "I've dressed a lot of wounds in my time as a galley slave and later in Naples. That's how I paid for my freedom and my family's as well. The head wound doesn't amount to much. The young man threw up his arms to protect his skull when Ursus hurled him into the wall after taking the girl away. He saved his head but dislocated his shoulder, wrenched his knee, cracked his collarbone and broke his arm instead."

"You've patched up quite a few of us," said the man called Crispus. "You've a reputation as a clever doctor. That's why I sent Ursus to bring you here at once."

"And he confessed along the way that he was ready to kill me yesterday."

"Yes, he told me about that. He thought he would be saving all of us. But I know you, Glaucus. I know what a good man you are and how you love Christ. I explained that your accuser had to be a liar."

"I took a demon for an angel," Ursus said with a sigh.

"We'll talk about that later." Glaucus shrugged. "Now let's take care of this young man's injuries."

The pain, Vinicius realized, was sharp and piercing because the physician was resetting his broken and dislocated bones, and he kept losing consciousness even though Crispus bathed his face with water. This may have been a blessing because he felt nothing when Glaucus set and bound his fractured upper arm and immobilized his leg, wrapping each of them tightly in splints made of small, partly hollowed boards.

But when the surgery was finished and consciousness returned for a longer moment, he saw that Ligia was also there, standing beside his cot. She was holding a small copper pail, out of which Glaucus was sponging his face and head, but at first he took her for a dream or a hallucination.

"Ligia," he managed to whisper after a long pause, and he watched as the pail trembled in her hands.

"Peace be with you," she said. When she looked at him, her eyes were full of sadness, her voice was low and gentle, and her face showed both pity and sorrow.

He, in turn, stared at her as if to fill his eyes and stamp them with her portrait so that her image would remain under his eyelids long after he closed them. She had lost weight and color. Her whole face seemed smaller. She was thinner and much paler than before, even though a slight flush mounted under the fixed intensity of his stare. He watched the sweep of her dark brown hair and looked with remorse at the shapeless tunic of a laboring woman on her frail body. Two thoughts bored into him like a surgeon's probes: One was that he still wanted her and always would; the other told him clearly that he alone was responsible for her drawn, pale look and the wretched poverty around her. It was he who had driven her out of the safe and comfortable home where she was loved and cared for, threw her into this miserable hovel, and dressed her in that beggar's robe of dark wool. And because he wanted to wrap her in cloth of gold and shower her with jewels, he groaned with pity, shame, remorse and such gripping sorrow that he would have thrown himself at her feet and begged for forgiveness if he was able to move.

"Ligia," he said, managing to control his voice, "you didn't let them kill me."

"May God bring you safely back to health," she answered with an ineffable sweetness.

No medicine would have helped him more, Vinicius was certain.

He was aware of all the harm he had already brought her, as well as all he had barely failed to inflict. He forgot about the strange Christian teachings that may have spoken through her. He heard her only as a woman he loved above all else, and he searched her words for some special warmth, caring and affection for him. He was stunned by the degree of goodness and compassion in her; he didn't think anything like it was possible for human beings. And just as moments earlier he had given way to pain, now a sudden flood of tenderness sapped his returning strength. He felt powerless and helpless, as if he were spinning in some unknown void; but he also felt calmed and soothed, happy and content. He was convinced in that moment of hallucinatory weakness that a loving deity had appeared before him.

Meanwhile Glaucus finished washing the blood off his head and smeared the cuts and scrapes with a healing ointment. Ursus took the pail from Ligia's hands, and she reached for a cup of water mixed with wine and brought it to his mouth. Vinicius gulped it down thirstily and felt considerably better. The worst of the pain was already gone. His open wounds had stopped bleeding and were beginning to close under the bandages. He was awake, aware, and conscious of everything around him.

"Let me drink some more," he said.

Ligia left the room with the empty cup while Crispus talked briefly with Glaucus and came to the bedside.

"God didn't let you commit an evil act, Vinicius," he said quietly, "but kept you alive so that you might think about what you almost did. Man is mere dust before him, and he delivered you into our hands with nothing to help you. The Christ we worship commands us to love even enemies. We dressed your wounds and we'll pray for your full return to health, just as Ligia told you, but that's as much as we can do for you. Be well, then, and ask yourself if it's right for you to continue persecuting this child whom you robbed of her family and home, and to bring harm to the rest of us who repaid your violence with charity and goodness."

"You're going to leave me here?" Vinicius asked, alarmed.

"We've no choice. We have to leave this house. The city prefect will come after us. The man you brought with you has been killed. You are a wealthy and influential man and you have been injured. It's not our fault, of course. We didn't do anything to cause it to happen. But we're the ones who'll have to bear the brunt of the law."

"Don't worry about any prosecution," Vinicius said. "I'll protect you from that."

Crispus didn't want to tell him that they were less concerned about the prefect and the city watch than about protecting Ligia from his violent attentions.

"Your right hand is fine, my lord," he said. "Here is a stylus and some writing tablets. Write to your servants to bring a litter for you this evening to take you home where you'll rest more comfortably than in these poor surroundings. We rent these rooms from a widow who'll be along quite soon. Her son can take your message. As for the rest of us, we'll have to find shelter somewhere else."

Vinicius felt the blood ebbing from his face. He knew these men wanted to cut him off from Ligia, and he might never see her again if he lost her now. He grasped the fact that some mysterious outside force had created an insurmountable barrier between Ligia and himself and that he would have to find new ways to win her, but he had no time to look into that just now; the realization was too sudden for any serious thinking. He also understood that his promises might not mean much to these cautious people; he could swear to return her immediately into Pomponia's keeping, and they would have the right to distrust everything he said. And yet, he knew, that was exactly what he could have done! He could have gone to Aulus and Pomponia, sworn to them that he wouldn't plague Ligia any longer, and they would have sought her out on their own and brought her home again.

No. His promises would be worthless here. No oath of his would stop them from taking her away, especially since he was not a Christian, whom they might believe. All he could swear on were the immortal gods in whom he didn't place much trust himself and whom the Christians viewed as corrupted and malignant spirits.

He was desperately anxious to convince Ligia and these strange new guardians of hers that he could be trusted, but he needed time for that and there wasn't any. He also wanted to be near her for a few more days. Like a drowning man who clutches at a plank or a broken oar, he clung to the idea that he might come up with something useful if he had those days, or he might think of some important thing to say that would bring them closer together, or some unexpected stroke of good luck might intervene on his behalf with the other Christians.

He lay still for a while, gathering his thoughts.

"Hear me, you Christians," he began reasonably and firmly. "I was at Ostrianum with you last night, and I listened to some of your teaching. It's all very strange to me and I don't understand it, but you've convinced me by the way you act that you're good, honest people. Tell your widowed landlady to stay put. She'll be quite safe here. Nobody will trouble her or you, I'll make sure of that. Let me stay here with you for a few more days. Ask your friend Glaucus, who seems to know how to get a sick man on his feet again, if I can be moved anywhere just now. I have broken bones that need time to knit. That's why I'm staying here unless you throw me out by force."

His bruised, battered ribs made him short of breath, and he had to pause.

"No one is going to force you into anything, my lord," Crispus said. "We'll just remove ourselves."

But the young Roman was unaccustomed to having his wishes questioned, and his brows drew together in an angry frown.

"Wait," he said. "Let me catch my breath. Now listen to this. Nobody will miss Croton in Rome, because everyone knows he was about to go to Beneventum where Vatinius hired him to fight in the arena. Nobody saw him and me go into this building except one Greek who works for me and was with us last night in Ostrianum. I'll tell you where he lives, and you can have him brought here. I'll order him to keep his mouth shut about everything. I'll write a note to my household that I've also gone to Beneventum. If that Greek has already notified the prefect, I'll testify that I killed Croton myself, and it was he who broke my arm, so you won't be blamed. I swear to you by the spirits of my departed parents that this is what I'll do. So stay here too! You'll be safe! Nobody will touch you! And now go and get that Greek for me. His name is Chilon Chilonides."

"In that case Glaucus can stay with you, my lord," Crispus nodded, still troubled about the offer and stubborn to the end. "He and the widow can nurse you back to health."

The young man's frown sharpened and his brows narrowed dangerously but he restrained himself.

"Listen to me, old man," he said, "and pay close attention. You seem like a decent fellow, but you're not telling me what you really think. You're afraid I'll summon my slaves and have them abduct Ligia. Isn't that correct?"

"Yes," Crispus said with a touch of sternness.

"Then note that I'll be talking to Chilon in front of you. You'll all hear what we say. I'll write the instructions for my household in front of you as well, letting my people know I've left the city so they won't expect me. Nor will I find any other messengers here except one or another of your own people. So . . . think carefully about this. Think, and don't provoke me anymore. Do not make me angry."

But his own features were convulsed with anger; the need to plead, beg or explain was abhorrent to him.

"Did you think," he burst out, "that I'd deny why I want to stay here? Of course it's to see her! Any fool would know that, no matter what I said! But I'll never try to take her by force again."

Soft for a moment as he made that promise, his voice sharpened coldly. "And here's something else you ought to know, Crispus. If she doesn't stay, I'll tear off all these bandages and dressings, and refuse any food or drink you feed me, and may my death be charged to your account. Did you dress my wounds just so I could suffer? Why didn't you have the human decency to kill me?"

Anger and weakness exhausted him. He was whiter than the worn, threadbare sheets on which he was lying. Ligia, who heard this whole conversation from the other room and who had every reason to suppose Vinicius would do exactly as he said, was suddenly afraid. His death was the last thing she would ever wish. Wounded and defenseless, he inspired only pity in her; she neither thought about fearing him nor felt any fear of anything he might do, and she had gone through a mystical transformation of her own. Since her escape from him she had been living among people whose every moment passed in religious fervor, who existed in a state of permanent spiritual exaltation, who built their lives on sacrifice and giving, and who practiced self-denial and mercy without limit. She became so imbued with this powerful new spirit that it replaced everything she had lost. It was now her home, her family and all her hope for future happiness in this world and the next. It also made her into one of those inspired Christian women who later changed the conscience of the world. The role that Vinicius played in her destiny had been too important for her to forget him; his intrusion into her existence was too significant to deny. She thought about him for days at a time and prayed for a chance to treat him according to Christ's law, offer him kindness in return for his persecution, repay his evil with her own loving goodness, break him, win him for Christ and save him. And now it seemed to her that this was such a moment; her prayers had been heard and were answered.

"Crispus!" she hurried to him as if propelled by a holy vision, her voice not her own. "Let him stay among us, and we'll stay with him until Christ makes him well."

The old presbyter hesitated only for a moment. He was used to seeking God's guidance in everything; her exalted state reminded him that she could be serving as the mouthpiece of a higher power. Shaken, he bowed his head.

"Let it be as you say," he assented.

Crispus' quick surrender made a strange and powerful impression on Vinicius who didn't take his eyes off Ligia for a moment. It struck him that the Christians treated her with the obedience and respect due a Sybil or a holy priestess, and he began to feel this respect rising in himself. A sense of awe entered the love he felt, so close to adoration that the very idea of loving her started to seem like an impertinence or an imposition. Nor could he come to terms with the thought of their role reversal: His life was now under her control, not she under his. He was no longer the driving and directing force in their relationship; on the contrary, sick and battered as he was, he was transformed into a helpless and defenseless child, secure in her care. With anyone else he knew, such dependence would be unendurable. It was, in fact, an unforgivable insult for a young patrician and quite intolerable for a man as self-driven, proud and self-assured as he.

With her, however, he felt no sense of degradation or reduction. He was neither humiliated nor diminished. Indeed, he felt grateful.

Nothing like this had ever troubled his sense of self before; such a surrender of his natural role would stun anyone who knew him. He was perfectly aware that only the day before he would not have given a passing thought to such outlandish notions. He suspected they would amaze him even now if he tried to perceive them clearly. But he didn't want to question any part of this unbelievable experience or undermine the vast new joy that filled him. He was merely happy and content to be there with her.

He couldn't even tell himself exactly what he felt. Yes, there was gratitude—he had no trouble identifying that—but there was also another feeling, so new for him he could barely acknowledge it. Humility, a state of being totally foreign to him, joined the love and awe he felt for this girl. He was, however, so exhausted by the emotional upheavals of a moment earlier that he couldn't speak and could only thank her with his eyes. He was overjoyed that he could stay with her and see her every day; he would be able to look at her tomorrow just as he did today, and perhaps long after that as well.

Something else happened to him then, something so totally beyond the bounds of his experience that it shattered his own vision of himself. He, the ruthless and remorseless soldier, the fearless commander, was suddenly afraid. Ligia brought him another cup of water fortified with wine. He seized it, gulped it down, and felt an urge to close his hand on hers, as he had done at every other opportunity to touch her. But he was suddenly so anxious that these new perceptions should go on and that he should never let go of the little he had managed to gain, he didn't dare.

And this, he told himself in utter confusion, was the same Vinicius who at that famous banquet at the Palatine had crushed her lips with his greedy mouth, without a single care how she felt about it, and who swore he would drag her by the hair to his bed or order her flogged.

‹ 3 I ›

ONE OTHER THING that worried Vinicius was the possibility of help coming from the outside too soon. Chilon might have already run to the prefecture about his disappearance or passed the word to Vinicius' freedmen, in which case the civil guard could burst in at almost any moment. It passed through his mind that in that event he could order Ligia picked up and locked in his house, but he knew he wouldn't even try it. True, he was ruthless, dictatorial, impatient and indifferent to the rights of others; he took what he wanted, and he could be utterly merciless about it. But he was neither as cruel and corrupt as Nero nor as vicious and malignant as Tigellinus. Army life had given him a strict sense of order, narrowed his notions of fair play and justice, and left him with just enough conscience to know that such a deed would be beneath contempt. Fury might cause him to do it if he were fit and in full command of his mind and body, but right now he was helpless on his back, unable to move and in the grip of gentler thoughts and feelings. His one immediate worry was that no one should intrude himself between him and Ligia.

He was surprised that neither Ligia nor Crispus asked for guarantees; in their place he would have demanded a hostage. But from the moment she took his part, deciding for all of them that they would stay together, none of the Christians said one word about looking for another hideout, as if they were certain that an unknown, supernatural force would come to their aid if they needed help. Vinicius, who had lost his ability to judge between what was actual and what defied logic since he heard the apostle preaching in the graveyard, wasn't ready to dismiss miraculous interventions. His boundaries of reality had been blown sky-high; the worlds of hard fact, superstition and spiritual mysteries became inextricably tangled and confused in his direct, sharply delineated mind. But looking at the matter soberly, he reminded them about the Greek informer and once more demanded that Chilon be found and brought there.

There was some discussion. A few others entered, among them the apostle Peter who found a quiet seat behind the trestle table, but it was Crispus who made the decision, and Ursus got ready to look for the Greek. Vinicius could tell him where Chilon kept his lodgings, since he had been sending slaves there for weeks before the night at Ostrianum, but the slippery Greek was very seldom there unless it suited him to be found. He scribbled a few words on a wax tablet and gave it to Crispus.

"I've written to him," he said, "because he's a sly, suspicious fox and might not want to come. He's done that before. Whenever he thought I'd be angry with him, he'd have somebody tell my people that he wasn't home."

"I'll bring him here whether he wants to come or not," Ursus said, "as long as I find him." He threw on a cloak and hurried out.

It wasn't easy to find someone in Rome even with good directions, but Ursus knew the city inside out. Moreover he possessed the sharp tracking instincts of a forest dweller, so it didn't take long for him to find Chilon's lodgings. Once inside, however, he failed to recognize him. He had seen him only once, and that was in darkness. Besides, no one would recognize the convincing, self-assured persuader in the cringing, terrified old Greek who whined at the door.

Chilon was quick to realize that Ursus was looking at him without recognition, and he breathed a little easier. Vinicius' tablet, when he read the message, settled him even more; at least the tribune didn't think he had sold him out and led him like a goat to slaughter. The Christians, he decided, didn't kill the tribune because he was too important. Few people in the city would dare to lift a hand against such a rich, powerful and influential person. Good, Chilon assured himself, he'll shield me, too, if I need protection. He would hardly summon me like this to be killed.

Encouraged, he tried a question: "Tell me, my good man. Didn't my friend, the noble Vinicius, send a litter for me? My legs are so swollen I can hardly walk."

"No litter," Ursus said. "We'll have to go on foot."

"And what if I won't?"

"Don't do that, please." Ursus wasn't threatening, but it was clear an argument was useless. "Don't refuse. You have to come, so you'll go either way."

"Yes, I will, but only because it suits me. No one could force me otherwise, because I am a free citizen and a personal friend of the city prefect. As a thinking man I'm also armed with ways to counteract coercion, and I know how to change people into animals or trees. But I'll go, I'll go! Just let me throw on a warmer cloak and a deeper hood, or we'll never get out of this quarter where I'm just too well known for my acts of goodness. Every slave along the road would stop us to kiss my hands."

He changed his mantle to a fuller one and put on a deep Gallic hood, fearing that Ursus might recall his features when they came into better light outside.

"Where are you taking me?" he asked as they walked along.

"They call it the Trans-Tiber."

"I haven't been in Rome long so I haven't been there, but even across the Tiber, I expect, are people who love goodness."

Ursus was a simple, primitive man, but he wasn't stupid. He was there when Vinicius said that the Greek was with him at Ostrianum and that later on he watched him and Croton going into the building.

"Don't lie, old man," he admonished Chilon. "You were with Vinicius at Ostrianum last night and near our gate this morning."

"Ah!" said the Greek. "So your house is in the Trans-Tiber? As I said, I'm new in Rome, and I still don't know the names of all the city quarters. Yes, my friend! Of course I was at your gate. Where else would I beg Vinicius by all the holy virtues not to go in there? And do you know why I went to Ostrianum with him? I've been working for a while now on converting him, and I wanted him to hear the first of the apostles. May the light shine in his soul, as in yours! You're a Christian, aren't you? And you want the truth to prevail over falsehood, don't you?"

"I do." The Lygian's voice was humble.

Now Chilon was in full stride and firmly in control. "Vinicius is rich. He's a friend of Caesar's. He listens to the prompting of bad spirits more often than he should, but God help us all if a single hair should fall from his head. Caesar would avenge him on all the Christians."

"We are defended by a stronger master," Ursus said.

"Quite right! Quite right!" But a fresh anxiety stirred and alarmed the Greek. "What do you people have in mind to do with Vinicius?"

"I don't know. Christ orders us to be merciful."

"You couldn't have said it better! Never forget it either, or you'll sizzle in Hell like a stuffed sausage in a frying pan."

Ursus sighed. He was a terrifying man in the first flush of fury, but Chilon thought he would be able to mold him anytime he wished into just about anything he wanted. To find out now what had gone wrong in Ligia's abduction, he put on his gravest and most severe voice.

"How did you people cope with Croton?" he demanded. "Tell the truth and don't whitewash anything."

Ursus sighed again. "Vinicius will tell you."

"I take it, then, you knifed him or clubbed him down, is that it?"

"I had just my hands."

The Greek couldn't resist a gleam of admiration for the superhuman strength of the barbarian. "May Pluto take— Ah! I meant to say, may Christos forgive you."

They walked in silence for a while, then Chilon turned again to the subdued barbarian.

"I won't give you away," he assured him, "but watch out for informers and the night watch."

"I fear Christ," the humbled giant said, "not the city guard."

"And quite right too! Murder is the worst of all sins, and most of the time it's a pretty serious crime as well. I'll pray for you, but I'm not sure even my prayers will work unless you vow right now never to touch anyone again, not even with a finger."

"As it is," Ursus said with a sigh, "I've never killed anybody because I wanted to."

But Chilon wanted to lay some solid groundwork for his future safety no matter what happened. He pressed Ursus to make his vow at once, and he went on denouncing the evils of murder. He also tried to question Ursus about Vinicius, but the Lygian gave reluctant answers, saying that Vinicius would tell the Greek what he ought to hear. Talking like this, they made the long trip from the Suburra to across the Tiber and found themselves in front of the building where Vinicius had disappeared that morning. Chilon's heart quaked with fear once again. It seemed to him that Ursus was throwing greedy glances at him.

"Dead is dead," he murmured to himself. "What's the difference how he feels about killing me if he goes and does it? I'd much rather see him hit with lightning, along with all the Lygians. Oh, do it for me, Zeus, if you can!"

Mumbling about the hazards of the evening chill, he burrowed deeper into his Gallic cloak. I'm safe, he told himself. Nothing's going to happen. But his knees quivered when he thought of facing those mysterious people he saw in the graveyard. When he and Ursus finally crossed the passageway and the first enclosure and found themselves near the little garden, he slowed down and then stopped.

"Let me catch my breath," he said. "Otherwise I won't be able to speak to Vinicius and guide him to salvation."

He heard singing coming from the cottage. "What's that about?" he asked.

"You say you're a Christian"—the Lygian wagged his head—"and you don't know we always sing in praise of our Savior after we eat a meal? Miriam must've gotten back with her boy and got the dinner ready. The apostle may also still be there. He comes to see her and Crispus every day."

"I see, I see! Well, never mind, it must've slipped my mind. Take me straight to Vinicius, if you will."

"They're all together in the one big room. The rest are just sleeping cribs, big enough for a pallet and no more. Let's go in, though. You can rest inside."

They entered the dimly lit room. The sky was black with clouds, the dark winter evening merely deepened the gray gloom inside, and the pale glow of a few oil lamps did little to dispel the twilight. Vinicius didn't recognize the hooded shape of Chilon; no light came near his face. Rather, he assumed it was the Greek because he tried to disguise himself. Chilon, in turn, catching sight of the cot and Vinicius on it, headed straight for him without a glance at anybody else, as if the wounded man was his best guarantee of safety.

"Master! My lord!" he cried, pressed his hands together as if in dire mourning. "Why wouldn't you listen to my pleas?"

"Shut up and listen!" Vinicius snapped coldly.

He fixed his eyes on Chilon's with a hard, penetrating glare and started speaking slowly, stressing each word as if to chisel it deep into the Greek's memory and making sure he took everything he said as a direct order and didn't doubt anything about it.

"Croton attacked me, understand? He tried to rob and kill me. I killed him instead. And these good people took care of the wounds I received in my struggle with him."

Chilon grasped at once that if Vinicius was telling him such a blatant lie, it had to do with some arrangement he had made with the Christians. In other words he wanted his lies believed.

"He was a scoundrel to the bone!" he cried, raising his eyes skyward as if appealing to an absent witness. Neither surprise nor doubt flickered on his face for even a moment. "Didn't I warn you not to trust him, sir? All my good teaching bounced off his ears like dry peas rattling off a wall. Hell doesn't have torments bad enough for him! If a man can't be honest, he must be a scoundrel, and who but a scoundrel would rather not be an honest man? But to attack his own benefactor, and one as generous as yourself, moreover . . . O gods!"

He recalled suddenly that he claimed to be a Christian while on his way to the house with Ursus, so he clamped his mouth shut.

"If it weren't for my dagger," the patrician added, "Croton would have killed me."

"I bless the moment I advised you to bring at least a knife!"

But Vinicius turned a sharp, questioning eye on him. "What did you do today?" he demanded.

"I? Today? Didn't I tell you, sir, that I was making vows for your recovery?"

"And that's all you did?"

"That's all! I was just getting ready to visit your lordship when this good man came along and told me you wanted to see me."

"Here's a wax tablet." Vinicius glanced at his message to his household freedman. "You'll take it to Demas, my freedman not the baker you told me about. I write here that I've gone to Beneventum. Confirm that to Demas on your own any way you like. Tell him I received an urgent summons from Petronius and set out this morning—*this morning*," he stressed. "To Beneventum. Understand?"

"How could I fail to understand you, my lord, when I waved goodbye to you this morning at the Capena Gate? Of course you left! Why else would I be as grief-stricken as I am? In fact, if your munificence doesn't soothe my grief, I'll choke to death on my own tears like Aedon, the wretched wife of Zethos, who was turned into a nightingale."

Sick as he was, and used to the Greek's agility, Vinicius couldn't suppress a smile of amusement, and he was also pleased to have his thoughts followed so exactly.

"In that case I'll add an order to give you something for your pain," he said as he reached for his tablet. "Bring me a light."

Relaxed and now quite at ease about his current prospects, Chilon reached for one of the small tallow lamps that hung around the walls. But when the light fell fully on his face, with the hood slipped off his head and shoulders, Glaucus leaped from the bench on which he was sitting and faced him in two strides.

"Don't you know me, Cephas?" he demanded.

Chilon raised the light, took one look and almost dropped to the floor along with the lamp. Bent almost double with terror, he started to moan: "It was not I! It was some other man! Have mercy!"

Shaken with his remembered horrors, the old physician turned to the others grouped around the table. "That is the man who sold me and all my family to the slavers and death!"

One quick glance showed Chilon that Vinicius cared less about what had happened than the astounded Christians. The injured tribune knew the story quite as well as they, and the only reason he hadn't put Glaucus' and Chilon's tales together was that he kept losing consciousness while his bones and wounds were reset and dressed, and didn't catch the name. But this brief moment was enough for Ursus. The doctor's stricken cry when the lamplight fell on Chilon's frightened face struck like a thunderbolt tearing through darkness. He leaped at the Greek, seized him by the shoulders, and bent his spine back toward the floor.

"That's the man who told me to murder Glaucus!" he shouted.

"Mercy!" Chilon moaned. "I'll give you . . . My lord!" He craned his neck toward Vinicius. "Save me! I trusted you, I was faithful to you. Intercede for me! I'll carry your message! My lord! Oh, my lord!"

"Bury him in the garden." If he could, Vinicius would have shrugged; mercy was an outlandish concept to his way of thinking, and the treacherous Greek deserved everything he got. "Somebody else can carry my message."

His words rang like a death knell in Chilon's trembling ears, and the Greek felt his bones starting to creak in Ursus' terrifying grip. His eyes were watery with tears and bulged with pain.

"By your own god, have mercy!" he howled. "I'm a Christian! *Pax vobiscum!* Yes, I'm a Christian . . . and if you don't believe me, baptize me again! Do it twice, ten times, as many as you like! You've got it wrong, Glaucus! Let me talk, explain! Make me a slave but don't kill me! Oh, have pity on me!"

Stifled by pain, his voice gradually faded into nothing, and then the apostle Peter rose behind the table. The old man's palsied white head trembled on its neck, swayed and nodded for a time, his eyes closed in thought, and then it sank slowly to his chest. The others whispered. When he looked up again, he spoke into a breathless silence.

"And the savior said unto us," he murmured, "'Caution your brother if he errs against you, and forgive him if he shows contrition, even if he sins and shows remorse seven times in a single day.'"

This time the silence seemed deep enough to go on forever. Glaucus had clutched his face in both hands, as if unable to look into his own remembered agony, but at last he dropped them.

"Cephas," he said. "May God forgive you for what you did to me, as I forgive you in Christ's name."

Ursus dropped the Greek and also stepped away. "Let the Savior have mercy on you as well," he said, "as I forgive you."

Down on the floor and propped on his elbows, the Greek squirmed in terror, darting blind glances everywhere at once like a netted animal and expecting death to strike from any direction. He could believe neither his eyes nor his ears; it never even occurred to him that anyone would spare him. But no one touched him. No one moved against him. The terror started to recede, as slowly and as steadily as an ebbing tide, and only his blue-gray lips still quivered with fear.

"Go in peace!" the apostle told him.

Chilon scrambled to his feet, but he couldn't speak. He still edged instinctively toward Vinicius, as if he thought he would be safe under his protection. It didn't dawn on him yet—he simply hadn't had the time to give it a thought—that this man who had used him and was thus an accomplice in his evildoing damned him without a qualm, while those against whom he was being used forgave him everything. That realization would come later in its own good time; for now, his blind, staring eyes revealed only the shock of stunned disbelief. He had already grasped that he was forgiven, but he could hardly wait to get away from these frightening, unfathomable people whose goodness terrified him quite as much as any cruelty would. Sure that some fresh, unimaginable thing would happen if he stayed there a moment longer, he hurried to Vinicius.

"Give me your message, lord!" he stuttered. "Let me take your tablet!" Plucking the wax tablet from the sick man's hand, he bobbed a hasty bow to him, another to the Christians, and scurried from the room.

Out in the little garden the remaining hairs quivered on his head, because he was convinced that Ursus would charge out after him and murder him in the encompassing darkness. He would have run for his life, but Ursus suddenly appeared before him, and his legs seemed to turn to stone.

"Urbanus . . . in the name of Christ . . . " Chilon threw himself facedown on the ground and started to sob.

"Don't be afraid," Ursus said, trying to calm him. "The apostle told me to lead you out into the street so you don't get lost in all these corridors. And if you're too weak to make it home alone, I'll take you there."

Chilon looked up. "What's that? You're not going to kill me?"

"No, I won't!" Unbelievably, the huge barbarian's voice sounded reassuring. "But if I squeezed you too tight back there, I ask that you forgive me."

"Help me up," said the Greek. "You're sure you won't kill me? Just get me out into the street, then. I'll go from there on my own."

Ursus lifted him as lightly as if he were a feather and set him on his feet. Then he led him through the passageways and the central courtyard. "I'm done for!" Chilon muttered every step of the dark way until they finally emerged into the alley.

"That's far enough." Chilon mopped his forehead. "I'll go alone from here."

"Peace be with you then," Ursus said.

"And with you! And with you! Just let me catch my breath."

But Chilon couldn't draw a lungful of air until the Lygian left him in the alley. Then he filled his chest with a long, slow breath. His fingers fluttered along his hips and belly as if to make sure he was still alive, and he bolted rapidly on. But after a few dozen paces he stopped, puzzled and bewildered.

"Why didn't they kill me?"

No matter what he had learned from Euricius about the Christian teachings or what he remembered from his talk with Ursus that time by the river or what he saw and heard in the Ostrianum graveyard, he couldn't find an answer.

‹32›

VINICIUS WAS ALSO puzzled by what he had just witnessed. He was no less amazed than Chilon to see him walk away. He was surprised to have his own attack repaid with care and kindness instead of swift, retributory justice. He attributed it in part to the Christians' strange beliefs about love and mercy, in a larger part to Ligia, and in no small part to his own standing and importance.

But what they did with Chilon defied all he had ever heard about human nature and all natural laws; forgiveness played no part in the world he knew. Like Chilon, he also asked himself why they didn't kill him. The Greek deserved to die. They would never be caught. Ursus could simply drop him in a hole or fling him in the Tiber. Street robberies and murders, some of them done at night by Caesar and his cronies, were now so commonplace and so many corpses floated in the river each morning that no one even cared how they got there. The way Vinicius saw it, the Christians should have murdered Chilon; he saw no reason for the Greek's being allowed to live. True, mercy wasn't totally unknown in the Roman world; the Athenians had a temple dedicated to it and resisted the importation of gladiator fighters for quite a few years. It also happened now and then that conquered peoples found mercy in Rome itself; Calicratus, the captured king of the Britons in the time of Claudius, came to Rome in chains and now lived there freely on a handsome pension. But wreaking personal vengeance was not only morally justified throughout the civilization of the time but was also legally accepted and socially correct in the Roman empire; it was doing the right thing, as Vinicius and everybody saw it. Abandoning it went against everything the young man believed.

Yes, he did hear in Ostrianum that people were supposed to love even enemies, but he took that for some odd, far-reaching philosophic notion that played no practical role in real life. It occurred to him that Chilon was allowed to live because the time may have been wrong for murder. This could be some special season for the Christians—like ritual fasting or a festival observance or an unpropitious phase in the lunar cycle—when it was inappropriate for them to kill anyone. He had heard there were entire nations that couldn't even make war in forbidden months. But why didn't they simply turn the Greek over to official justice? Why did the apostle say that even a seven-time offender must be forgiven each of the seven times? And why did Glaucus tell the Greek, "May God forgive you as I do"?

This was beyond Roman comprehension. There could be no worse injury, pain and suffering than what the Greek had inflicted on Glaucus, and yet he forgave it. Vinicius thought about what he would do to someone who, for example, caused the death of Ligia, and he was seized by a seething fury. There were no torments in the young tribune's imagination that he wouldn't inflict in revenge.

And Crispus forgave it!

And Ursus also forgave the Greek, although he could kill anyone he pleased in and around the city and get away with it; all such a strangler had to do was go to Nemea, kill and replace the reigning titleholder of the Nemean games, and become the "Rex" or champion of the sacred grove where Hercules throttled the lion. That was how this position was achieved, and no one could or would touch a Nemean champion until he was killed in turn by his own replacement. Could any living champion beat the man who broke Croton's back? If there was such a man, Vinicius hadn't heard of him.

Vinicius could see only one answer to all these questions: These people didn't kill because they had a vast new goodness, which had never existed in the world before. They offered so much love to others that they forgot their own needs, put their own happiness behind them, ignored their worst calamities, misery and misfortunes, and lived for all mankind rather than for just themselves. But why? For what gain? Their reward for all this made little sense to Vinicius. He had heard it preached at Ostrianum, and it was something of a revelation. He was dazed and dazzled by it as a mystical experience. He could agree with some aspects of their faith on a philosophic plane, but down here on earth these strange human beings combined the cruel everyday reality with the hardships of self-deprivation, stripping themselves of every comfort and delight for the sake of others. They were doomed to wretchedness, misery and failure.

Other than amazement, his strongest feeling about the Christians was pity, shaded with contempt. He saw them as a flock of sheep that must be devoured sooner or later by the wolves. All his basic instincts, all that made him Roman, rebelled against feeling respect for those who let themselves be eaten.

One thing struck him forcibly about them after Chilon left. Some vast inner joy bloomed in each of them and lighted up their harrowed faces.

The apostle placed an arm on Glaucus' shoulder and said: "Christ triumphed within you."

He, in turn, looked up with so much trust, happiness, gratitude and delight shining in his eyes, it was as if he had been granted a bounty beyond reckoning.

Vinicius, who found and understood such joy only in retribution, stared at him as if he had gone mad. But when he saw Ligia—a king's daughter even though a barbarian—run up to this man who looked like a slave and press her lips reverently to his hand, he boiled with outrage. The world was standing on its head, he thought. He felt as if every natural law had been violated and all order had left the universe.

Then Ursus returned and told how he took Chilon out into the street, how he, too, forgave him, and how he asked to be forgiven for bruising his ribs. The apostle then blessed him, too, and Crispus declared this a day of triumph. Hearing what he had witnessed hailed as a victory, Vinicius lost the thread of his thought and drifted away.

When Ligia handed him a cooling drink a short while later, he kept her for a moment and asked: "Did you also forgive me?"

"We're Christians," she answered. "We're not allowed anger in our hearts."

"Ligia," he told her then, "whoever he may be, this god of yours, I'll sacrifice a hundred oxen to him just because he is yours."

"You'll please him more," she said, "when you learn to love him in your own heart."

"Just because he's yours," Vinicius said again, but in a fading voice. Feeling weak again, he let his eyes fall shut.

Ligia walked away, but she was back quite soon and leaned over him to see if he was sleeping. Vinicius sensed her nearness, looked up and smiled at her, and she touched his eyelids lightly with her hand as if to urge him back to his dreams. A sense of deep tenderness and sweetness settled upon him along with his sickness; he felt warm and as if drifting like a leaf. Night was already well along, he was parched with fever, but he stayed awake and followed Ligia with his eyes wherever she moved.

He did slip at times into a dreamlike, semiconscious state in which he saw and heard everything around him, but it was set against a

backdrop of memory and imagination where reality clashed with
fever and delirium: an old abandoned cemetery, a temple like a tower
with Ligia as its priestess. He saw her luminous on the rooftop, a lute
in her hands, singing her nightly chant to Luna like the moon
priestesses he had known in the East. He saw himself creeping up to
seize her, with his last ounce of strength crawling up a narrow stairway that spiraled toward her, while Chilon snaked behind him.
"Don't do this, my lord," the Greek was panting at his heels. "That's
a priestess whom *he* will avenge."

Vinicius didn't know who "he" might be. He knew, however, that
he was on his way to commit a sacrilege. A deep fear reached for him
with an icy hand as if his love for her were a profanation. When he
did finally reach her at the balustrade that circled the rooftop, an
apostle with a silver beard stood suddenly beside her. "Don't presume
to touch her," he commanded, "because she is mine."

They left him on his knees, reaching after them and pleading to be
taken with them, and walked into the sky on a road of moonlight.

He woke then, conscious and aware, and stared straight ahead. The
night outside was cold, and the room was chilly. Only a few coals still
glowed in the raised stone hearth, but they cast a cheerful light on the
group of Christians who clustered around it. Vinicius watched their
warm breaths cooling into mist. The apostle sat in the center, with
Ligia huddled on a footstool at his knee. Glaucus, Crispus and
Miriam sat together before them, while Ursus crouched on one edge
of the group and Miriam's son, Nazarius, on the other. The boy was a
sweet-faced child with long black hair falling to his shoulders.

The old apostle was murmuring something in a low voice, and
Ligia was looking up at him and listening. Vinicius watched him with
superstitious awe, not much less chilling than the fear in his interrupted visions. It crossed his mind that his delusions had divined the
truth and that this ancient visitor from a distant country was going to
take Ligia far away from him and lead her into the unknown where he
couldn't follow. He was sure the old man was talking about him,
probably conspiring to throw up new walls between him and Ligia.
He couldn't imagine that anyone would talk about anything else just
now, so he grasped and focused all of his attention and started to listen.

But he was disappointed. The apostle was talking once more about
Christ. "These people live by that name," Vinicius decided, puzzled
about such reverence. The old man told the story of how the temple
guards seized Christ in the olive orchard.

"Then came the temple guards and servants," he related, "and the Savior asked whom they were seeking there. 'Jesus of Nazareth,' they told him, and when he said to them, 'I am he,' they threw themselves facedown on the ground before him and didn't dare raise their hands against him. They asked again, and once more he told them, 'I am he,' and it was then that they seized him."

Here the apostle paused and warmed his hands at the dwindling fire. "It was a cold night, like this one, but I felt as if my heart had burst into flames," he told them. "I drew a sword to defend him and cut off the ear of one of the soldiers. I would have fought for him harder than my life, but he told me to put up my sword. 'Am I to turn away this cup which my Father gives me?' he asked, and then they took him and bound him with a rope."

He paused again and pressed both palms against his forehead as if to push back a rush of memories before going on. But Ursus couldn't wait for more. He jumped up, stirred the embers in the hearth so that a bright new swarm of sparks shot out into the gloom and a flame leaped up, then sat down and cried: "Ah, if I had been there!"

He broke off because Ligia signaled for him to be quiet. But he went on breathing noisily and deeply, and it was clear that his simple feelings were in turmoil. On the one hand he loved the apostle; he would kiss the ground he walked on. But on the other hand he would never give up the fight as Peter had. Oh, if he had been there that night! If someone had dared to lay a finger on the lamb while he was around, he would have knocked the stuffing out of all those soldiers, temple guards and servants! His eyes filmed over with longing as he thought about it. He would not just fight for the Savior by himself— oh, no. He would have all the Lygians running to help, lads as big as barns and as tough as nails. But then he became confused, because this would go against the Savior's will and interfere with the salvation of the world.

Peter dropped his hands and resumed his tale, but Vinicius, burning with fever, slipped back into dreams. What he was hearing now flowed into the story he had heard at Ostrianum, the one where Christ appeared to the fishermen on the shore of the inland sea. He saw the wide waters and the fishing skiff that carried both Peter and Ligia. He swam behind them as hard as he could, but he couldn't reach them; the pain in his broken arm made him slow and weak. A storm erupted. The waves blinded him. He started to drown. But Ligia knelt before the apostle, who then turned the boat around and held out an oar. Vinicius grabbed it; they helped him aboard, and he lay exhausted in the boat.

Then he was standing, looking back toward the way they had come, and saw many others swimming in their wake. The waves swept over them, foaming around their heads. Some went down, drowning, only their reaching hands showing above the water. But Peter saved them all, pulling them out one after the other and taking them aboard, and the boat grew miraculously larger. Soon it was carrying greater multitudes than at Ostrianum. Still more came aboard, and Vinicius worried that they would swamp the vessel. But Ligia calmed him down and pointed to a light on the distant shore to which they were sailing. A luminous figure stood within that light, and Vinicius saw the storm around him dwindling and abating. The apostle had related at Ostrianum how Christ showed himself to the fishermen, and now that incandescent figure was the goal toward which Peter steered. The core of light expanded as they drew near it, the winds and waves died down, and the calmness spread across the water. The crowds were singing. The scent of sandalwood deepened in the air. A vivid rainbow rose out of the sea and pulsed above it like a giant heart, and then the boat beached gently. Ligia took his hand.

"Come," she said. "I will take you to him." She led him to the light.

He woke again. Reality was drifting back, but he was slow to focus his attention and the dream continued a while longer. He was still on that shore, alone in the multitudes; he peered around looking for Petronius without knowing why, but he couldn't find him. Nor was there anybody left within the light from the hearth. They had all gone to bed, and the wavering firelight kept him awake. The olive embers cast a meager glow, subdued in the ashes, but a bright new flame danced on a handful of kindling tossed onto the coals.

In its light Vinicius saw Ligia sitting at his bedside. Joy, gratitude and pity swept through him together. She had been up all night at the cemetery, then spent the day looking after him. The rest of them were gone, resting and asleep, and only she stayed up to watch over him. It wasn't hard to guess how tired she must be; her eyes were closed, and she sat as if carved from stone. Vinicius couldn't tell if she was sleeping or merely deep in thought. He watched her clean, quiet profile, the long lowered lashes, the hands folded gently in her lap, and a wholly new idea of beauty struggled to life in his pagan head. Beauty, by Greek and Roman definitions as he knew them, was proud of its challenge to the senses, naked and unashamed, hedonistic and delighting in physical perfection. But now it took on a new meaning that went beyond the sensual. There was, he thought, surprised, another kind of beauty in the world: a crystal purity that contained the soul.

He couldn't quite bring himself to name this new perception or see it as Christian, but Ligia made it impossible for him to think of it as separate from the faith she followed. The one thing sprang out of the other and made it what it was. It came to him that if she still sat watching over him while all the others went to bed, this, too, was part of the mystical experience that made her a Christian. This thought disturbed him. He was beginning to admire this teaching, but he would rather that she be near him because she was in love, was pleased with his beauty, admired his body, and wanted him, like other Greek and Roman women he knew.

Suddenly he thought that if she were like all his other women, something would be lacking. The notion left him gasping with surprise, and he couldn't understand what was happening to him. He was adrift among new feelings, thinking in terms quite foreign to the world he lived in, and found himself astonished at each turn.

She opened her eyes and saw him watching her. She moved closer to him.

"I'm here with you," she said.

"I saw your soul," he said.

"Where?" Ligia smiled.

"In my dreams."

‹ 3 3 ›

HE WAS WEAK but clearheaded when he woke the next morning. His fever was down. Waking, he thought he heard a whispered conversation, but when he opened his eyes he saw no one near him. Ligia was also gone, but he saw Ursus stooped over the hearth. The Lygian giant had raked aside the pale gray ashes and was now blowing on a few live coals, although it seemed more like a blacksmith's bellows than a man's mouth and lungs. Vinicius looked at his massive back with the keen, appreciative eye of an arena enthusiast; he noted the cyclopean neck, the colossal torso, and upper legs as thick as a pair of tree trunks. This, he remembered, was the man who had literally crushed Croton the day before, and he offered silent thanks that he was still alive.

Mercury be thanked he didn't twist my neck, he thought. By Pollux! If the Lygians are all like him, the Danube legions may have a bad time with them someday.

"Hey there, slave!" he spoke.

Ursus looked up from the hearth with a smile that was almost friendly. "God give you health and a good day, sir," he said pleasantly. "But I'm a free man, not a slave."

Vinicius was pleased. He was curious about Ligia's homeland and wanted to question Ursus about it; talking to a free man, even though a plebeian, was less distasteful for a Roman of patrician rank than talking to a slave, who wasn't even recognized as a human being.

"You don't belong to Aulus Plautius, then?"

"No, sir. I serve Callina, as I served her mother, but of my own free will."

Here he hunched over the hearth again to blow new life into the embers and toss in some kindling. "There are no slaves among us," he said, looking up.

But Vinicius had only one interest: "Where's Ligia?"

"She just left, sir. I'm to make your breakfast. She watched over you all night."

"Why didn't you help and take a turn?"

"That's what she wanted," Ursus said. "I do what she says." Then his eyes grew sad. "If I didn't, sir," he added contritely, "you wouldn't be alive."

"You're sorry, then, that you didn't kill me?"

"No, sir. Christ forbids killing."

"What about Atacinus? How about Croton?"

"I couldn't help it," Ursus muttered; he stared at his fists as if unable to explain their actions. His soul, he seemed to say, was a Christian one, but his hands remained pagan.

Then he put a pot on the fire, squatted by the hearth, and lost himself in thought staring at the flames.

"It's your fault anyway, sir," he said at last. "You shouldn't have raised your hands to my king's daughter."

This blunt, simple speech—short on servility and long on directness—enraged Vinicius at first. His pride was outraged. His Roman and patrician dignity seethed that a commoner, and a barbarian at that, dared to speak to him almost as an equal, and chided him as well. This was unheard of! It was one more surprise to add to all the unparalleled and abnormal things that had happened since he went with Chilon to Ostrianum. But he had neither the will nor his own slaves around him, so he fought the urge to react as he should have, both by law and custom. Moreover he wanted to hear more about Ligia's life, and his curiosity prevailed over pride.

Calm again, he started questioning Ursus about the Lygians' war on Vannius and the Suevi. Ursus was happy to talk, but he didn't have much to add to what Vinicius already knew from Aulus Plautius. He wasn't at the final battle, because he had gone with Ligia and her mother to the camp of Atelius Hister, and all he knew was that the Lygians beat the Suevi and their allies. His king was killed in that battle, however, shot by a Yazigian archer. Soon afterward the Lygians heard that their neighboring Semonones set their forests on fire; they hurried home to punish the invaders, while the two royal hostages stayed behind with Hister. The Roman general treated them like royalty, but when the mother died, he didn't know what to do with the little princess. Ursus wanted to take her north to the Lygian country, but it was a long, dangerous journey through lands infested with wild beasts and swarming with fierce tribesmen. Hearing at last that a Lygian embassy was in Pomponius' camp on the lower Danube, offering an alliance against the Marcomanni, Hister sent Ligia to them, but no Lygian envoys were there when she and her suite arrived. Pomponius brought them to Rome as part of his triumphal victory celebration and placed the child in the keeping of his sister, Pomponia Graecina.

Vinicius knew much of this already, but he was glad to hear it again. It flattered his pride that she was a princess. His boundless vanity about his own family's history and position enjoyed this first-hand confirmation of Ligia's royal origins. As a king's daughter she could take a high place at Caesar's court, equal to the first families in Rome, especially since her father's people had never fought the Romans. True, they were barbarians, but they were not to be taken lightly on that account; Atelius Hister himself made note in his writings of their "uncountable multitudes of warriors."

Ursus confirmed this when Vinicius asked about his country.

"We live in the far timberlands," he said, "but no one has ever been to the end of our forests, and we have a lot of people. There is also a lot of rich, wooden towns in our woods, because whatever the Semnones, Marcomanni, Vandals and Quadi pillage all over the world, we take away from them. They know better than to come after us, so it's peaceful up there. But when the wind is right, they set our border trees on fire. No, we're not afraid of them, nor do we worry much about the Roman Caesar."

"The gods gave Rome dominion over all the world," Vinicius spoke sternly.

"The gods are demons," Ursus shrugged. "And where there are no Romans, there is no dominion."

He fed the fire and went on as if speaking to some vision of his own.

"That time when Caesar took Callina into his house, when I thought she'd be harmed in some way, I had it in mind to go north again and bring the Lygians down to help our princess. And they would come too. They're good people even if they're pagans. Maybe I'd be that 'bearer of good tidings' the great apostle talks about. Why not? Somebody has to tell them. Christ was born far away, and they have never even heard of him. But I'll do that anyway someday. I'll ask Callina to let me go home as soon as she is safe and back with Pomponia."

His mind, straightforward and uncomplicated though it was, seemed as fixed on Christ as the other Christians and always came around to him again.

"Why not?" he muttered, staring into the fire. "He knew better than I where he should be born. But if he had come into the world in our forests, things would've been different. We wouldn't have killed him. We'd have looked after the infant, made sure he never ran short of venison or mushrooms or beaver pelts or amber. . . . He'd be comfortable with us. If he needed something, we'd just take it from the Suevi or the Marcomanni for him."

He stirred the homemade brew he had put on the fire and drifted into thought, letting his memory take him to his forests. It was only after the liquid had bubbled and began to hiss, and he'd poured it out to cool in a shallow bowl, that he spoke again.

"Glaucus said for you not to move, sir. Not even your good hand. So Callina told me I should feed you."

Vinicius didn't argue. It never even occurred to him to question her wishes. She might have been Caesar's daughter or a goddess: Her whim was his law. Ursus squatted beside him, dipped the warm brew from the bowl with a smaller cup, and handed it carefully to his mouth. He was so concerned to do it right and his sky blue eyes were so full of caring that Vinicius couldn't believe this was the raging Titan who only yesterday had crushed Croton, roared at him like a hurricane, and would have torn him to pieces if Ligia hadn't stopped him. This was also the first time Vinicius ever gave a thought to what a commoner, a servant, or a barbarian cared about.

Ursus was a clumsy nurse, however, no matter how caring. The cup disappeared in his massive fingers, leaving no room on the rim for the young man's mouth.

"It's a lot easier to drag a bison from a thicket," he grumbled in concern.

Vinicius grinned, amused by the Lygian's dogged persistence, but the mention of the animals intrigued him. He had seen the terrible horned aurochs in the circus and knew they came from the northern forests. Even the best of the *bestiari* in the arena were afraid of them, and only elephants matched their size and power.

"You mean you've tried to throw such beasts by the horns?" he asked, astonished.

"I was scared my first twenty winters," Ursus said with a shrug, "but it didn't bother me much after that."

He returned to feeding the brew to Vinicius, even clumsier than before. "I'd better ask Miriam or Nazarius to do this," he muttered.

Then Ligia leaned out to them from behind a screen. "I'll help in a moment," she said.

She came out of the sleeping space almost at once, ready for bed in a short light tunic closed tightly across the breast, the kind known as a *capitium* in the ancient world, and her hair was loose on her back and shoulders. Vinicius, whose heartbeat quickened at the sight of her, started chiding her for going so long without rest.

"I was about to do that"—her voice had a merry ring—"but first I'll take over from Ursus here."

She took the cup, sat on the edge of the cot and started to feed Vinicius, who felt both humbled and delighted. Warmth came to him from her body when she leaned toward him, her loose hair drifting about his chest, and he was sure all color drained from his face. Desire seized him and swept him into a whirlpool of confused emotions, but he was also sure that this was a dear, inestimably precious person, more important to him than all else on earth. Wanting her as a lover, he now also loved her like a caring husband. Up to this moment he felt and acted like every other man or woman of his place and time: a self-willed, uncompromising egotist, blind to any feelings but his own and concerned only with his own pleasure or advancement. Now he also began to care about her as a human being.

He loved looking at her. Being with her was a joy to him, but he was worried she would overtax her strength. "That's enough," he said, refusing the nourishment. "Go to sleep, my goddess."

"Don't call me that," she said. "It's wrong for me to hear it."

But she was smiling at him as she said it. She was no longer sleepy and didn't feel tired; she said she'd stay with him until Glaucus came later in the morning. He listened to her musical voice, totally enthralled, gripped in a sense of rising, thankful joy, and searching for some way to show her that he was grateful.

"I didn't know who you were," he said after a long silence. "But now I know I took the wrong road to reach you. So I'll tell you now: Go home to Pomponia Graecina. You can be sure no one will raise his hand against you from now on."

Her face saddened. Her soft, resigned voice was almost a sigh: "I would be happy to see her even from a distance, but I can never go back to her again."

"Why is that?" Vinicius was surprised.

"Acte lets us know what happens at the Palatine," she told him. "Didn't you hear what Caesar did after I escaped? Just before he left for Naples he called in Aulus and Pomponia, thinking they had helped me, and threatened them with his most severe displeasure. It was good that Aulus could remind him he'd never spoken a lie in his life, and then he swore he and Pomponia neither helped me nor knew where I was. Caesar believed him. Later he forgot all about it. Our elders here advised me not to write to Mother so that she'd always be able to swear she hadn't heard from me or knew where I was. Perhaps you won't understand this, Vinicius, but we're not allowed to lie even if our lives depend on it. That's our law, and we must bend all our wishes to it, so I haven't seen Pomponia since I left her house. All she hears about me is an odd word here and there that I'm safe and well."

Tears showed in her eyes because she missed her home, but she became calm and at peace again quickly. "I know Pomponia misses me as well, but we have our consolations."

"Yes," Vinicius murmured. "Christ is your consolation, but that's something I don't understand at all."

"Look at us, then. See us as we are. We do not have conflict, pain or suffering among us, and if they come, they are changed into joy. Death itself, which for your people is the end of life, is merely the beginning of ours, a change for the better in everything, the quiet after the storm, peaceful and eternal. Think what it means to live according to a teaching that commands compassion even for an enemy, forbids every lie, frees your spirit forever from every form of anger and offers inexhaustible happiness at the end."

"I heard this in Ostrianum," Vinicius agreed. "I also saw how your people treated me and Chilon. When I think about that, I still feel I'm dreaming and that I shouldn't trust my eyes and ears. But tell me something else: Are you happy?"

"Yes!" she said firmly. "It isn't possible to be unhappy when you're with Christ."

"And you wouldn't want to go back to Pomponia?"

"With all my heart. And if that's God's will, I shall."

"That's why I'm saying this: Go home, and I'll swear on my household gods that I won't trouble you."

She thought for a long moment. "No," she said at last. "I can't. I love them too much to place them in danger. Caesar doesn't like the Plautius family. If I went home, he'd know about it before very long. You know how quickly news travels through Rome. Slaves tell one another everything that happens, and Caesar would hear it from his. The least he would do to Aulus and Pomponia would be to take me away again."

"Yes." Vinicius frowned. "That could happen. If for no other reason, he'd do it just to impose his will. It's true he has quite forgotten about you, preferring to think that I'm the offended party and not he. But maybe . . . Well, what if he took you from Aulus and gave you to me? Then I'd just take you back to Pomponia."

Her smile was even sadder then. "Vinicius, would you really want to see me at the Palatine?" she asked him.

Pain shot into his temples as he ground his teeth. "No. You're right. I spoke like an idiot."

Suddenly he saw a darkness about his world; a pit of ugliness opened up before him. He was a patrician, a military tribune, a man of immense power of his own, and yet all Roman power resided in the hands of a single maniac whose whims and malice could never be foreseen. Only people such as these Christians could live without his shadow over them, unafraid of him, not taking him into account in everything they did. This whole existence, along with all the heartaches, pains and separations that went with living in such a world, was meaningless to them, and death itself was nothing. Everyone else, the highest and the lowest, was mentally on his knees before the madman in the Palatine one way or another.

The full inescapable and degrading horror of his times lay suddenly before Vinicius with all its loathsome depth and all-pervading fear. He couldn't bring Ligia back to Aulus in case the monster remembered her again and vented his frightful anger on people she loved. Nero would forget it the moment he did it, but the damage would have been done. Vinicius was certain the same thing would happen to Ligia and himself along with the others if he married her at once. It struck him like a stunning blow that life was intolerable under these conditions. The world had to change and become transformed into something new, or life could no longer be endured. He also grasped a truth that had eluded him only moments earlier: Only the Christians could be happy in such times. Above all, he was revolted that his own mistakes had made such a tangled mess of his life and Ligia's that there was practically no way to get things right again.

Grief struck him like a fist. "There's more joy in your life than mine," he said. "Do you know that? You have your Christ here in this hovel, among these wretched people. All I had was you, and since you vanished I've been like a starved, homeless beggar praying for the end. You mean more than all the world to me. I searched for you because there was no way I could live without you. Believe me, there were no more banquets for me and precious little rest. Only the hope of finding you kept me from throwing myself on my sword. But now

I'm afraid to die because I'd never see you again. I'm telling you the purest truth I know. I can't think how I can live without you, and all that has kept me alive was the hope of finding and seeing you again.

"Do you remember our talks in the Plautius house?" His voice was urgent but also filled with loss. "One day you drew a fish in the sand, and I didn't know what it meant. Do you remember how we threw the ball? I loved you even then more than my own life, and you, too, started to feel I loved you. Then Aulus came with his warnings about chills and shadows, and we never finished saying what we had started. Pomponia told Petronius on our way out that God was one, all-powerful and all-forgiving, but it never dawned on us that your god is Christ. Listen, I'm ready to love him if he gives you to me, although he seems like a god of slaves, foreigners and beggars.

"You sit here beside me"—passion gripped his voice—"but you're thinking only about him. Think of me, too, or I'll begin to hate him. You're the only divinity I worship. I bless your parents and the land you come from. I'd like to kiss your feet, burn sacrifices to you and offer you my prayers. You're three times a goddess, as far as I'm concerned. You don't know, you simply can't imagine how I love you."

His face was white and strained, and he brushed a hand across his damp forehead. His nature didn't understand opposition, and he observed no limits in either love or fury. He spoke like a man carried away by feeling, who no longer cared how his words were taken, but he spoke with the honesty of absolute conviction. She could feel the pain, the craving, the naked lust and the unrestrained adoration that had built up in him and now burst from him in an avalanche of words. They struck her as blasphemous, yet her heartbeat suddenly quickened and her breathing increased sharply under the constraining tunic, as if her body wished to break free of it. She couldn't help feeling sorry for him in his misery. She was touched by his respect and consideration for her. She felt she was loved and adored beyond any limits, and she also recognized the influence she held over this dangerous and unbending Roman. He was now hers absolutely and humbled beyond anything his kind of man usually permitted. It was this humbling of his overwhelming pride, the first step before looking into the truth, that made her so happy.

She remembered him at his best, the magnificent, beautiful Vinicius who seemed like a pagan god in the Plautius gardens as he told her about the power and beauty of love and churned her dreamy musings into something vital and disturbing that she had never felt in the childlike innocence of those days. He was the same man whose kisses she remembered from the Palatine and from whose arms Ursus had snatched her as if from a fire. Only now that haughty face was soft with pain and worship, the eyes begged under a pallid forehead; and he was hurt, broken in all his hopes for love but still loving her, brought down from the Roman pedestal of his insolence, humbled and adoring. This, she realized, was all she wanted from him in those greener days; she would have loved him with all her heart if he had been able to be like that for her, and this made him even dearer to her now.

She knew there might come a time when this love of his would engulf her and carry her away, and then she felt the same thing he had just a moment earlier. A pit yawned suddenly before her. She stood poised on the edge of an abyss, and she couldn't understand how this had come about. Was this why she had turned her back on Pomponia's home? Is this what she had fled from? Did she hide all this time in the most wretched quarters of the city because of this? And who was this Vinicius anyway? An Augustan, a soldier and one of Nero's courtiers who had taken part in all his craziness and debauchery, as proved by that banquet she could not forget.

How could she trust him? Her thoughts and feelings were in violent collision. Didn't he go with all the others to the pagan temples? Make his sacrifices? Bow to the dissolute animalistic deities, in which perhaps he didn't believe but which he honored in public anyway? He said he loved her, and perhaps he did. But he had hounded her all this time to make her his slave, turn her into his concubine, and drag her into that dreadful and degrading world of opulence, excess, viciousness, obscenity and indulgence that challenged God's anger and cried for retribution. He seemed changed in a way, he wasn't quite the same, but hadn't she just heard him say he would hate Christ if she thought more about him than Vinicius? It seemed to Ligia that love for anyone other than Christ was a sin against him and his teaching, and when she realized that such contradictory feelings could take root in the depths of her soul, she became frightened of her future and disturbed by the promptings of her own desires.

In this moment of inner confusion Glaucus came into the room to change the sick man's dressings and check on his health. Annoyance and impatience flashed at once across Vinicius' face. He hated this intrusion into his talk with Ligia and answered Glaucus' questions with something like contempt. He quickly realized that Ligia would see through him and lose whatever illusions she might have had about the changes in his ruthless, single-minded nature wrought by what he'd heard in Ostrianum. Yes, he was different now, both of them could see that, but only to the extent that it affected Ligia. Beyond that solitary feeling he stayed what he was. His heart, she knew, beat with the same harsh, selfish, predatory rhythm as before. He would always be a Roman, as much a preying animal as the she-wolf that had suckled Romulus and Remus. He was no more capable of grasping the full import of Christ's gentle teaching than of ordinary human gratitude.

She left, full of anxiety and turmoil. The heart she offered Christ daily in her prayers was as clean and clear as a teardrop, but now this clarity was clouded and confused. A poisonous insect had slipped into the flower and was buzzing there. Sleep brought no rest. Tired as she was after two sleepless nights, she tossed in a nightmare. She was at Ostrianum. Nero was trampling across crowds of Christians in a rose-wreathed chariot and galloping behind him was a swarm of dissolute Augustans, noisy priests of Cybele, half-naked dancers and gladiators. Vinicius seized her in his arms, crushed her against his chest and whispered, "Come with us."

FROM THAT TIME ON she didn't come as often into the common room and seldom went near his cot. But this didn't help her peace of mind or dispel her fears. She could feel Vinicius' pleading eyes on her wherever she moved. She saw that he considered any word from her an act of grace, almost like a blessing, that he was tormented but didn't dare to complain in case it upset her or she thought less of him, and that he only cared about her happiness and well-being.

This brought remorse. She pitied him and was sorry for him. The more she tried to stay out of his way, the more upset she felt for causing pain in any way at all, and this pity and guilt endeared him to her even more. She was no longer at peace; she argued with herself. She told herself she should always be with him, first because God wished her to give good for evil, and then to bring him to that teaching through conversation and explanation. Her conscience pointed out at once, however, that she was lying to herself; it was the magic of his love for her that drew her so powerfully toward him.

She was distraught. Her inner conflicts mounted daily. She felt trapped, and the more she struggled, the more tightly she became ensnared. She could not escape. She had to admit to herself that seeing him became more important to her every day, and she took fresh pleasure in his voice each time she heard it. It took all her willpower to suppress what she really desired and not spend all her time perched on the side of his cot. He beamed with joy each time she came near him, and this made her very happy. One day—and this had never happened to her before—she found traces of tears in his eyes. She wanted to kiss them dry. Feeling panicky and full of self-contempt and recriminations, she cried through the night.

He was as patient with her as if he had sworn to be forbearing in all things. Whenever anger, disdain or impatience glinted in his eyes, he mastered them quickly and then looked at her uneasily as if wanting to apologize.

This moved her more than anything. No one had ever loved her so totally. She felt both guilt and delight when she thought about it, and she watched for anything about him she could love in return. Vinicius was indeed changing every day whether he knew it or not. He was less haughty when he talked to Glaucus. To his surprise, sometimes it occurred to him that this poor slave healer was a human being, as was the old, foreign-born Miriam, who showed him such care, and Crispus, whom he always saw buried in his prayers. It was a startling thought, nevertheless he had it.

He became fond of Ursus. They talked all day long. Vinicius couldn't hear enough about Ligia, and the giant never ran out of stories. Moreover, performing all the small tasks necessary at a sick man's bedside, Ursus began to exhibit a kind of attachment. Vinicius always thought of Ligia as a being of another order, someone unique and unrelated to anyone else and superior to everyone around her, but now he started looking at ordinary people as if they were human, and he saw them with slightly different eyes. They were not dust or dirt under his boots. Their poverty no longer placed them beneath notice. Their unimportant lives didn't make them automatically sub-human like stray dogs or vermin. He could actually feel an unusual interest in them, which was amazing in itself. They showed him facets of character and humanity he had never imagined their kind could possess.

Nazarius was the only one he couldn't abide. The boy had the outrageous gall to fall in love with Ligia. He forced himself to be civil to him as long as he could, but one day, when the boy brought Ligia a pair of quail he had bought at the market with his own earned money, the dam broke. Vinicius gave way to ancestral rage: The haughty spirit of his Quirite forbears, for whom foreigners were nothing more than insects, broke into the open. He turned white as a sheet when he heard Ligia's thanks.

"How can you stand to have him bring you things?" he demanded when the boy left to get water for the birds. "He's a foreigner! Don't you know the Greeks equate Jews with dogs?"

"I don't know how Greeks feel about anyone," she replied, "or what they call the Jews. But I know Nazarius is my Christian brother."

He saw reproach cloud her eyes, and he ground his teeth in anger, because his outburst had shattered an illusion for them both. He had suppressed the Roman in himself for so long that she was beginning to forget about it, while he was beginning to question it and recoil from that darker side. He clenched his teeth to keep himself from saying that he would have had that kind of brother flogged to death or sent to the chain gang in his Sicilian vineyards.

But he had mastered even this fundamental outrage. "Forgive me," he told her. "For me you're always a king's daughter and the adopted child of Aulus and Pomponia."

He overcame his own ingrained beliefs to such a degree that when the boy came back, he promised him a pair of peacocks or flamingos from the gardens of his city compound, once he returned home.

Ligia could see these struggles and understood how much it cost him to fight against himself. Her heart went out to him each time he won such victories. When it came to Nazarius, however, the struggle cost him much less than she supposed. Vinicius could be outraged by the boy's presumption but he couldn't feel jealous. Miriam's son didn't mean much more than a dog to him. Besides, he was a child, and his love, if he was even aware of it, was a mixture of worship and childish fascination.

The young tribune fought a longer and far harder battle against surrender to the veneration these people bestowed on the name of Christ and his cult. The struggle was all the more intense because he couldn't share it but could only fight it out in silence within himself. On one hand, it was Ligia's faith, so he was ready to accept it without further question. Moreover, the more his body healed, the better he remembered a long string of astonishing events that had occurred since that night at Ostrianum and all the startling new concepts and ideas that had entered his head since then, and he was stunned by the superhuman power of the faith that transformed men's spirits so totally and profoundly. He came to the realization that nothing like it had ever existed in the world before, that it was greater than his understanding, and he began to think that if it ever became the law for all men everywhere, investing all mankind with love and forgiveness, there'd be the dawn of an era comparable to the most ancient times, the eons before Jupiter's ascension when Saturn ruled the world.

He didn't doubt Christ's supernatural origins; the Greek and Roman gods scattered their half-human progenies everywhere in all kinds of guises. Nor did he question the idea of a resurrection or doubt the other miracles on which Christians doted. He heard an eyewitness whose obvious truthfulness and abhorrence of lies placed him beyond doubting. Moreover civilized Roman skepticism allowed questions about the gods but not about miracles, which were part and parcel of the lives of men and gods alike.

All this combined to make a riddle that he couldn't solve because this picture had another side. The whole religion challenged the laws of nature and overturned the established order. It was clearly so impossible in universal practice and so lunatic in theory that every other outlandish rite seemed logical beside it. Romans and the many peoples of the world could be corrupt and evil, which Vinicius and everyone else accepted, but the order of things that regulated life was proper and correct. What more could anybody want as long as the ruling Caesar was a decent, reasonable man or the senate consisted of Stoics like Thrasea instead of degenerate libertines and toadies? The Roman peace, he argued, created and maintained all civilization. Roman rule was good for everyone, the conquerors as well as the conquered. Social divisions were correct and fair. Meanwhile this teaching, as he understood it, would overturn the natural order of things in the world, topple dominion and authority, and make all men equal.

What would it do, for example, to the existence and supremacy of Rome? Would Romans cease to rule? Give up their imperial destiny? Accept the conquered herds as their human equals? The patrician's mind couldn't accept that. It went against everything he knew or imagined, uprooted all his values, dismissed his heritage and his way of thinking, and overturned all he believed about life and the world. He couldn't see how he would be able to exist if he became a Christian. Everything within him fought against acceptance of this new religion, which he admired on one level as much as he feared it on another. Finally, convinced that it was all that stood between him and Ligia, he started to hate it.

At the same time, he knew, this faith gave Ligia her inexpressible new beauty, the deep inner glow that opened his heart to admiring and respecting her, added devotion to his physical desire, and in his eyes turned her into the extraordinary being he valued above all else.

It was then that he wanted to love Christ, for he knew he would have to make his choice someday and throw himself into one ocean or the other. It didn't matter to him which he chose right now, but he already knew he could never be neutral or indifferent. Meanwhile he was adrift between the two opposing currents, propelled by two colliding and contradictory tides. He hesitated, couldn't make a choice, questioned his own judgment, challenged his thoughts, distrusted his feelings, and did his best throughout to show a silent respect for this deity he couldn't understand, because it was Ligia's.

She saw what was happening to him, how he strained and struggled with himself and how his Roman arrogance fought against the teaching. It just about broke her heart, because it was such an insurmountable barrier for him, but she was also moved by his willingness to try. She was grateful for the silent respect he showed Christ.

She thought of Aulus and Pomponia and Pomponia's single source of sorrow: her grief that she and Aulus could never be together after death. She understood something of Pomponia's sadness and her frequent tears. She, too, had found a dear being she would lose for all eternity. She deceived herself at times, thinking that he might yet open himself to Christ and embrace his truth, but she also knew this was an illusion. She knew him too well by now. Vinicius as a Christian was an impossible idea; the two images simply couldn't exist side by side in her imagination. If the thoughtful and enlightened Aulus couldn't become a Christian under the influence of the wise and excellent Pomponia, how could Vinicius do it? There was no hope for him. He would never know salvation. That was the only outcome she could see, and her pity for him made him all the dearer.

Thinking about this frightened her. This grim, irrevocable verdict that rang with the finality of doom didn't thrust her away from him or make him ugly in her eyes, as it should have. On the contrary, she was alarmed to note, she felt more her compassion for him. She wanted to reach out to him no matter what happened and talk to him about his eternity of darkness. She tried only once. Sitting beside him, she told him there was no life outside the Christian teaching. He raised himself up on his good arm, laid his head on her knees and said, "You are life!"

And suddenly she couldn't breathe. She became disoriented. A strange, wonderful shudder ran through her. She caught Vinicius by the temples with both hands, wanting to raise him up, but this bowed her toward him and she pressed her lips against his hair. They stayed like that as if fixed in time for a precious moment: locked in a common struggle against their mutual intoxication with each other, and lost in their love.

She broke free and fled. Her blood seemed on fire and her senses reeled. But this was the proverbial drop that filled the cup beyond overflowing. Vinicius had no idea what price he would end up paying for that happy moment, but Ligia knew at once that she was the one who needed help. Confused and torn between conflicting feelings, she burst into tears. She couldn't sleep that night, despising her weakness, praying, yet sure she would not be heard, thinking herself contemptible and unworthy to beg Christ's forgiveness. She slipped early out of her *cubiculum,* found Crispus and led him to the wilted arbor in the little garden; she poured out her troubles to him, and pleaded for him to let her go away. She could no longer trust herself, she told him. She couldn't keep denying her love for Vinicius. Staying with him in Miriam's house, breathing the same air, was impossible for her.

Crispus was stunned. He was an old, judgmental man, fanatical in his religious fervor. He could see why Ligia had to leave the house, but he saw all love other than spiritual as profane and couldn't forgive her descent into carnality. He was appalled. He was the one who had looked after her since her escape, confirmed her in her faith, and came to love her as the pure and undefiled offering he reserved for God. He saw her as a virginal white lily rising from sound Christian soil, unpolluted by any earthly matter; he couldn't understand how she could find room anywhere within her for a lesser love. He wanted to offer her to Christ like a jewel, as something precious fashioned for His glory by Crispus' own hands. The disappointment left him shocked and bitter.

"Go beg God to forgive your sin," he groaned. "Do it before the demons that possess you complete your destruction and you deny the Savior! God died on the cross for you, to ransom your soul with his blood, but you preferred the love of a man who wanted your body. God's miracle saved you from him, but you reach out to that son of darkness and soil yourself with lust. What is he? A friend and servant of the Antichrist, his partner in debauchery and crime. Where do you expect him to lead you if not into the pit, that foul Sodom where he lives that God's just anger will scorch any day? I tell you, you'd be better dead than let that serpent crawl into your breast. I'd rather have the walls of this house tumble on your head than have the slimy beast soil you with its venom."

Then he was ranting, swept away by his own fanatical devotions— not merely angry with the girl but disgusted with all things natural to a human being, loathing humanity itself, and full of bitter contempt for the frailty of women. Scratch a woman, he seemed to be saying, and you'll always find Eve and the origins of sin. It meant nothing to him that the girl was untouched in any way, or that she had tried to escape from that love and confessed it with humility, regret and contrition. Crispus saw her as a fallen angel; he wanted to lift her to the highest peaks of religious fervor, the plane of dedication where only love for Christ existed, and she fell in love with an Augustan! Just thinking about it made his blood run cold, not to mention the revulsion and the disappointment. No! He couldn't forgive that! Never! His own words burned his lips; their horror seemed to scorch and blister his mouth like hot coals. He struggled for a moment to hold them back, shaking his bony fists before the terrified young woman.

Ligia knew she deserved some blame but nothing like this. She thought that leaving Miriam's home would be a victory over temptation and reduce her guilt. But Crispus turned her into dust in her own eyes; he cheapened everything about her and made her feel contemptible beyond anything she ever imagined. The old presbyter was like a father to her since her escape from the Palatine, and she went to him hoping for some compassion and advice, but rather than help her and fortify her determination, he merely destroyed her.

"Let God take my pain and my disappointment in you," he went on, merciless to the end. "Let him give you justice. You have chosen to disappoint the Savior himself! You've thrown yourself into a quagmire, and its foul stench has poisoned your soul. You could have offered it to Christ like a pure vessel, a precious cup, saying, 'Take it, Lord, and fill it with your grace,' but you preferred to give it to the devil. May God forgive you and find some mercy for you. But I . . . as long as you crawl in the mud with serpents . . . I, who picked you as one of the elect . . . the chosen few—"

He broke off then, catching sight of two men coming toward the arbor. One, he saw through the tangle of dead ivy vines and evergreen, was the apostle Peter. The other's face was partially hidden in a goat's hair cloak, the kind worn by Syrian mountaineers, seafarers and soldiers. At first Crispus took him for Chilon.

Catching bits and pieces of his jeremiad, they came into the arbor and sat down on a stone bench to listen. There Peter's stooped companion dropped his cloak and showed his gaunt old face, wizened as a turtle's, a scaly bald head with clumps of tight white curls clinging to the temples, watery red-rimmed eyes and a crooked beak of a nose. Ugly enough to be grotesque, he seemed on fire with zeal, and Crispus recognized him as Paul of Tarsus. Ligia threw herself on her knees before Peter and pressed her small head silently into the folds of his robe.

"May your souls be at peace," Peter told them. He noted the girl's anguish. "What has happened here?"

The grim old presbyter burst at once into the whole story while Ligia clutched the apostle's feet in terrified despair, as if he was the only refuge she could hope to find. Ah, Crispus cried, shaking with indignation. He had had such hopes for Ligia. He wanted to give her to Christ as pure as an unshed tear, but she defiled herself with an earthly love. Ah, and for whom? For a Roman. For one of the patricians. For a cruel, lustful profligate who indulged himself in all the depravities of the Roman world. The apostle heard him out quietly to the end, put his gnarled old hand on the girl's bowed head, and raised his own sad eyes to the quivering old priest.

"Haven't you heard, Crispus," he asked, "of the wedding feast at Cana, where our beloved master blessed the love between men and women?"

Crispus' shaking arms fell and hung uselessly at his sides while be gaped at the apostle with shock in his eyes.

"Do you imagine, Crispus," Peter went on after a short silence, "that Christ would turn his back on this gentle child, as fresh and pure as one of the lilies of the fields? He who let Mary of Magdala kiss his feet? He who forgave the whore?"

Ligia was racked with sobs. She wept and clutched the apostle's worn feet all the harder, weak with relief that she hadn't turned to him in vain. He stooped and turned her shining, tear-stained face toward him.

"As long as the man you love is blind to the truth," he told her, "you should avoid him, to keep yourself from stumbling into error. But pray for him. Loving is not a sin. The fact that you've done all you can to escape temptation just adds to your merit. I tell you then, my child: Don't cry and torment yourself, because the grace of the Redeemer has not been taken from you. Your prayers will be heard, and days of joy will follow."

He placed both hands on her hair, raised his eyes and prayed quietly for her, while his face seemed to glow with an unearthly gentleness and kindness.

Crispus was crushed. "I sinned against mercy." His voice was humble and contrite. "I thought she was denying Christ by giving way to an earthly love . . ."

"I denied him three times," Peter interrupted. "Yet he forgave me and let me be a shepherd to his flock."

". . . because Vinicius is an Augustan," the humbled presbyter said, trying to justify himself, "one of the masters of the Roman world—"

"Christ has moved harder hearts than his," Peter said.

"And I am the living witness," the dwarfed, ugly Paul of Tarsus added quietly, pointing to himself. "No one did more than I to root out and destroy the light of his teaching. I'm the executioner and tormentor of his people. I'm the one who had Stephen stoned. And yet our Master picked me to spread his word throughout the earth, as I've done in Judea, in Greece, on the islands, and in Rome as well when I was imprisoned the last time. And now that Peter called me, here I am again to bend this proud head of mine before him, and scatter the seeds of his truth on this rocky soil. Barren and hard it may be, but he will enrich it so that it'll flower forever."

He rose and turned to go, and Crispus saw the hunchbacked, crooked little man for what he really was: a giant who would shake the earth, possess all the lands, and seize the hearts and souls of all their people.

"HAVE MERCY ON ME, *carissime*," Petronius wrote soon after Vinicius returned to his own home. "Try to be less laconic in your letters and leave epigrams to the Spartans and to Julius Caesar. If you were at least able to say as he did, 'I came, I saw, I conquered,' I might appreciate the brevity of your style. But what you tell me in effect is: 'I came, I saw, I ran,' and that needs explaining. It isn't like you to end things that way. Nor can you merely mention in passing that you were injured and that some strange things happened. I couldn't believe my eyes when I read that your Lygian squeezed the life out of Croton as easily as a Catalan mastiff throttles mountain wolves in the Iberian passes. This fellow is worth his weight in gold, and he could be Caesar's darling anytime he wished. I'll have to see him when I'm back in town and have him cast in bronze; Copperbeard will burst with curiosity when he hears it's from a live model. A really fine athletic body is becoming rare in Italy and Greece; Germans are big, but it's more fat than muscle, and you can forget about the East. Find out from him if he's an exception or if there are more like him in his country. You and I might find ourselves obliged to fund public games someday, and it'd be good to know where to look for the finest bodies.

"The gods of the East and West be praised that you've escaped alive from such hands. You survived probably because you're a patrician and an ex-consul's son, but everything else you mention is simply amazing. I've never heard anything like that business with the Christians at the cemetery or the things you said about them and their treatment of you. And what about Ligia's new escape? Where is she? And why do I sense vast anxiety and sadness in your note? Enlighten me since there are many things that confuse me about your situation. I can't make head or tail of the Christians or you or your Ligia. None of you makes sense. Life bores me, as you know, and I neither care nor want to know about it; I'm usually quite indifferent to whatever doesn't affect me directly, but don't be surprised by so many questions. After all, I am somewhat responsible for everything that happened, so I have a right to know.

"Write in full and quickly since I don't know when we'll be together again. Fresh whims dart everywhere at once through the imperial skull, and they're as unpredictable as the winds in spring. We're still in Beneventum, but Nero wants to sail directly to Greece and not stop in Rome. Tigellinus whispers in his ear that the Roman mobs will miss him so much they'll start rioting if he stays away, but what he really means is they'll miss their free circuses, bread and oil. I can't tell which notion will prevail; if it's Greece, then we might also go to Egypt. I'd insist you join us, because our amusements and the journey would be a tonic in your current state, but we might be gone by the time you get here. Give some thought to resting for a time in your Sicilian holdings rather than sitting fruitlessly in the city; you'll recover quicker. Write to me immediately, tell me everything, and stay well. By Pollux, I don't know what to wish you nowadays so I don't enclose any wishes this time."

It took Vinicius a long time to answer. He lacked the energy and interest. What good would it do to write? What could it explain? How would it solve any part of his complex problem? Everything seemed so futile and hopeless. He felt so dull and listless. Life as he knew it had lost all its meanings. Nothing he wrote would convince Petronius or even make the slightest sense to him; they could never be close again after what had happened.

Vinicius couldn't even explain things to himself. Home again from across the Tiber, back in the luxury of his pleasure-laden villa in the Carinnae, he rested for a day or two among the comforts and attentions of his frightened household, but this contentment was illusory at best. He felt as empty as if he hung suspended in a void, indifferent to everything that moved him or absorbed him until then. The central core of his whole existence dimmed to such a point that life itself became unimportant. Everything he used to care about was now too trivial to focus his attention, or vanished altogether. He saw himself as a hamstrung thoroughbred whose vital tendons were severed without warning; fate had reached out to him, cut through the cords that linked him to his former life and didn't replace them with ties to another. His reaction to going to Greece or Beneventum—and also the first clear, straightforward thought he had for days—was a wry "What for? What good will it do me?" He never imagined there might come a time when he'd resent being with Petronius or that he could be bored by his eloquence and wit, blind to the brilliance of his exposition, and deaf to the exquisite care and aptness with which he phrased and expressed his thoughts, but now the idea of traveling to see him struck him as a waste.

Solitude also began to sap him, however. Everyone he knew was dancing attendance on Caesar in Beneventum, so he stayed at home, alone with thoughts and feelings he couldn't understand, and with no one to talk to even if he wanted to. Now and then it occurred to him that if he could talk it out with someone, he might come to grips with his puzzling new reality and place his life in order. He hoped a letter to Petronius would help him clarify his thinking whether or not he actually sent it, so a few days later he wrote a reply.

"You ask for a full account, so I comply," he started. "But I don't know if I can make things any clearer for you since I can't unravel all these knots myself. You know about my stay among the Christians, about the way they treat their enemies, the kindness with which they nursed me back to health, and finally about Ligia's latest disappearance. True, they had every right to think of me and Chilon as enemies; but no, I wasn't spared just because I'm a consul's son. They treat everyone the same and pay no attention to social distinctions. They forgave Chilon, after all, even though I urged them to break his neck and drop him in a hole somewhere in their garden. They are a totally new kind of human being, and their religion is like nothing else the world has ever seen. Anyone who'd judge them by our standards would miss by a mile. I'll just say that I couldn't have gotten better care if I was laid up in my own house, looked after by my own family or household. I have more comforts here, that goes without saying, but nothing like their goodness, concern and attention.

"Ligia, you should know, is like the others in that respect. The care she gave me couldn't have been more loving if she was my sister or my wife. Joy overwhelmed me at times when I thought about it, because I was sure that only love gave so much tenderness. I read it in her face and in the way she looked at me now and then, and when that happened—if you can believe it—I was far happier among those plebeians, in the drab little room where they cooked, ate and lived together, than anywhere before. No, I wasn't wrong about that. I could tell she loved me. Even today I can't think of it any other way. And yet she left Miriam's house in secret, and I can't think why.

"Did I write that I offered to take her back to Aulus and Pomponia? Well, I did. She refused because of the danger of slaves' gossip reaching the Palatine, in which case Caesar would simply have her seized and taken back again. But she knew I wouldn't hound her anymore, that I've given up all thoughts of violence toward her, and that since I can't stop loving her or even live without her, I'd bring her into my house only as my wife. And yet she fled from me. Why? I was no longer any threat to her. If she didn't love me, she could simply have said so and I wouldn't have bothered her again. Ah, I tell you, it's more than I can understand.

"I met a strange man the day before she vanished, a certain Paul from Tarsus, who talked to me about Christ and his teaching. He spoke with such power and conviction that every word seemed to shatter the foundations of all our beliefs. He also told me, after Ligia vanished: 'When God lifts your blindness and reveals his light, you'll know she did the right thing and then perhaps you'll find her.'

"I've been puzzling over these words as if they were a Delphic oracle. Once in a while I seem to see some light. They love mankind. We trample it and rule it. I belong to that world of violence and corruption they reject, and so she fled from me, from our gods, and from all our cruelties, because she can't share that kind of life with me. They see it as vicious. You'll say that if she could simply tell me 'No,' she had no reason to run from me again. But what if she loved me? What if she was running from her own love for me? Whenever I think of this, I feel like sending my slaves to shout 'Come back, Ligia' through all the tenements in the city.

"All this defies rational explanation, and I am starting to give up trying to solve this bewildering puzzle. I wouldn't have forbidden her to worship her Christ in our home! I'd have been glad to raise an altar to him in my atrium. I mean, why not? What harm could one more household deity do to anybody? What's so strange about worshiping a new god, even though I don't have much use for any of the old ones? And besides, this Christ of theirs could be a real divinity. Christians don't lie, I know that for a fact, and they all say he rose from the dead. A mere man wouldn't be able to do that. That Paul of Tarsus, who's a Roman citizen but also a Jew, is familiar with old Hebrew writings, and he says their prophets have foretold Christ's coming for thousands of years. All these things border on the fantastic, but aren't we constantly puzzling over every new discovery? People are still talking about Apollonius of Tyana, aren't they?

"Paul confirms there's only the one true god, not a whole crew of them, and that makes sense to me; I think Seneca believes the same thing, and there were other monotheists before him. There certainly was a Christ. He did exist. He did let himself be crucified to save the world, and he did rise up from his grave. All this is verified by witnesses, and I don't see any reason to argue with anyone about it or refuse to raise an altar to him in my house—if I'd raise one to Serapis, for example. Nor would I have a problem renouncing other gods since no rational person believes in them anyway. But I don't think this would be enough for the Christians, and here's where all my good intentions fall apart.

"It's not enough, you see, to honor Christ with rituals and worship. You have to live according to his teaching, and that's like coming to the edge of an ocean and being told to go across on foot. It's deeds, not words, that matter to these people. They'd be unable to believe me if I swore I'd do it, Paul said so himself. You know how I love Ligia and there's nothing I wouldn't do for her, but can I lift mountains? Could I hoist Vesuvius on my shoulder if she asked me? Or hold Lake Thrasymene in the palm of my hand? Or make my eyes as blue as a Lygian's? I'd try anything she wished, but they're beyond my powers.

"I'm not a philosopher, Petronius, but neither am I as much of a fool as you've thought at times. I don't know how the Christians manage their lives among us, but I can tell this much: Rome's power and dominion end wherever their teaching finds a foothold. Life as we know it loses all its meaning. There's no longer a difference between the conqueror and the conquered, the rich and the poor, the master and the slave. Christianity means the end of all authority, of government, of Caesar, of the laws, and of established order as we know it. Instead there is Christ. There is an instant sense of mercy never found anywhere before. What follows is such superhuman goodness that it overturns everything we know about mankind and about our own Roman character as well.

"I wouldn't give a tinker's cuss for Rome and all its grandeur if I had Ligia in my house, but that's another story. The whole world could go hang as long as she was mine and we were together! But it's not enough to say such things to these Christians. You have to feel what they feel. You have to know there is nothing better than this Christ of theirs and have no room for anything else in your heart and soul, and this I can't do! Can you understand it? There's something in me, some deep-seated Roman instinct, that rebels against such outlandish notions. I could praise Christ to the skies and follow all their rules but I'd be doing it only out of love for Ligia. I know by everything that makes me what I am that I'd be totally opposed to such ideas if it weren't for her. I'm quite amazed that this Paul of Tarsus could grasp it so clearly, but so did that other old magician, the fellow named Peter who was Christ's disciple and is the most revered man among them even though he's just a lowborn commoner. And do you know what they're doing about it? They're praying for me and asking for something they call 'grace' to touch me, but I'm just getting more anxious and upset, and long for Ligia all the more.

"As I wrote earlier, she disappeared without a word, but she left me a cross made from two ivy twigs. I found it near my bed when I woke up. I have it here among my household gods, but I can't understand why I think of it as holy. I look at it with awe as if it were a god. I love it because she made it with her own two hands, and I hate it because it keeps us apart. At times I think it's all some kind of witchcraft. That magician Peter is said to be just a common fisherman, but he's far greater than Apollonius and all the other wonderworkers before him, and I'm beginning to believe he cast a spell on me, Ligia, Pomponia and everybody else.

"You note anxiety and sadness in my last letter. I'm sad because I lost her once again, and I'm uneasy because I feel different. I tell you frankly there's nothing more at odds with my character than this Christian teaching, but I simply can't tell who I am since I brushed against it. Is this love or magic? I don't know! Circe, the enchantress who bemused Odysseus, changed human flesh when she touched it and turned men into swine, but I feel as if they've changed my soul! Only Ligia could have done that to me, or rather Ligia and that strange path she follows."

What he wrote next unsettled him so much he was ashamed to see it on his tablets. "Just imagine this: No one expected me when I came home. My household thought I was in Beneventum and wouldn't be back for months, so I found total chaos in the house. The slaves were drunk. They were having an orgy on my dining couches. They expected death to come stalking in among them sooner than seeing me, and they would have been less terrified if it did. You know what an iron grip I keep on my domestics, so everything alive threw itself on its knees before me, and some of them even fainted out of terror. My first normal instinct was to call for whips and branding irons, but can you guess what I did instead? I was ashamed to flog them, if you can believe it. I actually felt sorry for those miserable wretches. My grandfather brought some of the old slaves from beyond the Rhine in the time of Augustus Caesar, though I can't imagine why I thought of that.

"Anyway, I did nothing to them. I locked myself alone in my library. I started thinking that after everything I saw and heard among the Christians, I could no longer treat my slaves as I did before. I saw them as people. They crept about like shadows around the house for a few days, thinking I was holding off on their punishment until I came up with something really frightful, but I did nothing to them simply because I couldn't force myself to do it! On my third day home I called them all together and said I forgave them; they were to make amends by faithful and devoted service. They couldn't believe it. They all threw themselves on their knees, burst into tears, stretched their arms toward me and called me their own beloved master, their true lord and father . . . and—believe me or not—I found myself as moved as never before. I swear I could see Ligia's face before me, as grateful as those weeping slaves, and thanking me for what I'd just done. I even felt tears gathering in my own eyes.

"I tell you freely I am lost without her. I feel deprived of everything that matters, and I'm far more unhappy than you suppose. But an astonishing thing happened regarding those slaves I forgave. Far from making them insolent, lazy or rebellious, as we always supposed leniency would do, my act of mercy made them more eager to please than any punishment could have done, no matter how dreadful. They never served me as well out of fear as they have from this new gratitude of theirs. They seem to guess my thoughts and anticipate all my wants and wishes, and they race each other to do everything cheerfully and gladly. I mention this only because I told Paul, the day before I left the Christians, that the world would fall apart with such soft rules as his, like a cooper's barrel when the iron hoops are removed, and he said: 'Love binds mankind together more powerfully than terror.' I'm starting to think this could be true in certain circumstances.

"I tested this idea on my creditors and debtors who came running over as soon as they heard about my return. You know I've never been harsh or tight-fisted in my business dealings, but I always treated shopkeepers with disdain, keeping them in their place, as I learned from my father. Well, this time, seeing their shabby cloaks and hungry faces, I felt the same strange pity I felt for the slaves. I gave them a good dinner and talked with them, called some of them by name, asked about their wives and children. And I saw the same grateful tears in their eyes. Moreover I was suddenly quite sure that Ligia could see this from wherever she was, that she approved of it and that it made her happy. I don't know if I'm losing my mind or if love has turned everything upside down inside me, but I keep thinking that she can see everything I do, and I'm afraid to do anything to hurt her or offend her.

"That's how it is, Caius! They've altered my soul. Sometimes I feel good about it, but then I worry that I've lost my manhood, and that I've been stripped of all my former drive, energy, forcefulness and power. I'm afraid I might no longer be fit to exercise authority, judge and command others, take my place in council, enjoy our normal pleasures or even fight in wars. What could this be but witchcraft and black magic? I tell you, I've been made over so completely, it occurred to me even before I left the company of the Christians that if Ligia was as dissolute, self-centered and available as Nigidia, Poppea, Crispinilla or any of our other high-society divorcees, I wouldn't be able to love her as I do. Imagine this: I love her for the differences between her world and ours, not for what we share. You can surely see the chaos this creates within me, the darkness in which I live, how hard it is for me to find the right road and how far I am from knowing what to do.

"If life can be compared to a stream, Petronius, mine flows dark and heavy with anxiety. I live only on the hope of seeing her again. I feel that this has to happen before very long, but what if it doesn't? What will become of me in a year or two? I can't even begin to guess, but I won't leave Rome right now or join you anywhere. I can't bear the thought of being among our fellow augustians. My one relief is that she's somewhere near and that perhaps I'll hear some news about her from Paul of Tarsus or Glaucus, the doctor who promised to look in on me.

"No! I wouldn't leave Rome if you made me governor of Egypt! Since I am telling you so much that's unbelievable, I might as well add that I ordered a tombstone carved for our old slave Gullo, the one I killed in blind rage the night we lost Ligia. It's only now I remember how he used to carry me on his back, play with me as a child, and taught me to notch my first arrow. I don't know why I keep remembering him with pity and remorse.

"If you're surprised by what I've written here," Vinicius concluded, "then let me tell you I'm no less astonished. But I am telling you exactly how things are and how I feel. Be well and good-bye."

‹36›

THIS TIME PETRONIUS didn't send an answer, apparently expecting Nero to order a return to Rome almost any day. The expectation also ran like fire through the city and drove the rabble wild with joy in anticipation of free grain and oil and the customary games in the arena. The port of Ostia was piled with supplies in preparation for Caesar's official generosity, and in due course the emperor's freed-man, Helios, went to the senate to announce his imminent return.

But Nero took his time. He and his court boarded a fleet of galleys near Cape Misenum and sailed slowly north toward Rome and Ostia, going ashore to rest or stage theater performances in every sizable coastal town. At Minturnum, where Nero gave another public con-cert, they stayed the best part of two weeks, while Nero wondered about returning to Naples until spring, which came early and was particularly warm this year.

All this time Vinicius stayed shut up in his house, thinking about Ligia and all the other matters that crowded his mind, upsetting his feelings and plans. Glaucus called on him a number of times, which delighted him because he had a chance to talk about Ligia. The doctor couldn't tell him where she was but assured him that the Christian elders took good care of her. Once, however, moved to pity by the young tribune's obvious suffering, he told him how the apostle Peter had admonished Crispus for his condemnation of Ligia's earthly love.

Hearing this, Vinicius turned as white as his sheets. He, too, thought at moments that Ligia cared for him, but he was just as quick to fall into uncertainty and doubt. Now he was hearing his best hopes confirmed by a virtual stranger, and a Christian at that. His first thought was to run to Peter and pour out his grateful thanks. But when Glaucus said Peter was out of the city, teaching in the country-side, Vinicius begged him to bring the apostle to the house.

"I'll make rich men out of all the poor of your community," he promised. If Ligia loved him, the last barrier between them was as good as gone, he was sure. "I'll become a Christian any time you say."

But Glaucus told him it wasn't quite that easy. Baptism alone wouldn't guarantee Ligia to Vinicius. "You also have to have a Christian soul," he said.

Again, as in the past, any contradiction was likely to infuriate Vinicius, but this time he understood that Glaucus spoke to him as a Christian and said only what he should be saying. He was still unable to perceive the deepest change within him, but he was starting to concede there was such a thing as another point of view. In the past his yardstick for anything was how well it served him; now he was slowly accepting the idea that other eyes saw things differently, other hearts might respond to different truths and feelings, and what suited him best wasn't necessarily what was right.

He felt powerfully drawn toward Paul of Tarsus, whose words both fascinated and alarmed him. He composed arguments he could cite to disprove his teaching the next time they met; he fought him bitterly in mental debates that left him strangely unsatisfied and unsure; but he could hardly wait to see and hear the ugly little man again. Paul had gone to Aricium, however, and no one knew how long he would be away. Glaucus' visits also became rare as the young man's bones knit together and his health improved, and Vinicius was left quite alone.

On his feet again and strong enough to travel, he went back to haunting the narrow lanes and alleys across the Tiber and the back streets adjoining the slums of the Suburra, hoping to catch at least a glimpse of Ligia somewhere in the distance. When this also failed, he started to get both annoyed and bored. His old impatient and demanding nature surged back to life and flooded him like a returning tide. He told himself he had been a fool. Why stuff his head with things that made him unhappy? Why not live life as he understood it and take from it whatever he could? He was determined to drive Ligia from his mind or at least fill his days with pleasure beyond whatever he might feel for her. It was his last chance, he knew, to remain what he was, and he threw himself into his old ways with a ruthless drive and blind, single-minded passion.

As it happened, Rome itself seemed to summon him. Winter was over. Pleasure and excitement were restored to the city as the vacationing high society returned from their country manors. The dull, gray days of winter, which had made Rome seem like a depopulated graveyard, brightened and warmed at the prospect of the emperor's return, and Rome got ready to mark that homecoming with an all-out, festive celebration. Spring was on its way. The warm Mediterranean winds swept out of Africa, and the snows vanished from the peaks of the Alban hills. Violets bloomed again in the city gardens; a hot new sun shone on the crowds that reappeared in the Forum and on the Field of Mars; and the Appian Way, the time-honored favorite for drives in the country, filled again with richly ornamented chariots. Young women were once more slipping from their homes, under the pretext of visiting the temples of Juno in Lanuvium or Diana in Aricium, and looking for fresh thrills beyond the city walls, while pleasure parties started traveling to the Alban hills.

It was here, among a swarm of superb racing chariots, that Vinicius saw Chrysothemis driving her own trap, drawn by four matched Corsican ponies, and with a pair of prize Molossian greyhounds running before her. Surrounded by a crowd of young men and aged senators whose various duties kept them in the city, she rode while tossing bright, teasing smiles and taps with a golden whip everywhere around her. Catching sight of him, she welcomed him aboard with all the others and took him home to a dinner that lasted all night.

Vinicius got so drunk he didn't even know how he was taken home, but he remembered he became so angry with her when she started asking about Ligia that he emptied a full flagon of Falernian wine over her head. He was still angry about it when he was sober the next day. The day after, however, she seemed to have forgotten all about the insult, called for him at home, took him with her for another ride along the Appian Way and then stayed for supper at his house, where she confessed she was bored with both Petronius and his freed lute player and was interested in finding a new lover.

They went about together for a week, but the relationship didn't hold much promise. Neither of them mentioned Ligia since the incident with the Falernian wine, but Vinicius couldn't rid himself of her anyway. He felt that she was always near and watching, that she was sad to see him so debased; and he hated himself both for this sadness and the guilt it brought him. He was actually relieved when Chrysothemis threw her first jealous tantrum after he bought himself two Syrian dancing girls, and he drove her out of his life without another thought.

He went on indulging himself a while longer, steeping himself in wine and women as if to spite Ligia, but no amount of pleasure could drive her from his head. He simply couldn't stop thinking about her and soon realized that nothing else mattered to him but her. She was the source of all his instincts, evil along with good, and everything else was merely tasteless boredom. He saw himself as nothing more than a desperate beggar no matter what distractions he bought for himself, and at last all sense of pleasure went out of his life, leaving only weariness, disgust and self-contempt.

This puzzled him more than anything. He couldn't understand it. He never questioned his right to amuse himself in any way he pleased and always took whatever gave him pleasure as the ultimate good. Now all his choices paled. His self-assured, careless arrogance, so totally oblivious to anything but himself, gave way to a mindless, moribund torpidity that stayed with him even after Caesar and his court finally returned to Rome and life in the city roared with new excitement.

But he no longer cared about anything. Nothing moved him. Nothing drew his interest. He didn't even go to see Petronius until the latter sent his own litter for him with an invitation. Greeted with open arms, he couldn't summon enough energy for more than forced, fumbling answers to Petronius' questions until at last his long-suppressed thoughts and feelings burst out of him in a torrential stream of words. He gave a detailed account of his search for Ligia, his time with the Christians and everything he saw and heard among them. Once again he poured out all the doubts and fears that troubled his mind and undermined his spirit, the emotional chaos in which he was living, his inability to think rationally and calmly, to judge things as they were or to distinguish between right and wrong.

"Nothing appeals to me anymore," he muttered. "There is nothing for me to enjoy. I don't know where to stand on anything or what to do about it."

He was as ready to worship Christ, he said, as to persecute him. He understood the sublime nature of his teachings even as he loathed them. He knew that he would never possess Ligia, not entirely, because Christ would always claim his share of her. His life, he said, had turned into endless drab days without joy or pleasure, a living death; he had lost all hope for happiness and faith in his future.

"I feel like a blind man stumbling in the darkness," he cried out at last, "and I can't find the way!"

Petronius stared at the young man's grimly altered features; he noted the jerking hands, the strange groping gestures, as if Vinicius were really lost in some impenetrable night and seeking a way out, but he could think of nothing that might help. He rose suddenly, went near to Vinicius and started fingering the hair above his ears.

"Do you know you have some white hairs on your temples?" he asked.

"Could be," Vinicius muttered. "It wouldn't surprise me if they all turned white before very long."

They sat in silence. Petronius was a rational, thinking man who often turned his mind to contemplating life, human nature and the soul. The existential circumstances of the life around such men as he and Vinicius could be classified in terms of happiness or misfortune, but their personal inner lives were generally calm, predictable and undisturbed. Just as a thunderbolt or an earthquake could topple a temple, so some external calamity could end their existence, but in its overall sense, life as they knew it unfolded in a simple and harmonious pattern, free of complications. But now Vinicius was introducing something altogether different, delving into matters that no one had looked into before and posing questions Petronius had never considered. He was intelligent enough to sense their importance, but even his sharp intellect could supply no answers.

"It must be witchcraft," he said after a long silence.

"That's what I thought, too," Vinicius said. "It occurred to me that we were both under some kind of spell."

"What if, for example," Petronius offered, "you went for help to the priests of Serapis? You can be sure there are as many fakes among them as in all the priesthoods, but a few of them have plumbed some peculiar mysteries."

Troubled, Vinicius rubbed his forehead. "Spells!" he muttered. "Witchcraft! I've come across wizards who got rich by calling up dark, unearthly powers. I've seen others who used magic against their enemies. But Christians live in poverty, forgive their enemies, preach goodness, mercy and humility, so what would they get out of casting spells? It doesn't make sense."

Petronius was starting to get annoyed that he couldn't come up with any answers, but this was more than he wanted to admit.

"It's a new sect," he said just to say something. "By Aphrodite!" he exclaimed after a while. "By the divine dweller of the sacred groves in Paphos! How all this gloom poisons the sweetness of living! You admire these people's charity and goodness, but I say they're evil because they're the enemies of life, like death and diseases. We've enough plagues among us as it is without these damned Christians! Just add it all up: sickness, Caesar, Tigellinus, Nero's poetry, cobblers who lord it over the descendants of the Quirites, freed slaves who sit in the senate. Enough of this, by Castor! That is a destructive and disgusting sect! Did you try to shake yourself free of this introspective mourning and taste a bit of life?"

"I tried it," said Vinicius.

"Ah, you sly devil!" Petronius burst into happy laughter. "News travels fast among the slaves. You stole my Chrysothemis, didn't you?"

Vinicius shrugged as if the reminder filled him with distaste.

"No matter." Petronius was equally indifferent. "As a matter of fact I really ought to thank you. Now I can send her a pair of pearl-sewn slippers, which means 'go and good-bye' in my amatory lexicon. I've two reasons to be grateful to you: One is that you refused my gift of Eunice, and the other is that you've freed me from Chrysothemis. Hear me out. What you see before you is a man who rose in the morning, bathed, feasted, possessed Chrysothemis, wrote satires and sometimes even prose mixed with poetry, but who was as bored as Caesar and often gave way to gloom. And do you know why? Because I searched for something far away that lay close at hand. A beautiful woman is always worth her weight in gold, but one who also loves you is absolutely priceless. Not all the ill-gotten riches of Cornelius Verres, the Sicilian *praetor* who sold justice to the highest bidder, could get you such a precious combination. Well, now my life is filled with happiness, like a cup that overflows with the finest wine on earth, and I drink until my arm grows numb and my lips turn pale. Nothing else concerns me in the slightest, I don't give a hoot about the future, and that's my latest view of life and living."

"What's new about this? That's what you've always thought."

"But now it has a context."

He called for Eunice. She came at once, dressed in flowing white, more like a golden-haired love goddess than a former slave.

"Come to me!" Petronius opened his arms to her, and she ran to him, perched on his knees, wound her arms about his neck and pressed her head against his chest. A deep flush spread across her cheeks and her eyes misted over with joy, and Vinicius saw the two of them less as lovers than as a sculpted pair representing happiness and love. Petronius took a handful of violet blooms from a shallow bowl on a side table and started to scatter them over her head, her breast and her sleeveless gown.

"Happy is the man," he said, "who discovers love locked within such beauty." He bared her shoulders. "I sometimes think we're a pair of gods. See for yourself. Did Praxiteles or Miron or Scopas or even Lysias ever create such perfect lines . . . so warm, so rosy and so full of love? Does Paros or Mount Pentelicus yield such flawless marble? There are lovesick men who kiss away the rims of a vase, but I'd rather find my rapture where it really lies."

He started to brush his lips along her neck and shoulders. She began to tremble. Her eyelids fluttered with tremors of delight that defied description, and Vinicius felt his own heart beat a little faster.

"Think." Petronius lifted his own finely chiseled face and looked at Vinicius. "What are your gloomy Christians beside this? If you can't see the difference, then you really do belong among them. But this sight ought to cure you."

Vinicius breathed the scent of violets that permeated the room, and his face lost color. He thought that if he could tease Ligia's naked shoulders with his lips the way Petronius brushed his along Eunice's, the joy he'd experience would seem sacrilegious, and he wouldn't care if the whole world tumbled in ruins after that. Accustomed by this time to swift understanding of everything that moved him, he noted that even now all he could think about was Ligia.

"Divine one," Petronius said, turning to Eunice, "order garlands for our heads and have our breakfasts served."

She left at once, and he turned again to Vinicius. "I wanted to free her," he confided, "but she wouldn't even hear of it. She said, can you imagine, she'd rather be my slave than Caesar's wife. I freed her anyway, without telling her. The prefect did it for me as a favor so she didn't have to be there to see it done. Nor does she know she'll inherit this house and all the jewels other than my gemstones when I die."

He rose and walked up and down the room for a while. "Love changes everyone in one way or another," he said, "and it changed me as well. I used to like verbena, do you recall? But Eunice prefers the scent of violets, so I also became fond of it, and we've been breathing violets since the start of spring."

He paused in front of Vinicius. "How about you?" he asked. "Is sandalwood still your favorite?"

"Leave me alone!" the young man snapped.

"I wanted you to take a good look at Eunice, and I am telling you about her only to suggest that you, too, may be searching for something far away that is close at hand. Perhaps you have someone in your slave quarters whose simple, loving heart longs for you alone. Use it like a balm. Heal your wounds. You say that Ligia loves you? Maybe so. But what kind of love denies its own fulfillment? Does that suggest it's real? Doesn't it mean there is something stronger? No, my dear boy, Ligia isn't Eunice."

"It's all the same torment." Vinicius waved his hand, resigned and fatalistic. "I watched you kissing Eunice, and I thought that if Ligia ever bared her shoulders like that for me, I wouldn't care if the earth split under us afterward! But then I felt as if I were about to rape a vestal or profane a goddess. Yes, Ligia isn't Eunice, but I see that difference differently from you. Your love changed your nose, so you'd rather smell violets than verbena. Mine changed my soul, so no matter how I want her and how much it costs me, I'd rather have Ligia as she is than any other woman."

"In that case you've nothing to complain about." Petronius shrugged. "But I don't understand it."

"Yes! That's it!" Vinicius spoke with the urgency of fever. "We can no longer understand each other!"

There was another silence.

"May Hell consume those Christians of yours!" Petronius burst out at last. "They've snatched all real meaning from your life and wrecked your peace of mind. To Hell with them all! You're wrong about their teaching. It's not a boon to mankind! On the contrary! What counts is whatever makes men happy, and that's a sense of beauty, love and power, which they dismiss as trivial and corrupting. You talk about their mercy and forgiveness, but where's their sense of justice? If we're to repay evil with good, what shall we use to pay for decency and goodness? And if the payment is the same for both, why should anyone bother to be good?"

"The payment's not the same. But it starts in the afterlife, according to their teaching."

"That's still to be seen—if it's possible to see anything with dead eyes—so I won't argue about that one way or the other. But what do they all amount to in the meantime? They're weak, impotent and helpless. True, Ursus strangled Croton, but he has fists of iron. The rest of them, however, are puny, mealymouthed crybabies, and the future doesn't belong to the weak."

"Their lives begin with death," Vinicius said.

"That's like saying days begin with sunset. Are you still planning to seize Ligia and carry her off by force?"

"No. I can't repay her goodness to me with violence. I swore I'd never do that again."

"Are you planning to become a Christian?"

"I'd like to, but their teaching violates everything I believe."

"Can anything here help you forget about Ligia?"

"No."

"Then travel!"

Just then the slaves announced that breakfast was served, but it struck Petronius that he had hit upon a good idea, and he continued talking about travel as they made their way to the dining room.

"You've covered a bit of the world but only as a soldier, marching in double time to where you had to be without halting anywhere for long. Come with us to Greece. Caesar hasn't given up that trip. He'll stop everywhere along the way, sing, gather laurels, loot the temples, and eventually return to Italy in triumph. It'll be something like Bacchus and Apollo traveling together in a single person. All the Augustans, both men and the women, and the music of a thousand lutes! By Castor, it'll be worth remembering! The world has seen nothing like it up to now."

He stretched out beside Eunice on the dining couch while slaves placed a wreath of anemones on his head.

"What have you seen while serving with Corbulanus?" he went on. "Not a thing. Did you make a thorough tour of all the Greek temples, as I did, going from one guide to another for two years? Have you been to Rhodes to see the site of the Colossus? Did you visit Panopeus in Phocis to look at the clay into which Prometheus breathed life when he stole fire from the gods and created man? Or Sparta, to see the eggs laid by Leda after Zeus seduced her in the form of a swan? Have you been to Athens to look at the famous Sarmatian breastplate made out of horses' hooves? Or to Eubea to inspect Agamemnon's ship? Have you seen the drinking cup molded from the left breast of Helen of Troy? Or Alexandria or Memphis or the pyramids or the hair that Isis tore out of her head in mourning for Osiris? Did you ever listen to the moans of Memnon? It's a big world out there, my lad; everything doesn't end just across the Tiber. I'll go with Caesar for now, but when he comes back, I'll leave him and go on to Cyprus, because my golden-haired goddess wants us to sacrifice doves to Aphrodite in Paphos, and you may as well know her wish is my law."

"I am your slave," Eunice murmured.

He laid his flower-wreathed head in her lap and smiled up at her. "In that case I'm the slave of a slave girl," he told her. "I adore everything about you, my divinity, from head to toe."

He turned once more to Vinicius. "Come with us to Cyprus. But first, don't forget to pay a call on Caesar. It's bad that you still haven't been to see him; Tigellinus can use this to cause you some trouble. He has nothing personal against you, but he's not fond of you if for no other reason than that I'm your uncle. We'll say you were sick. We must also give some thought to what you'll tell Nero if he asks about Ligia. It might be best just to shrug it off and say you kept her until she bored you and then packed her off. He'll understand that. You can also tell him that illness kept you home, that you were in fever out of disappointment from missing his marvelous performance in Naples and that it was only the hope of hearing his voice again that brought you back to health. Don't be afraid to stretch the truth as much as you like. Tigellinus swears he'll come up with something to amuse him that'll be not only vast in scope but also sufficiently vulgar. I'm afraid he'll undermine me before very long. . . . I'm also worried about your state of mind."

"Do you know there are people who don't worry about Caesar one way or another?" Vinicius asked. "It's as if he didn't even exist for them."

"Yes, I know. Your Christians."

"Yes. Only they. While for the rest of us, life is merely one uninterrupted fear."

"Don't bother me with your Christians." Petronius flipped his hand in annoyed contempt. "I don't want to hear any more about them. They're not afraid of Caesar because he probably hasn't even heard of them. Either way he knows nothing about them and couldn't care less if they were a pile of dead leaves. But I tell you they're a bunch of worthless, mealymouthed nonentities. You sense it yourself. You know it deep inside you. We both know you do. If all your instincts find them so repugnant, it's clear proof they're beneath your notice. You're made of different clay, so don't give them another thought or waste more of our time on them. You and I know how to live and die, which is enough for Romans, but nobody knows what they're able to do."

These words struck a powerful chord in Vinicius, and when he got back home he began to think that perhaps the Christians' kindliness, charity and mercy did indeed denote an intrinsic weakness. It seemed to him that strong, proud, spirited and high-minded people—in other words the only kind of people valued by a Roman—wouldn't be so eager to forgive. It occurred to him that this could be the cause of his repugnance to their gentle teaching.

"We know how to live and die," Petronius had told him. But all that Christians knew was how to forgive; they could feel neither real love nor hatred.

‹37›

CAESAR WAS ANGRY to be back in Rome and a few days later the idea of going off to Greece inflamed him again. He even issued a decree announcing the journey and assured the city that he wouldn't stay away too long and that public matters wouldn't be jeopardized by such a short absence. Then, with an entourage of Augustans, including Vinicius, he went to all the temples of the Capitol to make sacrifices for a successful trip.

But as he entered the temple of Vesta on the second day, something happened that changed all his plans. Nero didn't care much about the gods but he was superstitiously afraid of them all, and the mysterious Vesta frightened him so much that he went into an epileptic fit at the sight of her image and the sacred fire. His hair rose in terror, his jaws locked, and he toppled backward into the arms of Vinicius, who happened to be standing right behind him. He was immediately taken out into the fresh air and carried to the Palatine, where he recovered soon enough, but he stayed in bed for the rest of the day. He did manage to announce to the astonished courtiers that the stern goddess had given him a secret warning against leaving Rome as soon as he proposed, and his anticipated journey was indefinitely delayed. An hour later city criers were telling the mobs all over the city that Caesar couldn't leave them because he knew how much they would miss him; like a good, loving father who didn't want to add to his children's sadness, he would stay with them to share all their joys and problems.

The crowds were delighted. The public games would go on as scheduled, and the free distribution of cornmeal would take place as usual. The mobs thronged to the gates of the Palatine to howl cheers for their loving Caesar, while he interrupted his dice game long enough to tell the Augustans the delay was only temporary.

"I had no choice," he said. "The trip had to be put off for a little while. Egypt can wait, and so can my rule over all the East. It's all

been prophesied so it's bound to happen, and that goes for my journey to Greece as well. In the meantime I'll have a new channel cut
across the isthmus of Corinth, and I'll have such vast monuments to
myself raised when we get to Egypt that the pyramids will seem like
mere child's play. I'll order a new Sphinx, seven times bigger than the
one that stares into the desert outside Memphis, but it'll have my
face. Future generations will talk about nothing else but that Sphinx
and me."

"Your poetry has already given you a monument for the ages,"
Petronius assured him. "Not merely seven times loftier than the
Sphinx but three times seven greater than the pyramid of Cheops."

"And my singing?"

"Ah! If only humanity could build you a statue like the one to
Memnon and it had your voice instead of that hollow booming that
comes from that one at sunrise! The shores of Egypt would swarm
with ships on which three-quarters of mankind would listen to your
songs for a hundred centuries!"

"Yes!" Nero loved the image. "But who can build such a thing
these days?"

"At least you can have a basalt mountain carved into a statue of
yourself as a chariot driver."

"True! I'll order it at once!"

"All mankind will weep in gratitude."

"And when I'm in Egypt, I'll marry the goddess Luna who is now a
widow. Then I'll really be a god."

"And the rest of us can marry all the stars and create a new Nero
constellation. You can have Vitelius marry the River Nile and breed
hippopotami. And you can give the desert to Tigellinus so he can be
the king of the jackals."

"What about me?" asked Vatinius. "What do you see me doing in
Egypt?"

"Apis bless you!" Petronius made a sly, glib reference to the jackal-
headed god who barked at the moon. "You gave us such a spectacle at
Beneventum that I must wish you only the best I can. You can sew
boots for the Sphinx whose paws get stiff with the cold at night.
Then you can make sandals for all the colossi that line the avenues
leading to the temples. Each of us can have his own line of work over
there, doing what we do best. Domitius Afer, for example, whose
honesty is a byword, can be the tax collector. I like it, Caesar, when
you dream of Egypt. I'm only sorry you decided to defer the trip."

Nero sighed, as if the matter lay beyond his powers. "Your mortal eyes didn't see a thing, of course," he said. "The gods make themselves invisible to anyone they want to. But Vesta herself appeared beside me when I visited her temple and whispered, 'Put off the journey,' right into my ear. She startled me so much that I actually fainted, although I should be grateful for such obvious caring among the gods about my welfare."

"We were all startled," Tigellinus said at once. "And the vestal Rubria also swooned in terror."

"Ah, Rubria," Nero said, momentarily distracted. "What a snowy neck she has."

"But she blushes every time she sees you, divine Caesar."

"True! She does! I noticed it myself." Nero's mad green eyes glinted for a moment, as if the dissolute chief priestess of Vesta, pledged theoretically to purity but as profligate as any other woman in society, might help him get over his superstitious awe. "Strange, right? A vestal virgin . . . hmm. There's something of the goddess in all of those vestals, and Rubria is really very beautiful."

His mind took off on another tangent. "I wonder why people fear Vesta more than the other gods. What's behind all that? I was afraid myself, even though I'm the supreme pontiff of all religions. All I remember is that I fell over backward and would have crashed to the floor if someone hadn't caught me. Who did that, by the way? Who caught me?"

"I did," said Vinicius.

"Ah, it was you, you 'fierce son of Mars?' Why didn't you go with us to Beneventum? Somebody told me you were ill, and it's true you look somewhat different. Ah, but I also heard Croton tried to kill you. Is that true?"

"Yes, Caesar. He broke my arm but I managed to defend myself."

"With a broken arm?"

"I got some help from a barbarian who proved more powerful than Croton."

Nero gaped, astonished. "More powerful than Croton? You must be joking. Croton was the strongest man alive. Now the Ethiopian Syphax is the strongest."

"I tell you, Caesar, I saw it with my own eyes."

"Where is that pearl, then? Is he now the ruling champion of Nemea?"

"I don't know where he is, my lord. I lost track of him when it was all over."

"Don't you even know where he's from?"

"I was hurt . . . that broken arm, you know, sir. So there was no time to question anyone about him."

"Find him for me, will you?"

"I'll take care of that for you, Caesar," Tigellinus offered.

But Nero went on talking to Vinicius. "Well, thanks for catching me, anyway. I might have cracked my head on that marble floor. You used to be good company, I remember, but you've turned into a bit of a savage under Corbulanus, and I don't seem to see you very often." Another thought glimmered in his head just then, and his eyes glinted with interest. "And how's that girl of yours? The one with narrow hips that I got for you from Aulus and Graecina?"

Vinicius hesitated, thrown off stride and wondering how to answer, but Petronius stepped in to help at once.

"I'll bet he's quite forgotten her, my lord. Just look at how bewildered he is. Ask him how many other girls he's had since then, but I won't guarantee you'll get a better answer. The Vinicci make fine soldiers but even better roosters. They need a whole henhouse. Punish him for it, Caesar, and don't invite him to that feast Tigellinus promises to give in your honor on the ponds of Agrippa."

"No, I won't. I expect, Tigellinus, there'll be whole a flock of pretty women there."

"Could we run short of Graces, sire," Tigellinus said, bowing with an obsequious smile, "when the god of love himself is going to be there?"

"I'm bored with Rome!" Nero groaned. "Bored beyond endurance! I stayed here only as a favor to the goddess but I can't stand this city. I think I'll go to Antium. I simply can't breathe in these narrow streets, I suffocate among those tumbling houses and those stinking alleys. That reeking air invades even my house and gardens. Ah, if only an earthquake would level this damned Rome! If some angry god would raze it to the ground! Then I'd show you how to build a city fit to rule the world and be my capital."

"Caesar," Tigellinus offered, smooth as silk, "you say, 'If only some angry god would destroy the city.' Isn't that right, my lord?"

"It is. And what of it?"

"Well . . . aren't you divine?"

But Nero, bored with talk, only flipped his arm and yawned in dismissal. "We'll see how you'll amuse us on Agrippa's ponds," he said wearily. "But then I'll definitely go to Antium. Yes, I will. You're all too small to understand I must have greatness around me everywhere."

He closed his eyes as a sign that he wanted rest, and the Augustans began to leave the chamber. Petronius walked out with Vinicius.

"So you've been summoned to Nero's fun and games," he observed. "Copperbeard may have talked himself out of his epic journey, but he'll go madder than ever here in Rome, making himself at home all over the city. There ought to be enough craziness even for your distraction. Try to forget your problems. Ah, what the devil! We've conquered the whole world so we've a right to amuse ourselves! You, Marcus, are a very beautiful young man, and I imagine that's partly to blame for my fondness of you. Ah, by Diana of Ephesus! If you could just see your own stern Quirite face, that single black line of eyebrows, so obviously patrician! You made the rest of that jumped-up Augustan herd look like a mob of freedmen. No question about it! If it weren't for that absurd Christianity, Ligia would be waiting in your house right now. Try all you want to prove they aren't the enemies of life and all humanity, but you'll be wasting your time. Yes, they treated you quite well, I expect, so you can be grateful to them if you wish, but if I were in your place, I'd soon hate their deadly, self-denying dogma and look for my pleasures where they are, right here on earth among us. You're a beautiful young man, I repeat, and Rome is full of easy divorcees."

"I'm just surprised you can still be bothered with all that trivial, self-indulgent nonsense," Vinicius replied. "I would've thought you'd be tired of it long ago."

"And who told you I'm not? I've been bored with it for years, but I'm quite a bit older than you, my lad. Besides, I've other pleasures and distractions, which you lack. I love books, and you don't. I'm fond of poetry, which bores you. I love artwork, gemstones, and many other things that you don't even see. I get backaches that don't bother you. And, finally, I've discovered Eunice, while you've found nothing comparable for yourself. I'm comfortable at home among my art treasures, but I'll never make a lover of beauty out of you. I know that life will never offer me anything I haven't had before, but you aren't even aware that you're still expecting new discoveries and still searching for some fresh sensations. With all your courage and all your disappointments, Marcus, you still cling to life as if it held some hidden promises and meanings. I think if you were to die today, you'd be unpleasantly surprised that it's time to go, while I'd accept death as something necessary and natural, knowing there are no pleasures in this world that I haven't tasted.

"I'm in no rush to die," he went on, "that goes without saying, but

I'm not going to hold back either when the moment comes. All I care about is that I manage to amuse myself until the end. There is such a thing in this world as a merry-minded skeptic. The Stoics are stupid, as far as I'm concerned, but Stoicism does, at least, discipline the soul. Your Christians, on the other hand, fill the world with gloom, playing the same role in life as rain does in nature.

"Ah, but do you know what I heard?" A wry smile flickered briefly across his handsome face. "Tigellinus plans to line the banks of Agrippa's ponds with pleasure tents staffed by the best of our society women in the role of harlots. I should think you'll find at least one beautiful enough to take your mind off your troubles. They'll even have young girls there, making their debut in society so to speak—as water nymphs! Ah well, that's our imperial Rome for you. Still, the weather's getting warmer every day; the south wind will take the chill off the water and the goose pimples off those naked bodies. And you, my dear Narcissus, won't find one who'll turn you away; you can be sure of that even if they are vestals."

Vinicius started slapping his own forehead like a man obsessed with a single thought. "It's just my luck," he said, "to have found one who does."

"And who's to blame for that if it's not your Christians? What can you expect from people who pick a cross, the most despised object in the empire, for their symbol? Listen to me now! Greece was beautiful and created wisdom. We invented power. But what can such a teaching give the world? If you know, do me the kindness and enlighten me because, by Pollux, it defies my imagination."

Vinicius shrugged, unconvinced. "It seems as if you're afraid I'll become a Christian."

"I'm afraid that you'll wreck your life! If you can't be Grecian, then try to be Roman. Rule and exploit. All our mad excesses make some sort of sense simply because that's their guiding principle. I despise Copperbeard because he's merely a fake, artificial Greek, but I'd grant him full rights to his craziness if he thought of himself as a real Roman. Promise me one thing, will you? Stick your tongue out at any Christian you find in your house. If it's that doctor, Glaucus, he won't even be particularly surprised. And now go back home. I'll see you on the ponds of Agrippa."

⟨38⟩

RANKS OF PRAETORIANS kept the gaping crowds out of the woods that spread beside the ponds of Agrippa so that nothing would intrude upon Caesar's pleasures, but vast throngs flocked there anyway, simply to be near. This, by all accounts, was to be the spectacle of the era, beyond anything in the city's history, and everybody who was anybody in Rome, whether by virtue of wealth, mind or beauty, hurried to be there. Tigellinus wanted to console the emperor for the disappointment of his deferred journey into Greece, to surpass anyone who ever hosted Nero, and at the same time to prove that no one could create more for his amusement. To this end, even while he was with the emperor in Naples and then at Beneventum, he got things under way and issued streams of orders so that the feast wouldn't lack for rare animals, the most exotic plants and birds, and rich furnishings and hangings rushed from every corner of the world. The revenues of entire provinces went to satisfy the craziest whims and notions, but Caesar's powerful favorite didn't have to worry about that. His influence on Nero crept upward day by day. He may not have been the courtier Nero liked the most, but he was fast becoming the man most necessary to him. Petronius would always stand head and shoulders over him in polish, mind and wit. Nero was still more likely to listen to him than Tigellinus and feared his disapproval in matters of good taste.

But Petronius had a powerful handicap. He was a victim of his own superiority to Caesar. His eloquence and intelligence far surpassed the emperor's, while the coarse and cruel Tigellinus made Nero feel at home. Even the title of *arbiter elegantiarum* generally accorded to Petronius grated on Nero's vanity. After all, shouldn't it be his? Who had a better right to the last word on all that was beautiful and artistic? Moreover Tigellinus was shrewd enough to know his own shortcomings. He could see he would never be able to compete intellectually or artistically with a Petronius or Lucanus, or anybody

else of distinguished talent, birth or learning, so he chose to compete
with assiduous service and with such extravagance that even Nero's
torpid imagination would be struck by it.

He ordered the banquet set on a colossal raft made of gilded logs,
edged throughout by rare shells and conches plucked from the Red
Sea and the Indian Ocean, and glowing pearly white or rainbow, all
the colors of the spectrum. Oases of palms, lotus pools and groves of
blooming roses transformed the giant raft into a floating island,
bright with the glittering arcs of perfumed fountains and loud with
the cries of richly plumed birds in gold or silver cages. Rather than
block the diners' view with tent walls, Tigellinus had only the purple
top of a Syrian tent raised over the couches on slim silver poles, while
the tables glowed with Alexandrine glass, cut crystal and priceless sil-
verware looted from Italy, Greece and Asia Minor. Gold and silver
cables anchored this verdant artificial island to a fleet of boats, shaped
like fish, swans, seagulls and flamingos. Naked youths and girls of
extraordinary beauty sat at painted oars, with their hair styled either
in the Eastern fashion or held in a golden net.

When Nero finally arrived with Poppea and all the Augustans and
took his place under the purple tent top, the boats stirred, the oars
struck the water, the golden cables tightened, and the whole floating
banquet sailed across the ponds. It was immediately surrounded by
smaller rafts and boats, full of nude girls playing harps and zithers;
their pale pink bodies seemed to drink in the blue of the sky and
water, streaked with the gold reflections of their instruments, and
projected their own glow like many-colored flowers.

Music and songs burst out of all the groves and the fantastic buildings raised for the occasion and hidden in the thickets. The woods
rang with the cry of the horns and trumpets, the whole countryside
resounded with song, and the echoes spread the music.

Nero loved it. He didn't stint on compliments for Tigellinus.
Flanked by Poppea and Pythagoras, he was especially pleased when
swarms of naked slave girls, dressed in green fishnetting to imitate
the glistening scales of mermaids, appeared among the boats. But
while he praised Tigellinus, he kept a cautious eye on Petronius, anxious for his judgment.

The arbiter, however, said nothing until Nero turned to him directly.

"To my mind, my lord," he said at last, "ten thousand naked bodies
have less effect than one."

But Nero liked the novelty of this floating orgy. The dishes offered at the tables were as fantastic as he normally expected, but the variety served by Tigellinus would have stunned the imagination of Apicius, the most notorious epicure in the reigns of Augustus and Tiberius. The same went for the many kinds of the finest wines. Otho, Poppea's former husband, who liked to serve eighty different wines at his splendid banquets, would drown himself in shame, Nero was quite sure, if he could see this extravagant display.

Only the so-called beautiful people of Rome, the exquisite Augustans, reclined beside the tables with their women, but Vinicius' striking looks put them all to shame. The young man's face and body used to bear the hard stamp of the career soldier, too threatening for an aesthete's notions of patrician beauty, but now he seemed gentled and transformed. Pain, illness and anxiety had refined his features, as though a sculptor's skilled hand had given him the last necessary polish. His skin, once scorched by campaign suns, had lost its windswept harshness, retaining only the light golden glints of Numidian marble. His eyes had grown larger and deeper with sadness. Only his powerful torso kept its massive shape, as if created for a soldier's breastplate, but the magnificent, subtly sculpted head looked as if it belonged to a young Greek god. Petronius had spoken from experience when he said that all the most distinguished women of society were his for the asking, including the vestals. All of them eyed him now, including Poppea and Rubria, who was there at Nero's insistence.

The wines, chilled in vats of snow that running couriers carried from the mountains, soon inflamed the diners, heating their minds and bodies. The shoreline thickets disgorged fresh swarms of boats shaped like grasshoppers and dragonflies; the smooth silvery surface of the water began to look as if swarms of brightly colored insects had settled on it amid floating flowers. White doves and shrill, exotic birds from Africa and India circled above the boats, held captive by sky blue cords or strands of silver wire.

It was unusually warm for a day in early May, even though the sun was already well into the afternoon, and the heat pulsing from sated and wine-sodden bodies soon brought to mind the swelter of summer. The oars beat the surface of the pond in time to the music, creating waves that sent the great raft rocking in the water; but the air above it was breathless and still, so that it seemed as if the groves and thickets on the banks were awed into stillness by what was happening on the pond. The great raft sailed through the water hour after hour, inscribing loops and arabesques on the agitated surface and carrying an ever noisier cargo of swilling banqueters. The drunken diners had long ceased to pay attention to the seating order; they staggered to their feet, peered about for fresher company and plunged beside whatever man or woman they fancied the most, even though the feast had barely come halfway to the end.

Caesar himself was the first to break the seating rule, ordering Vinicius to trade places with him so that he might start whispering into Rubria's ear, and the young tribune found himself lying beside Poppea. She stretched her full white arm toward him, asking him to tighten the fastenings of an armlet that had come undone, and when he did this with unsteady hands, she shot him a long glance from under her lashes, as if she was suddenly ashamed of her own warm feelings, and she shook her head briefly as if in regret.

The sun, meanwhile, grew larger, flushed a deeper crimson and sank slowly behind the crowns of the trees. By this time most of the dinner guests were completely drunk. The raft was now circling near the wooded shore, where groups of men disguised as fauns and satyrs piped on flutes and whistles and shook tambourines, while young girls, stripped to represent tree and water nymphs, gleamed whitely among clumps of trees and flowers. Darkness came at last, greeted by wild shouts from under the tent top and drunken cheers to Luna, and the groves glittered suddenly with a thousand torches. Streams of light fell from the temporary brothels scattered along the bank; fresh throngs of naked women, the wives and daughters of Rome's finest families, poured out on the terraces, crying out and gesturing their open invitations to the banqueters.

The raft slid into the bank at last. Caesar and the Augustans threw themselves into the groves and vanished in the brothels, in the tents hidden within the thickets, and in the artificial groves scattered among the woodland springs and fountains. Madness seized everyone. No one knew where to look for Caesar. There was no longer any way to tell the senators and knights from dancers and musicians. Howling fauns and satyrs chased the screaming nymphs. People started whipping the lamps and torches with bundles of dry stalks to put out the lights, and then darkness gripped the groves. From everywhere in the spreading shadows came wild shouts, shrill bursts of laughter, urgent whispers and panting breath. Rome had indeed never seen anything like this before.

Vinicius was nowhere near as drunk as at the banquet in the Palatine when Ligia was present. But even he was dazzled and inflamed by everything he saw around him, and wild madness seized him along with all the others. He burst into the trees and ran with the rest, peering about for the prettiest tree nymph he could find. Whole flocks of them raced past him, crying out and singing, pursued by fauns, satyrs, senators and knights, and trailed by the music. At last he caught sight of a swarm of girls led by one dressed as the goddess Diana, and he swerved toward them for a better look. But suddenly he lost his breath and his heart hammered in his chest. The lithe, inviting goddess with the horns of the moon shining on her forehead reminded him of Ligia.

The nymphs danced around him, like a wreath of wildly animated flowers, then whirled away like a herd of does, wanting him to follow.

But he stood still. His heartbeat had quickened, and his breath hissed heavily in his throat. Seen at close range, Diana proved to be nothing like Ligia, but the effect of his first mistake drained him of all strength. He was immediately seized by a desperate yearning. He longed for Ligia beyond hope or dreams of possession. His love for her filled him so completely that it felt like a tide bursting through his chest. She never seemed as dear to him or less sullied than in these groves of debauchery and madness. A moment earlier he was set to throw himself into the mindless cesspool of unbridled senses; now he felt repugnance and was choked with loathing. He felt a sudden need for fresh air to breathe and for the sight of stars not hidden by the branches of the ghastly grove, and he turned to run.

He had barely taken the first few strides when a veiled figure rose out of the darkness and leaned with both hands against his chest; the heat of her whisper swept across his face. "I want you. . . . Come! Nobody will see us. Hurry!"

Vinicius jumped like a man woken from a dream. "Who are you?"

"Guess."

Her arms pulled his head powerfully toward her, her lips closed on his through the tissue of her veils, and she jerked away from him only for air to breathe.

"This is a night of love," she gasped, struggling for a breath. "A night of total rapture. . . . A night of the senses . . . ! Everything is allowed tonight. . . . You can have me!"

But that kiss burned like a red-hot brand on Vinicius' mouth. It disgusted him. His mind and spirit had flown somewhere else, and there was no one else for him but Ligia anywhere in the world.

"Whoever you are," he said, pushing her aside, "I love another. I don't want you."

But she only pulled his head closer to her own. "Lift my veils!" she ordered.

Leaves rustled just then in the nearby myrtles. The veiled figure whirled away and vanished like an apparition, and only a quick burst of laughter ringing in the darkness indicated that she had been there. That laughter seemed oddly malevolent and threatening.

Then he was looking at Petronius.

"I saw and heard it all," Petronius said.

"Let's leave this place," Vinicius said in answer.

They did so at once. They said nothing to each other all the way back to the city, and it was only when they stood in Vinicius' atrium that Petronius asked: "Do you know who that was?"

"Rubria?" Vinicius gave an involuntary shudder at the thought of sacrilege with a vestal.

Petronius dropped his voice. "Vesta's fire is no longer sacred because Rubria lay tonight with Caesar. You"— he lowered his voice even further—"were with the Diva Augusta, the divine Poppea."

Neither had anything to say after that. But then Petronius added, in shrugging explanation: "Caesar couldn't hide his lust for Rubria, so maybe Poppea just wanted to pay him back in kind. I broke in on you because I was afraid you'd turn her down. And if that happened after you saw her face and knew who she was, nothing would save either of you—either you or Ligia."

But Vinicius finally had enough. "To Hell with you all! I'm sick of Rome, Caesar, orgies, the Augusta, Tigellinus and the rest of you! I'm strangling among you! I can't live like this, do you understand?"

"Vinicius!" Petronius was truly alarmed and concerned. "You're losing your grip, your sense of perspective! You've lost the power of judgment!"

"I love only one woman!"

"So what?"

"So I don't want any other love. And I don't want any more of your life, your pastimes, your debaucheries or your crimes!"

"What's the matter with you, man? Are you now a Christian?"

But the young man only seized his head in both hands and started to say over and over as if in despair: "Not yet! Not yet!"

❰ 3 9 ❱

Petronius went home highly displeased and shrugging in defeat. Even he grasped at last that he and Vinicius no longer understood each other and their lives had split into different courses. He used to have a powerful influence over the young soldier. Vinicius had modeled himself on him for years; he was the young man's chief mentor and exemplar. Often enough one of his ironic quips either halted Vinicius in his tracks or pushed him deeper into an idea.

None of that existed anymore; the last threads of their similarity had parted. Petronius didn't even try to get things back to where they were; he was convinced that all his clever witticisms and ironic comments would bounce off the steep, slippery walls that love and the unfathomable Christian world had created between them, and any effort to knock down those barriers would be a waste of time. The worldly skeptic understood that he had lost the key to this mind and spirit. He was annoyed but also increasingly alarmed as he reviewed some of the night's events.

"If he is more to Poppea than just a passing fancy," he mused in concern, "and if she still wants him, then only one of two things can happen: Either Vinicius gives in, in which case he'll be caught in some accidental trap and nothing will save him, or he puts her off. If that should happen—which is very likely, the way he is these days—he'll be lost for sure. Moreover I'll probably share his fate, if for no other reason than that we're related. Poppea would turn on our entire family and put her influence behind Tigellinus."

Either way there were no quick solutions. Petronius had a great deal of courage and no fear of dying, but since he expected nothing after death, he saw no point in hurrying it along. He gave the problem long and careful thought and decided that a lengthy journey for Vinicius could be the answer. "Ah," he muttered grimly, "if I could give him Ligia for a traveling companion, he'd go like a shot!" He didn't expect any trouble convincing the young man. Then he'd feed the rumors in the Palatine about Vinicius' illness and avert danger for both of them.

"The Augusta can't really tell if she was recognized or not," he mused. "She could suppose she wasn't, in which case her vanity wasn't hurt too badly. But the next time could be altogether different, and that's what we must prevent."

Time was important. Petronius played for time. Tigellinus knew absolutely nothing about art or beauty, and his influence would dwindle into nothing once they set out for Greece. Petronius had no doubt he would triumph over all his challengers once Caesar launched himself into that deferred pursuit of Greek adulation that he craved. The problem was to retain his influence on Nero until then.

Meanwhile he determined to keep a close eye on Vinicius and urge him to go traveling. He spent more than a dozen days wondering if he shouldn't get Caesar to expel the Christians by decree, driving them out of Rome the way Claudius had expelled the Roman Jews not long ago. Ligia would leave with them, and Vinicius would be sure to follow. Why shouldn't Nero do it? There would be more room in Rome with the Christians gone. Since the night of the floating orgy, Petronius saw Nero every day, either in the Palatine or at private gatherings; it wouldn't be difficult, he knew, to slip the notion into Caesar's ear, especially since he never turned down an idea that would hurt somebody or lead to their ruin. He would give a banquet for Caesar in his house and plant his project there. Caesar might even entrust him with carrying out the edict.

"In which case," he mused in anticipation, "I'd ship Ligia to some place like Baiae, with all the care due a lover of Vinicius, and let them love each other there and play at being Christians as much as they like."

He called on Vinicius almost every day. Despite all his Roman egotism, he couldn't shake his fondness for the young tribune or his attachment to him, and he urged him to leave Rome at once. Vinicius kept to his own house, pretending to be ill, and didn't show himself at the Palatine, where new whims and notions were appearing by the hour. Finally Petronius heard from Caesar himself that he intended to go to Antium in three days no matter what happened, and he brought this news the next morning to Vinicius.

But the young man merely showed him a list of those invited for the trip to Antium, which one of Nero's freedmen had delivered at daybreak.

"My name is on it," he said. "So is yours. You'll find the same thing waiting for you at home."

"If mine wasn't on it," Petronius observed, "that would suggest it's time for me to die. But I don't expect it before the trip to Greece. Nero will need me too much there."

He looked over the list and shook his head sadly. "What a pity, though. We've just come back to Rome, and it's already time to go off again. But if we must, we must! This isn't just an invitation, it's an order."

"And what if somebody refused to obey it?"

"He'd get an order to take a longer trip, the kind from which you don't return. What a pity you refused to leave while there was still time. Now you have no choice. You have to go to Antium."

"I have to go to Antium. . . ." Vinicius grimaced with loathing and contempt. "Just look at the horror of the times we live in and what slaves we've become."

"You've just caught on to that?"

"Far from it. You call Christianity the enemy of life because it fetters the human sense of joy. But what about the chains we wear every day? You said the Greeks gave us wisdom and created beauty while we invented power. So where's this power of ours?"

"Get Chilon to philosophize with you," Petronius snapped coldly. "I've no time for such games today. By Hercules! I didn't create these times, and I won't be held responsible for them. Let's talk about Antium. Get it into your head that you're in worse danger there than if you tried your hand with that Ursus who throttled Croton. And yet you have to go!"

Vinicius shrugged, indifferent. "What's new about danger? We grope in the shadow of death all the days of our lives, and somebody sinks into it every other minute."

"Do you want me to list everyone who was smart enough to survive Tiberius, Caligula, Claudius and now Nero? Some are in their nineties! Just look at Domitius Afer, to give one example. He has reached a ripe old age even though he was a thief and a cutthroat all his life."

"That's probably how he did it," Vinicius said with a shrug.

He started to look at the invitation list. "Tigellinus," he snapped. "Vatinius. Sextus Africanus. Aquilinus Regulus, Suilius Nerulinus, Eprius Marcellus and so on! What a foul collection of scoundrels and toadies! And just think: They rule the world! Aren't they better suited to trundle some Syrian or Egyptian deity through the marketplaces, tell fortunes, strum lyres, or dance on the tightrope?"

"Or exhibit trained apes, dogs that bark out numbers, or donkeys that blow air through a flute," Petronius added. "It's all quite true, but we're talking about something urgent. Get a grip on your mind and start listening to me. I have spread the word at the Palatine that you're ill and can't leave your home, but here's your name on the invitation anyway. That means someone thinks I'm lying and did it on purpose. Nero wouldn't care if you came or not. For him you're just a soldier without a glimmer of art, poetry or music anywhere in you. He might talk to you about chariot racing, but that's all. No, your invitation must have come from Poppea's fingers, and that means she's serious about wanting you."

"That's risky business for an empress."

"Risky indeed. She could lose it all. But Poppea calculates all her risks precisely. May Venus light some other fires in her as soon as she can, but as long as she still fancies you, you're walking on eggshells. She has lost some of her novelty for Copperbeard. He's far more interested these days in Pythagoras or Rubria, but his vanity would demand the most frightful vengeance on you both."

"I didn't know who she was that time in the woods," Vinicius said. "But you were there. You heard what I told her. I don't want her. I love another woman."

"And I beg you by all the lesser gods not to abandon the last shreds of reason left you by those Christians. How can you hesitate when your only choices are instant disaster or the faint possibility of survival? Didn't I tell you that if you slight Augusta you'll be lost? By Hades! If you're sick of life, then slit your wrists or throw yourself on your sword, and be done with it! It could prove an easier death than what you'll get if you offend Poppea.

"Ah"—he shrugged mechanically—"it used to be much more pleasant to talk with you when you could see reason. What bothers you about it so much, anyway? What will you lose by it? Will it put an end to your love for Ligia? And bear in mind that Poppea saw her at the Palatine. It won't take her long to put two and two together and identify her rival. And once she's done that, once she realizes you rejected her imperial favors for a fugitive barbarian, she'll turn over every stone in the empire until she gets her hands on the girl. You'll bring destruction not just on yourself but on Ligia too. Do you understand?"

Vinicius listened, but his mind was clearly somewhere else. "I have to see her," he said at last.

"Who? Ligia?"

"Ligia."

"Do you know where she is?"

"No."

"Then how will you find her? Are you going to start combing old cemeteries and the Trans-Tiber all over again?"

"I don't know what I'll do, but I have to see her."

"Good. Do it. She may be a Christian, but she might have a better hold of reality than you, and she's sure to show it where your survival is concerned."

Vinicius shrugged. "She saved me from Ursus."

"In that case, hurry. Copperbeard isn't going to delay his trip, and he can issue death sentences in Antium as easily as here."

《40》

VINICIUS DIDN'T GIVE much thought to what Petronius told him because his mind was totally absorbed with Ligia. All he could think about was seeing her and searching for a way. Then something happened. Chilon came unexpectedly to see him the next day, an event that promised to put things right again.

He came in rags, with signs of hunger on his face, as gaunt in misery as he could ever get and with his wretched cloak hanging in strips and tatters, but the household slaves were still under orders to let him in at any time of day and didn't dare stop him, so he stumbled straight into the atrium.

"May the gods give you immortality," he whimpered to Vinicius. "And may they share their power over the world."

Vinicius' first thought was to have him flung out of the house. Then it crossed his mind that the Greek might know something about Ligia, and his eagerness to know overcame revulsion.

"Ah, it's you, is it?" he asked. "What's your story these days?"

"An unhappy one, great son of Jupiter," Chilon sighed. "True virtue is in scant demand these days, and a true sage must be content to buy a sheep's head from a butcher once in five days so he may gnaw on it in some attic and drink his own tears. Ah, my lord! Everything you gave me went to buy scholarly books at the Atractus bookstore; then I was robbed and ruined altogether. The slave girl whom I bought to transcribe the fruits of my learning ran off with whatever I had left of your munificence. I am a beggar now, but it occurred to me that I might come to you, splendid Serapis! To you, whom I love and adore as a god and for whom I risked my life."

"So why did you come? And with what?"

"For help, great Baal! And all I bring is my misery, my tears, my devotion, and some bits of information I gathered as a labor of that love. You recall, my lord, what I once said about that thread from

Aphrodite's girdle that I gave to the slave girl of the divine Petronius, the one who wanted to win a reluctant lover? Well, I stopped by there recently to see if it helped her. And you, son of the Sun, who knows everything that happens in that household, also know what Eunice is in that house today! Well, sir, I still have one such thread. I saved it for your lordship."

His teeth snapped shut at the look of fury he saw gathering in Vinicius' face, and he hurried to forestall the outburst.

"I know where the divine Ligia is staying!" he rushed to explain. "I'll show you the alley and pinpoint the house, my lord."

It took a moment for Vinicius to smother the sudden rush of feeling that seized him at this news. "Where is she?" he said.

"With Linus, their chief priest. She's there with Ursus but he works at night. He's still with that miller whose name is the same as that of your butler. Yes, the miller Demas. He won't be home if you surround the house at night. Linus is an old man . . . and besides him there are only two old women in the house."

"How do you know all this?"

"You recall, my lord, that the Christians had me in their grasp, but they let me go. Glaucus is wrong to think that I'm the cause of all his misfortunes, but he's convinced himself of that, poor fellow, and believes it to this day. But still they set me free! So don't be surprised, my lord, that gratitude filled my heart. I am a man of the old ways and virtues, following the old customs. Was I to turn my back on my friends and benefactors? Wouldn't it be the grossest heartlessness not to ask about them, find out how they're doing and what's happening with them, and also where they live? By Cybele of Pessina," he swore, naming the town in Galatia near Phrygia Major where the corn goddess was worshiped like Astarte, who in turn was noted for ritual prostitution. "I'm not capable of a deed like that. I was afraid at first that they had misread my motives and misunderstood all my good intentions. My love for them proved greater than my fear, however, especially since they're so quick to forgive every kind of injury. But my foremost thought, my lord, was of you! Our last expedition ended in defeat, and how can such a son of Fortune as yourself make his peace with that? So I prepared your victory. The house stands alone. You can have your slaves surround it so tightly, that a mouse wouldn't squeak through between them. Oh, my lord! My lord! It's purely up to you if that peerless princess finds herself in your house tonight. But if that should happen, give a thought to my father's poor and hungry son, who may have played a role in making you happy."

A rush of blood swept through the tribune's head. An irresistible temptation seized and shook everything that made him what he was. Yes! This was it! This was the surest way, and this time it was foolproof! Who would manage to take Ligia from him once he had her here? And once he turned Ligia into his lover, what choice would she have but be one as long as she lived? And to perdition with those gloomy teachings! To Hell with them all! What would those Christians matter to him, with their mercy and their contemplative mourning, after that? Wasn't it time to shake himself free of them? To forget all that? To start living once more like everybody else?

How Ligia might respond to this or how she'd reconcile her fate with her religion didn't matter to him. Such things carried no weight whatsoever! What counted first and foremost was that she would be his—and before the morning. Moreover who could say if that faith of hers would stand up to the magnificence of the world she would enter and to the joys and raptures she would experience? And all of this, he knew, could begin to happen before the night was over. All he had to do was hold Chilon until nightfall and give the necessary orders. And then endless joy.

"What has this life been for me?" he had to ask himself. He listed its contents: "tormenting thoughts, unsated lust, and questions without answers."

It was time to cut loose from it all, and this was the way. It crossed his mind that he had sworn to her he would never use violence with her again, but what did he swear on? Not on the gods, because he no longer believed in them. Not on Christ, because he still didn't believe in him. Besides, if she felt herself injured in some way, he'd make it up by marriage.

Yes, that he had to give her because she saved his life. He recalled the day he broke into her refuge with Croton. He saw again the vast fist of Ursus trembling above his head, and he remembered everything that followed. He saw her leaning over his cot, dressed in her slave tunic, full of charity and loved by everyone around her. His eyes shifted to his household gods and fixed themselves on the small twig cross she had given him just before she vanished. Was he to pay for that with a fresh assault? Was he to drag her by the hair to his bed? And how was he to do that when he not only wanted her but loved her, and loved her for what she was? Suddenly he felt it wouldn't be enough just to have her with him in his house. He wanted more than just crushing her in his arms. His love demanded infinitely more. He wanted her consent, her love given freely, and her commitment to complement his own. Blessed be this roof, he cried silently, the moment she steps under it of her own free will. Blessed be the moment, blessed be the day, blessed be the life thereafter. Their happiness would be immeasurably greater in such event and as immutable as the sun. But taking her by force would destroy it all. It would be like murdering happiness, and not merely killing it but also turning it into something foul, loathsome and repugnant: the utter ruin of all he loved and wanted.

Terror convulsed him at the thought. He glanced at Chilon. The Greek was peering into his eyes intently. He thrust a hand inside his filthy rags and scratched himself uneasily as he eyed Vinicius. The young tribune saw him then as something inexpressibly revolting and wanted to grind his head under his boot as he would do to household vermin or a poisonous snake. But he already knew what he had to do, and since he never did anything by halves, throwing himself into everything with total conviction and driven to exaggeration and excess by his Roman ruthlessness, he had a frightening answer for the anxious Greek.

"I won't do what you suggest," he said to him coldly. "But so you don't leave without the reward you earned, I'll have three hundred lashes laid on your back in my sweating chamber."

Chilon grew white. The determination he saw in the young tribune's classically beautiful face was so chilling and so bereft of feeling that he couldn't hope the promised payment was just a cruel joke. He threw himself at once on both his knees, scrunched into a ball and started whimpering in a broken voice.

"Why, king of the East? For what, you pyramid of mercy, grace and kindness? Have pity, you colossus of compassion! I'm old, poor and hungry. I did so much for you. And that's how you thank me?"

"As you thanked the Christians," Vinicius said and called for the *dispensator*, the head of his household, who as the atrium supervisor dispensed the discipline among the other slaves.

But Chilon wasn't done. He leaped in one bound to the tribune's knees and clutched them in a spasm of terror. His face looked like a death mask.

"Lord, my lord!" he howled. "I'm old! Fifty, not three hundred! Fifty will do! One hundred, not three! Have mercy! Have mercy!"

Vinicius kicked him aside and snapped out an order. Two powerful Quadi slaves ran into the atrium behind the supervisor, seized Chilon by the tufts of his remaining hair, twisted his own rags around his head and dragged him outside.

"In the name of Christ!" Chilon howled from the doorway to the corridor.

Vinicius was alone. His savage order excited him and quickened his breathing. He took his time about restoring order to his mind and calming his senses. He felt a vast relief. The victory he had won over himself gave him new hope. It seemed to him that he had just taken a great stride toward Ligia and that something good would happen to him in return. It didn't occur to him at first how unfairly he had treated Chilon, inflicting such severe punishment for a service he had always rewarded before. He was too much a Roman to feel another's pain or to clutter up his mind with one worthless Greek; and even if such thoughts did occur to him, he would have felt fully justified in ordering a whipping for a scoundrel.

But he was thinking only about Ligia. "I won't repay your goodness with my evil," he was saying to her. "You'll be grateful to me if you ever hear how I dealt with a wretch who wanted me to raise my hand against you."

Then he paused, wondering if Ligia would approve of what he had done to Chilon. Her faith demanded mercy and forgiveness. Her fellow Christians forgave the same creature, although they had a far heavier score to settle with him. That desperate "In the name of Christ" rang out at last in the tribune's soul. He remembered that Chilon saved himself from Ursus with just such a cry and decided to suspend the rest of his whipping.

He was about to call his *dispensator* when the man appeared on his own. "The old man fainted," he reported. "Or maybe he's dead. Am I to keep whipping?"

"Bring him around and fetch him here before me," Vinicius ordered.

The *atriensis* vanished behind the screen, but Chilon's return to consciousness must have been a hard one. Vinicius waited a long time, starting to get impatient, when the slaves finally brought the Greek and backed out of the atrium at their master's signal.

Chilon looked as gray as a sheet of canvas, and threads of blood trickled down his legs to the mosaic on the atrium floor. He was fully conscious and threw himself on his knees as before.

"Thank you, great lord!" he cried and stretched his arms in the Roman gesture of adoration, subservience and worship. "You are great and merciful."

"Know this, you dog," Vinicius said. "I let you go for the sake of that Christ whom I owe my own life."

"I'll be his servant from now on, my lord! His and yours!"

"Keep quiet and listen. Get up! You'll go with me and show me the house where Ligia is living."

Chilon leaped to his feet as ordered, but the effort drained the last of his physical resources. He lost whatever color he had in his face, and his voice grew faint.

"I'm really hungry, lord," he groaned. "Oh, I'll go . . . I'll go. But I'm too weak to move. . . . Feed me at least the scraps from your dog's bowl, and I'll go!"

Vinicius ordered him fed, threw him a gold piece and had a new cloak draped over his shoulders. But Chilon was too weak to go even after eating. The bloody whipping and the days of hunger had robbed him of all strength, and his wispy hair rose on his head in terror in case Vinicius took his weakness for some new resistance and ordered a resumption of the lash.

"Just let this wine warm me up a bit," he whimpered through clattering teeth. "I'll be able to go at once, even to the far ends of greater Greece."

Some strength returned to him in a short while, and they left together. They walked a long time. Like most of the Christians, Linus lived in the slums across the Tiber, and not too far from the house of Miriam. But Chilon could point out a little house at last, surrounded by a wall covered with ivy.

"Here it is, lord," he said.

"Good," said Vinicius. "Now make yourself scarce, but note one thing more. Forget you ever served me. Forget where Miriam, Peter and Glaucus are living. Forget this house and everything else you know about any Christians. Come to my house once a month, and Demas, my freedman, will pay you two gold pieces every time you show. But if you go on spying on the Christians, I'll have you whipped to death or turn you over to the city prefect."

Chilon bowed almost to the ground. "I'll forget," he promised. But when Vinicius vanished beyond a turn in the alley, he stretched both his fists after him, shook them in hatred and grated out: "By the goddess of death and all the furies, I will not forget!"

Then he collapsed again.

⟪41⟫

WITH CHILON NO LONGER on his mind, Vinicius went directly to the house of Miriam. The boy Nazarius was startled when he came across him at the gate, but the young tribune threw him a pleasant greeting and asked to be taken to his mother's home. There, besides Miriam, he found Peter, Glaucus, Crispus and also Paul of Tarsus who had just come back from preaching in Fregellae. Surprise and perhaps shock as well showed in their faces as he walked in among them.

"I greet you in Christ's name, whom you worship," he said coming in.

"May he be praised forever," they chorused in reply.

"I saw how good you really are," he said. "I sampled your kindness. I come as a friend."

"And we, too, greet you as a friend, my lord," Peter said. "Sit with us and share our supper as our guest."

"Gladly. But first I have something to tell you, Peter, and you, Paul of Tarsus, so you'll know I'm being honest with you. I know where Ligia is hidden. I've just come from the house of Linus that is near here. I have the right to take her, given to me by Caesar. I've close to five hundred slaves in my various houses in the city. I could throw them around that house and take her by force, but I didn't do that and I won't."

"The Lord will bless you for it," Peter said, "and cleanse your heart and soul."

"Thank you, but hear some more. I held back from violence even though I live in agony and longing. In other times, before I was with you, I would have taken her and kept her by brute force. But your goodness and your creed changed something inside me, even though I still don't share your faith, and I can no longer resort to violence. I don't know how it happened, but that's how it is. So I come to you as Ligia's guardians, taking the place of her parents, and I ask you to let me marry her. Let her be my wife, and I swear to you that she'll be free to worship Christ as always. Moreover I'll start to learn his teaching myself."

He spoke with his head raised proudly like a Roman and with determination ringing in his voice, but he was greatly moved and his legs trembled in the folds of his Augustan cloak. Stillness spread across the room when he finished speaking, and he broke out again as if anticipating denial.

"I know everything that is standing in the way," he said. "But I fear losing her more than I fear blindness. I love her more than my life. I'm not yet a Christian, but I'm neither your enemy nor Christ's. I want there to be only truth between us so you'll be able to trust me. My life's at stake here but I'm not trying to take advantage of it. Somebody else might ask for an immediate baptism, but I want enlightenment. I believe that Christ rose from the dead. I know this from eyewitnesses to his resurrection who live their lives in truth. I believe because I saw it for myself that your faith breeds goodness, justice and compassion, and not the crimes of which you're suspected. I don't know much else about it, but what I gathered from the way you are, from Ligia and from talking with you. And yet I'll say again that something changed in me because of your teaching. I used to rule my household with an iron fist. I can no longer do that. I had no sense of pity, but I have it now. I used to love all the delights of the flesh, but I ran away from the ponds of Agrippa because I couldn't breathe in that obscenity. I put my trust in might and now I've renounced it. Believe me, I don't recognize myself in what I've become. I can't stand the orgies. I've lost my taste for wine. I'm sick of songs, zithers, garlands, naked bodies, and everything else about Caesar's court. Above all, I'm sick of all the crime.

"When I think," he went on, "that in comparison Ligia is like the fresh clean snow on the mountaintops, I love her all the more. When I remember she is as she is because of your religion, I love that religion and want it for myself. But because I can't grasp it, can't really comprehend it, I can't tell if I could live within it the way you do. I don't know . . . I can't be sure . . . my nature would accept it. And so I live in doubt and torment as if in a dungeon."

Here his brows drew together in a painful frown, his face flushed, but he went on speaking, hurrying ever faster and with rising fervor.

"Look at me! I'm tortured both by love and darkness. I've been told there's no room in your faith for life, human pleasures, happiness, the laws, the natural order, authority or respect for Rome. Is this true? I'm told you're all mad. So tell me, what do you bring the world? Is it a sin to love? Is it wrong to feel joy or want to be happy? Are you the enemies of life? Does a Christian have to be a beggar? Must I renounce Ligia? What is the core of your creed, the cornerstone of all your beliefs? What you say and do are like crystal waters, but what's at the bottom of the pool? You can see I'm honest. Bring light to this darkness! Because this is something else that I've been asked about you: 'Greece gave the world wisdom and beauty, Rome created power, but what do they offer?' So tell me, what's your gift? If your doors guard enlightenment, then open them to me!"

"We bring love," said Peter, but Paul of Tarsus added a grim warning: "If I speak with the tongues of men and of angels but have not love, I am like sounding brass."

The sight of the young man's anguish moved the old apostle; he glimpsed a troubled soul, like a shackled bird straining toward the sun and the open air, and he stretched his arms toward Vinicius.

"Knock and it shall be opened," he said gently. "God's grace is near you, and so I bless you and your soul, and I bless your love, in the name of the Savior of mankind."

Then something happened that amazed them all. Vinicius had been speaking at a high pitch of excitement all along, but now he stepped toward the old apostle, fell on his knees before him and seized both his hands. Then this haughty scion of the Quirites, who had never thought of foreigners as human, pressed the old Galilean's fingers to his lips.

Peter was clearly pleased. He understood that the seed of truth had once again fallen on fertile soil and that his net had caught yet another soul. The other Christians were also delighted, glad to see such respect shown to God's apostle.

"Glory be to the Lord on high!" they cried out.

Vinicius rose, his face alight with joy. "I see that happiness can live among you after all, because I am happy. I've no doubt you'll prove other things to me as well. But it won't happen here in Rome. Caesar is going to Antium, and I must go with him. You know to disobey his orders means death. But come with me. Spread your teaching there. You'll be in a lot less danger than I; with such vast crowds around, you'll be able to preach your faith even in Caesar's court. I hear Acte is a Christian, and there are more of you among the praetorians; I saw, Peter, how the soldiers knelt before you at the Nomentan Gate.

"Look now," he went on, pleading but insistent. "I've a villa in Antium. We can all gather there to hear your instruction right under Nero's nose. Glaucus told me you'd go to the ends of the earth to save a single soul, so do for me what you've done for others, all those for whose sake you came all the way from Judea, Peter. Don't leave my soul in darkness."

They started to discuss his appeal at once, glad to see their creed winning another victory and excited about the effect the conversion of such a highborn Augustan, a member of one of the most ancient Roman families, would have on the pagan world. It didn't even occur to them to refuse Vinicius. They were ready to go anywhere for a new adherent; indeed, that's what they had been doing from the moment of their master's death.

But Peter couldn't go. He was now the shepherd of the entire flock, responsible for the whole community.

"How about you then, Paul?" Vinicius asked.

Paul of Tarsus nodded. He was always traveling. He had just come back from Aricium and Fregellae, and was now getting ready for a long journey to the East to visit the Christian chapels in Corinth on Achea, and he could catch a ship in Antium that might carry him to the Achean Sea.

Vinicius thanked him, although he was disappointed that Peter couldn't go. He had become attached to the old apostle. But he had one more thing to ask him.

"I know where Ligia lives," he said. "I could go there on my own, as I should anyway, to ask if she'd have me for a husband once I've become a Christian. But I'd rather have your permission first. Let me talk to her. Perhaps you can even take me to her. I don't know how long I'll have to stay in Antium. It's worth remembering that nobody near Caesar is sure what the next day might bring, and Petronius has already warned me that I'm in some trouble. Let me see her first. Let me fill my eyes with her one more time and ask if she's willing to forget my misdeeds of the past and share whatever goodness the future may hold for us together."

Peter smiled kindly. "Who could deny you such simple joy, my son?" he asked. "Especially since you seek it in a righteous way."

Vinicius bowed over the old man's hands again. He was too moved to speak. The apostle placed both his hands on the tribune's temples.

"And don't be afraid of Caesar," he said while nodding quietly. "Not a hair will fall from your head, take my word on that."

He asked Miriam to fetch Ligia but not to tell her whom else she would find among them so that the girl might be even more delighted by being surprised.

It wasn't far, so Miriam was soon on her way back again, and everyone gathered in the room caught sight of her among the myrtles beyond the small window, leading Ligia by the hand. Vinicius wanted to run out and greet her in the garden, but the sight of this beautiful young woman whom he loved so much made him too weak to move. His heart was hammering in his chest. He could barely breathe and his legs were trembling under him. He was, he knew, a hundred times more stirred than the first time he heard Parthian arrows whirring past his ears.

She, on her part, ran in expecting nothing out of the ordinary, then stood stock still at the sight of him. Her face flushed deeply, grew correspondingly pale, and then she turned her startled and frightened eyes on all the others there. All she could see around her, however, were gentle, smiling faces and devoted glances.

"Ligia," the apostle Peter said, coming up to her. "Do you still love this man?"

Neither she nor anyone said anything for a protracted moment. Her lips began to tremble like a guilty child's who has to take the blame.

"Answer me," said Peter.

She slid to her knees beside the apostle. Her voice was humble, fearful and obedient.

"Yes, I do," she said.

Vinicius was already on his knees beside her, and Peter placed both of his old worn hands on their bowed heads and said:

"Then love each other in the Lord and to his greater glory, because your love is blameless."

⟨42⟩

WALKING WITH LIGIA in the little garden, Vinicius told her everything he had confessed to the apostles a short while earlier. His quick, heartfelt phrases revealed his inner turmoil, the changes within him, and the unfathomable longing that shrouded his life since he had left Miriam's house after his recovery.

He admitted he had tried to forget her but couldn't do it. She was always with him, night and day. She filled all his thoughts. The little ivy cross she had twisted for him before she disappeared reminded him of her each time he glanced at his household deities, and he found himself looking at it as if it were holy. His love for her was stronger than any other feeling and it took him over entirely.

"Others have the Fates spinning the threads of life," he told her, "but mine is twisted out of sadness, remorse, love and longing."

Yes, he had acted badly, but it was out of love. He loved her in the Plautius home and at the Palatine, and when he watched her listening to Peter at the Ostrianum and when he came with Croton to carry her off and when she watched over him and when she vanished from him. Chilon had told him where she was living and urged him to seize her, but he preferred to go to the apostles and ask for instruction in the faith.

"I bless the moment I thought of it," he said, "because here I am. I'm with you and near you. And surely you won't run from me again as you did at Miriam's?"

"It wasn't you I ran from," Ligia said.

"Why did you, then?"

She fixed her deep blue eyes on him for a moment and then looked away. "You know why," she said.

Joy silenced him. It took a while before he could speak, and then he told her how—gradually, slowly, in intermittent flashes of realization—he had come to understand who and what she was, and that she was like no other woman in Rome except perhaps Pomponia. He told it badly, stumbling from one thought and image to another, because he couldn't quite explain it even to himself.

"What it is," he said, "is that you bring another kind of beauty to the world, a kind that never existed before. It isn't something monumental. It's not for pedestals. But it's something holy."

Then he told her what filled him with the greatest joy: that he loved her even though she had resisted him and that she'd have his full respect when she was his wife. Out of words at last, he caught her hand and stared at her, entranced and overjoyed as if she were his rediscovered life. He repeated her name as if to make sure she was really there.

"O Ligia, Ligia . . ."

At last he started questioning her about her own feelings. She told him she loved him back when they were in the Plautius home and that she would have announced it to her guardians and begged them to forgive him if he had taken her there from the Palatine.

"I swear to you," he said, "it didn't even cross my mind to steal you from Aulus and Pomponia. Petronius will tell you someday. I told him even then I loved you and wanted to marry you. 'Let her anoint my doors with wolves' tallow,' I told him, 'and sit at my hearth.' But he laughed at me and planted the idea in Caesar to have you taken away as an imperial hostage and given to me. I don't know how many times I cursed him in my bitterness, but maybe it was a lucky stroke of fate, because I wouldn't have met the Christians otherwise, or understood you."

"Believe me, Marcus," Ligia said. "It was Christ's way of bringing you closer to him."

Vinicius looked up, surprised. "That's true!" His voice rang with feeling. "Looking for you, I discovered Christians. Every step led closer. . . . I was stunned by what I heard Peter say in Ostrianum. I'd never heard anything like it before. Were you praying for me?"

"Yes," Ligia said.

They strolled past the ivy-covered arbor and came to the spot where Ursus had throttled Croton and raised his fist over Vinicius' head.

"I'd have died here," the young man said, "if it wasn't for you."

"Forget about it," Ligia urged. "And don't hold it against Ursus."

"Would I want any harm to come to him when he was only defending you? I'd give him his freedom on the spot if he were a slave."

"Aulus and Pomponia would have freed him a long time ago if he'd ever been one."

"Do you remember," Vinicius asked, "that I wanted to return you to them? You said then that Caesar would find out about it and turn his anger on them. Well, now you'll be able to see them whenever you want!"

"What do you mean, Marcus?"

"I said 'now,' but I meant after we are married. It'll be quite safe then. If Caesar asks what I did with the hostage he gave me to keep, I'll say I married her and that she visits Aulus and Pomponia with my full consent. He won't stay long in Antium anyway, because he's anxious to go to Greece, and I won't have to see him every day. I'll be baptized as soon as Paul of Tarsus teaches me your faith; then I'll come straight back here, regain the goodwill of Aulus and Pomponia the moment they're back from Sicily—which should be any day. Nothing more will get in the way. I'll ask for you formally, lead you to my house and sit you by my hearth. Oh, *carissima! Carissima!*"

He lifted his arms as if calling on the skies to witness what he said, and she raised her own glowing eyes to his.

"And then I'll say: 'Where you go, Caius, there I go, Caia.'"

"No, more than that!" he cried. "I swear to you, Ligia, no woman was ever as honored and respected in her husband's house as you'll be in mine."

They walked in silence for a while, in love and quite unable to contain their joy, so beautiful that they seemed like a pair of deities, as if spring had brought them to the world along with the flowers. They stopped beside the cypress that grew at Miriam's door. Ligia leaned back against the trunk, and Vinicius turned to her again.

"Have Ursus get your things from Aulus' home," he said, his voice quavering slightly. "Send him to Pomponia for all your childhood toys and have them brought to my house."

This was the ritual that preceded marriage and signified that the bride was ready for her husband's bed; it meant that the married woman who taught her what to do had done all her work, that she, too, was now an aware woman, and that the toys were passing to her own child whenever it was born.

"I'm not quite ready for that," she said, flushing as deeply as a rose or a reddening dawn. "And that's not the custom."

"I know," he nodded. "The *pronuba* usually brings them after the wedding night, but do it for me now. I'll take them with me to Actium to remind me of you."

He pressed his hands together like a pleading child and went on repeating: "Do it for me, *carissima!* Do it for me! Pomponia will be back in town any day."

Ligia flushed an even deeper crimson at the mention of the marriage tutor. "Let Pomponia do as she thinks best," she said.

They were quiet again for a while, too much in love to talk. Ligia stood with her back pressed against the tree trunk, her white face glowing like a flower in the leafy shade, her eyes cast down, and her breast rising and falling swiftly with suppressed emotion. Vinicius flushed and grew pale by turns. They could hear the beating of their hearts in the warm stillness of the afternoon; in their absorption and intoxication with each other, the little gray myrtle patch seemed like a garden of love.

Miriam showed in the door just then and asked them to come in for supper. They took their places at the table among the apostles, who watched them with joy, seeing a new generation that would keep, preserve and help to spread their faith after they were dead. Peter blessed and broke the bread. Peace was on all their faces. Some deep, unspoken happiness seemed to fill the room.

"Look now," Paul said at last to Vinicius. "Are we the enemies of life and joy?"

"I know the truth about that now," the young man replied, "because I've never been as happy as with you."

‹43›

THAT EVENING, walking home through the Forum, Vinicius caught sight of Petronius' litter carried by eight Bithynian slaves near the opening of the Tuscan Way. He motioned them to stop and went near the curtains.

"Pleasant dreams!" he cried, laughing at Petronius who had dozed off inside.

"Ah, it's you, is it?" Petronius came awake. "I must have nodded off a bit. I spent the whole night at the Palatine, and now I'm looking for something to read in Antium."

"Going through the bookshops, are you?"

"I don't want to turn my library upside down, so I'm getting fresh reading matter for the road. I hear Musonius and Seneca both published something new. I'm also looking for a piece by Persius and a special edition of Virgil's *Ecologues* that I never got. Dear gods, am I tired! My arms and hands are numb with stretching for all those scrolls on the storage pegs. . . . Ah, but you know how it is in bookstores. This and that catches your eye, and then you want to see some other thing. I've been to Avirnus' bookshop, to Atractus' bindery on the Argiletum, and to the Sozius brothers' on the Vicus Sandalarius. By Castor, how I need some sleep!"

"You were up at the Palatine, then? Let me ask you, what's the word from there? Or better yet, why don't you send your litter and the book tubes to your house without you and walk home with me? I want to talk to you about Antium and something else as well."

"All right." Petronius stretched and climbed out of his litter. "You know, of course, that we're off to Antium the day after tomorrow?"

"And how am I supposed to know that?"

"What planet are you living on? Am I the first to tell you? That's what it is, though; be ready by first light the day after tomorrow. Oiled beans didn't help our singer, a silk scarf didn't do any good around his thick neck, and Copperbeard has lost his precious voice.

He's as hoarse as a creaky door, so there's no time to waste. He curses Rome by all that's holy and unholy, complains about the air, and he'd like nothing better than to tear down the whole city or burn it to the ground. He can't wait to get to the sea. He says the stench from the alleys will drive him to his grave. Wholesale sacrifices for the restoration of his voice were made today in all the city temples, and I pity both the city and the senate if that voice doesn't come back soon."

"There'd be no point in the trip to Greece," Vinicius said, grinning and nodding, "if he couldn't sing."

Now Petronius laughed, amused at the irony. "What? Is that the only talent our divine Caesar has at his command? He'll perform at the Olympic games, act out his epic poem on the burning of Troy, hurtle around the track in the chariot races, give concerts with the lyre, compete as an athlete and leap with the dancers, and win all the prizes. Do you know how that posturing ape got a sore throat? He had this notion yesterday to outdance our Paris, so he regaled us with the ballet of Leda and the swan, sweated like a pig and caught a bad chill. Ah, you should've seen him! He was as wet and clammy as a fresh-caught eel. He switched masks back and forth, twirled like a spinning top and flung his arms around like a drunken sailor until I thought I'd throw up at the sight of that huge jouncing belly and those skinny legs. Paris worked two weeks to show him all the steps, but can you imagine that fat clown as Leda, or Zeus in swan's form? Some swan, I tell you! But he wants to mime the whole thing in public, first in Antium and then after we've returned to Rome."

"There was a lot of harsh comment about his public singing," Vinicius observed. "But to think that a Roman Caesar would put on a mime! That ought to be too much even for the Romans."

"My dear fellow"—Petronius flipped his hand, dismissing the comment—"Rome will put up with anything, and the senate will vote a public day of thanksgiving for the divine Father of the Country."

After a wry, thoughtful pause, he added: "And the rabble will swell up with pride to see their Caesar clowning for their amusement."

"Tell me," Vinicius said, "whether it's possible for us to sink any lower."

Petronius shrugged, as if this was nothing. "You stayed home, thinking about your Ligia and your Christians, so you probably haven't heard what happened a few days ago. Nero married Pythagoras, officially and in public! The emperor played the role of the blushing bride! You'd think that's as much insanity as anyone could take. But what's to be said? The priests came as ordered and performed the marriage with all the rites and trimmings. I was there. I watched it. It takes a lot to shake my self-control, believe me, but even I thought the gods would show us some sign of their anger. That's if there are any gods left anywhere at all. . . . But Nero doesn't believe in any gods, and he's quite right in that."

"That makes him the high pontiff of all the religions, a god and an atheist all in one," Vinicius remarked.

Petronius started laughing, pleased with the wit in the observation.

"Exactly! It hadn't crossed my mind, but that's a mix the world hasn't seen before."

He halted for a moment and built on the thought: "Moreover this high priest who doesn't believe in the gods and this god who laughs at the other deities is also totally scared of them as an unbeliever."

"Which we know by what happened that time in Vesta's temple," the young tribune said.

"What a world, eh?" Petronius shook his head.

"The world is what Caesar makes it," Vinicius said, leading them both into his house. "But it won't last much longer."

Once in his atrium Vinicius called out lightly for dinner to be served. He turned to Petronius. "No, my friend," he added. "This world must be made over or born again in another form."

"We won't renew it," Petronius observed. "If for no other reason than that men live like mayflies in the time of Nero. Or like butterflies. All's well as long as they can bask in the sunshine of imperial favor, but let the first cold breeze come fluttering their way, and that's the end of it whether or not they like it. By Mercury, son of Jupiter and Maia! I often wonder how a man like Lucius Saturninus could survive for ninety-three years among us. How did he outlive Tiberius, Caligula and Claudius? No matter, though. Will you let me send your litter for Eunice? I've somehow lost my need for sleep, and I'd like to enjoy myself a little. Order some zither music to go with our dinner, and then we'll talk about the trip to Antium. You, in particular, need to think about it."

Vinicius ordered a litter sent for Eunice but said he wouldn't waste his time thinking about Antium. "That's for those who can't live without Caesar's favor," he said. "The world doesn't end with the Palatine, especially for those who have other things in their hearts and minds."

He was so offhand and amused about it and he spoke so lightly that Petronius stared at him in alarm. "What's wrong with you today?" he asked after a while. "You're acting like a boy."

Vinicius laughed. "I'm happy, that's all. And I've brought you here to tell you something special."

"And what might that be?"

"Something I wouldn't trade for the whole empire."

He sat down, stretched his arm along the back of his chair, and propped his head on it.

"Do you recall," he said, his face alight and smiling, "when you first saw that lovely, godlike girl in the Plautius garden? The one you called as fresh as the light of dawn and the epitome of spring? Do you remember that Psyche, that matchless beauty brighter than all young girls in Rome and all your goddesses as well?"

Petronius watched him as if wondering if he had lost his wits. "What are you trying to say?" he asked at last. "Of course I remember Ligia."

"I'm engaged to her."

"You're what? When did that happen?"

Vinicius jumped to his feet and called his head servant. "Have all the household slaves assembled here at once," he ordered. "Quickly now! Every last one of them!"

"You're engaged to her?" Petronius repeated.

The vast atrium of Vinicius' house started to fill with people before Petronius got over his shock and amazement. Old men came panting at a run, along with all the hurrying younger men and women, and the small serving lads and errand girls, filling the atrium tighter by the moment. The corridors, known as *fauces,* rang with calls in many languages. At last the whole household was crowded into the atrium and lined up along the walls and between the columns. Vinicius took his place near the *impluvium.*

He turned to his freedman Demas and said, "Those who have served here twenty years or more are to report to the city prefecture tomorrow. They'll be given their freedom. Those who have served less will get three gold pieces and double rations for a week. Send word at once to all the country work farms and punishment camps to suspend all sentences, unshackle the chain gangs, and make sure everyone is well fed from now on. Know, all of you, that this is a joyful day for me, and I want to see joy everywhere in this house."

The amazed slaves stood speechless, stunned, as if unable to believe their ears. Then all their arms jerked upward together. "A-a-ah, master!" they cried out as one. "A-a-ah!"

They tried to crowd around to thank him and kneel at his feet, but he waved them off. They hurried away, still not quite able to believe what they had seen and heard, and their delighted voices rang throughout the house from the roof beams to the deepest cellar.

"I'll have them all gather in the gardens tomorrow," Vinicius continued, "and scrawl signs in the sand. Ligia herself can free those who draw the fish."

Petronius never wondered about anything for long since little still surprised him. "A fish? Aha, I remember what Chilon said about it. That's the Christians' sign."

He stretched out his hand to Vinicius. "Joy, like beauty, lives in the eye of the beholder. Congratulations, lad. May Flora"—amused as ever, he called on the flower goddess whose spring rites were celebrated with particular license—"strew petals at your feet for many years to come. I wish you everything you wish for yourself."

"Thanks," Vinicius said. "I thought you'd try to talk me out of it, and that would have been time wasted, as you see."

"I? Talk you out of it?" Petronius frowned slightly. "Far from it. In fact, I'll tell you straight off it was the best thing to do."

"Ah, you twirling weathercock," Vinicius mocked, laughing at Petronius. "You change with the wind. You crowed me quite a different tune when we were leaving Aulus and Pomponia, remember?"

Petronius kept his unshakable poise, calm and detached in all circumstances when not aloof and scathing with contempt.

"Not at all," he said, his voice cool and steady. "I haven't changed my mind." After a moment, when a deeper chill edged into his tone, he waved a wry dismissal as if it all were totally unimportant.

"My dear boy," he said. "Change is everything in Rome! In fact, everything is always being changed and changing. Men change wives. Wives change husbands. Why shouldn't I change my mind if I feel like it? Listen, it almost happened that Nero married Acte; it wouldn't have taken much, you know, the way that man loved her. And the historians were already searching for a royal pedigree. But Nero changed his mind, or rather Poppea did the changing for him, and what's the result? He doesn't have a decent wife and we a decent empress. By Proteus and his ocean wilderness, I'll change my mind whenever it suits my needs or convenience. But if you're referring to what I said about Ligia's lineage and her barbarian background, you can be sure her blood is bluer than the bloodlines concocted for Acte. We had that poor Greek dancing girl related to the kings of Pergamus, if you can believe it. But you watch out for Poppea when you're in Antium. She never forgives."

"I wouldn't waste a thought on her," Vinicius said lightly. "A single hair won't fall off my head in Antium."

"If you think you can still surprise me with anything you say, you're riding the wrong mare." Petronius grew coolly watchful and polite. "But would you mind telling me what makes you so sure?"

"Peter told me."

"Ah!" The irony lay heavily on Petronius' voice. "The apostle Peter! You've heard this personally from the apostle Peter. Well, that beats all arguments, of course. It ends the need for any discussion. But do allow me to take certain precautionary measures just in case the apostle Peter turns out to be a false prophet. We wouldn't want the apostle Peter to look like a fool, in which case he might lose your trust—which, incidentally, can be very useful to the apostle Peter."

"Do as you like," Vinicius said with a shrug. "I trust him. And if you think you'll undermine him for me, mouthing his name like that, then I have a surprise for you."

"Then I've just one more question: Are you now a Christian?"

"Not yet. But Paul of Tarsus is coming with me to explain Christ's teaching, and then I'll be baptized. Because what you said, about Christianity being an enemy of life and happiness, isn't true."

"All the better for you and Ligia," Petronius replied. Then he shrugged and muttered as if to himself: "It's quite amazing, though, how those people manage to get converts and how that sect is spreading."

"That's right!" The young man's enthusiasm would have done justice to a real Christian. "There are thousands and tens of thousands of them in Rome, in the Italian cities, in Greece and in Asia. There are Christians in the legions, among the praetorians, and even in Caesar's palace. It's a religion for everyone: slaves, citizens, the well off and the poor, commoners and patricians. Do you know that some of the Cornelius family are Christians, that Pomponia Graecina is one, that Octavia may have been one, and Acte is one for sure? Yes! This creed is sweeping through the world, and it's the only one that can change it. Don't shrug. Who knows if you won't turn to it yourself in a month or a year?"

"I?" Petronius was both scornful and amused. "Never, by all the shades of Lethe! Not if it held all the truth and wisdom of men and gods alike. That would take an effort, and I don't like to expend myself. It calls for self-denial, and I don't care to deny myself anything. With your flash and fire, your hot blood, your impulsiveness and your restless nature, something like this was bound to happen to you. But I? I've my gems, my cameos, my vases and my Eunice. Why would I need religion? I don't believe in Olympus, but I've created a godlike existence for myself at home. And I intend to flourish comfortably until the end of my appointed time or until Caesar orders me to slit my wrists. I'm too fond of violets and soft dining couches. I even like our gods, as figures of speech. I love Greece, where I intend to go with our overweight, spindly-legged, incomparable, divine Caesar, our Hercules of the heavy-handed sentence, our all-highest Nero!"

The thought that he might accept the ragtag faith of Galilean fishermen was so absurd that Petronius fell into high good humor and sang a few bars that celebrated a famous murder-suicide in the times of Caesar:

> I'll sheathe my bright sword in a sheaf of myrtle
> As did Harmodius and Aristogiton.

He cut it short when the *nomenclator* announced Eunice. They sat down to dinner, heard a few songs sung by the zither player, and Vinicius told about Chilon's visit. "It was then, while he was being whipped, that I got the idea of going straight to the apostles."

"Not a bad thought since it worked." Petronius felt sleep stealing over him again and kneaded his forehead. "I'd have given Chilon five gold scruples rather than a whipping, but since you chose the lash, you should've had him flogged to death. Who knows how high a man like that can rise nowadays? There might come a time when senators bow and scrape before him, as they do with our distinguished knight of the cobbler's awl, the noble Vatinius."

Soon afterward he and Eunice took off their dining garlands and set out for home, and Vinicius made his way to his library to write a note to Ligia.

"I want this letter to say good morning to you when you open your lovely eyes, my adored divinity," he wrote. "That's why I write today although I'll see you tomorrow. Caesar is off to Antium the day after tomorrow, and I—God pity me!—must go with him as ordered. I told you that to disobey him would be to risk death, and I wouldn't dare die at this moment. Still, if you'd rather have me stay, just send one word and I won't stir from here, and it'll be up to Petronius to find a way of averting danger. Today, on this day of joy, I've spread some happiness among my slaves, and those who have served twenty years or more will get their freedom at the prefecture tomorrow. I think you'll approve, my dear, since this seems to go with your gentle creed, and I did it all for you, anyway. I'll tell them tomorrow that you're the one to whom they owe their freedom, their gratitude and their praises.

"For my part, I'm glad to be a slave to happiness and to you, and God grant that I'm never a free man again. Damn Antium and all other journeys! I'm happy three and four times over that I'm not as smart or knowledgeable as Petronius and don't have to go on the trip to Greece. Meanwhile, thinking about you will ease the separation. I'll jump on a horse every chance I get and gallop to Rome so I might thrill my eyes with the sight of you and delight my ears with your voice. Whenever I can't break free, I'll send you a slave with a letter and inquiries about you. I bless you, my goddess. I kiss your feet, beloved. Don't blame me for calling you a goddess, and I won't do it any more if you say I shouldn't, but I still can't think of you in any other way. I send you greetings from your future home with all my heart and soul."

‹44›

ALMOST EVERYONE in Rome knew that Caesar wanted to stop in Ostia on the way, to see the world's biggest ship that had just brought grain from Alexandria, and then go on to Antium by the coastal Via Littoralis. The orders had gone out several days before, and thick avid crowds started gathering at first light by the Ostia Gate. This was, in part, curious local rabble but also newcomers from all the nations of the world, all anxious for a glimpse of the imperial entourage, of which the Roman mobs never had enough.

The road to Antium was an easy one. The town itself, consisting of magnificent palaces and villas, contained every comfort, enough to satisfy even the most jaded and demanding tastes. But Caesar had the habit of bringing everything he liked wherever he went, including musical instruments, household furniture, statues and mosaics, which were set up whenever he stopped to eat or rest even for a moment. This meant that whole brigades of servants went with him everywhere, as well as his praetorian bodyguard and all the Augustans, each of whom had his own swarms of slaves around him.

Earlier that morning herdsmen from Campania, trousered in goatskin leggings and with sun-scorched faces, drove five hundred she-asses through the gate so that Poppea might have her supply of bathing milk when she got to Antium. The mob took a huge delight in the way their ears flopped about in the cloud of dust, in the hiss and crack of the drovers' whips, and in the herdsmen's shouting. A gang of sweepers ran to clean the road behind the herd and sprinkle it with spruce needles and flowers; and the growing crowds took pride in repeating that all these blooms, picked from private gardens all over the city or bought for top prices from peddlers at the Mugian Gate, would sheet the highway all the way to Antium. The mob swelled as the morning passed. Whole families clustered along the way as if for an outing, laying out their food as they waited and spreading picnic baskets on the dressed stone blocks for a new temple to Ceres, the goddess of good harvests. Others grouped around loudmouthed know-it-alls who lectured them on Caesar's many journeys and traveling in general, while seamen and long-service soldiers told amazing tales about far-off countries they had heard of on distant voyages and campaigns, even though no Roman had ever set foot there. The common townsfolk, for whom the Appian Way was the farthest limit of traveling from home, listened with bug-eyed wonder to astounding myths of India and Arabia, to tales of ghosts that lived in the British archipelago where Briareus, the hundred-armed giant, guarded old Saturn in an island dungeon, to stories about the unexplored countries of the north, frozen seas, and the dreadful roaring with which the sun sets in the Western Ocean beyond the Pillars of Hercules that guarded their own Mediterranean Sea.

If even Tacitus and Pliny could believe such stories, it wasn't hard for the rabble to swallow them. There was also a lot of lively speculation about the giant ship that Caesar was to inspect in Ostia. Rumor had it that she brought four hundred passengers and a like-sized crew, whole herds of wild beasts for the summer spectacles in the arena, and enough grain to last them all two years. Such stories added to Nero's popularity with the common masses; to them he was the good Caesar, even though he was also a bit of a joke, since he not only fed the people but gave them entertainment.

Meanwhile a troop of Numidian cavalry clattered into view, swathed in yellow cloaks with scarlet sashes, and with huge golden loops dangling from their ears. Like most of the praetorian guard, they were mercenaries; the inhabitants of the Italian mainland were exempt from military service since the time of Augustus Caesar, unless they volunteered. The sun caught in the points of their bamboo spears, blazed on their golden earrings, and gleamed in gold reflections on their broad, black faces. Detachments of praetorian infantry threw a double cordon down the street from both sides of the gate. The avid crowds pressed forward nonetheless, eager to see the wagons piled high with tents, either in the three imperial colors of purple, red and violet or hand-stitched snow-white Egyptian linen; and the drays heaped with Oriental carpets, tables carved from cedar, slabs of mosaic flooring, pots and pans of the imperial kitchens, cages of exotic eastern, western and southern birds whose brains and tongues were destined for Caesar's table; flagons of wine and baskets of fresh fruit. Hundreds of slaves came on foot behind them, carrying objects that might be chipped or broken in the carts, such as rare vases and statuary of Corinthian bronze. Each throng of slaves, watched over by slave masters with long, lead-tipped whips and separated by troops of praetorian infantry and horsemen, carried different treasures. Some bore the Etruscan vases; others were assigned to Greek pottery or gold drinking vessels or silver chalices or Alexandrian glassware. The passage of these hundreds of men and women, each clutching some rare object with utter devotion, seemed like a solemn religious procession, especially when Caesar's own musical instruments and those of the court musicians went by. The mobs gaped at harps, at Greek, Hebrew and Egyptian lutes, at lyres, zithers, trumpets, flutes and cymbals, and at the long, curved warhorns of the legions known as the *buccina*. Staring at the river of shining instruments, each richly glowing in the sun with gold, brass, copper, mother-of-pearl and jewels, the gawkers could have thought that Bacchus or Apollo was setting out on a journey around the world. Then came magnificently decorated platforms loaded with acrobats and dancers, chorus girls posing in groups with wands in their hands, and slaves meant for more personal services. These were young boys and girls, picked for their beauty throughout Greece and in Asia Minor, as cherubic as Cupids, either long-haired or with clusters of ringlets held in golden nets, with their lovely faces thickly coated with cosmetic grease so that the hot, Campanian winds wouldn't do them damage.

Then again came a praetorian company of blue-eyed, Germanic Sugambrii from beyond the Rhineland: huge bearded men with red or yellow hair, as massive as battering rams behind their Roman eagles. Standard-bearers known as *imaginarii* bore those eagles before them, along with brass numerals and inscriptions on overhead tablets, the images of various Roman and Germanic gods, and a bust of Caesar. Their thick, sunburnt forearms, as corded and as powerful as catapults and fit for the heavy weapons with which such guards were armed, showed under their armorplate and leather. The ground seemed to sink under their heavy, measured tread, as if they were war machines rather than men in armor. They marched past, glaring with disdain at the gaping masses, each of them seemingly aware of the power they were capable of using even against the Caesars and apparently forgetting that most of them had come to Rome in chains.

The main part of the ten praetorian cohorts, whose job was to guard the city and keep a tight grip on its population,' had stayed in their camps, and Caesar's picked bodyguard detachments were relatively small. Behind them came lion tamers from India and Arabia, leading tigers and lions trained to draw a chariot in case Nero wished to imitate Dionysus and have a pair of them harnessed to his own. They held the huge cats on steel chains and collars so tightly wound with irises and roses that it seemed as if the beasts had only flowers to hold them in check. Tamed by expert trainers, the animals looked at the crowds with sleepy green eyes, once in a while lifting their huge heads to draw a snarling breath, sniff the human stenches, and lick their chops with their abrasive tongues.

Still to come were Caesar's chariots and carrying chairs of various dimensions, gleaming in gold and purple, studded with pearls and overlaid with ivory or glittering with jewels; then marched another company of praetorians in Roman legionary armor, this one composed of Italian volunteer guardsmen; and at long last a swelling tide of cheers announced Caesar's arrival.

The apostle Peter had never before seen a Roman Caesar, so he was also standing in the crowd with Ligia and Ursus. The girl was thickly veiled to escape attention in that jostling and excited mob, even though Ursus guaranteed the best possible protection. Right away the gigantic Lygian hoisted a slab of quarried stone for Peter to stand on; he plowed like a ship through the waves of people with the huge boulder hefted overhead. The crowd growled and muttered, unwilling to give way, but the sight of the colossal slab he picked up, a weight that four of the strongest men among them couldn't manage to shift, brought cheers of admiration.

Meanwhile Caesar appeared before them. He drove alone in a great gold cart drawn by six white Idumean stallions shod with golden horseshoes. The ceremonial carriage was shaped like an open tent, with the side sheets raised so that he could be seen and admired from front, sides and rear. Although it was large enough to carry several people, Nero drove alone through the city, with only two misshapen dwarfs crouching at his feet, so as not to share the crowd's attention with anyone else. He wore a glittering amethyst-colored toga over a white tunic, and the reflection stained his face with a purple flush. A laurel wreath lay stiffly on his head. He had put on much weight since his last appearance in the streets of Rome. His face had ballooned. His jowls were thick and bloated. His double chin had acquired a third one, so that his pouty mouth, which always lay too near his nose, seemed to be gouged right under the nostrils. His fat white fingers fiddled constantly with the thick silk scarf he always wore around his fleshy neck, and his pudgy hands bristled with tufts of ruddy hair at the wrists and knuckles, looking like bloodstains. Someone had told him that hairy knuckles prevented tremors in the fingers, disastrous for a lutist, and he refused to let his depilators touch them. Weariness and a dull, unmitigated boredom spread across his face along with his usual overwhelming vanity and self-adoration.

In all of its parts, it was the face of a cheap, vulgar clown who was also mankind's most terrifying monster. Riding along, he turned his head slowly from side to side, slitting his small eyes from time to time to focus his attention, and he listened eagerly to how he was greeted—and what greeted him was a storm of cheers.

"Hail, divine Caesar!" howled the mobs. "Hail, emperor and conqueror! Hail, peerless . . . Apollo!"

A smile flitted across his face as he listened to these roars of adulation, but a sullen cloud spread over it from time to time as well. The Roman mob also loved to jeer. Confident in its numbers, the rabble showed no restraint with even the greatest military heroes, hurling their biting comments at leaders it truly loved and honored. Everyone still remembered how the mob greeted Julius Caesar when he and his legions entered Rome after conquering Gaul. "Here comes the bald whoremaster," they cried, laughing and howling with pride in his well-known amatory conquests. "Romans, hide your wives!" Nero's enormous vanity, however, couldn't stand the slightest criticism, and he could hear voices shouting; "Hey, Copperbeard! Are you taking your flaming chin out of the city in case it sets the town on fire?"

The howling fools didn't know the terrible prophecy they were uttering, even though Caesar was inclined just then to let the insult pass. He wore no beard, having offered it in a golden tube as a sacrifice to the Capitoline Jove; but other hecklers, well hidden behind the piles of stone and around the sides of the temples, shouted other comments. "Matricide!" they yelled, linking his name with other famous mother killers of mythology and history: "Nero! Orestes! Alcmeon!"

"Give back the royal purple!" others cried. "Where's your wife, Octavia?"

Poppea, whom the rabble hated and who rode in her litter just behind her husband, drew a storm of jeers. *"Flava coma!"* the mob howled as her litter passed, using the term for the cheapest streetwalker. Nero's trained ears, pitched to songs and music, caught every such jibe, and then he raised his polished emerald to his eye as if to see and remember whoever did the shouting. In one such moment his glaring eye rested on the apostle Peter.

Their glances locked for a while—the one mild and curious, the other venomous and bitter—and no one in that vast gathering of people or within Caesar's brilliant retinue realized that the two most powerful rulers of mankind were looking at each other just then. Nor did it even occur to anyone that one of them would soon be gone, vanished into darkness like a gory nightmare, while the other, the old man in the worn gray cloak of slaves and wanderers, would seize possession of the city and the world and hold them forever.

In the meantime Caesar had ridden past, and now eight gigantic Africans came by carrying Poppea in a splendid litter. Like Nero, she was dressed in imperial purple. Remote, indifferent, as still as a statue and with a thick layer of makeup painted on her face, she looked like a beautiful but malignant deity carried in a ritual procession. Another swarm of servants, men as well as women, trailed in her wake, along with a whole column of wagons loaded with utensils and supplies that had to do with her appearance and comfort.

The sun was well into the afternoon by the time the Augustans started to ride by. It was like a serpentine passage of splendid and glistening exotic creatures, dazzling with gems and color, and seemingly endless. The languid Petronius, greeted with friendly shouts, had himself carried in a litter with his beautiful golden-haired slave. Tigellinus drove a pony cart, a sort of miniature war chariot or *quadriga*, with white and purple plumes tossing on the heads of the little horses. He kept jumping up and craning his neck toward Nero, to see when Caesar might signal him to join him in his carriage. The fickle mob applauded Licinianus Piso, laughed at Vitelius and jeered at Vatinius, and tossed a few cheers to Vestinius. It ignored the two consuls, Licinius and Lecanius, but the Roman rabble was fond of Tullius Senecio for some unknown reason and greeted him warmly.

There seemed to be no way to count that vast court. It was as if everything in Rome that was rich, splendid and distinguished was moving to Antium. Nero never traveled anywhere with less than a thousand wagons and a retinue the size of an imperial legion, which in his time always numbered twelve thousand men. The curious rabble pointed fingers at the phenomenally rich old Domitius Afer, the corrupt former governor of Sicily who advertised his prices in his court of justice, and at the venerable Lucius Saturninus who had survived three Caesars. They saw Vespasian, who hadn't yet gone campaigning in Judea from which he would return only to become their Caesar; they saw his sons and young Nerva, and Lucan and Annius Gallo with Quinitianus, and it was as if their future had appeared before them, although they didn't know it. There was no way to list all the women famous for their riches, beauty or debauchery.

The mob's eyes swung from celebrated faces to the equipage, the chariots and horses, and to the outlandish costumes of the countless slaves who came from every nation. There was something to fascinate everyone in this avalanche of opulence and power. It more than dazed the eye, it also stunned the senses with its glittering brocades of dazzling violet and purple, glaring gold, precious stones, mother-of-pearl and ivory. It seemed as if the sun's rays were pouring into this confluence of splendor and melting within it. And although there was no lack of poverty in the rabble and there were people with starved eyes and shriveled bellies all along the route, the spectacle set fire to them as well. For some it may have been a raging lust for something that might approximate such a life, and an envious craving for some similar leisure, luxury and possessions. But for most it inflamed their pride in being part of Rome, part of the overwhelming and eternal might that the whole world supported and before which all peoples everywhere knelt in submission. No one throughout the world could doubt that this ordained eternal sovereignty would span the centuries and last beyond the end of every other nation. Nor did anyone dream of anything in the world that might be able to resist it.

Vinicius, who rode a chariot near the end of the Augustan procession, caught sight of the apostle and Ligia, whom he hadn't expected to see at all. He jumped out of the chariot, threw the reins to the driver and plunged into the crowd.

"You've come then?" His face was still aglow with the joy with which he greeted them, but his words stumbled hurriedly like a man with no time to waste. "I can't thank you enough, love of my life! God himself couldn't send me a better omen. I won't be gone long, though. So keep well. I'll post relays of Parthian horses all the way to Antium so I can race back every chance I get, and sooner or later I'll find a way to leave with permission."

"You keep well, too, Marcus," Ligia said and then added softly: "And may you walk with Christ and open your soul to what Paul can tell you."

He was delighted to see she cared how quickly he became a Christian.

"*Ocelle mi!*" he said. "Let it happen just as you describe it. Paul prefers to travel with my household, but he's there somewhere, coming to be my teacher and companion. But lift your veil, will you? Let me see you once more before I go. Why are you hiding anyway?"

She raised the veil and showed him her bright face and her laughing eyes.

"Is the veil so bad?" she teased him a little.

"Bad for my eyes," Vinicius sighed. "They'd rather see you than anything." He turned to Ursus: "Look after her as if she were the apple of both your eyes," he told him, "because she's my princess now as well as yours."

He caught her hand and kissed it, causing some amazement among the rabble who couldn't understand why a magnificent Augustan would show such respect to a poorly dressed girl who looked like a slave.

"Keep well," he said again, and he ran to his chariot. Caesar's parade left him far behind, and he had to hurry to catch up. Peter blessed him with a small, secret sign of the cross, while the good-hearted, simple Ursus started singing his praises straightaway, happy that his young lady was grateful to hear them.

The procession wound slowly out of sight, disappearing in a cloud of gold-speckled dust, but they went on looking after it until the miller Demas, the same one who employed Ursus between dusk and dawn, came up to them, kissed the apostle's hand and asked them all to take a light supper at his house. They had spent most of the day at the gate, he reminded them, while his home was just a few blocks away behind the Emporium.

They followed him home, rested and refreshed themselves at his table, and it was late in the evening before they started back to the Trans-Tiber quarter. Wanting to cross the Tiber by the Emilian bridge, they walked along the Clivus Publicus that cut across the Aventine between the temples of Mercury and Diana. The apostle Peter looked down from the ridge at the vast structures looming everywhere around him and at the others that dwindled and vanished in the distance. Plunged into worried thought, he contemplated the immensity and sheer might of this inimitable city where he had come to spread the word of God. Up to this time he hadn't grasped the essence of Rome's dominion. He had seen Roman rule and the legions in the various countries through which he had traveled, but these were little more than the limbs of the Colossus he saw for the first time today, personified by Caesar. The boundless city—so ravenous, predatory and insatiable, and at the same time so vicious, unbridled and rotten to the core—seemed unassailable in its crushing power; the Caesar who murdered his own mother, wife and brother, trailed by a spectral convocation of as many victims as the vast court that traveled behind him; the vain, debauched buffoon who was also lord of thirty legions and, through them, of the earth; the courtiers gleaming in their gold and scarlet, not sure if they would survive the day but nonetheless more powerful than kings. All of it added up to some infernal kingdom, a source of boundless and malignant evil. His simple, unsophisticated mind couldn't understand why God would grant such staggering omnipotence to Satan, how he could surrender the earth to be crushed, trampled, twisted inside out and throttled, ravaged as if by hurricanes, scorched with the flames of hellfire and squeezed dry of its blood and tears.

Fear stirred in his apostolic heart when he thought about this. He doubted his powers. "Lord," he addressed his master in his mind and spirit, "what can I do in this city where you've sent me? How shall I begin? It holds the seas and all the lands between them. It rules all the creatures on earth and under water. Thirty legions guard its other kingdoms. And what am I, Lord? A fisherman from a lake. How shall I start here? How can a man like me hope to overthrow such evil?"

He tilted his trembling white head toward the sky, praying and crying out to God with all his heart but racked with doubt and fear.

Suddenly Ligia's voice broke into his prayers. "The city seems on fire," she said.

He looked. It was a strange sunset, unusual in the way it lit up the sky. Half of the sun had already sunk behind the Janiculum and hung there like a glowing buckler, while the sky above the city pulsed with crimson fire. From where they were standing they could see far into the distance. Slightly to the right lay the elongated walls of the Circus Maximus, with the tiered palaces of the Palatine above it. Straight ahead, across the Forum Boarium and Velabrum, they saw the summit of the Capitol with the temple of Jupiter above it. But now these walls, columns and temple roofs seemed to be sinking into the fiery gold and crimson glow, as if engulfed and consumed by flames. What they could see of the distant river looked as if it flowed with blood. And as the sun dipped lower behind the hill, so the sky glowed redder, more like a reflection of a raging holocaust, and a violent, all-consuming light grew and spread until it covered the seven hills and spilled down the slopes over everything around them.

"It looks as if the whole city is on fire," Ligia said again.

"God's anger hangs above it," Peter said, and he covered his eyes.

⟨45⟩

"FLEGON, THE SLAVE who brings you this letter," Vinicius wrote to Ligia, "is a Christian, thus he'll be one of those who'll receive his freedom from your hands, my dearest. He is an old and trusted servant of our house, so I can write freely, without fear that this note might fall into hands other than yours.

"I write from Laurentum, where we've halted because of the heat. Otho once owned a magnificent villa here, which he gave as a present to Poppea, but even though she divorced him to marry Caesar, she thought it proper to keep it anyway. Compared to you, the women who surround me these days are as shallow as pools of muddy water. When Deucalion, the son of Prometheus, created a new mankind after the Flood by breathing life into a variety of pebbles, he must have used pure crystal for your type because you're an entirely different human being. I love and worship you so much I want to write only about you, and it's an effort to tell you about the journey, about whatever is happening with me nowadays or about court news.

"This is the latest: Poppea gave Caesar a surprise boating party, inviting only a few of the Augustans, but Petronius and I were both told to be there. After breakfast we rowed in golden barges on a sea so calm it seemed asleep, and as blue as your eyes, my goddess. We did the rowing ourselves, since it apparently flattered Poppea to have only consuls or the sons of consuls working her oars. Caesar stood at the tiller in a purple toga and sang a hymn to the sea he had written the night before, while Diodorus helped him compose the music. Other boats, full of slaves from India trained to play on conches, provided the chorus, and dolphins played in the sea around us as if really lured out of the depths by the music. But all I could think or care about was you, wanting to take that music and that sunny sea and give them to you.

"Would you like us to live near the shore someday, my empress, my own dear Augusta? Far from Rome? I've an estate in Sicily where the almond groves come to the water's edge, and when they bloom pink in springtime, the branches almost dip into the waves. That's where I'll love you and pay worship to the creed Paul is about to teach me, because I already know it doesn't stand against human joy and pleasure. Is that what you'd like too?

"But before I hear the answer from your sweet lips, let me tell you what else happened in that boat. Once we were well away from shore, we saw a sail in the distance, and there was an argument as to whether it was an ordinary fishing boat or the great ship from Ostia. I was the first to identify it, and Poppea said that eyes as sharp as mine must be able to pierce all disguises. Then she suddenly veiled her face and asked if I'd be able to tell who she was even through such a barrier. Petronius quipped at once that even the sun is invisible behind a cloud. But she laughed, said that only love could blind a man like that, and made a show of teasing me about all the lovers I supposedly have among our highborn ladies. She named one after the other, turning it into a sort of pretend guessing game about my current love throb, and finally she named you. She raised her veil as she did that and probed my face with eyes as sharp as icepicks. In just that moment Petronius rocked the boat, diverting everyone's attention, and the danger passed. I'm really grateful to him because he saved the day. I had controlled myself well enough throughout, answering her calmly, but if she had said one derogatory or hostile word about you, I'd have had a real struggle not to smash her head with one of her golden oars.

"You remember the story of what happened at the ponds of Agrippa? The one I told you in Linus' house the night before I left Rome with Caesar? Petronius is afraid for me and begs me not to offend Poppea's vanity, but he's no longer able to tell how I think so he can't understand that there's no love for me but you. There's no joy, love or beauty for me without you, and Poppea fills me with loathing and contempt. You've changed my soul so much and taken it so far from where it was before that I'd be unable to go back to my former life even if I wished to.

"Don't be afraid, however, that something bad might happen to me here. Poppea isn't really interested in me. She certainly doesn't love me. She couldn't care for anyone, she doesn't know how. She just wants to spite her straying husband. Caesar is still largely under her influence, and maybe he even still loves her in some way, but he no longer hides any of his escapades and affairs from her and doesn't care what she thinks about them. Moreover, just to set your mind wholly at rest about me, Peter himself told me not long before I left not to fear Caesar. He said that not a single hair would fall from my head, and I believe him. Some hidden voice keeps whispering to me that every word he utters is a prophecy. And since he blessed our love, my own dearest Ligia, then neither Caesar nor all the powers of Hades—no, not even Providence itself!—will ever take you away from me. I know what Heaven feels like when I think about this, because only Paradise can bring such a calming joy.

"Do I offend you as a Christian by what I say about Providence and Heaven? Forgive me if that's so. I don't mean to make light of them. I've yet to be purified by baptism, but my heart is like an empty cup that Paul is filling with your faith, all the more dear to me because it is yours. Grant me at least some merit in that I've emptied this cup of all it held before, that I don't begrudge it, and that I thrust it forward eagerly like a thirsty traveler at a wayside spring.

"My days and nights in Antium will pass in listening to Paul preaching. He won over all my people so completely in just the first day of travel, not merely as a man of miracles but as an almost supernatural being, that they cluster around him at all times. I saw happiness shining in his face yesterday, and when I asked the cause, he said: 'I'm planting seeds.' Petronius knows he is with my people and also wants to meet him, and as does Seneca who heard of him from Gallo.

"But the stars are growing pale, dearest Ligia. The morning star is burning ever brighter, and the dawn's rosy light will soon spread on the sea. Everything and everyone around me is still fast asleep, but I can't close my eyes with loving you and thinking about you. Greetings to you, *sponsa mea,* along with the sunrise!"

《46》

A FEW DAYS LATER he wrote to her again, but this time from Antium.

"Dearest! Were you ever in Antium with Aulus and Pomponia? If you weren't, I'll be delighted to show it to you sometime. The villas run along the shore all the way from Laurentum, one next to the other, and Antium itself is an endless row of palaces and porticoes whose columns are reflected in the water on a clear, calm day. I also have a home on the beachfront here, with an olive grove and a cypress wood spreading behind the villa, and when I think that this will be your home as well, then the marbles seem to glow whiter for me, the shade is more soothing, and the sea is bluer.

"Oh, Ligia! How good it is to be alive and in love! Old Menicles, who is my overseer here, planted whole fields of irises just beyond the myrtles, and when I look at them, I think of the Plautius home, your pool, and the gardens where I sat with you. You, too, will be reminded of home by these irises, and I'm sure you'll fall in love with Antium and this villa.

"Right after coming here, Paul and I sat a long time together over breakfast, talking about you, and then he started teaching. I listened for hours. I wouldn't be able to tell you what I thought and felt even if I could write like Petronius. All I'll say is I had simply no idea the world could hold a form of joy, beauty, happiness and peace that no one ever saw on earth before. But I'm saving all that for my talk with you, the first chance I get to go to Rome.

"Tell me this much, however: How can the same planet be the home of three such men as Peter, Paul of Tarsus, and our emperor? I ask because after a day with Paul, I spent the evening in the company of Nero. You can't imagine how insane he is or the madness of our life around him. First he read his own epic about the fall of Troy. Then he started wailing that he never saw a great burning city. He said he envied Priam of Troy who was able to watch the firestorm that turned his native city into smoking embers. He called him the happiest man in history. 'Just say the word, divinity,' Tigellinus said at once, 'and I'll take a torch, and you'll see Antium in flames before the night is over.'

"But Caesar told him not to be so stupid. He said, 'Where would I come for the sea air to soothe my precious voice, which is a gift from the gods that I must protect for the sake of all humanity? Isn't it Rome that causes all the damage? Isn't it the stink from the Suburra and the foulness of the Esquiline that make me so hoarse? And, anyway, wouldn't the sight of burning Rome be a hundred times more tragic and inspiring than a mere Antium?'

"Everyone said at once what an unheard of tragedy it would be to see the city that conquered all the world turned into a heap of dead, graying ashes. His Trojan epic, Caesar said at once, would then overshadow Homer. He started to talk about how he would rebuild the city and how mankind would praise this incomparable achievement for ages to come, and all his drunken guests shouted: 'Do it! Do it!' And he just said: 'I'd have to have far more loyal and devoted friends for that.'

"I confess he worried me at first, *carissima*, because you're in Rome. I laugh about it now, of course. Caesar and his cronies may be off their heads, but not even they would dare such an act of madness. Even so, every man worries about his most precious treasure, and I wish you and Linus didn't live in a narrow alley across the Tiber, a poor, crowded quarter inhabited for the most part by unimportant immigrants from abroad. No one would care much if their hovels burned or be concerned about them.

"The way I see it, the Palatine itself wouldn't be good enough for you, so I'm concerned that you shouldn't lack for any luxuries or objects you've been accustomed to having from childhood. Move to the house of Aulus and Pomponia, dearest Ligia. I've thought a lot about this. Ursus and Linus could be with you and also be safer. If Caesar was in Rome, the news of your return could indeed reach the Palatine through gossiping slaves, attract his notice, and bring down his anger on you for daring to defy him. But he'll stay a long time in Antium, long enough for the slaves to find fresher gossip before he's back in Rome. Besides, I live in hope that you'll be in your own new home in the Carinnae before Nero sees the Palatine again.

"I bless the hour and the day when you finally step across my threshold. And if that happens by the will of Christ, whose faith I want to follow, then may his name also be blessed forever. I'll serve only him, shedding my blood and even dying for him if I must. No, I've said it badly. We'll serve him together, you and I, as long as we live. I love you and long for you with my whole heart and soul."

⟨47⟩

A FEW DAYS AFTER THAT, Ursus was drawing water from the well in Linus' back garden, hauling the double amphora by hand on a knotted rope and feeling pleased with everything he could see around him. He hummed a low, strange-sounding Lygian song as he glanced at Ligia and Vinicius who stood together like two beautiful white statues, a loving sculpture, holding hands in the falling twilight. Not even the whisper of a breeze mussed their robes in the evening stillness, alight with red-gold streaks among the purpling shadows, and the two of them appeared even whiter against the dark cypresses and myrtle.

"Is it safe for you to come here, Marcus," she asked, "without Caesar's knowledge?"

"Nothing will happen to me, my love," he assured her. "Caesar announced that he'll be unavailable for two days, locked in with Terpnos to compose some new hymns to sing. Whenever he does that he loses touch with reality and forgets everything else around him. Besides, what do I care about Caesar when I'm here with you? I couldn't wait to see you, and the past few nights I couldn't even sleep. When I did doze off now and then out of sheer exhaustion, I'd jerk awake, suddenly quite sure you were in some kind of danger. Or I'd dream that somebody stole the relay horses I left between Rome and Antium. Nobody did, and I galloped here faster than an imperial courier. I just couldn't stand it without you any longer, my own dearest love. I love you too much to stay away."

"I knew you'd come," she said. "I had Ursus running twice to the Carinnae to ask about you in your house. He and Linus both laughed at me for that."

It was easy to see that she did expect him; in place of the dark, coarse work clothes she normally wore among her fellow Christians, she had put on a soft, snow-white *stola*, flowing in delicate folds from her shoulders to just above her sandals. Her bare arms and head were like spring blossoms rising through the snow. A sprig of pink anemones lay scattered in her hair.

Vinicius pressed his lips to her hand, and then they sat together on a stone bench set among the grapevines. Leaning into each other's shoulders, in silence they watched the sunset whose last golden glow reflected in their eyes. Both felt the magic of the evening stealing over them and let it enchant them.

"How peaceful it is here," Vinicius said softly. "And what a lovely world this is after all. What a warm and clear night it's going to be. I've never been so happy. Tell me, Ligia, why was I blind for so long? I never imagined such love was possible. I thought it was all lust and fire and excitement, but it's much more than that. I see now that one can love with every breath and heartbeat, be totally immersed in another being, and yet feel as peaceful and serene as if it were all a gentle, uninterrupted dream or even the carefree sleep of death itself. I see the silent trees and feel the stillness and quietness in myself. I can understand how there can be a form of happiness no one knows about. Now I know why you and Pomponia always have such serenity about you. . . . Yes! That comes from Christ."

She pressed her beautiful face against his shoulder. "Marcus, my dear . . ." she began and couldn't go on. Her voice faded in the rush of joy, gratitude and a feeling that now she was truly allowed to love, and happiness filled her eyes with tears. Vinicius drew his arm around her slight, slim body and hugged her gently for a silent moment.

"Ligia," he said at last, and for the first time with a Christian's reverence: "Blessed be the moment I first heard his name."

"I love you, Marcus," she answered as softly.

Then both were quiet again, saying nothing, their words hushed by the magnitude of feeling. The last lilac glimmers slipped off the cypress trees that were turning silver in the moonlight.

"I know," Vinicius said after a long while. "I read the questions in your eyes the moment I came in and kissed your sweet hands. Do I understand Christ's teaching? And have I been baptized? Yes and no. I understand the creed and believe the teaching, but I've not yet been baptized. Paul told me himself: 'I've shown you the truth. You now know that God came down to earth and let himself be crucified to save all mankind. But let it be Peter who baptizes you. He was the first to bless you and stretch his hands over you.' I also wanted you, my dearest love, to be there to see it and for Pomponia to be my godmother. That's why I'm still not baptized, though I believe in the Savior and his way.

"Paul," he went on, "convinced and converted me. How could it be different? How could I fail to believe that Christ walked among men? Peter knew him and was his disciple. Paul saw him when Christ spoke to him on the Damascus road. How can I doubt he is God when he rose from the dead? They saw him in the town, on the lakeshore and on the mount, and these were witnesses who never told a lie. I believed it when I heard Peter at Ostrianum. I told myself back then that every man alive would have to be branded as a liar before I could doubt him, and he said, 'I was there. I saw.' But I was afraid to accept your faith. I thought it took you from me. I thought it did not contain beauty, happiness or truth. Now that I understand and accept Christ's message, what kind of man would I be if I didn't want truth to conquer lies, love to replace hatred, goodness to rule the world in the place of evil, loyalty and devotion to be the way rather than bad faith, and mercy to be our guide in place of retribution? Who'd choose something different or want anything else? And this is the basis of Christ's teaching.

"Other philosophies call for justice," he conceded, "but yours is the only one that brings compassion to the human heart. Moreover it makes the heart as true and pure as yours and Pomponia's. I'd have to be blind not to see it. And when, in addition, Christ the God gives eternal life and offers such inexhaustible joy that only God can offer, what more could a human being need?

"If I asked Seneca why he promotes virtue when vice pays so much better, I doubt he'd be able to give me a reasonable answer. But I know why I must be ethical and decent. Love and goodness come from Christ, and only he can help me find life after death, find happiness, find myself again, and find you, my dearest.

"How could I not love and accept a faith that offers truth and abolishes death at the same time?" It seemed so obvious that there wasn't even a note of conjecture in the young man's voice. "Who wouldn't take goodness over evil? I thought this new religion was a threat to joy, but Paul convinced me it not only doesn't take anything away but adds immeasurably more. There's so much for me to think about I can hardly make room for it in my head. But I feel it's right because I've never been happier, and I couldn't be even if I carried you off by force and had you in my house all this time.

"A moment ago," he said quietly, nodding all the while, "you told me you loved me. Not all the might of Rome would've dragged those words out of you before. Ligia, my love! Reason itself tells me this is the best faith. The mind accepts that it comes from God. The heart feels its truth. Who could resist such a combination?"

Ligia listened, her blue eyes fixed on his. Moonlight turned those eyes into flowers, mystical and profound and as shining with love as real flowers with dew. "Yes, Marcus!" she said, pressing closer to him. "That's what we are given."

They felt immensely happy in that moment. They understood what they could truly share. They were united in their love but also joined together by another power, irresistible but supremely gentle, one through which love itself became something endless, lifted beyond change, immune to disappointment or betrayal and even death. They could be certain they would never stop loving and being loved, never be another's no matter what happened, and this awareness filled their hearts completely. A great unspoken peacefulness flowed into them out of this certainty and knowledge.

Vinicius felt that this love was not just different in being absolute and endless but that it also was totally new, something mankind had never known before. Everything came together for him then. He could see this love in Christianity, in Ligia, in the dreamy quiet of the clear starry night, with the moonlight on the cypress trees. The entire universe seemed filled with this love.

He was overcome with feeling, and his voice trembled slightly when he spoke again.

"You'll be the center of my soul," he said, "dearer to me than everything in the world. Our hearts will beat as one. We'll share the same prayer and gratitude to Christ. Oh, my sweet love! What could be better than to live together, worship the same gentle God together, and know that death won't be the end of it? That we'll open our eyes again into another light, as if only after a brief, blissful dream? I'm only surprised it took me so long to grasp it. And do you know what I'm beginning to think? No one will be able to resist this teaching. In two or three hundred years the whole world will come to it and love it. No one will even think about Jupiter. There'll be no gods other than Christ and no temples except his. How else can it be? Who'd willingly abjure his own happiness? Ah, listen, I heard the dispute between Paul and Petronius, and even though Petronius finally said, 'That isn't for me,' he couldn't answer any of the questions."

"Tell me what Paul said."

"It happened one evening in my house. Petronius started off in a light, slightly joking manner as he always does, and Paul said to him: 'You are a rational man, Petronius. So how can you say Christ couldn't have risen from the dead when you weren't there to see it?

But Peter saw him. John saw him. I met him on the Damascus road. First prove that we are liars and then dismiss our story.'"

"What did Petronius say?"

"He said he wouldn't doubt anything he heard. Nothing would surprise him. Life was full of inexplicable matters, defying all logic, which reliable people witnessed and reported nonetheless. But it's one thing, he said, to discover a new foreign god and quite another to accept his creed. 'I don't want to hear anything that might change my life,' he said, 'or undermine its beauty. It doesn't matter if our gods are real. It's enough they are beautiful, that we have a pleasant time with them, and that we're free to live in any way we please.'"

"And how did Paul answer?"

"Paul said, 'You reject a philosophy of mercy, love and justice, Petronius, to live without care. But how carefree are you, my lord, when neither you nor the most powerful and richest man among you can go to sleep at night sure he won't be ordered to die in the morning? You want to keep your pleasures, but wouldn't you feel more secure in all your joys if Caesar lived by a rule that commands justice and compassion? Wouldn't life seem easier and more cheerful then? As for art and beauty, if you could build so many priceless monuments and temples for the gods of vengeance, adultery and deceit, how much could you achieve in honor of the one true God who is the God of love? You're pleased with life because you're rich and free to indulge all whims, but you could be poor and abandoned just as easily, even though you come from a distinguished lineage. The world would be a brighter place if all men were Christians. In your city,' Paul said, 'even wealthy parents sometimes give up their children, send them to foster homes and call them *alumni*, because raising them at home creates too many problems. You, too, my lord, could have been such an unwanted child. But if your parents lived by our rule, this could never happen.'"

Ligia, a rare alumna whose life was happy with her foster parents, nodded quietly, and Vinicius went on with what Paul had said.

"He asked if it wasn't better to trust a wife or husband in a marriage knowing he or she would never break the faith than live in our dissolute Roman way. 'Look at the life around you,' he said to Petronius. 'See the corruption, turpitude, self-indulgence and faithlessness everywhere you look. Men trade their wives and women take new men like shopping at a fruit stall. You're amazed yourselves when you come across a woman you call *univira*. But those who carry

Christ in their hearts will never betray their husbands, any more than a Christian man could betray his wife. What can you be sure of? Not of those who rule you. Not of your fathers, wives and children. And certainly not your servants. The whole world trembles before you and you live in fear of your slaves, because you know they could rise up against your tyranny any day and unleash a bloody holocaust among you as they've done before. You're rich, but you don't know if tomorrow you'll be ordered to give up your riches. You're still young, but one man's whim can end your life in moments. You love, but faithlessness and deceit always wait in ambush. You take pride in your villas and surround yourself with objects of beauty, but tomorrow you could be forced to finish out your days on the barren beaches of Pandataria like all the other exiles. You have a thousand servants, but each of them can kill you at any time. And if that's so, how can any of you be at peace, know true happiness, or enjoy your lives?

"'But I,' he said, 'preach love. I bring a faith that orders kings to care for their subjects, commands compassion between slaves and masters, lets the servants serve out of affection, assures everyone of justice and forgiveness, and promises an everlasting joy in the hereafter. How then, Petronius, can you claim that this faith is a threat to life when it makes it better? You know you'd be a hundred times happier and more secure if such a faith ruled the world as completely as Rome does today.'

"That's what Paul said, my dearest, and that's when Petronius said, 'That's not for me,' pretended to be sleepy and went home. Leaving, he said he'd rather have his Eunice than a new religion. 'But, my dear Judean,' he added as he went, 'I wouldn't want to fence with you on a public rostrum.' I heard Paul with every fiber of my heart and body. Each of his words found an instant echo in my mind and spirit. When he talked of women, I worshiped the faith that made you what you are. And then I thought: Here is Poppea who betrayed two husbands for Nero. Here's Calvia Crispinilla, Nigidia, and just about every other woman I know in our society except for Pomponia, who sell themselves to the highest bidder, trading in vows and promises like peddlers at a fish stall. And there is only the one, my own Ligia, who'll never leave me, who'll never deceive me, and who won't ever choke our marriage hearth with ashes even if everything else I trust turns sour and dies. So I asked myself, how can I repay her except with my own love and my own devotion? Did you sense this when I was in Antium? Did you hear me talking to you constantly as if you were there? I love you a hundred times more, my wonderful Ligia, because you ran from me at the Palatine. I'm through with Caesar. I want no part of him, his pleasures or his music. All I want is you. Say just one word, and we'll leave Rome at once and settle somewhere else."

She looked distantly at the silver tops of the cypress trees, remote and dreaming and still snuggled warmly into his shoulder. "I'd like that, Marcus," she said after a pause. "You wrote me about Sicily, where Aulus and Pomponia want to retire soon—"

"That's right, my love!" Vinicius broke in happily. "The two estates are near. It's a glorious coast and has an even milder climate and warmer nights than Rome, both open and fragrant. . . . Life and joy mean the same thing there."

Then he began to muse about the future.

"One can forget all of the world's cares in a place like that. We'll walk and rest in the shade of our olive groves. Oh, Ligia! What a wonderful life it will be for us, full of love and healing. To walk together, look together at the sea and sky, worship the same loving God together, and do good everywhere and treat everyone fairly and with mercy."

Quiet again, they looked into the future while his arm tightened around her and she nestled closer. Moonlight flashed on his gold signet ring, the badge of his knighthood. Everyone in this poor workmen's quarter was now fast asleep, and not a single murmur broke the silence.

"You won't mind," she asked, "if I see Pomponia?"

"Mind?" He laughed. "Of course not. They'll come to see us and we'll visit them. Would you want us to take Peter with us? He's worn out with work and age and deserves to rest. Paul will also visit when he can. He can convert Aulus Plautius, and we'll start a Christian colony the way old soldiers plant new settlements abroad, bringing the Roman way to the far boundaries of the empire."

Ligia took his hand and tried to raise it to her lips, but he took hers instead. "No," he whispered as if happiness were a panicky small bird, too easy to startle, and he was anxious not to frighten it away. "No, Ligia. I'm the one who worships and reveres you. It's up to me to kiss your hands in homage."

"I love you," she said.

But he had already pressed his lips to her open palms, white as jasmine petals. All they were aware of for a while was the quick and strong beating of their hearts. With no wind in the evening air, the cypresses stood as still as if they, too, were breathless.

Suddenly the silence cracked around them; a booming roar, as deep as a roll of subterranean thunder, sent a cold shudder through her body.

"It's just the lions," Vinicius said, and he got to his feet. "In the arena pens."

They listened for a time. The first roar found an echo in another, and then a third, a tenth, coming from every quarter of the city and from all directions. There could be thousands of lions in the city at any one time, penned near the arenas. Sometimes at night they padded to their bars, leaned their huge heads against them and voiced their fierce longing for freedom and the desert. This was one such time. The roaring passed from one animal to another in the nighttime stillness until the whole city echoed with their thunder. There was something so desolate and threatening in the savage voices that they blew apart her clear and untroubled vision of the future, and Ligia's heart constricted in some strange fear and sadness.

But Vinicius only tightened his arm around her. "Don't be afraid, my love," he said. "It isn't long until the summer games, so all the pens are crowded."

The lions' roar swelled and rumbled everywhere around them and followed them to the house.

《48》

MEANWHILE IN ANTIUM, Petronius scored almost daily victories against the resident Augustans who competed with him for Caesar's smiles and favor. Tigellinus lost whatever influence he had. Ruthless and calculating as he was, he could make himself indispensable only in Rome where it was just a matter of getting rid of people who seemed dangerous or plundering their property or playing politics and staging public spectacles of mind-boggling extravagance and vulgarity, or satisfying Nero's monstrous whims.

But in Antium, where the classic porticoes and palaces were reflected in the calm blue mirror of the sea, Caesar lived the life of a Hellenic artist. Poetry readings and discussions of their form and structure were his daily fare. Music, the theater, literature and everything else that Greek taste and genius had given to the world absorbed the court from morning to night, and Tigellinus didn't know anything about them. The witty, urbane, subtle and eloquent Petronius, so much more knowledgeable and refined than Tigellinus and the other courtiers, had a clear advantage. Caesar sought his company, solicited his opinion, asked for advice about his own creations, and showed a livelier friendship than ever before. It began to seem to everyone that his hold on Caesar was now unbreakable and that their friendship, always a matter of Caesar's whim and fancy, had finally stabilized and might last for years. Even those who hadn't cared much for the exquisite Epicurean now flocked to him, anxious to be friendly. Some of them were even secretly quite pleased that the advantage had gone to Petronius. True, he saw through all their flatteries, knew the worth of their artificial smiles, and took his sudden popularity with a skeptical smile of his own. But he was either too lazy or too civilized to go after former enemies and detractors, and didn't use his power to damage or destroy anybody. He even had some moments when he could have ruined Tigellinus, but he preferred to make a fool of him and expose his ignorance and crudeness.

Six weeks went by without a death sentence and back in Rome the senate breathed easier. Amazing tales ran through Rome and Antium about the unbelievable refinements practiced by Caesar and his favorite in their dissipations. Everyone would much rather have an artistically besotted Caesar than a bestial one, as he would have been under Tigellinus' guidance. Tigellinus himself almost went out of his mind with worry, practically ready to admit defeat, because Caesar kept saying there were only two true Hellenes in Rome, only two great souls in his court and empire who understood each other—himself and Petronius.

Petronius' amazing smoothness and dexterity convinced everyone that his influence on Caesar would surpass and outlive all others. No one could imagine how Nero would manage without him, with whom he could talk about poetry, music and chariot racing, or at whom he'd glance to judge the effect of his own creativity. Meanwhile Petronius did not seem to care where he stood with Nero or attach any great importance to his new position. As always, he was forgetful, lackadaisical, lazy, indifferent, skeptical and witty. Sometimes he seemed to be laughing at the whole court, at Caesar, at himself and at life in general. Occasionally he dared to criticize Nero to his face, but just as the shocked listeners thought he had gone too far or that he was writing his own epitaph and digging his own grave, he flavored his criticism with a deft complimentary phrase, turned insult to flattery, and came out ahead. About a week after Vinicius came back from his trip to Rome, Nero read some excerpts from his *Troyad* to a select circle, and when the shouts of rapture and amazement rang through the room, he turned a questioning eye as usual on Petronius.

"Mediocre versifying," Petronius said, dismissing it. "Fit only for the fire."

Sheer terror gripped everyone in the room and robbed them of breath, because no one had chided Nero in that tone since childhood, or for such a reason. Tigellinus' face glowed with savage joy while Vinicius turned as pale as a sheet. He was convinced Petronius must be drunk, even though he never drank more than he could handle.

"Really?" Nero's honeyed tone, usually the signal of mortal danger, couldn't hide the quiver of wounded vanity. "What do you think is so bad about it?"

"Don't trust their judgment." The bystanders were stunned as Petronius savaged Nero. "They don't know anything about the craft of writing and understand even less about literary genius. What's so bad, you ask? Well, I'll tell you: Nothing, if it was written by Virgil,

Ovid or even by Homer! But coming from you? You're not allowed the luxury of such sloppy writing. You're too good for that. The fire you describe doesn't burn enough; your flames aren't hot enough to be convincing. Don't pay attention to Lucan's flatteries; I'd call him a genius if those were his verses. But you? You're far too great. When a man is as gifted by the gods as you, we have a right to expect perfection. But you're too lazy. You don't try hard enough. You'd rather take a nap after breakfast than get down to work. You're capable of creating the greatest masterwork of all time, something the world has never seen before. So that's why I tell you to your face: Write something better than the best because you can do it!"

He spoke as if he couldn't care less, both chiding and amused, but Nero's eyes fogged over with delight.

"The gods did give me some slight talent," he murmured at last. "But they gave me something even more important: a true judge, a real connoisseur, and a friend who never tells me anything but the truth."

He thrust his pudgy, ruddy-haired fist toward a golden candelabrum that he had stolen when he was last in Delphi, but Petronius plucked the poetry from his fingers before he could set the papyrus on fire.

"No, no!" he said. "Even something as unworthy of your gifts as this belongs to all mankind. Let me keep it for you."

"In that case"—Nero rose and threw his arms around the adroit arbiter of good taste and beauty—"let me send it to you in a special cylinder of my own design."

He thought about Petronius' comments for a while, then nodded and said: "Yes. You're quite right, of course. My burning of Troy doesn't glow enough. My fire isn't hot enough. I thought it would do just to equal Homer, but I should do better. I've always had a problem with timidity in my estimation of myself. You've opened my eyes, Petronius. But do you know the cause of the trouble here? When a sculptor wants to carve a statue of a god, he looks for a model, and I had no model. I never saw a conflagration that destroyed a city, and that's why my description falls short of the truth."

"I'll just add this much, then." Petronius dropped another compliment edged with irony that Nero wouldn't catch. "You have to be a truly great artist to understand the importance of a model."

But Nero was deep in thought, turning something over in his mind.

"Tell me just one thing more, Petronius," he said as if not quite sure what answer to expect. "Are you ever sorry that Troy was destroyed?"

"I? Sorry? No, by the lame husband of Venus. Not at all! Troy burned because Prometheus stole fire from the gods and the Greeks decided to make war on Priam. If there'd been no fire, Aeschylus couldn't have written his *Prometheus,* and Homer couldn't have written the *Iliad* if there was no war. I think it's better to have both *Prometheus* and the *Iliad* than to preserve some backwater little town, probably dull and dirty, where some godforsaken provincial governor would be sitting on his hands today and wasting your time by bickering with the local judges."

"That's what we mean by clear and logical thinking," Caesar sighed and nodded. "No sacrifice is too great for poetry and art. How lucky for the Greeks that they could supply material for Homer's *Iliad.* How wonderful that Priam could actually watch the flames which devoured his city. But I've never even seen a whole town on fire."

No one knew what to say after that until Tigellinus broke into the silence.

"As I've already told you, Caesar," he reminded him quickly, "I'll set fire to Antium if you give the word. Or better yet, if you're sorry to see the end of these palaces and villas, I'll burn the fleet in Ostia. Or I'll put up a wooden town in the Alban foothills, and you can toss the torch into it yourself! Is that what you'd like?"

Nero merely threw him a contemptuous glance. "You want me to look at some burning wooden market sheds?" he snapped. "Your mind has lost whatever inventiveness it had, Tigellinus. Moreover it's clear you don't value my talents or my *Troyad* if you think a real sacrifice for their sake, I mean a real city, would be too much for them."

Tigellinus stumbled back, shocked and lost for words, while Nero shrugged as if to change the subject.

"Summer's coming," he said wearily and sniffing the fresh sea air. "How that damned Rome must stink already . . . and yet I'll have to go back there for the games. . . ."

"Caesar." Tigellinus stepped forward suddenly, his eyes sharp and gleaming. "Spare me a moment after you've dismissed the others."

An hour later, walking home with Petronius from Caesar's villa, Vinicius confessed just how alarmed he had been by his criticism of Nero's Trojan epic.

"You gave me a bad moment there, my friend," he said.

"And why's that?"

"I thought you were too drunk to know what you were doing, and cutting your own throat. Remember that you're trifling with death when you're teasing Caesar."

"That's my arena." Petronius shrugged, unconcerned one way or another. "It amuses me to think that I'm the best gladiator in that circus. Look how it all ended. My influence went sky-high again, just in that one evening. He'll send me his verses in a library tube, and I'll bet you anything it'll be just as costly as it'll be vulgar. I'll have my medic keep laxatives in it. But I played that little game for another reason. Seeing how well it works, Tigellinus will rush to imitate me, and I can imagine what'll happen when he tries to think. It'll be as if a bear tried to walk a tightrope. I shall laugh like Democritus when he discovered atoms. I might be able to ruin Tigellinus if I really put my mind to it, and then I'd make myself the praetorian prefect in his place and get a good hold on Copperbeard himself, but I can't be bothered. I'd rather put up with the life I have, and that includes Caesar's versifying."

"You're really something!" Vinicius laughed in admiration. "Imagine being able to wring flattery out of a bad review. But is his poetry really that awful? I don't know the first thing about it."

"It's no worse than others'. Lucan has more talent in one finger, but Copperbeard has something too. First and foremost, there is his genuine love of poetry and music. In two days we'll be with him to hear the music to his hymn for Aphrodite, which he's finishing today or tomorrow. It'll be a small group. Just you, me, Tullius Senecio, and young Nerva. As for his verses, well, I don't really use them for the same effect that Vitelius gets with a flamingo feather in his *vomitorium* after a full banquet. Some of it is eloquent. Hecuba's lines are really quite moving. She complains about the agonies of childbirth, and Nero manages to find some apt expressions, probably because he agonizes over every couplet. Sometimes I'm sorry for him. By Pollux! What a strange mix he is! Caligula was totally around the bend, but even he wasn't such a freak."

"Who can tell where Copperbeard's lunacy will take us?" Vinicius shook his head.

"No one, and that's the point. There might be things still ahead of us that'll strike people dumb with horror when they think about them hundreds of years from now. But that's what makes life with Nero interesting. That's what fascinates me. And even though I'm as bored at times as Jupiter Hammon in the desert sands, I think I'd be a hundred times more bored with any other Caesar. Your Judean Paul has a nice touch with words, I grant him that freely, and if that's the

kind of missionary who'll be spreading that new creed of his, then
our gods had better get serious about it or they'll wind up in storage.
It's quite true that we'd all feel safer with a Christian Caesar. But
your Tarsus prophet missed the point with me. He didn't think that
taking chances puts spice in one's life. If you don't gamble, you don't
lose, but neither do you win. Life on the razor's edge has its own
peculiar fascination and gets rid of all the nonessentials. I've known
some young patricians who became gladiators of their own free will.
I, as you put it, play games with my life, and I do that because I enjoy
it. Your Christian virtues, on the other hand, would in one day bore
me even more than one of Seneca's discourses, and that's why Paul
wasted his eloquence on me. He ought to understand that my type of
person will never accept his teaching.

"You, on the other hand," he said with a smile, "are a different
story. With your makeup there'd be only two ways to go. You'd either
loathe the very name of 'Christian' like the plague, or you would
become one. For my part, I agree with them, but they make me yawn.
So instead we live our lunatic existence, rushing headlong into the
abyss. And if there's some dark mystery coming from the future or if
something gives way under us or crumbles beside us, then that's fine
with me. If there's one thing we all do well, it's dying. But in the
meantime we shouldn't make our lives more difficult than they have
to be or fill our heads with the hereafter until we are in it. Life exists
for its own sake and serves its own purpose. It doesn't have to serve
death as well."

"And yet I have to pity you, Petronius."

"Don't pity me more than I do myself. You used to have a good
time among·us, and you missed Rome when you were fighting in
Armenia."

"I still miss Rome today."

"Yes! Because you fell in love with a Christian vestal who sits
across the Tiber. This neither bothers nor surprises me. What I do
find peculiar is that this so-called religion of love—which, in your
case, is shortly to be crowned with a marriage wreath and which you
call an ocean of happiness and joy—makes you look so sad.
Pomponia Graecina seems to be in perpetual mourning, and you
haven't smiled since you became a Christian. Don't try to tell me that
it's a happy creed! You came back from Rome even gloomier than
you were before. If that's what your Christian loving is about, then—
by the curly locks of Bacchus!—I don't want any part of it."

"That's something different," Vinicius replied. "I won't swear by any part of Bacchus but I will swear on my father's soul, that I've never even sampled the kind of happiness that fills my life today. But I miss Ligia terribly, and whenever I'm away from her, I have this strange feeling that she is in danger. I don't know what it is or where it might come from, but I sense it the way one can sense a storm before it breaks."

"In two days I'll get you permission to leave Antium for as long as you want," Petronius promised. "Poppea seems to have calmed down. As far as I can tell she's no longer a threat to you or Ligia."

"She was questioning me today about my day in Rome even though I kept the trip a secret."

"She may have had you followed. But even she has to watch her step with me now."

Vinicius halted then.

"Paul said that God sometimes sends a warning but doesn't allow belief in omens, so I've been trying not to believe in one. I can't do it, though. I'll tell you what happened, just to ease my mind. We sat together one night, Ligia and I, talking about our future. It was a beautiful night, as clear as this one. All the stars were out. I can't tell you how peaceful it was and how happy we were. And then the lions started roaring. It's an everyday thing in Rome, I know, and yet I've not been able to find any peace since then. I keep hearing it like a threat, or a promise of a terrible misfortune. You know I don't panic easily, but the way I felt then, it was as if anxiety and fear filled the entire night. That feeling, call it a premonition or whatever, came on me so unexpectedly that I keep hearing that sound all the time, and I can't shake the thought that Ligia is in some terrifying danger, like maybe from those lions. So I'm in real torment. Get me that permission to leave or I'll go without it. I can't just sit here anymore. I tell you, I can't!"

Petronius merely started laughing.

"Things haven't come to such a pass among us," he said, "that sons of consuls or their wives get thrown to the lions. You can die in just about any other way but not that one. Who knows if those were lions, anyway? The German aurochs can roar just as loud. As for me, I laugh at all omens. Last night was just as clear as this one and full of falling stars. A lot of people might have felt queasy, but I just thought that if mine were up there among them, then at least I'd have a lot of company in the afterworld!"

Then he was quiet again, thinking for a moment. "Besides," he said, "if your Christ could rise after dying, he ought to be able to save you from death as well."

"It could happen," Vinicius said, looking at the star-studded sky.

‹49›

NERO PLAYED AND SANG his hymn to Aphrodite, the "Queen of Cyprus," which he'd written and composed himself. He happened to be in good voice that day and felt that his music really gripped and swept away his audience. This sense of power transformed the sounds he made into something greater and filled him with such blissful admiration of himself that he seemed inspired. He grew pale in the end out of sheer emotion. For the first time in his life he didn't even want to hear the praises and applause but sat bowed over his zither, clutching it to his chest.

"I'm tired," he said at last, rising suddenly. "I need air. Tune the zithers while I go outside."

He wrapped a silk scarf around his throat and beckoned to Vinicius and Petronius who sat in a corner. "You'll both come with me," he said. "Give me your arm to lean on, Vinicius. I'm too spent, too shaken. And you, Petronius, talk to me about music."

They went out on the palace terrace, paved with alabaster slabs and sprinkled with aromatic saffron.

"Here I can breathe more freely," Nero said. "I'm filled with sadness even though I know that the small sample I sang and played for you is more than adequate for public performance. It will be the greatest triumph a Roman ever had when I bring it to the stage."

"You can perform it here, in Rome and in Greece as well," Petronius said. "I admired you with my whole heart and mind, divine one."

"I know you did. You're too lazy to dream up praises that you don't feel. You're as honest and sincere as Tullius Senecio, but you know infinitely more. Tell me what you thought about the music."

"When I hear poetry, watch you drive your chariot in the circus, see a beautiful statue, temple or painting, I feel that I can grasp the totality of it all and that my admiration embraces everything these things have to offer. But when I hear music, and especially yours, I see fresh beauties and delights opening up before me one after another. I run behind them, catch them, savor them, but still more come before I can absorb them, quite like the waves of the sea that come on and on endlessly and forever. So I'll just say this much: Music is like a sea. We stand on the beach and see into an infinite distance spreading out before us, but we can never see the other shore."

"Ah, what a profound analyst you are!" Nero said.

They walked along the terrace in silence for a while, Petronius on one side of Caesar, Vinicius on the other, and only the scattered dry saffron stalks rustled underfoot.

"You expressed my own thoughts exactly," Nero said at last, "which is why I always say that you're the only man in Rome who can understand me. Yes, that's my view of music. When I play and sing, I see things I never knew existed in my empire or anywhere on earth. I'm Caesar! The world belongs to me, and I can do anything I want! Yet music shows me new kingdoms, new mountains and seas, and reveals new raptures I never imagined. Even my mind can't grasp them totally or even name them, but I feel them with all my senses. I feel the presence of the gods. I see Mount Olympus. Strange winds come from the supernatural and carry me away. I glimpse through a mist an unknown vastness as bright as a sunrise. . . . The universe quivers with sound around me." A genuine amazement put a powerful tremor in his voice. "I tell you . . . I, god and emperor as I am, feel at such times as insignificant as a speck of dust. Can you ever believe that?"

"Yes," Petronius said. "Only a great artist can feel small beside his art—"

"This is a night for honesty," Caesar told him, "so I am opening up my soul to you as to a friend, and I'll tell you more. . . . Could you ever think of me as stupid or blind? Do you think I don't know what they write about me on the walls in Rome? That they call me a matricide and wife killer, and think me a monster of cruelty just because I allowed Tigellinus to dispose of a few of my enemies? Yes, my dear friend, they call me a monster, and I know it well! They've almost convinced me of my own cruelty to the point that I sometimes ask myself if I am a monster! But they don't understand that cruel deeds don't necessarily make a cruel man. . . . Ah, no one will ever know how music transforms me. You yourself, my dear friend, won't believe perhaps that when music moves my soul, I feel as gentle as a child rocking in a cradle. I swear to you by the shining stars above us that I am telling you nothing but the truth. People don't know how much goodness there is in my heart and what treasures I discover in it when music unlocks the doors and lays them before me."

Petronius didn't have the slightest doubt that Nero spoke with utter sincerity just then. Music did have the power to bring out the best in him, buried as it was under mountains of self-love, self-indulgence and crimes beyond counting.

"People have to know you as well as I do," he said. "Rome has never been able to appreciate you."

Caesar hung heavily on Vinicius' arm, as if bowed down under the weight of terrible injustice.

"Tigellinus told me they're whispering to one another in the senate that Terpnos and Diodorus play the zither better than I do. They won't even grant me that much! But you don't lie. You always speak the truth. So tell me honestly, are they really as good as I or better?"

"Far from it. Your touch is softer but has greater power. In you, one hears the artist. In them, skilled professionals. Indeed, hearing them makes it easier to understand just who and what you are."

"Let them live, then. They'll never know what you did for them just now. Besides, if I sent them to the block, I'd just have to get others to replace them."

"And people would say your love of music drives you to destroy it. Never kill art for art's sake, O divine one!"

"How different from Tigellinus you are!" Nero said. "But I'm an artist in everything, you see, and because music takes me into new dimensions I never knew existed, leading me into regions I don't rule and offering thrills I never found among ordinary people, I can't live just another ordinary life. Music tells me that there are extraordinary levels of existence, and I search for them with all the power the gods bestowed on me. I sometimes think that to scale these new Olympian heights I must do something no man ever did before. I must rise above merely human notions of what is good and evil and surpass every other man in both. I know people also think I am going mad. But that's not madness, that's my search! And if I am going mad, it's out of boredom with the ordinary and my impatience to find what I'm looking for. I search. I must keep searching. I know you understand. And that's why I must be greater than any man, because that's the only way to be the greatest artist."

He dropped his voice so that Vinicius wouldn't be able to hear him. He leaned toward Petronius, and started whispering straight into his ear.

"That's the main reason I condemned my mother and wife to death," he breathed hoarsely. "Did you know? I wanted to lay the greatest sacrifice any man could make at the gates of the unknown new world. I expected something extraordinary to happen afterward. I thought some door would open on some great mystery. Let it be either too wonderful for human comprehension or too horrifying, I don't care as long as it's uncommon and awesome. . . . But the sacrifice wasn't great enough. It seems more is needed to open that transcendental door. . . . So now let things happen as they will."

"What's going to happen?"

"You'll see. You'll see. Sooner than you think. Meanwhile bear in mind that there are two Neros, not just one. One is as everybody sees him, the other is the artist known only to you. And if he kills like the plague and revels like Bacchus, it's because he's choked by the flat, one-dimensional commonness of the ordinary world and wants to decimate it, winnow it like chaff, even if it takes fire and iron to do it. . . . Oh, how stale, dull, vapid and prosaic this world is going to be when I'm no longer here! No one, not even you, my dear friend, has an inkling of what an artist I truly am. Not yet. But that's exactly why I suffer so, why my soul is as dark and melancholy as these bleak cypresses before us. It's hard for one man to carry the burden of the greatest power and the greatest talent."

"I feel for you, Caesar," Petronius said smoothly. "So does the earth and the sea and all the creatures of the sky and water . . . not to mention Vinicius who adores you as he would a god."

"I've always liked him too." Nero smiled and squeezed the young tribune's shoulder. "Even though he serves Mars rather than the muses."

"I rather think his first allegiance is to Aphrodite," Petronius said. Suddenly he decided to settle his nephew's problems at one stroke and at the same time rid him of all the dangers that could threaten him. "He's as head over heels in love as Troilus with Cressida. Allow him, my lord, to go back to Rome, or he'll dry up with longing. That Lygian hostage you gave him has been found, you know, and he left her in the care of a certain Linus while he came to Antium. I didn't mention it before because I didn't want to intrude on your creative moments while you were in the throes of composition, working on your hymn, and that takes precedence over everything. The fact is that Vinicius wanted her for a concubine, but when she proved as virtuous as Lucretia, he fell in love with her virtue and wants to marry her. She's a king's daughter, so there's no harm in it. But he's a real soldier. He sighs, groans, suffers and withers on the vine as he waits for his emperor's permission."

"The emperor doesn't pick his soldiers' wives. Why does he need my permission?"

"As I've said, my lord, he simply adores you."

"All the more reason to let him have his marriage. She's a pretty girl, I recall, but narrow in the hips. Augusta Poppea complained to me that she cast a spell on our child in the Palatine gardens. . . ."

"And I told Tigellinus, as you may recall, that gods are beyond the reach of witchcraft. You remember, divine one, how dumbstruck he was and how you shouted 'Habet,' as if he were a beaten gladiator needing the last stroke?"

"I remember." Nero nodded briefly and turned to Vinicius. "Do you love her, as Petronius says?"

"I do, my lord!"

"In that case I order you to go to Rome tomorrow, marry her at once, and don't let me see you without a wedding ring."

"Thank you, my lord! With all my heart and soul!"

"Oh, how pleasant it is to make people happy." Caesar sighed, dramatically content. "I wish I could spend my life doing nothing else."

"Grant us one more favor, divine one," Petronius said quickly. "Announce your will before the Augusta. Vinicius wouldn't dare marry anyone for whom she doesn't care. One word from you, however, will remove the Augusta's doubts, especially if you make it clear that he is marrying by your direct order."

"So be it," Caesar said. "I can refuse nothing to you and Vinicius."

He turned back to the villa and the others followed, thrilled by their success. It took all of the young tribune's discipline and will not to throw himself on Petronius in gratitude, because now all threats and obstacles seemed out of the way.

Nerva and Tullius Senecio were chatting with Poppea in the villa's atrium while Terpnos and Diodorus were tuning the zithers. Nero marched straight to a chair inlaid with tortoiseshell and whispered something in a Greek slave's ear. The page left at a run and returned with a golden casket from which Nero lifted out a magnificent necklace of polished pink opals.

"Here are some jewels worthy of this evening," Caesar said.

"They're as brilliant as the light of dawn," Poppea observed, sure that the necklace was for her.

Caesar played with the large rosy stones for a moment, holding them up to the evening light and then lowering them again, and passed them to Vinicius.

"Give this from me to the Lygian princess I'm ordering you to marry," he commanded.

Poppea's angry and astonished glance swung from him to Vinicius and finally rested coldly on Petronius. But he was leaning across the arm of his chair and fingering the carved back of a harp beside it as if he wanted to fix every detail in his mind.

Vinicius thanked Caesar for his gift and joined Petronius in the corner, out of the others' hearing.

"How can I thank you for what you did for me today?" he asked.

"Sacrifice a pair of swans to the muse of music, praise Caesar's songs and laugh at the omens. I trust that lion roars won't disturb your sleep from this moment on. Or your Lygian lily's."

"They won't," Vinicius said. "I have no more worries."

"May Fortune smile on you both. But now brace yourself because Caesar is picking up a lute. Hold your breath, listen, and weep with admiration."

Caesar did indeed grasp a lute and lifted his eyes to the ceiling. All talk ceased in the room and everyone sat as if turned to stone. Only Terpnos and Diodorus stirred anxiously, watching his lips and glancing at each other, poised to accompany him the moment he started.

Suddenly shouts and running footsteps erupted in the entryway, one of Caesar's freedmen peered through the parted curtains, and the consul Lecanius pushed in close behind him.

Nero frowned.

"Forgive me, divine Caesar!" the freedman cried, out of breath and panting. "Rome is on fire! Most of the city is already burning!"

The news brought everybody leaping to his feet. Even Poppea rose and stared uncertainly at Caesar.

"O gods!" he said gratefully and laid his lute aside. "I'll see a burning city and finish my *Troyad*."

He turned to the trembling consul. "If I leave at once, will I be in time to see the fire?"

Lecanius was as white as the alabaster walls. "My lord," he stammered, "the whole city is a sea of flames. People are suffocating by the hundreds in the smoke and throwing themselves into the fire in madness of despair. . . . Rome is perishing, my lord!"

"*Vae misero mihi!*" Vinicius cried in the sudden silence. He threw off his toga and hurled himself out of the palace, dressed only in his tunic.

Nero lifted his eyes and arms in an actor's stance and started declaiming: "Woe to you, Priam's holy city!"

‹50›

VINICIUS BARELY TOOK the time to order a few slaves to follow him. He leaped on his horse and galloped like a madman down the dark streets of Antium to the Laurentum road.

The appalling news stunned him and hurled him into a state of mindless frenzy so that he couldn't tell at times what was happening with him or around him. He had a grim notion that disaster crouched on his horse behind him, lashing him along with the animal, and shouting "Rome is burning!" as it drove them both toward the fire. He galloped blindly, dressed only in his tunic and with his head down on the horse's neck, oblivious of anything in the way. In that calm, starry night and in the moonlit silence, horse and rider seemed like phantoms escaped from a dream. The Idumean stallion flew like an arrow, its ears pressed back and its neck stretched forward, passing the still black cypresses and the white villas gleaming in the shadows. The hoofbeats clattered on the stone pavement slabs, waking the dogs, who barked at their passage and then lifted their muzzles and howled at the moon.

The slaves who rode far lesser horses were soon left behind, and Vinicius galloped through slumbering Laurentum like a malignant spirit. He turned toward Ardea where he had posted remounts to shorten the time on his rides between Rome and Antium, as he had also done in Aricium, Bovillae and Ustrinum. Knowing that he had fresh horses waiting all along the road, he drove his mount until it dropped.

Beyond Ardea it seemed to him that the sky to the southeast carried a reddish glow. Could that be dawn? The day came early in July and it wasn't long until morning. But Vinicius decided it was the glare of a conflagration, and a howl of rage and anguish burst from him. "The whole city is a sea of flames," Lecanius had said, and for a while it seemed that he'd go truly mad. He lost all hope of saving Ligia or even getting to the city before it burned to a heap of ashes. Frightful images created by his mind flew before him like a flock of nightmares, shrill with despair and fury. He didn't know where in the city the fire had begun, of course, but he thought the Trans-Tiber might have been the first to feed the flames with its warren of rickety wooden houses, lumberyards and slave sheds.

Fires broke out almost every day in Rome, along with violence and looting, especially in the slums that teemed with an impoverished, half-savage population, in large part barbarian. What could be happening now in a place like the Trans-Tiber, swarming with rabble drawn from every corner of the world? An image of Ursus flashed across his mind, but what could even a Titan do against a holocaust? Fear of a slave rebellion was another nightmare that had choked Rome for years. The times of Spartacus weren't that far back in history. Hundreds of thousands were said to be dreaming of another rising against their tormentors, and what better opportunity would they have than the death of Rome? War could be raging right now in the city alongside the fire. War, slaughter, massacre . . . perhaps the praetorians had attacked the city on Caesar's orders and were murdering the population he despised.

Sheer terror gripped Vinicius at this thought. He was suddenly remembering all the talk about burning cities that had occupied Nero and his court for some time with a strange persistence. He recalled his complaints that he was forced to describe a historic holocaust without ever having seen one, his contemptuous reply to Tigellinus who offered to burn down Antium or a makeshift wooden substitute, and finally his constant whining about Rome and its stinking slums. Yes! That was it! Caesar must have ordered the burning of Rome. No one else would dare. And only Tigellinus would carry out such a terrible command. And if Rome was burning on its emperor's order, who could be sure the whole population wouldn't be slaughtered too? Not even this was beyond that monster! What lay ahead then—what it had to be—was a flaming holocaust, a slaves' revolt and a wholesale massacre; and Ligia was trapped in the midst of it!

Vinicius' groans blended with the wheezing grunts of the exhausted horse. Charging all out along a rising road all the way from Ardea, the animal was running with the last of its strength. Vinicius was now stretched full length on the stallion's back, his fists in its mane, and ready to gnaw the animal's neck with his rage and anguish. Who'll carry Ligia out of that fire storm? Who'll save her?

In that moment another rider dashed past at breakneck speed, heading the other way, toward Antium. He cried "Rome is dying!" as he galloped by. "Gods!"

The hoofbeats drowned the rest, but the last word jarred Vinicius back to reality. Gods, yes. Or rather, God! He looked up and raised his arms to the starry sky. "No, not you whose temples are on fire," he started to pray. "But *you!* You who suffered! You who are merciful and know human pain and anguish! Show the compassion that you came down to earth to teach mankind. If you're what Paul and Peter say you are, save Ligia for me. Take her in your arms and carry her out of the fire. Give her to me, and I'll pour out my blood for you in return. If you won't do it for me, then do it for her. She loves and trusts you! You promise life and happiness after death, and this won't pass her by. But she doesn't want to die just yet. Let her live. Lift her up and take her out of Rome. You have the power . . . or don't you want to do that?"

He stopped then, afraid that if he went on, he'd start voicing threats. He didn't want to anger God at the time he needed mercy and grace the most. Just the thought of it frightened him so much, he started flogging his horse anew, to drive even the possibility of a threat from his thoughts, and especially since he saw the white walls of Aricium glowing before him in the moonlight.

He was halfway to Rome. A moment later he was galloping past the temple of Mercury that lay in a grove just before the town. Word of the disaster must have spread here already because there were crowds in and around the temple. Flying past, he saw throngs of people on the steps and among the columns, hurrying with torches, anxious to put themselves under the protection of the god. Nor was the road as clear now as it had been back at Ardea. Most of the crowd headed for the grove along the smaller side roads, but clusters of people also stood on the highway and struggled to get out of the way of the charging horseman. The town itself buzzed with excited voices like a roiled beehive.

Vinicius burst in among the houses like a hurricane, bowling over several people on the way and trampling some others. "Rome's burning! The city is in flames!" The shouting was now everywhere around him. "Save Rome, all you gods!"

The horse stumbled before the inn where Vinicius kept one of his relays and slid back on its haunches when the rider reined it in sharply with a powerful hand. The slaves Vinicius posted there stood waiting in the doorway, as if expecting their master's arrival, and raced to bring the remount. But he had caught sight of a ten-man troop of praetorian cavalry, which was apparently riding with reports to Antium. He ran to them for answers.

"Which part of the city is on fire?" he shouted.

"Who are you?" demanded the troop leader.

"Vinicius, military tribune and Augustan! Answer if you want to keep your head on your neck!"

"It started in the market sheds around the Circus Maximus, my lord. By the time we were sent with dispatches, all of the city center was on fire."

"And the Trans-Tiber?"

"The fire hasn't gotten there yet, but it's leaping from one quarter to another. There's just no stopping it. People are dying everywhere from the heat and smoke, and all rescue is hopeless."

The slaves brought Vinicius his fresh horse just then. He leaped on its back and galloped on at once. He was riding now toward Albanum, passing Alba Longa on the right along with its scenic lake. The highway climbed a mountain at this point, hiding Albanum and the far horizon, but Vinicius knew that once he reached the crest he would see not just Bovillae and Ustrinum, where he had remounts waiting but also Rome. Beyond Albanum the Appian Way ran through the flat lowlands of Campania, with nothing to block the view other than the high-arched aqueducts that brought the city's water.

"I'll see the fire off the crest," he kept muttering, and he started to whip his horse again.

But before he reached the top of the mountain he smelled smoke on the wind, and a reddish glow edged the peak with crimson and gold.

"That's the fire," he groaned.

The night had been ebbing for some time. The first light of dawn had brightened into sunrise, and all the other hilltops nearby glowed with the same pink and golden fires. This could be daybreak as easily as reflected fires. But when Vinicius finally burst onto the ridge line he saw a terrifying sight: All the low country as far as he could see had vanished under one vast cloud of smoke that hugged the earth and swallowed all the towns, the aqueducts, the villas and the trees. Beyond it, at the far end of the terrible gray plain, the seven hills of the city lay burning.

This fire didn't take the form of a single pillar of flames and smoke, as happens with one building. Rather, it was a burning river or a long wide ribbon glowing with all the colors of a hellish sunrise. Above it rose a solid wall of smoke—in places an impenetrable black, elsewhere rose-colored or a bloody red. It squirmed and coiled like a massive serpent, bulging out or narrowing, twisting and stretching, spilling out and whirling. At times the fire itself seemed to shrink under the weight of this colossal monster and seemed as thin and narrow as a stream of embers; then it would throw its glaring light into the boiling black coils overhead and turn its lower layers into a sea of flames. Both the smoke and the fire filled the sky between the horizons, as far as the eye could see in any direction, and blotted out everything beyond them. The Sabine hills were totally invisible.

At first glance Vinicius was convinced that the whole world was burning, not merely the city, and that nothing would escape alive from the holocaust.

The wind blew ever stronger from the direction of the fire storm, carrying the acrid stench of burned wood, soot and ashes, which started to obscure even nearby objects. It was now full daylight, and the sun lit up the hilltops around Alban Lake, but through the haze of ashes the bright golden rays seemed rusty and sick. As Vinicius came down the mountain road, the smoke lay thicker, and it was harder to see through. The little town was completely smothered in the thick gray haze. The streets were full of anxious people, and it was frightening to imagine what was happening in Rome since even here people were finding it difficult to breathe.

Despair seized him again, and the hair on his head stood up in terror. He tried to comfort himself as best he could. It was impossible, he thought, for the whole city to burn all at once. The wind blew from the north, didn't it? It drove the smoke this way, so the north side should be clear. The Trans-Tiber lay across the river. It might have escaped destruction. And anyway, it would be enough for Ursus to get Ligia out through the Janiculum Gate for both to be safe. Moreover it was impossible for the whole population to perish at once and hardly likely that the city which ruled the world would vanish off the face of the earth along with all its people. Even in towns taken by assault, when wholesale massacre and pillage rage beside the fires, some inhabitants survive. So why should Ligia be so sure to die?

"God is protecting her," he assured himself. "The God who triumphed over death in his own behalf."

With such thoughts flashing through his mind, he started to pray fervently again, but old habits die hard. Used to the Roman way, he offered Christ great gifts and sacrifices in exchange for mercy.

Once through Albanum, most of whose population had climbed trees and rooftops to watch the terrible spectacle in Rome, he steadied a little and regained some of his normal coolness under pressure. He recalled that Ligia was not merely in the hands of Ursus and Linus but also looked after by the apostle Peter, whom he regarded as almost supernatural. Fresh hope poured into him at this thought. Ever since he had heard Peter speak at Ostrianum, he thought of him as almost a being from another planet, an entity beyond his grasp or comprehension. Every word uttered by this ancient man was either true or a prophecy of a truth to come. The more he got to know him in Miriam's house and later, the more he was convinced, and his faith in him was now beyond question. It was quite simple really: If Peter blessed his love and promised him Ligia, there was no way Ligia could perish in the fire. The city could turn into ashes, but not a single spark would singe her clothing.

The wild, sleepless night, the chaotic gallop, and the kaleidoscope of terrible impressions and emotional upheavals combined to throw the young tribune into a strange fervor, an exaltation beyond the bounds of ordinary reality where anything could happen. Peter could simply make the sign of the cross over the flames, part them with one word, and they would all pass untouched through the avenue of fire. Moreover Peter could read the future, so he was sure to have foreseen this disaster, warned the Christians, and led them out to safety well ahead of time. And if so, how could he fail to save Ligia, whom he loved as if she were his own child?

Vinicius grew more optimistic by the minute. If they had run from the city, he might find them in Bovillae, he thought. Or somewhere on the road. Any moment now that sweet, beloved face might show in the smoke that spread thickly across all Campania.

This seemed all the more likely when he started meeting growing swarms of people who had escaped the fire and were headed for the Alban hills to get beyond the smoke. The highway was so crowded before he reached Ustrinum that he had to slow to a walk. The fugitives came on foot with bundles on their backs, with mules and packhorses loaded with possessions, in heaped carts and wagons, and finally in litters borne by slaves. Ustrinum was so packed with refugees from Rome that it was almost impossible to squeeze through the crowds. Fugitives swarmed in the market square, jammed the streets, and clustered among temple columns. Others put up tents to shelter entire families. Yet others camped in the open, shouting, calling on the gods or cursing their fate.

It was hard to get any answers in that atmosphere of terror. People either refused to talk at all or met Vinicius with blank, horror-stricken stares, babbling that the city and the whole world had come to an end. Fresh crowds of men, women and children poured in from the direction of Rome, adding to the shouting and disorder. Families were split up, lost in the chaos. Desperate women looked frantically for strayed children. Men battled each other for camping space. Bands of half-wild Campanian shepherds pushed into the small town, eager for news and whatever they might steal in the confusion. Gangs of runaway slaves and gladiators of every nationality started breaking into the homes and villas in the town and fighting the soldiers sent out to protect the residents.

But at last Vinicius was able to get some news. He caught sight of Junius, a senator he knew, outside a hostelry surrounded by a troop of Batavian slaves. Junius had some detailed information. The fire, he confirmed, broke out near the Circus Maximus, close to where the Palatine approaches the Caelian heights, but then it spread with unbelievable speed to the city center.

"Not since the time of Brennus," said the senator, naming the leader of the Gauls who had defeated the Romans at the River Allia, "has Rome suffered such a terrible disaster. The Circus is gone, along with all the homes and shops around it. The Aventine and Mount Caelius are in flames. The fire swept around the Palatine and reached the Carinnae—"

Then Junius broke down. He owned a magnificent compound in the Carinnae, full of priceless artworks that he loved. Mindless with grief, he seized a handful of dirt, poured it over his head, and started to moan.

"Get hold of yourself!" Vinicius shook him by the shoulders. "My house is also there. But if all else is going up in smoke, then let it burn too!"

Then he remembered that he had advised Ligia to go to the house of Aulus and Pomponia. "What about the Vicus Patricius?" he asked.

"In flames," Junius said.

"And the Trans-Tiber?"

Junius threw him an astonished glance and clutched his aching head. "Who cares about the Trans-Tiber?"

"I do!" Vinicius shouted. "More than all the rest of Rome together!"

"Maybe you'll get there through the Via Portuensis. I don't know. . . . The heat will choke you if you try the route along the Aventine. . . . The Trans-

Tiber? I really can't tell. The fire hadn't got across the river when I left, but only the gods know if it reached there now."

Junius hesitated for a moment, peered around, then clutched at Vinicius.

"I know you won't give me away," he said in a low, hushed voice, "so I'll tell you something. This is no ordinary fire. The Circus could've been saved, but people were stopped from putting out the flames. There were a thousand voices shouting 'Death to fire fighters' when the fire spread to the homes and shops. I heard them myself. . . . There are unknown men running through the city and throwing burning torches into buildings. . . . Moreover the rabble is up in arms everywhere, yelling that the city was torched by somebody's command. That's all I'm going to say, but you get the picture. Ah, what a heartbreak for me, for you, for us all! What an utter waste! There's no way to describe what's going on there. People are burning to death, choking in the smoke or murdering each other in the crush. This is the end of Rome!"

He went on repeating: "Ah, what a disaster . . . what a disaster . . . what a terrible calamity for us all," but Vinicius leaped back on his horse and pushed on down the Appian Way.

But now it was less a ride than a desperate struggle against a tide of carriages and people fleeing from the city. Rome lay in plain sight before him, swept by a monstrous hurricane of fire. A searing heat welled out of the smoke and from the sea of flames whose roar and hissing drowned the screams of thousands.

« 5 I »

THE CLOSER VINICIUS GOT to the city walls, the clearer it became that the trek to Rome had been easier than reaching the center of the city would be. Thick with people, the Appian Way became more of an obstacle than a highway. The farms, temples, gardens, fields and graveyards on both sides of the road had become bivouacs. In the temple of Mars, lying right next to the Appian Gate, the mob broke down the doors to find shelter for the night. Others fought for possession of the bigger tombs in the cemeteries.

All the disorder of Ustrinum was just a foretaste of what was taking place within the city walls. There was no respect of any kind for laws, position, family ties or class privileges. Slaves could be seen beating Roman citizens with cudgels. Large gangs of gladiators, drunk on wine looted from the Emporium, rampaged with wild yells through the roadside campgrounds, trampling the terrified people, robbing them and chasing them away. Thousands of barbarians, held for sale in slave sheds throughout Rome, had broken out to freedom. The fire and the destruction of the city signaled the end of their slavery and also their hour of vengeance. Now they howled with joy, ripping the clothes off desperate refugees and dragging off the younger women, while the ruined citizens, who had lost everything in the flames, stretched their arms to the gods, begging for help and rescue. Running beside these marauders were older slaves who had been in Rome for years, naked derelicts and paupers dressed only in loincloths, and nightmare creatures from the back alleys who were almost never seen in the streets in daylight and whose existence in the city was hard to imagine.

Mobs of enslaved Asiatics, savage Africans, wild Germans, Greeks, Trachians and Britons raged and shrieked in every language known to man, unchecked and sure they were now free to extract payment for their years of suffering and pain. Praetorian helmets glinted above the heaving mass, bright in the harsh light of day and the conflagration, as soldiers fought pitched battles here and there against the crazed rabble, while the gentler population sought shelter behind their backs. Vinicius had seen towns taken by assault, but he had never witnessed such a spectacle of rage, agony, despair, savage pleasure, madness, unleashed bestiality and demented chaos. And above this swaying, roaring sea of maddened human beings, the seven hilltops of the world's greatest city burned on, sending its fiery breath into this convulsion and blanketing it with layers of smoke that obscured the sun.

It took the greatest effort, with his life at risk at every step, for the young tribune to reach the Appian Gate, but here he realized he would never get into the city through the Capena quarter, and not just because of the human logjam. The scorching heat just inside the gate made the air quiver. Moreover the new bridge at Porta Trigenia, across the river from the temple of the Bona Dea—the good goddess of chastity and felicity worshiped by Roman women—had still not been built, so there was only one way to cross the Tiber. He had to push through to the Pons Sublicius, which meant riding around the Aventine through a part of town that was now an ocean of flames.

This, he knew, was quite impossible.

He had to backtrack to Ustrinum, leave the Via Appia, ford the river below the city and reach the Via Portuensis that led straight into the Trans-Tiber. Even this wasn't easy because the chaos on the Appian Way increased by the minute. Cutting through with a sword might have been the quickest way, but Vinicius left Antium unarmed, galloping out in what he wore at Nero's soiree.

At the springs of Mercury he caught sight of a praetorian centurion he knew, who was at the head of several dozen soldiers fighting off the fugitives to protect the temple. The centurion didn't dare disobey an Augustan tribune, and one quick order put him and his men under Vinicius' command. Putting aside for the moment Paul's instructions about love for his fellow man, Vinicius cut through the crowds with a hurry that proved deadly for several people who didn't get out of the way in time. A shower of stones and curses followed him and his galloping detachment, but Vinicius paid no heed to either. He pressed on, anxious to break into the clear. This called for the greatest effort and endurance. People who had already set up their campsites didn't want to give way to the soldiers and cursed them and Caesar at the top of their lungs. In some places they even stood their ground against the praetorians. Vinicius heard them cursing Nero as an arsonist. Death threats were hurled at him and Poppea. Shouts of "buffoon," "mountebank," and "matricide" echoed everywhere. Some people howled about dragging him to the Tiber where the foulest criminals were drowned. Others raged that Rome had been patient enough with such a monstrous Caesar. It took no great stretch of the imagination to see that an all-out rebellion could burst at any moment if the mobs found a leader they could follow.

Meanwhile their fury and despair turned on the praetorians, who found it harder to force their way through the press of people. Their path was blocked by bales of belongings hastily dragged out of the fire, barrels and crates of food, heaps of whatever costly furniture could be saved, household utensils, cradles, piles of bedding, carts, wagons and litters. Hand fighting broke out here and there, but the praetorians made short work of the unarmed rabble. Forcing their way to the Via Latina, they cut across the Numitia, Ardea, Lavinia and Ostia highways, circled innumerable villas, gardens, burial grounds and temples, and at last reached the township of Vicus Alexandri where they crossed the Tiber. The going became easier and there was less smoke. Fugitives—and there were enough of them even there—told Vinicius that only a few sections of the Trans-Tiber were on fire as yet but that nothing could stop the conflagration since the fires were being set on purpose and the arsonists kept fire fighters away, claiming they were acting under orders.

The young tribune no longer doubted it was Caesar who had ordered the burning of the city, and the vengeance that the mobs demanded seemed right and just to him. What more could have been done by Mithridates or any other of Rome's most implacable enemies? It was clear treason. The lunacy had gone too far. It had become too monstrous to endure. The craziness now made human life unendurable. Vinicius was convinced Nero's last hour had come, that the rubble into which the city was turning must and should fall on that abominable buffoon and bury him along with all his crimes. This could be just a matter of hours if the desperate people found a man bold enough to lead them. And why shouldn't it be he?

Daring and vengeful thoughts flashed through his mind, and it all made sense. The Vinicius family was a household word. His family had produced Roman consuls for several centuries, and all the outraged people needed at this time was a well-known name around which to rally. It had been touch and go only recently when the vicious prefect, Pedanius Secundus, sent four hundred slaves to their deaths for a single murder. Outright rebellion and civil war had hung in the air. So what might happen now in the face of the most calamitous disaster in Rome's eight hundred years? Whoever sounds the call to arms in the name of the old spirit of the Quirites, Vinicius was certain, will topple Nero and assume the imperial purple.

Who would do that better than he? He was a veteran soldier; hardier, braver and younger than other Augustans, a born commander and an experienced leader. True, Nero held command over thirty legions on the far-flung borders of the empire, but wouldn't those legions and their generals be outraged at the burning of Rome and all its temples? And if that happened, Vinicius could be Caesar.

And why not? Weren't there rumors among the Augustans that some fortune-teller prophesied Otho would be emperor? How was he worse than Otho? Maybe Christ with his divine powers would help him, he thought, and perhaps all this was his inspiration anyway. "Let this be true!" Vinicius cried silently. He would settle with Nero for all the threats to Ligia and for his own anguish, bring a rule of truth, compassion and justice, extend Christ's teaching from the Euphrates to the misty shores of Britain, and at the same time dress Ligia in imperial purple and make her mistress of the world.

But these thoughts that burst within his head like a shower of sparks hurled from a flaming building also died like sparks. First he must save Ligia. He could see the disaster firsthand now. Fear gripped him again when he looked at the raging sea of flames and the mountains of smoke. His trust in Peter's mystical ability to save and protect Ligia fell apart in the face of this terrible reality. Despair clutched at him once more, stayed with him all the way on the Via Portuensis that led straight into the Trans-Tiber, and didn't leave him until he was inside the gate. There he was told what he already knew from the refugees: The best part of the quarter was still free of flames even though the fire had spread across the river in several locations.

The Trans-Tiber was just as choked with smoke and crowded with escaping people, however, and the going was even harder than before, because the fugitives had more time to try to save more of their possessions and the narrow little streets were jammed from wall to wall. The main harbor road was completely blocked with salvaged furniture, and huge piles of it were stacked around the Naumachia Augusta. Smoke lay so thickly in the smaller alleys that access was hopeless. Their inhabitants fled from them by the thousands. Frightful sights met Vinicius on his way. Time and again two human tides collided in a narrow passage and fought to the death. People battered and trampled one another. Families got lost. Desperate mothers looked for missing children. Vinicius blanched with horror at the thought of what must be happening nearer to the fires. In all the screams and yelling it was impossible to question anyone about anything or even to understand the shouts. New clouds of smoke roiled over from across the river every now and then, so thick and heavy that they rolled like boulders along the cobblestones, and so black and dense that they covered buildings, people and all else with an impenetrable darkness as if it were night. The fire generated its own winds, blowing the clouds apart just enough for Vinicius to keep moving on, working his way closer to the alley where Linus lived.

The swelter of a hot July day augmented by the scorching heat of the fire storm that raged across the river became unendurable. Smoke burned his eyes, and his lungs fought for air. Even those locals who stayed in their houses, hoping the river would hold back the flames, began to leave, and the crowds of refugees were swelling by the hour. The praetorians who came with Vinicius fell behind, and he went on alone. Someone in the tightly packed mob wounded his horse with a hammer, and the animal started to jerk its bloody head, rearing up and refusing to obey its rider. His rich tunic also betrayed him as an Augustan, and a roar of furious shouts burst out around him.

"Death to Nero! Death to his fire starters!"

It was a dangerous moment, because several hundred fists reached for Vinicius, but the panicked horse carried him away, trampling some people, while a new wave of black smoke plunged the street into murky twilight.

He realized he would never get through on horseback. He jumped off his mount and ran the rest of the way on foot, squeezing and slipping along the walls and sometimes halting until the worst of the fleeing mob had gone by.

He knew that all these efforts were probably in vain. Chances were that Ligia was no longer in the city. She might have managed to escape to the countryside. It would be easier to find a pin in the sea, he thought, than to find her in this chaos. But he was determined to make sure and to get to the house of Linus at all costs. He ripped off a part of his tunic, covered his nose and mouth, and ran on.

The nearer he got to the river, the more frightening the searing heat became. The fire, Vinicius knew, had broken out in the Circus Maximus, so he supposed at first that the heat came from the glowing ruins of that giant structure, along with the Forum Boarium and the lumberyards of the Velabrum quarter that adjoined the circus and must have burned down as well.

But the furnace heat was too close, almost beyond bearing, and at last one of the fleeing people pointed to the source. "Don't go near the Cestius bridge," croaked the last of the fugitives, an old man who limped by on crutches. "The whole island is burning!"

He could have no illusions now. The fire was across the river, and the Trans-Tiber was as good as burning. At the turn toward the Jewish Quarter, where Linus lived, the young tribune saw flames within the smoke. More than just the island was on fire. The Vicus Judaeorum was engulfed as well, or at least the far end of the little street where Ligia was staying.

Vinicius suddenly remembered that Linus' house stood in a little garden and that there was a small open field between it and the Tiber. The fire could halt there for a moment. Thus he still had hope. Each gust of wind carried not just smoke but whirling swarms of sparks that could set fire to the end of the alley already behind him and cut off his retreat, but he kept on running.

At last he caught sight of the cypress trees looming out of the smoke that shrouded the garden. The homes beyond the open field were already blazing like piles of cordwood, but Linus' small compound was still untouched by fire. Vinicius tossed a grateful glance at the sky and leaped toward the garden even though the air was so hot it blistered his skin.

He kicked open the garden gate and stumbled inside. There was no one there. The house seemed abandoned.

Maybe they've been overcome by smoke, he thought. He shouted: "Ligia! Ligia!"

Nobody answered. Only the grim roar of the nearing fire thundered in the silence.

"Ligia!"

Suddenly his ears caught the gloomy subterranean sound he had heard in the garden once before. The nearby burning island housed animal pens next to the temple of Asclepios. It had apparently caught fire, and the trapped caged beasts, among them the lions, were roaring in terror. Vinicius shuddered from head to heel. Once again when all his thoughts were locked around Ligia, those dreadful voices were making themselves heard like a strange foreshadowing of a threatening future.

This was only a fleeting thought; there was no time for more. The roar of the fire, so much more terrifying than the lions, was pressing and immediate. Ligia hadn't answered his shouts, but she could be in the threatened building, either unconscious or overcome by smoke. Vinicius broke into the house. The little atrium was dark with smoke, but there was no one in it. Groping for doors to the sleeping rooms, he caught sight of a flickering oil lamp, saw the traditional niches of the household gods and the cross with the small flame dancing under it. It flashed through the young convert's mind that the cross sent the light to help him find Ligia, so he snatched up the lamp and started searching for the sleeping alcoves.

He found one. It was empty, but Vinicius was sure it was Ligia's because her clothes hung from nails in the wall, and thrown across the cot was a *capitium*, a tight-fitting shift that women wore next to the body. He kissed it and buried his face in it, then threw it across his shoulder and went on, but there was no one anywhere in the house, not even the cellar. Ligia, Linus and Ursus must have gotten away, along with everybody else from that part of town.

"I'll have to look for them in the crowds beyond the gates," he told himself.

Nor was he especially surprised to have missed them on the Via Portuensis. They could have left the Trans-Tiber in the opposite direction, heading toward the heights of Vatican hill. Either way, he thought with immense relief, they're safe from the fire. He had seen the dreadful dangers that faced the refugees, but he took comfort in Ursus' superhuman strength. He'll see them through, he thought, if anybody can.

"Once I get away from here," he said, "I'll go across the grove of Domitius to the gardens of Agrippina. I'm sure to find them somewhere along there. The smoke is not so bad out that way since the wind is blowing from the Sabine hills."

It was high time to think about his own safety, however, because the fires roared ever closer, spewing from the island. Billows of smoke were choking the better part of the yards and alleys around the house. He had been lighting his way in the murky twilight with the little lamp, but a violent backdraft blew it out, plunging him into darkness. Outside again, Vinicius set off at a dead run for the Via Portuensis, the way he had come, and the fire storm raced after him like a greedy monster. He felt the hot lick of its breath, and sparks rained on his hair and neck. His chest heaved with the smoke around him. His tunic was already smoldering in several places, but he ran on, paying no attention, afraid he'd suffocate. As it was, he had a burned sour taste in his mouth, soot clogged his nostrils, and his lungs and throat were as raw as if they were burning. Blood pounded in his head, and he started to see everything in flashes of scarlet. "This fire is alive!" he told himself, wondering if he shouldn't simply throw himself down in the crimson dust and let it devour him.

He ran on, starting to feel the effort. Sweat poured down his neck, shoulders and back, hot as boiling water. He had wrapped his head in Ligia's shift, or he wouldn't have been able to breathe at all. If it weren't for that and for her name that he kept repeating like an incantation, he knew he would have fallen. A few moments later he started to lose his sense of direction. He wondered where he was. He didn't recognize the passages around him. Consciousness came and went. All he knew was that he had to keep moving because Ligia waited for him in the fields outside as Peter had promised. Then suddenly he knew with the feverish certainty of a deathbed vision that he had to see her, marry her and die.

By this time he was running like a drunken man, staggering from one side of the alley to the other. All of a sudden everything changed around him. Everything that was merely smoldering in the vast inferno that gripped the sprawling city burst into a single sheet of flames. All the smoke vanished, swept away by a searing windstorm, and the colossal force of unleashed, scorching air hurled an infinity of sparks down the long, narrow tunnel in which he was moving.

Vinicius was running in a cloud of fire, but with the smoke gone he could see ahead. Right at the point when he felt himself falling, he caught sight of blank walls, the end of the alley, and knew that if he was able to round the corner, he'd outrun the fire. Then he was past the corner, swerving down the road that led to the gates, the Via Portuensis, and the Codetan Fields beyond. The fire cloud was gone. If he could reach the harbor road, he knew, he'd be safe even if he were to fall unconscious in the gateway.

But he couldn't see the end of the road. A thick gray cloud obscured it. If that's smoke, he thought, I'm dead. I won't get through. Running with the last of his strength, he was naked because he had ripped off his smoldering tunic and had Ligia's shift wrapped around his head. Closer now, he saw that the gray cloud was stone and mortar dust, not smoke. He heard shouts and voices. That's the rabble looting homes, he thought, but at least they're people. They can help.

He ran toward them, shouting, and this was his last effort. Everything around him was blood-red. He seemed to be looking through a scarlet haze. He could no longer breathe; his lungs were burning as if they had caught fire. His bones felt like liquid, and he fell.

But he had been heard, and two men ran toward him carrying gourds of water. He was still conscious enough to grasp a water gourd with both hands and gulp down half of it.

"Thanks," he managed, then made another effort. "Get me up on my feet, and I'll make it the rest of the way alone."

The men, he could see now, were laborers, not looters. One bathed his head with water. They raised him up and carried him to the rest of their group, which formed a small, worried circle around him, looking him over carefully for any major damage.

This anxious care surprised him. "Who are you?" he asked.

"Workmen," one of them said. "A wrecking crew. We're knocking down these buildings to make a firebreak. We're trying to keep the harbor road clear."

"You helped me just in time," Vinicius said. "I owe you my life. I had already fallen."

"We have to help everyone we can," several voices said. "We have no choice."

Vinicius had time to peer more closely at the surrounding faces, so different from the animal masks of the mobs he had seen all day. He knew what they were.

"May . . . Christ repay your kindness," he said.

"Praise be to his name," they murmured in a quiet chorus.

"Linus?" Vinicius tried to ask, but that's all he managed. He didn't hear the answer, whatever it was. Drained of all strength, physically and emotionally exhausted, he slipped into darkness. He regained consciousness only in the clear, open space of the Codetan Fields, looking up at a cluster of men and women resting in the gardens.

"Where's Linus?" he asked again.

No one said anything for a moment, and then Vinicius heard a voice that sounded familiar. "He went out through the Nomentan Gate two days ago. He's in Ostrianum. Peace be with you, mighty king of Persia!"

Vinicius sat up. He saw Chilon standing over him.

"Your house is sure to have burned down, my lord," said the Greek, "because the Carinnae is a mass of flames. But you'll always be as rich as Midas, won't you? What a calamity, eh? The Christians, great son of Serapis, have long been saying that this city must perish by fire. But Linus, along with the daughter of Jupiter, is in Ostrianum. Ai, but what a shame, eh? I mean about the city?"

"You saw them?" Vinicius felt weakness creeping over him again.

"I saw them, my lord." The Greek's voice carried a strange note of triumph, and his wizened face twisted in a gap-toothed smile. "I saw them both, Osiris. Praise be to Christ and all the other gods that I'm able to bring you this good news. I owe you something, don't I, for all your great kindness. And I swear by this burning Rome that I'll pay you back."

It was already evening, but the twilight was as bright as day because the fires raged even more fiercely than before. It seemed as if it wasn't just a few separate districts that lay engulfed in flames but that the whole city burned from end to end, like one vast funeral pyre. The sky hung like a crimson lid on the horizon, and a bloodred night was settling on the world.

⟨ 5 2 ⟩

THE FIERY GLOW of the burning city filled the night sky as far as the eye could reach. A great full moon rolled out from behind the hills, caught fire from the glare, and hung like a vast copper-colored eye above the perishing capital of the world. Pink stars blinked in the reddish depths of space, but the earth below was brighter that night than the skies above it. Rome lit up the entire Campania like a giant bonfire. Its bloodred light bathed the hills, temples and country villas, the aqueducts that ran toward the city from the nearby mountains, and the swarms of people who had climbed into the aqueducts for shelter or to watch the fire.

Meanwhile the terrible elemental force swept through new quarters by the hour. There was now no doubt in anybody's mind that the fresh outbreaks bursting into life in areas far removed from the original blaze were being set on purpose, the work of unknown hands acting under orders. The flames rolled like lava down the hills on which Rome was built, covering the crowded space below, jammed as it was with five- and six-floor tenements and dwellings, full of sheds, shacks, market stalls and portable wooden stages thrown up everywhere for every kind of spectacle or performance, packed with lumberyards and storage bins for oil, grain, almonds, hazelnuts and pine nuts, the staple fodder of the poorest people, and bales of used clothing sometimes given by imperial order to the masses that swarmed in these warrens. Reaching this wealth of combustible material, the fire burst into a rapid series of violent explosions that swept through whole streets at a time in a matter of moments.

The refugees who camped beyond the walls and the spectators on the aqueducts could guess what was burning by the form and color of each fresh eruption. The intense heat within the blazing city, set like a bowl among its seven hills, hurled fiery columns high into the air. Millions of burning nuggets, red as coals, whirled into the skies like an uncountable swarm of glittering fireflies, and they either burst there with a crackling rattle or swept on, carried by the wind, to descend on other parts of the city, on the aqueducts, and on the fields around them. Any thought of fighting the inferno made no sense, and the chaos in and around the city deepened by the hour. On one side of the walls, people were pouring out through every gate, running for their lives; on the other side, curious thousands came running from every town and village for miles around, including the primitive, half-wild mountain shepherds who saw a chance to loot.

"Rome is perishing!" was a constant cry, and in those days the fall of the city meant the end of all authority and the dissolution of all ties that held mankind together. The rabble, composed for the most part of slaves and new arrivals for whom Roman rule had no special meaning in itself and who stood to lose nothing but their chains in its disappearance, started to get dangerous. Violence, robbery and murder spread rapidly. Only the awesome spectacle of the dying city seemed able to distract them from launching an all-out massacre, which was sure to erupt as soon as Rome turned to a heap of rubble.

Hundreds of thousands of slaves seemed to be waiting only for a leader and the command to start. The name of Spartacus, whose terrible rebellion shook the empire in its time and threatened Rome itself, sounded everywhere among them, while the citizens clustered together and armed themselves with whatever they could lay their hands on. There was no Spartacus now, but hair-raising tales sprang up at every gate. Some of the fugitives insisted that Jupiter himself was out to destroy the city, ordering Vulcan to burn it down with subterranean fires. Others claimed this was Vesta's vengeance for Nero's seduction of her priestess Rubria. Either way, there was nothing to be done about it except besiege the temples and pray for the gods' forgiveness, and the thousands of refugees who believed these stories made no attempt to save or rescue anything. The most widely rumored source of the catastrophe, however, was Nero's wish to burn down the slums of the Suburra so that he might have cleaner air to breathe, and to replace Rome with a new city to be named Neronia.

A howling rage swept over the ruined and dispossessed Romans at this thought, and if a new Roman leader did appear among them, it would have been just as Vinicius had supposed: Nero's last hour would have struck immediately, years earlier than it was destined to do.

Rumors and speculations fed on each other as voraciously as the conflagration. Some people argued that Caesar had gone mad and that he would order the praetorians and gladiators to charge whoever escaped from the fire and slaughter the entire population. Others swore by every god and goddess that all animal pens had been thrown open at Copperbeard's command, and wild beasts were rampaging through the city, attacking the people. Some claimed to have seen lions with flaming manes and herds of elephants and aurochs who gored and trampled everyone they saw. As it happened, there was some truth to that: Elephants in a number of pens scattered throughout the city did panic and stampede at the sight of the approaching fire; they battered their way out into the open and ran in terror down the streets, away from the flames, smashing everything in their path.

Rumor had tens of thousands killed by the flames alone, and this, too, had some basis in fact. Deprived of all they owned or of someone who was precious to them, many people threw themselves into the fire out of sheer despair, not wanting to live. Smoke overtook and suffocated others. In the city center—the teeming quarters bounded by the heights of the Capitoline and the Quirinal, the Viminal and Esquiline hills, and the Palatine and Caelian hills—the fire broke out in so many places simultaneously that some fleeing crowds ran unexpectedly into another wall of flames and died hideous deaths, trapped in the storm of two conflagrations.

Terrified, bewildered and lost in the chaos, people didn't know where to go or how to get there. The streets were blocked, piled high with abandoned furniture and objects, and in some places utterly impassable. Those who tried to wait out the blaze in the open where the fires presumably would have nothing to attack—such as city squares and marketplaces, where the Flavian amphitheater would be built afterward, near the Temple of the Earth, the Portico of Livia, up around the temples of Juno and Lucina and between Clivius Vibrius and the old Esquiline Gate—found themselves ringed by walls of flame and died of the heat. Hundreds of charred bodies were found afterward in places the fire never reached; the wretched victims had ripped up paving slabs here and there and tried to bury themselves in the soil to escape the broiling heat around them.

Almost no family that lived in the central quarters escaped without losing someone, whether burned or lost and crushed to death in the panicked crowds. The grief-stricken howls of distraught women, half-mad with despair, rang along all the walls, at every gate and on each road beyond them.

If all respect for human ties and authority withered in the fire, so did faith in the established gods. Some old men among the howling thousands still begged for divine compassion from the Roman gods, stretching their arms toward the temple of Jove the Liberator and crying out: "You are the city's savior. Save it and your altar." But for the most part the old gods took the brunt of the people's anger and despair. In the minds of the populace, the original divinities of the founding fathers were entrusted with the happiness and safety of the city; but they had proved helpless, and the mobs turned in panic to the foreign deities. It happened that when a company of Egyptian priests appeared in the Via Asinaria, carrying a statue of Isis saved from the temple near the Caelian Gate, the rabble hurled itself into the procession, harnessed itself to the wagon and hauled it all the way to the Appian Gate, where it enthroned the cat goddess in the temple of Mars—the god of war, who embodied Rome's authority and power—and beat up his priests in the process.

Serapis and Baal suddenly had masses of new adherents. So did Jehovah, whose followers spilled out of the back alleys of the Suburra and the Trans-Tiber quarters, creating an uproar in the fields beyond the walls with their chants and shouting. But there was a strange note of triumph in their supplications; they seemed aglow with a secret pleasure, so that while some citizens joined their choruses, praising the Lord of the world, others were enraged by this jubilation and tried to silence them by force. Elsewhere clusters of men in the prime of life, gnarled oldsters, and women and children of all ages sang strange, solemn hymns that no one understood, except for the recurring reference to days of wrath and judgment and "the coming of the Lord."

Hearing all this and seeing this restless, sleepless human tide made it seem as if the burning city stood in the center of a stormy sea.

But nothing helped, not hymns, blasphemies or despair. The disaster seemed as total, absolute and irreversible as destiny itself. Near Pompey's amphitheater, stores of hemp and cord used in great quantities in all the circuses and arenas to operate mechanical devices of all kinds suddenly caught fire, along with the adjoining warehouses of pitch and other lubricants used to grease the ropes, and a terrifying new spectacle dazed the frightened masses. All of the city nearest to the Field of Mars burned for several hours with such a bright, pale yellow light that it seemed to the horrified spectators, numb and half-dead with terror as they were, that the natural order of night and day was suddenly reversed and the sun glowed at midnight.

But then a single bloodred glare consumed all the other colors of the holocaust. Flames shot out of this scarlet ocean into the sky in colossal pillars and fountains, erupting into fantastic crowns and plumes at their summit, where the wind seized them, turned them into golden threads, wild manes and cascades of sparks and debris, and swept them into the plains of Campania almost as far as the Alban hills.

The night grew brighter by the hour. The air itself seemed saturated with fire, infused with infernal light. The Tiber flowed like glowing, red-hot lava, a river of flames. The ruined city had turned into a living hell. The conflagration seized ever widening spaces, stormed the hills, and devoured the flat plateaus between them. It raged, roared and thundered, and ravished the slopes and valleys.

‹ 5 3 ›

THE WEAVER MACRINUS, to whose cottage the Christians brought Vinicius, washed him, gave him some clothes and fed him, and the young soldier recovered all his strength practically at once. He insist- ed on searching for Linus straightaway, not waiting until morning. Macrinus, who was also a Christian, confirmed what Chilon had said: Linus, along with a senior priest named Clement, had gone to Ostrianum where the apostle Peter was to baptize a group of con- verts, having left his house in the care of a certain Gaius about two days ago. Vinicius was convinced that Ligia and Ursus hadn't stayed home and that they had also gone to Ostrianum.

This gave Vinicius a feeling of immense relief. Linus was old, hard- ly able to make the long trip beyond the Nomentan Gate every day. It made sense that he would find temporary quarters near Ostrianum in the house of some fellow Christian and that Ligia and Ursus would stay with him. This meant they hadn't even been in the city when the fires started, and they were not in any danger since the flames never got to the far side of the Esquiline. Vinicius saw Christ's hand in all of this and believed himself under God's particular protec- tion. He swore with all the love and fervor within him to devote the rest of his life in payment for the favor.

This made him all the more eager to go to Ostrianum, find Ligia and Linus and Peter, and take them to some far-off estate of his, maybe in Sicily, where they would all be safe. Why stay here? Rome would be just a heap of ashes in a few more days, a vast gray ruin haunted by a maddened rabble. In Sicily they would have the peace- fulness of the countryside around them, live blessed by Peter under Christ's protection, and have cohorts of disciplined slaves to guard them. All he had to do now was find them.

This wouldn't be easy. He remembered how hard it was to get from the Appian Way to the Trans-Tiber and how he had to swing far across open country to reach the harbor road. He decided to circle the city in the opposite direction. Going along the river on the Via Triumphatoris, he could get as far as the Aemilian bridge; from there he would go past Mount Pincius and the gardens of Pompey, Lucullus and Sallust, edging along the Field of Mars to the Nomentum highway. This was the shortest route, but Macrinus and Chilon advised another. True, the fire hadn't yet broken into that part of the city, but all the streets and markets were sure to be jammed with fugitives and everything they carried. Chilon thought it better to take the grazing fields below the Vatican as far as the Flaminian Gate, cross the river there, and then go on past the gardens of Acilius, following the far side of the city walls all the way to the Porta Salaria. Vinicius thought about this for a moment and agreed.

Macrinus had to stay home and watch over his house, but he found a pair of mules that would be useful later on for Ligia. He wanted to add a slave for further protection, but Vinicius didn't think they'd need one. If the need arose, he'd simply take charge of the first praetorian troop he came across, as he did before.

Moments later he and Chilon set off through the Janiculum district to the Triumphal Way. The open fields were thick with refugees here as everywhere, but they pushed through without a lot of trouble since the greatest mass of the fugitives was pouring out toward the sea by the harbor road. Once past the Gate of Septimus, they made their way between the river and the magnificent gardens of Domitius, whose towering cypresses glowed as red in the firelight as if it were sunset. Their path was getting easier all the time; the fugitives thinned out very quickly, and soon all they had to struggle against were waves of country folk heading for the city. Vinicius urged his mule along as best he could, while Chilon kept close behind, muttering all the way.

"So the fire's behind us now," he murmured, wriggling his shoulders. "It feels nice and warm. O Zeus, if you don't swamp those fires with a cloudburst, it'll be a sign that you've turned your back on Rome just as I'm doing. There's nothing men can do to put out that bonfire. Imagine, such a mighty city. It had all of Greece and the entire world jumping at its orders, and now the first ragtag Greek that comes along can roast his beans in its ashes! Who'd ever think of that! Well, Rome's gone for good, and good riddance to it. Soon there won't be any Romans either to lord it over everybody else. . . . And whoever wants to kick the ashes once they're cold will be welcome to them. . . . Oh, gods, imagine dancing on the ashes of such a worldshaking colossus! What Greek or even barbarian would ever expect it? But here it is, and you can kick the ashes to your heart's content, because ashes are ashes, no matter whether they're left behind by camping shepherds or a burning city. Sooner or later the wind will blow them all out of sight forever."

He kept twisting around to stare at the walls of flame behind them, and his face revealed an evil satisfaction.

"Going, going, gone!" he muttered with pleasure. "The world won't see any more of it. And where's mankind going to send its grain, its oil and all its money from now on? Who'll be there to squeeze gold and tears out of it? Marble doesn't burn, but it crumbles nicely. The Capitol will turn to dust, and the Palatine will be a pile of rubble. O Zeus! If Rome was a shepherd, the rest of mankind was just a flock of sheep, and every time the shepherd got hungry, he slaughtered one of them, ate it and offered you the fleece. Who'll be the slaughterer now, you lord of clouds and thunder? To whom will you give the whip? Because Rome is burning. It's cooked good and proper. . . . It couldn't burn better if you set it on fire with one of your thunderbolts."

"Keep going!" Vinicius urged the Greek. "What are you doing back there anyway?"

"I'm weeping over Rome, my lord!" Chilon sniffed. "Ah, that such an awful thing could happen to Jove's city!"

They rode in silence for a while, listening to the dull roar of the burning city and to the flapping of birds' wings overhead. The pigeons that nested in vast numbers in the small towns and villas throughout Campania, along with all kinds of field birds from the coast and the nearby mountains, must have confused the vast red glow with sunrise and headed blindly toward the fire.

"Where were you when the fire started?" Vinicius broke the silence.

"I was on my way to see my friend Euricius who had a stall near the Circus Maximus, my lord. And I was just meditating on Christ and his teaching when I heard people shouting 'Fire! Fire!' A lot of people came running to look or help, but I didn't stay around too long. Once the fire took hold of the circus and then all those other fires started all over the place, I had to think about myself."

"Did you see anyone tossing lighted torches into the buildings?"

"Ah, what didn't I see, grandson of Aeneas! I saw men hacking their way through the crowd with swords! I saw pitched battles and human entrails trampled in the dust. You'd have thought, my lord, that barbarians had taken the city and were massacring the people.

People thought the end of the world had come. Some lost their heads and just stood there, waiting for the fire. Some went mad. Others howled with terror. But I also saw some who danced with joy, because the world is full of evil men, my lord, who can't appreciate your gentle Roman rule and those just laws that give you the right to strip them of everything and take it for yourselves. People just don't know how to make their peace with the will of the gods!"

Vinicius was too absorbed with his own thoughts to note the Greek's bitter irony. He shook with terror at the thought that Ligia could have found herself trapped in that hellish chaos, crushed in those streets where people trampled on others' entrails, so even though he'd already questioned Chilon ten times about everything the old man might know, he had to ask again.

"And you saw them at Ostrianum with your own eyes?"

"I saw them, son of Venus! I saw the maiden and the good Lygian and the saintly Linus and the holy Peter."

"Before the fire?"

"Yes, before the fire."

But something about this didn't sound right. Chilon could be lying. Vinicius stopped his mule and glared at the Greek. "What were you doing there?"

Chilon lost a bit of his aplomb. Like many others he thought the end of Rome also meant the end of Roman sovereignty and power, but here he was, face to face and alone with a Roman tribune who had once threatened him with terrible retribution if he went on spying on the Christians and especially on Ligia and Linus.

"Why won't you believe that I love them, my lord?" he asked. "Yes, I was at Ostrianum. Why not? I'm at least half a Christian. Pyrrho taught me that goodness is worth more than wisdom, so I'm getting fonder of good people all the time. Besides, my lord, I'm a poor man, and I was often hungry while you were in Antium. There I'd be, slumped over my books, and there'd be a cold wind howling through my empty belly. So I'd sit by the wall in Ostrianum, and the Christians would drop a few pennies in my old tin cup. They may be poor themselves, but they give more to the poor than the rest of Rome together."

That seemed close enough to the truth to satisfy Vinicius, and he asked no more.

"So you don't know where Linus is staying out there?" he said far less fiercely.

"You punished my curiosity once before, my lord," Chilon reminded him. "And cruelly at that."

Vinicius said nothing.

"Lord," Chilon said after a while, "you wouldn't have found the young lady without me that other time. Will you forget about me if we find her again?"

"You'll get a house with a vineyard in Ameriola."

"Thank you, Hercules! With a vineyard? Thank you! Thank you! Oh, yes, with a vineyard!"

They were now passing the hills of the Vatican, which glowed a somber red with reflected fire, and they turned right beyond the artificial lake where sea battles were staged. Once past the Vatican pastures they would be at the river, and once they crossed the Tiber they could turn toward the Flaminian Gate.

But Chilon suddenly reined his mule. "My lord!" he cried. "I have an idea!"

"Speak up, then."

"Right there, lord, beyond the Janiculum and the Vatican, past the gardens of Agrippina, there's an excavation where they have the sand and gravel for the foundations of Nero's Circus. Now listen to this, my lord! As you know, the Trans-Tiber is full of Jews, and they've been very hard on the Christians lately. You recall the uproar they caused in the time of the divine Claudius and how he finally had to drive them out of Rome? Well, since they've been back and feeling safe under the protection of the divine Augusta, they've been harder than ever on the Christians. I've seen it! I can swear to it! There's been no edict against the Christians, at least not yet, but the Jews denounce them to the prefect for all kinds of things—saying they kill children, worship an ass, and practice rites that haven't been approved by the senate. And they beat them up, too, and attack their prayer houses and hound them so fiercely the Christians have to hide from them."

"What are you after, Chilon?" Vinicius snapped, impatient. "Where are you heading with all this?"

"Where am I heading? While the Jews' temples are out in the open all over the Trans-Tiber, my lord, the Christians have to hide theirs. They gather in empty sheds and abandoned quarries outside city walls. Those who live in the Trans-Tiber chose the one I've just been talking about. Now that the city's burning, they're sure to be praying. We'll find whole swarms of them underground if we look there.

So I suggest that we stop there on our way. And that's where I'm heading!"

"But you've just said that Linus went to Ostrianum!" Vinicius cried, angry with impatience.

"And you, great lord, just promised me a house with a vineyard in Ameriola," Chilon countered, "so I'm going to look for the young lady wherever she might be. They might have gone back to the Trans-Tiber once the fires started. . . . They could've gone around the city just as we are doing. . . . I mean, Linus has a house there, doesn't he? He might've wanted to see if it was all right. And if they did, then I swear to you by Persephone, my lord, that we'll find them in those underground excavations. Or we'll hear something about them."

"You could be right." Vinicius nodded. "Lead the way."

Chilon turned left toward the hillside without another word.

The slope hid the fires for a moment, so they were suddenly plunged into shadows even though the surrounding heights were alive with light. They turned left past the circus and slipped into a narrow gorge where there was no light of any kind, but Vinicius caught sight of gleaming lanterns at the other end.

"There they are!" Chilon hissed. "There'll be more of them tonight than ever, because all their Trans-Tiber prayer houses are either burned or choked with smoke. Like everything else there."

"Yes," said Vinicius. "I can hear them singing."

The sound of singing came to them out of a tunnel cut into the hillside, and lanterns vanished into the dark hole one after another. More quiet human shapes emerged from side passages, and soon Vinicius and Chilon found themselves walking with a great many other people.

Chilon slid off his mule and beckoned to a skinny lad who was walking nearby.

"Hold our mules, will you?" he said and tossed him the reins. "I'm a priest of Christ and a bishop too. You'll have my blessings and for-giveness for your sins."

Then he joined Vinicius.

After a moment they pushed into the mouth of the cave with a group of others. They followed a dark tunnel, barely lit by the pale glow of hand lamps and little portable lanterns, until they came to a wide stone cavern.

This was where the circus pavement slabs must have been quarried, because the cavern walls were made of fresh-cut stone. Torches burned here, as well as hand-carried lamps and lanterns, and the light was better. Vinicius could see a whole throng of people kneeling with upraised arms. He didn't see Ligia, Linus or the apostle Peter anywhere, but all the faces around him were solemn with feeling. Some showed fear. Others, hope. All were hushed with quiet expectation. The torchlight glinted in the whites of upraised eyes. Sweat beaded foreheads as white as chalk. Some sang hymns, others beat their chests, yet others gasped the name of Jesus as if they were in the grip of fever. It was clear they expected something extraordinary to happen at any moment.

Then the hymns died down.

Crispus, whom Vinicius recalled from his stay at Miriam's, suddenly appeared above the assembly in a niche gouged out of the cavern wall by the removal of a giant boulder. His face was pale, stern, fanatical and judgmental. He seemed half delirious as he scrawled his blessings in the twilight air. All eyes fixed upon him anxiously, as if hoping for some encouragement and consolation, but what the people heard was a ranting, hurried voice, thick with foreboding.

"Repent your sins!" he boomed. "The time is upon us! God has unleashed the fires of his wrath on that town of murder and corruption! The hour of his judgment is at hand, the time of doom and anger. . . . The Lord said he would come again, and now you will see him! But this time he won't be coming as the sacrificial lamb who offered his blood to redeem your sins but as a terrible judge who will throw the sinners and the unbelievers into eternal darkness! Woe to the world! Damnation to the sinners, who will find no mercy! I see you, Christ! I see you! The stars are raining down upon the earth, the earth splits and trembles and the dead are rising, and you are coming to the sound of trumpets amid your legions of avenging angels, with thunderbolts and lightnings. . . . I see you, Christ! I hear you!"

Silent now, he cocked his head and appeared to listen, his eyes fixed blindly on some terrible immensity that only he could see. Then the cavern began to echo with a deep, subterranean thunder, and another and another, on and on, pounding like a drum. Whole streets of burned-out buildings were crashing to the ground in the flaming city, sending reverberations deep under the surface. Most of the gathered Christians took these unearthly sounds for the end of the world. Their faith in the Second Coming was so much a part of their reality, along with their expectation of a final judgment, that the destruction of Rome in a fiery holocaust was all the proof they needed.

Fear of God seized all of them. "Judgment Day!" shrill voices cried. "It's coming!"

Some hid their faces in their hands, convinced that the earth would split open around them and infernal beasts and demons would leap out of the abyss and devour all sinners.

"Have mercy, Christ!" they cried. "Be merciful, Redeemer!"

Others beat their chests and confessed their sins or threw themselves into each other's arms so as to have some loving person near in their final moments. But there were also others who showed no fear; their faces, bright with unearthly smiles, shone with joy, as if they were about to ascend to the heavens. Some fell into religious ecstasy and broke out in a babble of strange tongues. "Sleepers, awake!" some voice boomed out of the darkest recess of the cave, and Crispus shouted, "Keep watch! Witness his coming!"

From time to time a deep silence fell on everyone, as if in breathless expectation of whatever was about to happen. The distant thunder of collapsing structures, tumbling in what seemed like whole districts at a time, resounded in the sudden hush, and then the moans, cries and prayers broke out again.

"Have mercy, Redeemer!"

Crispus began to shout again: "Renounce your earthly goods, because soon there won't be a foot of ground beneath you! Renounce those dear to you, for the Lord will show no mercy to those who loved their wives and children more than him. Cursed be those who care more for God's creatures than for their Creator! Woe to the rich and powerful! Woe to those who love the pleasures of the flesh . . . man, woman and child!"

A rumbling tremor shook the quarry with greater violence than before. Everyone threw himself facedown on the ground, arms spread wide in the shape of a cross to ward off the demons. There was the sound of panting breaths, terrified whispers of "Jesus, Jesus, Jesus!" and, here and there, the tearful wail of children.

And then a quiet voice spoke from high above the dark, prostrated mass: "Peace be with you!"

It was the voice of the apostle Peter, who had stepped into the cavern a few moments earlier. All fear vanished at the sound of his voice, just as a frightened flock is calmed when it sees the shepherd. The people rose everywhere around him. Those who were near him gathered at his knees as if seeking shelter.

"Lift up your hearts," he said, stretching his hands over them. "Why are you so troubled? Which of you can guess what will happen at the final hour? Yes, the Lord punished Babylon with fire, but you who are washed clean by baptism and redeemed by the blood of the

Lamb will find only mercy, and you will go to him with his name on your lips when your moment comes. Peace be with you!"

After hearing Crispus' grim and merciless voice of doom, this fell on the gathering like a soothing balm. Instead of cowering in fear, they felt comforted by God's love for them. This was the Christ they had come to honor and adore: the mild and patient Lamb whose mercy soared a hundredfold above the worst that any man could do, rather than the stern and unforgiving judge. Peace came to them all. Hope and gratitude filled them and lifted their spirits. "We are your sheep!" they cried. "Lead us to your pastures!"

"Don't leave us in the hour of wrath!" cried those who were nearer, kneeling at his feet.

Vinicius joined them, caught up the edge of his ragged cloak and bowed his head before him.

"Help me, master," he said. "I looked for her in the smoke and fire and in the crowds as well, but I can't find her anywhere. I trust in you. I believe that you can give her back to me again."

Peter placed his hand on the young man's head. "Believe and follow me," he said.

‹54›

ROME KEPT ON BURNING. The Circus Maximus tumbled into ruins; soon afterward entire blocks and streets collapsed into rubble. Pillars of fire shot briefly into the sky after each cave-in. The wind, shifting all the time, blew with hurricane force out of the sea and carried flame, hot coals and charred embers to the Caelian, Esquiline and Viminal heights, although some attempts were being made to halt and fight the fire.

Tigellinus arrived from Antium on the third day and ordered rows of homes leveled on the near slopes of the Esquiline to form a firebreak. But this was just a stop-gap measure, designed to save the remnants of the city. Whatever was already burning was quite beyond saving. It was also time to decide how to cope with the disaster's other consequences. Incalculable wealth had perished right along with Rome. Everything its inhabitants possessed had gone up in flames, and hundreds of thousands of beggared people were camping outside the walls with nothing to eat. Vast stores of food had burned in the city, and with the chaos and collapse of all administrative functions, no replacements were brought in. The desperate masses grew hungry by the second day. No relief orders went to Ostia until Tigellinus took charge of the firefighting, and in the meantime the dispossessed were becoming dangerous.

Crowds of women lay siege to the house on Aqua Appia where Tigellinus had set up his temporary quarters; they howled for bread and shelter from morning to night. The whole praetorian corps was marched in from the great walled camp between Via Salaria and Via Nomentana to keep some kind of order, but they barely managed to hold the throngs at bay. In some places the hard-bitten mercenaries fought for their own lives against enraged armed mobs. Elsewhere, unarmed crowds pointed at the burning city and shouted, "Isn't that enough? Do you have to murder us as well?"

They rained shrill curses on Caesar, the Augustans and the prefect's soldiers. Their rage swelled by the minute as the hours passed. Watching the thousands of campfires glittering around the walls at night, Tigellinus thought of them as the siege fires of a hostile army.

Ground flour was carted in at his command, not just from Ostia but from all the surroundings towns and villages, along with every loaf of baked bread that could be seized throughout the territory, causing the most chaotic uproar yet. It was still night when the first of the wagon trains reached the Emporium, but the starved people pulled down the main doors on the Aventine side and seized the whole supply in minutes. It was a hellish scene in the red glare of the conflagration: Mobs fought like wild beasts for every loaf and trampled stacks of them underfoot, while the entire space between the granary and the arches of Drusus and Germanicus was littered with ripped flour sacks and turned as white as snow. The pandemonium lasted until soldiers occupied the surrounding buildings and scattered the crowds with catapults and arrows.

Not since Brennus and the Gauls set fire to the city had Rome seen such an unparalleled disaster, and that one wasn't quite as terrible as this. At least the Capitol had escaped destruction at the hands of Brennus. This time it burned, gripped in a wreath of fire. The marble didn't actually burst into flame, but when the wind blew the flames apart at night, showing a momentary glimpse of its crowning temple, the rows of columns under the lofty portico of Jupiter pulsed and glowed as red as burning coals. Moreover Rome's population at the time of Brennus was a single, homogeneous entity, disciplined and devoted to their gods and city; now the immense crowds of slaves and freedmen camped around the walls babbled in all the languages of the world, not restrained by any sense of civic pride or duty and ready to turn on all authority under the pressure of its needs and hunger.

In some ways the immensity of the holocaust itself served as a restraint; it was so terrifying that it robbed the rabble of the will to act and cowed it into a sort of bewildered submission. Disease and famine, sure to follow the fiery disaster, could prove quite as devastating, especially since the scorching summer heat filled the cup of misery to the brim. It was impossible to breathe the burning air, hot from the sun and fire.

Night brought no relief. On the contrary, it created its own kind of hell, although at least it hid the sweltering human sea that spread around the city. But daylight painted a demonic picture of a vast metropolis spewing smoke and flames amid its hills like a colossal volcanic eruption, while sprawled around it as far as the Alban hills was one vast, immeasurable bivouac of lean-to shacks, tents, camp-fires, carts, barrows, litters, makeshift stalls and crude brushwood shelters, choked with an impenetrable cloud of dust and smoke. The merciless July sun burned as red as fire on the roaring human masses, loud with shouts, threats and curses and filled with fear and hatred.

It was a monstrous hodgepodge of humanity, mostly at its worst. Men, women and children were indistinguishable in their misery. Genuine descendants of the founding Quirites jostled for space with Greeks and the shaggy-haired, pale-eyed people of the north, Africans and Asians. Roman citizens, slaves, freedmen, gladiators, peddlers, artisans, peasant serfs and soldiers massed into a single human sea washing like a tide against an island of fire.

All kinds of rumors swept across this human sea, the way winds send breakers surging across a beach. Some were good, others threatening. People claimed that huge cargoes of grain and clothing were to be stockpiled in the Emporium for free distribution. Others insisted that all the provinces of Africa and Asia were to be looted by Caesar's order, and the collected treasure would be divided among everyone in Rome so that each man could build a new house of his own. But there were also tales that all the water in the aqueducts was poisoned, because Nero wanted to annihilate the people as well as their city so that he would be able to move to Greece or Egypt and rule the world from there.

Each rumor swept rapidly through the rabble with the speed of lightning; each gripped its own credulous supporters, causing wild outbursts of hope, anger, fear or fury. At last a kind of fever seized the swarming thousands: The Christian belief that fire would come down from the skies to destroy the world and that the end was near claimed new adherents every day among these worshipers of the pagan gods. People lost their minds or sat slumped in numb hopelessness and indifference. Some saw the gods among the red-tinted clouds, peering down at the end of life on earth; they either cursed them or begged for mercy with outstretched arms.

Meanwhile the soldiers kept tearing down the buildings along the edges of the Esquiline and Caelian hills and through the Trans-Tiber, so that most of it survived. But the main and richest portions of the city collapsed in flaming ruins, along with priceless works of art and vast treasures gathered through centuries of triumphant conquest, magnificent temples, and the most precious monuments of Rome's past and glory. It was expected that only a few outlying districts would escape destruction and that hundreds of thousands would be left without shelter.

And then a fresh rumor swept the homeless masses: The soldiers, it was said, weren't wrecking all those dwellings to contain the fire; the so-called firebreaks were just another way to ensure that the city vanished without a trace. In each report Tigellinus begged Caesar to hurry his arrival so that his presence might calm the desperate population, but Nero took his time. He set out only when the flames engulfed the huge *domus transitoria*, the city's hostel for visiting dignitaries. Then he moved with all the speed possible for his enormous entourage so he wouldn't miss the high point of the fire.

⟨ 5 5 ⟩

THE FIRE REACHED the Via Nomentana, swung with the wind toward the Via Lata and the Tiber, swept around the Capitol, engulfed the Forum Boarium, and roared back to the Palatine, destroying everything it had missed before. Tigellinus mustered all his praetorians in preparation for Nero's imminent arrival and dispatched one courier after another to assure him that the spectacle would be at its best when he finally got there.

But Nero wanted to reach Rome after dark. That would give him the most satisfying and inspiring view of the dying city. With this in mind, he halted near Alban Lake to practice a variety of poses, expressions and gestures. He summoned the tragedian Aliturus to coach him in his tent, arguing fiercely about whether he should raise both his arms while crying out to Heaven, or merely one, letting the other hang limply at his side with the lute in his hand. The verse in question was "O sacred city, which men had thought more lasting than Mount Ida, the hiding place of the infant Zeus, enduring and eternal," and it was the most important question in the world to him.

He was still unsure about it when he set out at nightfall on the last stage of his journey. He questioned Petronius as to whether he should insert a few soaring blasphemies at this point, bearing in mind the tragedy of the moment and the requirements of artistic realism.

"I mean," he argued, "wouldn't it be natural for Priam to curse the gods at this point? Wouldn't such bitter words burst spontaneously from any man forced to look at the destruction of his patrimony?"

At last, near midnight, he came close to the city walls, along with his immense following of courtiers, senators, nobles, knights, freedmen, slaves, women and children of both sexes.

Sixteen thousand praetorians massed around him in full battle order to assure his safety and keep the raging populace at a proper distance. The people howled, hissed and hurled curses at him but didn't dare actually attack him. In fact there was even a flurry of applause from the worst and lowest of the rabble, which had nothing to lose in the fire and everything to gain from the expected bounty of free grain, oil, clothing and liberal gifts of money.

The blare of massed battle horns and trumpets, blown at Tigellinus' order, finally drowned out all the yells, curses, hisses and applause, and Nero halted for a moment at the Ostian Gate.

"Here I am," he declaimed, "the homeless ruler of a homeless people! Ah, where shall I rest my wretched head this night?"

He climbed partway up the incline of the Clivus Delphini, a section of the Sacred Way that wound toward the Capitol, and then ascended a stairway built for the occasion to the top of the Appian aqueduct. Crowding behind him were all the Augustans and a choir of singers who carried zithers, lutes and other instruments.

All of them held their breaths, eyes fixed upon Caesar, waiting to hear him make some unforgettable pronouncement they would do well to remember for their own survival. But he stood mute: silent, ceremonial in his purple toga and gold laurel wreath, staring into the raging power of the flames. When Terpnos handed him a golden lute, he lifted his eyes to the fire-drenched sky as if for inspiration.

The people pointed him out from a distance: a bloodred apparition in that tragic light. Beyond him, in the distance, the flames hissed like serpents, and the holiest of Rome's heritage turned into heaps of ashes. The temple of Hercules, raised by Evander, burned like a giant torch. So did the temple of Jupiter Stator, the city's founding deity, and the one to Luna built by Servius Tullius, the sixth king of Rome, and the palace of Pompillius Numa, who was the second king. On fire was the sanctuary of Vesta, dedicated to all the Roman household gods. The Capitol glowed red under its fiery mane. The whole historic past that gave Rome its soul was burning away, and Caesar, lute in hand, stood with the face of a tragic actor and with no thought of his stricken nation; he was tuned entirely to how he stood, the pathos of each word he uttered, and how best to describe the catastrophe before him in order to attain the greatest admiration and bring the most applause.

He loathed this city. He hated everyone who lived there. He was enraptured that he could finally see a tragedy similar to the one he had written about. The poetaster was overjoyed; the declaimer felt himself inspired; the thrill-seeker feasted on the terrifying spectacle and mused that even the fall of Troy was nothing in comparison with the destruction of this gigantic city. What more could he demand? Here was Rome, master of the world, burning like a pyre, and there he stood on the arches of an aqueduct, a golden lute in hand, seen and admired by all, magnificent and poetic. Somewhere below him in the darkness, a mass of people seethed and muttered like a distant storm! But let them! What did the people matter? Centuries would pass, thousands of years would flow by, and mankind would remember and honor the poet who sang about the fall of Troy on this amazing night. Who was Homer beside him? Who was Apollo himself with his hollow lute?

He raised his arms, struck a chord and intoned in Priam's tragic words: "O home of my fathers, my most precious cradle!"

In the open air, his voice seemed strangely weak, pale and uncertain against the booming roar of the fire and the distant growl of the thousands massed in the plain below, while the accompaniment sounded like the buzzing of a fly. But the senators, officeholders and Augustans gathered on the aqueduct bowed their heads in mute admiration. He sang on and on, striving for an ever sadder note. The choir repeated the last few lines while he caught his breath; then he tossed the tragedian's trailing cloak off his shoulder with a gesture taught by Aliturus, plucked the lyre and went on. When he came to the end of what he had composed, he started to improvise, searching for lofty comparisons in the sight before him, and his fleshy, flushed face quivered and became transformed. The destruction of his native city left him quite unmoved, but he was swept away by the pathos of his own performance. Intoxicated by the sound of his own voice, he let the lute clang to the ground, threw his cloak tragically around him and remained as fixed as if he'd turned to stone, much like the mournful figures of Niobe in the forecourt of the Palatine.

A storm of applause broke into the silence after a hushed moment, and a howl of outrage answered from the masses. No one there doubted any longer it was Caesar who ordered the city burned to create a spectacle he might serenade. But Nero merely turned his hurt eyes upon the Augustans and smiled with resignation like a deeply and unjustly injured man.

"See how the Romans appreciate me and poetry," he said with a sigh.

"The scum!" Vatinius cried. "Have the praetorians charge them, my lord!"

Nero pondered briefly, then turned to Tigellinus. "Can I count on the troops?" he asked. "Will they remain loyal?"

"Yes, divinity!" the prefect assured him.

"You may trust in their loyalty," Petronius said coldly, "but not in their numbers. Stay where you are for now, because it's safer here. But something must be done to pacify these people."

Seneca and the consul Licinius agreed. Meanwhile fury swelled in the crowds below. The people armed themselves with stones, tent poles, planks ripped out of wagons and any piece of iron they could find. A few moments later several cohort commanders rode up to report that the massed mobs were pressing their lines so hard the praetorians had great difficulty keeping their formations. Having no orders to attack, they didn't know what to do.

"Ye gods!" Nero said. "What a night! Flames on one side and the fury of a human ocean on the other!"

He started searching at once for the best metaphors to illustrate the danger of the moment, but the pale faces and worried glances he saw around him suddenly frightened him.

"Give me a dark cloak with a hood!" he shouted. "Is there really going to be a battle?"

"My lord," Tigellinus quavered, "I've done what I could! But the situation's getting dangerous. . . . Speak to the people, highness, and promise them something."

Nero, however, didn't want to get closer to the mobs than he already was. "I?" he cried dramatically. "You want the emperor himself to speak to the rabble? Let somebody else do it in my name. Who'll do it?"

"I will," Petronius said calmly.

"Go then, my friend! You're always there when I need you most. . . . Go and promise them anything you can think of!"

The look Petronius turned on Nero's entourage lay between indifference and contempt. "You senators," he said coldly, "those of you who happen to be here . . . and also Piso, Nerva and Senecio . . . follow me!"

He moved slowly off the aqueduct. Those he had called to follow did so with some hesitation, but they quickly took some courage from his calmness. Once he stood on firm ground under the arches of the aqueduct, armed only with a reedlike ivory cane he used occasionally for walking, he ordered a white horse brought to him at once. He mounted and led his cavalcade through the deep ranks of praetorian infantry toward the vast mobs howling in the darkness.

Coming up on them, he forced his horse among them. All he could see around him in the lurid light were raised fists that clutched every sort of weapon, raging eyes, sweating faces, and roaring, foam-flecked mouths. The maddened waves coiled and beat around him, and beyond them swirled a sea of bobbing, moving, terrifying faces.

He kicked his horse into the thick of the howling rabble; poles, wagon chains, pitchforks and even swords whirled above his head, and fierce fists clutched at him and his horse's bridle. But he pressed on—unmoved, indifferent and contemptuous—riding deeper into the furious mob. Once in a while he lashed some particularly persistent fellow with his ivory cane as if this were merely an ordinary crowd, through which he would force his way in the same demanding and expectant manner, and this calm self-assurance started to puzzle and surprise the mob. Then they recognized him.

"Petronius! Petronius! It's the arbiter," several voices shouted, and then his name boomed out all around: "Petronius! Petronius"

The wild swirl of enraged, glaring faces became less dangerous and threatening as the name spread wider through the crowd. The roar lost some of its ferocity. The exquisite patrician never made an effort to please the common rabble, but he had long been the people's favorite among the Augustans. He had a reputation for careless generosity and humanity, almost never noted in the ruling class, and the rabble thought him a friend of the people. His popularity soared immeasurably since the Pedanius Secundus affair when he spoke against the savage verdict that sent all the slaves of the murdered prefect to mass execution. Slaves, in particular, loved him from that moment, ready to worship him the way oppressed and bitterly mistreated people turn to anyone who shows them even a shred of compassion. Curiosity also played its part in this special moment; everyone thought Nero had sent him as his personal spokesman and wanted to know what Caesar had to say.

He took off his white, purple-edged toga, the mark of the highest-born patrician, and started whirling it overhead, signaling that he wished to speak.

"Silence! Silence!" voices began shouting everywhere at once and the vast throngs grew silent. He squared his shoulders and lifted his head.

"Citizens!" He spoke firmly and calmly, his strong voice carrying far. "You who are near, tell those who don't hear me what I have to say. And I want all of you to start acting like human beings, not a pack of wild beasts in the arenas. And at once!"

"We're listening!" screamed the mob. "We hear you!"

"Hear this, then! The city will be rebuilt, top to bottom. The gardens of Lucullus, Maecenas, Julius Caesar and Agrippina will be turned over to you for your use anytime you please. Starting tomorrow there'll be free distribution of corn, wine and oil, so much that each of you can stuff his belly until he chokes! Then Caesar will stage such games for you as the world has never seen, along with gifts and banquets. You'll be richer after the fire than you were before!"

He heard a deep growling mutter all around him, spreading out from the center like ripples when a stone is tossed into a pool. As word reached those too far to hear him, shouts broke out and grew. Some were still angry but some were approving. Suddenly all of the pent-up rage, fury and hope came together in a single, universal and colossal roar:

"*Panem et circenses!* Give us bread and circuses!"

Petronius draped his toga around him and sat listening calmly, as still and remote in his snow white clothing as a marble statue. The frightful howl grew and swelled, now roaring even louder than the fire, breaking out at the farthest reaches of the immense human mass and booming out of its darkest depths.

"Bread and circuses!"

But Caesar's messenger apparently had something more to say because he sat waiting. He raised his hand and signaled for silence.

"You'll have your bread and circuses!" he said with disdain. "That's your Caesar's promise. Now give a cheer for the man who feeds you, clothes you, puts a roof over your miserable heads and fills your leaky pockets! And then go to bed, you vulgar scum, because it's not long until sunrise!"

He turned his horse around and rode out toward the praetorians, hitting the heads and faces of those in the way with light taps of his ivory staff. When he reached the foot of the aqueduct, it seemed that another kind of riot was about to break out at the top. Nero's court didn't understand the roar of the mob demanding bread and circuses; they took it for a fresh outburst of fury, and the Augustans were now close to panic. No one expected Petronius to come back alive, so when Nero caught sight of him, he ran to meet him at the head of the stairway.

"Well?" he asked, his face white with fear. "What's going on there? What are they doing? Has the battle started?"

Petronius took a slow, deep breath, as if to fill his lungs with cleaner air.

"By Pollux!" he drawled. "They sweat and stink, that's what they're doing! Bring me some smelling salts, somebody, or I'll faint."

He turned to Caesar. "I promised them grain, oil, access to the gardens and some games," he said. "They all adore you again. You can hear them cheering, although you never saw such ugly, chapped lips. Ugh!" He shuddered slightly. "Gods, how these common people stink!"

"I had the praetorians ready!" Tigellinus tried to focus some credit on himself. "I'd have silenced them forever if you hadn't calmed them. It's a pity, Caesar, you wouldn't let me use the necessary force."

Petronius threw him a calm, disdainful glance, as if aware of things beyond this moment. "Nothing's lost yet," he said with a shrug. "You might get your chance tomorrow."

But Caesar was listening only to himself. "No, no, that's all over now," he said. "I'll have the gardens open to them and order the feeding. Thank you, Petronius! I'll give them games! And I'll give a public performance of this anthem I sang for you here."

Too moved to say much more just then, he rested his hand on Petronius' shoulder until the onrush of relief and gratitude had time to abate.

"Be honest with me, though." He turned to what really mattered to him, now or ever. "What did you think of me as an epic singer?"

"I thought you were worthy of the moment, just as the moment was worthy of you," Petronius said quietly, looking steadily at the conflagration. "But let's keep watching a while longer and say good-bye to life as we knew it. Farewell, ancient Rome!"

‹56›

MEANWHILE, ON THE OTHER SIDE of the burning city, the words of the apostle Peter calmed the frightened Christians. Judgment Day, in which they all fervently believed, didn't seem about to fall on them straightaway, and the end of the world wouldn't come just yet.

They began to think they might live to see the end of the reign of Nero, whom they believed to be the Antichrist, before they witnessed God's retribution for his crimes and their own end as well. Much encouraged, when the prayers were over they started to leave the caverns and disperse, going to their temporary shelters and even back to the Trans-Tiber itself. The wind had changed there, the fire that had been set in several widely scattered places had turned back toward the river, and the devastation grew no wider.

The apostle also left the quarry, along with Vinicius and Chilon, who trailed behind them, praying silently as he made his way through the long dark maze of the buried tunnels. The young tribune didn't dare interrupt his prayers; he walked in silence for a while, although he kept begging mutely with his eyes and shook with anxiety.

But there was no way to question the apostle. People kept flocking around him in the tunnels to kiss his hands or the edges of his cloak; mothers held out their children to him; others knelt in the darkened corridors, held their lanterns over their heads and asked for his blessing; and many others sang loudly as they walked behind them. Nor was it any better in the gully outside. It was only when they came to the flat open country, with the flaming city before them, that the apostle blessed it with a threefold sign of the cross and turned to Vinicius.

"Don't worry," he told him. "It's not far from here to the ditchdigger's hut where we'll find Linus, Ligia and her faithful servant. Christ means her to be yours and has kept her for you."

Vinicius swayed then and had to lean against a boulder. His strength had been sapped by his headlong gallop from Antium, his struggles beyond the city walls, and his search for Ligia among the hot billows of suffocating smoke. Lack of sleep and terrible anxiety drained him even further. Hearing that this dearest and most precious person was near and that he was about to see her nearly knocked the last of his strength from him. He felt so weak that he slid down at the apostle's feet, clasped his knees in silence and stayed like that, unable to speak.

But the apostle rejected any show of gratitude or worship for himself. "It's Christ you must thank and worship!" he said. "Not me! Never me!"

"What a great god!" Chilon said behind them. "But what am I to do with those two mules we have waiting over there?"

"Rise and come with me," Peter said, and he took Vinicius' hand.

Vinicius rose. Tears glinted in his eyes in the red light of the conflagration. His face was pale with feeling. His lips were moving slightly as if praying.

"Let us go," he murmured.

"What about the mules, then?" Chilon asked again. "Maybe the prophet would rather ride than walk?"

Vinicius had to pause to think of an answer. He had no idea. But the quarryman's hut stood a stone's throw away, as the apostle said.

"Take them back to Macrinus," he told Chilon.

"Forgive me, great lord, if I remind you about the house in Ameriola." Chilon nudged the young man's memory. "It's easy to forget something that trivial in the face of such a terrible disaster."

"You'll get it."

"I've never doubted it, great grandson of Pompilius Numa! But now that the apostle heard you promise it, I won't even mention the vineyard it's supposed to have. *Pax vobiscum*. I'll find you later, my lord. *Pax vobiscum*."

"And peace be with you," Peter and Vinicius replied together.

Then both turned right, heading for the sandpits, and Chilon turned left toward the city.

"Master," Vinicius said as they walked, "baptize me so I can truly call myself a Christian. I love him with all the power of my soul. Wash me free of sin because my heart is ready. I'll do whatever he commands us, and you can tell me what I may do beyond that."

"Love all men like your brothers," the apostle told him. "That's the only way to serve him."

"Yes! I understand that now. And I also feel it deep inside me. I believed in the old Roman gods when I was a child but I never loved them. But I love him, and I'd be overjoyed to die for him."

He stared into the red sky overhead, gripped by a soaring passion. "Because he's the one and only God!" he went on. "Because he's the God of mercy and compassion! Even if the whole world should burn down, not just this one city, I'll still worship him and be a witness to his truth."

"And he'll bless you and yours," finished the apostle.

They had turned into another gully where a pale light glimmered at the other end.

"That's the quarryman's hut." Peter pointed. "That's where we took shelter when Linus fell ill while we tried to get back across the Tiber."

Soon afterward they were there.

The hut was actually a cave dug into the closed end of the narrow passage, with a single wall across its mouth built of mud and reeds. The door was closed, but the fire-lit interior showed through the hole that served as a window. A gigantic figure loomed out of the shadows before them to ask who they were.

"Christ's servants," Peter said. "Peace be with you, Ursus."

Ursus stooped to clasp the apostle's knees, then recognized Vinicius.

"And you're here, too, master?" he asked, pleased to see him. He seized the tribune's wrist and kissed his hand like a loyal servant. "Blessed be the Lamb for the joy you'll bring to Callina."

He stepped back and threw open the door. They went in. Linus lay ill on a straw pallet, his face gaunt and his forehead as yellow as old ivory. Ligia sat by the hearth holding a string of small fish apparently meant for supper. Sure it was Ursus coming in, and too busy with the fish to look up, she paid no attention. But Vinicius stepped close, spoke her name and stretched his arms toward her. She jumped up then, joy and surprise flashing across her face, and ran into his open arms without a word, like a lost child who suddenly finds her father or mother after days of fear and disaster.

He threw his arms around her and pressed her to his chest with the same depth of feeling he would show if she were saved for him by a miracle. Breaking his hold he took her face in his hands, his fingers at her temples, and kissed her eyes and forehead. He hugged her again, repeating her name. Then he kissed her hands and pressed his head to her knees, happily greeting and adoring her. His joy, he knew, was as boundless as his luck and love.

He began to tell her about his wild ride from Antium and how he had looked for her outside the walls in all the smoke and in Linus's

home; how worried and afraid for her he had been all that time; what
agonies he had gone through until the apostle told him where she
was.

"But now that I've found you," he said, "I won't leave you again.
Not with that fire and those crazed mobs out there. People are killing
one another right outside the walls. The slaves are going wild. There's
murder and looting. God only knows what other disasters are going
to fall on Rome. But I'll save you, dearest, and all the rest of you as
well. Listen, my love! Why don't you all come with me to Antium?
We'll get a ship there and sail to Sicily. My estates are yours, you
know that, and so are my villas. Hear me now! In Sicily you'll find
Aulus and Pomponia. I'll take you to her and then ask her for you
properly, as it should be done. Surely you're no longer afraid of me,
carissima. I'm not yet baptized, but you can ask Peter if I didn't tell
him while we were on our way here that I want to be a true follower
of Christ. I asked him to baptize me at once, right in this quarryman's hut if need be. Trust me. All of you can trust me."

Ligia's face seemed aglow with joy as she listened to him. All of
the people in the hut had lived for years in uncertainty and fear, first
because of the hostility of their fellow Jews—Christianity was a dangerous revolutionary threat to their religion and their way of life—
and now because of the conflagration and its various expected
consequences. Moving to Sicily would open a new peaceful era in
their lives and put an end to all such mental turmoil. If Vinicius had
wanted to take her alone, she might have refused; she wouldn't want
to leave Peter and Linus behind. But didn't he invite them all? Didn't
he say, "All of you come with me. My lands and villas belong to you
all"?

She then did what Roman brides did only at the marriage altar. She
took his hand to kiss it in a sign of acceptance and submission and
said: "Your hearth is my own."

She didn't know how the others would take this declaration.
Would Peter think it too forward and immodest? What would Linus
say? Would Vinicius find it premature? She flushed deeply and stood
in the firelight with her head cast down, but a quick glance at her
lover's face quickly reassured her. All she could see there was total
adoration.

"Rome burns by Caesar's order." Vinicius turned to Peter. "He was
complaining even back in Antium that he'd never seen a great city
destroyed by a fire. If such a monstrous crime was not beyond that
man, just think what he might do next. Who knows if he won't call

out the army to slaughter all survivors? Who can tell what kind of decrees and persecutions will come after the fire, or if this catastrophe won't unleash rebellion, civil war, massacres and famine? Protect yourselves from all that, and let's protect Ligia! You can wait out the storm in Sicily and come back when things quiet down again to continue your work in what's left of Rome."

Some wild, distant shouts full of fear-crazed fury broke out outside just then, coming from the direction of the Vatican plantations as if to confirm Vinicius' premonitions. Then the quarryman who owned the hut ran in and hastily barred the door.

"They're slaughtering each other near Nero's circus!" he shouted. "The slaves and gladiators are massacring the people!"

"You hear him?" asked Vinicius.

"The cup of evil is full to the brim," the apostle said, nodding, "and fresh calamities will spill over us like a raging sea. Take this girl whom God has destined for you"—he turned to Vinicius—"and carry her to safety. And let Linus, who is ill, and Ursus go with you."

But Vinicius wouldn't dream of turning his back on Peter, whom he'd come to love with all his passionate and impulsive soul. "I swear to you, master," he cried out, "that I won't leave you alone in this danger!"

"The Lord will bless your good intentions," the apostle told him. "But haven't you heard that Christ told me three times on the shores of the Sea of Galilee that I was to be a shepherd to his flock?"

Vinicius had no reply.

"No one entrusted you with anybody's care," Peter went on quietly, "and yet you say you won't leave me behind to be destroyed. Think then, how can I abandon all the people Christ placed in my keeping? He didn't leave us when a sudden storm caught us in an open boat and made us weak with fear. So how can I, his servant, fail to follow my master's example?"

Suddenly Linus lifted his gaunt, illness-ravaged face and smiled at Peter. "And how am I not to follow your example, master?"

Vinicius started to rub his head like a troubled man who struggled mutely with himself, battling his best intentions. Then he caught Ligia's hand and turned to the others.

"Listen to me!" he said with the harsh determination of a Roman soldier. "Hear me, Peter! And you, Linus! And you, too, *carrissima!* I said what reason prompted. But you all follow another kind of logic, one that requires obedience to the Savior's will rather than your own safety. I didn't understand that, but I do now. I spoke according to the rules of my old nature, not yet able to see the other truth beyond it, even though it wasn't my own safety I was concerned about. But because I love Christ and want to be his servant, I kneel before you now and swear what the commandment of love and sacrifice demand. I won't leave my brothers in their hour of danger!"

He knelt then, gripped by a vast inner exaltation, and raised his eyes and arms to the unseen sky.

"Do I finally understand you, Christ?" he cried out. "Am I worthy of you at last?"

His arms and hands were trembling. His eyes gleamed with tears. His body quivered with love and dedication. The apostle Peter picked up a clay water jug and stepped quietly toward him.

"I baptize you in the name of the Father and of the Son and of the Holy Ghost," he said in a ringing, ceremonial voice. "Amen!"

Vinicius' fervor swept across them all. It seemed to them that some unearthly light was filling the small room, that they were hearing music from another world, that the cavern roof had parted overhead and rows of angels drifted down toward them, and that a great cross glowed in the firmament above them while two hands, pierced and bleeding, were scrawling a blessing.

Meanwhile the howls of fighting people and the roar of flames boomed in the outside air.

‹57›

TENS OF THOUSANDS of people were camping in the magnificent gardens thrown open to them by Caesar, once owned by Domitius and Agrippina. They camped on the Field of Mars, in the gardens of Pompey, Sallust and Maecenas, under temple porticoes, in ball courts, in the delightful suburban summer homes of the rich and in cattle pens. The peacocks, flamingos, swans, ostriches, gazelles, African antelopes and deer that served as living ornaments in the parks and gardens went into the cooking pots of the squatting rabble. Shiploads of food came in such quantities from Ostia that one could walk dry-shod across the moored rafts and boat decks from one bank of the Tiber to the other. Grain was sold at the unbelievably low price of three sesterces, and the poor didn't have to pay for it at all. Vast loads of wine, olive oil and chestnuts were brought to the city; huge herds and flocks of sheep and cattle were driven in each day from mountain pastures. The homeless beggars who skulked before fires in the back alleys of the Suburra and who starved in normal times now lived far better than they had ever hoped.

The specter of famine dwindled and disappeared, but it was far more difficult to deal with the robbery, violence and looting. Criminals of all kinds felt right at home under the open skies; they exclaimed their admiration for Caesar whenever he appeared and grabbed everything they wanted. Since all authority had vanished in the chaos and there weren't enough armed troops in place to impose any kind of discipline on the unleashed rabble, the things that happened in and around the city inhabited by the dregs of humanity defied imagination. Each night saw pitched battles, mass murders and the wholesale rape of women and young boys. Hundreds of people died every day in the fighting around the cattle pens at the Mugian Gate where the cattle herds were driven from throughout Campania. The banks of the Tiber were piled high each morning with corpses that no one bothered to collect for burial, and they stank and rotted in the scorching heat. Disease swept through the campgrounds and threatened to decimate what was left of the population.

Meanwhile the city burned on. It was only on the sixth day that the fire reached the cleared spaces of the Esquiline, where a vast number of homes had been pulled down for a fire break, and the conflagration slowed and ceased to spread. The scorched debris still pulsed with such a fierce red glow that no one could believe the catastrophe was over. Indeed, the conflagration flared up again on the seventh night, bursting out suddenly in the structures owned by Tigellinus. But it soon died down again for lack of fresh fuel. Only the gutted buildings collapsed on themselves for some time thereafter, hurling up sheets of flame and pillars of sparks. Gradually the glowing ruins started to darken on the surface. The bloodred light seeped slowly out of the night skies after sunset, and the sharp blue tongues of flame licked the heaps of burned charcoal and cinders and flickered throughout the scorched black wasteland after dark.

Four of Rome's fourteen administrative districts survived in some fashion, the Trans-Tiber among them. The rest were gone, devoured by the fire. When at last the heaped piles of scorched and gutted rubble began to cool under drifting ashes, the vast space between the Tiber and the Esquiline turned into a uniform gray plain, as grim and lifeless as a cemetery. Skeletal black chimneys stood among the ruins like funeral pillars among graves. Groups of grieving people drifted like ghosts among the columns in the daytime, searching for scraps of their lost possessions or the bones of vanished kin. At night only homeless dogs howled among the ashes and rubble of their former homes.

Despite the spectacular generosity with which Nero tried to soothe the furious population, he could not still their rage or silence the curses of the dispossessed. Only the mobs of cutthroats, thieves and beggars had anything to be pleased about, free as they were to eat, drink and pillage. But people who lost their loved ones along with everything they owned weren't likely to be satisfied with access to imperial gardens, handouts of free wheat or promises of further gifts and games. The catastrophe was just too incredible and overwhelming.

For those who still nourished some faint spark of patriotism and affection for their native city, rage gave way to despair as they heard that Caesar planned to build a new city from the ruins of their ancient *Roma* and call it Neropolis, so that even Rome's name would vanish from the earth. The tide of hatred that loomed and swelled around Nero frightened this Roman Caesar who depended on the goodwill of the rabble more than any emperor before him. No matter how the Augustans flattered him or how many lies he heard from Tigellinus, he was terrified of losing the mobs' volatile support in his grim life-or-death struggle with the old patrician families and the senate, whom he could terrorize so utterly only because the mobs always stood behind him.

The Augustans were no less alarmed because death and destruction might fall on them any day if Rome turned against them. Tigellinus made plans to bring in a few legions from Asia Minor; Vatinius, who giggled stupidly even when his face was slapped, lost all of his humor; and Vitelius couldn't even eat. Others began to plot how to avert the danger since none of them doubted that they would be doomed right along with Nero. Only Petronius stood a chance of coming out alive if their detested Caesar were swept away; no one else among the Augustans could count on living longer than a moment after Nero fell. They knew that all of Nero's madness and depravity, along with the monstrous crimes he committed any time he pleased, were popularly ascribed to their corrupt influence and their evil prompting. They were hated almost as much as he.

How were they to save themselves? Whom could they blame for starting the fire? On whom could they turn the fury of the people? They knew they had to clear Nero of responsibility for the catastrophe before anyone would believe they weren't to blame. Tigellinus met for hours with Domitius Afer to find a way out. He even turned for advice to Seneca, although he hated him almost as much as he did Petronius. Poppea, who understood that the fall of Nero would mean her death as well, sought ways and means among her confidants and the high priests of Rome's influential Jewry, making no secret of the fact that she had been a Jehovah worshiper for years. Nero scrambled about for his own solutions, leaping from one terrible extreme to another and usually making a fool of himself. He swung between utter terror and infantile amusement, but always whined and looked for someone else to blame.

One day he took part in a long and fruitless bickering debate with his closest courtiers, held in Tiberius' old palace that had survived the fire. Petronius held that the best thing would be to get away from all the turmoil around them, go to Greece and then to Egypt and Asia Minor. The trip had been planned for a long time, after all. Why put it off? Rome, he pointed out, was too grim to be amusing nowadays and far too dangerous as well.

Caesar seized on that idea with enthusiasm, but Seneca thought for a while about it and then shook his head.

"Leaving is easy," he said. "But coming back later would be a lot harder."

"By Hercules!" Petronius snapped, impatient. "We can come back at the head of the Asian legions."

"That's it!" Nero cried.

But Tigellinus started to argue against it. He was unable to think of anything himself, and if he had had Petronius' idea, he would have pushed it for all he was worth as their best salvation. But he was desperate that Petronius shouldn't prove himself again as the only man who could save everyone in moments of crisis.

"Hear me, divine one!" he burst out. "That's deadly advice! We'd have a civil war on our hands before we got to Ostia. Who knows if some surviving minor descendant of the divine Augustus wouldn't declare himself emperor, and what would we do if the legions ranked themselves behind him?"

"We'll just make sure Augustus has no living kin," Nero said. "There are few of them as it is, so getting rid of the last one won't be a big problem."

"Yes, we could do that," Tigellinus agreed. "But will that suffice? My spies reported just yesterday that the crowds are saying a man like Thrasea ought to be the emperor."

Nero bit his lip.

"Ingrates!" he snapped after a while, and he raised his eyes as if appealing to the skies for justice. "They never have enough! We've given them all the grain they want, and they have plenty of charcoal now to bake their wheat cakes. What more do they need?"

"Vengeance," Tigellinus said.

There was a moment of dull, worried silence, but suddenly Nero raised an arm and started to declaim: "Hearts cry for vengeance, and vengeance seeks a victim!"

Forgetting everything and delighted with himself, he turned a radiant face to the others. "Hand me a tablet and a stylus!" he cried out. "I must note this line! Lucan never composed anything this good. And did you notice how quickly it came to me?"

"O incomparable one!" several voices chorused.

Nero scribbled the line on a tablet. "Yes, vengeance needs a victim," he went on. "What if we spread the word that it was Vatinius who burned down the city? Wouldn't he fit nicely as a sacrificial victim?"

"Who am I for such a role, divinity?" Vatinius cackled weakly.

"True! We need someone a lot more important. How about Vitelius?"

Vitelius grew pale but laughed anyway. "My fat would probably start up a new fire."

Nero had something else in mind. He searched for a scapegoat who would really satisfy the angry population, and then he thought he found one.

"Tigellinus," he said after a while. "It was you who set Rome on fire."

The Augustans shuddered. Everyone realized that the joke was over, and what came next would be very serious. Tigellinus' face narrowed into a snarl like the muzzle of a dog that was about to bite.

"I did," he said coldly. "At your orders."

They stared at each other like two threatening demons. The silence stretched into such utter stillness that everyone could hear the buzzing of flies across the atrium.

"Tigellinus," Nero murmured then. "Do you love me?"

"You know I do, my lord."

"Then why don't you sacrifice yourself for me?"

Tigellinus wore a bitter smile. "Why do you hand me such a sweet cup to drink, my lord," he asked coldly, "when you know I don't dare touch it? The people growl and mutter. Do you want the praetorians to turn on you as well?"

An icy terror gripped the gathering for a breathless moment. Tigellinus was the prefect of the praetorians, who marched at his orders. His words were nothing less than an open threat. Nero grasped the fact as swiftly as everyone else, and his face turned as yellow as a soiled sheet.

Just then, however, Epaphroditus, one of Caesar's freedmen, slipped into the room with an announcement that the divine Augusta had some visitors in her apartments whom Tigellinus ought to hear.

Tigellinus bowed to the emperor and left, his face calm and heavy with contempt. He had shown his teeth. He had made it clear who and what he was and what he could do. Fully aware of Nero's basic cowardice, he knew this master of the world would never dare raise his hand against him.

Nero sat quietly for a while but then saw that the others expected some comment. "I've raised a viper at my breast," he said.

Petronius shrugged as if to say it wasn't hard to cut off such a viper's head.

Nero noticed the gesture and turned eagerly toward him. "You've something to say? Advise me! I trust you more than anyone because you've more brains than all the rest. And besides, you love me!"

Petronius was at the point of saying, "Make me the prefect of the praetorians, and I'll give Tigellinus to the mob and pacify the city in one day." But then his natural indolence got the better of him. Being the prefect meant taking care of thousands of public affairs and practically carrying the whole weight of the empire. What did he need that for? Wasn't it better to read poetry in his delightful library, gaze on beautiful statuary and vases, hold Eunice's lovely body against his chest, kiss her coral lips and run his fingers through her golden hair?

"My advice is to go to Greece," he said.

Caesar was disappointed. "I expected something more from you. The senate hates me. Who'll guarantee they won't rise up against me the moment I leave? They'll name someone else the emperor. The people were loyal to me once, but today they'd go with the rebels. . . . By Hades! If only the senate and the mob had only one head!"

"Permit me to say, divinity"—Petronius showed a wry, mocking smile—"that if you want to keep Rome, you must keep a few Romans."

Nero's voice turned to a complaining whine: "What's Rome to me? Why do I need Romans? Greeks listen to my art. Here all I have is treason. Everyone turns against me! Even all of you are ready to betray me! I know it! I know! You never even think what posterity will say about you for abandoning such an artist as myself."

He suddenly thought of something and struck his own forehead. "That's the truth! With all these worries I've forgotten who and what I am!"

He turned to Petronius as radiant as if he had no worries whatsoever.

"The people growl and mutter," he said eagerly, "but what if I took my lute and went to the Field of Mars and sang for them the same hymn I sang for you during the fire? Well? Don't you think I'd move them all to tears, the way Orpheus used to fascinate wild beasts with his music? What do you think, Petronius?"

It was Tullius Senecio who broke in with an answer. Bored and impatient and anxious to get back to the slave girls he had brought from Antium, he wanted to go home.

"No question about it, Caesar," he said quickly. "If they would just let you start."

"Ah, so let's go to Greece!" Nero cried, disgusted with it all.

In that moment Poppea swept into the room, with Tigellinus striding close behind her. All eyes fixed on him, surprised by his triumphant face; no one remembered any conqueror riding to the Capitol with such immense confidence and pride.

"Hear me, Caesar!" He spoke slowly, savoring each word and measuring its effect, and each one fell with the sharp precision of a sword stroke ringing as harsh as iron. "I've found the answer! The people want vengeance and a victim, yes, but not just one. They need hundreds of them. We will give them thousands! Did you ever hear, my lord, about a certain Chrestos, the one crucified by Pontius Pilate under Tiberius Caesar? Or about the Christians? Haven't I been telling you about their crimes, their foul rituals and their prophecies that the world would end in a fire storm? The people hate them and suspect them of the worst. No one has ever seen them in our temples because they think our gods are evil spirits. They don't go to the stadium because they despise horse and chariot races. No Christian ever applauded you or called you a god. They are the sworn enemies of mankind, of Rome and you as well. The people mutter and snarl against you, but it wasn't you who ordered Rome burned, nor was it I who did it. . . . The people want vengeance, do they? So let them have their vengeance. They want blood and circuses, so let's give them both. They suspect you, so let's turn their anger and suspicion elsewhere. Let's give them the Christians."

At first Nero listened with surprise, then with rising interest and amazement. But as Tigellinus went on and he grasped the gist of what he was hearing, his vain actor's face began to change, flashing in turn with grimaces of anger, sorrow, sympathy and outrage. At last, as if unable to bear it any longer, he leaped to his feet, let his toga fall in a heap around his feet, raised both his arms in a mute appeal like a tragic mime and stood like that in histrionic silence.

"O gods!" he cried at last, posturing like an actor. "Great Zeus, Apollo, Hera, Athena, Persephone and all you other immortals! Why didn't you help us? What did our unhappy city ever do to those inhuman criminals that they should burn it down so cruelly?"

"They're the enemies of all mankind," Poppea said coldly. "And especially yours!"

"Justice!" shouted others. "Give them Roman justice! Punish the fire setters! The gods themselves cry out to you for vengeance!"

Nero dropped tragically into his chair and let his head hang down upon his chest in silence as if what he had just heard was simply too terrible for human understanding.

"What punishments fit such awful crimes?" he asked at last, flapping his arms helplessly as if lost for words and groping for ideas. "What torments can pay for such depravity? Ah!" he cried dramatically. "The gods will help me! They'll inspire me! All the powers of Hell will come to my aid, and I'll give our people such a spectacle they'll think of me with gratitude for ages to come."

Petronius' forehead clouded with concern. He saw the danger that would hang over Vinicius, whom he cared about so much, over Ligia and over all the people whose creed he rejected but whose innocence lay beyond a doubt. He could sense the beginnings of the bloody orgies that his aesthetic principles couldn't bear. "I must save Vinicius," he told himself quietly. "He'll go mad if something happens to that girl of his." He knew he was about to start the most dangerous game he had ever played, but that consideration outweighed all the others.

"Well, so you've found your scapegoats." He smiled with contempt. He kept his tone light, careless and amused, as he always did when criticizing or ridiculing some crude notion advanced by Caesar or one of the Augustans. "Good for you! You can send them into the arenas or dress them in 'shirts of pain.' My congratulations! But take another look at what you are doing. You have the might, the authority and the praetorians, so can't you at least be honest with yourselves when no one else can hear you? Fool the people all you want, but must you fool yourselves? Throw the Christians to the mobs, condemn them to whatever tortures amuse you, but have the courage to admit it wasn't they who burned down the city! Pshaw!" He grimaced with disgust. "You call me the arbiter of good taste, so let me tell you I despise amateur theatrics, and all this smells of the tent shows at the Porta Asinaria, where tenth-rate actors play gods and kings for the amusement of country clodhoppers and then go off to eat raw onions and gulp sour wine or dodge kicks and cudgels. Be real kings and gods if that's what you want because you have all the power you need for it!

"As for you, Caesar," he said directly to Nero, "you threatened us with the judgment of the ages, but think of the verdict they'll send down on you. By the divine Clio, muse of theater and music, think of your own image. Here's Nero, the ruler of the world, who burned down Rome because he was as mighty here on earth as Zeus on Olympus. Here's Nero, the poet, who loved poetry so much he sacrificed his own native city for it! No one did or dared anything of that kind since the beginning of mankind.

"By the nine muses!" he appealed. "I beg you not to turn your back on such immortal glory, because generations would sing about you until the end of time! How would Priam, Agamemnon, Achilles or even the gods ever be able to compare with you? It makes no difference if it's good or bad to burn down Rome like that. What counts is that it's unusual and magnificent! Besides, the people won't turn on you. That's a lie. Show the courage of your convictions. The only thing to fear is some act unworthy of your greatness! Your only danger is that future generations might say: 'Nero burned Rome. But as a timid emperor and a mediocre poet he didn't have the greatness to stand by his act. He denied it out of fear and threw the blame on the innocent.'"

Normally, whatever Petronius said had a strong effect on Nero, but he had few illusions this time about coming out on top. He was aware that he might be able, with luck, to save the Christians, but it was far more likely he would doom himself. The chance of saving Vinicius, however, along with his love of playing for high stakes, prompted this all-or-nothing gamble, and he didn't hesitate for a moment. "The dice are rolling," he told himself while Nero gaped, confused. "Let's see if this sick ape will worry more about his own skin or go for the glory." In his heart of hearts, however, he thought cowardice would win.

A deathly silence followed his appeal. Poppea, along with everybody else, fixed her eyes on Nero's in breathless fascination while he pursed his lips and curled them up almost to his nostrils, as he did whenever he had no idea what to do. At last, however, uncertainty and displeasure flickered in his face.

"My lord!" Tigellinus read the signs and leaped for advantage. "Let me leave! When you're not only urged to risk your divine person but are also called a timid Caesar, a mediocre poet, an arsonist and a tenth-rate clown, my ears just can't listen!"

"I've lost," thought Petronius.

He turned coldly on Tigellinus and stared at him with the contempt of a great, civilized patrician for a vulgar pickpocket.

"You are the posturing clown I had in mind," he said, "because that's what you are even at this moment."

"How so?" Tigellinus snarled. "Because I don't want to listen to your insults?"

"No. Because you claim to love Caesar without limits, but just a few moments ago you threatened him with your praetorians, which all of us understood just as well as he."

Tigellinus never thought Petronius would dare throw such cards open on the table. The specter of a palace revolution was never mentioned aloud before any Caesar since too many of them had perished at the hands of the praetorians. His face turned as gray as a winding-sheet; he lost his composure and gaped openmouthed in numb consternation. But this was Petronius' last victory over his competitor as Poppea played her hand in support of the dumbstruck prefect.

"My lord," she snarled. "How can you permit such a thought to even cross someone's mind, far less hear it uttered in your presence?"

"Such insolence should be punished at once!" Vitelius shouted, glad to expose someone else to danger. "Punish him, my lord!"

Nero pursed his mouth again, blinking and unsure, then fixed his glassy nearsighted eyes on Petronius.

"Is this how you repay the friendship that I had for you in the past?" he asked.

"If I'm wrong, then prove it and I will stand corrected," Petronius said quietly. "But I say only what my love for you commands me to say."

"Punish the insolence!" Vitelius howled again.

"Do it!" urged other voices.

The atrium filled with sound and motion as people started to edge away from Petronius. Even Tullius Senecio, his old companion at the court, and young Nerva, who always showed him a very lively friendship, took care to step away. Quite isolated now and with no one near him on the empty left side of the atrium, Petronius stood alone with a quiet smile. He ran his fingers through the folds of his toga as he waited for Caesar to say or do something.

"You want me to punish him," Caesar said at last. "But he's my friend. My beloved companion. So even though he stabbed me through the heart, let him know that this heart knows only . . . forgiveness."

"I've lost the game," Petronius acknowledged to himself. "And now I'm lost as well."

Caesar rose. The meeting was over.

‹58›

PETRONIUS SET OUT for home, while Nero and Tigellinus went to the atrium of Poppea where the men with whom the prefect had been talking earlier were still waiting for them. There were two Trans-Tiber rabbis in tall miters and long, ceremonial robes, a young scribe who served them, and the old Greek Chilon. At the sight of the emperor, the two spiritual leaders blanched with emotion, raised their open palms to the height of their shoulders, and bowed their heads into their hands.

"Hail to you, king of kings and ruler of rulers," they chorused, "Caesar and protector of the chosen people, lion among men, whose reign is like the light of the sun, like the lofty cedars of Lebanon, like a freshwater spring, like a palm, and like the healing balm of Jericho—"

"You don't call me god?" Nero interrupted.

The two priests blanched even whiter than before.

"Thy words, O lord," the leader spoke again, "are as sweet as a cluster of ripe grapes or like honeyed figs, since Yahveh filled your heart with kindness and goodness. . . . Yet even though the Caesar Caius, the predecessor of your father, was a cruel tyrant, our emissaries didn't call him god, choosing death over sacrilege to the temple."

"And I expect Caligula fed them to the lions."

"No, king of kings. The Caesar Caius feared the wrath of Yahveh."

With this, both priests raised their lowered faces. Confident in the might of their Jehovah, they could look boldly into Nero's eyes.

"Are you here to accuse the Christians of setting Rome on fire?" Caesar asked.

"We, my lord, accuse them only of being enemies of the temple, of mankind, and of you and Rome, and they have long been threatening the city and the world with fire. The rest you'll hear from this man we've brought whose lips cannot lie, since the blood of the chosen people flowed in his mother's veins."

"Who are you, then?" Nero turned to Chilon.

"Your humble worshiper, divine Osiris. And a poor Stoic too."

"I hate the Stoics!" Nero said. "I hate Thrasea, Musonius and Cornutus. I loathe what they say. I detest their contempt for art, their self-imposed poverty and their sloppy clothes."

"My lord, your teacher Seneca owns a thousand tables made of lemon wood. Just say so, radiant one, and I'll immediately own twice that many. I am a Stoic only because I have to be. My poverty is by no means self-imposed. Dress my Stoicism in a wreath of roses and place a jug of wine in front of it, and I'll sing you hymns in praise of hedonism louder than all the Epicureans together."

Nero, who rather liked being addressed as "radiant one," grinned at the old Greek.

"I like you!" he said.

"This man is worth his weight in gold!" Tigellinus cried immediately.

"Add to this weight substantially, my lord," Chilon shot back at once, "or any breeze is likely to carry it away."

"True." Caesar nodded, eying the thin Greek. "You'd hardly match Vitelius on the scales."

"True again, you silver-browed apotheosis of the mighty Zeus." Chilon sighed. "It's a good thing my wits aren't made of lead."

"I see *your* temple doesn't mind calling me a god."

"My temple, O immortal one, is contained in you! That's the temple the Christians blaspheme against, and that's why I hate them."

"What do you know about them?"

"Ah!" Chilon groaned. "May I weep, divinity?"

"No," Nero yawned. "Tears bore me."

"How right you are, light of the world! Eyes that have glimpsed you once ought to be dry forever after. Protect me from my enemies, great lord!"

"Tell us about the Christians." Poppea was impatient to get to the point.

"As you wish, great Isis. I have devoted myself to philosophy from my earliest years, searching for the truth. I looked for it among the divine sages of antiquity, in the Academy of Athens, and in the Serapeum of Alexandria too. Hearing about the Christians, I thought they were some new school where I might pick up a few grains of wisdom, and so I got to know them, much to my misfortune. The first Christian whom an ill wind blew my way was a Neapolitan physician by the name of Glaucus. It was from him I learned they worship a certain Chrestos, who promised to exterminate all mankind and destroy every city in the world, but he would spare them if they helped him kill every man alive. Or to put it in its proper philosophic form, all the children of Deucalion, son of the great Prometheus who stole fire from the gods, from whom derive all the men and women born after the Flood, which is to say the whole new race of men. That's why, great lord, they hate all humanity, poison wells, and blaspheme against Rome and all the temples where we worship the ancient Roman gods. Chrestos was crucified, but he promised he'd come back once Rome was destroyed by fire, and then he'd give them dominion over all the earth."

"Now the people will know why Rome was destroyed," Tigellinus added.

"Many already know it, lord," Chilon said, "because I preach the truth to them in the parks and gardens and the Field of Mars. But if you hear me out, you'll understand why I want judgment against these people. Glaucus, the medic, didn't let on to me at the start that their creed commands hating people. On the contrary, he told me Chrestos was a good god and that the basis of his teaching is brotherhood and love. My sentimental heart couldn't resist such a philosophy, so I loved Glaucus like a brother and gave him my trust. I shared each crust and every penny with him, and do you know, my lord, how he paid me for it? On the way from Naples to Rome, he knifed me and sold my beautiful young wife Berenice to slavers. Ah, if only Sophocles knew the life I've lived. . . . Ah! But what am I saying? I'm heard by someone better than Sophocles."

"Ah, the poor man!" Poppea murmured.

"He who has seen the face of Aphrodite, my lady," Chilon said, "can never be called poor, and I behold her at this very moment. But in those days I sought my consolations in philosophy. Reaching Rome, I tried to find the Christian elders for justice on Glaucus. I thought they might pressure him into giving back my wife. I've met their high priest, and another one named Paul who was jailed here for a time but is now at liberty. I know the son of Zebediah and Linus and Cletus and a lot more besides. I know where they lived before the fire and where they meet now. I can show you one underground cavern in the Vatican heights and one graveyard on the Nomentum road where they get together for their obscene rituals. I saw their apostle Peter there. I saw Glaucus murdering children so Peter would have fresh blood to sprinkle on the heads of his followers. I saw Ligia, the one brought up by Pomponia Graecina, who boasted that even though she couldn't bring any innocent blood to the ritual, she caused the death of a child since she put a spell on your daughter, O great Osiris and Isis!"

"Do you hear this, my lord?" Poppea demanded.

"Can this be?" cried Nero.

"I could have forgiven them my own suffering," Chilon went on mournfully, "but when I heard what she did to you, O illustrious ones, I wanted to knife her! But the noble Vinicius loves her and got in my way."

"Vinicius? But didn't she run away from him?"

"She did, but he went on looking for her anyway because he just couldn't live without her. I helped him for a miserable beggar's wage, and I pointed out the house in the Trans-Tiber where she lived. We went there with your favorite wrestler, Croton, whom Vinicius hired as a bodyguard. But Ursus, Ligia's slave, throttled Croton. That's a terrible man, my lord, who twists the heads off bulls like poppy heads. Aulus and Pomponia always loved him for it."

"By Hercules!" Nero was impressed. "A man who could strangle Croton ought to have a statue in the Forum. But you're wrong there, old man. Vinicius killed Croton with a knife. He told me himself."

"That just shows how people lie to the gods, my lord. I saw with my own eyes how Croton's ribs cracked in that monster's grasp, and then how he felled Vinicius. He'd have killed him, too, if it weren't for Ligia. Vinicius was ill a long time after that. They nursed him back to health, expecting he'd turn Christian out of gratitude. And that's just what happened."

"Vinicius is a Christian?"

"That he is, my lord."

"So maybe Petronius is another?" Tigellinus broke in eagerly.

Chilon began to squirm and twist his hands. "I am amazed by your perspicacity, my lord." He shot a series of quick, worried smiles toward Tigellinus. "It could be! Oh, yes, it could be!"

"Now I understand why he was so anxious to protect the Christians," Tigellinus said.

But Nero burst out laughing. "Petronius, a Christian? Petronius, an enemy of life and the flesh? Don't be such idiots and don't expect me to believe such nonsense, or I'll stop believing everything else you say."

"The noble Vinicius is definitely a Christian, though, my lord," Chilon babbled swiftly. "I swear it by the radiance that flows from your godhead. It's the truth! Nothing disgusts me more than lies, I swear it! Pomponia is a Christian, and so is little Aulus and Ligia and

Vinicius. I served Vinicius faithfully, but Glaucus had him whip me even though I'm old. And I was ill and hungry at the time as well. I swore by Hades I'd never forgive him. Avenge my wrongs on them, my lord! Do so, and I'll give you their apostle Peter and Linus, Cletus, Glaucus, Crispus and all of their elders. I'll lead you to Ligia and Ursus. I'll point them all out in hundreds and thousands. I'll take your men to all the prayer houses and graveyards where they gather. There won't be room enough for them in all your prisons when I'm finished with them! You'd never find them without me! So far I looked for solace from my troubles only in philosophy. Let me find it now in your royal favor! I'm old. Life has passed me by. . . . Let me start living and find a little peace!"

"You want to be a Stoic with a full belly, is that it?" Nero grinned.

"He who serves you, my lord, lives well," Chilon said.

"You've got that right, philosopher."

Nero was still unsure, musing about all the possibilities, but Poppea never lost sight of a chance for vengeance. Her interest in Vinicius was just a passing whim, spurred largely by jealousy, anger and hurt pride; but the young man's indifference struck a bitter blow, touched her far deeper than she would admit even to herself, and filled her with implacable ill will. The mere fact he would rather have some other woman was enough to call for retribution. As for Ligia, alarmed by her beauty, she hated her at first glance. Petronius could talk Nero into thinking her hips were too narrow, but Poppea couldn't be fooled that easily. One glance had been enough to know that this northern girl was her only true competition in Rome and that she could very well come out the winner in a real challenge. The moment was quite enough to condemn the girl.

"My lord," she prompted, "avenge our dead child!"

"You must hurry, though!" Chilon urged. "Hurry! Otherwise Vinicius will hide her! I'll show you where they've moved after the fire."

"I'll give you ten men," Tigellinus said, "and you can go at once."

"My lord"—Chilon wouldn't dream of facing Ursus with a mere squad of praetorians—"you never saw Croton being crushed by Ursus. If you gave me fifty men, I'd only point out the house from a distance. But if you don't jail Vinicius as well, I am a dead man."

Tigellinus shot a glance at Nero. "Wouldn't it be best, divine Caesar, to take care of the nephew and the uncle at one stroke?"

Nero pondered briefly.

"No," he said. "Not yet. Nobody would believe that Petronius,

Vinicius and Pomponia set Rome on fire. Their homes were too beautiful for that. . . . The mobs need other victims just now. Their turn will come later."

"Then give me soldiers, my lord, to protect me," Chilon begged.

"Tigellinus will give some thought to that."

"You can join my household for the time being," the prefect told Chilon, who breathed a sigh of vast relief and whose face shone with joy.

"I'll point out all of them!" he cried hoarsely. "Only hurry! Hurry!"

HAVING LEFT CAESAR, Petronius had himself carried to his house in the Carinnae, which escaped the fire since it was surrounded on three sides by gardens and had the open space of the small Cecilian Forum before it. This stroke of luck merely added to his reputation as especially blessed by Fortuna, the goddess of good fortune, whose firstborn son he was said to be by other Augustans. That reputation had soared particularly high through Caesar's recent friendship and added to the envy of Nero's other intimates who had lost everything they owned in the conflagration.

But now this lucky son of Fortuna had reason to wonder about the changeability of his supposed mother; she seemed more like Chronos, the original creator, who devoured his children.

"If my house had burned down," he observed to himself, "along with all my gems, artwork, Etruscan vases, Alexandrine glassware and Corinthian bronzes, Nero might be able to forgive me. By Pollux! And to think it was entirely up to me to be the praetorian prefect at this very moment. I could denounce Tigellinus as the arsonist he is, dress him in a 'shirt of pain' and throw him to the mobs, save the Christians and rebuild Rome as well. Who knows if decent people wouldn't have a better life thereafter? If nothing else, I should have done it for Vinicius. If the job carried too much work, I could pass it on to him and make him the prefect. Nero wouldn't even bother to object. Let Vinicius baptize all his praetorians afterward, if that's what he felt like. Let him baptize Caesar. What would I care one way or the other? In fact a pious, merciful and virtuous Nero might have been amusing."

This idea was so entertaining that he began to smile, but his thoughts quickly veered into another channel. It suddenly seemed to him that he was still in Antium, debating Christianity with Paul, and that the Christian missionary was making good sense.

"You call us enemies of life," he heard the preacher saying. "But wouldn't your life be safer and surer, Petronius, if Caesar were a Christian?"

"By Castor!" he swore to himself. "No matter how many Christians they end up slaughtering here, Paul will soon replace them, because if the world can't exist on villainy and crime, then he wins the argument. But what if it can? The scum has certainly settled at the top. I've learned a lot in life, but I didn't learn how to be a blackguard or a big enough scoundrel to survive, and that's why I'll soon be obliged to slit my own wrists. But that's how it would've ended anyway, and if not precisely this way, then something similar. I'll miss Eunice, of course, and my Myrrhene vase, but Eunice is free and the vase goes with me. Copperbeard won't get his hands on it no matter what happens! I'm sorry about Vinicius. He deserves a lot better than he's about to get. Yes, the last few years were a little less boring than before, but I'm quite ready. There is a great deal of beauty in the world, but most people are so contemptible it's not worth mourning the loss of one's life. He who knew how to live ought to know how to die. And even though I was an Augustan, I was a freer man than they could ever imagine."

He shrugged. He focused for a moment on his fellow courtiers. There they were, thinking his knees were quivering with terror and all his hair was standing erect on his head; and here he was, on his way home to take a bath in violet-scented water, to be massaged by his loving, golden-haired Eunice, and then to listen with her, after supper, as sweet-voiced singers harmonized Anthemioses' hymn to Apollo.

"I said it myself," he recalled. "There's no point in giving any thought to Death, because she'll come calling with or without our help."

He thought it would be truly marvelous if there were such a thing as the Elysian fields, with their wandering shades of the departed. "Eunice would join me there in time, and we'd drift together through fields of asphodels. The company would certainly be better than here. What buffoons! What clowns! What cheap country jugglers! What drooling peasants without a touch of taste, polish, elegance or culture! Ten arbiters of taste wouldn't be able to civilize those primitive 'Trimalchios.' By Persephone! I've had enough of them!"

He was suddenly aware of the gulf between those people and himself. He knew them inside out, of course. He had long known what to think of them. And yet they seemed far beneath him now and more contemptible than ever. Really, he thought, I have had enough!

But then he focused on his situation. All his shrewdness and experience told him that his doom was likely to be deferred for a while. Nero couldn't resist the temptation to mouth a few lofty phrases about friendship and forgiveness, and that tied his hands to some extent. He would have to search for an excuse, and that might take quite a bit of time. "First he'll create a spectacle out of the Christians," Petronius concluded. "And only then will he turn his thoughts on me." And if that's the way it was, there was no point in worrying about it or changing his life-style. The danger was far more pressing for Vinicius.

Determined to save the young man, he turned his thoughts to Vinicius the rest of the way home.

The slaves trotted smartly, carrying his litter through the gaunt, gray landscape of the Carinnae, among the scorched rubble and skeletal chimneys, but he ordered them to run all out to get him home as fast as possible. Vinicius had lost his home in the fire and was staying with him. Luckily, he was in.

"Did you see Ligia today?" Petronius asked as soon as he saw him.

"I've just come back from her."

"Pay attention to what I have to say and waste no time on questions. I've just come from Caesar's. They've decided to blame the Christians for burning Rome. That means persecution and extermination; the hunt will start any moment now. Take Ligia and run for it. Head north across the Alps or to Africa, it doesn't matter where, just get her away. And hurry! It's a lot closer to the Trans-Tiber from the Palatine than from here."

Vinicius was too much of a soldier to ask many questions. He listened with narrowed eyes, his face tensed and dangerous in total concentration but quite without fear. It was clear his first reaction to danger was to fight.

"I'm on my way," he snapped.

"One word more. Take gold, arm yourself, and bring some of your people. Make sure they are Christians. If need be, fight for her and get her away!"

Vinicius was already through the atrium doors. "And send me a slave with news!" Petronius shouted after him.

Then, left alone, he started pacing among the columns that lined his atrium walls, pondering what would happen. He knew that Ligia and Linus had gone back to where they lived in the Trans-Tiber before the fire, since that house survived along with most of the quarter, which was unfortunate. It would have been far more difficult to find them in the crowds. But since no one at the Palatine knew precisely where to look for them, Vinicius was sure to get there before the praetorians. It also occurred to him that Tigellinus would want to catch as many Christians as he could with one massive throw, so he'd have to stretch his net across all of Rome, thinning out his praetorians into small detachments.

"If they don't send more than ten men after her," he thought, "that Lygian giant will be enough to crack all their necks. Not to mention Vinicius coming with armed help."

That made him feel better. True, armed resistance to the praetorians was as good as going to war with Caesar. Petronius was also quite aware that if Vinicius got away, escaped Caesar's vengeance, the blame would likely fall upon him, but that was the least of his concerns. Indeed, the thought of muddying the waters for Nero and Tigellinus pleased him and amused him. He decided to spare neither men nor money for such a good goal; and since Paul of Tarsus converted most of his slaves in Antium, he could be sure they'd fight to the death defending the Christian girl.

But Eunice slipped into the atrium just then, and all his ponderings and worries vanished. He forgot all about Caesar and his own fall from grace. He gave no more thought to the worthless, contemptible Augustans, the hunt for the Christians, Ligia and Vinicius, and looked at her with the admiring eyes of a connoisseur whose pleasures come from beauty, and of a lover nourished by that beauty. She wore a translucent violet robe known as a *coa vestis*, through which her body gleamed like a pale rose; she looked as beautiful as a goddess. Feeling herself admired, loving him with all her heart and soul and always eager for his touch, she flushed with joy as if she were an innocent young girl rather than his mistress.

"What have you to tell me, my nymph?" he asked gently.

"My lord." She inclined her golden head toward him. "Anthemios has brought his singers and wants to know if it's your wish to hear them today."

"Let him wait. He'll sing to us at supper. Imagine! We are surrounded by rubble and ashes, and we'll be listening to a hymn in praise of Apollo! Ah, by the sacred grove of Paphos! When I see you in that *coa vestis*, I feel as if Aphrodite veiled herself with a strip of sky and stands here before me."

"Oh, my lord!" breathed Eunice.

"Come to me, Eunice. Put your arms around me and give me your lips. . . . Do you really love me?"

"I couldn't love Zeus more." She pressed her lips to his and trembled in his arms.

"What if we had to part?"

She stared fearfully into his eyes. "Why, my lord? How?"

"Don't be afraid! It might be I'll be obliged to take a long journey."

"Take me with you, then."

But Petronius suddenly changed the subject. "Tell me, do we have asphodels on our garden lawns?"

"All the lawns and cypresses are yellow from the fire, the myrtles are leafless, and the garden looks dead."

"All of Rome looks dead, and it'll be a real cemetery before very long. There'll be an edict soon against the Christians, along with persecutions in which thousands of people will be killed."

"Why will they be punished, my lord? They are good, quiet people."

"That's why."

"So let's go to the seashore. Your eyes, my lord, don't like to look at bloodshed."

"Very well. But right now I must bathe. Come later to the anointing room and oil my shoulders. Ah, by Aphrodite's girdle! You've never looked this beautiful before. I'll have a bath made for you in the shape of a seashell, and you'll lie in it like a precious pearl. . . . But come later, will you?"

He went to bathe. An hour later, dressed in wreaths of roses and their eyes dimmed with sensuous pleasure, he and she rested behind a table spread with golden dishes. They were waited on by small boys dressed as Cupids, while they sipped wine from crystal goblets and listened to the harps and voices of Anthemios' singers. Why would they care that skeletal chimneys loomed out of the ruins everywhere around them or that gusts of wind scattered the ashes of Rome around their villa? They were absorbed in their own happiness and thought only about love that transformed their lives into a godlike dream.

Before the hymn had come to an end, they were interrupted by the slave in charge of the atrium.

"My lord"—his voice shook with worry—"there's a centurion and a company of soldiers at the gate. He demands to see you."

The song died at once, and the harps were silenced. Anxiety spread to everyone, since Caesar seldom used praetorians to send messages to friends. Their coming usually meant bad news, times being what they were. Only Petronius showed no trace of worry.

"They could at least let me finish my supper in peace," he said in the bored, weary voice of a man who is constantly being interrupted. Then he nodded to the *atriensis*. "Let them in."

The slave vanished behind the draperies. A moment later came the dull thud of heavy military footsteps, and an armed centurion marched into the chamber. Petronius knew him slightly. His name was Aper. He wore full battle armor and an iron helmet on his head.

"A message from Caesar, my lord," he said, holding out wax tablets.

Petronius stretched his white arm for the tablets, glanced at them and passed them to Eunice as if they were nothing.

"He'll be reading a new song out of his *Troyad* tonight and calls me to hear it," he said.

"My only job was to deliver the message," the centurion said.

"Very well. There won't be an answer. But why don't you rest here with us for a bit, centurion, and drink a cup of wine?"

"Thank you, noble lord. I'll be glad to drink to your good health, but I can't stay because I'm on duty."

"Why did they use you for a messenger instead of sending a slave?"

"I don't know, my lord. It could be because I was coming this way anyway. I've a job out here."

"I know." Petronius nodded. "You're after the Christians."

"That's correct, my lord."

"How long ago did the hunt begin?"

"Some units went to the Trans-Tiber before noon."

The centurion shook a few drops of wine on the floor in honor of Mars, then drained the goblet. "May the gods give you whatever you wish, my lord," he said.

"Keep the cup."

The officer saluted and went out, and Petronius signaled to Anthemios to resume the concert. So Copperbeard is playing games with me and Vinicius, he thought when the harps sounded again. I know what he's up to. He wants to alarm me by sending a centurion. They'll be questioning him tonight about my reaction.

"No, no, you cruel and malicious ape," he murmured softly to himself. "You won't get much pleasure out of that report. I know you won't forget your hurt pride, I know that I'm doomed, but if you think I'll plead for mercy, beg you with my eyes or show any fear or contrition, you've a surprise in store."

"Caesar writes: 'Come if you wish,' my lord," Eunice said. "Will you go?"

"I'm in fine form and excellent humor," Petronius said. "Amused enough even for his verses. I'll go, all the more since Vinicius can't."

Indeed, when they had finished dining and he took his usual after-dinner walk, he placed himself in the skilled hands of his various slave girls who dressed his hair and arranged the proper folds in his toga. He had himself carried to the Palatine an hour later, as exquisite as a pagan idol.

It was late, the evening was warm and quiet, and the moon shone so brightly that the lampadari who walked before his litter put out their flaming torches. Groups of excited people, tipsy on cheap wine and wreathed in ivy and honeysuckle garlands, weaved down the streets or stumbled in the ruins, waving myrtle and laurel boughs plucked from Caesar's gardens. The abundance of free grain and the prospect of spectacular public games delighted the mobs. Some of the crowd were dancing. Others sang love songs or ballads about the balmy night that seemed to be created for the pleasure of the gods themselves. Several times the slaves had to call for room for the litter of the honorable Petronius, and the crowds gave way and cheered their favorite Augustan.

He, in the meantime, thought about Vinicius and wondered why he had had no message from him all day. He was an egotist, very much an Epicurean in his attitudes, but he had spent so much time recently with Paul of Tarsus and Vinicius, hearing about the Christians, that he had changed a little without even being aware of it. It was as if some unknown breeze had blown from them to him, carrying strange seeds. Other people, not merely himself, started to interest him, and he had always been fond of Vinicius anyway, having loved his mother, his own sister, very much. Moreover, having taken a hand in his affairs, he watched them now with the absorption of a rare theatrical performance, anxious to see it through the final act. He went on hoping that Vinicius had managed to reach Ligia before the praetorians or that he had freed her by force and got her away to safety. But he wished he knew more of what actually happened in case he was obliged to answer some questions.

They halted before the palace of Tiberius, and he stepped from the litter and entered the atrium that was already crowded with Augustans. Yesterday's friends, surprised he had been invited, played it safe by avoiding him. He moved calmly and carelessly among them, as exquisite, free, at ease and self-assured as if he were still able to dispense great favors. He noted with amusement that some of his cautious former friends now looked as if they were wondering whether they hadn't stepped away from him too soon.

Caesar pretended not to notice him and ignored his bow under the guise of being absorbed in conversation, but Tigellinus stepped up to him with an ironic smile.

"Good evening, arbiter of taste," he said. "Are you still saying the Christians didn't set fire to Rome?"

Petronius shrugged and patted the prefect indifferently on the shoulder, as if the all-powerful Tigellinus were no more than a common freedman.

"You know as well as I do what to think of that," he said.

"I wouldn't dare match your wisdom or experience," Tigellinus said sarcastically.

"And you're right as far as that goes. Otherwise you'd have to say something that makes sense after Caesar reads his new passage from the *Troyad*, instead of shrieking like a brainless peacock as you always do."

Tigellinus gnawed his lips with anger. He was upset that Nero chose this night to read his new verses because that opened an arena in which he couldn't compete with Petronius. Indeed, while the reading went on, Nero kept shooting glances at Petronius from sheer force of habit, trying to gauge the effect of his recitation from the expressions he caught on the arbiter's face. Petronius, in the meantime, listened with close attention, raising his eyebrow now and then or nodding briefly or leaning forward as if to make sure he had heard a phrase correctly. Then he praised or corrected a given line or passage, and suggested changes or a better choice of words for added polish. Even Nero felt that the others' ecstatic exclamations were wholly self-serving, while this man really cared about poetry for its own sake and was the only expert; he could be sure his verses were worth praising if Petronius praised them. He let himself be drawn gradually into a discussion, disputing certain points, and when Petronius questioned the need for a particular line, Nero said to him:

"You'll see why I use it when you hear the last canto."

Ah, so I'll live long enough to hear the last canto, Petronius thought, while others worried that having so much time to mend his position, Petronius might very well return to Nero's good graces and perhaps even topple Tigellinus.

The Augustans started edging up to him again, but the evening ended on a sour note. As they were saying good night, Nero looked at him through narrowed eyes glinting with spite and malicious pleasure and asked: "Why didn't Vinicius come with you?"

If Petronius knew that Ligia and Vinicius were safely out of the city, he would have said: "He married, by your permission, and left town." But noting Nero's strange equivocal smile, he said: "Your invitation didn't reach him, divine one."

"Tell him I'll be glad to see him soon," Nero said. "And remind him for me not to miss the games where the Christians will be the star attraction."

These words alarmed Petronius. He thought they related directly to Ligia. Once in his litter he ordered his slaves to take him home even faster than they had that morning, but this wasn't easy. A thick crowd stood before Tiberius' palace—as drunk, unruly and noisy as before, but now they were neither dancing nor singing; on the contrary, the sullen, seething throng seemed ready to explode with outrage. Some distant shouts Petronius didn't understand echoed in the background; as they grew and neared and became stronger and distinct, they turned into one vast savage howl:

"Christians to the lions!"

The courtiers' richly ornamented litters pushed their way through a caterwauling mob that swelled with new arrivals from the burned-out streets, wanting blood, mad with hatred, swarming and repeating: "Christians to the lions!"

The news flew from mouth to mouth. The hunt had been on since midday, crowds of arsonists had been caught already, and soon the shrieks and howls echoed through all the old streets and the newly laid-out avenues, in the alleys buried in the rubble around the Palatine, on all the seven hills and in all the gardens the length and breadth of Rome.

"Christians to the lions!"

"Cattle!" Petronius muttered with contempt. "The people are worthy of their Caesar."

No, he thought, there was no future here. This kind of world couldn't go on much longer. A society based on brute force and violence, on cruelty beyond anything possible among the barbarians, and on such universal viciousness and debauchery, could not survive forever. Rome ruled mankind, but it was also its cesspool and its seeping ulcer. It reeked of death and corpses. Death's shadow lay over its decomposing life. It was said often among the Augustans—although Petronius never understood it more clearly than now—that the triumphal chariot on which Rome stood garlanded with conquests, dragging whole flocks of captive nations in the dust behind it, was heading for the edge of a cliff and the abyss below. All that passed for

life in this capital of the earth seemed suddenly like some kind of mad
processional for capering buffoons, a dance of mindless clowns, and a
bloody orgy that had to end by its own excess.

It came to him that only the Christians offered a new foundation
for civilization, but he assumed there wouldn't be a trace of them left
on earth before very long. And what would happen then?

"The dance of the clowns will go on, prancing after Nero. When
Nero goes, there'll be another like him or even a worse one, because
none other is possible with such a people and such an aristocracy.
There'll be other orgies, each uglier and more vile than the one before.
But they have to end sometime. No one can live at such a pitch of vile-
ness forever. Rest must come if only out of sheer exhaustion."

Petronius felt immensely weary, drained by such conclusions. Was it
worth living, unsure of being able to survive beyond the next moment,
only to look at such reality? The spirit of death was no less beautiful than
the spirit of dreams, and both had wings at their shoulders.

The litter halted before his own doors, which a watchful gatekeeper swung open at once.

"Has the noble Vinicius returned?" Petronius asked.

"Yes, my lord. Just now."

So he didn't get her back, Petronius thought grimly. He threw off
his toga and ran into the atrium. Vinicius sat on a three-legged stool,
his face buried in his hands and his head hanging almost to his knees,
but he looked up at the sound of the footsteps. His face was as set
and gray as stone, and his eyes seemed to burn with fever.

"You got there too late?" Petronius asked.

"Yes. They took her before noon."

Neither said anything for a time. Then Petronius stirred. "Have
you seen her?"

"Yes."

"Where is she?"

"In the Mammertine."

Petronius shuddered. The prison of the Mammertine lay like a
stain on the city's history, with row after row and layer after layer of
dungeons where countless enemies of the state had been starved to
death. Vinicius caught his worried glance and shook his head.

"No. They didn't throw her in the Tullianum"—he named the
deepest dungeon, the one reached only through a grating in the floor
above. "I bribed the keeper to give her his own room. Ursus lies at
the door and guards her."

"Why didn't he defend her?"

"They sent fifty soldiers. Besides, Linus stopped him."

"Did they get Linus too?"

"Linus is dying. They left him alone."

"What do you want to do?"

"To save her or die with her. I'm also a Christian."

Vinicius spoke calmly, but there was something so heartbreaking in his voice that Petronius felt the touch of genuine compassion.

"I understand," he said. "But how will you save her?"

"I've bribed the keepers. First, so they'd protect her from brutality, and then, so they wouldn't hinder her escape."

"When's that to happen?"

"They said they can't give her to me now because they're afraid of getting caught. They'll let her go later when the prisons fill up with people and they lose count of whom or what they have there. But that's only the last resort! First it's up to you to save her and me! You're Caesar's friend! He gave her to me himself! Go to him and save us!"

Instead of answering, Petronius snapped an order to a slave who came back at a run carrying two hooded capes and a pair of military swords.

"Cloak and arm yourself," Petronius told Vinicius. "We're going to the prison. You'll pay the keepers one hundred thousand sesterces or twice that much or five times what they want to let Ligia go at once! This is your last chance! As for what I can do, I'll give you your answer on the way."

A moment later they were in the streets.

"Now listen," said Petronius. "I didn't want to waste time saying this before. As of today I am out of favor. My own life hangs by a thread, and that's why I can't do anything with Caesar. Even worse, I'm sure he'd do the opposite of anything I asked. Do you think I'd have advised you to run for it with Ligia if there was something I could do for you? Caesar's fury will turn on me the moment you escape! He'd sooner do something for you than for me these days, but don't count on that. Get her out of prison and run! Nothing else can help you. If you fail, we'll think about some other means. In the meantime, you had better know that Ligia wasn't seized merely because she's a Christian."

"What else could it be?"

"Poppea. Did you forget that you humiliated our divine Augusta? That you rejected her? And she knew very well that you repulsed her for the sake of Ligia, whom she's hated from the first time she saw her. She tried to have her destroyed once before, remember? The time she called her a sorceress who bewitched her child and caused her to die? You can be sure Poppea is behind all this. She never forgives. How else can you explain that Ligia was jailed first? Who in the Palatine would know where she'd be staying? And yet the praetorians went straight to Linus' house as if someone had pointed the way. They must have had spies trailing her for months. I know I'm shredding the last of your hope and tearing you apart, but you've got to know that if you don't set her free at once, before they get the idea that you'd even try, you will both be lost."

"I understand." Vinicius spoke with the hard finality of a closing tomb.

It was late and the streets had emptied, but a drunken gladiator lurched suddenly before them and fell against Petronius.

"Christians to the lions!" he howled in a hoarse, wine-logged voice, breathing thick fumes into Petronius' face and leaning on his shoulder.

"*Mirmillo.*" Petronius called him by the name given to Thracian swordsmen who fought in the arenas against the net and trident. "Take my advice and find another road."

The drunken fighter only seized him by the other shoulder. "Shout with me or I'll twist your neck!" he roared. "Christians to the lions!"

These murderous howls had finally exhausted the patrician's patience. He had been deafened by them from the moment he left the Palatine but ignored them as beneath his notice. This was the limit. The huge clenched fist shaking in his face pushed him over the edge.

"My friend," he said quietly. "You reek of wine and you are in my way."

With this he thrust his short sword to the hilt in the gladiator's chest, let him fall, and took Vinicius' arm as if nothing happened to interrupt what he had been saying.

"This is what Caesar said to me today: 'Tell Vinicius for me not to miss the games at which the Christians will be the main attraction.' Do you understand what this means for you? They want to amuse themselves with your agony. It's all prearranged. Perhaps that's why you and I still haven't been jailed. If you don't manage to get her out at once . . . well, I don't know. Acte might intercede, but will that be enough? There's a chance Tigellinus might trade her for your Sicilian holdings. It's a slim chance, I know, but you can try."

"He can have everything I own," Vinicius said simply.

It wasn't far to the Forum from the Carinnae, and they were soon there. The night was growing pale, and the peaks of the crenelated fortress loomed out of the shadows. But Petronius turned toward the prison gate, threw a sharp glance at the walls around it and stopped where he was.

"Too late," he said. "Praetorians . . ."

Twin ranks of soldiers lined the whole outside perimeter of the prison compound. The graying twilight silvered their iron spear points and gleamed on their helmets. Vinicius' face shone as white as marble.

"Let's go on," he said.

A few moments later they stopped before the wall of praetorians. Petronius, who had an extraordinary memory and could name not only all the officers but also most of the rank-and-file guardsmen, soon spotted a cohort colonel he knew and beckoned him over.

"What's happening here, Niger?" he asked. "Did they send you to protect the prison?"

"That's right, my lord. The prefect thought there might be an attempt to free the fire setters."

"Do you have orders to keep out visitors?"

"No, my lord. Friends will be coming to see the prisoners, and we'll catch more Christians."

"In that case, let me in," Vinicius said. He squeezed Petronius' hand and embraced him briefly. "Go and see Acte. I'll come by for news."

"Come when you can."

But in that moment the sound of singing rose from behind the walls and from the deep subterranean dungeons almost at their feet. The hymn was soft and barely audible at first, but then it swelled and grew, gathering up a choir of men's and women's voices along with the trilling of imprisoned children so that the whole prison resounded like a giant harp.

There was, however, neither sorrow nor despair in the sudden music. It rang with joy. Its cry was triumphant. The soldiers stared at one another with open amazement. The first gold and rosy glints of dawn appeared in the sky.

‹60›

"CHRISTIANS TO THE LIONS!" rang without end through all the quarters of the city. Not only was there no doubt anywhere from the start that they were the true cause of the disaster, but everyone wanted to believe them guilty since their punishment would provide superb entertainment.

The ruin of Rome, however—as everyone believed with extraordinary promptness—couldn't have been so catastrophic unless the gods were angry, and so propitiatory offerings were ordered in all the temples. The senate dipped into the sacred books of the Sybillae to stage the ceremonial public sacrifices to Vulcan, Ceres and Proserpine, the god of fire and the goddesses of fruitfulness and darkness. Matrons prayed to Juno, the mother of all the gods, and marched in procession to the sea for water with which to bathe her statue. Housewives prepared ritual feasts and vigils for the lesser gods. All of Rome strove to cleanse itself of sin and to placate the immortals on Olympus, and in the meantime broad new avenues were laid out in the ruins. Ground was already being cleared for the foundations of splendid palaces, villas and new temples. But first and foremost, a vast wooden amphitheater was built at record speed, to provide the arena for the Christians' torment.

Right after the decision in Tiberius' palace, orders went out to all the overseas proconsuls to supply vast numbers of wild beasts for the arena. Tigellinus emptied all the pens and cages on the Italian mainland, down to the smallest city. His orders set the entire population of coastal Africa on a gigantic hunt. Fleets of ships brought tigers and elephants from Asia, crocodiles and hippopotami from the Nile, lions from the Atlas mountains, wolves and bears from the Pyrenees, wild dogs from Hibernia, mastiffs from the Epirus, bisons from Germany and the huge ferocious wild bulls known as aurochs that terrorized the forests of the north. The sheer number of the condemned promised a spectacle never seen before, dwarfing all other slaughters ever staged. Caesar determined to drown the memory of the fire in such wholesale bloodshed that even Rome would be drunk with it, so the coming carnage looked like a splendid show.

Delighted mobs helped the city watch and the praetorians in hunting down the Christians. This was easy work since whole groups of them camped in the gardens along with everybody else and didn't try to hide who and what they were. Surrounded, they offered no resistance; they merely knelt, sang their joyful hymns and let themselves be dragged away without any struggle. But their meekness merely enraged the mobs, which didn't understand its source; the persecutors took this mild acceptance of oppression for depravity and a persistent dedication to the forces of evil.

Madness seized the crowds. It happened that the blood-mad mobs tore the Christians out of the hands of the praetorians and ripped them apart with their bare hands. Women were dragged to prison by the hair. The skulls of children were smashed on cobblestones. Thousands of people ran howling through the streets, hunting day and night for victims in the rubble, chimneys and cellars. Bonfires blazed at night outside every prison where drunken bacchanalia erupted in wild songs and dances, while the revelers listened with anticipation to the fierce, thundering roars of caged beasts of prey that echoed through the city. Then came a heat wave of unbelievable proportions, with nights so hot and humid they seemed suffused with blood and the choking violence of chaos.

All pity died. It seemed as if people forgot how to speak and remembered only the one, endless exclamation: "Christians to the lions!"

The exorbitant cruelty was met by an equally determined martyrdom. The Christians were going to die willingly, and some even sought death until their superiors told them it was a sin. Their elders ordered them to meet only outside the city, in the subterranean caverns along the Appian Way and in the country vineyards of Christian patricians, none of whom had been arrested until then. Everyone at the Palatine was aware that Flavius, Domitilla, Pomponia Graecina and Vinicius belonged to the Christians; but Nero didn't think the masses would believe such people would burn Rome, and since the point of the manhunt was to convince the people, their deaths were deferred. Some of the Augustans thought they were saved by Acte, but they were wrong. She could save no one. She lived in isolation, abandoned, forgotten, and tolerated only if she stayed out of Nero's and Poppea's sight. Petronius did go to see her on Ligia's behalf after he left Vinicius at the Mammertine, but she could offer him no more than tears and pity.

She did, however, go to see Ligia in the prison, bringing food and fresh clothes. She helped convince the bribed keepers they should spare the prisoner from their own abuse.

Petronius couldn't rid himself of the idea that he was to blame for Ligia's situation. If it weren't for him and his idea of taking her from Aulus and Pomponia, most likely she would never have met Poppea and would have avoided prison. Moreover, wanting to win his duel with Tigellinus, he spared no effort and left nothing to chance. Within days of her arrest he called on Seneca and Domitius Afer, on Crispinilla through whom he sought to influence Poppea, on Terpnos and Diodorus and the beautiful Pythagoras, and finally on Paris and Aliturus whom Nero seldom denied anything. Through Chrysothemis, who was now the mistress of Vatinius, he tried to win even that crude and greedy debauchee's support, showering him and all the others with promises and money.

But all these efforts failed. Seneca lived in dread for his own day-to-day survival and argued that while the Christians might be innocent of arson, they ought to be exterminated anyway for the good of Rome, thus rationalizing in advance the carnage to come. Terpnos and Diodorus took the money and did nothing for it. Vatinius ran to Caesar to denounce Petronius for attempted bribery. Only Aliturus, who was at first hostile toward the Christians but now felt some pity, dared to mention the imprisoned girl and intercede with Caesar, but Nero told him bluntly: "Do you think I lack the spirit of Brutus, who founded the Republic? If he could sacrifice his children for the good of Rome, can I do less with mine?"

When Petronius heard about this, he gave up all hope. "Now that he's found a comparison with Brutus," he said with resignation, "he'll never relent."

He went on worrying about Vinicius. Caring for him and looking at things in his own Roman way, he thought the desperate young man might take his own life. "Right now," he told himself, "he's kept alive by everything he does to help her and by the horror of seeing her in prison. That's what keeps him going. But what if nothing helps and he loses the last spark of hope? By Castor! He won't live without her. He'll throw himself on his sword."

Petronius found it easier to accept such an end to living than to grasp the kind of suffering and love that could cause death by his own hand.

Meanwhile, Vinicius was also doing all he could think of or imagine. He called on the Augustans he despised, crushing his pride and begging them to save Ligia. Using Vitelius as a go-between, he offered all his Sicilian estates to Tigellinus, along with anything else the prefect might want. But Tigellinus declined, probably not to jeopardize his standing with Poppea. To prostrate himself before Caesar and beg Nero's pity would have led nowhere, but he was ready to do even that.

"And what will you do if he refuses?" Petronius demanded, alarmed about the outcome. "Or worse yet, if he answers you with some gross gibe or an obscene threat?"

The answer was clearly seen on the young tribune's suddenly pinched face, in the grimace of pain, and in the glint of murder that flashed in his eyes.

"There you are!" Petronius pointed as an explanation. "That's why I advised against it. That'll slam the gates on all possible avenues of rescue."

But Vinicius brought himself back under control and rubbed a numb hand along his sweaty forehead. "No," he murmured. "No! I'm a Christian!"

"And you'll forget it when the time comes just like you forgot it a moment ago. You have the right to doom yourself, but you've no right to doom her as well. Remember how they killed the daughter of Sejanus in the Mammertine and what they did to her before they killed her."

He knew he wasn't wholly honest when he spoke like that. He was far more concerned about Vinicius than he was about Ligia. But he also knew that nothing would keep the young tribune at a greater distance from a fatal step than the thought he might be adding to her irrevocable doom. As hindsight would later show, he was right in another supposition: The emperor's circle expected a visit from the dangerous young soldier and made appropriate plans to ambush Vinicius.

Meanwhile, the agonies that racked the young man passed every boundary of suffering known to men.

From the moment Ligia was taken to prison and the aura of her future martyrdom brushed her with its unearthly glow, he started to think of her in yet another way. Love turned to reverence. He not only loved her a hundred times stronger but found himself adoring her in an almost spiritual sense as if she were a being touched by God and not of this plane. The thought that he might lose her, that this twin entity he loved as a woman and venerated as a religious symbol might die in the arena, and might have to suffer other agonies far more excruciating for her than merely dying, froze his blood. Roman law forbade the execution of virgins and children; Sejanus' twelve-year-old daughter, condemned to die with all her family by an earlier Caesar, was raped by her jailers before she could be legally beheaded. Petronius resurrected this horror in his mind.

All his thoughts—his mind and his spirit—turned into a single constant groan. His senses were reeling. It seemed at times as if explosions were erupting in his skull and that they'd either obliterate his feelings or blow him apart. He lost his grip on reality. He stopped trying to connect with the world around him. He ceased to understand why this merciful, loving Christ—this God!—failed to help his followers, why the sooty walls of the Palatine weren't caving in on themselves, burying Nero, the Augustans, the camps of the praetorians, and the whole monstrous city of violence and crime. He thought this was the way things ought to be, that nothing else should be allowed to happen and that everything he saw around him was just a horrible nightmare crushing his spirit and sending his mind howling.

But it was not a nightmare, not a dream. The roar of wild beasts told him this was really happening. The thud of axes, out of which rose the new arenas, was the true, undisputable reality, not any illusion. The howling mobs and the crowded prisons were its confirmation. His faith in Christ trembled and turned to fear at such times, and this fear was possibly the worst of his torments.

And in the meantime Petronius was telling him to remember what Sejanus' child went through before she died.

« 61 »

EVERYTHING FAILED, despite all his efforts. Vinicius fell so low that he sought help from Caesar's and Poppea's freedmen and slave women, paid for their empty promises and bought their goodwill with costly gifts. He found Poppea's first husband, Rufius Crispinus, and got him to write a letter to his former wife. He gave his Antium villa to Rufius, her son by that marriage, but this only angered Caesar who hated his stepson. He sent a special courier to Spain, begging help from Otho, Poppea's second husband. He offered all his property and himself as well to anyone he thought might have some influence on the vengeful empress, until he realized that he had become a joke among the Augustans who were playing with him for their own amusement. He would have done better, he thought, if he had pretended he didn't care about Ligia one way or another.

The same thought occurred to Petronius. Meanwhile the days rushed past. The amphitheaters were ready. People were already getting their *tesserae*, or free season passes, to the morning shows, but this time the matinees were to take all day. The sheer number of victims and the variety of torments planned for them promised to stretch the entertainments into weeks and months. The prisons were so full that the praetorians no longer knew where to jail the Christians, and fever raged in the crowded cells, threatening to sweep the city. The burial pits, or mass graves in which slaves were buried, started overflowing, and the fear of plague added to the hurry.

Vinicius saw and heard it all, and his hopes burned down to cinders. While there was time left, he could fool himself that he would be able to find some way and do something, but time had run out. The games were beginning. Any day now Ligia could find herself in a holding pen whose only gate led to the arena. Vinicius couldn't guess which of the circuses would be her destiny and started touring all the amphitheaters and arenas, bribing the beast-keepers and the guards and binding them to promises they would never honor. It came to him now and then that he worked only to make her death easier and her end less frightful. That's when he felt that his skull held burning coals rather than a brain.

He had no thoughts beyond that, no aims and no goals. He saw no reality for himself beyond her death and planned nothing more than to die beside her, the two of them together. His one fear was that his pain would snap his life too soon and that he would die before they faced the terrible arena.

Petronius and his few remaining friends also thought that he would step into the realm of shades almost any day. Life had no meaning for him now. The young man's face turned a waxy gray, like the death masks people hung in the alcoves of their household gods. A numbed surprise seemed frozen in his features, as if he couldn't understand what happened and what it could mean. When someone spoke to him, he clutched his head with a mindless, automatic gesture, his eyes full of questions, and stared back in terror. He spent his nights in the Mammertine, watching with Ursus at her door until she ordered him to rest. Then he would go home and pace the atrium floor into the late morning.

He also prayed. The slaves would come across him kneeling with outstretched arms or with his face pressed to the marble floor. He called on Christ. There was no other hope. All else had failed and only an act of God could save and rescue Ligia, and so Vinicius beat his head on the stone pavement slabs and begged for a miracle.

But he kept his wits enough to know that Peter's prayers would mean more than his. Peter had promised Ligia to him. Peter baptized him. Peter himself could make miracles, so let him show the way, bring some relief, and help him understand what he couldn't fathom.

He set out to find him. The few Christians still at large hid Peter even from one another, in case some weak soul among them gave way and betrayed him either on purpose or against his will. Quite consumed by his efforts to set Ligia free, and needing all his concentration to stay sane in the savagery of the persecutions, Vinicius had lost sight of the apostle. He had met him only once since his baptism, and that was before the arrests began. He went to see the quarryman in whose hut Peter had baptized him and learned where to find him. Peter, the quarryman told him, would be in the vineyard owned by Cornelius Pudens past Porta Salaria, where the remaining Christians had gathered for prayer.

"He's sure to be there," the quarryman insisted. "Let me take you there."

They went that night at twilight, got across the walls, and made their way through a corridor of sandpits and winding, reed-choked gullies to the untended vineyards, which had the still, hushed look of a wilderness far off the beaten track. The meeting, as they saw by the flicker of carefully hidden lanterns, was taking place in the winery where the grapes were pressed. The murmur of prayers led them to the door.

Barely able to make out dim shapes in the pale lamplight, Vinicius saw several dozen people inside praying on their knees. It was a low, sad chant rather than a prayer, a sort of litany murmured by a leader, in which the chorus of men's and women's voices repeated "Christ have mercy on us" in a mournful cadence. Heartrending grief, anxiety and complaint underlay this murmur.

Peter was there. He knelt in front, praying before a wooden cross nailed to the wall. Vinicius recognized his white hair and thin upraised hands. His first thought was to burst through the gathering, throw himself at Peter's feet and shout: "Help me!" But his body failed him. His knees bent under him, either from exhaustion or from the solemnity of prayer, and he slid to his knees just inside the entrance, groaning through clenched teeth: "Christ have mercy on us!"

If he had been truly conscious of everything around him, he would have known he was not the only man who sobbed out his prayer; everyone else had brought his or her own pain, bewilderment and fear. There wasn't one man or woman there who hadn't lost someone precious to him or her. And when the best and bravest of the Christians were already jailed, when each moment brought fresh news about the tortures and bestiality they suffered in prison, when the disaster reached such vast, unimaginable proportions—and, finally, when only this meager handful of Christ's followers was left— there wasn't one survivor whose faith didn't falter. "Where is Christ when we need him?" they asked themselves, giving way to doubt. "Why does he permit evil to triumph over good?"

Meanwhile they prayed, having nothing else. They begged for mercy to end their despair. No matter how shaken in their faith they were, each of them still carried the spark of hope that Christ would come, destroy their oppressors, hurl Nero into the abyss and set his rule over all mankind. Their eyes were still fixed with hope on the sky, their ears were still straining for the sound of angel choirs and trumpets, and their voices still trembled in prayer.

Fervor gripped Vinicius. He felt the same sense of exaltation that had swept over him in the hut of the quarryman. Each time he chorused "Christ have mercy on us" with the others, he felt more certain that he would be heard. How could Christ refuse them? They were calling out in darkness, out of the abyss, from the depths of anguish. Peter himself was calling. Any moment now the skies would rip asunder, the earth would shudder down to its foundations, and he would come in a blinding light with stars at his feet, bringing love and justice, gathering his faithful worshipers to him and letting Hell devour their oppressors.

Vinicius hid his face in both hands and crouched close to the ground. The air was suddenly hushed around him, as if fear had stifled all the murmured prayers. Something, he knew, was about to happen. A miracle was coming. He was sure that when he looked up again and opened his eyes, he'd see a blinding light and hear a voice that turned hearts to water.

But the silence went on, ending at last in a woman's sobs.

He looked up, eyes fixed on space, understanding nothing. There was no great light. A few stray tongues of pale yellow flame flickered in the lanterns, while silvery moonlight seeped in through the ventilation hole in the roof and ceiling. The people who knelt near him held their weeping eyes fixed as blindly as his own on the wooden cross. He heard other sobbing. He could hear the short, soft signal whistles with which the sentries checked on one another outside.

Then Peter rose from his knees and turned to face the others.

"Children," he said. "Lift up your hearts to the Savior and offer him your tears."

Then he was silent.

"I am a widow," a woman's voice broke in suddenly, spilling immeasurable pain and sorrow. "I had just one son to take care of me in my old age. Give him back to me, O Lord!"

There was another silence in which nothing stirred. Peter looked out over his kneeling flock, troubled and unsure, and suddenly as old, bowed and helpless as an ancient crone.

"The hangmen raped my little daughters," groaned another voice, "and Christ let it happen."

"There's just me left to look after my children now," complained a third. "Who'll feed them when they drag me away as well?"

"Linus," said a fourth, "was dying, but they took him anyway and stretched him on the rack."

"The praetorians will get us when we go back home," said a fifth. "Where are we to hide?"

Words fell like stones in the hush of the night; each dull, despairing groan was an accusation. The old fisherman closed his eyes and bowed his trembling head over all this suffering and pain. No one said anything for another long moment after that, and only the cautious whistling of the sentries came from beyond the shed.

Vinicius struggled to his feet, wanting to claw his way through the throng and demand a miracle since only a miracle could reverse the terrible decree. But then he faltered. An abyss yawned suddenly at his feet and turned his legs to stone. What, he thought, if the apostle confessed his own helplessness? What if he admitted that the Caesar of Rome was mightier than Jesus of Nazareth? The hair lifted on his head in terror, because if that should happen, then the abyss would swallow and devour not only the last remnants of his hope but also himself, Ligia, his love for Christ, his faith and all he lived by. There'd be nothing left but death and darkness without end.

Peter started talking. He began so low that hardly anyone heard him in the beginning.

"My children!" he said. "I was there when they crucified the Master. I heard the mallets pounding in the nails. I saw them raise the cross and fix it in the ground so that the multitudes could watch him die . . ."

Step by step and word by word he led them through the Passion.

". . . I saw them thrust the lance into his side, and I saw his death. Going home from the cross I cried out in torment just as you are crying. 'Lord,' I wept, 'what will become of us without you? You are God! Why did you let this happen? Why did you die? We believed your kingdom would come, why do you break our hearts?'"

Fear by fear and sorrow by sorrow, he took them to the Resurrection.

". . . And he, our Lord and God, rose on the third day and was among us, and then went up into his kingdom as bright as the sun. . . . And we, seeing ourselves as men of little faith, fortified our hearts and have been sowing his seeds from that day on."

Here he stopped and turned toward the woman whose complaint came first.

"Why do you ask so much?" His voice was firmer, stronger. "God gave himself to torture and death, and you want him to turn them away from you? Oh, people of little faith! Haven't you grasped his teaching? Is this the only life he promised you? He comes to you now and says: 'Follow in my footsteps.' He lifts you up to him, and you clutch at the ground under you and cry, 'Master, save me!'

"I'm dust before God," he thundered now. "But for you I'm God's apostle and his deputy on earth. I tell you in Christ's name you've nothing to fear! Life waits for you, not death. Joy without end, not torments. Song waits, not tears and moaning. Thrones wait for you, not slavery!"

He seemed to grow and spread, majestic in his great simplicity.

"I tell you as God's apostle, widow," he said, "that your son won't die but will be born in glory to a new life, and you will be together. I tell you, father, whose innocent daughters they've soiled, they'll be as unblemished as the lilies of Hebron when you meet again. I say in Christ's name to all you mothers who'll be torn away from your orphaned children, all you who'll lose your fathers, all who cry for pity, all who'll witness the death of those they love, all who are sick at heart, unfortunate and fearful, and I say again to you who must die: You will wake as if from a dream into eternal light, and the Son of God will shine in your night. In Christ's name, let blindness fall from your eyes and let your hearts be free!"

He raised his open palms as if in command, and fresh blood seemed to fill all his veins and a shudder moved along his bones. This was no longer a stooped and troubled old man who stood before them, unsure of what to say. It was a giant, an embodiment of power, who lifted them out of the dust and sent their spirits soaring.

"Amen!" many chorused.

A light seemed to glow and spread from his eyes. A sense of holiness, majesty and power flowed from him. People bowed before him. When the last amen died away, he spoke again.

"Sow your seeds in tears so you may harvest joy. Why do you fear evil? The God who lives within you soars above this earth, this Rome and all the walls. Stones will run with tears, blood will soak the sand, your bodies will fill graves beyond overflowing, but I say you'll conquer! The Lord is marching on this lair of pride, murder and oppression, and you are his legion! And just as he ransomed the world from sin with his own blood, so he wants you to give your blood and suffering for this city's sins! These are his words! He speaks through my lips!"

Arms thrown wide, he stood with an upraised face and eyes fixed on the space above him, and everyone grew so still it seemed as if all hearts had stopped beating. They felt he was seeing something their eyes couldn't see. His features softened, shifted. They became ecstatic. He stood in silence as if struck dumb by immeasurable bliss.

"You're here, Master!" he said at last. "You show me your ways.

But how is it, Christ? Why do you want this seat of Satan for your capital, not Jerusalem? It's here, then, you want to build your church, out of all the blood and all the tears? Is this where your eternal kingdom is to stand? Where Nero rules today? Oh Master, Master. . . . Am I to watch over your flocks from here? And you command these frightened, timorous people to build the foundations of your universal church out of their own dead bones? And am I to rule their spirits, and all the peoples of the earth?

"Power flows from you," he went on, "to fill the fearful hearts! I hear your command! I'll be their shepherd until the end of time! Glory be to your will! You send us out to conquer in your name! Glory! Glory! Hosanna! Hosanna!"

Those who were numb with fear rose from their knees, captured by his vision. Faith flooded the doubting. Some chorused "Hosanna!" Others cried *"Pro Christe!"* Bright summer lightning flashed in the clear sky and lit up the shed. They showed pale faces, swept by a wave of feeling, silent and expectant.

Deep into his vision, Peter prayed quietly a long time and then seemed to wake.

"See how the Master conquered your doubts," he said, turning his inspired, glowing face toward the gathering. "Go now and conquer in his name!"

Although he already knew they would conquer and that something lasting and eternal would rise from their blood and tears, his voice shook nonetheless when he began to bless them.

"Blessed be your suffering, my children," he told them, scrawling the sign of the cross in the air above them. "Blessed be your death and your life everlasting."

But no one wanted to leave him just yet. They surged around him, crying out, "We're ready now! But you take care, holy one! Hide yourself! You're Christ's deputy, ruling in his name!"

They clung to his robes, wanting to protect him, He placed his hands on their heads as he went among them, blessing each of them like a father who sends his children on a distant journey.

They started to hurry out into the open then, anxious to get home and to the prisons and arenas. Their minds had broken away from earthly concerns. Their thoughts lifted toward eternity. They walked as if entranced or dreaming, to pit their spirits and their faith against cruelty and power.

Nereus, the vineyard steward of Cornelius Pudens, led Peter to his house along a hidden path, trailed by Vinicius in the moonlit night. When they came to Nereus' hut, Vinicius ran and threw himself at the apostle's feet.

Peter recognized him. "What do you need, my son?"

Vinicius didn't dare ask for anything after what he had heard. He merely threw his arms around Peter's feet, pressed his forehead to them and broke out in tears.

"I know." Peter nodded. "They took the girl you love. Pray for her."

"Master!" Vinicius groaned, clutching his sandals. "Master! I'm dust to him, but you knew Christ himself! You plead with him for me! You intercede!"

He was shuddering like a leaf, unable to cope with his pain. He beat his head on the ground before the apostle. Peter alone had the power, he knew. He had seen it. Peter would bring Ligia back to him.

Peter was moved. He could feel the pain. He thought of Ligia, who had thrown herself at his feet in much the same way, pleading for mercy after Crispus flayed her with his accusations. He had raised her up and comforted her, he remembered. He stooped and helped Vinicius to his feet.

"Of course I'll pray for her," he said. "But remember, son, what I told the others. God himself suffered on the cross. And don't forget that life everlasting begins after this one."

"I know!" Vinicius struggled to speak, gulping air as if he couldn't breathe. "I heard you. But . . . I can't. If Christ needs blood, ask him to take mine. I'm a soldier, master! Let him give me three times the pain meant for her. I'll bear it. But let him save Ligia! She's just a child, master, and he's mightier than Caesar. I believe it! Mightier than all the Caesars! You loved her yourself, master. You gave us your blessings! She's still only an innocent child!"

He dropped to the ground again and pressed his face to Peter's knees. "You knew Christ, master! You knew him. He'll listen to you. Intercede for her!"

Peter closed his eyes and prayed.

The summer lightning flashed again in the nervous sky, and Vinicius, his eyes fixed on the apostle's lips, waited for the verdict that meant life or death. It was so quiet they could hear the quail chirping among the vines and the dull thud of treadmills.

"Vinicius," the apostle said at last, "do you believe?"

"Master," the young man answered, "would I be here if I didn't?"

"Then believe until the end because faith moves mountains. Believe

Christ can save her even if you see her under an executioner's sword or in a lion's jaws. Believe and pray to him, and I will pray with you."

He faced the sky then. "Merciful Christ," he said. "Look down at this heartsick soul and comfort it. Temper the storm to what the lamb can bear. As you once asked your Father to turn away the cup of bitterness, so turn it now from this man who serves you! Amen!"

Vinicius stretched his arms toward the stars and groaned through his prayer: "I'm yours to command, Christ! Take me in her place!"

The sky in the East began to turn pale.

62

VINICIUS LEFT THE APOSTLE and hurried to the prison with renewed hope. Fear and despair still screamed in the depths of his innermost being, but he suppressed their cry. It seemed impossible that God would ignore the intercession of his own deputy and the power of his supplications. He was afraid not to hope and feared losing his power to believe.

"I'll trust in his mercy," he told himself, "even if I see her in a lion's mouth."

Cold sweat broke out on his temples at this thought, and everything within him shook, but he clung to his faith. Each of his heartbeats had become a prayer. Faith could move mountains, he told himself, because he felt a new power within him he didn't have before. He felt strong enough to try almost anything, which would have been impossible only yesterday. It was as if the times of terror were over and evil had vanished. Whenever desperation shrilled again within him, he brought to mind what he had seen that night and the venerable holy face lifted toward the sky in prayer.

"No!" he assured himself. "Christ won't refuse his first disciple and the shepherd of his flock. Christ won't refuse and I won't lose faith."

He hurried to the prison as if he were the bearer of good news, but there he ran into something new and unexpected. The praetorians detailed to guard the Mammertine all knew him by this time and seldom hindered him in any way, but this time the gates remained chained and the guard commander shook his head as he came up to him.

"Forgive me, noble tribune," the centurion said, "but I have orders not to let anyone in today."

"What orders?" Vinicius felt the blood drain from his face again.

The praetorian gave him a sympathetic glance. "Caesar's orders.

There's a lot of sickness in the prison. Maybe they're afraid visitors will spread disease."

"These orders are just for today, you said?"

"We change the guard at noon."

Vinicius said nothing. He bared his head. The small felt skullcap he wore seemed suddenly as heavy as lead. The centurion stepped a little closer.

"Steady, sir," he murmured. "Ursus and the keepers are watching over her."

He leaned forward and with one swift motion scrawled the shape of a fish on the pavement slab with his long Gallic sword.

Vinicius threw him a sharp glance. "And you're a praetorian?"

"Until they throw me in there." The centurion jerked his head toward the prison walls.

"I also worship Christ."

"I know, sir. Praise be to his name. I can't let you in, but if you write a letter, I'll see that she gets it."

"Thank you, brother."

He shook the soldier's hand and went away. His skullcap no longer seemed made of lead. The morning sun had climbed above the prison walls, and its fresh new light encouraged Vinicius. The Christian soldier had confirmed the power of Christ. He halted after a few steps and fixed his eyes on the pink clouds above the Capitol and the temple of Jupiter the Lawgiver.

"I didn't see her today, my lord," he murmured, "but I believe in you."

Petronius waited for him at home. Turning night into day in his usual manner, he had come back from the Palatine not long before, but long enough to bathe and have himself massaged before sleep.

"I've news for you," he said. "I was at Tullius Senecio's this morning, and Caesar was also there. I don't know what popped into Poppea's head, but she brought her little Rufius with her. Perhaps she wanted to appeal to Nero's artistic sensibilities with the child's beauty. Unfortunately the little tyke fell asleep during the recitation, just as Vespasian did the other time, and Copperbeard hit him with a goblet. He cut him badly and Poppea fainted. But everybody heard Caesar snarl: "I've had my bellyful of this roadside whelp!" And that's as good as a death sentence, as you know."

"God's justice hangs above Augusta," Vinicius said, nodding. "But why are you telling me this?"

"I say it because you and Ligia are both the victims of Poppea's vengeance. Perhaps now she'll be too full of her own troubles to hound you as fiercely. She might be more willing to listen to reason and let me influence her. I plan to see her and talk to her tonight."

"Thank you. That's good to hear."

"And you go to bathe and get a little rest. Your lips are blue, and you're just a shadow of what you used to be."

But Vinicius had more pressing matters on his mind. "Did anyone say when the first morning games would start?" he wanted to know.

"In ten days. But they'll use up the other prisons first. The more time we have, the better. Nothing is lost yet."

The truth was, of course, that there was no longer any hope for Ligia, and Petronius knew it. Once Caesar found the lofty answer he gave to Aliturus, a way to compare himself with Brutus, the girl was doomed, and nothing could help her. Pity for Vinicius also drove him to hold back what he heard in Senecio's house, that Caesar and Tigellinus planned to pick the most beautiful Christian girls for their own amusement before they were sent into the arenas and give them out to their other cronies. The rest were to be raped on the day of the games by the animal-keepers and the praetorians.

He knew that Vinicius wouldn't want to live once Ligia was killed, and he did his best to keep his hopes going. Compassion was a part of it, but he also had an aesthetic reason. It seemed important to this lover of the exquisite that if Vinicius was to die, he should do it proudly, like a Roman, in the full flower of his youth and beauty, not like a gray shadow drained by sleeplessness and pain.

"I'll say it to Augusta more or less like this," he remarked. "*Save Ligia for Vinicius, and I'll save your Rufius.*' And I'll really give some thought to that. One word planted at a proper moment in Copperbeard's ear can save or doom anyone. In the worst scenario we'll gain a little time."

"Thank you," Vinicius said again.

"You'll thank me best if you eat and rest. By Athene! Odysseus kept sleep and food in mind at the worst of times! I expect you spent the whole night in the prison?"

"No. I tried to go this morning, but there's a new order not to let anybody in. Find out for me, Petronius, if that's just for today or if it's to continue through the start of the games."

"I'll find out tonight and tell you tomorrow. But now, even if the sun were to vanish forever in the land of shadows, I'm off to bed, and I advise you to do the same."

They parted, but Vinicius went into the library to write his letter to Ligia. When he was done, he took it to the prison and handed it to the Christian officer, who took it inside at once. He was back soon afterward with greetings from Ligia, and he promised to bring out her own letter later in the day.

Vinicius didn't want to go all the way home again, so he sat down on a boulder to wait for her message. The sun had climbed high in the sky, and the Forum's usual crowd flowed down the Clivus Argentarius, the street of the silversmiths and money-changers. Peddlers hawked their goods. Fortune-tellers clutched at passersby. The more settled of the citizenry gathered soberly around the speakers' platforms to gossip about fresh news or to hear whatever orator happened to be haranguing the crowd. Groups of idlers looked for shade under temple porticoes as the day grew warmer, driving out flocks of doves that whirled into the sky with a great rush of wings, gleaming in the sunlight like feathery white balls thrown into the sky.

The sharp morning light, the rising heat, the rumble of voices and his own exhaustion settled on Vinicius. His eyes blinked and closed. The rattle of dice and the monotonous calls of the *morra* players around him rocked him into sleep. The sentries' measured tread quickly sent him under. He tried to lift his head a few times, staring at the prison, then rested it against a rockface, sighed like a child after a bout of weeping and fell fast asleep.

Dreams came at once. He gave way to visions. He thought he was carrying Ligia at night through some unknown vineyard while Pomponia Graecina carried a torch ahead. A far-off voice, not unlike Petronius', cried "Turn back!" behind him. But he paid no attention and followed Pomponia to a hut where Peter the apostle waited on the threshold. "We've come from the arena, master," Vinicius told Peter, "but we're unable to wake her. Will you wake her, please?" But Peter shook his head. "Christ will do that," he said.

Then the dream blurred. He saw another orgy. Nero and Poppea were holding little Rufius, whose forehead ran with blood. Petronius was trying to stanch the flow and wash the wound. Tigellinus was scattering ashes on the banquet tables, richly set with a variety of dishes; Vitelius gorged himself on all the food at once, while a swarm of other Augustans sprawled on dining couches. Ligia was resting at his side. Lions were padding among the tables with blood dripping off their tawny manes. She begged him to get rid of them, but he couldn't do it. He was too weak to stir. Then the nightmare plunged into total chaos and gave way to darkness.

The glare of the heat and a sudden uproar that broke out beside him pulled him out of his sleep. He rubbed his eyes. The street was jammed with people, but two runners dressed in yellow tunics parted the crowds with long bamboo canes, shouting for room for a magnificent litter carried by four muscular Egyptians. Some white-robed stranger was sitting in the litter, his face hidden by rolls of papyrus clutched in front of his eyes.

"Make room for the noble Augustan!" the runners shouted.

The street was so crowded, however, that the litter had to pause and halt for a moment right beside Vinicius. The distinguished passenger dropped his reading matter and thrust his head impatiently through the curtains.

"Drive this scum aside!" he shouted. "And be quick about it!"

He caught sight of the young tribune, pulled his head swiftly back behind the curtains and hid his face again behind the papyrus.

Vinicius stared and rubbed his eyes once more, certain he was dreaming.

The man he saw was Chilon.

It all lasted only a fraction of a moment. The runners cleared some space, and the Egyptian bearers got ready to move. But Vinicius suddenly understood much that had confused and puzzled him earlier. He stepped up to the litter.

"Greetings to you, Chilon!" he said.

"Greetings, young man," Chilon answered loftily, trying to look much calmer than he felt. "Don't hold me up. I'm in a hurry to call on my friend, the noble Tigellinus."

Vinicius clutched the edge of the litter, leaned forward and stared straight into Chilon's eyes. "You betrayed Ligia?" he asked in a low voice.

"Help, Colossus of Memnon!" cried the frightened Greek.

He could see no threat in Vinicius' eyes, so his fright passed quickly. He was, he remembered swiftly, under the protection of Tigellinus and Caesar himself, that is to say, the two greatest powers on earth before whom everything alive trembled in the dust. Moreover he had strong slaves around him, while Vinicius stood before him unarmed and alone, with a gaunt, harrowed face and a body stooped with pain.

What can he do to me? he thought. I'm safe. He's helpless. I am the Augustan! He fixed his pale, red-rimmed eyes on the young patrician as all his insolence and effrontery returned.

"You had me whipped when I was dying of hunger," he whispered.

Both were quiet for a moment. "I wronged you, Chilon," Vinicius said at last in a dull somber voice.

"Ha!" The Greek lifted his chin proudly in the air and snapped his fingers with disdain, indifference and contempt.

"My dear fellow," he said loud enough for everyone near to hear, "if you've a petition, bring it to my house on the Esquiline early in the day where I receive guests and clients after my morning bath."

He flipped his hand, signaling his Egyptians to pick up the litter, while his runners waved their bamboo canes and shouted in chorus:

"Make way for the litter of the noble Chilon Chilonides! Make room there! Give way!"

63

IN A LONG, hurried letter written in her cell, Ligia said her final good-byes to Vinicius. She knew by then that no more visitors could enter the prison and that the next time she saw Vinicius would be from the arena. She asked him to find out when her turn would come—and to make sure to be there!—because she wanted to look at him once more before she died.

Her letter showed no fear. She wrote that she and all the others couldn't wait to stand in the arena; they longed for the liberation they would find there. Expecting that Aulus and Pomponia would come back to Rome, she asked that they, too, be there on her day. Each word rang with the joy of a soaring spirit, full of exaltation; each showed the severance of all ties with the world that all the condemned lived by in their cells; and each brimmed with faith that all the promises would be kept beyond the grave.

"Whether Christ frees me now or after death," she wrote, "he promised me to you through his apostle. Therefore, I am yours."

Don't pity her, she begged him. Don't let his grief undercut his faith. Death cut no bonds with her. She was his forever. With heart-breaking, childlike trust she assured Vinicius that she'd tell Christ, immediately after her death in the arena, that she left her betrothed, Mark, in Rome and that he longed for her with all his heart. She thought Christ might allow her soul to return to visit for a while, long enough to tell him that she lived, that she was beyond all memory of suffering and that she was happy. The entire letter breathed happiness and faith beyond measuring. But she had one request of an earthly nature. She asked that he claim her body in the *spoliarium*—the pits in which the bodies of dead beasts and slain gladiators waited for mass burial—and bury her as his wife in his family's tomb, where he would also lie some day.

He thought his heart would break as he read the letter. He couldn't understand how anyone could throw her to the lions or how

Christ could fail to show pity on her. All his faith and trust rested on that. He went home to write in reply that he would wait each day by the dungeon walls until Christ crumbled them and gave her back to him. He told her to believe God could do that even in the circus, that the great apostle begged him for it fervently and that she would soon be free. The Christian centurion was to give her the letter the next day.

But when Vinicius went to the prison the next morning, the centurion left the ranks, led him aside and said:

"Hear me, sir. Christ tested you, and now he shows his grace. Last night Caesar and the prefect sent their freedmen here to pick out some Christian virgins for their beds, and they were asking about the girl you love. But our Lord touched her with the fever that's killing the condemned in the Tullianum, so they let her be. She was already unconscious by nightfall yesterday, blessed be the Savior's name! The sickness saved her from rape and humiliation, maybe it can save her from death as well!"

Vinicius felt so weak, he had to lean on the centurion's iron shoulder plates.

"Thank the Lord's mercy," the soldier continued. "They brought Linus here and tortured him, but seeing he was dying anyway, they let him go. Maybe now they'll let you have your young lady, and Christ will make her well."

The young tribune stood silent and staring at the ground a while longer.

"That's how it is, centurion," he said softly. "Christ saved her from shame. He'll save her from death."

He sat until nightfall under the prison walls. When he got home that night, he sent his slaves for Linus and had him moved to one of his country villas.

Hearing about all this, Petronius also decided to act at once. He had already been to see Poppea, now he went again. He found her at little Rufius' bedside. The child's skull was fractured, and the little boy kept losing consciousness. Terrified and desperate, his mother fought to bring him back to life, wondering perhaps if she was saving him for a much more brutal and violent death. She was so totally engrossed by her own suffering, she didn't even want to hear about Vinicius and Ligia, but Petronius added to her terror.

"You've angered an unknown god," he told her. "You, Augusta, worship the Hebrew Jehovah, but the Christians say that Chrestos is his son. Think, then, if you're not being punished by the angry father.

Who knows if what happened here isn't just their vengeance and if Rufius' life doesn't depend on what you do next."

"What should I do?" Poppea was desperately afraid.

"Placate the angry god."

"How?"

"Ligia is sick. Influence Caesar or Tigellinus to give her to Vinicius."

The look she gave him was a blend of anger, self-pity and despair. "Do you think I still can?" she asked bitterly.

"Then try something else. If Ligia gets well, she'll go to the arena. Go to the vestals and arrange for the *Virgo Magna* to be near the gates of the Tullianum when they're taking the prisoners out to execution. Ask the chief vestal to order the girl freed. She's allowed to do that. She won't refuse you, and not even Caesar can object."

"And if Ligia dies of that prison fever?"

"The Christians say Christ is a vengeful god, but he's also fair. Your good intentions could be enough for him."

"Let him give me a sign he'll save Rufius!" Poppea had to bargain.

"I'm not here as his representative, Augusta," Petronius reminded her. "I'm just here to tell you to be on good terms with all the gods, the Roman and the foreign ones alike."

"I'll go!" Poppea's voice expressed defeat and surrender.

Petronius drew a long, slow breath. He had gotten through at last.

Back with Vinicius, he didn't even bother to explain how he had won over the implacable Poppea. "Ask your god," he told Vinicius, "to keep Ligia alive through that prison fever. If she doesn't die, the chief vestal will order her freed at the gate. Our Augusta will write to her in person."

But Vinicius' eyes were burning with their own kind of fever. "Christ will free her."

Meanwhile Poppea tried to do even more than Petronius had asked her. She left her child's bedside. She would have been ready to sacrifice white bulls by the hundreds to every god and idol in the world if that would save Rufius. She left the boy in the keeping of her old nurse, Sylvia, and had herself carried to the vestals' temple in the Forum.

Nothing could have saved her child, however. The verdict had fallen in the Palatine. Poppea's litter had hardly cleared the main gate when two of Caesar's freedmen pushed their way into Rufius' sickroom. One threw himself at the old nurse, hurled her down and stuffed her mouth with bedding. The other seized a copper statuette of the Sphinx and stunned her with one blow.

Then they went to Rufius. The feverish, barely conscious boy didn't understand what was happening. He smiled at them. He tried to focus his luminous eyes on them as if to know who they were. But they stripped a sash off the nurse, wrapped it around his throat and strangled him quickly.

He cried out just once, calling for his mother. They wrapped the little body in a sheet, took it out, mounted ready horses and galloped all the way to Ostia where they weighed it down and threw it into the sea.

Poppea didn't find the chief vestal at the temple. The *Virgo Magna* and several other vestals were at a banquet given by Vatinius, so the empress hurried back to the Palatine. She found the empty bed and the cold corpse of Sylvia and went into shock. She fainted. Revived, she started to scream, and her wild screams echoed all night and through the next day.

On the third day Caesar ordered her to attend a banquet. She came dressed in her amethyst tunic and sat beside him: stony-faced, as still as a statue, silent, golden-haired, beautiful, foreboding and as malignant as the angel of death.

⟪64⟫

BEFORE THE FLAVIANS raised the Colosseum, Rome's circuses were built mainly of wood, and most of them burned down along with the city. But Nero ordered several new ones for the promised games, including a gigantic one whose massive timbers, cut on the slopes of the Atlas Mountains, began arriving by sea and up the Tiber just as soon as the flames died down and the ashes cooled. Because these games were supposed to tower over all the spectacles that had ever gone before, not just in cost and splendor but in the number of victims, this vast new amphitheater housed enormous cages for the wild beasts and their human prey.

Thousands of workmen labored day and night. Artisans of all kinds worked around the clock to build and decorate the colossal structure. People told wonders about the huge sums spent on the richly decorated seating and supporting arches, inlaid with bronze, amber, ivory, mother-of-pearl and rare tortoiseshell brought from overseas. Iced water, piped straight from the mountains, was to run in special conduits along the rows of benches, cooling the air pleasantly even in a heat wave. A vast purple *velarium* was to provide the shade. Arabian scents and aromatic oils were to be burned in censers placed between the benches. High in the rear were sprinklers to cool the spectators with mists of saffron and verbena water. The famous builders Severus and Celer used all their skills to raise an amphitheater greater than all others and able to accommodate more of the avid, thrill-seeking populace than any of the rest.

With all this expected so many weeks before, huge crowds stood waiting at the gates on opening day, massing since dawn on the morning of the first performance, and listening with mouth-watering pleasure to the roar of the lions, the hoarse cough of the panthers and the baying of the killer dogs. The keepers starved the animals for two days, teasing them by dragging slabs of bloody meat before their cages, goading them into a frenzy of hunger. This deadly uproar was so loud at times that people couldn't make themselves heard outside the gates, while the more imaginative among them turned pale with fear.

Sunrise brought a fresh and different sound. Calm, soaring hymns rose from the circus grounds, surprising the assembled gawkers.

"Christians!" the mobs muttered, staring at one another in anticipation. "That's the Christians."

As it happened, great crowds of them were brought over in the night from the prisons, coming from all holding jails at once rather than from one at a time as was first planned. The jostling rabble knew that the games would go on for weeks, even months. They speculated whether there would be time to finish off all those meant for this day's show before the day ended. The singing chorus was so large, with so many men, women and children gathered in the cages that it seemed unlikely one day would be enough to slaughter them all. Experts insisted that if they were sent into the arena as many as one or two hundred at a time, the animals would be so sated and tired by the killing they'd never maim and devour them all by nightfall. Others claimed that too many victims at a time would spoil the show. Large numbers distracted from the appreciation of the finer points and ruined the effect.

As it came closer to the time for the gates to open, when the crowds would pour into the long interior corridors known as *vomitoria*, the mood of the waiting mass lifted, became livelier, and the arguments spread to include a thousand other matters related to the spectacle ahead. Some people argued that the lions did a better job of ripping up a victim; others favored the tigers. Bets were made. Every wild beast seemed to have its supporting faction. Hot arguments raged about the gladiators who were to fight in the arena prior to the Christians, and again there were instant factions for every kind of fighter. Some swore by the Semnones who lived between the Elbe and Oder rivers in the German forests. Others bet on the Gauls or lauded the Thracians or argued the merits of sword fighters against the *retiarri* who fought with net and trident.

Groups of these trained, disciplined professionals started arriving early in the morning, marching in small troops or sizable detachments from the various gladiator schools under their sword masters. Not wanting to waste their strength before the combat, they came without their heavy fighting armor; some walked quite naked, wearing wreaths of flowers in their hair and carrying green branches. As handsome as young gods in the sharp, early morning light, their muscular oiled bodies hard and as smooth as marble and full of life and power, they sent the populace roaring with enthusiasm. Rome worshiped strength and beauty in the human body. Many of the fighters were known in the city. Shouts of "Hail Furnius!" burst from the crowd and echoes of "Hail Leo!" "Hail Maximus!" "Hail Diomedes!"

Young girls shot them glances full of love, and they sought out the prettiest and joked with them in passing, as if they had nothing to trouble their minds. "Give us a hug before death comes to do it," they called out, and wafted their kisses through the air. Then they vanished through the gate, many of them never to step out again.

The crowds had other arrivals to distract them. Behind the gladiators came the *mastigophori*, wielding whips and scourges; their job in the arena was to lash the fighters and goad them to fury. Then came the mule-drawn platforms piled high with stacks of crude wooden boxes that turned into the *spoliarium;* the sight of so many coffins thrilled the waiting masses who judged the vastness of the spectacle by the number of prospective victims. Next came a swarm of men costumed as Mercury or Charon who finished off the wounded, then those who kept order in the circus and assigned the seats, then throngs of slaves who carried food and cooling drinks among the stalls, and finally the praetorians whom every Caesar liked to have at hand in the circus.

At last the gates swung open. The crowds burst inside and pushed through the tunnels. Such huge numbers were waiting to get in that they poured in for hours, amazing everyone that one amphitheater could contain the gathered rabble. The animals picked up the fresh human scent and roared all the louder, matched by the uproar of the arriving throng who sounded like a storm at sea as they took their seats.

Finally the city prefect came with the *vigiles* of the city watch, and then began an endless stream of litters bearing senators, consuls, magistrates, court criers and other officials, palace officers and public officeholders, senior praetorian commanders, patricians, and beautifully gowned ladies of the court.

Lictors, carrying burnished execution axes wrapped in scourging rods, marched before some of the civil dignitaries, signaling their power and importance. Others brought crowds of slaves. The sunlight gleamed and glittered on the gilded litters, on the white and richly colored robes, on the plumes, earrings, jewels and tiaras, and on the steel of the axes. The circus boomed with the shouts of the gathered masses greeting the powerful or distinguished. Other praetorian detachments arrived through the morning.

Last to appear were the priests of the various temples, and only then came the litters of the sacred vestals preceded by lictors. Only Nero's absence held up the start of the games, but he was anxious to captivate the crowds and made sure not to keep them waiting. He arrived soon after with Poppea and all the Augustans.

Petronius came with the rest of the court, bringing Vinicius with him in his litter. Ligia was ill, he knew, but he wasn't sure she'd be spared from the opening games; access to the prisons had been so heavily restricted in the last few days, with guards forbidden to talk to the keepers or answer any questions about the prisoners, that Vinicius had no one he could ask about her. Conscious or not, she could be thrown to the lions anyway; the beasts wouldn't care. But because the victims were to be sewn into animal skins and sent into the arena whole groups at a time, no one could tell one from another or see if this or that individual was among the rest.

This helped the rescue plans Vinicius had put together at such cost. He bribed all the keepers. He paid off everyone who worked in the circus. The beast masters were to hide Ligia in some out-of-the-way corner of the amphitheater and turn her over after dark to one of the young patrician's loyal country tenants, who would smuggle her out of the city and take her at once into the Alban hills. Let in on the secret, Petronius advised the young man to come openly and visibly to the circus and then slip away just before the entrance, make his way quickly to the holding pens and personally point out Ligia to the keepers so there would be no mistake.

The keepers let him in through their own side door, and one of them, named Cyrus, took him to the Christians.

"I don't know if you'll find what you seek, my lord," he said on the way. "We've been asking around for a girl named Ligia, but nobody tells us anything. Maybe they don't trust us."

"Are there a lot of them?"

"So many that some will have to keep until tomorrow."

"Are there any sick people among them?"

"Some. But none that can't stand on their own two feet."

He unlocked a door, and Vinicius stepped into a vast, dark cellar, so low the stone foundation arches brushed his head and lighted only through the iron gratings that led to the arena.

He could see nothing in the sudden darkness.

He heard the low, steady drone of murmuring voices, but whatever loud sounds there were came from the amphitheater.

He peered blindly through the murky twilight until his eyes grew accustomed to the shadows, and then he saw himself surrounded by strange furry creatures, more like animals than people, who looked like wolves and bears.

These, he knew, were the Christians sewn into the hides of animals they would face in the arena, but it was hard to tell one from another. Some stood erect, pressed against the others. Others knelt and prayed. Here and there long hair hung from under an animal disguise, showing the victim was a woman. Mothers who looked like she-wolves clutched children sewn into wooly lambskins.

The white faces that peered in the gloom out of the shaggy masks were bright with anticipation, sunny and untroubled, and the eyes sparkled with hot, feverish joy. It was clear that a single thought glowed in all these minds, one that made these people different from all others and consecrated them to another world, which took all fear and pain out of anything that might happen to them or around them and let them long for the suffering they expected. Some, questioned about Ligia, stared back with dreamy eyes and didn't even answer. Others smiled quietly, laying a cautionary finger on their lips or pointing to the bars and the streams of sunlight that flowed in through them. Only some children sobbed occasionally, frightened by the roaring and the strange animal skins worn by their parents. Walking beside Cyrus, Vinicius stared into the exalted and enigmatic faces, searching for someone he knew and asking questions, now and then tripping on the bodies of those who had fainted for lack of air in the stifling heat. Pushing on through the dark, dense clusters of the waiting victims, he thought their dungeon had to be as vast as the amphitheater itself.

Suddenly he stopped. One voice seemed familiar, and he turned and pushed back toward the barred grating. A beam of sunlight fell on the speaker's emaciated face, glaring fanatically under the skinned muzzle of a wolf. The tribune recognized the unforgiving Crispus.

"Repent your sins," he boomed, "because the time has come! He who thinks death alone will wash him clean of his transgressions, commits yet another, and he'll be cast down into everlasting fire. Each of your sins added to Christ's torments and kept them alive, so how dare you think your deaths will pay for his! The righteous and the sinners will die alike today, but the Lord will know his own. Woe to you, because the lions will claw and gnaw your bodies, but they won't settle your account with God or tear up your sins. God showed enough compassion in letting himself be nailed to a cross, but from now on he'll be only a stern, uncompromising judge who won't leave any sin or sinner unpunished. You've blasphemed, those of you who thought you'd pay for all your faults with the agonies of dying. You've challenged God's justice, and you'll be doomed for it! There will be no more mercy, because the hour of God's anger is upon you! You are about to stand before the awesome judge who'll spare none but the most righteous among you. Repent, I say, because the gates of Hell yawn open before you, and you're all damned, men along with women, and parents with their children!"

Fanatical, unappeased and merciless even in the face of the death that was about to fall on all these people, he shook his bony hands over their bowed heads, while they beat their chests and prayed for forgiveness. "Let us repent our sins!" a few voices cried after he was done, and then only the frightened wails of the children broke into the silence, along with the dull thudding of struck breasts and pounding fists.

Vinicius felt as if his blood had suddenly turned to ice. All his hopes were resting on Christ's mercy, and now he heard that a terrible judgment was about to come, bereft of compassion, and that not even death in the arena would move God to pity. It came to him at once that Peter would have spoken differently, taking another tone with those about to die, but the shock remained. Crispus' harsh, damning zealotry filled him with as much horror and dismay as this dark, barred dungeon, the place of the coming martyrdoms that shone beyond the grating, and the crowd of victims costumed for their terrible performance.

Cold sweat burst out across his forehead. He gulped the vile air, choked, and felt as if he were being strangled. The heat and the stench of all the animal hides and close-packed human bodies made it hard to breathe. Everything around him added up to one frightful and compelling image, a hundred times more horrifying than the bloodiest battle in which he had ever fought. He was suddenly afraid he'd collapse and fall, like those whose bodies tripped him as he pushed his way back across the cellar, still searching for Ligia.

Time was running out. He knew the iron grilles that led to the arena would lift at any moment. He started shouting for Ligia and Ursus. Someone, he hoped, might know them, even if they weren't there.

Someone did. A man sewn head to foot into a bearskin tugged his sleeve at once. "They've stayed in prison, master. I was the last to go and I saw her on the cot behind me."

"Who are you?"

"I'm the quarryman in whose hut the apostle Peter baptized you, my lord. They jailed me three days ago, but I'll die this morning."

Vinicius breathed deeply, suddenly relieved. Coming in, he had wanted to find Ligia. Now he thanked Christ that she wasn't here. "That's a sign of mercy," he assured himself.

But the quarryman was tugging again at his toga. "Do you recall, master, how I led you to the winery where Peter was preaching?"

"I remember."

"I saw him later, the day before they jailed me. He blessed me and said he'd be in the circus to bless all the dying. I'd like to be looking at him as I go and see the sign of the cross. It'll make dying easier. So if you know, master, tell me where he is."

Vinicius dropped his voice.

"He's with Petronius' household, disguised as a slave. I don't know where they'll sit, but I'll go up into the stands and see. Look for me when you come out into the arena. I'll rise and turn my head in their direction, and then you'll find him with your eyes."

"Thank you, my lord. And God's peace be with you."

"May the Savior show you his compassion."

"Amen," the quarryman said.

‹65›

VINICIUS LEFT the holding pens and went up into the amphitheater where he had a seat beside Petronius among the other Augustans.

"Is she there?" Petronius asked him.

"No. She was left in the prison."

"Listen, here's a thought I had. Look at Nigidia as we talk as if we were discussing her hair. . . . Chilon and Tigellinus are looking this way. . . . Here it is: Have Ligia put into a coffin and taken out for burial like any other corpse. You've enough imagination for the rest."

"Yes," Vinicius said.

But Tullius Senecio leaned over and interrupted them. "Do you know if they're going to arm the Christians?" he asked.

"We don't know." Petronius shook his head.

"I'd rather they armed them," Tullius went on. "Otherwise the arena looks too soon like a slaughter yard. But what a superb amphitheater this is!"

What lay before them was indeed an outstanding sight. The lower rows, closest to the barrier, were packed with togas and shone as white as snow. Caesar sat in a raised, gilded box, wearing a diamond collar and a gold crown shaped like a laurel wreath. The grim and beautiful Poppea sat beside him. The vestals sat next to them on both sides, flanked in turn by high imperial officers, senators with broad purple stripes edging their cloaks and togas, senior military commanders in gleaming armor—in short, everything in Rome that was magnificent, powerful and rich. The knights, that is to say the members of the Equestrian Order, sat further along, while high behind them rose the dark mass of the common people, a sea of agitated heads in motion under long hanging garlands of roses, lilies, grapevines, ivy and honeysuckle that stretched from all pillars.

Everyone in the crude, noisy ragtag masses jammed into the circus, talked in loud voices, called out to others, sang, burst out laughing at some witty comment passed among the rows, and stamped their feet,

impatient for the show to start. The pounding sounded like an uninterrupted roll of thunder, and the city prefect gave the signal for the
games to start. He had already circled the arena with a glittering retinue, and now he rose and waved a scarf toward the low barred open-
ings of the holding pens. A long, satisfied "A-a-a-a!" broke from ten
thousand throats.

Most games began with hunters going after wild beasts of one kind
or another, using native weapons; barbarians from Africa and the
north were especially worth watching. This time there were going to
be more than enough animals on show, so the spectacle opened with a
peculiar game of blindman's buff known as *andabates*. The gladiators
fought each other in helmets without eyeholes, striking blindly at
unseen opponents. More than a dozen of them came into the arena
and started flaying about with their swords, while the *mastigophori*
moved them toward one another with long-handled pitchforks. The
more discerning among the spectators treated such tasteless buffoon-
ery with contempt, but the rabble loved the clumsy stumbling, roaring with laughter whenever one contestant backed into another. They
howled "Right! Left!" and "Straight ahead!" to confuse the fighters,
but several pairs managed to come to close quarters and men started
dying. Relentless battlers tossed away their shields, clutched each
other's left wrist so as not to separate again, and fought to the death
with the other hand. When a man fell wounded, he raised his thumb
and begged mutely for his life, but the rabble usually cried for death
so early in the games, especially when it came to the *andabates* who
fought with hidden faces and had no recognizable identity.

More men fell. The number of fighters dwindled until only two
remained on their feet. The goaders pushed them at each other so
that they fell, grappled and rolled together in the sand, stabbing each
other until both were dead. Loud shouts of *"Peractum est! It is done!"*
swept through the stands while slaves dragged out the corpses and
young boys raked the bloody sand and sprinkled it with saffron.

Now a more serious contest would take place, one that intrigued
not merely the rabble but the discerning connoisseurs as well. Young
patricians often bet such enormous sums on their favorites that they
gambled away all but the clothes they wore. Wax tablets were now
passing from hand to hand as the players scribbled the names of their
champions and the sums they staked. Most people bet on the *spectati*,
known gladiators who had fought before and won several victories,
but there were many who went for the long odds, putting large sums

on unknown newcomers to make a huge profit. Everyone gambled. Rome was mad with gambling. The emperor was a player. All the priests were gamblers. The vestal virgins, senators and knights placed and took bets just like the common people. The avid rabble staked their own freedom if they ran out of money, selling themselves into slavery if they lost. The whole amphitheater now waited nervously for its champions, with pulses racing in fear or anticipation. Many made loud promises to the gods if they'd support their favorites.

Then came the shrill, blood-chilling blare of trumpets. A profound, expectant hush settled on the circus. Thousands of eyes fixed on the massive portals and on a man dressed like Charon, the gatekeeper of the underworld, who marched up to it and struck it three times with a mallet as if summoning those who stood behind it to their deaths. The doors swung open, baring a dark interior, and the gladiators slowly spilled out of it into the bright arena. They marched in troops of twenty-five, divided into their specialties and nations: Thracian *mirmillons*, swordsmen who fought against the net and trident in helmets shaped like fish; the Gauls and Semnones, all heavily armored and with only their elbows and knees exposed; and finally the *retiarii* who swung their long weighted nets in one hand and carried a three-pronged spear in the other.

Applause broke out in the open benches and burst into a storm that swept the amphitheater from the rafters to the arena floor. Wherever the eye fell there were flushed faces, gaping mouths and clapping hands. One vast, uninterrupted shout rang on and on as the gladiators circled the arena. They marched like athletes, striding in cadence with a powerful military step, glittering with their weapons and richly decorated armor. They halted in formation before Caesar's podium—proud, unaffected by anything around them, and magnificent. A horn blew for silence, and they lifted their clenched right fists toward Caesar, fixed their eyes upon him, and chanted out in slow, measured voices:

"Hail, Caesar! We who are about to die salute you!"

They broke apart at once, taking their positions in the arena, and prepared for combat. They were to fight each other in detachments, one school against another, but single combat was allowed to the most famous swordsmen so they could display their strength, dexterity and courage. Now, too, a single champion stepped out from among the Gauls, well known to circus-goers as Lanio the Butcher, who had won many victories. In his huge, heavily visored helmet and thick body armor encasing his massive chest and back, he looked like a gigantic gleaming beetle against the sunlit yellow backdrop of the sand. A famous net-and-trident man named Calendio, known for as many victories, was to fight against him.

"Five hundred sesterces on the Gaul!" howled a voice as the betting started.

"Five hundred on Calendio!"

"By Hercules! Make it a thousand!"

"Two thousand!"

In the meantime, the heavily armored Gaul advanced slowly to the center of the arena and began a gradual retreat. He held his sword thrust out toward his opponent, his head hunched and lowered, as he watched the nimble netman through the holes in his iron visor. The *retiarius*, as lithe as a dancer and naked except for a strap around his hips, seemed like a beautiful marble statue set in nimble motion, circling swiftly around his ponderous opponent and twirling his net gracefully above him. His trident moved up and down, always aimed at the eyeholes of the swordsman's visor, and he chanted the derisive little ditty the netmen always sang to their challengers.

"Non te peto, piscem peto;
Quid me fugis, Galle?"

Delighted, the crowd roared back in chorus: "I am fishing, I'm not fighting; why, Gaul, are you running?"

But the Gaul had no intention of running. Having assessed the netman he hadn't fought before, he halted and held his ground, turning only enough to keep his enemy in front. There was now something terrifying in his posture and the huge armored head, and the audience knew it. Some cold malignant force gathered behind those eyeholes, as if this heavy, bronze-encased body was coiling all its strength for a single leap that would decide it all.

Meanwhile the netman darted toward him and then skipped away, feinting and stabbing so swiftly with his trident that few people could follow the movements. The clang of the arrow-tipped tines on the swordsman's buckler was heard several times, but the Gaul didn't even sway, showing his great strength. His whole being seemed focused on the net rather than the trident, and the net circled constantly above him like a threatening bird.

The audience held its breath, watching this contest of master gladiators. Lanio saw his chance and hurled himself at his opponent; moving just as swiftly, the netman whirled under his sword and tossed the net. The Gaul swung to face him and caught it on his shield, then both leaped back to stalk each other again.

"*Macte!*" the crowds shouted. "It's a draw!" New bets were made in the front rows closest to the barrier. Caesar hadn't paid much attention until now; he was too busy talking with the vestal Rubria. But now he swung his head toward the arena.

They were fighting with the same skill and precision as before, so perfect in their movements it seemed as if they didn't care about life or death but only to display the mastery of their craft and the range of their knowledge. Lanio escaped the net twice more and started backing off toward the edge of the arena. Those who bet against him urged him to attack, afraid that he'd rest a little there.

"Attack!" they howled. The Gaul obeyed and charged. The net-man's arm suddenly spouted blood, and his net hung limp.

Lanio bounded forward, aiming the last stroke, but Calendio leaped to life again. The limp net and the useless arm were only a feint to draw the Gaul forward. The netman twisted away from the sword thrust, jabbed the shaft of the trident between Lanio's knees, and tripped him in the sand. The Gaul tried to heave himself to his feet again, but the deadly mesh hissed through the air and snared him so tightly that every kick and struggle entangled his arms and legs even more. Meanwhile the tines of the trident flashed time and again and nailed him to the ground.

The Gaul made one more effort. Pushing up with one arm, he tried to tear himself free with the other and get to his feet, but he couldn't do it. He managed to lift a numb, lifeless hand toward his head but was no longer able to pick up his sword, and he fell on his back. Calendio pressed his neck to the ground with his trident, leaned on the shaft, and looked up toward Caesar's loge.

The crowds went wild. The whole amphitheater shook with their roar and applause. For those who bet on Calendio, he was now a greater man than a Caesar, and this helped to dampen their thirst for Lanio's blood. After all, hadn't he spilled it to make them rich? Swayed by almost any whim, the will of the people underwent a shift. Signals for life and death fluttered on all the benches, split just about equally between the death stroke and mercy, but the netman looked only at Caesar and the vestals to see what they wanted. Caesar didn't care for Lanio, which was bad luck for the gladiator. He had bet against him at the last games before the fire and lost a large sum of money to Licinius; so now he stretched his hand out of the box and turned his thumb downward. The vestals immediately did the same.

Calendio knelt on the chest of the fallen Gaul, drew a short knife out of his belt, bared Lanio's throat and drove the thick, triangular blade in up to the hilt.

"*Peractum est!*" sounded again through the amphitheater.

Lanio jerked and quivered for a while like a slaughtered ox, plowing up the sand with his heels, then stiffened and lay still.

No "Mercury" needed to make sure he was dead by poking him with a red-hot iron, and he was soon dragged out of the way. Some other pairs fought each other, and then came the time for the grand melee, or battle of detachments. The rabble took part with its eyes, hearts and souls: howling, roaring, whistling, clapping, laughing, goading the fighters and going mad itself. In the arena the gladiators fought like wild beasts in two hostile cohorts. Breastplates clanged together. Bodies strained and grappled. Bones snapped. Ribs cracked. Muscular limbs creaked in their joints. Swords sank into chests and bellies, and graying lips spewed blood over the sand. Such fear-crazed panic seized some dozen novices toward the end that they broke free of the bloody chaos and tried to run for it. But the *mastigophori* drove them back into the battle with long, lead-tipped whips. Broad, dark stains spilled across the sand. Heaps of stripped and armored bodies lay scattered like corn shucks. Those who were still alive fought each other across stacks of corpses, tripped on shields and armor, cut their legs on smashed weapons and fell in their turn. The howling masses went deliriously wild. Swept away by the blood and slaughter, they panted for more death, gulped it down by the mouthful, stuffed their eyes with it and filled their lungs with its exhalations.

At last all but a few of the losers lay dead in the sand. A small number of wounded dragged themselves into the middle of the arena and knelt there swaying, lifting their arms to the people and begging for mercy. The winners were crowned with laurel wreaths and held olive branches as a sign of peace. A short intermission brought a moment's rest, but Caesar's order turned it into a feast. Perfumes burned in the vases, and clouds of incense wafted from the censers. The sprinklers bathed the populace with a gentle shower of saffron and violet-scented water while the attendants carried cooling drinks, roast meats, cakes, wine, fruit and oil among the rows of benches.

The common crowds gorged themselves, babbled, argued, and yelled cheers for Caesar to prompt him into even greater generosity. When their thirst and hunger were sated for the moment, slaves swarmed through the circus with baskets of gifts. Small boys dressed as Cupids tossed presents by the handful to the cheering masses, but fierce fights broke out in the stands when free lottery tickets were thrown to the rabble. People pushed and shoved, kicked and clawed, knocked each other down, trampled on each other, screamed for help, leaped across rows of seats and suffocated in the press of bodies, because a winning number could give them a house with a garden, a slave, rich clothes, or some rare animal they sold back to the amphitheater at full price. This caused such chaos that the praetorians had to restore order, and people with broken arms and legs were carried out after every distribution. As usual, some were dead, trampled to death or suffocated in the crush.

The wealthier patrons took no part in these fights for tickets, and the Augustans in the lower benches found it more amusing this time to poke fun at Chilon. The wretched Greek did all he could to show he could watch the fighting and bloodshed as well as anyone, but he failed badly. No matter how he frowned, gnawed his lips, clenched his fists or drove his nails into his palms, his Greek tradesman's nature quailed at the sight of blood, and his personal cowardice made him want to vomit. He was as pale as a corpse, his lips were blue with terror, his forehead was beaded with sweat, his eyes retreated deep into his skull, his teeth clenched and rattled, and his body shook as if he were about to have a fit. He managed to get himself more or less under control once the fighting ended, but the Augustans' gibes sent him into panic, and he made a desperate effort to give back as good as he got.

"Hey there, Greek!" Vatinius seized Chilon by the beard and gave it a tug. "So you can't take the sight of torn human skin?"

"My father didn't stitch leather for a living," Chilon snarled and bared his last two yellow teeth, "so I can't mend it either."

"Macte! Habet!" several voices shouted. "Well parried!"

But others went on jeering.

"It's not his fault he has a cheese in his chest instead of a heart!" cried Tullius Senecio.

"It's not your fault you have a clown's bladder on your neck instead of a head!" Chilon shot back.

"Why don't you turn into a gladiator? You'd look good with a net in the arena."

"If I caught you, I'd net a stinking tickbird!"

"And how will it be with the Christians?" asked Festus Ligurius. "Why don't you turn into a dog and bite them?"

"Because I wouldn't want to turn into your brother."

"Ah, you Moesian leper!"

"Ah, you Ligurian mule!"

"You've got the itch, that's clear, but don't ask me to scratch it."

"Scratch your own! But if you pick off your pimples you'll be losing your best parts."

So they snarled at him, and he snapped back like a rabid dog while they laughed and jeered. Nero clapped, egged them on and kept repeating *"Macte!"* Petronius strolled near after a while and tapped the Greek's shoulder with his ivory cane.

"That's all very well, philosopher," he said, "but you've made one mistake. The gods made you a petty pickpocket, but you've become a demon. That's why you won't last."

The old man glared at him with his bloodshot eyes but somehow couldn't find an insulting answer. He kept quiet for a time, then forced out a mutter.

"I'll last," he said.

‹66›

THE TRUMPETS SIGNALED the end of the intermission. People began to leave the aisles where they had gathered to talk and stretch their legs. Movement erupted everywhere at once, along with the usual quarrels about taken seats. Senators and patricians returned to their places. Talk quieted down, and the amphitheater settled slowly into some form of order. Out in the arena a few more circus hands appeared to rake the last of the blood-soaked sand and bury the traces.

The Christians were next.

Because this was a new kind of spectacle for the common masses and no one knew how the Christians would behave, everyone was curious and a bit uneasy. The crowd was now moody and subdued, expecting to see quite unimaginable sights but also grim and hostile. These Christians they were about to see had set Rome on fire and burned all its treasures! And didn't they drink the blood of infants, poison public fountains, cast spells on all mankind and indulge in the foulest rituals? No retribution could be harsh enough for such malignant felons, and no amount of hatred was too much. If anyone was worried about them, it was to make sure their punishment would be terrible enough to fit all their crimes.

The sun had climbed high into the sky and its red beams seeped through the overhead *velarium*, filling the amphitheater with a gory light. The sand glowed like fire. Something ominous seemed to come from the bloodred stain on the glowering faces and the empty sands of the arena, soon to be filled with human agony and the savage fury of wild beasts. Death and terror seemed to hover in the crimson air. The crowds, usually raucous and amused, waited in grim, unforgiving silence. Hatred turned them sullen.

Suddenly the prefect gave the sign, and the same old man who had summoned the gladiators to their deaths in his Charon costume paced slowly across the arena. There was total silence in the circus; no one made a sound as he struck the doors three times with his mallet.

A threatening growl swept through the amphitheater. "The Christians! The Christians!"

The iron gratings screeched upward, baring their dark caverns. The *mastigophori* let out their usual cry.

"Into the sand with you! Out, into the sand!"

In what seemed like a single moment the whole arena filled with groups of strange woodland creatures dressed in animal skins, as if for some sylvan pagan celebration. All of them ran quickly, moving with a sort of feverish anxiety into the middle of the ring, where they knelt down in rows, one next to the other, and stretched their arms upward.

The crowd took this for a plea for mercy and roared with anger. "What cowards! Kill them all! No mercy!" Feet pounded, whistles shrilled. Drained wine cups and gnawed bones fell on them like hail. "Bring on the beasts! We want the animals!"

Then something happened that was so unusual it caused the shouting to die away and mouths to fall open in astonishment along all the benches. Singing came suddenly from the midst of the doomed shaggy herd, a hymn that burst out and swelled: A great paean of joy and expectation rang out for the first time in a Roman circus.

"*Christus regnat!*"

Amazement gripped the crowd.

The victims sang with eyes raised to the *velarium*. They were white-faced and filled with some uplifting powerful emotion. Everyone understood that these people did not beg for mercy; indeed, they didn't even seem to see the amphitheater, the crowds, the senate or Caesar. "*Christus regnat!*" rang out ever louder. At the top of the rows of benches, people began to ask what was going on and who this *Christus* was who reigned on the lips of those about to die.

Meanwhile another cage was opened and packs of wild dogs swarmed into the arena. Starved, red-eyed, tawny mastiffs from the Peloponnesus, huge striped hounds from the Pyrenees and Hibernian wolfhounds raced around the sand, barking and baying fiercely, teeth bared and flanks caved in with hunger. Their howls and whining seemed to fill the bowl of the circus to the brim. The Christians finished singing and knelt without moving as if turned to stone, merely repeating in a groaning chorus: "*Pro Christo! Pro Christo!*" while the dogs caught the scent of humans under the animal skins and milled about, confused by their stillness, not daring to charge them. Some rose on their hind legs and clawed at the barriers as if they wanted to get in among the spectators; others ran around barking furiously, as if chasing some invisible quarry.

The crowds lost patience and turned ugly. A thousand voices screamed maledictions, howled, barked and bayed like hounds, and shouted "Kill!" in every language of the Roman world. The circus shook to the roar of curses. The frenzied dogs began to leap at the kneeling people and then backed off, snapping their teeth and snarling, until one of the mastiffs suddenly lunged forward, drove his fangs into the shoulder of a kneeling woman and dragged her under him.

As if this were a signal, the pack hurled itself into the breech in dozens and tore into the Christians. The gallery quieted down, stopped howling and watched the scene below with greater attention. The quavering men's and women's voices still cried out their plaintive *"Pro Christo! Pro Christo!"* amid the snarls and growling, but the arena was now a heaving, tumbling mass of dogs and mutilated prey. Blood stained the sand in streams. The dogs fought each other for bits of human offal. They tore bloody arms and legs out of each other's jaws. The stench of blood and ordure filled the amphitheater. The kneeling figures who were left soon vanished under the swarming mass.

When the Christians first ran into the arena, Vinicius rose and turned to where Peter sat, hidden among the household of Petronius, keeping his promise to the quarryman. He sat down again and slumped like a dead man, his face set and somber, watching the terrible spectacle with dull, lifeless eyes. At first he was terrified the quarryman might have been wrong and that Ligia was among the victims. But when he heard the voices crying out *"Pro Christo!"* and when he saw the ordeal of so many people dying for their God, witnessing his truth, he gave way to another feeling. The real meaning of the sacrifice pierced him sharper than the worst imaginable pain, yet he could not refute it: If Christ himself died a terrible death, if a thousand others were dying in his name and a sea of blood was spilling in the sand, one more drop was insignificant, no matter how precious, and to beg mercy for one individual was a sin. That thought flowed to him out of the arena, entering his consciousness with the moans of the dying and the reek of their blood. He went on praying silently, whispering through parched lips: "Christ! Christ! Even your apostle prayed for her!"

Then he lost touch with his surroundings and drifted into his own agonized reality, not sure where he was. All he knew was that the blood rose in the arena like a gathering wave and became a tide that would swell and tower above everything, spilling out of this amphitheater to drown Rome itself. He neither heard nor saw anything beyond that; he was deaf to the howling dogs and the screaming people. He didn't even hear the Augustans near him calling out: "Chilon's fainted!"

"Chilon's fainted!" Petronius repeated, turning toward the Greek.

The old man had indeed collapsed. White as a sheet of canvas, he sat with his head thrown back and his mouth wide open, looking like a corpse.

Then a fresh flock of victims sewn into skins and pelts ran into the arena and knelt like the others. The spent dogs didn't bother them, however. Only a few threw themselves on the ones kneeling nearest. The rest lay panting, their bloody jaws agape, their flanks heaving as they gulped air.

Alarmed by what they couldn't understand but drunk on blood and driven into frenzy, the crowds were now screaming for the lions.

"Give us the lions! The lions! Let the lions loose!"

The lions had been scheduled for the next day, but circus crowds imposed their will on everyone, including the emperor. Only the mad and unpredictable Caligula ever dared to thwart them, sometimes ordering them lashed into submission, but even he gave way most of the time. Nero, who loved applause more than anything, always gave them everything they wanted. Moreover he was anxious to pacify the rabble enraged by the fire and to turn the blame on Christians.

He signaled his assent, and the howling mob quieted down at once. The cage gates creaked open. The lions stirred. The dogs huddled together, crouched and whining softly at the far edge of the ring. The huge beasts strode regally into the arena one after another, seeming to roll like enormous objects: gigantic, tawny monsters with huge shaggy heads, dangerous and disdainful. Even Caesar turned his bored face toward them, raising his polished emerald to his eye for a better look. The Augustans greeted them with appreciative applause. The massed city rabble on the higher benches counted them on their fingers, shooting avid glances at the rows of Christians to see how they'd react. They merely knelt with upraised arms and went on repeating their *"Pro Christo! Pro Christo!"*—which puzzled most people and irritated all.

The lions were hungry but in no hurry to rush at their prey. The reddish glare in the arena dazzled them at first, so they blinked sleepily as if contemplating something strange and new. Some stretched their long yellow bodies lazily. Others yawned, displaying their terrifying teeth. At last the reek of spilled blood and the sight of the mangled corpses littering the sand started to take effect. Their movements became nervous. Their manes stiffened. Their nostrils sniffed the air with a hoarse, growling sound. One of them suddenly lunged at the corpse of a woman with a ripped-off face and started licking the clotted blood with his coarse, barbed tongue. Another neared a Christian who hugged a small child sewn into the pelt of a fawn.

The child wept and screamed, shaking with sobs and terror, and clung with a convulsive death grip to its father's neck. The father, wanting to keep the child alive a little longer, tried to pry its hands off his neck and pass it on to others who knelt farther off. But the child's screams and the father's movements enraged the animal. It gave a short, abrupt roar, smashed the child with one blow of its paw, and crushed the father's skull in its jaws.

At this, all the others leaped on the Christians. A few women shrieked, unable to contain their terror, but their screams were drowned in the storm of applause that burst from the stands.

The applause soon faded, giving way to eager fascination with the sudden horror on the sands of the arena: heads vanished inside gaping jaws, rib cages were split apart and thrown wide like portals with a single blow, and eviscerated hearts and lungs spilled onto the sand. Bones crunched and crackled in the massive jaws. Some of the lions seized their prey by the trunk or torso and bounded with them across the arena, as if looking for a quiet spot where they might devour them out of sight. Others grappled and wrestled with each other, filling the amphitheater with thundering roars. People rose in their seats. Others pushed down the aisles for a better view, squeezed and packed together to the point of suffocation. It seemed as if enthusiasm would hurl this human mass onto the sand to wreak their carnage along with the lions. The sounds were then inhuman shrieks, sometimes a hurricane of clapping, sometimes the roars, growls, grinding of gnashed teeth and howls of the mastiffs, and sometimes only moaning.

Caesar was paying close attention, the emerald at his eye. Petronius wore a look of disgust and contempt. Chilon had been carried out of the circus sometime before. Fresh throngs of victims streamed out of the cages, whipped into the arena.

The apostle Peter looked down at this ongoing stream of sacrifice from the top of the amphitheater, the very last row. No one looked at him. All eyes were fixed on the spectacle. He rose. And just as he had blessed those in Cornelius' winery who were about to be arrested, scrawling the sign of the cross over them, so now he blessed those dying in the jaws of animals, hanging the cross over their blood, their torture, their dead bodies turned into shapeless lumps of meat, and their souls that lifted from the blood-stained sand. Some of them raised their eyes to him, saw the cross and smiled, their faces momentarily alight. He thought his heart would break.

"Master!" he cried within himself. "Your will be done, because it's for your glory and your truth these lambs of mine are dying! You made me their shepherd, so I pass them to you. You count them, Master, and heal their wounds, soothe their pain, and give them even greater happiness with you for the torments they endured here."

He said farewell to them, one throng after another, sending them off with the sign of the cross and such love as if they were his children. He knew he was passing them directly into the hands of Christ.

Suddenly Caesar ordered something new. Whether he merely wanted to make sure the spectacle exceeded everything seen in Rome before or because he was totally immersed in it himself, he whispered a few words to the city prefect who went at once to the holding cages. Even the people were surprised to see the gratings lift and wondered what could possibly come next. Every kind of meat-eating beast of prey bounded into the arena. Tigers from the Euphrates, Numidian panthers, bears, wolves, hyenas and jackals turned the arena into a single heaving mass of striped, yellow, tawny, gray, brown and dappled pelts. All of it convulsed, roiling in a chaotic jumble of wild animals, rolling spines and backs. The spectacle lost the appearance of reality. It became something that combined an orgy of blood, a terrifying dream, and the hideous nightmare of a madman's mind. It was too much. The crowd could take no more. Into the sound composed of roaring, howls and grunting came shrill outbursts of hysterical laughter; here and there on the gallery benches women spectators who were unable to bear any more began to scream. Faces grew dark, and people began to feel fearful and uneasy, as if in the presence of something unimaginable but frightening. Many scattered voices started to shout: "Enough! Enough!"

But it was easier to let in the animals than to drive them out. Caesar, however, saw a unique opportunity to clean out the arena and distract the crowd with a fresh amusement. Every aisle in the circus filled with gleaming black cohorts of Numidian archers, bows in hand, exotic in their plumes and the gilded hoops they wore in their ears. The people guessed at once what was about to happen and greeted them with loud shouts of pleasure. They, in turn, lined the rim of the arena, notched their arrows, and began to shoot into the swarms of beasts.

This was indeed a new spectacle and an excellent distraction. The lithe black bodies leaned back to the pull of the bow and sent shaft after shaft. The growling twang of bowstrings and the hiss of flying arrows pierced through the howls of animals and the people's cries of admiration. Wolves, bears and panthers fell dead to the ground, along with whatever human beings were still alive in the arena. A wounded lion snapped around here and there, his muzzle streaked with rage, trying to rip out the buried shaft with his gaping fangs or grind it to splinters. Others groaned with pain. The smaller predators ran in blind panic back and forth across the arena or threw themselves head-first into the closed gratings. The missiles streaked on and on through the air until everything alive in the arena stopped quivering in the last of its death throes.

Hundreds of slaves swarmed into the arena armed with spades, shovels, brooms, wheelbarrows, hampers for carting out the entrails, and huge sacks of sand. One wave followed another, and the whole ring filled with a frantic bustle. The corpses, blood and ordure were soon cleared away. The floor of the arena was turned over, raked smooth, and covered with a thick layer of fresh sand. A flock of Cupids ran in, scattering rose and lily petals, and every kind of bloom. The censers were lit again, and the *velarium* was taken down because the afternoon sun had now dipped low. The people peered at one another in anticipation, wondering aloud what else they'd see that day.

What they saw defied all expectations. Caesar had left the podium sometime earlier and now appeared in the flower-strewn arena, dressed in a purple mantle and a crown of golden laurel leaves, and carrying a silver lute. Twelve singers bearing zithers paced solemnly behind him, while he advanced with a majestic tread into the center of the ring, bowed several times to the audience, lifted his eyes to the sky and waited as if for inspiration.

Then he struck the strings and began to sing his hymn to Apollo.

"O radiant son of Latona,
Ruler of Tenedos, Chios and Chrysos,
Are you the one who kept watch over sacred Troy
And turned it over to the Argive fury?
Are you he who suffered holy altars,
That blazed eternally to your glory,
To be soiled with the blood of Trojans?
Old men lifted their trembling arms to you,
O far-ranging archer of the silver bow.
Mothers raised tear-filled cries to you
From the depths of their breasts,
Begging your mercy for their young.
A rock would feel compassion at this lamentation,
But you, O Smintheus, felt less than a stone!"

The hymn turned slowly into a mournful, pain-filled elegy. The circus was hushed. Caesar himself had to stop, too moved to continue singing, but he resumed after a brief moment.

"Could your divine lyre drown the hearts' lament
And the cries of pleading,
When even today the eye brims with tears
Like a dew-filled bloom at this mournful music,
Which resurrects that day of fire, calamity and doom
From the dust and ashes?
Smintheus, where were you then?"

Here his voice quavered and his eyes grew wet. Tears showed in the eyes of the vestals. The crowds made no sound until he was done and then erupted with a storm of clapping that went on and on without pause.

Meanwhile the sound of creaking cartwheels came from the outside through the *vomitoria* that had been thrown open to admit fresh air, and the bloody remnants of the Christians—men, women and children—were carted off to the terrible *puticuli*, or pits of corruption.

The apostle Peter seized his trembling head with both hands and cried out within him:

"Master! Master! Whom did you make the ruler of this world? And do you still want to build your capital here?"

‹67›

THE SUN SUNK in the West and seemed to melt into the evening glow. The spectacle was over. The crowds started to leave the circus through all the tunnel corridors at once, pouring into the city. Only the Augustans took their time, waiting for the human tide to pass, and in the meantime they left their seats and crowded at the podium where Caesar returned to hear himself praised. The common masses hadn't skimped on clapping when he finished singing, but he wanted more. He expected frenzy, enthusiasm that bordered on madness, and he was annoyed. It didn't help that the Augustans sang his praises now or that the vestals kissed his hands as if he were a deity or even that Rubria bowed her head so low while she paid him homage that her reddish hair brushed against his chest. Nero was disappointed, and he couldn't hide it. He was also surprised and alarmed that Petronius kept a stony silence. A few flattering words of praise that also pinpointed a special quality in his hymn would be a great comfort to him just now. At last, unable to stand it any longer, he beckoned the arbiter over to the podium.

"Say something," he urged when Petronius stepped into the box.

"I'm silent because I can't find the words," Petronius said coldly. "You surpassed yourself."

"That's what I thought too. But what about the crowd?"

"Can you expect appreciation of poetry from such mongrels?"

"So you also noticed they didn't thank me as much as they should have?"

"You chose a bad moment."

"How was it bad?"

"Minds reeling with the stench of blood can't pay enough attention."

Nero clenched his fists. "Ah, those Christians! They burned Rome, and now they're hurting me as well! What else can I concoct to pay them back for that?"

Petronius noted he had taken the wrong road and that his words brought the opposite result from the one he wanted. He had to point Nero's thoughts in a new direction.

"Your hymn is marvelous," he whispered into Nero's ear. "But I have one suggestion. The fourth line in the third stanza leaves something to be desired."

Nero flushed with shame, as if he had been caught in a shameful act, and glanced fearfully around.

"You catch everything!" he whispered back. "I know. . . . I'll change it. . . . But nobody else noticed, did they? And you . . . you'd better not tell anyone—if you love the gods . . . and if you like living."

Petronius frowned as if too bored and weary to care any longer.

"You can have me condemned to death, divine one, if I'm in your way," he said, staring directly into Caesar's eyes. "But don't try to frighten me with death, because the gods know best if I'm afraid of it."

"Don't be angry." Nero paused, then muttered, "You know that I love you."

A bad sign, thought Petronius.

"I wanted to ask you to a feast tonight," Nero went on, "but I'll lock myself in my rooms to polish that damn line in the third stanza. You noticed, that's to be expected, but who else? Seneca and perhaps Secundus Carinas might have caught it too. I'll get rid of them at once."

He called Seneca and told him to pack for a mission. He was to go with Acratus and Secundus Carinas to all the towns and villages on the Italian mainland and then to all the other provinces as well. They were to squeeze as much money as they could out of the cities, hamlets, noted temples, and everywhere else money could be found, seized or extracted. Seneca knew at once he was to play the role of pillager, bandit and sacrilegious looter, and he refused straight out.

"I'm going to the country, my lord," he said. "I'll wait for death there. I'm old, too old for all this, and my nerves are gone."

Seneca's Iberian nerves were better than Chilon's Greek ones, but it was true that his health was poor; he was as drawn and frail as his former shadow, and his hair had recently turned completely white.

Nero gave him a calculating glance and thought he might not have to wait too long for him to die.

"I don't want to send you on a journey if you're ill," he said, "but I can't let you settle in the country. I'm too fond of you for that. I'd miss you if you weren't in Rome. So instead of waiting for death in the country, you'll lock yourself in your house and and wait for it there."

He laughed. "Sending Acratus and Carinas alone after tribute is like sending wolves to bring in the sheep," he said. "So whom should I send to keep an eye on them and watch over the money?"

"Give me the job, my lord," said Domitius Afer.

"Hardly!" Nero laughed. "I've no wish to draw Mercury's anger on us all, and you'd shame even him with your thievery. I need some Stoic like Seneca or like my new friend and philosopher Chilon." He peered around. "What happened to him, by the way?"

Chilon, who had recovered in the fresh air outside and who had returned to hear Caesar's singing, edged closer at once.

"I'm here, radiant offspring of the sun and moon. I was ill, but your singing made me well."

"I'll send you to Greece," Nero said, amused. "You must know how much they have in every temple down to the last penny."

"Do so, Zeus, and the gods will pay you such a tribute it'll shame everything they've ever given anyone before."

"But"—Nero grinned—"I wouldn't want you to miss the pleasure of the games."

"O Baal!"

Chilon lost his glib tongue for a moment. The other Augustans started laughing, glad that Caesar's humor had improved.

"No, my lord!" they cried. "Don't deprive this heroic Greek of seeing the games. Don't let him miss the rest of the entertainment!"

"Do deprive me, lord, of seeing these cackling Capitoline geese, whose brains wouldn't fill an acorn cup if they were lumped together," Chilon answered back. "I'm writing a hymn of praise to you in Greek, great son of Apollo, and I want to spend a few days in the temple of the muses to beg for inspiration!"

"Oh, no!" Nero cried. "You want to worm your way out of the games! But you won't succeed!"

"I swear to you, my lord, I'm writing a hymn!"

"Then watch the games in daytime and write your hymn at night. Look for your inspiration in Diana right here in Rome. She is Apollo's sister, isn't she?"

Chilon hanged his head, glancing with anger at the others who went on laughing at him. Caesar turned to Senecio and Suilius Nerulinus.

"Imagine," he said with a sigh. "We managed to dispose of only half the Christians meant for today's performance."

Old Aquilus Regulus, who was an expert on everything to do with circuses, thought a while and said:

"Those spectacles *sine armis et sine arte*, where untrained people appear without weapons, last almost as long and entertain far less."

"I'll order them armed," Nero said.

The superstitious Vestinius had been pondering something and now shook his head.

"Did you notice they see something as they die?" he asked in a hushed voice full of wonder. "They stare and don't seem to suffer. . . . I'm sure they see something."

He raised his head and peered at the sky where the night began spreading its own star-spangled *velarium*. The others answered him with laughter and joking speculations about what the Christians might see as they died. Caesar signaled to his slave torchbearers and left the amphitheater, followed by the vestals, senators, officials and all the Augustans.

The night was warm and clear. Crowds were still milling around the gates, wanting to see the emperor's departure, but they were quiet and strangely sullen, gloomy and ill-tempered. There was some clapping here and there, but it died down at once. At the *spoliarium*, the creaking wagons continued to cart away the bloody remnants of the Christians.

‹68›

PETRONIUS AND VINICIUS made their way home in silence. When they were close to the villa Petronius turned to the younger man.

"Have you given any thought to what we talked about?" he asked.

"I have," Vinicius said.

"Can you believe that this is now a matter of the utmost importance to me as well? I have to free her just to defeat Caesar and Tigellinus. It's like a challenge now that I have to win. It's like a game where I have to triumph even if it costs my neck. . . . What we saw today only confirmed me in this enterprise."

"May Christ repay you!"

"You'll see for yourself."

This brought them to the doors of the villa, and they stepped out of their carrying chair. At that moment a dark form loomed toward them.

"Is the noble Vinicius here?" asked a young boy's voice.

"Yes," said the tribune. "What do you want?"

"I am Nazarius, son of Miriam. I come from the prison. I've news of Ligia for you."

Vinicius leaned his forearm on the young boy's shoulder and stared into his eyes by the light of the flaming torches, but he couldn't speak a word. Nazarius, however, guessed the one question that hung on his lips.

"She's still alive," he said. "Ursus sent me, my lord, to say she prays in her fever and calls out your name."

"Glory be to Christ," Vinicius said. "He can return her to me."

He took Nazarius into the house and into the library where Petronius joined them a few moments later.

"Her sickness saved her from being molested," the boy said, "because the hangmen were afraid to touch her. Ursus and Glaucus, the doctor, watch her day and night."

"Does she still have the same guards?"

"Yes, and she's in their room. Those who were in the lower prison have all died of fever or suffocated from lack of air."

"Who are you?" Petronius interjected.

"The noble Vinicius knows me. I'm the son of a widow in whose house Ligia stayed."

"And a Christian too?"

The boy threw a quick, questioning glance at Vinicius, but seeing he was bowed in prayer, he lifted his head and said: "I am."

"Then how are you free to walk in and out of the prison?"

"I hired myself out, my lord, to carry out the dead. I did that so I could help my brothers by bringing in the news from the city."

Petronius started looking at the boy with greater attention, noting the beauty of his face, the sky blue eyes and abundant hair.

"Where do you come from, lad?" he asked.

"I'm a Galilean, my lord."

"Would you like Ligia to be free?"

The boy raised his eyes. "Even if I was to die right afterward."

Suddenly Vinicius finished praying. "Tell the keepers to put her in a coffin as if she were dead. You pick out some helpers who'll carry her out at night. Near the burial pits you'll find some men with a litter; let them have the coffin. Promise the keepers enough gold from me that each will fill his cloak."

His face changed as he spoke, its apathetic lifelessness gone. Hope resurrected his decisiveness and energy. He was again a soldier. Nazarius seemed to glow with joy.

"Let Christ make her well," he cried, lifting his hands to heaven. "Because she will be free!"

"Do you think the guards will go along with this?" Petronius asked.

"They, my lord? Yes, as long as they know they won't be caught and tortured."

"That's correct," Vinicius confirmed. "The keepers were willing to let her escape. They'll be all the more willing to have her carried out as dead."

"It's true they've a man who burns the corpses with a red-hot iron to see if they're dead. But he takes just a few sesterces to leave the face untouched. For one gold *aureus* he'll just brand the coffin."

"Tell him he'll get a capful of *aurei*," Petronius said. "But are you sure you'll find the men to help you?"

"I can pick out the kind who'd sell their wives and children if the price was right."

"Where will you find them?"

"Right there in the prison or almost anywhere in town. Once the keepers are bribed, they'll let me bring in anyone I want."

"In that case you'll bring me as one of your hired hands," Vinicius said.

But Petronius was determined that this shouldn't happen. The praetorians might recognize him even in disguise, and all would be lost.

"You'll go neither to the prison nor the burial pits," he insisted. "It's essential that everyone, including Caesar and Tigellinus, be convinced she's dead. Otherwise they'd order an immediate search. We can avoid suspicion only if we stay in Rome when your men take her out to the Alban hills, or even to Sicily. Only after a week or two you'll fall ill, call Nero's physician, and he'll order you to take a cure in the hills. Then you'll be reunited. As for what happens later . . ."

His mind focused elsewhere for a moment, and then he waved his thoughts aside. "Times might change," he said.

"May Christ watch over her, " said Vinicius. "You talk about Sicily, but she's sick and the trip might kill her."

"So for the time being we'll hide her somewhere closer. The fresh air alone will cure her once we've plucked her out of the Mammertine. Don't you have some tenant in the mountains you can trust?"

"Yes, yes, I have one!" Vinicius said quickly, anxious to get started. "There's a loyal man near Corioli who carried me in his arms when I was a child, and he's still fond of me."

Petronius handed him a set of writing tablets. "Write him to be here tomorrow. I'll have a courier on his way at once."

He called for the *atriensis* and gave him the necessary orders. A short while later a mounted messenger galloped into the night, heading for Corioli.

"I'd be more content if Ursus could go with her." Vinicius was voicing some of his concern, but Petronius would have none of it.

"My lord," Nazarius pointed out, "that man is stronger than any man alive. He can rip out the bars and follow her on his own. There's this one window, high on a sheer wall, that no one guards below. I'll bring Ursus a rope, and he'll do the rest."

"By Hercules!" Petronius exclaimed. "Let him break out any way he pleases, but not with her! And not until two or three days later, or they'll track him to her hiding place. By Hercules! Do you want to doom yourself as well as her? If you even breathe a word to Ursus about Corioli, I wash my hands of the whole affair."

The others saw the point and said nothing more. Nazarius got ready to leave a few moments later, promising to be back at daybreak. He thought he'd settle with the keepers that night, but first he wanted to visit his mother who was still free but worried about him in those dreadful times. As for a helper, he decided not to look for one in town but to bribe one of those who worked with him carrying out the dead. Leaving, he stopped suddenly and drew Vinicius aside.

"My lord," he whispered, "I won't mention a word of this to anyone, not even my mother, but the apostle Peter promised to look in at our house after the circus, and I want to tell him everything."

"You don't have to whisper in this house," Vinicius said. "The apostle Peter was at the amphitheater among Petronius' people. Besides, I'll go with you."

He called for a slave's cloak and then they left.

Petronius sighed with deep satisfaction. I'd have been glad at first if she had died of the fever, he thought; that would have been the least of the blows that could strike Vinicius. But now it has become something else. Now I'd offer a gold tripod to Asclepios to have her recover.

"Ah, you copper-bearded ape!" he mused. "So you want to amuse yourself with a lover's pain. And you, divine Augusta Poppea, first you envied the girl's beauty, and now you'd like to devour her raw because your Rufius died. And you, Tigellinus, you want to see her destroyed out of spite for me! But we'll see about that. Take it from me, you'll never set your eyes on her in the arena, because she'll either die her own death or I'll rip her out of your jaws like a bone from a dog, and you won't even know how any of it happened. Whenever I look at you afterward, I'll be able to say: Here are the fools outwitted by Petronius."

Pleased with himself, he passed into the dining room where he sat down to supper beside Eunice. While they dined, the lector read to them from the *Idylls* of Theocritus. Clouds piled in the sky outside, driven by the wind from the direction of Soracte, and a sudden storm broke the silence of a soft summer night. Thunder rolled now and then on the seven hills as they lay beside each other at the table, listening to pastoral poetry about the love of shepherds told in the melodious, songlike Doric dialect of old Greece. Then they prepared to make their calm, languorous way to bed.

But first Vinicius returned, and Petronius went out to see him. "Well?" he asked. "Did you come up with some new idea? And did Nazarius go to the prison?"

"Yes," the young man said. Rain had soaked his hair, and he was combing it forward with his fingers. "Nazarius went to make his deal with the keepers, and I talked with the apostle Peter. He ordered me to pray and believe."

"That's good. If all goes well, we'll be able to get her out tomorrow night—"

"My tenant should be here by dawn with his people."

"It isn't far. Now go and get some sleep."

But Vinicius knelt in his sleeping room and prayed.

At sunrise, as expected, the tenant Niger arrived from near Corioli, bringing what Vinicius had requested: mules, a harnessed litter, and four loyal men he picked from his Britannic slaves. Anticipating some need for secrecy, he left them at an inn in the Suburra.

Vinicius went out to meet him. He had been up all night, praying, and Niger was alarmed and moved to see how drawn he was. Kissing his hands and eyes, as an old household servant and now a country leaseholder could do, he worried aloud about his young master.

"My dear boy, are you ill? Or is it your worries that sucked all the blood from your face? I didn't recognize you at first glance."

Vinicius took him to an inner colonnade, a covered Greek portico known as a *xystos* and used for exercise, and told him the whole plan. Niger paid close attention, but great emotion showed in his ruddy sunburned face that he didn't even bother to hide.

"Then she's a Christian?" he cried out.

He started peering carefully into the young man's face, as if in search of something, and Vinicius guessed what the countryman was seeking.

"Yes," he said. "I, too, am a Christian!"

Tears gleamed suddenly in Niger's eyes. He was silent for a moment, perhaps too moved to speak, and then he lifted up his arms in joy.

"Thank you, Christ, for letting the blind see and for opening the one pair of eyes I care about the most in all the world," he said. He clasped his hands around his young master's head and began to kiss his forehead as he would a son's.

Soon afterward Petronius brought Nazarius. "Good news!" he called out when still at some distance, and it was good indeed. First, Glaucus guaranteed that Ligia would live, even though she was ill with the same fever that had killed hundreds of people every day in all the prisons. Nor would there be the slightest problem with the keepers and the man who tested corpses with a red-hot iron. Arrangements had also been made for a helper named Attis.

"We've drilled holes in the coffin," Nazarius said, "so she'll be able to breathe. The whole danger is if she should moan or make some sound as we're taking the coffin past the praetorians. But she's very weak, and she's been lying with her eyes closed all day. Besides, Glaucus will make her a sleeping draft from the herbs I brought in from the city. The coffin lid isn't nailed shut. You can lift it easily and put the sick woman in the litter. Just have a long sandbag ready to take her place in the coffin."

Vinicius was as pale as a sheet as he listened, but he focused his attention so sharply on each word that he seemed able to anticipate what Nazarius was about to say.

"Are they taking out any other corpses tonight?" Petronius asked.

"Twelve people died last night," the boy said, "and more than a dozen others will be dead by this evening. We have to go with the rest of the corpse carriers, but we'll drag our pace and fall behind. At the first turn in the road my comrade will start limping badly and get even further behind the rest. You wait for us at the small temple of Libitina. I hope God gives us the darkest night there is."

"He will," Niger said, nodding. As a country man he knew about weather. "Last evening was clear and then there was the storm. Today the sky is clear again, but it's hot and muggy. There'll be rain and thunder every night from now on."

"Do you carry torches?" asked Vinicius.

"Only in front of the column. Just to make sure, you should be at Libitina's temple as soon as it's dark, even though we usually bring out the corpses just before midnight."

Then they were quiet. The only sound was Vinicius' rapid breathing.

Petronius turned to him. "I said yesterday that you and I ought to stay at home, but now I don't see how I'd be able to stand the suspense myself. We'd have to be more careful if this was an escape, but since they're carrying her out as dead, no one should have even a glimmer of suspicion."

"I've got to be there," Vinicius said. "I want to take her from that coffin myself."

"And I guarantee her safety once she's in my house near Corioli," Niger said.

« 69 »

THEIR TALK ENDED THERE. Niger went to the inn in the Suburra to collect his people. Nazarius went back to the prison, with a satchel of gold hidden in his tunic. For Vinicius there began a day of restlessness, anxiety, nervousness and feverish impatience.

"Our plans should go well because they're well thought out," Petronius assured him. "We couldn't have arranged it all any better than we have. You'll have to go on pretending to be sad and worried and wear a dark toga when you're out in public. But don't miss the circuses. Let them see you there. . . . The plans are good so there shouldn't be any disappointments."

Then the last possible question flashed across his mind. "Are you absolutely sure this tenant of yours can be trusted?"

"He is a Christian," Vinicius said simply.

Petronius stared at him, surprised for a moment, then started wondering aloud, as if trying to explain something to himself.

"By Pollux!" He shrugged, bemused. "How that thing is spreading! And how it clings to people's souls. With this kind of terror most people would forswear all the Roman, Greek and Egyptian gods at once. This is very strange, very curious. By Pollux!" he swore again. "If I believed that anything under the sun still depended on our gods, I'd promise six white bulls to each of them and twelve to the Capitoline Jove. But you should also promise something to your Christ."

"I've given him my soul," Vinicius said.

They parted. Petronius went back to his sleeping quarters. Vinicius went to watch the prison from a distance and then made his way to the far slopes of the Vatican, to the hut of the quarryman where Peter had baptized him. It seemed to him that Christ would hear him sooner in this place than elsewhere, so he found it, threw himself on his knees inside it and focused all the power of his tortured soul in a prayer for mercy. Such was the depth of his complete immersion that he forgot where he was and what was happening with him.

A blare of trumpets coming from the direction of Nero's amphitheater roused him after midday. He went out of the hut and blinked sleepily around like a man waking from a dream. The air was like a glowing furnace. There was no sound other than the intermittent brassy trumpet calls and the shrill, never-ending chatter of locusts and crickets. The day was parched and steamy, thick with heat and moisture. The sky above the city was still a clear blue, but low on the horizon dark clouds massed above the Sabine hills.

Vinicius went home, where Petronius was waiting for him in the atrium.

"I've been to the Palatine," he said. "I showed myself there on purpose and even played a few hands of dice. Anicius is giving a banquet tonight and I said we'd be there but only after midnight because I need my sleep. I intend to go, and it would be a good idea if you went as well."

"Has there been any news from Niger or Nazarius?" Vinicius had to know.

"No. We probably won't see them until midnight. Have you noticed there's a rainstorm coming?"

"Yes."

"Tomorrow's spectacle is to be of Christians and crucifixions but perhaps the rain will get in the way."

He drew closer and tapped his nephew's shoulder. "But you won't see her on a cross," he told him, "just in Corioli. By Castor! I wouldn't trade the moment when we set her free for all the gemstones in Rome! And it isn't long to wait, evening is almost here."

Evening was indeed drawing near, and the clouds that now covered the horizon brought darkness to the city earlier than they would normally expect. A heavy rainstorm burst overhead just after the sunset; the downpour turned into steam on the sun-drenched pavements that had been sweltering in the heat all day, and filled the streets with a thick white fog. After that came brief alternating spells of misty calmness and short, violent showers.

"Let's hurry," Vinicius urged at last. "There'll be more. The storm might make them move the corpses earlier tonight than usual."

"It's time!" Petronius agreed.

They wrapped themselves in hooded Gallic cloaks and slipped into the street by the small garden gate. Petronius also armed himself with the short, curved Roman dagger called a *sica*, which he always carried on his night adventures.

The streets were empty, swept clean by the storm, and the city looked abandoned and devoid of people. Lightning ripped through the clouds now and again, casting its sharp white glare on the walls of newly built houses or those in construction, and splashing on the wet stone slabs underfoot. By that light they saw the mound and the tiny temple of Libitina above it, and a cluster of mules and men at the foot of it.

"Niger!" Vinicius called out quietly.

"I'm here, master!" The voice came through the rain.

"Is everything ready?"

"Yes, dear lad. We were here as soon as it got dark. But get under the overhang of the mound here, or you'll get soaked through. What a storm, eh? I think it'll hail."

Niger's prediction came true almost at once. Hail rattled down out of the clouds, coming at first in a gust of granules and then in a blast of pellets hitting as hard as if from slingshots. The air chilled at once. Hidden under the wall of the escarpment, sheltered from the wind and the icy missiles, they talked in low voices.

"Even if someone sees us here," Niger said, "nobody will think much of it. We look just like anyone else trying to wait out the storm. But I'm afraid they might put off carrying out their dead until tomorrow."

"It won't hail for long," Petronius observed. "It never does. And we have to wait here at least until first light."

And so they waited, listening for the sound of the approaching column of carriers and corpses. The hailstorm passed swiftly, but then another downpour started up and rustled in their ears. A sharp whistling wind also rose at times; it brought the stench of putrefaction from the reeking pits, where the decaying dead were piled one upon another close under the surface.

Suddenly Niger said: "I see some light flickering through the fog . . . and there's another . . . and two more. Those are men with torches!"

He turned quickly to his waiting men. "Watch sharply now!" he ordered. "Make sure the mules don't make a sound!"

"They're coming!" said Petronius.

Niger began to cross himself and pray. Meanwhile the grim procession drew gradually nearer; it came abreast of Libitina's temple and slowed to a stop. Petronius, Vinicius and Niger backed as far as they could go into the shadows of the temple mound and watched in silence, uneasy about this unscheduled halt and why it was made. But the carriers stopped only to tie rags over their mouths and nostrils because the stench near the burial pits was beyond enduring, and then they picked up the stretchers with the coffins and trudged on again.

But one coffin, the last to reach the mound, stayed where it was near the little temple along with its carriers.

Vinicius leaped toward it, with Petronius, Niger and two of his Britons running behind him, while the two slaves brought up a covered litter. Before any of them reached the grounded stretcher, Nazarius' stricken voice cut through the rain-filled darkness.

"My lord!" he cried. "They moved her and Ursus to the new prison on the Esquiline! We're carrying someone else! They took her away before midnight!"

Home again, Petronius looked as grim as thunder and didn't even try to comfort Vinicius. Nobody had to tell him that getting Ligia out of the underground dungeons of the Esquiline was impossible; it wasn't even something to imagine. He guessed that she was moved from the diseased cellars of the Mammertine so she wouldn't die of the fever that raged in the Tullianum dungeons and so avoid the end planned for her in the arena. This proved to him that she was watched and guarded closer than the others.

He felt sorry for her, and he pitied Vinicius with all his heart and soul. But he was racked by yet another thought: He had never failed before in something he attempted; for the first time in his life he had lost a challenge.

"It looks as if Fortuna is turning her back on me," he muttered, surprised and annoyed. "But the gods are wrong if they think I'll agree to a life like this."

He glanced at Vinicius, who was staring at him with wide, empty eyes.

"What's wrong with you?" Petronius asked. "Are you ill?"

The young man answered in a strange, high voice, as strained and halting as if he were a child:

"I still believe that he can bring her back to me," he said.

The final thunders of the storm subsided above the city.

‹70›

THREE DAYS OF RAIN—an unheard-of phenomenon in Rome in the summer—along with unexpected hailstorms, caused an interruption in the games. People became frightened. Vintners predicted a poor harvest at grape-picking time, and when one afternoon a thunderbolt struck and melted the bronze statue of Ceres on the Capitol, sacrifices were ordered in the temple of Jupiter Salvator. The priests of Ceres launched a rumor that the gods were angry because Rome wasn't punishing the Christians fast enough, and the mobs howled for the resumption of the games no matter what the weather. Joy swept the city when word came at last that the games would start again after a three-day break.

Beautiful weather also reappeared. Thousands of people filled the amphitheater the night before the games, and Caesar also arrived early with the vestals and the court. The spectacle was to start with combat among the Christians, armed and equipped like gladiators, but they were a great disappointment. They threw down their nets, tridents, spears and swords, and started hugging, encouraging and strengthening one another to endure the suffering and death. The crowds were outraged and deeply offended. Some cursed them for cowards without spirit, others claimed they refused to fight because they hated people and tried to deprive the rabble of the thrills it got watching displays of courage. At last, when the Christians all knelt and began to pray, real gladiators rushed in on Caesar's orders and slaughtered them in minutes.

After the corpses had been dragged away, the crowds were treated to a series of mythological tableaus created for them by the emperor himself. They watched Hercules in flames on Mount Oeta. Vinicius grew numb at the thought that this would be Ursus, but the man who burned to death on the pyre was a Christian he had never met.

The next tableau, however, struck hard at Chilon whom Caesar wouldn't excuse from the games. It showed the death plunge of Icarus and Daedalus—both of whom, according to mythology, tried to fly on wax wings that melted in the sun—and the old Greek knew the victims very well. Picked for the role of Daedalus was Euricius, the man who revealed the sign of the fish to Chilon; playing Icarus was Quartus, his son. Both were hoisted on cranes high above the circus and then dropped to fall. Quartus struck the sand so close to Caesar's elevated box that his blood splashed not merely the outer decorations but the purple-lined loge as well. Chilon didn't see the body strike the ground—he had closed his eyes—but when a little later he saw splashes of blood right beside him, he almost fainted again.

The scenes changed swiftly. The violent deaths of young girls, after being raped by gladiators costumed as wild beasts, delighted the rabble. They watched animal rites associated with priestesses of Cybele and Ceres. They watched the deaths of the Danaïdes, the daughters of Danaus who conspired to murder their father and who were thrown to the beasts; the fate of Dirce, punished for her cruelties by being tied under a wild ox and raped until dead; and the passions of Pasiphaë, in love with a bull, who later gave birth to the Minotaur. They saw young girls, barely out of childhood, torn apart by mustangs.

The crowds clapped and cheered each of these imperial inventions. Nero, proud of himself and thrilled with the applause, hardly ever took his emerald from his eye as he observed the white bodies quivering in convulsions or raked apart with irons.

Next came tableaus drawn from the city's history, and so the crowds could watch Mucius Scaevola, who burned off his right hand when captured by Etruscans. The stench of burned flesh filled the amphitheater, but the Christian whose arm was clamped to a flaming tripod stood like the real Scaevola in Porsenna's tent: eyes fixed on the sky, without a sound of pain, and with blackened lips murmuring a prayer.

The usual noon break started when he was finished off and his body dragged to the *spoiliarium*. Caesar, the vestals and the Augustans left the amphitheater and went to a gigantic scarlet tent, set up for his pleasure, where he and his guests feasted on a superb noon meal. Most of the masses followed his example, poured out of the circus and sprawled in picturesque clusters around the tent, either to stretch their cramped limbs or eat from a variety of dishes that slaves carried by Caesar's kind orders. Only the most avid went down to the arena, fingered the bloody sand, and gave their expert views on what had taken place and what was still about to happen. Soon even they were gone, anxious not to be late for the food outside; only a handful remained scattered throughout the circus. It wasn't curiosity that held them there, however, but sympathy for the next victims.

Crouched behind barriers or the lower benches, they watched as the arena was smoothed out again and then filled with holes, dug in rows next to each other and covering the whole expanse of the sand so thickly that the lead row lay only a dozen paces from the emperor's podium. From outside came the hum of massed human voices, shouts and cries and clapping, and the slaves worked in a feverish hurry to set the stage for some new kind of torture as an entertainment. Suddenly all the holding pens were thrown open at once, and swarms of Christians, each one naked and staggering under a wooden cross, were driven into the arena out of every opening. They streamed out across the sand, covering it completely.

Old men ran bowed under the beams, grown men and women with loose hair with which they tried to hide their nudity, barely grown boys and girls and even little children. Most of them, like their crosses, were garlanded with flowers. All of them missed death on opening day because there hadn't been time enough to throw them to the wild dogs, lions and beasts, and this was how they were to die today. The circus hands lashed them without mercy, forcing them to line the crosses in rows beside the holes and stand next to them. African slaves seized them eagerly, stretched them on the timbers, and nailed their hands to the crossbeams with lightning speed, so that the crowds could find all the crosses raised when they came back to their seats after the midday break. The booming sound of mallets echoed through the stands of the amphitheater, spilled into the open space outside and seeped into the tent where Caesar entertained his cronies and the vestals. They lay drinking wine, poking fun at Chilon and whispering curiously irreligious matters to their sacred virgins, while work in the arena went on at frantic speed: Iron spikes plunged into hands and feet and shovels whirred, filling up the holes under the raised crosses.

Crispus, however, was still on the ground, among the victims who awaited their turn. The lions hadn't had time to devour him, so he was to be crucified. Always ready for death, he was delighted that his hour was coming. He seemed a different man. His gaunt, dry body was stripped completely naked except for an ivy garland wrapped around his hips and a wreath of roses clamped above his eyes. Those eyes burned with the same old zeal, and the same grim, unforgiving face peered from under the roses. Nor had his heart changed in him. Just as he hurled threats at his brethren in the holding pens, frightening them with damnation and the wrath of God, so he was thundering against them today instead of giving hope and consolation.

"Praise the Savior for letting you die the same death as his!" he cried. "Maybe this will pay for some of your sins. But tremble before his anger, because there can't be the same reward for righteousness as for evil!"

His voice rang out against the thud of hammers that drove nails into hands and feet. Ever more crosses rose in the arena. He turned to those who still stood on the ground, waiting beside their timbers.

"I see an open sky," he said, "but I also see the gaping pit. . . . I don't know myself how to account for my life before the Lord, although I believed and I hated evil. But it's not death I fear! I fear resurrection! It's not the torture I'm afraid to face but the final justice, because the day of wrath and judgment is upon us!"

Suddenly a calm and solemn voice called out from the nearest benches.

"Not wrath but mercy, happiness and salvation, because I say to you that Christ will take you unto him and set you on his right. Trust and believe because Paradise is opening up before you."

All eyes lifted at once toward the benches, and even those who were already hanging on their crosses raised their pale, tortured heads and started to look at the man who spoke. He came down to the lowest barrier and began blessing them with the sign of the cross.

Crispus stretched out his hand, as if about to hurl a scathing admonition, but he caught sight of the man's face. His arm dropped, and his knees buckled under him.

"The apostle Paul!" he whispered.

To the amazement of the circus hands, all those who were not yet crucified knelt at once, and Paul of Tarsus turned toward Crispus.

"Don't threaten them, Crispus, because they'll be with you in Paradise today. You think they could be damned? But who'll damn them? Will it be the God who gave his only son for them? Will it be Christ who died for their salvation, as they die for the glory of his name? How can damnation come from the source of love? Who'll be the accuser of those whom God picked for his own? Who'll call this blood accursed?"

"Master," the old priest said, "I hated evil."

"Christ taught us to love all men even more than to hate wrongdoing, because his creed is love, not hatred."

"I've sinned in the hour of my death," Crispus said, and he started to beat his breast in contrition.

Just then an usher ran up to Paul and demanded to know who he was. "And by what right do you speak to the condemned?"

"I am a citizen of Rome," Paul told him calmly, and he turned once more to Crispus. "Have faith and believe, you servant of God, because this is a day of forgiveness."

Two black slaves came up to Crispus to stretch him on his cross, but he threw one more glance around the arena and cried out: "Brothers, pray for me!"

His stony features lost their usual grimness. A peaceful sweetness settled on his face. He stretched his own arms along the crossbeam to speed up the work and prayed fervently to the sky above him. He didn't seem to suffer any pain. No spasm passed across his face as the nails sunk into his hands; no tremor touched his body as they nailed his feet. He prayed as they lifted up his cross, prayed when they set it in the hole and tamped down the earth around it. Only when the crowds started pouring back into the circus with their shouts and laughter did the old man's brows draw sharply together as if he was angry, as if the pagan mobs disturbed his peace and the ineffable sweetness of his death.

All the crosses had been raised by then, so that a forest of human bodies nailed to timbers seemed to fill the entire arena. Sunlight lay on the crossbeams and on the martyrs' heads, but bars of shadow darkened the arena under them, forming a dense latticework of darkness in which the sand gleamed like a yellow stain. The pleasure of such spectacles allowed the crowds to enjoy the sight of long, protracted dying, but no one had ever seen so many crosses together so thickly before. They were packed so tightly into the arena that the circus hands could barely squeeze between them. Mostly women hung in the outside rows; but Crispus, as a leader, looked down from a gigantic cross, festooned with honeysuckle and planted almost within reach of the imperial box.

None of the victims had died as yet, although some of those crucified the earliest were unconscious. None of them moaned and no one begged for mercy. Some of them hung with heads leaning on shoulders or dangling on their chests, as if they were sleeping; others seemed lost in thought; yet others were gazing at the sky while their lips moved in prayer. There was something threatening in this ghastly forest; a sense of foreboding came from the spread-out bodies; and a terrible accusation lay in the victims' silence. The crowds that had poured back into the amphitheater with loud shouts and laughter, sated with food and pleased with everything around them, grew silent, unable to decide which body to look at and confused about what to think. The suspended, rigid bodies of the naked women no longer stirred their lust. No one made bets on who would be the first to die, as people usually did when there were fewer victims in the arena. And it looked as if Caesar was bored himself; he turned his head, his face dull and sluggish, and plucked at his collar with listless fingers.

Suddenly Crispus, who hung with closed eyes as if either unconscious or dead, opened them wide and fixed them on Caesar. His face was so implacable in its condemnation and his eyes glared with such a raging fire that the Augustans started whispering to each other and pointing with their fingers. Even Nero noticed him and lifted his emerald to his eye with a sleepy gesture.

Complete silence settled on the circus. The audience fixed its eyes on Crispus, who tugged at his nailed right hand as if to tear it free. His chest expanded suddenly, his ribs stood out, and he began to shout.

"Matricide!" he cried down to Nero. "Woe to you! You're doomed!"

The Augustans held their breath, too terrified to move when they heard this deadly insult hurled at the ruler of the world before the crowd of thousands. Chilon froze as if already dead. Caesar jerked as if he had been stabbed, and the emerald slipped out of his fingers.

The crowd also sat in a breathless, dumbstruck hush as Crispus' voice boomed and swelled across the amphitheater.

"Woe to you, wife-killer, murderer of your own brother! Tremble, Antichrist! The bottomless pit is opening up before you, death reaches out for you, and your grave awaits you. Woe to you, living corpse, because you'll die in terror and you'll be damned forever!"

Unable to free his hand and stretched out horribly in his agony, he was terrifying in his raging zeal. Bony as death itself, even though he was still alive, and as implacable as fate, he let his white beard shake above Nero's podium, scattering rose petals from the wreath tilted on his head.

"Woe to you, murderer! Your measure has brimmed over and your time is coming!"

His body strained once more so that it seemed he would rip his right hand away from the crossbeam and shake his fist at Caesar. But suddenly his skeletal arms appeared to stretch even longer, his body sagged downward, his head fell forward on his chest, and he died.

Within the forest of crosses, the weaker victims also began dying.

CHILON WAS TERRIFIED. "*Domine,*" he begged some nights later at the banquet table, "let us go to Greece. The sea is like a sheet of glass or a bowl of oil. The waves seem asleep. Apollo's own glory waits for you there. Triumphs and laurels wait. People will deify you, and the gods will welcome you among them as one of themselves. But here, my lord—"

He broke off and couldn't go on because his lower lip trembled so violently that his words turned into a babble without meaning.

"We'll go after the games are over," Nero said. "I know some people are already saying the Christians are harmless. '*Innoxia corpora,*' they call them, innocence in the flesh. If I went away now, everybody would start to say it. What are you afraid of, anyway, you withered old toadstool? I thought Vestinius was the superstitious one."

He frowned but peered at Chilon with expectant eyes as if anxious for an explanation. His air of indolent indifference, he knew, was a fraud, and he was just as worried as the Greek. That last show in the arena was a shock. The curses of the crucified old Crispus had sent him into a panic. He couldn't sleep that night out of shame and rage, not to mention terror. And now Vestinius was also squirming worriedly and shooting anxious glances left and right as if expecting ghosts.

"Listen to this old man, my lord," he said in a portentous voice. "There's some mysterious power around those Christians. . . . Their god gives them an easy death, but he can be an unforgiving one."

"I've nothing to do with those games," Nero said at once. "Tigellinus is running them, not I."

"That's right!" Tigellinus broke in, hearing Caesar's answer. "I'm in charge of them. I'm doing it all, and I laugh at all the Christian gods. Vestinius, my lord, is just a pig's bladder stuffed with superstitions, and this Greek hero is ready to drop dead of fright at the sight of a barnyard hen defending her chicks."

"True!" Nero said. "But from now on have their tongues cut out or stuff their mouths with something."

"We'll stuff them with fire, lord." Tigellinus laughed.

"Gods help me!" groaned Chilon.

The prefect's contemptuous self-assurance bolstered Caesar's shaken confidence. He snorted with laughter and pointed at the terrified old Greek.

"Behold the heir of Achilles!" He grinned in derision, because Chilon really looked desperate with fear. The last of his hair had turned completely white, and his face mirrored immense anxiety, foreboding and dread. At times he looked comatose, as if he'd been drugged and only half-aware of anything around him. He was confused. Questions baffled him. At other times he would fly into a towering rage and lash out at anyone without caring about the consequences, so Nero's other cronies preferred to give him a wide berth.

Just such a moment had come on him now.

"Do what you want with me!" he cried in despair, snapping his fingers to show he didn't care. "But I won't go to another of those games!"

Nero gave him a brief speculative glance and turned to Tigellinus.

"Make sure this Stoic is close to me when we're in the gardens," he remarked. "I want to see what he thinks of our illuminations."

Tigellinus grinned, and Chilon felt the lick of yet another fear, one that didn't need any explanation. The danger that rang in Caesar's voice was unmistakable.

"Lord," he groaned, "I won't see anything. I can't see at night."

"The night will be as bright as day," Nero said with a ghastly smile.

Then he turned to some of the other Augustans and started chatting about the chariot races he wanted to stage toward the end of the games.

But Chilon wasn't left alone for long. Petronius came over and tapped him on the shoulder. "Didn't I say you wouldn't be able to stand the consequences?"

"I want to get drunk," Chilon said.

He stretched his quivering arm toward a bowl of wine, but his hand shook so hard he couldn't get it to his mouth. Vestinius took it from him and put it aside. Then he leaned over, pushed close and peered into Chilon's face.

"Are the Furies after you?" he asked, both frightened and curious. "Are they? Eh?"

The old man stared at him blindly for a while, his mouth hanging open as if he didn't understand what he was being asked.

"Well? Are the Furies hounding you?" Vestinius said again.

"No," Chilon muttered. "But there's a night before me."

"What night? Gods help you, man! What do you mean, night?"

"A terrible night. A night without end. And there's something moving in it and coming toward me. What is it? I don't know, but it scares me."

"I always knew they were witches!" Vestinius was both frightened and excited. "Do you have any dreams?"

"I don't sleep. I didn't think they'd punish them like that."

"Are you sorry for *them?*"

"Why do you have to spill so much blood? You heard what that man said on the cross, didn't you? Woe to us!"

"Yes, I did hear," Vestinius murmured quietly. "But they burned the city."

"That's a lie!"

"And they're the sworn enemies of mankind."

"That's a lie!"

"They poison the water."

"That's a lie!"

"And they murder children."

"That's a lie!"

"How? What do you mean?" Vestinius was astonished. "You said all that yourself when you informed on them to Tigellinus!"

"And that's why there's this night around me and death comes toward me. It sometimes feels as if I'm already dead and so are the rest of you."

"What? No, no! They're the ones who die, we're the ones who live. But tell me one thing: What do they see when they're dying?"

"Christ."

"Is that their god? Is he powerful?"

Chilon had regained some control over himself, recalled where he was, and answered the question with another: "What are those 'illuminations' Caesar talked about?"

"Oh, that. Haven't you ever seen them? They're known as *sarmenticii* or *semaxii*. What happens is they'll dress the felons in 'tunics of pain,' well soaked in pitch and pine sap, tie them to upright timbers and set them on fire. I just hope their god doesn't unleash some new calamity on Rome. *Semaxii!* That's a terrible way to die."

"It might be better," Chilon said. "At least there won't be blood.

Tell a slave to hold a cup to my mouth. I want to drink, and I'm spilling all the wine because my hand is shaking with old age."

The others at the table were also talking about the Christians, and old Domitius Afer thought they were a joke.

"There are so many of them," he mocked, "they could start a civil war, and you must remember there were some fears they might defend themselves. But they die like sheep."

"Let them just try something else!" Tigellinus said.

"You're wrong," Petronius spoke out suddenly. "They do defend themselves."

"With what?"

"With endurance."

"That's a new way of doing it."

"It certainly is. But can you say they die like common criminals? No! They die like victims, as if the real criminals were those who condemned them. In other words we and the Roman people."

"What drivel!" Tigellinus sneered.

"*Hic abdera!*" Petronius quoted the proverb about fools. "There speaks the stupidest man of all."

The others were struck by the accuracy of his other observation and started looking at one another in surprise. "It's true," they said, nodding. "There's something very special and peculiar about the way they die."

"I tell you, they see their god!" Vestinius cried from farther down the table.

"Hey you, old man!" Several of the Augustans turned with curiosity to Chilon. "Tell us, what do they see?"

The Greek choked and spluttered wine all over his tunic. "Resurrection," he said finally. Then his whole body began to quiver and shake so violently that those who sat near him burst into gales of laughter.

‹72›

THERE WERE MANY NIGHTS that Vinicius didn't go home at all, but Petronius didn't want to know where he was or what he was doing. It occurred to him that the young soldier had some new plan of rescue and that he was working on freeing Ligia from the dungeons on the Esquiline, but he didn't want to bring bad luck to the attempt by asking questions. This refined, civilized and educated skeptic had also become slightly superstitious about certain matters. Since his failure to rescue Ligia from the Mammertine, he ceased to believe in his star, in his ability to control his fate or trust in his luck.

Nor did he place much faith in whatever Vinicius had in mind to do. The prison on the Esquiline, built in a hurry on the cellars of buildings torn down to create a fire break, wasn't as terrible as the old Tullianum next to the Capitol, but it was a hundred times better guarded. Petronius understood quite well that Ligia was moved there only so that she wouldn't die in the Mammertine and miss the arena, and it was logical she would be guarded like the apple of the keepers' eye.

"It looks as if Caesar and Tigellinus have her reserved for some unique spectacle more dreadful than the rest," he told himself at last. "And it'll be easier for Vinicius to die in the attempt than to set her free."

Vinicius also doubted his chances for success. The way things were now, only Christ could free her. All the young tribune wanted was to find a way into the prison so that he could see her. He kept thinking that Nazarius managed to slip into the Mammertine by getting hired to bring out the dead, so he decided to try that route himself. Bribed with a vast sum, the overseer at the burial pits let him join his carriers, whom he sent every night for corpses at the prisons. The danger that he might be recognized was slight. The dark of night, a slave's costume, and the dim lighting in the dungeons were his best protection. Besides, who would ever think to look for a patrician, a member of the original Roman aristocracy whose father and grandfather had been consuls, among graveyard workers, exposed as they were to the foul exhalations of the dungeons and the putrid pits? Or that he'd take a job doing what only slavery or utmost poverty forced others to do?

When the time came, he was glad and grateful to twist a loincloth around his hips and wrap his head in rags soaked in turpentine, and go with a group of others to the Esquiline.

His heart was pounding, but the praetorians didn't create any problems. All the bearers carried special passes that a centurion checked by lantern light, and a short while later a great iron gate opened up before them. Inside, Vinicius stepped into a broad, vaulted cellar, beyond which lay passages linking it to others. A feeble light wavered in a few tallow lamps and showed a dim interior filled with human beings. Some of them lay curled against the walls, either dead or sleeping. Others surrounded a large tub of water, set in the middle of the floor, and drank from it as if they burned with fever. Yet others crouched with their elbows on their knees and their heads held numbly in their hands, while sleeping children pressed against their mothers. All he could hear around him were dull groans, the loud hurried breathing of the sick, some sobs and weeping, the whisper of prayers, hymns murmured in an undertone, and the keepers' curses.

The dungeon, full of gasping people, stank like an open grave. Its murky depths were an agitated clutter of dark human shapes; nearer, the flickering small flames lit up terrified bloodless faces, caved-in with hunger and with eyes that were either lifeless and remote or burning with fever, with blue-gray lips and matted hair, and with streams of sweat pouring down their foreheads. Sick people cried and mumbled incoherent pleas in the dark corners, others called for water, and others begged to be taken out and killed.

It was hard for Vinicius to remember this was a far less awful prison than the old Tullianum. His legs trembled under him. His chest gasped for air. His hair rose on his head at the thought that Ligia was somewhere in this pit of misery, and a shout of despair died stillborn in his throat. Anything was better than these frightful cellars with their reek of corpses. The amphitheater, the fangs of wild beasts and the crosses would be a relief.

Pleading voices begged from all sides: "Take us to our deaths!"

Vinicius dug his nails into his palms because he felt his strength draining out of him and thought he might collapse. He wanted to die. Everything he had gone through until now—all his love and suffering—turned into a single longing for oblivion.

Suddenly he heard the overseer of the burial pits speaking right beside him. "How many corpses do you have tonight?"

"Must be a dozen," said one of the turnkeys. "But there'll be more by morning. There's already quite a few in their death throes in the corners."

The keeper started to complain about the women who wouldn't give up their dead children but hid them to keep them out of the burial pits a bit longer. You couldn't tell the dead from some of the living, he said, except by the smell.

"It stinks in here anyway," he said, "but that makes it worse. I'd rather be a slave in a hard labor camp than guard these dogs that rot while they're still breathing."

The overseer of the burial pits consoled him that his work wasn't any better.

Vinicius got a grip on himself, reclaimed his hold on reality and began to think clearly. He couldn't see Ligia anywhere in the gloom, and it occurred to him he might not find her until she was dead. There were more than a dozen of these cellars here, connected by newly excavated passages, and the burial crew entered only those where there were dead bodies to take out. He was suddenly afraid that all these desperate efforts would prove futile.

But his bribed employer brought him unexpected help: "You have to get the corpses out as soon as they're dead," he told the turnkey. "They spread the plague faster than anything. If you don't, you'll all die here along with your convicts."

"There's only the ten of us for all these cellars down here," the turnkey complained, "and we have to get some sleep sometime."

"So I'll leave you four of my men. You sleep, and they'll patrol the cellars and look for the dead."

"You do that, and we'll toss down a few cups tomorrow. Let your men take every corpse to inspection, because we have new orders to cut their throats before they leave here. And then straight to the pits with them!"

"Good enough," the overseer said. "And we'll drink to it."

He detailed four men to stay behind, Vinicius among them, and set the others to loading the stretchers.

Vinicius took a grateful breath. At least he knew that now he'd be able to find Ligia. He began with a thorough search of the first of the many cellars. He peered into all the dark corners where the flickering lamplight barely reached. He checked every sleeper. He looked at the worst of the ill who had been dragged into a special corner of their own, but he didn't see Ligia anywhere. The second and third cellars yielded the same dispiriting result.

Meanwhile, the hours crept on. It got to be late. The dead were taken out. The turnkeys, slumped in the connecting passages, fell asleep. The children were quiet at last, worn out by their tears, and the only sounds in the subterranean warren were the gasping breaths of exhausted sleepers and now and then the whisper of a prayer.

Vinicius brought a lighted taper into the fourth cellar, much smaller than the others, lifted it overhead and started peering around him through the gloom. Suddenly his nerves jumped and his body quivered. He glimpsed a gigantic form crouched under a heavily barred hole high up in the wall and thought it was Ursus.

He blew out the light at once and made his way nearer. "Ursus?" he asked. "Is that you?"

The giant turned his head toward him. "Who are you?"

"Don't you recognize me?" the young man asked.

"How can I? You blew out the light."

Just then Vinicius caught sight of Ligia lying on a cloak spread next to the wall and went down on his knees quietly beside her.

"Praise Christ!" Ursus recognized him. "But don't wake her, master."

On his knees, Vinicius stared at her through tears. He could see her face, pale as alabaster even in the gloom. He saw her wasted arms. Love seized him with a tearing pain that shook him to the depths of his being; he was so full of pity, worship and adoration for this girl, he loved her so much, that he threw himself facedown beside her and started to kiss the edge of the cloak on which she was lying.

Ursus watched him a long time in silence but finally intruded.

"Master," he said, plucking at his tunic, "how did you get here? Did you come to save her?"

Vinicius sat up and struggled for a while longer with his shaken feelings.

"Tell me how!" Ursus said. "I thought you'd find a way. I can think of only one. . . ." He turned his eyes to the grated opening, then muttered as if answering himself. "Yes! But they have soldiers there."

"A hundred praetorians," Vinicius confirmed.

"So . . . we won't get through!"

"No."

The Lygian rubbed his forehead and asked again: "How did you get here, sir?"

"I've a pass from the overseer of the burial pits—" Vinicius began, but then he broke off as if a new idea had flashed through his head.

"By the Savior's suffering!" he spoke rapidly. "I'll stay here. Let her take the pass, wrap her head in rags, throw that cloak across her shoulders and go in my place. There are a few half-grown lads in the burial detail, so the praetorians won't notice the difference. And once she gets to Petronius' house, he'll save her!"

But the Lygian let his head droop onto his chest. "She won't go, master. She loves you. Besides, she's too ill to stand."

Then after a moment's silence he added : "If you and the noble Petronius couldn't save her, master, who'd be able to do it?"

"Only Christ."

They were both silent after that. It occurred to the simple Lygian that Christ could save them all anytime he wanted, that he could rescue the whole community. If he didn't do it, then it was time to suffer and be killed. He didn't mind that so much for himself, but he was racked with pity for this child who grew up in his care and whom he loved more than his life.

Vinicius knelt again beside Ligia. Moonlight seeped through the barred hole into the dungeon and lit up the gloom better than the single tallow wick that still flickered feebly above the door.

All of a sudden Ligia opened her eyes and laid her hot palms on his hands.

"I see you," she murmured. "I knew you would come."

He seized her hands, pressed them to his breast, his heart and his forehead, then raised her slightly from her bedding and leaned her against his chest.

"I'm here, my love," he said. "May Christ guard you and save you, my beloved Ligia!"

He could say nothing more because his heart seemed to howl within him with love and agonizing pain, and he didn't want to add his suffering to her own.

"I'm ill, Mark," she said. "I'll die either here or in the arena. . . . But I prayed to see you once more before that happened, and you came. Christ heard me!"

While he still couldn't trust himself to speak and only pressed her to his chest in silence, she went on.

"I'd see you through the window at the Tullianum, and I knew you were trying to come to me too. And now the Savior gave me a lucid moment so we can say good-bye. I'm going to him, Mark. I am almost there. But I love you and I always will."

Vinicius broke through his grief, stifled his pain and fought to keep his voice quiet and controlled.

"No, my love," he said. "You won't die. The apostle told me to believe and promised to pray for you. He knew Christ. Christ loves him and won't refuse him anything. . . . If you were going to die, Peter would never order me to trust in Christ's goodness. He said, 'Keep trusting!' No, Ligia! Christ will take mercy on me. He doesn't want your death, he won't let it happen. . . . I swear to you on the Savior's name that Peter prays for you every day!"

They sat in silence then. The tallow wick sputtered out above the doorway, but moonlight was now streaming into the subterranean vault through the opening. A child wailed in a corner across the room and was quiet again. From outside came the voices of some praetorians who had come off guard and were throwing dice against the prison wall.

"Mark," Ligia said. "Christ said to his father, 'Take this bitter cup away from me,' but he drank it all. He died on the cross, and now thousands are dying in his name. So why should he spare me alone? Who am I, Mark? I heard Peter say that he, too, will die a martyr. What am I beside him? I was afraid of suffering and death when the praetorians came for us, but I no longer fear anything. What is there to fear? Look at this terrible prison and remember I'm going to Heaven. Think of what I'm leaving and where I am going. This is the place of Caesar, but in the other place is the Savior, full of love and mercy, and there is no death. You love me, so just think how happy I will be. And think, my dearest Mark, that you'll join me there!"

She paused for breath and a moment's rest, and then she raised his hand to her lips.

"Mark!"

"What, my love?"

"Don't cry for me. Remember you'll be coming there to me. I didn't live long, but God let me have your soul. So I want to be able to tell Christ that even though I died and you watched my death and were left to suffer and grieve for me, you never once blasphemed against his will and that you still love him. And you will love him, won't you? You will accept my death with humility and patience? Because then he'll reunite us, and I love you and want to be with you. . . ."

Once more her breath failed her, and he could barely hear the last of her words.

"Promise it to me, Mark!"

Vinicius pressed her to him with shaking arms. "By your saintly head, I promise!" he said.

Her face brightened then and seemed to glow in the light of the moon. She kissed his hand again.

"I am your wife," she whispered.

The gambling praetorians got into a noisy argument beyond the wall, but Ligia and Vinicius forgot about prisons, guards and the earth itself. Their souls had come together. They heard angel voices. They began to pray.

FOR THREE DAYS, or rather for three nights, nothing disturbed their peace. When the usual prison chores were done—that is to say, when he had stacked the dead away from the living and separated the dying from the sick, and when the tired turnkeys lay down to sleep in the corridors—Vinicius slipped into Ligia's dungeon and stayed there until the first light of dawn glimmered between the bars. She would lay her head on his chest, and they talked softly about love and death. Step by step in all their words and thoughts, and even hopes and wishes, they moved further away from life and lost the sense of living. Both were like voyagers whose ship had sailed beyond sight of land and were now a part of the infinite horizons that opened before them. Unconscious of the change, both cut their ties with everyday reality, turning slowly into quiet, disembodied spirits in love with each other, adoring Christ, and ready to fly away. Only occasionally the old pain erupted and shook him like a windstorm; once in a while hope still flashed like lightning, coming from love and faith in the crucified God. But each day severed more of his connections with the world, and he surrendered to the idea of dying. When he left the prison in the morning, he looked at the city, at the outside world, at people he knew and at everything relating to life and living, as if they were a dream. Everything seemed foreign, empty, trivial and remote. Even the fear of physical agony ceased to bother him; it was just a stage to be crossed with the mind focused on something else and eyes fixed elsewhere. It seemed to both of them that they had already stepped into eternity.

They talked about love and how they would live together, but only beyond the grave; and if once in a while their thoughts touched earthly matters, it was only like people getting ready for a great journey who talked about their travel preparations. As for the rest, it all slipped away, lost in the stillness that surrounds two lone, forgotten pillars in a wilderness. All that concerned them now was whether Christ would let them stay together. Since every moment strengthened that conviction, they loved him all the more as the precious link that united them and as the source of endless happiness and eternal peace. The dust of the earth drifted away from them while they were still alive. Their souls became as clean and pure as tears. Heaven began for them on that prison pallet, in the grim shadow of death in the arena and in the midst of misery and terror, because she took him by the hand and led him to the source of eternal bliss as if she were already holy and redeemed.

Petronius found himself astonished by the rising peace he saw in Vinicius and by the strange new light he glimpsed in his face. He even thought at times that Vinicius must have found some fresh means of rescuing the girl, and he was upset not to be included.

"You've changed," he said at last, unable to stand it. "Whatever it is, don't keep it a secret because I want to help. So have you come up with something new?"

"I have." Vinicius nodded. "But there's nothing more you can do for me. After her death I'll make a public admission that I am a Christian and follow after her."

"So you've given up all hope?"

"On the contrary. Christ will give her back to me and we'll never be apart again."

Petronius started striding up and down the atrium, annoyed and disappointed.

"You don't need your Christ for that," he snapped impatiently. "The Greek Thanatos can do as much for you. One angel of death is much like another."

Vinicius smiled sadly. "No, my dear friend," he said. "But that's something you refuse to grasp."

"And I don't want to, either. This is no time for debates. Do you remember what you said when we failed to rescue her from the Mammertine? I lost all hope, but you said, 'Christ will return her to me.' Well, let him do it. If I threw a precious vase into the sea, none of our gods would be able to hand it back to me. But if yours can't do better, I don't see the point of worshiping him rather than the old ones."

"But he will give her back to me," Vinicius said.

Petronius shrugged. "Are you aware the Christians are to serve as torches in Caesar's gardens tomorrow?"

"Tomorrow?" Vinicius echoed.

His heart seemed to leap in pain and terror at the speedy approach of terrible reality. He thought this might be the last night he would ever spend with Ligia. He said a hasty good-bye to Petronius and hurried to the overseer of the burial pits for another pass. But here he was bitterly disappointed. The overseer wouldn't give him one.

"Forgive me, my lord," he said. "I did what I could for you, but I can't risk my life. Tonight is the night they'll be taking the Christians to the gardens. The prison will be full of officials and soldiers. If someone recognized you, that'd be the end for me and my children."

Vinicius understood that any further urging would be a waste of time. But he thought the soldiers who had seen him there before might let him in without a pass, so when evening came he put on his coarse workman's tunic, wrapped his head in rags and reported at the prison gate. That night the praetorians were checking the passes more carefully than ever. Moreover he was recognized by their commander, the centurion Scevinus, a fierce disciplinarian who was devoted body and soul to Caesar. Some last stray sparks of pity for human misery must have been glowing in his armored chest, however, because instead of striking his shield and calling out the guard, he took Vinicius by the arm and led him aside.

"Go home, my lord," he said. "I know who you are, but I'll keep quiet about it or you'll be lost at once. I can't let you in, but go on your way, and may the gods send you some kind of peace."

"You can't let me in," Vinicius said, "but let me stay here so I can see those you're taking out."

"I've no orders against that," Scevinus said.

Vinicius found a place before the gate and waited for the condemned to be led outside. At last, close to midnight, the prison gates swung wide and the prisoners started to emerge, coming in long lines of men, women and children surrounded by heavily armed troops of praetorians. The night was very bright under a full moon that lit up their bodies, not merely their faces. They walked in pairs, like mourners in a funeral procession, in a deep silence interrupted only by the clang and rattle of weapons and armor. So many were led out, he thought there would be no one left in any of the dungeons.

He recognized Glaucus, the physician, close to the end of the procession, but neither Ligia nor Ursus was among the condemned.

‹74›

NIGHTFALL WAS STILL to come when the crowds started pouring into Caesar's gardens. They came singing and dressed as if for a celebration, wearing wreaths of flowers, in a jovial mood and mostly drunk, flocking to see a superb new spectacle. The shouts of *"Semaxii! Sarmenticii!"* rang on the Via Tecta, on the Emilian bridge and from across the Tiber, on the Triumphal Way, from around Nero's amphitheater, and all the way to the slopes of the Vatican. People burned at the stake had been seen in Rome before, but never in such numbers.

Wanting to be finished with the Christians once and for all and also to stop the epidemic that was spreading from the prisons all over the city, Caesar and Tigellinus ordered all dungeons emptied so that a mere few dozen prisoners were left in the jails, all of them destined for the close of the games. The result was that the crowds were dumbstruck when they passed inside the garden gates. All the main avenues and paths along the leafy groves and all the walkways that ran through the meadows and beside the ponds, ornamental pools, thickets, lawns and flower beds were thickly studded with tall, pitch-smeared stakes, each with a Christian fastened near the top. Seen from one or another of the rolling hillocks, with the view unobstructed by the trees, rows upon rows of flower-wreathed posts and bodies stretched into the distance, running across the hills and clearings, garlanded in myrtle leaves and ivy. They stretched so far that while the nearer ones looked as tall as ships' masts, those in the distance seemed no bigger than grounded javelins. Their numbers surpassed every expectation; it was as if an entire nation had been staked out for the amusement of Caesar and the city. Throngs of gawkers stopped before one post or another as the shape, age or sex of the victim captured their attention; they stared at the faces, wreaths and ivy garlands, and then moved on, asking in amazement: "Could there have been so many guilty ones? And how could Rome be burned

down by toddlers who can barely walk?" The astonishment changed
gradually to uneasiness.

Night had come. The first of the stars glittered in the sky. A slave
with a lighted torch stationed himself next to every victim, and when
trumpets sounded all over the gardens, signaling the start of the spectacle, they set the bottom of each post on fire. Pitch-soaked straw
hidden under the flowers caught quickly; the blaze flamed brightly,
twisted through the garlands, and leaped toward the legs of the victims. The crowds grew quiet. The gardens rang with one vast, protracted moan and long cries of pain. Some of the victims fixed their
eyes on the starry sky and began to sing hymns in praise of Christ.
The throngs gawked and listened. Even the most hard-hearted of
them cringed with horror when shrill children's voices screamed
"Mama! Mama!" from the smallest stakes. Even the drunkest of the
rabble shuddered at the sight of the little bodies writhing in the flames
and the small, innocent faces twisted in pain or choking in the smoke
that began to suffocate the victims. The flames crept upward, on and
on, burning through ever more garlands of ivy and roses.

Light blazed above the main avenues and the pathways; it glowed
among the groves, meadows and flower beds. The water in the artificial lakes and ponds burst into its own fiery illumination, the shrubs
and leaves turned pink with reflected light, and the night turned as
bright as day. The reek of burning flesh filled the entire park, but at
that moment slaves started sprinkling myrrh and aloes into special
censers set between the stakes. Shouts broke out here and there in
the crowd, but it was impossible to say if they expressed compassion,
awe, pleasure or delight. They swelled by the moment along with the
flames that gnawed the posts, crept up to the victims' chests and
shriveled their hair, covered their scorched, black faces and leaped
ever higher, as if to affirm the power and triumph of those who
ordered them lighted.

Caesar appeared among his people at the very start of the spectacle, driving a magnificent racing chariot drawn by four white horses.
He was dressed as a circus charioteer wearing the colors of the
Greens, which he and his court backed at the hippodrome. Behind
him came other chariots full of richly costumed courtiers, senators,
priests, and naked women representing the drunken rites of Bacchus,
all wearing wreaths in their hair, clutching jugs of wine, and for the
most part drunk and howling like banshees. Riding beside them were
musicians dressed as fauns and satyrs and playing on zithers, eight-
string lutes, pipes and hunting horns. The wives and daughters of

Rome's high society drove in other chariots, half-naked and as drunk as the rest, surrounded by runners who shook long, jingling staves festooned with bells and ribbons, pounded tambourines and scattered petals and flowers.

The glittering cavalcade moved forward, shouting *"Evoe!"*—the shout of joy that opened the festivals of Bacchus—and rolled along the broadest avenue among the billows of smoke and the human torches. Caesar drove at a snail's pace; flanked in his chariot by Chilon and Tigellinus, and he planned to amuse himself with the old Greek's terror. He looked enormous, blinking his puffy little eyes as he savored the sight of the burning bodies and cocked a careful ear to the shouts and cheers. Standing high in his gilded chariot, surrounded by the vast, bowing human tide and wearing the gold wreath of a racing champion, he towered over his court and the masses like a monstrous giant. His thick, fleshy arms—held high to grasp the reins—looked as if raised in blessing. A smile flickered on his face and in his narrowed eyes, and he shone above the people like a sun, or like a terrible god who was both magnificent and mighty.

From time to time he halted for a better look at a young girl whose breasts were starting to shrivel in the flames or at the twisted face of a little child, and then rode on, drawing his frenzied and demented retinue behind him. Now and then he bowed solemnly to the masses or leaned back, hauled on his gilded reins and talked to Tigellinus. At last he halted by the fountain at the intersection of two avenues, stepped from the chariot, signaled his followers to gather around him and mingled with the crowds.

Shouts thundered. Applause greeted him. The drunken revelers, nymphs, senators, Augustans, priests, fauns, satyrs and praetorian guardsmen surrounded him at once in a delirious, enthusiastic circle and he walked around the fountain with Tigellinus on one side and Chilon on the other. Several dozen human torches blazed around this fountain, and he stopped before each of them, commenting on the victims or jeering at the Greek, whose face showed utter and absolute despair.

At last they came to a tall mast wreathed in myrtle boughs and bindweeds. The flames had only just begun to lick the victim's knees, but his face was invisible at first because the burning green boughs obscured it with smoke. In a while, though, a fresh night breeze blew the smoke away and uncovered the head of an old man with a long white beard hanging to his chest.

Chilon seemed to shrivel and twist into a ball like a wounded reptile. His mouth gaped in a cawing screech, more animal than human.

"Glaucus!" he croaked. "Glaucus!"

Glaucus looked down at him from the burning post. He was still alive. Pain raked his face, and he was straining forward as if to take one last long look at his tormentor, the man who betrayed him, robbed him of his wife and children, set an assassin on him, and when all this had been forgiven in the name of Christ, thrust him once more into the hands of torturers. No one had ever wronged another man worse than he had been wronged. No one had ever suffered more cruelly at another's hands. And now the victim was burning on a pitch-smeared stake while his tormentor was standing below.

Glaucus' eyes never left Chilon's face. Smoke hid them now and then, but Chilon saw them fixed on him every time a breeze blew the smoke away. He leaped up, tried to run but couldn't. His legs were suddenly like lead. Some unseen hand seemed to grip him with superhuman strength and hold him before this pillar of flames, unable to move. He turned to stone, petrified with terror. All he felt—all that he could feel—was something bursting within him, tearing, giving way; something welled over, spilled and overflowed. He knew he couldn't stand more blood and suffering around him, that his life was ending, that everything about him was vanishing in the night along with Caesar, the court and all the massed people. He crouched in the middle of an endless, terrifying darkness in which he could see only the eyes of this martyr, summoning him to judgment.

That head strained toward him, dipping lower and lower, and the eyes kept looking.

Those nearest them saw that something special was taking place between them, and the Augustans crowded forward, looking for amusement, but their laughter froze.

Chilon's face was horrifying, twisted in such agony and terror as if the tongues of flame were licking his own flesh. Suddenly he lurched forward, stretched his arms upward to the sufferer and screamed in a frightened, panic-stricken voice:

"Glaucus! In Christ's name! Forgive me!"

Silence gripped everyone. A shudder ran through everybody near, and all eyes were fixed on the tormented old man on the stake as if they had a will and power of their own. The head of the martyr nodded slightly or seemed to be nodding, and a moan drifted down from the top of the mast.

"I . . . forgive you."

Chilon hurled himself facedown on the ground howling like an animal, clawed up a fistful of earth in each hand and poured them over his head. Meanwhile the flames shot upward, embraced Glaucus' chest and face, unwound his myrtle crown, and caught the ribbons at the top of the stake, which suddenly blazed with a great bright light.

When Chilon rose a short while later, his face looked so different that the Augustans thought they were seeing another man. His eyes burned with the zeal of revelation. His wrinkled forehead radiated a transcendent power. Stumbling and decrepit only a moment earlier, the Greek now seemed like a man possessed or like a priest who had glimpsed his god and wanted to proclaim a new truth to the world.

"What's wrong with him? He's gone mad!" several voices growled among the Augustans.

He turned his back on them, raised his right hand to demand attention and started to shout loud enough for all the rabble to hear him, too, not just the court and Caesar.

"People of Rome!" he cried. "I swear by my own death that innocent people are being killed here! The man who set fire to the city . . . is there!"

He pointed his finger at Nero.

There was a moment of stunned, breathless silence. The courtiers turned numb. Chilon kept standing with his trembling arm stretched out and pointing at Caesar. Suddenly pandemonium broke out all around. The crowds surged toward him like a wave struck by a sudden wind, the better to see him. Some people shouted "Get him!" Others screamed "Gods help us!" The rabble erupted with shrill, hissing whistles. "Redbeard!" they howled. "Matricide! Arsonist!" The uproar swelled by the minute. The naked bacchantes ran for the chariots, screeching to high heavens. A number of stakes burned through just then and fell to the ground, hurling showers of sparks and adding to the chaos. The dense, teeming mob broke into mindless panic, swept over Chilon and carried him away into the depths of the park.

The torches were now toppling everywhere, crashing across the avenues and pathways, and choking them with sparks and the stench of burned wood and flesh. Lights dimmed and died. Darkness gripped the gardens. Worried, dispirited and frightened, the rabble choked the gates trying to get out. The story of what happened passed from mouth to mouth, exaggerated and distorted. Some people said Caesar fell into a dead faint. Others claimed he confessed to burning down the city. Another story had him falling ill and being whisked away like a corpse in his golden chariot.

Some scattered voices started to argue in sympathy with the Christians. "They didn't burn down Rome, did they? So why so much blood, torture and injustice? The gods won't stand for it. They're sure to want vengeance, and what kind of offerings will placate them now?"

More and more people talked about *"innoxia corpora,"* the phrase that summed up the personification of harmlessness and goodness. Women took loud pity on all the children thrown to the wild beasts, nailed to the crosses, and burned to death in the hellish gardens! Then their pity changed to curses hurled furiously at Caesar and Tigellinus.

There were also those who halted suddenly in their pell-mell rush to ask themselves or others: "What kind of god is it who gives such strength in the face of death? And who makes people oblivious to torture?"

They went home wondering and thoughtful.

‹75›

CHILON WANDERED, lost in the park, for hours afterward. He didn't know where to go or where to turn for help. Once more he felt like a sick, helpless, enfeebled and useless old man. He tripped over burned but recognizable human bodies, stumbled into the husks of burned-out stakes that sent hot sparks swarming after him, or sat on the ground staring blindly at whatever lay in front of him, only half-aware of what he was seeing.

It was almost completely dark in the gardens now. Only a pale moon flitted among the trees, throwing its hesitant light onto the roads and pathways and the charred timbers across them, and on the shapeless entities, unrecognizable as human, that were the incinerated victims. The old Greek thought he saw the face of Glaucus in the moon, with his eyes still fixed on him intently, and he did what he could to hide from the light. At last, however, he left the shadows and found himself moving against his will, as if propelled and guided by mysterious forces. Some unknown power was directing him back to the fountain at which Glaucus died.

Suddenly a hand fell on his shoulder from behind.

The old man spun around. He saw an unknown man. "Who's there? Who are you?" he shouted in terror.

"I'm the apostle," the man said. "Paul of Tarsus."

"I'm cursed . . . damned forever! What do you want with me?"

"I want to save you," the apostle said.

Chilon staggered back against a tree. His legs wobbled under him, and his arms hung limp and useless at his sides.

"There's no salvation for me," he said in a dull, somber voice as heavy as lead.

"Did you hear that Christ forgave the thief who was crucified beside him?"

"And did you hear what I did?"

"I saw your suffering," Paul said. "And I heard you witness to the truth."

"Oh, master . . ." Chilon groaned.

"And if Christ's servant forgave you in his hour of torment, how can Christ not do so?"

Chilon clasped his head like a madman. "Forgiveness? Forgiveness for me?" He started to moan like a man who had finally come to the end of his strength and could no longer struggle against his suffering and pain.

"Lean on me," Paul said. "And come with me."

He put his arm around him and led him toward the crossroads, guided by the rustle of the fountain, which seemed to weep in the silent night over the martyrs' bodies.

"Our God," he said again, "is a God of mercy. If you were to throw stones into the sea, could you ever fill it? I say to you that Christ's mercy is like the sea, and all the sins and faults of all the people will sink in it like stones. And I say it's like the sky that covers all the mountains and lands and seas, because it's everywhere and there's no end to it. You suffered at Glaucus' stake, and Christ saw your suffering. You said, 'He is the man who set Rome on fire,' without fear of what may come tomorrow, and Christ noted that. You're free of malice. You've shed lies and evil. There's only boundless remorse and sorrow in your heart. . . . Come with me and listen to what I say, because I also once hated him and persecuted those he chose to be his disciples. I neither wanted him nor believed in him until he showed himself to me and called me to him. He's been the source of my love ever since and its only object. He let you suffer heartache, pain and fear to call you to him. You hated him and he loved you. You sent his worshipers to be tortured, but he wants to forgive you and save you."

A vast sobbing racked the devastated man as if his soul were ripped in two, and Paul possessed him, took control of him, and led him like a captive. After a while he spoke again.

"Follow me, and I'll take you to him," he said. "Why else would I have come to you? He ordered me to harvest people's souls, so that's what I do. You think you're damned, and I say to you: Believe in him, and you will be saved. You think you're hated, and I say he loves you. Look at me! Without him, all I had was malice in my heart, and now his love is enough to serve as my father, mother, and all the riches and kingdoms of this world. He is the only refuge. Only he will credit your remorse, take note of your misery, ease your fear and lift you up to him."

Speaking like this, he brought Chilon to the fountain whose silvery arcs could be seen gleaming in the moonlight from a long way off. It was quiet there with nothing else to see because the garden slaves had already cleared away the charred stakes and the martyrs' bodies. Chilon moaned and threw himself on his knees, hid his face in his hands and remained as still as the night around him, while Paul raised his face toward the stars and began to pray.

"Master," he said, "look down on this sufferer. See his remorse, count his tears and torment! Forgive him, Lord of mercy, who spilled your blood for our sins. By your own suffering, death and resurrection, forgive him!"

He was silent for a long time after that, but he continued to pray and look at the stars. Then the man who knelt at his feet emitted a moaning cry.

"Christ! Christ! Forgive me!"

Paul stepped up to the fountain, dipped both hands into it, and brought the water to the kneeling sufferer.

"Chilon," he said. "I now baptize you in the name of the Father and of the Son and of the Holy Ghost. Amen!"

Chilon looked up, spread his arms wide, and stayed like that as if carved in stone. The moon poured its light on his white hair and his equally white face, as still as if it already belonged to the dead. Time passed. Roosters began to crow in the great aviary of Domitian's gardens but he remained kneeling like a graveside statue. At last he roused and turned to the apostle.

"What am I to do before I die?" he asked.

"Believe and serve the truth."

They left together. The apostle blessed him once more at the garden gates, and they parted there. Chilon insisted they go their own ways since he expected after what happened that Caesar and Tigellinus would be hunting for him. He was right. When he arrived home he found the house surrounded by praetorians. They seized him, commanded by Scevinus, and dragged him off at once to the Palatine.

Caesar had gone to bed, but Tigellinus was still waiting for him.

"You've committed treason"—his voice was calm but menacing and malignant—"and you'll pay for it. But if you speak out in the amphitheater tomorrow and say you were mad and drunk and that it was the Christians who set Rome on fire, you'll just be flogged and exiled."

"I can't do that, my lord," Chilon murmured quietly but firmly.

Tigellinus stepped up to him, as slow and sinister as a creeping reptile. His voice was as soft as Chilon's but ominous and thick with anger.

"What do you mean you can't, you Greek dog? Weren't you drunk? Don't you understand what'll happen to you? Look over there!"

He pointed to the corner of the atrium where four Thracian slaves waited by a long wooden bench, clutching ropes and sharp iron tongs.

"I can't, my lord!" Chilon said.

Rage shook the prefect, but he controlled himself. "You saw how the Christians died," he said. "Is that what you want?"

The old man raised his gray, wasted face. His lips moved quietly for a while.

"I, too, believe in Christ," he said.

Tigellinus gaped at him as if he'd gone mad. "You *have* gone crazy, you sick dog!" he snarled and suddenly all his pent-up fury broke free and spilled out. He threw himself on Chilon, seized him by the beard, knocked him to the floor, and started to kick him, while flecks of foam trickled from his mouth.

"You'll take it back!" he raged. "You'll take it all back!"

"I can't!" Chilon answered from under his boots.

"Hurt him!" the prefect roared.

The Thracians leaped up at the order, clutched the old man and dragged him to the bench, where they tied him down and started cracking his thin arm and leg bones. But he kissed their hands with humble gratitude when they were fastening him to the bench for torture, and then he closed his eyes and lay as still as if he were dead.

He was still alive when Tigellinus leaned over him and demanded: "You'll recant?"

His gray lips barely moved. His whisper was so hushed that Tigellinus almost didn't hear him.

"I . . . can't!" he said.

Tigellinus waved the torturers away and started to pace up and down the atrium. Anger and helplessness struggled in his face. Then he seemed to think of something else, because he called the Thracians back to the torture table.

"Rip out his tongue," he said.

‹76›

THE DRAMA *Aureolus* was usually staged in such a way that the scenery opened to create two separate spectacles, the lesser of which showed a crucified slave devoured by a bear. After what happened in Caesar's gardens, the normal staging was changed to a single scene so that the greatest possible audience could see the bloody climax. The animal role was usually played by an actor sewn into a bearskin, but this time the show was to be fully realistic with a real live bear and a real crucifixion.

The idea came to Tigellinus as he was torturing Chilon. Caesar announced at first that he wouldn't come but Tigellinus, now his reigning favorite, made him change his mind. He explained that after the fiasco in the gardens it was essential for the emperor to show himself in public. He also guaranteed that the crucified slave wouldn't attack him as Crispus had done. The rabble showed signs of being somewhat jaded with mass exterminations, sated with horror and tired of the bloodshed, but they were lured to the amphitheater by an announced free distribution of new lottery tickets, gifts, and a night of feasting, since this show was to be staged at night in a brightly lighted amphitheater.

The lure worked as expected, and the huge structure was packed from top to bottom as soon as it got dark. Every Augustan came, led by Tigellinus, not so much to see the show as to demonstrate their loyalty to Caesar and gossip about Chilon who was the talk of Rome. They whispered to one another that when Caesar arrived home from the gardens, he went mad with rage and couldn't sleep all night. He was racked by terrifying visions, which was why he announced his imminent departure to Greece the first thing the next morning. Others disagreed, holding that now he would be more implacable than ever against the Christians. Nor was there any shortage of cowards who thought that Chilon's accusation, hurled into Nero's teeth before the rabble, could bring the worst possible consequences.

There were others who felt the stirrings of human decency and pleaded with Tigellinus to stop the persecutions.

"Look where it's led you," said Barcus Soranus. "You wanted to satisfy the mob's lust for vengeance and prove the Christians guilty by sheer retribution. But what you've achieved is just the opposite."

"That's right!" Antistius Verus added. "Everyone's whispering that they're innocent. If that's supposed to be political dexterity, then Chilon was right when he said all your brains would fit in a nutshell."

"Is that so?" Tigellinus turned his cold eyes on Barcus Soranus. "People also whisper that your daughter, Servilia, hid her Christian slaves from Caesar's justice. And they say the same about your wife, Antistius."

"It's a lie!" Barcus Soranus was immediately alarmed.

"My wife's the victim of slander!" Antistius Verus was just as worried and shaken. "Those divorced hags of yours want to bring her down because they hate her virtue!"

But the rest wanted to talk only about Chilon.

"What happened to him?" Epius Marcellus wanted to know. "He handed them all to Tigellinus and went from real rags to some riches. He could've lived the rest of his life in comfort and had a splendid funeral, a fine tomb and a graveside statue at the end. But no! All of a sudden he throws it all away and dooms himself as well. Really! He must've lost his mind!"

"His mind's not the problem," Tigellinus said with a shrug. "He just became a Christian."

"Chilon? Impossible!" Vitelius said.

"And didn't I warn you?" Vestinius threw in with his furtive, superstitious air. "I said, 'Kill all the Christians you like but don't provoke their deity.' That's no joking matter! Look at what's happening! I didn't light any fires in Rome, but if Caesar would let me, I'd sacrifice a hundred oxen to their god at once. And everybody ought to do the same, because, as I'll repeat, this god is no joke! Remember I said this."

"And I said something else," Petronius remarked. "Tigellinus laughed when I said they were defending themselves in the circus, but I'll say more. They're winning!"

"How? What? What do you mean?" several voices questioned.

"By Pollux! If a creature like Chilon couldn't hold out against them, then who can? If you think that each spectacle doesn't create new Christians, you should start ladling soup in the public kitchens or get jobs as barbers. That way you might find out what the people think and what is happening all over the city."

"And that's the pure truth!" Vestinius cried, swearing by the sacred night-shift of Diana.

Barcus grew serious. "What are you leading up to?" He turned to Petronius.

"I'll end where you started. There's been enough bloodshed!"

"Ai!" Tigellinus mocked him with a pointed smile. "Just a little more!"

"If you don't have the head to grasp this," Petronius shot back, "try using the knob on your cane!"

Caesar's arrival put an end to their conversation. The drama started as soon as he and Pythagoras took their places in his loge, but no one among the Augustans paid much attention to *Aureolus* because Chilon was all they could think about. The bored masses hissed the play, yelled insults at the court and demanded the scene with the bear. Used to seeing cruelty and bloodshed, that's all they had come for; the play wouldn't have held them in the amphitheater if it wasn't for the promised gifts and the condemned old man.

The awaited moment came at last. Two arena workers carried in a wooden cross, low enough for a rampant bear to reach the victim's chest, and then two others brought Chilon, or rather dragged him in since all the bones in his legs had been crushed and he couldn't walk. He was thrown down and nailed to the cross so quickly that the curious Augustans couldn't get a good look at him. It was only when the cross was raised and tamped in its posthole that all their eyes fixed on him.

Few could recognize the former Chilon in this naked old man. Not a drop of color remained in his face after the tortures ordered by Tigellinus, and only a crimson stain clotted his white beard where his tongue had been torn out of his mouth. All his bones protruded as if he had been flayed. His skin seemed transparent. He looked much older, almost a doddering parody of age. Where his sharp, hungry and uncertain eyes had always gleamed with malice and suspicion, darting anxious glances out of a frightened, calculating face, he now wore the pained but gentle smile of a dreaming man or of someone dead and beyond all fears. Perhaps this confident and untroubled peace came from his recollection that Christ forgave the thief crucified beside him. Or perhaps he was already talking in his heart to the God of mercy, telling him, "Lord, I used to bite like a poisonous insect, but I was a famished beggar all my life, half-dead with hunger, kicked by everybody, always beaten and trampled, abused and tormented. I was poor and wretched, Lord, and there wasn't a single happy moment in my life, and now they've tortured me and nailed me to a cross. But you won't reject me! You won't push me from you. You'll accept me in the hour of my death."

His humble peacefulness was clear for everyone to see. No one laughed. There was something so quiet and gentle in this crucified old man, he seemed so age-worn, weak, helpless and defenseless—and his humility cried out so loudly for mercy and compassion—that people asked themselves, whether they were aware of it or not, how anyone could torture and crucify someone who was dying anyway. The crowds were silent. Vestinius twisted to the right and left of him among the Augustans, saying in a frightened whisper: "See? Look at how they die!" The rest of the court waited for the bear, wanting the spectacle to end as fast as possible.

At last the bear rolled into the arena, swaying his hunched head from side to side and peering up from under his lowered head as if making up his mind and looking for something. At last he caught sight of the cross and the naked body, ambled closer, rose on his hind legs, then let his paws sink down again and dropped to all fours. He hunkered down in the sand beside the cross, muttering and growling, as if some vestige of mercy had glimmered in his animal heart for this human being.

The circus crew yelled to excite the beast, but the crowds were silent. Chilon, meanwhile, slowly raised his head and let his eyes search among the benches until they fixed somewhere in the highest rows. He breathed more quickly, his skeletal chest moving with renewed life, and an astonishing change came over his face. A smile of ineffable joy lit up his solemn features, the blazing fires reflected on his furrowed forehead like sunlight, his head tilted back so that his eyes lifted toward the sky, and two great pent-up tears rolled slowly down his cheeks.

And then he died.

All of a sudden a deep and powerful voice rang out from under the *velarium:* "Peace be to the martyrs!"

The amphitheater lay in a stunned silence.

NOT MANY CHRISTIANS were left in the prisons after the spectacle of the living torches. Others suspected of practicing "the eastern superstition" were still rounded up now and then, but the manhunts caught fewer every day, barely enough to feed the next day's show, and the games began drawing to an end. The people had their fill of blood. Satiated to the point of boredom and indifference, the masses started to lose interest in the slaughter. Moreover the way in which the victims met their deaths made them uneasy. Nothing like it had ever been seen before, and it became both mystifying and frightening.

The rabble echoed the superstitious fears voiced by Vestinius, and something close to panic seized tens of thousands across the city. The mobs started muttering about the vengeful nature of the Christian god, and the tales became more fanciful every day. The typhus that broke out in the prisons spread into the city and fueled the general apprehension, while the frequent funerals seen all over Rome prompted urgent whispers that some new way must be found to placate the unknown and implacable deity. Sacrifices were made to Jupiter and Libitina. To make matters worse, more and more people started to believe that the strange, humble and unresisting Christians had no hand in burning down the city, that Rome was set on fire by the emperor's orders, and there was nothing Tigellinus and his henchmen could do to prevent it.

This was just the reason neither he nor Caesar would let up on the persecutions. New decrees continued the distribution of free grain, wine and oil to pacify the people; special relief measures were announced for homeowners to ease restoration; and the senate issued a new building code that specified the width of the streets and the materials to be used in the reconstruction to avert future conflagrations.

Caesar himself attended senate sessions, took part in meetings with the city fathers and worked to improve the lot of the people, but not even a shadow of relief fell on the condemned. The ruler of the world was determined to convince the city that such inhuman punishments could be inflicted only on the guilty. Nor did anyone in the senate speak out for the Christians. No one wanted to draw Caesar's baleful eye on himself. Moreover the thoughtful and far-seeing men in the assembly realized that the new faith threatened the basic principles of the Roman state. If Christianity were ever to triumph among them, Rome would fall.

Roman law dealt only with the living, however. The dead and the dying were turned over to their families, and Vinicius found some relief in that. If Ligia died, he would bury her in his family tomb and lie there beside her. He had no more hope of saving her from death. Immersed as he was in Christ and practically detached from all things related to this world, he dreamed of their reunion only in terms of life after resurrection. His faith had become so profound that this eternal life seemed far more real and compelling than the illusions of everyday reality by which he had lived so far. He was now living in a state of concentrated fervor, turning into a disembodied spirit while still alive and breathing; longing for his own final liberation, he wished it also for the other soul whom he loved above everything else on earth.

He imagined that he and Ligia would go hand in hand to Paradise, where Christ would bless them and let them live together in a light as bright and peaceful as all the sunrises and sunsets. His only pleas to Christ were to spare Ligia the tortures of the circus and let her die peacefully in prison; other than this he was sure beyond any doubt that he would die with her. He knew that he couldn't even hope she alone might survive the colossal slaughter. Peter and Paul both told him they, too, had to be martyred. The sight of Chilon on the cross convinced him that death could be sweet even after torture, and he wished it fervently for himself and Ligia as a longed-for change, transforming a harsh and sad reality into a better one.

At times he felt as though he were already living beyond the grave. The melancholy sadness that hovered over both their souls lost more of its scorching bitterness every day and gradually assumed a kind of serene, otherworldly surrender to God's will. In the past Vinicius had fought the current, struggling wearily against the running tide, but now he let the wave carry him away, believing that it would take him to eternal peace. He guessed that Ligia was preparing for death just as he was and that they were already joined together in spite of the prison walls that kept them apart. This thought made him happy.

And that's how it was. They were of like mind and together in spirit as if they still shared their thoughts for hours at a time each day. Ligia also wished and hoped for nothing this side of the grave. She looked at death as not merely liberation from the dungeons or refuge from Caesar and Tigellinus and not just as salvation but also as her wedding day. An earthly happiness would begin for her as well, for she would be united with Vinicius from that moment on, and so she looked forward to it like a bride.

This immense tide of faith that dwarfed reality, broke through all restraints and swept thousands of early Christians to life beyond death had also seized Ursus. He, too, couldn't make his peace for the longest time with the idea that Ligia had to die. But when each day's news of what was happening in the amphitheaters and gardens crept past the prison walls, when death seemed like the common, unavoidable fate of all the Christians—and one that was also their gate to immense happiness, greater than anything possible without it—he, too, didn't dare pray to Christ to deprive Ligia of this joy or at least to defer it for many more years.

His simple barbarian mind conceived the idea that the daughter of the Lygian king deserved more of this joy than commoners like himself and that she'd sit closer to the Lamb in eternal glory than he and his kind. He did hear something about all men being equal in the sight of God, but that didn't shake his conviction that she would be even happier than everybody else. After all, the daughter of the king of all the Lygians wasn't just some slave girl. He also expected that Christ would let him serve her as before.

As for himself, he had only one secret wish: to die on the cross like the Lamb. That seemed like too much joy to pray for, although he knew even the worst kinds of criminals were crucified by Romans. He thought he would most likely be killed by animals, which created his only fear and worry. He had lived from childhood in the vastness of the Lygian forests, hunting wild beasts of one kind or another long before he got to be a man and gaining quite a name for himself because of his superhuman strength. In fact he loved going one on one against wild bulls and bears so much that when he had to give it up later on in Rome, he would go to the animal pens and circuses just to look at the strange and familiar beasts. The sight of them roused his own killer instinct, however, and now he worried that when it came to meeting them in the arena, he'd forget he was supposed to die humbly like a Christian.

Even this, he thought, might be useful to Christ later on; indeed, he was sure he'd be able to serve the Redeemer a lot better than a great many of the other martyrs. He heard that the Lamb had declared war on Hell, and this included all the pagan gods the Christians believed to be evil spirits, and he thought the Lamb would find his enormous strength helpful in the fighting. There was no way for his simple, primitive mind to grasp that his disembodied soul might not be as powerful after death as he was right now.

Other than that, he prayed for hours at a time, looked after the other patients, helped the keepers, and did what he could to console his princess who had one regret: She complained now and then that she had had no time to fill her short life with as many good deeds as the renowned Tabitha, of whom she had heard from both Paul and Peter.

The keepers got to like him. His fearsome strength cowed them even in the dungeon—they knew no bars, chains or walls that could hold him if he got it into his head to batter his way out—but what impressed them most was his gentleness and kindness. They couldn't understand how he could be so cheerful and often questioned him about it, and they listened with unconcealed surprise when he explained what kind of life awaited him after his death in the arena. His conviction made his faith so real that it got them thinking.

What they learned was that joy could find its way even into dungeons where sunlight couldn't enter, and this was something new in their experience. When he urged them to believe in that Lamb of his, one or another of them would start pondering about his own life, seeing what miserable slavery it really was and how trapped they were until death finally put an end to it.

But this death, as they knew it, promised nothing new. At best it was something else to fear. Meanwhile this Lygian giant—and the girl who seemed so much like a flower tossed into dungeon straw—went toward it as joyfully as if it were the door to delights beyond reckoning.

‹78›

SENATOR SCEVINUS called on Petronius a few evenings later and launched into a long, meandering discourse about the difficult times in which they were living. He also talked at length about Caesar. Petronius liked him and was quite friendly with him, but Scevinus spoke so openly about dangerous matters that Petronius thought it best to be on his guard.

"The world's gone mad," the senator complained, "and it's going to get worse before it gets better. Who knows, we might end up with some disaster even worse than the burning of Rome."

He said that even the Augustans seemed to have lost heart, that Fenius Rufus, the deputy commander of the praetorians, could barely stand Tigellinus and his revolting orders, and that Seneca's entire family was outraged by Caesar's treatment of the old philosopher as well as the poet Lucan.

"The people are fed up with the way things are going nowadays," he said in conclusion. "And even the praetorians are restless and growling in their quarters. A lot of them are ready to back Fenius Rufus if something should change."

"Why are you telling me all this?" Petronius asked quietly.

"Why else? I'm worried about Caesar," Scevinus said quickly. "I've a distant relative among the praetorians, also named Scevinus, and that's how I know what's happening in their compounds. They're becoming angry. It's a serious matter. I mean, just look at Caligula, eh? He was another madman, and you know what happened! All of a sudden we had a Cassius Charea, didn't we? It was a dreadful thing, of course, and I'm sure there isn't a man among us who'd praise what he did. But Charea did free the world of a monster!"

"In other words," Petronius remarked, "you're saying 'I don't approve of Charea, but he was a fine man, and may the gods give us more like him.' Is that right?"

Scevinus quickly changed the subject and launched into unexpected paeans in praise of Piso. He lauded his family roots, his sense of decency and honor, his loyalty to his marriage vows, and finally his intellect, his powers of reason, and the odd way he had of winning the people.

"Caesar has no children," he said, "and everyone believes his heir should be Piso. There's no doubt everybody would back him, heart and soul, if he came to power. Fenius Rufus thinks the world of him. The whole Annaeus clan is devoted to him. Plautius Lateranus and Tullius Senecio would jump into fire on his behalf. So would Natalis and Subrius Flavius and Sulpicius Asper and Atranius Quinetianus and even Vestinius."

"If Piso's counting on help from Vestinius, he'll be disappointed," Petronius remarked. "Vestinius is afraid of his own shadow."

"Only where dreams and spirits are concerned," Scevinus replied. "Other than that he's a hardy fellow, and there are some sound reasons for making him a consul. And you shouldn't hold it against him if he's opposed to persecuting Christians since that is important to you as well."

"Not to me," Petronius said with a shrug, "but to Vinicius. I'd like to save one girl out of concern for him, but that's all. There's nothing I can do for him anyway since I fell out of favor with our Copperbeard."

"What do you mean? Haven't you noticed how Caesar comes up to you in public once again and strikes up conversations? And I'll tell you why. He's back to talking about that trip to Greece where he wants to sing some Greek hymns he composed. He's dying to go, but he also shudders at the thought of what those cynical Greeks might say about his singing. He can't make up his mind if he's about to face his greatest triumph or his worst disaster. He needs some expert guidance, and he knows he won't get it from anyone but you. That's why you're coming back into favor."

"Lucan can guide him. He's a fair poet."

"Copperbeard hates Lucan! In fact he's already marked him for a quick death sentence. All he's looking for is a good excuse, just as he's always looking for excuses. Lucan knows there is no time to waste."

"By Castor!" Petronius was amused. "Perhaps you are right. But I've an even quicker way to get back in Copperbeard's good graces."

"Such as what?"

"Such as repeating to him what you said to me just a moment ago."

"I didn't say a thing!" Scevinus cried quickly.

"Well now, let's see." Petronius squeezed the senator's shoulder. "You called Caesar a madman. You talked about replacing him with

Piso. You said, 'Lucan knows there is no time to waste.' What is it, *carissime*, that you're all so anxious not to waste time on?"

Scevinus turned as white as a sheet, and for a moment they stared straight into each other's eyes.

"You won't repeat it!" the senator said at last.

"By the divine hips of Aphrodite!" Petronius shook his head. "How well you know me! No, of course I won't repeat it, but I don't want to hear any more about it. You understand, I'm sure. Life's too short to bother with serious undertakings. But there's one thing I'd like you to do for me today."

"What is it?"

"Go to see Tigellinus and talk to him at least as long as you talked to me. The subject doesn't matter."

"But what's the point of that?"

"The point is that when Tigellinus says to me at some future time, 'You talked with Scevinus,' I'll be able to tell him 'So did you, and on the same day.' "

Scevinus nodded and snapped the ivory cane he held in his hand. "May whatever evil comes out of all this fall on this broken stick," he said. "I'll see Tigellinus, and then I'll go to the banquet at Nerva's. You'll be there, too, won't you? Anyway, good-bye for now. I'll see you at the circus the day after tomorrow. They'll be disposing of the last of the Christians. See you there!"

"The day after tomorrow," Petronius echoed when he was left alone. "That means there really is no time to waste. Copperbeard does need me in Greece, so maybe he'll listen."

He decided to play his final hand.

As it happened, Caesar demanded that Petronius be placed across from him at Nerva's banquet table that night so they could talk about Greece and the cities where he might expect the most successful concerts. He was especially worried about the Athenians and their sophistication. The rest of the Augustans paid close attention to everything Petronius said so they would be able to repeat it later as their own opinions.

"I think at times that I haven't lived," Nero said with a sigh, theatrical as ever, "and that I won't be born until I've gone to Greece."

"You'll be born to new glory," Petronius agreed, "and you'll become immortal."

"I believe I will. I just hope Apollo doesn't get too jealous. If I return in triumph, I'll offer him a sacrifice no god has seen before."

Scevinus quoted Horace:

"Sic te diva potens Cypri,
Sic fratres Helenae, lucida sidera,
Ventorumque regat Pater."

"The ship is ready in Naples," Caesar said. "If it wasn't for unfinished business, I'd sail tomorrow."

"Permit me, divine one, to add a happy note." Petronius rose slightly across the banquet table. "I'd like to give a wedding feast before we set sail, and you're the first man to be invited."

"A wedding? Whose?"

"The wedding of Vinicius and the daughter of the Lygian king who happens to be your official hostage. She also happens to be in prison just now, but that's not a problem. First of all, as an imperial hostage she can't be imprisoned. Furthermore, you yourself ordered Vinicius to marry her, and your decrees are as irrevocable as the will of Zeus. Therefore I expect you'll order her released immediately, and I'll turn her over to her future husband."

Petronius' calm, self-possessed and matter-of-fact tone left Nero somewhat shaken and confused, as always happened when someone took a direct approach with him.

"I know," he said, glancing down. "I've been thinking about her and that giant who strangled Croton. . . ."

"If that's so, then both of them are saved," Petronius said smoothly.

But Tigellinus came to his master's rescue at once. "The girl's in prison by Caesar's will," he said. "And as you said yourself, his decrees are irrevocable."

Everyone there knew the story of Ligia and Vinicius, and all were perfectly aware of the real issues between the praetorian prefect and Petronius, so they leaned forward eagerly, curious to see how the exchange would end.

"She is in prison by your error of judgment, Tigellinus, and through your ignorance of international law," Petronius said, and then he stressed, *"not* by the will of Caesar. You're a naive and foolish man, my dear fellow, but surely not even you would claim she set Rome on fire. And even if you did voice some such outlandish notion, Caesar wouldn't believe you."

Nero had time to get over his surprise and started blinking his nearsighted eyes, while an expression of indescribable cruelty and malice spread across his face.

"Petronius is quite right," he said.

Tigellinus looked at him in surprise.

"Yes, Petronius is quite right," Nero said again. "They'll open the prison gates for her tomorrow. As for the wedding feast, we'll talk about it in the amphitheater the day after tomorrow."

I've lost again, Petronius told himself.

He was so sure Ligia's life was about to end that he sent a trusted freedman to the amphitheater as soon as he got home, to make arrangements with the head of the *spoliarium* about Ligia's body, which he wanted turned over to Vinicius.

79

ROME SELDOM SAW night games before Nero's time; they were rarely staged novelties. But they became quite common during Nero's reign, both in the racetrack and in the arenas. The Augustans liked them because they often became all-night feasts and drinking orgies that stretched into morning. The common masses were getting bored with the relentless bloodshed, but when they heard that the games were ending and that the last of the Christians were to die in this final evening spectacle, uncounted thousands of them headed for the amphitheater at nightfall.

Not one of the Augustans dared miss this show. They guessed it wouldn't be an ordinary drama; Caesar, they knew, wanted to treat himself to a public performance of Vinicius' personal tragedy, so it would be something very special. Tigellinus was close-mouthed about the kind of martyrdom reserved for the young tribune's promised bride, but that merely heightened the excitement. Those who used to see the girl in the past at Aulus Plautius' home spun fantastic tales about how beautiful she was. Others debated whether they'd see her in the arena at all, since those who heard Nero's reply to Petronius at Nerva's banquet said it could be taken either way. Some simply thought Nero might give the girl to Vinicius or that perhaps he had already done so; they argued that as an imperial hostage she had a right to worship any god she pleased and that international usage placed her beyond any punishment.

The whole audience sat spellbound with curiosity, mystery and anticipation. Caesar himself arrived earlier than he usually did, and another barrage of speculation swept across the audience. No one doubted that something extraordinary was going to happen because he came not only with Tigellinus and Vatinius but also with Cassius: a huge, immensely powerful centurion whom Caesar brought only when he wanted a bodyguard beside him, as for example on his night forays into the Suburra. Moreover people were quick to note unusual security precautions in the amphitheater itself. The praetorian guard was far stronger than normal, and the troops were led not just by a centurion but by a tribune named Subrius Flavius, known for his unquestionable loyalty to Nero. It was immediately clear that Caesar wanted to protect himself against any possible outburst of despair by an enraged Vinicius, and excitement mounted even more.

By this time all eyes were focused intently on where the wretched young lover was sitting. He was very pale. Sweat beaded his forehead. Like everybody else, he didn't know what to expect, but he was shaken to the depths of his being. Petronius didn't know any details when he came home from Nerva's, so he told him nothing. He merely asked if he was ready for anything and if he'd be at the games.

Vinicius answered yes to both questions, but his flesh crawled because he knew Petronius would not ask unless he had a reason. His own existence had become a sort of half-life at best; he was immersed in the idea of his own death and accepted Ligia's death as well, since death was to be their liberation and their final union. But it was one thing, he realized, to think of it as a distant, peaceful descent into a gentle dream, and another to go and watch the brutal torture of someone dearer than life. All his old pain burned in him anew. The despair he managed to subdue screamed again inside him, and he wanted to rescue her no matter what the cost. He had tried since dawn to get into the holding pens to see if Ligia was already there, but the praetorians guarded every door under such strict orders that neither his pleading nor the gold he offered moved even those he knew.

Vinicius thought the anxiety would kill him before the spectacle settled his fears one way or the other. He clung to a shard of hope that Ligia wasn't at the amphitheater and all his frightful premonitions were without foundation. Christ, he told himself, could take her to himself in the prison, but surely he wouldn't let her suffer in the arena. Yes, he had bowed to his will in all things. Yes, he still believed. But now, when they finally drove him away from the holding pens and he returned to his seat in the amphitheater, and when the avid eyes that focused on him with such terrible curiosity made it so clear that his worst expectations could be justified, he started to beg Christ with the driven persistence of a threat.

"You can!" he whispered, crushing his hands together in a mindless spasm. "It is in your power!"

It had never crossed his mind before that this moment would be so terrible when it finally came. He had never thought reality would reassert itself with such crushing power. Quite unaware of what was happening to him, he was suddenly convinced his love for Christ would change to hatred and his faith to pure despair if he saw Ligia tortured before his eyes.

Blind terror fell on him and shook him with a numbing force. No, he didn't want to insult his God. He prayed. He needed Christ to make a miracle. He no longer begged him for her life. He merely wanted her to die before they dragged her into the arena.

"Grant me that much," he groaned silently inside, "and I'll love you even more than I have before."

At last his thoughts flew apart and shattered like waves hurled wildly into the sky by a storm at sea. He wanted vengeance. He craved other blood. He wanted to throw himself on Nero and strangle him in front of the watching thousands, but he also knew he was offending Christ once more and breaking his commandment.

At times lightning flashes of hope went through him that God's all-powerful, loving hand might still reach out and avert all these things that numbed his soul with horror. But this hope paled at once, snuffed out by boundless disappointment: This God who could destroy the whole circus and save Ligia with a single word had abandoned her even though she loved and trusted him with all the strength of her pure being. There she was, he thought, in a dark stone cage—sick, helpless, and at the mercy of dehumanized keepers, perhaps barely able to breathe—and here he sat, waiting without any means to help her in this hellish amphitheater, not even knowing what kind of torments they had dreamed up for her and what he would shortly see.

There was only one thing left for him. Like a man falling into an abyss who clutches at anything that grows on the edge, he seized on the thought that only faith could save her after all. That's all he had left! Didn't Peter say that faith could move mountains?

He forced himself into an utter, single-minded act of will, crushed his doubt, locked his whole being into a solitary phrase—"I believe!"—and waited.

But just as the string of a lute must snap when it is wound too tightly, so he cracked with effort. A corpselike pallor spread across his face, and his body stiffened.

God heard me, he thought. I've begun to die. Ligia must also have died, he thought. Christ is taking us.

The arena, the white togas of the innumerable spectators, and the lights of thousands of lamps and torches vanished before his eyes. But his collapse was merely a momentary illusion of relief. Awareness returned, drummed into his consciousness by the impatient stamping of the crowds around him.

"You're ill," Petronius said beside him. "Have yourself taken home!"

Indifferent to what Caesar might think or say, he rose to help Vinicius to his feet and take him outside. He felt a vast pity for the racked young man, along with an unbearable loathing and contempt for Nero who, with a look of satisfaction on his face, was peering at Vinicius through his emerald, studying his pain so that perhaps he might describe it later in some pathetic verses written for the sake of cheap applause.

Vinicius shook his head. He could die in this amphitheater, but he couldn't leave it. The spectacle was due to start at any moment.

In fact at almost that instant the city prefect threw out a scarlet scarf, the heavy portals in front of Caesar's podium creaked open at the signal, and Ursus stepped out of the darkness of the underground holding cell into the glaring lights of the arena.

The giant stood blinking for a while, apparently blinded by the sudden brightness, and then advanced into the center of the ring and looked around as if to guess what he would meet there. All the Augustans and most of the rabble knew this was the man who had crushed and strangled Croton, and a loud murmur swept all the benches at the sight of him. Rome wasn't short of gladiators who towered over ordinary people, but no one there had ever seen anything like this one. The massive Cassius who stood behind Caesar seemed like a mere wisp of a man in comparison. The senators, vestals, Caesar, Augustans and common masses looked with the breathless rapture of true connoisseurs at the colossal thighs, as massive as tree trunks, at the chest that seemed like two bucklers laid beside each other, and at the Herculean shoulders. The murmurs swelled in open admiration. There was no greater pleasure possible for these crowds than to watch such sinews at work, tensed in violent combat. Shouts broke out, along with feverish questions: Where did he come from? What tribe produced such giants? He stood like a naked stone colossus in the center of the ring, a look of troubled concentration on his sad, barbarian face. He saw only an empty arena around him and blinked his surprised childlike blue eyes at the massed spectators, at Caesar, and at the bars of the holding pens where he supposed his executioners were getting ready for him.

At the moment he stepped into the arena, his simple heart still contained some hope that maybe he would get to die on a cross. But when he didn't see one, or a hole dug in the sand to hold one, he concluded sadly that he wasn't worthy to die like the Lamb and that something else would rush out to kill him, most likely some beast. He was unarmed and decided he'd die as the Lamb commanded: with humility and patience. In the meantime he thought he would pray a little more to the Savior, so he knelt down, pressed his palms together and raised his eyes; the lights of stars flickered above the round rim of the amphitheater open to the sky.

The crowds didn't like this. They had had enough of Christians who died like sheep. They knew that if the giant didn't defend himself, the show would be pointless. Some started hissing. Others yelled for the *mastigaphori* to whip some fight into the colossus. But the noise soon died down, since nobody knew what kind of fate awaited the Lygian or whether he would choose to fight once he stood eye to eye with death.

They did not wait long.

An ominous blare of copper horns summoned their attention, the iron grille across from Caesar's podium grated open, and then—maddened by the howls of the beast-masters behind it—a monstrous German aurochs charged into the arena with a woman's naked body draped across its horns.

"Ligia!" Vinicius shouted. "Ligia!"

He dug his fists into his temples, his body convulsed like a man thrust-through with a spear, and he croaked over and over in an inhuman, rattling voice: "I believe! I believe! Christ! A miracle!"

He didn't even feel it when Petronius threw the folds of his toga over his head. The sudden darkness simply meant to him that he was blinded either by agony or death. He neither looked nor saw anything anyway. He had the sense of falling into some terrifying void, and not a single thought rang in his hollow head. Only his lips creaked on, repeating their delirious "I believe! I believe! I believe!"

Suddenly the amphitheater was as still as death. The Augustans rose to their feet as one because something extraordinary was taking place in the arena. The humble, unresisting Lygian caught sight of his princess roped to the horns of the forest monster, leaped as if scorched with fire, bowed his enormous shoulders and started to run aslant the arena toward the galloping wild bull.

A single sharp, astonished cry burst from every chest around the arena, and then there was a hollow, unbelieving silence. The Lygian had collided with the charging animal and seized it by the horns.

"Look!" cried Petronius, and he swept the toga from Vinicius' head.

He rose, his white face as colorless as canvas and tilted back as if his neck were broken, and fixed his glassy, barely focused stare on the scene below.

No one seemed to breathe. A fly's passing buzz could be heard in the utter silence. The crowds couldn't believe their eyes. Nothing like this had been seen in Rome since Romulus and Remus created the city.

The Lygian grasped the monster by the horns. His feet sank deep into the sand, buried above the ankles. His back bent like a bow, although what came to mind was the iron beam of a catapult drawn to hurl a boulder. His head disappeared, hunched between his shoulders. His muscles swelled until it seemed as if his skin would burst. But he had stopped the bull and fixed him in his tracks. Man and beast were locked together as still as a statue so that the breathless crowds thought they were seeing some classic myth drawn from the deeds of Hercules or Theseus, or an effigy in stone. This illusion of immobility contained an immense exertion of two straining forces. Like the man, the aurochs dug his hooves into the sand, and its dark, hairy bulk compressed into a giant ball.

Which of them would be the first to crack under the strain? Which would fall? No other question existed in the amphitheater. Rome could fall, its mastery of the world could disappear forever and their own fates could be hurled into the winds, but to the tense, absorbed and enraptured people this was all that mattered. This Lygian was now a demigod to them, worthy of statues and rituals of worship. Even Caesar rose. He and Tigellinus worked hard to create this astounding, monumental image, never expecting it would come to this. They knew the man's strength, at least by reputation, and they had a good laugh together as they picked the aurochs. "Let this Croton-killer try his hand against something his own size," they jeered, but now they gaped in utter amazement at what lay before them, as if they couldn't trust their eyes or the reality around them. All across the amphitheater people were on their feet, arms upraised like statues. Others dripped sweat as if they, too, were grappling with the monster. All that could be heard was the hiss of flames dancing in the lamps and the soft rustling of burned charcoal embers that fell from the torches. Their voices died stillborn on their lips, but their hearts were pounding as if to burst free and blow them apart. The struggle, everyone was sure, had lasted a century.

The man and the animal still stood locked together in their terrible exertion as if rooted deep in the ground.

Suddenly a hollow, groaning roar boomed in the arena. One vast cry swept the amphitheater, and then there was silence. Nobody could believe it. Could this be a dream? The monstrous head of the giant wild bull started to turn and twist in the iron fists of the barbarian.

The Lygian's face, neck, back, arms and shoulders were crimson with effort. His huge back curved deeper. It was clear he was reaching into his last reservoirs of strength and wouldn't be able to take the strain much longer. The whistling of his labored breath hissed through the grunting roars; these, the crowds could hear, were ever more pained and hollow. The beast's head twisted further, and his foam-streaked tongue lolled out of his maw.

Then the dry snap of parting bones crackled across the arena, and the animal toppled to the ground with a broken neck.

In one swift motion the giant tore the ropes off the aurochs' horns, lifted the girl in his arms and stood panting heavily. Blood flowed from his face, which was pale with emotion. His hair and shoulders were awash with sweat. He seemed barely conscious for an instant but then roused himself, looked up and turned his pleading eyes on the delirious people.

The amphitheater went mad.

Tens of thousands roared in a single voice that made the structure shake. Nothing had moved the crowds so much or carried them to such a pitch of feeling since the games began. Those in the upper rows bolted from their seats and pushed down the aisles for a closer look at the champion strongman. Countless stubborn and insistent voices cried out for mercy, soon changing into a single, uninterrupted roar demanding his freedom. They loved this giant now; he was priceless to them. To the massed, insensate rabble he was the most important man in Rome.

He grasped soon enough that the people were demanding he be spared and freed, but apparently he wasn't concerned only about himself. His eyes swept the rows for a while, and then he made his way toward Caesar's podium. He lifted the girl toward him in his outstretched arms and raised his pleading eyes as if to say, "It is she you should pardon! It is she you should save! I did it for her!"

Everyone understood what he was demanding. The unconscious girl looked like a mere child against his massive torso, and a tide of unaccustomed pity washed over the senators, nobles and the rest of the crowd. The hardest hearts were moved by the sight of the slight, white body, as lifeless and still as a miniature alabaster statue, and by the giant, whose devotion had freed her from terrible danger. To some it seemed as if a father was pleading for the life of his child. Compassion flamed among them and scorched them like lava. They had had enough blood, enough death, enough torture. Tear-choked voices pleaded for mercy for them both.

Ursus, meanwhile, circled the arena, cradling the girl on his forearms all the while, lifting her mutely to the crowds and pleading for her life with his eyes. Suddenly Vinicius jumped to his feet, leaped across the barrier into the arena, ran up to Ligia and threw his toga over her naked body. Then he ripped his tunic open across his chest, exposed the scars he had earned in the Armenian wars and stretched his arms wide to all the Roman people.

The crowds were swept away by a frenzy never before seen in an amphitheater. The rabble started to pound their feet on the floorboards and howl like madmen. Threats sounded in the voices that demanded mercy. The people were now doing more than siding with the athlete; they were also rising in defense of the girl, the soldier and their love.

Thousands turned on Caesar with clenched fists and with anger in their eyes, but he hesitated, unsure of what to do, and let the moment drag. He didn't really have much against Vinicius and didn't care whether Ligia lived or died, but he would rather look at her body gored by horns or ripped apart with claws. His inborn cruelty as well as his degenerate lusts and imagination found a strange pleasure in such sights. Now the mobs wanted to deprive him of it! Anger suffused his coarse, obese features at this thought. A boundless self-pride and an enormous sense of his own towering importance wouldn't let him surrender to the masses, but he was too much of a coward to resist their will.

He peered around him to see if at least some of his Augustans were holding their thumbs down in the sign of death. Petronius stood with his arm raised high, staring into his face as if daring him to risk a refusal. So did Vestinius, who could be moved by more than superstitions; he may have been terrified of ghosts and the supernatural, but he was fearless when it came to people and now demanded mercy. So did the senator Scevinus, so did Nerva, so did Tullius Senecio, so did the famous and revered old general Ostorius Scapula, so did Antistius, so did Piso and Vestus and Crispinus and Minucius Thermus and Pontius Telesinus and the one who counted the most among the common people, the admired Thrasea.

Annoyed and offended, the emperor snapped the emerald away from his eye with a gesture of petulant dismissal, and then Tigellinus suddenly leaned toward him. For him this was still a struggle with Petronius, and he wanted to hurt him.

"Don't give way, divinity!" he urged. "We still have praetorians!"

Nero turned his face to where the grim, loyal Subrius Flavius stood in command of his ranked praetorians and saw something he had never expected. The tribune's harsh old face was as stern as ever, but it was bathed in tears; he held his hand high and stretched, the thumb pointed upward.

The masses started to boil with fury. Clouds of dust rose from under their stamping feet and filled the amphitheater. More and more voices shouted threats and insults in the universal roar: "Copperbeard! Matricide! Arsonist!"

Nero slumped in fear. The amphitheaters belonged to the people, and they were the absolute masters in the circus. Other Caesars, especially the insane Caligula, sometimes ignored the will of the rabble but never without a riot and often with bloodshed. Nero was in a special quandary. First, as an actor and a singer, he needed their goodwill and applause; second, he had to have them on his side in his political struggle with the senate and the obdurate patricians; and finally, since the great fire of Rome, he would give anything to win them over and turn their anger onto others like the Christians. He understood at last that he could not hold them off much longer. They demanded action. A circus riot could easily spread across the city, with incalculable effect for Rome and himself.

He threw one more glance at Subrius Flavius, at the centurion Scevinus, a kinsman of the senator, and at the ready soldiers. All he saw were stern, demanding faces and grim eyes, unaccountably moved to mercy and compassion, fixed on him.

He gave the sign of mercy.

Applause burst out like a clap of thunder and filled the amphitheater from the topmost rows to the barriers at the rim of the arena. The crowds were now sure the condemned would be spared and freed since from this moment they came under the protection of the people, and not even Caesar would dare to pursue them after that.

80

FOUR BITHYNIANS carried Ligia carefully to Petronius' villa, with Ursus and Vinicius beside her, hurrying to get her as quickly as possible into the hands of a Greek physician. They walked in silence, unable to speak after the night's events. Up to this moment Vinicius seemed only half-aware of everything around him. His mind kept whispering that Ligia was saved, that she was no longer under the threat of prison or death in the arena, that their tragedies were over for all time and that he was now taking her home with him, never to be away from her again.

A new life seemed to be dawning for them both rather than just a return to reality.

He leaned over her open litter from time to time, to stare into her precious, moonlit face, which seemed asleep and dreaming. "She's here!" he kept saying to himself. "Christ saved her!"

He remembered that some unknown healer had come to the *spoliarium* where he and Ursus took her unconscious body and assured them that the girl would live. His joy made it almost impossible for him to breathe; he could barely stand on his own two feet and leaned heavily on Ursus as they walked. Ursus stared at the star-strewn sky and prayed.

The walls of newly built structures gleamed whitely in the moonlight in the streets around them, but the town seemed empty. A few small groups of people, crowned with wreaths and ivy, danced under the arches to the sound of flutes, making the best of a balmy night and the holiday atmosphere that swept the city when the games began. They were near to the house when Ursus finally stopped praying and started to whisper, as if afraid that he might wake Ligia.

"Our Lord saved her, master!" he murmured. "When I saw her on the horns, I heard a voice inside me. 'Fight for her!' it said, and I'm sure it was the Lamb himself. The prison took a lot out of me, but he let me have my strength when I had to have it, and he moved those cruel people to stand up for her. His will be done!"

"And may mankind praise his name forever," said Vinicius.

He could say nothing more. A tide of grateful tears was gathering inside him. He felt a near irresistible urge to throw himself on the ground and thank the Savior for his miracle and mercy.

They reached the house. They had sent a slave ahead to warn the household, and they all now poured into the street to welcome them home. Paul of Tarsus had converted most of these slaves back in Ancium, and the catastrophe that befell Vinicius was known to them. They were beside themselves with joy, seeing these sacrificial victims removed from Caesar's grasp and safe from his malice. They were even more delighted with the doctor's verdict. The slave Theocles, Petronius' personal physician, looked her over carefully, said she had no dangerous injuries, and announced she would be well in time, once she had recovered from the debilitation of her prison fever.

As it happened, she regained consciousness that very night. Her eyes opened on an exquisitely decorated bedroom, lighted with Corinthian alabaster lamps. She could smell verbena but had no idea where she was. The last thing she remembered was being bound to the horns of a chained wild bull. Now she was looking up into the adoring face of Vinicius, lit by a gentle multicolored glow. She thought they were no longer on the earth. She was still too ill to exercise much control over her thoughts, but it seemed natural to her that they had stopped somewhere on the road to Heaven so she could rest. She felt no pain and smiled at Vinicius, wanting to ask him where they were. All that breathed from her was a wavering whisper in which Vinicius heard only his name.

He knelt at her bedside and placed his palm gently on her forehead. "Christ saved you and gave you back to me," he said.

Her lips moved again in a whisper he didn't understand, and after a short while her eyelids flickered, her breast lifted in a gentle sigh, and she plunged into the deep, dreamless sleep that Theocles expected.

"After she wakes," the physician said, "she'll start to get well."

The learned Greek slave slipped in and out of the chamber several times to check on his patient, but Vinicius stayed beside her, praying at her bedside. Engrossed in his radiant and all-consuming love, he lost all track of time and place. The Greek doctor came in several times, and now and again the golden head of Eunice appeared between the curtains; and at last the screaming of the caged herons in the garden announced the sunrise. But Vinicius remained as he was, his mind detached from all earthly matters. Mentally kneeling at the feet of Christ, he was blind and deaf to everything else around him. His heart was filled with gratitude, and he kissed Christ's feet and worshiped him with all his thoughts and feelings. Enraptured to the point of ecstasy, it was as if he had been lifted to Paradise even though alive.

‹81›

NOT WANTING TO GOAD Nero into anger after Ligia's release at the extraordinary games, Petronius followed Caesar back to the Palatine with all the other Augustans. He wanted to hear what they had to say. He was especially curious about what Tigellinus might say about the girl. Both Ligia and Ursus had passed into the customary protection of the people, and no one could raise a hand against them without facing riots, but Petronius knew how he was hated by the all-powerful prefect of the praetorians. If Tigellinus still couldn't strike at him directly, he'd find some way to wreak his vengeance on his nephew.

Nero was angry and especially sensitive to imagined insults, because the spectacle didn't have the conclusion he had wanted. At first he wouldn't even look at Petronius, but the arbiter kept his elegant composure and walked up to him with all the freedom of an irreplaceable advisor.

"Can you guess, divine one," he remarked, "what just occurred to me? Write a song about a girl who at the command of the master of the world is freed from the horns of a wild bull and restored to her lover. Greeks are sentimental, and I'm sure such a song would enchant them."

Despite his sharp annoyance, Nero found himself taken with the thought. He liked it on two grounds: First, the theme was classic and much to his taste; and second, he'd be able to praise himself as the magnanimous ruler of the world.

"You're right!" He gave Petronius a long, careful look. "Perhaps you're right! But is it proper for me to sing about my own goodness?"

"You don't have to point to yourself by name. Everyone in Rome will guess what it's about, and news spreads from Rome all over the world."

"And you're quite sure they'll like it in Athens?"

"By Pollux!" Petronius swore.

He stepped aside and walked away contented. Nero's whole life consisted of twisting reality to suit his literary needs, and he wouldn't want anything to destroy his theme. This more or less restrained Tigellinus, but it did nothing to change his determination to send Vinicius out of Rome as soon as Ligia's health allowed it.

"Take her to Sicily," he urged Vinicius the next day. "The way things are now, you're both safe from Caesar. But Tigellinus will go to any lengths; he'll even try poison. If he doesn't do it out of hate for you, he'll certainly do it out of hate for me."

Vinicius smiled.

"She was on the horns of a wild bull," he said, "and yet Christ brought her through."

Try as he might to be uncritical of the young man's immersion in Christianity, Petronius found himself abrupt and impatient.

"So sacrifice a hundred bulls to him!" he snapped. "But don't ask him to save her a second time. . . . Do you remember what happened to Ulysses when he asked Eolus for a second helping of propitious winds? Gods don't like to repeat themselves."

"I'll take her to Pomponia Graecina," said Vinicius, "as soon as she's well."

"Good. Now is an especially good time for it because Pomponia is ill. I have it from Antistius, and they are related. So many changes will be taking place in Rome that everyone will forget about you, and nowadays those who have been forgotten are the lucky ones. May Fortuna smile on you like the sun in winter, and shade you in summer."

He left Vinicius to his happiness and went in search of Theocles to ask about Ligia's health.

She was no longer in any danger. If she had stayed buried in the dungeon, weak from her fever, then the foul air and harsh conditions probably would have killed her. But now she had the most painstaking care, and not merely comfort and abundance to meet any need, but opulence and riches. Two days after her recovery began, Theocles ordered her taken out into the garden daily where she stayed for hours at a time. Vinicius had her litter dressed in anemones and especially in purple irises to remind her of her home with Aulus and Pomponia. Hidden in the shade of the broad-limbed trees and holding hands, they talked about their past fears and suffering. Ligia said that Christ let him experience suffering to remake his soul and lift him toward him, and he agreed. He felt that nothing remained of the former proud, impatient and insolent patrician who had recognized no rights or laws other than his own.

There was nothing bitter about these recollections. It seemed to both of them that years had thundered past and lay far behind them. They felt a kind of peace they had never known before and were absorbed in their advance toward a new and blessed life. An unbalanced Caesar might be driving Rome toward its own madness and filling the world with terror, but they didn't fear him. The power that guarded them was a hundred times greater than all the Caesars; it was beyond human malice and madness, and held mastery over life and death.

One day, just before sunset, they heard lions and other animals roar in the distant pens. At one time these sounds filled Vinicius with fear and premonition. Now he and Ligia just smiled at each other and looked at the glow of the sunset.

Ligia was still very weak and unable to walk without help. Sometimes she fell asleep in the quiet of the garden, and he watched over her. Staring into her sleeping face, the unbidden thought came to him that this was no longer the Ligia whom he had met at the Plautius home. Prison and sickness had dimmed some of her beauty. When he used to see her with Aulus and Graecina, she was as breathtaking as a perfect sculpture and as lovely as a flower. Now her face was drawn and her skin seemed transparent; her features had acquired a translucent quality; her hands looked fragile and longer, being so very thin; her lips were pale, and even her eyes seemed to have lost most of the sapphire glow that made her so much like the embodiment of spring. The golden-haired Eunice who brought her flowers and rich embroidered covers for her feet looked like a living Aphrodite next to her.

Try as he might, Petronius was hard-pressed to discover her attraction and appeal in his aesthetic judgment. He shrugged. It crossed his mind that this Elysian spirit was hardly worth the effort, pain and torture that almost sucked the life out of Vinicius. But Vinicius was now in love with her soul and loved her all the more for her transformation, and it seemed to him as he sat watching over her that he was guarding and protecting the whole world.

‹82›

THE STORY OF LIGIA'S miraculous survival spread like wildfire among the scattered remnants of the Christians who had so far managed to escape the slaughter. The faithful started gathering to see this woman whom Christ's grace and bounty had touched so directly. First to come were young Nazarius and his mother Miriam, in whose home the apostle Peter was living in hiding. Then came many others. With Ligia and Vinicius and Petronius' Christian slaves, they all sat listening intently while Ursus told about the voice he had heard in the arena, the one that spoke in his soul and ordered him to fight the wild beast. They went away with new hope and a stronger faith, believing Christ wouldn't allow all his followers to be winnowed out before he came down to earth himself to render his judgment.

This faith gave them strength, because the persecutions were still going on. Whoever was rumored to be a Christian was seized at once by the city watch and thrown into prison. There were now fewer victims, because the bulk of the faithful were gone, caught and martyred; others had left Rome to wait out the storm in the distant provinces, or they hid themselves so carefully that they didn't even meet for communal prayer unless it was in hidden farms and homesteads, far away from the city. They were still watched and hunted, even though the games were now officially over, and they were either judged and executed on the spot or kept for future public entertainment. Nobody in Rome still believed it was the Christians who burned down the city, but they were declared enemies of humanity and the state, and the edict against them remained in full force.

It took a long time before the apostle Peter took the risk of appearing in Petronius' house, but one evening Nazarius announced he was coming. Ligia had almost totally recovered. She was on her feet and ran out with Vinicius to meet him, kiss his feet and lead him inside. He was greatly moved by the sight of them, all the more because so few remained from the flock Christ had given him to shepherd and over whose fate he shed so many tears.

"Master!" Vinicius told him. "The Savior gave her back to me, but you made it happen."

Peter shook his head. "He returned her to you because you believed and so that at least some might be spared who worship his name."

He must have been thinking of the other thousands he loved as his children who were torn by wild beasts, and of the crosses that studded the arenas and of the burning stakes, because his voice shook with enormous pity as he said it.

Ligia and Vinicius both noticed that his hair was now completely white. His whole body was stooped. His face held so much pain and such indelible sorrow it was as if he had suffered every agony inflicted on each victim of Nero's savagery and madness. Both understood that if Christ himself accepted death and torture, no one else could avoid the burden.

They knew it, but the sight of the apostle crushed by his age, suffering and hardships just about broke their hearts. Vinicius, who planned to take Ligia to Naples in a few days, where they would meet Pomponia and go on together to Sicily, begged him to come with them and leave Rome.

The apostle merely laid his cold, dry hand on the young man's head. "I still hear the words of the Master," he said, "when he said to me on the shores of the Sea of Tiberias: 'When you were young, you bound up your robe and walked where you wished; but when you are old, you'll stretch out your hands and another man will bind them, and he'll lead you where you have no wish to go.' It's right, therefore, that I should follow my sheep."

They didn't understand and watched him in silence.

"My work is almost done," he added. "But my rest and welcome wait only in my Master's house."

He blessed them. He asked them to remember him.

"I've come to love you both as a father loves his children," he told them. "And whatever you do in life, do it in God's name."

His trembling old hands shook over them, and they clung to him as if they were his children, feeling that this might be the last blessing he would ever give them. But they were destined to see him one more time.

A few days later Petronius brought threatening news from the

Palatine. One of Caesar's freedmen had been exposed as a secret Christian, and letters were found on him from the apostles Peter and Paul of Tarsus, and also from James, John and Joseph of Arimathea. Tigellinus had known for some time that Peter was in Rome, but he assumed he perished with the other thousands. Now it became clear that both chief priests of the new religion were still alive and at large in the city, and orders went out to find them at all cost, because their deaths seemed like the only way to stamp out the detested sect. Petronius heard from Vestinius that Caesar himself set a three-day limit for Peter and Paul to be under lock and key in the Mammertine, and whole companies of praetorians were sent into the Trans-Tiber to search every building.

Peter had to be warned. That night Vinicius and Ursus put on hooded cloaks and set out for Peter's hideout in Miriam's house, which lay at the far end of the quarter across the Tiber, almost at the foot of the Janiculum. They passed homes and houses surrounded by soldiers, guided by hooded men whom nobody seemed to know. Tension hovered in the quarter, and small crowds gathered to watch what was happening. Centurions were interrogating captured prisoners right out in the open, questioning them about Simon Peter and Paul of Tarsus.

Ursus and Vinicius got to Miriam's house ahead of the soldiers. Peter was still there, surrounded by a small group of the faithful that included Linus and Paul's helper Timothy. Nazarius led them all through a hidden passage to the garden gate, and then into an abandoned quarry a few hundred feet beyond the Janiculum Gate. Ursus carried Linus, whose bones, crushed in torture, hadn't had time to knit. Once they could feel themselves safe in the quarry tunnels, they squatted around an oil lamp that Nazarius lighted and started a whispered conference on how to save their beloved apostle.

"Master," Vinicius told him, "at dawn tomorrow Nazarius can take you out to the Alban hills. We'll find you there and take you to Naples, where I have a ship waiting to take us to Sicily. It'll be a happy day when you step across the threshold of my house and bless the hearth of my home."

The others were overjoyed to hear it. "Save yourself, our dear shepherd," they urged the apostle. "You can't survive in Rome! You are the last living witness to the truth, so help us preserve it. Don't let it die with us and you. Listen to us. We're begging you like children."

"Do it for Christ's sake!" others cried, clutching at his robes.

But Peter himself didn't know what he ought to do.

"Ah, my children," he answered, troubled and uncertain. "Who can tell when God decides to call us?"

He didn't say he would not leave Rome but struggled against the need to make a decision, since for a long time now he had found himself no longer certain about some things and even afraid. But why shouldn't he wonder? Why shouldn't he question his apparent failures? His flock was torn and scattered. His work was destroyed. The church, which had bloomed before the fire like a flowering tree, was a heap of ashes, turned into dust by the power of the beast. Nothing was left of it besides tears, memory, agonies and death. The seed had fallen on abundant soil, but Satan stamped it into the ground. Avenging angels didn't descend in legions to defend the dying, and Nero sat in glory over all the world, terrible and more powerful than ever, the true master of the lands and seas.

Many times already he had thrown up his arms, when there was no one near who could see him do it, and cried out: "Lord? What am I to do? How can I hold on? How can one old and helpless man fight the overwhelming evil that you allow to rule and triumph everywhere?"

As he cried like that from the depths of his inner pain, he also asked if he should leave the city.

"They're all gone now," he would say, "the sheep you told me to take out to pasture. . . . Your church is in ruins. . . . The rock on which you told me to build your capital is buried in mourning. So what is your command? Am I to stay here? Or am I to lead what's left of my flock so we may worship your name in hiding somewhere across the sea?"

He hesitated. He believed that the living truth would go on and be proved the stronger, but he thought at times that perhaps its time hadn't yet come and that light wouldn't dawn in the world until Christ returned on Judgment Day, coming in power and glory that extinguished Nero's.

Sometimes he thought that if he left Rome and the faithful followed, he would be able to take them home to the shaded groves of Galilee, to the stillness of the inner sea, and to the peaceful shepherds, as gentle as their flocks, who walked the hills that smelled of sandalwood and thyme. A longing grew in him for a resting place; the fisherman in him sighed for the quiet lake waters, and the Galilean longed for his native soil. More and more often tears gathered in his eyes.

But he would no sooner make that choice when doubt struck it down. He would feel the sudden fear of a mortal error. How was he to abandon the city where so much martyred blood sank into the soil? Where so many dying lips witnessed to the truth? Was he to be the only one who would step aside? And how would he answer when the Master said, "They died for their faith, and you ran away"?

Grief and anxiety gnawed at him day and night. The others—those torn apart by beasts, nailed to crosses and burned at the stake—were at rest, at peace. A single moment of agony brought them into the eternal tranquility of the Lord and peace without end. But he could not sleep. There was no rest for him. The pain he felt was greater than anything the torturers could devise for their suffering victims. Dawn was often glowing on the roofs around him when he was still crying out, imploring an answer: "Master! Why did you send me here? Why did you tell me to found your capital in this lair of the beast?"

He hadn't had a moment's rest in the thirty-four years since his master's death. Staff in hand, he had trudged around the world to "bring the good tidings." The hardships and journeys had sapped all his strength, and when he finally reached his goal, when he planted the glory of his Master's work in this capital of the world, one fiery breath of evil turned it into ashes, and he could see the battle would have to be fought again from the beginning. What a hopeless battle it must be! On one side stood the emperor, the senate, the people and the legions that grasped the world in a fist of iron, countless cities in countries beyond counting, and power never before seen among men; on the other side there was he alone, so weighed down by age and hardships that his trembling hand could hardly grasp his old traveling staff.

He doubted his ability to go on. Who was he to measure himself against the empire and the emperor of Rome? Christ's will, he thought in moments of despair, would take Christ himself to fulfill and impose.

The last loyal cluster of his followers begged him to save himself, and he saw all the questions that were never answered.

"Save yourself, rabbi!" they cried, huddling around him. "And lead us out of the lion's den as well!"

At last even Linus bowed his tortured, martyred head before him.

"Master!" he said. "It's you whom the Savior entrusted with his flock, but it is gone from here or will be gone tomorrow, so go where you might still find it. The word of God lives on in Jerusalem, in Antioch, in Ephesus and in other cities. What can you do in Rome?

Your death will only deepen the triumph of the beast. John's life span hasn't been ordained. Paul is a citizen of Rome and can't be punished without trial. But what'll happen when the rage of the beast is unleashed on you? Won't those who have started to doubt and fear also begin asking, 'Who stands above Nero?' You are our rock. God's church stands upon you. We'll die here, and you must allow it. But you mustn't let the Antichrist win over God's deputy, and don't return to Rome until the Lord has crushed those who cause this bloodshed."

"Look at our tears!" everyone there begged over and over.

Tears were also running down Peter's worn cheeks. He looked up after a while and stretched his hands over those who were kneeling round him.

"May the Lord's name be blessed," he said quietly. "And let his will be done."

‹ 8 3 ›

THE NEXT DAY, shortly before dawn, two dark forms appeared on the Appian Way and turned toward the plains of Campania. One was Nazarius. The other was Peter, who was leaving Rome and his persecuted brethren.

The eastern sky was already tinged a misty, pale shade of green, framed at the base by a sharper boundary of saffron. Branches with silvered leaves, the white walls of nearing villages, and the tall arches of the viaducts that ran across the plain toward Rome could be seen in the shadows. Gold seeped into the greenish sky and filled it with brightness, and then a reddening rosy glow bloomed in the East behind the Alban hills, painting them lilac and making them seem spun wholly out of light.

Dawn's pearly light trembled on the dew that clung to the leaves. The mists receded, opening a broader vista to the level plains, villas, cemeteries, small country towns and groves, and the white temple columns gleaming among the trees.

The road was empty. The farmers who brought produce to the city were still harnessing their carts. The clatter of the travelers' wooden clogs echoed in the silence, coming from the flagstones that covered the highway all the way to the hills. The sun rose to the mountain passes, and a strange sight bemused the apostle. It suddenly seemed as if the golden sphere had ceased to climb higher into the sky, that it slipped down the hillside straight ahead of them and was rolling down the road toward them.

Peter halted. "Do you see the brightness that's coming toward us?" he asked.

"I see nothing, master," Nazarius replied.

Peter shaded his eyes against the light. "Someone is coming to us in the glow of sunlight."

They heard no footsteps. The silence lay undisturbed around them. Nazarius merely saw the distant trees trembling as if brushed in passing, and the great light spread wider through the plain. But it was the apostle who alarmed him more.

"Rabbi!" he cried. "What's wrong? What's the matter with you?"

The traveling staff fell out of Peter's hand. His eyes were fixed immovably ahead. His lips were open, and his face reflected unbelievable surprise, immense joy, and rapturous exaltation.

Suddenly he threw himself on his knees, his arms lifted upward and stretched to the light, and his lips cried out: "Christ! O Christ!" His head beat against the dust as if he were kissing the feet of someone only he could see.

Then there was silence.

"*Quo vadis, Domine?*" his voice asked at last, punctured by his sobbing. "Where are you going, Lord?"

Nazarius heard no answer. But a voice of ineffable sweetness and abundant sorrow rang in Peter's ears. "When you abandon my people," he heard, "I must go to Rome to be crucified once more."

The apostle lay still and silent with his face pressed into the dust. Nazarius thought he had either died or fainted, but he rose at last, picked up his pilgrim's staff, and turned again toward the seven hills.

"*Quo vadis, domine?*" the boy asked like an echo of the apostle's cry.

"To Rome," Peter murmured.

Then he returned.

Paul, John, Linus and the other Christians were both surprised and alarmed to see him, all the more because the praetorians had surrounded Miriam's house at first light, just after he left, and searched for him. He answered all their questions with just a single phrase:

"I saw my Lord," he told them, radiant and at peace.

That evening and every evening thereafter he went to the Ostrianum cemetery to teach and baptize those who felt the need of Christ. Each time his crowds were bigger. It was as if new followers sprung from every tear, and each groan of pain in the arena found an echo in a thousand people. Caesar practically bathed in blood. Rome and the whole pagan world spun in a whirl of madness. Those who were finally sick of insanity as a way of life, those who were downtrodden and victimized, those who despaired, and those who lived lives of misfortune and oppression, and those who sorrowed and felt pain came to hear new stories about a God who let himself be crucified out of love for them. Finding a God they could love, they also found what no civilization of their time could give anyone: the happiness that can be found in love.

Peter understood that neither Caesar nor his legions would ever win out over the living truth. There would never be enough blood or tears to drown it. He also understood why God turned him back on the road. This city of vanity, debauchery and power was ready to fall into his hands and to become that double capital of both God and man, that would rule the spirit and the flesh throughout the world.

‹84›

AND FINALLY their time on earth ran out for both the apostles. Peter, so aptly named the fisherman of souls, ended his work by baptizing Processus and Martianus, the two praetorians who guarded him in the dungeons of the Mammertine.

Then came his time of suffering. Nero was away from Rome when the verdict came from his two freedmen, Helios and Politetes, whom Caesar left to administer the empire while he sang in Greece. The aged apostle was flogged, as the law required, and led the next day beyond city walls, out toward Vatican hill, where he was to be hanged upon a cross. The escort soldiers were surprised by the crowds that gathered at the prison gates and then followed the condemned all the way to the place of execution. In their view the crucifixion of a common man, and an unknown foreigner at that, shouldn't have aroused such interest. They didn't know that these crowds were the condemned man's coreligionists and not just curious gawkers, and that they hadn't come just to gape or gossip but to pay homage to their teacher and to be with him in his final moments.

Peter was led out of the prison sometime after noon, walking in the middle of a squad of soldiers. The sun dipped slightly toward Ostia, but the day was calm and the sky was clear. Peter wasn't forced to carry his own cross; no one thought he would be able to lift one at his age, nor was the customary wooden yoke locked around his neck. He walked alone, unbound, and his brethren could see him very well. Tears and sobbing broke out when they caught sight of his white head among the iron helmets, but their grief died quickly. The old man's face was so cheerful and untroubled, and it glowed with such immense confidence and joy, that everyone understood at once this wasn't a victim going to his execution but a conqueror marching to his triumph.

That is what it was for him and for them. The stooped, humble Galilean fisherman they were used to seeing walked straight and erect, full of dignity and taller than the soldiers, so that he seemed like a king surrounded by his people and his guard. No one had ever seen him with such majestic bearing. Proud, joyful voices broke out everywhere in the crowd: "There's Peter! Going to the Lord!" Everyone seemed to forget the hours of pain and the death that awaited him. They walked with calm but solemn dedication, full of inner peace, feeling that nothing equal to this moment had happened since that other death—the one on the Hill of Skulls outside Jerusalem. Just as that earlier death had redeemed the world, this one would redeem the city.

People along the way stopped what they were doing and looked in surprise at this beatific old man, while those who followed him put their arms around the gawkers' shoulders and said to them quietly: "See how he dies, this righteous man who knew Christ and preached love to the world." The bemused spectators walked away telling themselves that this man, at least, could never be one of the sinful.

All the shouts and yelling common to the streets died out along the way. The procession moved between new buildings, and past the white columns of freshly reconstructed temples that seemed to lift and support the deep blue infinity above them. They walked in silence. Only the murmur of their prayers and the clang and rattle of the soldiers' weaponry and armor broke in occasionally on the hush around them. Peter listened to this sea of prayer, and his face glowed with an ever greater joy, because he could never count the praying thousands. He felt that he had done his work after all. He knew that the truth he had preached all his life would flood the world and that nothing would be able to prevent it. He looked up into the infinite space above him.

"Master," he prayed. "You told me to take possession of this city that rules the whole world, and I've taken it. You told me to build your capital here, and I've built it. This is your city now, my Lord, and I'm going to you because I've worked hard and it's time to rest."

As he passed the temples he said to them: "You will belong to Christ."

Looking at the swarming masses of the Roman world that filled the crowded city streets and passed before his eyes, he told them quietly, "Your children will serve Christ."

He went on, knowing he had triumphed, conscious of how much he had accomplished, aware of his might, at peace within himself and wondrous to those around him.

The praetorians led him through the Pons Triumphalis, the bridge used by great conquerors who came to Rome to receive the welcome of the city, as if to pay their own accidental homage to his conquest. Then they took the road to the Naumachia, where sea battles and water spectacles were staged, and past the hippodrome that housed the chariot races. So many Christian converts came from the Trans-Tiber and joined the procession that the centurion who led the execution detail became alarmed. It dawned on him that he was escorting some high priest through a swarm of his followers, and he worried if he had enough soldiers close at hand.

But not a single angry shout came from the crowd. There was no hint of outrage. All the faces showed a deep awareness of the moment—solemn, uplifted and conscious of its greatness—along with the anticipation of the unexpected. Many among them recalled that the earth shook and the dead rose from their graves when Christ died on Golgotha, and some thought something of the kind would mark the passing of the great apostle. Others even wondered if Christ might choose the hour of Peter's death to come down from heaven and judge the world, and commended themselves to the Savior's mercy.

But nothing on that calm, quiet day suggested that the world was about to end. The hills looked as if they were resting and basking in the sun. The procession finally halted between the racetrack and the slope of Vatican hill. The soldiers began to dig a hole. Others put down the cross, mallets and spikes, and waited for the preparations to be completed. The crowds, as quiet and peaceful as before, dropped to their knees around them.

Sunlight bathed the apostle, enveloping him in white and golden lights, as he turned for the last time to look at the city. Far below him, the Tiber gleamed and glittered in the sunlight, and the green Field of Mars spread on the banks beyond it. Higher up rose the mausoleum of Caesar Augustus, the founder of the bloodstained Flavian dynasty; lower sprawled the monumental baths Nero had just started building; and lower still, the theater of Pompey. Then, shown in intermittent breaks between other monuments and buildings, was the Septa Julia, an endless vista of porticoes, temples, columns and great structures that rose many floors. But what really caught the apostle's eye, fixed far off in the distance, were the hills plastered with tenements and houses, and the gigantic, antlike, human swarm whose farthest reaches dwindled in the blue. A nest of evil, the apostle thought, but also a seat of power, madness but also order, the capital of the world and also mankind's most terrible oppressor, bringer of laws and peace, all-powerful, invulnerable and eternal.

Surrounded by soldiers, Peter looked at it and saw it as a monarch might see his kingdom. "You are redeemed and mine," he told it without words. And no one there, neither the digging soldiers nor the gathered Christians, guessed or realized that a real king of Rome was standing among them. Caesars would come and go, waves of barbarians would sweep down and then vanish, and ages would go by, but this old man would rule here without a moment's pause.

The sun moved deeper toward Ostia, crimson and enormous. All of the western sky was ablaze with a dazzling light. The soldiers turned to Peter to strip off his clothes. Praying, he suddenly stood erect and raised his right hand high into the air. The executioners halted, as if suddenly made timid by his commanding pose. The faithful also waited, thinking he would speak.

"*Urbi et orbi!*" he cried out, and then started to bless Rome and all the world in his last hour on earth.

He scrawled a cross in the air above the city, sending peace to the city and all the lands around it, and at the same time taking possession of them all in his master's name.

On the same beautiful evening another troop of soldiers led Paul of Tarsus along the Ostian Way to a settlement called Aquae Salviae. He, too, was followed by a crowd of converts. He enjoyed the privileges of a Roman citizen, and the soldiers didn't interfere when he stopped to chat with some he knew well.

Beyond the gates known as Tergomina he saw Plautilla, the daughter of the prefect Flavius Sabinus. Tears ran down her young face. He asked for her veil.

"Go home and be at peace," he told her, calling her a daughter of salvation. "Your veil will shield my eyes when I stand in the radiance of the Lord."

He went on, joyful and at peace, like a laborer who has worked hard in the fields all day and hurries home at sunset. His thoughts, like Peter's, were as calm and clear as the evening sky. His eyes rested quietly on the plains unfolding before him and on the Alban hills in the twilight. He recalled his journeys, hardships, work and struggles; he remembered all the churches he had founded in so many lands and beyond the seas, and counted his victories; he thought he had done enough to earn his rest. He, too, had done what he had been sent to do. The seed he sowed, he thought, had taken firm root in the soil, and no winds of terror would blow it away. He was leaving because his work was done. He was going, but he knew his truth would triumph and conquer the world, and a great sense of peace settled on his spirit and on his mind.

It was far to his place of execution. Evening began to fall. The mountains turned purple, and the foothills sank into the shadows. Flocks and herds trotted home. Here and there groups of slaves appeared in the fields, their work tools on their shoulders. Children stopped their games in the street to stare with bright curiosity at the soldiers who marched past their homes. There was a soothing sense of peace in the warm evening light and in the translucent air, and there was a harmony among all things on earth and in the sky. Paul heard it as the music of the world. Joy filled him at the thought that he had added a sound to this eternal harmony, one without which all of mankind was like sounding brass or a tinkling cymbal.

He recalled how he had taught love to people and how he had told them that even if they gave all their possessions to the poor and knew all the languages and plumbed all the mysteries and acquired all the knowledge in the world, they would be nothing without that love which is kind and gentle, which lasts and forgives, which harms no one and wants nothing in return, which endures with patience and trusts in all things, which takes all things into itself, and which endures beyond anything else on earth and in Heaven.

This was the truth he had spent his life teaching, and now he asked himself: What power can match it? Who can conquer it? How can any Caesar stamp it out, even with twice as many legions, cities, lands and seas, nations and possessions?

He was going to his reward like a conqueror.

He and the soldiers and the group around them left the highway shortly after that and turned east on a narrow path that led to the healing springs of Aquae Salviae. The sinking sun had turned the heather crimson. The centurion halted his troop at the mineral fountain, because this was to be the place of execution, and this was the time.

Paul tossed Plautilla's veil across his shoulder to use as a blindfold and looked for the last time at the immemorial fires in the evening sky. His eyes were full of peace. He prayed. Yes, the hour had come. His journeys through the world were over, but he could see a new highway stretching up through the blaze of nightfall. He repeated to himself the words he had written earlier in his cell, conscious of his work's completion and his approaching end:

"I've fought the good fight. I have run my course. I have kept the faith. The crown of the righteous waits for me in Heaven."

‹85›

ROME, IN THE MEANTIME, raged as madly as before. It seemed as if this city that had conquered the whole world was now tearing itself apart for lack of someone to lead it and direct it. Piso's conspiracy broke out even before the last hour came to the apostles, and the bloody harvest that reaped the highest heads in Rome was so overwhelming that even those who thought of Nero as a god now saw him as a god of death. Mourning consumed the city. Fear gripped the people and crept into their homes. But joyful garlands hung in all the doorways since no one was permitted to grieve for the dead. People asked themselves on rising in the morning whose turn would come next. The terrible procession of ghosts who trailed in the wake of Caesar grew longer every day.

Piso paid for the conspiracy with his head. So did Seneca and Lucan, Fenius Rufus and Plautius Lateranus, Flavius Scevinus and Afranius Quinetianus, and the dissolute Tullius Senecio, the boon companion of Caesar's most depraved debaucheries, and Proculus, Araricus, Tugurinus, Gratus and Silanus, Proximus, Subrius Flavius, who was once body and soul with Nero, and Sulpicius Asper.

Some fell as victims of their worthless natures, cowardice killed others, and yet others were condemned by their own riches or doomed by their courage.

The sheer number of conspirators terrified Caesar who packed the walls with soldiers, placed the city in a virtual state of siege, and sent centurions every day to the homes of suspects, ordering them to kill themselves or die in the dungeons. The condemned bowed and scraped before him to the last, flattered him in letters, thanked him for letting them commit suicide at home, and willed him a part of their properties so as to save the rest for their children.

It seemed toward the end that Nero went as far as he did on purpose, letting his madness rage unrestrained beyond any limit to see just how low society had sunk and how long Rome would endure a rule of blood and terror. The conspirators were followed to the block by their relatives, friends or simply men and women they happened to know. The patricians, nobles and leaders of the city who lived in the magnificent mansions built after the fire knew they would see a string of funerals each time they stepped into the street. Pompeius, Cornelius Marcialis, Flavius Nepos and Statius Domitius died for the crime of not loving Caesar as much as they should. Novius Priscus paid with his life for friendship with Seneca. Rufius Crispinus was condemned to live without fire or water, a sentence that deprived him of heat, light, cooked food, bathing, sanitation and everything else in Roman life that included water or a flame. His crime was that he had once been married to Poppea. The great Thrasea died because he was too decent and provided too much of a contrast with the murderous Caesar. Others were killed because they were patricians, descended from the founders of the city. Even the beautiful, implacable and unforgiving Poppea fell victim to one of Nero's momentary rages.

And the senate crawled before the terrible emperor, raised temples in his honor, sacrificed to the gods for the health of his voice, garlanded his statues, and assigned him an entire priesthood as if he were a god. The senators trembled as they went to the Palatine to applaud his singing and to go wild with debauchery beside him in orgies of naked flesh, wine and flowers.

Meanwhile, at the foundations of the city, among the masses closer to the streets and the blood-soaked earth, Peter's seed grew stronger and took deeper root.

‹86›

IT WAS AT ABOUT THIS TIME that Vinicius wrote from Sicily to Petronius. They knew in Sicily about the madness in the Palatine and what was happening in Rome. Carinas, Caesar's special tax collector, had been on the island on his way to Greece to loot the local treasuries and pillage the temples.

"You know Carinas, *carissime*," Vinicius wrote. "He's just like Chilon was before his death. . . . You ask if we are safe? I'll tell you simply that we are forgotten; let that be your answer. Right now, from the portico on which I am writing, I see our peaceful bay. Ursus is fishing on it from a boat. My wife sits beside me, spinning crimson wool, and I can hear our slaves singing in the shade of the almond trees."

He wrote about their peace, all the past pains and fears quite forgotten. He thanked Christ for his blessings in which he saw their destiny rather than in the spinning wheels of the Fates, and he mentioned the death of the two apostles.

"Peter and Paul are not dead," he wrote, "but born again in glory. We see them in spirit. If we cry for them, it's because we miss them, but we are happy for their happiness and joy."

He told Petronius once again about the Christian concept of the resurrection, about their peaceful lives, and about the love they practiced in their Christian household. The past seemed almost like a dream to him and Ligia now when they talked about it, although Vinicius would always think Christ rescued Ligia in the arena by a miracle of mercy. He urged Petronius to come to Sicily and see for himself how much ordinary, daily happiness could be found in becoming a Christian.

"We never had a god that we could love before," he wrote. "So people weren't able to love each other, and all unhappiness comes to us from that. Happiness, *carissime,* comes from love like light comes from the sun. But no one taught it to us."

He dismissed the Stoics and other contemporary philosophers; he referred to Paul of Tarsus and the question he posed to Petronius in Ancium—when the apostle asked, "What would Rome be like if Caesar was a Christian?" Writing of peace and his relationship with Ligia, he spoke of the beauties of spiritual love, and again asked Petronius to see their peace and happiness for himself.

"Compare your fear-lined delights, your concern for material objects when none of you is sure of his tomorrow, your orgies that seem like funeral suppers, and you'll find the answer. Come to our thyme-smelling mountains, to the shade of our olive groves, and to our ivy-covered coast. Peace waits for you here, the kind of peace you haven't known in years. And love waits for you here, in hearts that truly love you. You have a good and noble soul, Petronius. You deserve to be happy. Your brilliant mind can recognize the truth, and when you've seen it, you will come to love it.

"It's possible to hate it, *carissime*," he ended, "like Caesar and Tigellinus, but no one can be indifferent to it. So come, my dear Petronius. Ligia and I both hope to see you soon. Be well, be happy, and join us."

Petronius found this letter waiting in Cumae, where he had followed Caesar with other Augustans. His war with Tigellinus, which had lasted for years, was coming to an end. He knew now that he must lose, and he understood the reasons why. The lower Caesar fell each day into the role of an actor, a buffoon and a chariot driver, sinking deeper into the repulsive mire of gross debauchery and the most degrading of perverse corruptions, the less he wanted a refined, cultivated arbiter of taste. In fact Petronius had become a burden. If he kept silent, Nero took it as a reprimand. If he praised something, Nero heard it as irony and contemptuous gibing. The splendid patrician scratched open his most festering wound: his self-adoration; and he envied him everything he was.

Another reason his war must end in defeat was that the ruler of the world and his omnipotent minister began to eye his great wealth and his magnificent collection of artwork. Caesar craved them with the greed of lust. All that spared him up to this time was Nero's proposed singing tour of Greece, where his taste and familiarity with the arts and culture would be useful to him.

But Tigellinus advanced yet another pawn—the thieving, flattering, traveling tax collector and pillager of temples, the obsequious Carinas— and began to convince Caesar that the glib old looter knew more than

Petronius about art and beauty. As such he would be much better able to arrange the Greek games, concerts, receptions and triumphs.

From that moment Petronius was lost. Nero was afraid of sending him a death sentence in Rome, however. Both he and Tigellinus remembered uneasily that this supposedly effeminate aesthete, who "turned night into day," and who cared about nothing other than his pleasures, his art and his banquets, had been a ruthless and efficient proconsul in Bithynia and a hardworking, energetic consul in Rome as well. Much as they both either envied or detested him, they had a high regard for his abilities and thought he could accomplish anything he wished. The people loved him. The praetorians liked and respected him. No one among Caesar's closest circle could suggest how he would react at any given moment. The safest thing would be to lure him out into the provinces and get him there.

With this in view—and he was very well aware of what was going on—he was invited to go with Caesar to Cumae, and he went. Why? He didn't really know himself, and he didn't care. Perhaps it was too much trouble to refuse, because that called for open resistance. Perhaps to show a carefree face once more to Caesar and the Augustans and win one more duel with Tigellinus before he died.

But he no sooner set foot in his Cumae villa than Tigellinus charged him with high treason, citing his friendship with Senator Scevinus, who was the heart of the Piso plot. His Roman household was put under arrest. Praetorians surrounded his house as soon as he left it.

Petronius remained quite calm and unaffected when he heard about this. He smiled and was not even embarrassed before his guests in his luxurious Cumae country home and said he'd have to speak to Caesar about it.

"Copperbeard doesn't like direct questions," he said, "so you'll see how scatterbrained he'll get when I ask him if my Roman household was jailed on his orders."

Then he invited them to join him in a banquet "to celebrate a long journey I'm about to make," and that's when he received the letter from Vinicius.

He read it later in the evening.

Unlike his normal self, he thought about it seriously for several moments. Then his face relaxed into his usual pleasant expression, and he wrote back as follows:

"I delight in your happiness, dear ones, and I admire your kindness, since I didn't believe a couple in love could think about anybody else. And you not only think of me but want to invite me to Sicily, to share your hospitality and your Christ, who—as you put it—is so generous to you with his joys.

"If that's so, then worship him. I rather think that Ursus and the Roman people had more than a little to do with Ligia's liberation. I've even thought your kinship to Nero, through that granddaughter that Tiberius married off to another Vinicius, may have prompted him to stop your persecution. But if you think Christ did it all, so be it. Don't skimp on his offerings. Prometheus also sacrificed himself for mankind, but that's another story. And besides, Prometheus is supposed to be just a poetic concept, while credible witnesses told me they saw Christ with their own eyes. I agree with you that he must be the most honest of the gods.

"Yes, I remember what Paul of Tarsus asked me. I agree that if Copperbeard lived by Christian rules, I might have the time to visit you both in Sicily. Then we'd sit in the shade of the trees, by a woodland spring, and discuss all the gods and all the various truths, as the old Greek philosophers used to do. Today, however, I must say it briefly.

"There are only two philosophers that I care about, Pyrrho and Anacreon. You know what they stand for. The rest, along with the new Greek schools and all the Roman Stoics, you can have for the price of beans. Truth lives somewhere so high that even the gods can't see it from Olympus. You, *carissime*, think that your Olympus is a higher one, and you stand on it and cry down to me: 'Come up, and you'll see sights you've never seen before!' Perhaps so. But I say: 'My friend, I don't have the legs to climb mountains anymore,' and I think that when you've read this letter, you'll agree.

"No, happy husband of your sunrise princess, your creed is not for me. Am I to love the Bithynians who carry my litter? Or the Egyptians who stoke my bath furnace? Or Copperbeard and Tigellinus? No, by the white knees of the Graces. I swear I wouldn't be able to do it if I tried. Rome has at least a hundred thousand people with crooked shoulders, thick knees, dried-up thighs, bulging eyes or heads that are too large. Am I to love them too? Where am I to find that love when I don't feel it in me? And if your god wanted me to love them all, why didn't he make them as beautiful as Niobe's lost children, whose statues you admired at the Palatine? One who loves beauty can't love ugliness. It's one thing not to believe in our gods but another to love them for their beauty. And I love them as the great sculptors did; I see them through the eyes of Phidias, Praxiteles, Miron, Scopias and Lysias.

"No, my friend, I can't follow where you want to lead even if I wished to, and since I don't wish to, it's twice the reason. You believe, as Paul of Tarsus did, that once you've crossed the Styx into some joyful version of Elysian pastures, you'll see your Christ. Well and good! Let him tell you whether he'd let me in with my gems, my Myrrhenian vase, my Sosius first editions, and my golden-haired Eunice. I have to laugh when I think about it, because Paul himself told me we have to renounce everything for Christ, and that includes the wine and the roses. He did promise me other joys, but I had to tell him that I'm too old to try something new and that I'd always rather smell the roses than some dirty 'neighbor' from Suburra whom I'm supposed to love.

"This is why your happiness is not for me, my dears. But there is one more reason I've kept for the end. Old Thanatos is calling. Death beckons. You stand at the dawn of your lives, but my sun has already set and the night is near. In other words, *carissime*, I'm obliged to die.

"It's not worth discussing. It had to end like this. You know Copperbeard, so you'll understand. Tigellinus has beaten me at last, although perhaps it's only that my victories over him have ended. I've lived as I wanted, and I'll die in my own chosen way.

"Don't be distressed about it. No god ever promised me immortality so I'm not surprised. Besides, you're wrong to think that only your faith teaches one how to die at peace. Our world knew long before you that when the cup is drained, it's time to let it go and to do it pleasantly and with taste. Plato says that virtue is like music and the life of a wise man is always harmonious. If that's so, then I shall die a virtuous man, having lived in harmony with my world.

"I'd like to say good-bye to your divine wife, my dear boy, with the words I used when I met her in the Plautius home: 'I've seen many people, among many nations, but I've never met anyone like you.'

"So if the soul is something more than Pyrrho thinks it is, mine will fly your way as it heads for the underworld beyond the seas, and I'll perch near your home as a butterfly or—as the Egyptians prefer it—as a sparrow hawk.

"There is no other way in which I can be with you. In the meantime may Sicily be your gardens of the Hesperides, may all the field, woodland and water deities fill your paths with flowers, and may white doves nest in all columns."

‹87›

PETRONIUS WAS RIGHT in his expectations. Nerva, who was devoted and always well disposed toward him, sent word by a trusted freedman a couple of days later, reporting on everything that was taking place at court. Petronius' fate was already sealed there. Tomorrow evening, he was told, a centurion would call on him with orders not to leave Cumae and to wait for further instructions from Caesar. A few days later another messenger would bring his death sentence.

Petronius heard the freedman's news with unruffled calmness. "I'll have you take one of my vases to your master," he said. "And thank him for me from the bottom of my heart. I know now what I have to do."

Suddenly he started laughing like a man who had a good idea and couldn't wait to enjoy its full effect. That very evening his slaves ran through the whole summer colony, inviting the Augustan men and women who were in Cumae to a banquet at the magnificent villa of the arbiter of taste.

He spent the afternoon writing in his library, then bathed, ordered himself dressed so that he looked as exquisite and superb as one of the immortals, and made his way to his dining room to cast an expert eye on all the arrangements. He strolled into the gardens where small lads and beautiful young girls from the Greek islands were making rose wreaths for him and his guests.

No shadow troubled his face. He showed no trace of care. The only way his servants knew this banquet was special was that he ordered a rich bonus for those whose work he liked and a light scourging for those who didn't please him or who had earned some punishment and rebuke before. He was generous with the singers and musicians, whom he ordered well paid in advance. At last he settled in the garden under a leafy beech whose rustling crown let in broad shafts of sunlight that speckled the ground below.

There he called for Eunice.

She came, dressed all in white and with a sprig of myrtle in her hair, as breathtaking as one of the Graces. He seated her beside him, let his fingertips pass across her temples, and began to study her with the admiration of a connoisseur who sees a masterwork of sculpture emerge from under the chisel of an artist.

"Eunice," he said, "do you know you haven't been a slave for a long time now?"

She looked up at him with her quiet blue eyes and quickly shook her head. "I am one and always will be, master," she murmured.

He shook his head.

"You may not know it," Petronius went on speaking, "but this house, the slaves who are weaving roses over there, everything inside, and the herds and estates that go with this villa are yours from today on."

Eunice sat up suddenly and twisted away. "Why are you telling me this, my lord?" she asked in a worried voice. Then she leaned close and stared into his face.

She blinked in quick fear, and her face turned as white as her robe, while he went on smiling.

"Yes," he said quietly at last.

Neither of them said anything for a while, and only a slight breeze rustled among the leaves. Looking at her, Petronius could believe that he was really seeing a white marble statue.

"Eunice," he told her. "I want to die smiling and content."

The girl looked at him with a heartrending smile of her own. "I understand, my lord."

The evening guests gathered in large numbers. All of them had dined with him before and knew that a banquet in his home made even Caesar's feasts seem boring and barbarian. None of them could suppose this was the last time they would gather at his table. Many among them knew Caesar had turned against him and that Petronius was under a cloud; but this had happened many times before, and the smooth, polished arbiter never failed to soothe the situation—sometimes with just one daring word or a single skillful twist of the circumstances—and no one seriously believed he was in real danger. His cheerful face and his usual carefree, relaxed and unaffected smile dispelled whatever doubts anyone might have.

Eunice was also smiling. Petronius told her that he wanted to die without a care in the world, and she took every word he spoke as an oracular command. As beautiful as an Olympian dream, she was as serene that night as a real goddess, and there were some strange lights in her eyes that could be read as joy. Young lads, with their hair tied in golden nets, met the guests at the door of the banquet chamber, crowned them with roses and reminded them to step into the room with their right foot forward. The air in the room was lightly redolent of violets and the illumination came from multicolored Alexandrine lamps. Young Greek girls stood beside the reclining couches to sprinkle the diners' feet with perfume. The singers and the zither players waited along the walls.

Shining extravagance was the keynote of Petronius' table: its precious service and its costly settings were dazzling with riches, but here the glittering display was tasteful rather than jarring and oppressive, as if the opulence grew naturally out of its own profusion. Laughter and ease spread throughout the room with the smell of violets. Entering, the guests could feel relaxed and free; no threat or danger hung over them here as happened whenever they dined with Caesar, where insufficient rapture over some song or couplet could result in death. A sense of comfort, pleasure, ease and peace of mind came from the sight of muted lights, goblets wreathed in ivy, wines that lay cooling under layers of snow, and rare dishes. Talk spread, humming excitedly like bees on a flowering apple tree, broken at times by a burst of laughter, the murmur of praises, or the sound of a kiss planted with loud enthusiasm on some white arm or shoulder.

As they drank, the guests were careful to spill a few drops of wine as an offering to the household gods so that the deities would have the host in their care and keeping. It didn't matter that few of them believed in the gods. This was a sop to old Roman custom and their superstitions. Petronius lay beside Eunice, talking about the latest news from Rome, commenting on some scandalous new divorces, passions and love affairs, discussing the races at the hippodrome, the gladiator Spiculus who won some recent fame in the arena, and the latest books. Spilling his traditional drops of wine he said he did it only in honor of Aphrodite, the goddess-queen of Cyprus, saying she was the oldest and greatest of all the goddesses, and the only one who was truly immortal, commanding and eternal.

His conversation had the quality of sunlight, illuminating one subject after another, or of a summer breeze that stirs blooming flowers. At last he signaled to the choirmaster, the lutes sounded lightly, and young voices rose in harmony. Then dancers from Cos, born on the same island as Eunice, swayed among the diners, letting their rosy bodies gleam through transparent veils. An Egyptian soothsayer read fortunes in the glinting rainbow of reflected lights caught in a moving crystal prism.

When the guests had their fill of entertainment, Petronius rose slightly on his Syrian cushions.

"My friends," he said with hesitation, as if obliged to raise a tasteless matter. "I hate to ask for favors during dinner . . . but I want each of you to have the cup from which you spilled your offering to the gods and to my own good fortune."

Of gleaming gold and precious stones, and carved by great artists, Petronius' goblets were a rare treasure. And even though gift-giving was a common Roman practice, the diners were delighted. Some started to thank him and praise him. Others insisted that not even Jupiter was this generous with his guests while dining on Olympus. But the gesture was so totally out of the ordinary, exceeding any normal expectations for extravagance, that some of the guests actually started to refuse.

He merely held up a Myrrhenian bowl, a priceless artwork that caught the lights like a fiery rainbow.

"Here is the one I used to honor the Queen of Cyprus," he said, smiling with some private pleasure of his own. "Let no other lips touch it from now on, and let no other hand spill wine out of it to honor any other gods."

He hurled the treasure on the marble, saffron-sprinkled floor, where it smashed and shattered into fragments. The guests stared, amazed.

"Be glad!" he told them. "Don't look so surprised! Infirmity and old age make poor companions for our final years. But I'll give you some good advice and a fine example. You don't have to wait for them, you see. You can walk away before they come for you. And that's what I am doing."

"What *are* you doing?" asked troubled voices.

"What I love to do best: drink wine, enjoy myself, listen to music, caress the divine contours that you see beside me, and then go to sleep with roses in my hair. I've already made my valedictory to Caesar, but I'd be glad to read it to you if you'd like to hear it."

He drew a letter from under the purple bolster on which he reclined and began to read.

"I know, my Caesar, that you can't wait to see me and that your loyal heart misses me night and day. I know that were it up to you, you'd shower me with gifts, make me the prefect of the praetorians, and order Tigellinus to play the role for which the gods created him, namely to feed the mules on the estates you inherited after poisoning your sister Domitia. Forgive me, but I can't come to visit you just now, as I swear by all the ghosts in Hades, and that includes those of your murdered mother, wife, brother and Seneca as well.

"Life," he read on, "is a great treasure, my friend, and I knew how to pluck the most precious gems out of it. But there are also horrors in life that I can't endure. Oh, please don't think I was particularly offended when you killed your mother, wife and brother, burned Rome, and sent all the decent men of this empire to the underworld. No, you grandson of Chronos who devoured his children. Death is a part of our human heritage, and no one would expect you to behave in any other way. But to cripple my ears year after year, with listening to your songs, to watch your puny, skinny legs kicking about in a Pyrrhic dance, to hear your music, your recitations and your creaking epics—you poor, suburban versifier—proved too much for me and prompted me to believe I'd much rather die. Rome plugs its ears when it hears you, the whole world laughs at you, and I can't blush with shame on your behalf much longer. The howling of Cerberus, the two-headed dog that guards the gates of Hell, may remind me of you, but it won't hurt as much. I never had to pretend to be his friend, you see, and I don't have to apologize for his voice.

"Be well," he finished with his last advice, "but don't sing. Kill but don't write verses. Poison but don't dance. Burn cities but don't play the lyre. This is the last friendly bit of guidance you will ever get from . . . Petronius, the arbiter of taste."

The diners sat as still as stones, stunned by what they heard, because they knew this cruel blow would strike Nero harder than if he lost the empire. They also grasped at once that any man who wrote such a letter was as good as dead and they, too, might be in danger for hearing it read.

Petronius burst into a peal of laughter as if he'd merely played an innocent little joke.

"Be happy!" he cried out, letting his eyes rest on each of them in turn. "Don't be afraid. Nobody here has to advertise that he heard my letter, and I won't breathe a word of it, of course . . . unless I mention it to Charon as we cross the Styx."

He nodded to his Greek physician and stretched out his arm. The Greek moved at once, tightened a gilded thong on Petronius' biceps, and opened the vein inside the elbow. Blood spurted on the cushions of the dining couch and sprayed over Eunice who cradled his head.

"Master," she murmured, bowing over him, "did you think I'd let you go alone?"

"I hoped you would. You have much to live for."

"If the gods made me immortal," she smiled, "and Caesar gave me power over all the world, I'd still follow you."

Petronius smiled and raised himself enough to touch her lips with his. "Come with me, then," he said.

She stretched her arm to the surgeon, and a moment later her blood joined his.

Petronius signaled to the singers, and the sound of the lutes and voices rose again in the scented air. First they sang the tragedy of Harmodius, the famous Athenian who killed the tyrannical Hipparchus, and then Anacreon's pastoral tale of a gentle poet who found Aphrodite's cold and hungry infant crying at his door.

"Ah, how unfeeling are the gods," the poet sang, complaining that he pitied the weeping little creature and picked it up and warmed it and dried its small wings, and the ungrateful Cupid shot him with an arrow so that he never knew any peace thereafter.

Petronius and Eunice leaned against each other, listening and growing swiftly pale, and smiling as ethereally as a pair of deities.

He ordered more food and wine served when the singing ended and went on talking pleasantly about unimportant matters, the sort of easy and lighthearted trivia people talk about at dinner. Then he beckoned to the Greek and had him bind up the severed artery for a moment.

"I'd like to dream a little before I go," he said. "Thanatos is coming ... but I want to spend a little time with Hypnos."

He drifted off into a gliding sleep. When he opened his eyes again, Eunice's lifeless head lay on his chest like a pale flower, and he settled her peacefully on the bolster beside him so that he could see her and look at her once more and for the last time.

His artery was untied again.

The singers caught his glance and began another song by Anacreon, with the strings strumming softly so as not to intrude upon the words.

Petronius grew paler.

"Admit, my friends"—he started as the last notes of the music ebbed away—"that what dies with us here is ..."

He didn't finish. His arm tightened once more around Eunice, his head fell back into the cushions, and he died.

The dinner guests understood his unfinished message. Looking at the two exquisite white bodies, so much like an inspired work of art or a glorious sculpture, they knew that the last worthwhile quality had gone from their world, and this was its poetry and beauty.

‹Epilogue›

WHEN THE GALLIC LEGIONS revolted under Vindex—a name that in Latin meant "avenger"—no one thought the revolt would play much of a role in history. Caesar was only thirty-one. No one dared hope for an early end to the suffocating nightmare that convulsed the empire. The legions, as people told one another, rose in revolt several times before, but the outbreaks didn't unseat any other Caesars. In the reign of Tiberius, for example, Drusus pacified the Pannonian legions on the Upper Danube, and Germanicus ended the revolt of those on the Rhine.

"Who could rule after Nero," people asked themselves, "when nearly all the heirs of Caesar Augustus died out in *this* reign?"

Others, looking at the colossal monuments that depicted Nero in the form of Hercules, couldn't imagine a force that might topple so much might and power. There were also others among the people who confessed they missed him while he was away, because the rule of Helios and Politetes, whom he left to govern in his place, was bloodier than his own.

No one in Rome was sure of life and property. Laws gave no protection. Decency died out, along with human dignity. Families broke apart. The hope of something better couldn't even occur to the worthless and degraded people. They heard the echoes of Nero's triumphs in Greece, talked about the thousands of gold laurel wreaths he won on the stage and the thousands of competitors he surpassed. All the world seemed like a single orgy of posturing and bloodshed, and people started to believe in the end of seriousness and virtue. This, they could see, was the time to dance, sing and abandon all restraints; normal life thereafter would be an endless time of debauchery and bloodshed.

Caesar himself didn't give much thought to Vindex and his rebel legions. Indeed, he made it known he was pleased about it, because war and rebellion paved the path to new loot and booty. He didn't want to leave Greece at all, and set sail for Naples only when Helios warned him he might lose his empire if he delayed much longer.

He stayed in Naples. He sang and he played. He ignored the danger that seemed to loom larger with each piece of news. Tigellinus begged him to remember that the other army mutinies never had a general for a leader, while Vindex was descended from the former Aquitanian kings and was a famous and experienced military commander.

Fame and glory were Nero's own dearest goals, however, and he refused to stir from Naples.

"Greeks live here," he said. "Here I am heard by Greeks who alone know how to listen to music and who are the only people fit to hear my voice."

But when he heard that Vindex called him a mediocre artist, he left for Rome at once. The awful wound that Petronius had given his self-esteem healed a little during his Greek triumphs, but now it broke open afresh. He hurried to the senate to seek retribution for such a dreadful and unheard-of libel. But passing a roadside bronze statue of a fallen Gaul, struck down by a Roman, he took it for a lucky omen. If he mentioned Vindex and his legions after that, it was only to make jokes about them.

He returned to Rome in a celebration never before seen anywhere. He rode in the triumphal chariot of Augustus Caesar. One whole arch of the circus had to be torn down to give him free passage. The senate, the nobles and crowds beyond counting poured into the streets to welcome him. The walls shook with cheers.

"Hail, Augustus! Hail, Hercules" they shouted. "Hail, divine Caesar, the only true Olympian, the only Pythian . . . the immortal!"

Carried behind him were his laurel crowns and signs with the names of the master singers he had bested on the stage and the cities where he had won his most notable successes. Nero was drunk with the cheers, swept away by the tumultuous applause, and so moved he could hardly speak.

"Tell me," he stammered to the Augustans around him. "Did Julius Caesar ever have such a triumph in Rome?"

He couldn't understand how anyone would dare raise his hand against such a demigod and artist. He truly felt Olympian, beyond human reach, and safe from all judgment. The howling, enthusiastic crowds inflamed his madness so that it seemed as if not just the emperor and his city had lost their minds that day but the whole world as well. No one could see the abyss that yawned under the flowers and the piles of laurels. But that same evening, lists of his crimes appeared on the columns and the temple walls, along with threats of coming retribution and jeers at his singing.

A new popular saying flew from mouth to mouth, based on a play on the word *gallos* which meant both Gauls and roosters. "He sang until he woke the Gauls," people said and laughed, but the laughter soon gave way to fear. Frightening rumors took wing throughout the city and swelled to terrifying size. The Augustans worried. No one knew what to anticipate. People stopped talking to one another, afraid to express either hopes or wishes, and barely daring to think and feel.

In the meantime he lived only for his art, the theater and singing. He was absorbed by experiments with new musical instruments and a water organ that was being tested at the Palatine. In his childishly absurd imagination, incapable of either serious thought or meaningful action, he conceived the notion that his long-range plans for new spectacles and concerts would avert the danger. Instead of raising armies and means for defense, he worried about the precise word or phrase that best described the terror of the moment.

Those closest to him started to lose their minds, and some threw up their hands. Others believed he was merely trying to smother his own terror with his posturing and his recitations, and blinding himself and everybody else with his own illusions so that he wouldn't have to see the truth. Thousands of new plans flashed through his head each day. Sometimes he'd leap to his feet, ordering all-out war on the mutineers, and then he would have wagons filled with lutes while young slave girls were armed and transformed into Amazons.

He decided he would end the revolt of the Gallic legions by singing to the soldiers. He could already see the aftermath: thousands of rebel legionnaires won over by the beauty of his voice, flocking around him with tears in their eyes, while he hummed a soft victory song and led them into a new golden age for Rome and himself.

At other times he suddenly howled for blood, announced that he'd give up his Roman crown and be content with ruling as a governor in Egypt, or recalled the fortune-tellers who promised him a kingdom in Jerusalem. Or he would see himself as a wandering minstrel, earning his daily bread with his voice and music, and this sentimental fantasy moved him as none other could. Yes, he would trudge the roads and sing from city to city, admired and adored, while distant nations paid homage to him and hailed him as the greatest epic singer of all time, rather than as their Caesar and master of the world.

And so he raged and sang and strummed and changed his plans;

and rewrote his rhymes; and transformed his life along with the lives of everyone around him, into a mindless nightmare that was both frightful and fantastic; and turned the world into a howling joke composed of puffed-up phrases, cheap verse, moaning, tears and blood. Meanwhile, the threatening clouds that gathered in the West grew heavier and darker. The limit had been reached, and the cup was full. The tragic farce was about to end.

When he heard that Spain under Galba had joined the rebellion, he went mad with rage. He smashed goblets, overturned banquet tables and screamed out commands that even Helios and Tigellinus were afraid to put into effect. He wanted an immediate slaughter of all the Gauls in Rome, the city burned to ashes once again, all the wild beasts released into the streets, and his own capital moved to Alexandria.

Nothing, he thought, could be simpler, greater, and more astounding for sheer scope and drama. But the days of his unquestioned power were already over, and even his old accomplices were now regarding him as mad.

The sudden death of Vindex seemed to offer him a moment of reprieve. The Gallic legions were quarreling among themselves, and the balance of power shifted in his favor. New banquets, celebrations and death sentences were already posted in the Forum when a mounted messenger, riding a sweat-streaked horse, galloped in from the camp of the praetorians. The Roman garrison had raised the banner of revolt in the city itself and proclaimed Galba as their emperor.

Nero was sleeping when the courier came. Guards stood outside his doors at night, but none came running when he called for them. The palace was empty. Only a few slaves were still busy looting whatever came to hand when Caesar stumbled out into the corridors. They ran when they saw him, and he was left to wander alone through the palace chambers, filling the halls with shouts of fear and despair.

Three of his freedmen—Phaon, Sporus and Epaphroditus—brought him some needed help. They urged him to run for his life, telling him there was no time to waste, but he still toyed with fantasies and illusions. What, he asked, if he donned penitential robes and addressed the senate? Would the senate be able to resist his eloquence and tears?

"Would anyone in the world fail to be moved," he asked, "if I used all my dramatic speaking skills, all my erudition and all my acting talents?"

The least he'd get, he thought, would be the prefecture of Egypt.

Accustomed to flattery and lip service, the freedmen still didn't dare correct him; they merely warned that he'd be torn to pieces by the mobs before he reached the Forum, and they threatened to leave him, too, if he didn't mount a horse at once. Phaon thought they might hide him for a while in the freedman's villa beyond the Nomentan Gate.

They left almost at once, with cloaks thrown across their heads for disguise, and galloped across the city. The night grew less dark but the streets were filling up with people, all of them conscious of great events around them. Soldiers were marching everywhere, singly and in clusters. Quite near the praetorian camp, Caesar's horse shied away from a corpse, and his cloak slipped off his head just as a soldier was trying to get past him. The soldier looked up, annoyed, and recognized the emperor. But he was so shocked by this unexpected meeting that he presented arms while Nero galloped away. As they rode past the walled main camp of the praetorians, they could hear thundering cheers for Galba, and Nero suddenly realized that he'd be killed that night.

Fear and guilt took control of him. He started to say that he saw darkness waiting for him like a cloud, and there were faces peering from that darkness. He could see they were his mother, wife and brother. His teeth were clattering with terror, but he found something irresistible in that terrifying moment. He couldn't stop himself from posturing and acting. It seemed the height of tragedy to be the omnipotent ruler of mankind and to lose it all, and he played the role to the end. Quotations poured out of him like water. He wanted them all noted for posterity. Sometimes he longed to die and called for the gladiator Spiculus, who was known for his quick dispatch of victims. Sometimes he declaimed: "My mother, wife and father summon me to death!" Vain, childish hopes leaped up in his brain like fire and died just as swiftly. He knew death was coming, but he could not make himself believe it.

The Nomentan Gate was open and unguarded, and they galloped through. A while later they passed the Ostrianum, where Peter had preached and baptized. At dawn they were in Phaon's villa, and the freedmen no longer hid from him that he had to die. He ordered them to dig a grave for him and stretched out on the ground so they could take his measure. But panic seized him when he saw the earth thrown out of the hole. His quivering fat face turned a pasty white. Sweat beaded his forehead as thick as dew. He groped for delays. The moment wasn't precisely right, he said in his quavering histrionic voice. He offered more quotations. At last he asked that his corpse be burned rather than merely buried.

"Oh, what an artist dies here!" he cried out, as if still unable to believe it.

One of Phaon's runners arrived from the Forum at that very moment, with news that the senate had already passed sentence on Nero. The matricide would be executed in the old Roman way.

"And what way is that?" Nero's lips were now as pale as his face.

"They'll grip your neck in a vise and flog you to death," Epaphroditus barked. "And then they'll throw your body in the Tiber."

Nero bared his chest and looked up at the sky. "Ah, so it's time!" And then he said again, "Oh, what an artist dies here!"

More hoofbeats were coming at a gallop, heading for the villa. That could only be a centurion with a troop of soldiers coming for Nero's head. The freedmen were shouting for him to hurry. Nero put a dagger to his throat but only pinked himself with a trembling hand; it was clear he would never drive it into his own flesh. Suddenly Epaphroditus did the unexpected. He was Nero's most trusted confidential servant, loyal beyond question. He reached out, pushed the knife in up to the hilt, and Nero's eyes bulged out: terrified, enormous and frightful.

"You're to live!" the centurion said as he entered. "I bring you life!"

"Too late," Nero croaked, then added, "Ah, what loyalty."

Darkness settled on him at once. Blood gushed in a black stream out of the punctured neck and spattered the potted plants and flowers. His legs kicked the ground and he died. The faithful Acte wrapped him the next day in a costly shroud and burned him to ashes on a scented pyre.

So ended Nero, passing like a windstorm, a typhoon, a fire, a war and a plague. But Peter's church stands on the heights of the Vatican to this day, and it commands the city and the world. And near the old gate of Porta Capena stands a little chapel with a small tablet sunk into the wall. The writing is somewhat faint with age. It asks:

"Quo vadis, Domine?"

Historical Notes

In his justly famous novel *Quo Vadis?*, Henryk Sienkiewicz portrays a richly detailed and historically accurate picture of Rome in the time of Nero. The many names of individuals, places in and around Rome, and details of daily and political life that are found in the novel bring to life the city and its inhabitants of nineteen hundred years ago.

The setting of the novel was meticulously researched by Sienkiewicz. Before writing *Quo Vadis?*, he traveled to Italy several times to visit the museums and historic sites of ancient Rome. He was thoroughly familiar with the ancient sources of the period, especially Tacitus and Suetonius, as well as the works of contemporary scholars, in particular Fustel de Coulanges and Ernest Renan. His careful preparation has made *Quo Vadis?* an enduring masterpiece of the historical novel genre.

MAIN CHARACTERS

LIGIA, daughter of the king of the Ligians. The Ligians were a loose association of tribes which occupied the land between the Oder and Vistula rivers, or modern-day Poland. In 50A.D., the Ligians joined a confederacy of Germanic tribes in an attempt to overthrow a pro-Roman Germanic chief, Vannius. Roman policy prohibited interference in this internal squabble among the Germanic tribes, but they did demand a promise from the Ligians not to cross into Roman territory. Sienkiewicz's Ligia is the hostage who was given to the Romans as security of the Ligian pledge.

VINITIUS, MARCUS (Vinicius), son of Marcus Vinitius. His father was elected consul in 45A.D. after a distinguished military career. Marcus Vinitius, the Elder, married Nero's aunt, Julia Livilla, and was connected with court intrigue during the reign of Claudius, Nero's predecessor. The character in the novel, Marcus Vinitius, is presumably the son of this marriage and therefore a cousin of Nero.

PETRONIUS, GAIUS. Tacitus describes Petronius in his *Annals* as Nero's "Arbiter of Elegance," who was later forced to commit suicide in 66A.D. Petronius enjoyed a special friendship with Nero and was often consulted by the emperor on artistic matters. After the great fire of 64A.D., he began to lose favor with the emperor. Most scholars identify Petronius as the author of the ribald adventure story *Satyricon*.

NERO, LUCIUS DOMITIUS AHENOBARBUS, emperor of Rome, 54-68A.D. With the help of his mother, Agrippina, whom he later murdered, he became emperor at the age of seventeen. The notorious emperor of Rome was an able administrator in the first several years of his reign. His tyranny grew as he increasingly neglected matters of state to concentrate on his own personal artistic stature. Court intrigue and Nero's paranoia had increased dramatically by the time of the disastrous fire in Rome in 64A.D. Nero used the early Christians as scapegoats for the fire and initiated their bloody executions. In the last years of his reign, his fears and suspicions caused the execution (or suicide) of countless Roman aristocrats.

AULUS PLAUTIUS, consul 29A.D. During the reign of Nero, Aulus Plautius was living the quiet life of a distinguished Roman noble and military hero. He was well known as the conqueror of Britain.

POMPONIA GRAECINA, wife of Aulus Plautius. During the reign of Claudius (41-54A.D.), she was accused of being an adherent of a "foreign suspicion," which later tradition has identified as Christianity. She was acquitted in a "family" trial and given over to her husband. Throughout her life, she enjoyed a reputation for melancholy.

AUGUSTIANS, various Roman nobles in Nero's court. Nero surrounded himself with a grand and magnificent court which included many men and women from the most prestigious Roman families, as well as other clients, freedmen, slaves and assorted sycophants. The nickname Augustians was applied to his ever-present court. Famous Augustians included Petronius, Tigellinus, Seneca, and many others who also appear in Sienkiewicz's novel.

POPPAEA SABINA, Nero's second wife. Poppaea became Nero's wife in 62A.D. following his divorce and later murder of his first wife, Octavia. Nero's murder of Octavia was accompanied by the murder of other Claudian claimants to the throne. Under these circumstances, Poppaea wed Nero and brought with her a son, Rufrius Crispinus, by a previous marriage. She bore Nero a daughter, Claudia Augusta, who later died. Poppaea was killed by Nero in a fit of rage when he kicked her in the stomach.

PETER, Apostle of Jesus of Nazareth. Some historical evidence as well as centuries-old tradition place Peter in Rome at the time of the great fire in 64A.D. and subsequent persecutions. The story of the circumstances surrounding his martyrdom emerge from the very earliest of Church traditions and the location of his encounter with Christ and his execution site are venerated to this day.

PAUL, disciple of Jesus of Nazareth. Paul's proselytizing journeys were abruptly ended when he was arrested in 58A.D. in Jerusalem. He spent the next two and a half years in trials and prisons. He was finally brought to Rome in order to have his citizen's right to appeal heard by the Senate and the emperor, Nero. In 61A.D., he was acquitted and released by Nero, who at that time showed no animosity toward Christians. Tradition and legend surround the circumstances of Paul's re-arrest and martyrdom following the great fire in 64A.D.

ROME IN THE TIME OF NERO

Via Flaminia
Via Saleria
Ostrianum
Pincian Hill
Gardens of Sallust
Via Nomentana
Praetorian Guard Camp
Vatican fields
Gardens of Domitius
Old Servian Walls
TIBER
Campus Martius
Via Lata
Vicus collis
Viminalis
Quirinal Hill
Viminal Hill
Vicus Patricius
Via Tiburtina
Janiculum Hill
Via Triumphalis
Navilia
Vicus Longus
Subura
Clivus Suburanus
Esquiline
Capitol
Carinae
Gardens of Nero
Via Labicana
Forum
Nero's Domus Aurea
Via Merulana
Nero's Amphitheater
Via Aurelia
Trans-Tiber
Palatine
Via Asinaria
Circus Maximus
Caelian Hill
Via Portuensis
Emporium
Aventine Hill
Via Appia
Via Ostiensis

GATES
1. Asinarian
2. Caelemontan
3. Capenan
4. Esquiline
5. Flaminian
6. Salarian
7. Nomentanum
8. Septimian
9. Trigeminan
10. Viminal

BUILDINGS
I. Baths of Agrippa
II. Baths of Nero
III. Circus Flaminius
IV. Domus Augustus
V. Domus Tiberius
VI. Esquiline Prison
VII. Forum Boarium
VIII. Mamertine Prison
IX. Mausoleum of Augustus
X. Porticus Aemilia
XI. Theater of Pompey
XII. Velabrum

BRIDGES
A. Aemilian
B. Agrippaean
C. Triumphal (Neronian)

ROME AND CAMPANIA

Caere
Cures
ROME
VIA SALERIA
Corfinium
Sulmo
Ostia
Alba Hills
Lavinium
Aricia
Ardea
Antium
Satricum
VIA LATINA
VIA APPIA
A P E N N I N E S
Capua
Beneventum
Cannae
Cumae
CAMPANIA
Naples
VIA APPIA
to Tarentum
CAPRI

0 10 20 30 40 50
MILES

ALSO AVAILABLE FROM HIPPOCRENE BOOKS

ON THE FIELD OF GLORY
Henryk Sienkiewicz
Translated by Miroslaw Lipinski

After the tremendous worldwide success of his Trilogy, the Nobel Prize winner of 1905 set out to continue the story of Poland with a new trilogy. Sienkiewicz completed *On the Field of Glory*, the first volume, before his death in 1916. This passionate saga is set against the backdrop of the Turkish war in the seventeenth century, one of the most turbulent and critical periods of European history. Above it all is the tumultuous love story of Jacek and Anulka, one of Sienkiewicz's most lyrical.

This groundbreaking new English translation also includes a new epilogue narrating the events leading up to the glorious victory of the Christian forces led by King John Sobieski III. This epilogue has been carefully constructed by Miroslaw Lipinski, the translator, using historical accounts by Count John Sobieski (a distant relative of the king) and Count A.J. Orchowski.

278 pages • ISBN 0-7818-0762-X • $24.95hc

All prices are subject to change without prior notice. TO ORDER HIPPOCRENE TITLES: contact your local bookstore, call (718) 454-2366, visit www.hippocrenebooks.com, or write to: Hippocrene Books. 171 Madison Avenue. New York, NY 10016.